ABOUT TIME

THE UNAUTHORIZED GUIDE TO
DOCTOR WHO

1975–1979

SEASONS 12 TO 17

LAWRENCE MILES & TAT WOOD

Also available from Mad Norwegian Press...

THE ABOUT TIME SERIES
by Lawrence Miles and Tat Wood

About Time 1: The Unauthorized Guide to Doctor Who (Seasons 1 to 3)
About Time 2: The Unauthorized Guide to Doctor Who (Seasons 4 to 6)
About Time 3: The Unauthorized Guide to Doctor Who (Seasons 7 to 11)
About Time 4: The Unauthorized Guide to Doctor Who (Seasons 12 to 17)
About Time 5: The Unauthorized Guide to Doctor Who (Seasons 18 to 21)
About Time 6: The Unauthorized Guide to Doctor Who (Seasons 22 to 26,
the TV Movie; upcoming)

DOCTOR WHO REFERENCE GUIDES
*AHistory: An Unauthorized History
of the Doctor Who Universe* by Lance Parkin

Doctor Who: The Completely Unofficial Encyclopedia
by Chris Howarth and Steve Lyons

I, Who: The Unauthorized Guides to Doctor Who Novels and Audios
three-volume series by Lars Pearson

OTHER SCI-FI REFERENCE GUIDES
Redeemed: The Unauthorized Guide to Angel
by Lars Pearson and Christa Dickson

Dusted: The Unauthorized Guide to Buffy the Vampire Slayer
by Lawrence Miles, Lars Pearson and Christa Dickson

FACTION PARADOX NOVELS: THE COMPLETE SERIES
Stand-alone novel series based on characters and concepts
created by Lawrence Miles

Faction Paradox: The Book of the War [#0] by Lawrence Miles, et. al.
Faction Paradox: This Town Will Never Let Us Go [#1] by Lawrence Miles
Faction Paradox: Of the City of the Saved... [#2] by Philip Purser-Hallard
Faction Paradox: Warlords of Utopia [#3] by Lance Parkin
Faction Paradox: Warring States [#4] by Mags L. Halliday
Faction Paradox: Erasing Sherlock [#5] by Kelly Hale
Dead Romance by Lawrence Miles, contains rare back-up stories

Copyright © 2004 Mad Norwegian Press (www.madnorwegian.com)

Cover art by Steve Johnson.
Jacket & interior design by Christa Dickson (www.christadickson.com)

ISBN: 0-9725959-3-0
Printed in Illinois. First Edition: December 2004. Second Printing: March 2007

table of contents

How Does This Book Work? 5

Season 12

12.1 Robot. 7
12.2 The Ark in Space 17
12.3 The Sontaran Experiment 25
12.4 Genesis of the Daleks 31
12.5 Revenge of the Cybermen 42

Season 13

13.1 Terror of the Zygons 50
13.2 Planet of Evil. 57
13.3 Pyramids of Mars 64
13.4 The Android Invasion 74
13.5 The Brain of Morbius. 82
13.6 The Seeds of Doom 90

Season 14

14.1 The Masque of Mandragora. . . 98
14.2 The Hand of Fear 107
14.3 The Deadly Assassin 113
14.4 The Face of Evil 128
14.5 The Robots of Death. 137
14.6 The Talons of Weng-Chiang. . 145

Season 15

15.1 Horror of Fang Rock 157
15.2 The Invisible Enemy 164
15.3 Image of the Fendahl. 174
15.4 The Sun Makers 185
15.5 Underworld 191
15.6 The Invasion of Time. 200

Season 16

16.1 The Ribos Operation. 215
16.2 The Pirate Planet 226
16.3 The Stones of Blood 237
16.4 The Androids of Tara. 245
16.5 The Power of Kroll 250
16.6 The Armageddon Factor. 257

Season 17

17.1 Destiny of the Daleks 269
17.2 City of Death 280
17.3 The Creature from the Pit. . . . 291
17.4 Nightmare of Eden 299
17.5 The Horns of Nimon 307
17.6 Shada 314

table of contents

Essays

Does This Universe
Have an Ethical Standard? 9

Why Couldn't They
Just Have Spent More Money? 19

Which is Best, Film or Video? 27

How Badly Does
Dalek History Suffer? 33

September or January? 51

What Does Anti-Matter Do? 59

Where (and When) is Gallifrey? 65

Why Does Earth
Keep Getting Invaded? 75

Who Are All
These Strange Men in Wigs? 83

Is He Really a Doctor? 91

Does the Universe
Really Speak English? 99

Did Rassilon Know Omega? 117

Is This Really an SF series? 129

Cultural Primer #1:
Why *Top of the Pops*? 139

Bad Effects:
What are the Highlights? 147

When was *Doctor Who* Scary? 159

Cultural Primer #2:
Why *Blue Peter*? 167

Is This
the *Quatermass* Continuum? 177

Just How Involved
are the Time Lords? 193

How Might
the Sonic Screwdriver Work? 203

What Do the Guardians Do? 217

Cliffhangers: What are
the High and Low Points? 229

The Obvious Question:
How Old is He? 253

How Hard is it
to be the Wrong Size? 259

War of the Daleks: Should
Anyone Believe a Word of It? 271

When Did the Doctor
Meet Leonardo? 281

How Do You Transmit Matter? 301

What *Else* Didn't Get Made? 315

About Time prides itself on being the most comprehensive, wide-ranging and at times almost *shockingly* detailed handbook to *Doctor Who* that you might ever conceivably need, so great pains have been taken to make sure there's a place for everything and everything's in its place. Here are the "rules"…

Every *Doctor Who* story gets its own entry, and every entry is divided up into four major sections. The first, which includes the headings **Which One is This?**, **Firsts and Lasts** and **X Things to Notice**, is designed to provide an overview of the story for newcomers to the series (and we trust there'll be more of you, after 2005) or relatively "lightweight" fans who aren't too clued-up on a particular era of the programme's history. We might like to *pretend* that all *Doctor Who* viewers know all parts of the series equally well, but there are an awful lot of people who - for example - know the '70s episodes by heart and don't have a clue about the '60s. This section also acts as an overall Spotters' Guide to the series, pointing out most of the memorable bits.

After that comes the **Continuity** section, which is where you'll find all the pedantic detail. Here there are notes on the Doctor (personality, props and cryptic mentions of his past), the supporting cast, the TARDIS and any major Time Lords who might happen to wander into the story. Following these are the **Non-Humans** and **Planet Notes** sections, which can best be described as "high geekery"… we're old enough to remember the *Doctor Who Monster Book*, but not too old to want a more grown-up version of our own, so expect full-length monster profiles. Next comes **History**, which includes all available data about the time in which the story's supposed to be set.

Of crucial importance: note that throughout the **Continuity** section, *everything* you read is "true" - i.e. based on what's said or seen on-screen - except for sentences in square brackets [like this], where we cross-reference the data to other stories and make some suggestions as to how all of this is supposed to fit together. You can trust us absolutely on the non-bracketed material, but the bracketed sentences are often just speculation.

The only exception to this rule is the **Additional Sources** heading, which features any off-screen information from novelisations, writer interviews, etc that might shed light on the way the story's supposed to work. (Another thing to notice here: anything written in single inverted commas - 'like this' - is a word-for-word quote from the script, whereas anything in double-quote marks "like this" isn't.)

The third major section is **Analysis**. It opens with **Where Does This Come From?**, and this may need explaining. For years there's been a tendency in fandom to assume that *Doctor Who* was an "escapist" series which very rarely tackled anything particularly topical, but with hindsight this is bunk. Throughout its history, the programme reflected, reacted to and sometimes openly *discussed* the trends and talking-points of the era, although it isn't always immediately obvious to the modern eye. (Everybody knows that "The Sunmakers" was supposed to be satirical, but how many people got the subtext of "Destiny of the Daleks"?) It's our job here to put each story into the context of the time in which it was made, to explain *why* the production team thought it might have been a good idea.

Up next is **Things That Don't Make Sense**, basically a run-down of the glitches and logical flaws in the story, some of them merely curious and some entirely ridiculous. Unlike a lot of TV guidebooks, here we don't dwell on minor details like shaky camera angles and actors treading on each others' cues - at least unless they're *chronically* noticeable - since these are trivial even by our standards. We're much more concerned with whacking great story loopholes or particularly grotesque breaches of the laws of physics.

Analysis ends with **Critique**; though no consensus will ever be found on *any* story, we've not only tried to provide a balanced (or at least not-too-irrational) view but also attempted to judge each story by its own standards, *not just* the standards of the post-CGI generation.

The last of the four sections is **The Facts**, which covers ordinary, straightforward details like cast lists, viewing figures and - where applicable - the episodes of the story which are currently missing from the BBC archives. We've also provided a run-down of the story's cliffhangers, since a lot of *Doctor Who* fans grew up thinking of the cliffhangers as the programme's defining points. This gives you a much better sense of a story's structure than a long and involved plot breakdown (which we're fairly sure would interest nobody at this stage, barring perhaps those stories presently missing from the BBC archives).

The Lore is an addendum to the Facts section, which covers the off-screen anecdotes and factettes attached to the story. The word "Lore" seems fitting, since long-term fans will already know much of this material, but it needs to be included here (a) for new initiates and (b) because this is supposed to be a one-stop guide to the history of *Doctor Who*.

A lot of "issues" relating to the series are so big that they need forums all to themselves, which is why most story entries are followed by mini-essays. Here we've tried to answer all the questions that seem to demand answers, although the logic of these essays changes from case to case. Some of them are actually trying to find *definitive* answers, unravelling what's said in the TV stories and making sense of what the programme-makers had in mind. Some have more to do with the real world than the *Doctor Who* universe, and aim to explain why certain things about the series were so important at the time. Some are purely speculative, some delve into scientific theory and some are just whims, but they're *good* whims and they all seem to have a place here. Occasionally we've included footnotes on the names and events we've cited, for those who aren't old enough or British enough to follow all the references.

We should also mention the idea of "canon" here. Anybody who knows *Doctor Who* well, who's been exposed to the TV series, the novels, the comic-strips, the audio adventures and the trading-cards you used to get with Sky Ray ice-lollies, will know that there's always been some doubt about how much of *Doctor Who* counts as "real", as if the TV stories are in some way less made-up than the books or the short stories. We'll discuss this in shattering detail later on, but for now it's enough to say that *About Time* has its own specific rules about what's canonical and what isn't. In this book, we accept everything that's shown in the TV series to be the "truth" about the *Doctor Who* universe (although obviously we have to gloss over the parts where the actors fluff their

lines). Those non-TV stories which have made a serious attempt to become part of the canon, from Virgin Publishing's New Adventures to the recent audio adventures from Big Finish, aren't considered to be 100% "true" but do count as supporting evidence. Here they're treated as what historians call "secondary sources", not definitive enough to make us change our whole view of the way the *Doctor Who* universe works but helpful pointers if we're trying to solve any particularly fiddly continuity problems.

It's worth remembering that unlike (say) the stories written for the old *Dalek* annuals, the early Virgin novels were an honest attempt to carry on the *Doctor Who* tradition in the absence of the TV series, so it seems fair to use them to fill the gaps in the programme's folklore even if they're not exactly - so to speak - "fact".

You'll also notice that we've divided up this work according to "era", not according to Doctor. Since we're trying to tell the *story* of the series, both on- and off-screen, this makes sense. The actor playing the Main Man might be the only thing we care about when we're too young to know better, but anyone who's watched the episodes with hindsight will know that there's a vastly bigger stylistic leap between "The Horns of Nimon" and "The Leisure Hive" than there is between "Logopolis" and "Castrovalva". Volume IV covers the producerships of Philip Hinchcliffe and Graham Williams, two very distinct stories in themselves, and everything changes again - when Williams leaves the series, not when Tom Baker does - at the start of the 1980s.

There's a kind of logic here, just as there's a kind of logic to everything in this book. There's so much to *Doctor Who*, so much material to cover and so many ways to approach it, that there's a risk of our methods irritating our audience even if all the information's in the right places. So we need to be consistent, and we have been. As a result, we're confident that this is as solid a reference guide / critical study / monster book as you'll ever find. In the end, we hope you'll agree that the only realistic criticism is: "Haven't you told us *too* much here?"

And once we're finished, we can watch the *new* series and start the game all over again.

12.1: "Robot"

(Serial 4A, Four Episodes, 28th December, 1974 - 18th January 1975.)

Which One is This? The Target novelisation calls it *Doctor Who and the Giant Robot*, if that helps. The new Doctor has a go at being UNIT's scientific advisor (and finds he doesn't like it much), while Sarah Jane Smith gets to be the struggling female victim in an English home-counties remake of *King Kong*.

Firsts and Lasts It's the first outing for Tom Baker as the Fourth Doctor, of course, but this isn't the dawn-of-a-new-era we might expect. "Robot" was shown as the opening story of Season Twelve, but it was shot alongside the end of Season Eleven, so the old (Third-Doctor-era) *Doctor Who* production team is still in effect; this is the last story to have Barry Letts as its producer and Terrance Dicks as its script editor. As a result "Robot" finds itself sandwiched between the "modern Earth under threat" stories of the past and the "horror of outer space" stories to come, so the *real* Fourth Doctor era doesn't begin until the next story.

Still, at least here we see most of the props of Tom Baker's reign putting in appearances, including the scarf, the dependence on jelly babies and the insane stare. It's also the first appearance of Harry Sullivan, the Doctor's "backup companion" for the next year, while regular features which leave the series here include Bessie and UNIT HQ (neither of which turn up again until 20.7, "The Five Doctors").

In the same way that the first story of Jon Pertwee's run (7.1, "Spearhead from Space") broke new ground by being the first *Doctor Who* story shot entirely on grubby-but-costly-looking film, "Robot" breaks new ground by being the first story shot entirely on shiny-but-cheap-looking video, as by 1974 video cameras had become lightweight enough to allow the programme-makers to film all the exterior scenes on VT. Theoretically, this means that for the first time CSO effects can be used to make a monster look gigantic when it's *outside*, without the effect looking silly. (As it happens it looks quite silly anyway, but more on that later.)

Season 12 Cast/Crew

- Tom Baker (the Doctor)
- Elisabeth Sladen (Sarah Jane Smith)
- Ian Marter (Harry Sullivan)

- Philip Hinchcliffe (Producer, 4.2 to 4.5)
- Barry Letts (Producer, 4.1 only)
- Robert Holmes (Script Editor)

Four Things to Notice About "Robot"...

1. By this point, the audience is getting used to the idea that the Doctor can change his face every now and then. Previous "post-regeneration" stories at least *tried* to present the new Doctor as a figure of mystery, but here Tom Baker gets to mess around in his debut story safe in the knowledge that the viewers are going to be on his side. Apart from some quality clowning in the first episode, this leads to a scene that's destined to be recycled for later regenerations, and a sure sign that a change of lead actor is becoming as acceptable as a change of costume: this time the Doctor goes through the TARDIS wardrobe and picks out several other (odd) outfits before he settles on the now-familiar scarf-and-floppy-hat ensemble, giving Baker the chance to dress up and show off right from the beginning.

2. Indeed, it's the New Boy who gets all the good moments here. This is, famously, the story in which he describes himself as '*the* Doctor... the definite article, you might say'. He sets the tone for the rest of his performance when he emerges from the TARDIS dressed as a Viking, and the Brigadier points out that UNIT is supposed to be a security organisation, whereupon he replies: 'Do you think I might attract attention?' (Yet even so it's noticeable that while Pertwee made the programme "his" in his very first story, Baker still doesn't seem quite comfortable with the set-up by the end of "Robot". Well, he *is* trying to work with his predecessor's supporting cast.)

3. Though "Robot" doesn't hold a lot in common with the Fourth Doctor stories to come, in one way it *does* foreshadow the programme over the next year or two: its love of chunky monster costumes. Whereas previous seasons showed an interest in dinosaur puppets, wobbly spider props and creatures dressed up in excessive *Top of the Pops* video effects, "Robot" brings us... well, a

great big robot. Specifically, a juddering mass of pincers and shoulder-pads that has to be considered another medium-budget design success for the programme, even if its last stand is less than impressive. Every story in this season will feature monster outfits of some description, so it's no wonder that this is still considered the golden age of shambling things in latex and plastic.

4. No spotter's guide to "Robot" can possibly be complete without mention of the tank, known to *Doctor Who* fans everywhere as *that* tank. The climax of episode three sees the giant robot guarding the entrance to an 'atomic bunker', and the military calling in all available forces to dispose of it. This involves a tank rolling into view and preparing to open fire. What we *actually* see is an Action Man tank - or a G.I. Joe tank, if you're American - being pushed into the foreground, superimposed on top of the scenery through the magic of CSO. About as bad as effects ever get, this scene is brought to you by the same designer who presented us with an army of 10,000 toy Daleks in an ice-cave (10.4, "Planet of the Daleks") and the infamous tyrannosaurus / brontosaurus foreplay scene (11.2, "Invasion of the Dinosaurs", and see also **Bad Effects: What Are the Highlights?** under 14.6, "The Talons of Weng-Chiang"). The little doll of Sarah in the giant robot's hand deserves a mention, as well.

The Continuity

The Doctor The new Doctor is erratic and uncontrollable during his post-regenerative recovery period, as K'Anpo predicted [in 11.5, "Planet of the Spiders"]. To begin with, his memory's chronically impaired, but more tellingly he acts as if the people at UNIT are somebody *else's* friends and he's only there by accident.

When he starts to recover he's still noticeably more *alien* than his previous incarnation, showing no particular interest in human relations and treating the Think Tank crisis as if it's just something to stop him getting bored. Here he shows little or no interest in being a moral crusader, and comes across as some kind of a cosmic bohemian, with a need to travel and no real liking for UNIT.

He essentially kidnaps Harry Sullivan in the TARDIS, not warning the man about the consequences of going aboard, apparently just to prove a point [or because he needs people around him during his unstable period?]. Sarah Jane Smith is

the only person he seems to have any affection for. Initially he doesn't even seem to have an attachment to *her*, as he intends to leave Earth without even saying goodbye.

Whereas the Third Doctor acted with an air of authority, and seemed insulted whenever anybody questioned his judgement, the Fourth displays no interest in authority at all and gets his way just by confusing anyone who opposes him. It takes him a while to accept his new face, liking the nose but not being sure about the ears. He only seems to settle on his eventual "new look" when the Brigadier stops him trying on any more clothes [something similar happens in 24.1, "Time and the Rani"]. Here he sleeps on a table-top in the UNIT lab, not in the TARDIS.

The Doctor can type at ludicrous speeds, running off a letter in seconds. He can do calculations in his head that humans can't do without calculators, and karate-chops a brick into two pieces. [Although there's a "plunk" noise as the brick hits the floor, which may be the sound of the prop on which it was resting or may suggest that the brick itself is just balsa wood. It doesn't work when he tries to chop a *second* brick. The rather endearing fact that there are household objects lying around the lab, ready for experimentation, makes UNIT look like a sort of space-race-era version of CSI.] While recovering from the regeneration, the Doctor's left to mess around with the TARDIS for a short while, so it's at least *possible* that he might have all sorts of unseen adventures when he's still unstable [see 14.4, "The Face of Evil"]. If so then he must forget about them instantly, as he describes the others at UNIT HQ as coming to 'see me off' when they find him in the lab.

• *Ethics.* Here the Doctor's surprisingly quick to destroy the K1 robot, even though it's intelligent and developing a conscience. [He may not realise how advanced it is, since it menaces him whenever he meets it.] He values science as a quest for truth, and questions any use of it for more immediate ends, even apparently benign ones.

• *Inventory.* In the pockets of his new coat: jelly babies [see 10.1, "The Three Doctors"... did the Second Doctor stock this outfit?], a deck of trick cards, a scroll granting him with the freedom of the city of Skaro, honorary membership of the Alpha Centauri table tennis club [see **Planet Notes**] and a pilot's license for the Mars-Venus rocket run. He has an unfolding wallet full of IDs

Does This Universe Have an Ethical Standard?

Ethics and *Doctor Who*: big subject. Not least because we're dealing with over 150 separate "morality tales", spread over a twenty-six year period in which British society had to re-think most of its ideas about what was and wasn't acceptable anyway.

There *isn't* a solid, definite morality behind the Doctor's actions, (1) because such a thing would be impossible to maintain over so many seasons, (2) because of the BBC's eagerness to be non-denominational (and absolutely *not* allow the Doctor's companions to have "meaningful" conversations about God, the way the series' very first writer intended), and (3) because the deliberate absence of a proper "back-story" in the early episodes guaranteed a certain moral ambivalence on the Doctor's part.

Even from story to story, sometimes from episode to episode, his morals seem to waver. It *is* possible to squeeze all his actions into a single ethical code, with only one or two glitches, but that's not what concerns us here. In **How Does "Evil" Work?** (it's under 8.2, "The Mind of Evil", aptly enough), we dwelt on little things like the existence of the soul and What It Means to Be Bad in This Universe. In **How "Good" is the Doctor?** (under 25.1, "Remembrance of the Daleks"), we'll pause to think about the way the changing shape of the programme alters the nature of the Doctor's character. Here, we're going to talk about ethics: that is, how you're supposed to *behave* towards people, and whether *Doctor Who* is giving us a consistent message. Morality - the grounds for religion, beliefs, etcetera - can keep.

So. *Is* there a universal, ethical standard in this universe?

Right, crash-course on ethics in the world as we know it. Apart from "I'm right, you're wrong, die infidel", there are two standard positions on this, the Categorical Imperative and Utilitarianism. To summarise them in the kind of bonehead English that most scholars would find objectionable: the Categorical Imperative basically means "Do As You Would Be Done By", although the philosopher Emmanuel Kant spent a long time working on this to get it exactly right. Utilitarianism means "The Greatest Good for the Greatest Number", but even if we can agree on what "good" is, we still need a measure of how "great" a good is; an "ethical calculus".

Now, Utilitarianism is clearly at the heart of the Time Lords' actions. In "The Deadly Assassin" (14.3) we find out that their grand observation hall is called the Panopticon, a name which comes from a design of prison suggested by the eighteenth century philosopher and "father" of Utilitarianism, Jeremy Bentham. Bentham's Panopticon was, and this will be significant later, based on the idea that it's impossible to sin / try to escape / take crack / do anything else that's forbidden if someone can see you at all times. "Panopticon"... the name suggests "all-seeing". Bentham envisaged a great cylindrical building, with every cell visible from a central point, and there are some prisons built on this principle in Philadelphia and Illinois.

However, if you try taking Utilitarianism to extremes... well, there's a scene in Dostoievski's novel *The Brothers Karamazov* - and this will come up again in "Genesis of the Daleks" (12.4) - to the effect that a Utopia based on the deliberate torture of one individual might be worth achieving. Logically, the Greatest Good for the Greatest Number means that the perpetual sacrifice of one is acceptable, if it means the perpetual well-being of everyone else. For the Time Lords this isn't just theoretical, and many of their more questionable decisions are made with this logic in mind. Even apart from their later activities, they only achieved mastery of time when Omega was "sacrificed" to the black hole, and thereafter kept in pain for millennia (10.1, "The Three Doctors"). For our purposes it's a clue that Robert Holmes, who first brought the word "Panopticon" to the series, was aware of what he was suggesting in "Carnival of Monsters" (10.2) when he hinted that the Time Lords supervise the dignity and morality of sentient beings.

You can see the paradox. The Time Lords banned the Miniscope because watching inferior beings is demeaning, but what do *they* do all day? In '70s *Doctor Who* surveillance is an Orwellian nightmare, and being observed by "outside" beings as we go about our lives is the second scariest thing that can happen to you, after possession.

But the Doctor relies far less on any "calculus", on any rational system of how much sacrifice equals how much good, than he relies on sheer instinct. He rarely suggests that it's "good" for one life to be sacrificed in the name of billions, even if those who suicidally save the day are presented as all-round heroes. When he *does* go along with the idea that one life is worth less than millions, it's usually his own life that's being offered up. As a solo Time Lord he has no way of knowing the con-

continued on page 11...

and credit-card-like items, including a galactic passport [odd that he never carries an Earth-bound one].

He's still carrying a jeweller's eyeglass, and throws away some ball-bearings in a failed effort to trip up the robot. All sorts of other rubbish gets pulled out of his pockets at one stage, including a large toy bird [see 14.6, "The Talons of Weng-Chiang", for more on this], a pair of goggles, a yo-yo, a second wallet and something that looks remarkably like a packet of cigarettes.

The Doctor keeps the TARDIS key in his boot here [again recalling back to "Spearhead from Space"]. The sonic screwdriver can be turned into a sonic lance, and cut through locks, once a special attachment's fitted to the end. [This seems a more powerful version of the screwdriver, so it may have been upgraded at some point. Q.v. 9.2, "The Curse of Peladon".]

• *Background.* He indicates that he's met both Alexander the Great and Hannibal, though he could be either unstable or joking at the time.

• *Bessie.* This is the only occasion on which the Fourth Doctor drives his car. He leaves "her" on Earth when he goes off in the TARDIS, without displaying much affection for her. [This Doctor has lost his obsession with non-time-travelling vehicles. 26.1, "Battlefield" reveals that the Brigadier puts Bessie into storage until the 1990s.]

The Supporting Cast

• *Sarah Jane Smith.* Once the Doctor regenerates, she immediately accepts him as the same man [she is, of course, the only companion to have seen a regeneration *before* the Doctor's; "Planet of Spiders", again] and seems to see it as a personal duty to make sure he's well.

For the last time during her adventures with the Doctor, Sarah actively pursues her career as a journalist, investigating Think Tank because it's her job rather than because she thinks it's a threat to humanity. ["Terror of the Zygons" (13.1) sees her writing up a story, but only because she already happens to be involved in it.] However, she apparently sees her profession as an investigator dove-tailing with her "work" for UNIT. She still sees herself as a day-tripper in the TARDIS, not as a full-time companion to the Doctor. She's got her own car here.

• *Harry Sullivan.* UNIT's young Medical Officer [as mentioned in "Planet of the Spiders"], Lieutenant Sullivan is a well-meaning but boor-ishly old-fashioned public-school type who - curiously - doesn't seem to have been properly briefed on the Doctor's alien physiology. He doesn't know anything about the TARDIS yet [he's too posh to swap stories with Benton and the troops]. On the other hand, a crisis involving a giant robot and a disintegrator gun doesn't appear to surprise him at all, and he has no problem getting involved in a gung-ho UNIT undercover operation. He drives Bessie here.

• *UNIT.* Charged with the task of investigating the theft of the plans for a disintegrator gun, so the organisation's once again handling crises with an international dimension rather than specifically investigating the odd and the alien. The Brigadier has the power to fix up Sarah with a visitor's pass for Think Tank. UNIT HQ has a sick-bay.

On this occasion, the Brigadier seems to want the Doctor to brief the authorities on the crisis after the event, though obviously the Doctor isn't interested. The Doctor's also invited to the Palace, and he isn't interested in *that*, either. [Perhaps odd, since the Doctor's been so keen on hob-nobbing with royalty before now. This new incarnation is a lot less well-disposed towards formality.]

• *The Brigadier.* Fully named here as Alistair Gordon Lethbridge-Stewart. He treats the Doctor's regeneration with resignation. Despite these trying times, he's as bluff as ever and speaks of the British as if they're intrinsically more trustworthy than foreigners. He seems to know more than expected about the top secret disintegrator gun, understanding that it requires a 'focusing generator' as well as knowing the name and location of the only electronics factory which can provide one. He is - as ever - happy to tell Sarah the journalist everything that happens at UNIT as long as he says 'you realise of course, Miss Smith, all of this is top secret' afterwards. He just seems to want someone to talk to, and admits that he misses having the Doctor around. Sarah calls him a 'swinger', amusingly.

• *Benton.* Finally rewarded for being the second-most-reliable member of UNIT, Benton has been promoted from Sergeant to Warrant Officer [though he's still "Sergeant" on the end credits... for all we know, that's his name]. Technically the Brigadier should have a Major and a Captain under him, but the UNIT budget at present doesn't stretch to that. He's the one who gets this month's "point-out-the-obvious-solution-that-everyone's-overlooked" moment.

Does This Universe Have an Ethical Standard?

...continued from page 9

sequences of his actions, and mainly relies on hope. When he cites the "Law" of the Time Lords in "The Hand of Fear" (14.2) or presents a seemingly-spurious argument for stopping the Virus of the Nucleus in "The Invisible Enemy" (15.2), it sounds as if he's just using fragments of a code of conduct that he left behind when he left Gallifrey.

The other "standard" model, the Categorical Imperative, offers a bit more scope. "Do As You Would Be Done By", remember. While Kant wanted to provide an ethical standard based on respect for the souls of any people one might encounter (and this applies to disembodied intelligences and robots as well as people in the more conventional sense), here we have no need for divine agencies, Karma, or the threat of eternal damnation. Even though we know the Time Lords are watching, and even though they presumably know how things will turn out, we're supposed to act in a certain way because it's "right". Not because of a higher power with a big stick. Respect for others is to be learned, or acquired, autonomously.

So now we come to Kettlewell's robot. As we see in "Robot", K1 begins to develop an idea of "good" based not on what Jellicoe and Winters tell it, but on what capacity any given human has to understand its distressing neural imbalances. Sarah and Kettlewell are "good" because they empathise, whether they actually *do* anything or not. They want to help when the robot's in pain. The robot evaluates its own actions on whether people will suffer and how much "badness" will be prevented. There are other considerations, like retaliating when shot at, but these all develop from the basic experience of pain. Whether what *it* feels is in any way similar to what *we* feel is immaterial. The robot suffers hurtful effects from inner conflict, maps these onto other people and assumes their actions to be similarly motivated. It has, as child psychologists call it, a "theory of mind".

All *Doctor Who* monsters have this to some extent, even vegetables (the Krynoid, for instance). Only absolute reflex-driven beasts like Drashigs seem to lack it, and even then it's hard to tell. Aliens planning to take over the world must assume human thoughts to be analogous to their own for their fiendish plans to work. Disembodied forces, such as the Great Intelligence, can suffer even without a body in which to experience pain.

Anything capable of empathy is expected to understand that the same experience of "bad" applies to everyone else. If they *do* understand this, but cause suffering anyway, then they're in the wrong. Consider "The Savages" (3.9), in which Steven starts a revolution by making the guards understand what it feels like to be on the receiving end of a light-gun.

And when we look carefully at the few times that the matter's been explicitly talked about in the series rather than assumed, we find empathy right at the top of the ethical agenda. "The Two Doctors" (22.4) puts the motives of those who inflict pain under the spotlight. Androgums barely exist as moral agents; they're pure id, and live for self-indulgence. Dastari and Chessene are supposed to know better and are therefore morally culpable (whereas Shockeye isn't, and the Doctor butchers him like an animal... mind you, this *is* the Sixth Doctor we're talking about).

Think how often "emotional capacity" is used as the benchmark. The food being discussed by the Androgums is often produced by (arguably) cruel means, and in fact many of the examples given in the story are those used in the Voigt-Kampf Test of empathy in Philip K. Dick's *Do Androids Dream of Electric Sheep?* - filmed, sort of, as *Blade Runner* - in which the inability to flinch at the thought of lobsters being boiled alive is proof of not being human. Beings who lack the capacity to empathise have to be seen as less-than-complete moral agents. The Daleks are like a virus, but Davros (and humans) have the choice, and are therefore worse. In "The Robots of Death" (14.5), the robots - who are apparently incapable of empathy, except for the peculiar D84 - are merely used as weapons. (In English law, until 1811, a bull or dog that killed someone could be tried and hanged as a "deodand". But the principle of arresting all non-human killers was abandoned when steamrollers started appearing in court.)

A seemingly unlikely consequence of this is that the motivation of any act is a better indication of its being "good" than the consequences, however benign those consequences turn out to be in the long run. You can do the "right" thing even if it's a nasty thing to do to someone.

Our test-case, the K1 robot, is supposedly incapable of harming anyone but also seems to be programmed for self-preservation. This makes sense, for an experimental prototype which must

continued on page 13...

The TARDIS Costumes from the TARDIS wardrobe that the Doctor tries on, before he chooses his coat, hat and scarf: a Viking [probably an opera costume, since real Vikings wouldn't dress that way]; a story-book royal who looks as if he's stepped out of a deck of cards; and a Pierrot, thankfully without the make-up. When Sarah rushes to the doors of the departing TARDIS, the Doctor breaks off the dematerialisation halfway through, the first time this happens. [Previous "abortive" take-offs have been test-runs ending in comedy explosions; 7.1, "Spearhead From Space" and 8.1, "Terror of the Autons"].

The Non-Humans

• *Robot K1.* An eight-foot-tall machine-man weighing a quarter of a ton and with pincers for hands, built by Professor J. P. Kettlewell of Think Tank. An experimental prototype, it's ostensibly designed to help humans with tasks like mining and handling radioactive materials. It's also made out of what Kettlewell calls 'living metal', a substance he invented himself, so the whole robot grows like a living organism and is at least thirty feet high after it absorbs energy from the disintegrator gun. Though the Scientific Reform Society believes K1 to be incapable of human feeling, it has 'neural circuits' which allow it to develop something like a personality before long. Kettlewell calls the robot a "he", and says he gave it his brain-patterns, principles and ideals.

Though K1's prime directive tells it not to harm human beings, this obviously doesn't suit the plans of the SRS and the directive can be re-set, but the robot suffers pain when its principles cause conflict. Endearingly, it goes 'aaah!' and faints when it kills its creator. The Doctor, in a rare moment of Freudian insight, believes it to have a 'suppressed Oedipus complex leading to excessive guilt and over-compensation'. The robot's powerful enough to burrow into a high-security vault using sheer brute strength, while its senses can apparently detect specific human beings on the other side of solid objects.

[The implication is that K1 is a breakthrough, but nowhere does anybody state that there are *no* other intelligent robots on Earth. Since there are sentient computers on Earth as early as the 1960s - see 3.10, "The War Machines" and 10.5, "The Green Death" - this could be the first time that a machine-brain has been fitted inside a humanoid body, or more likely, the first time that a machine-

brain and machine-body have developed in tandem as part of an organic process. But even if it's got a male voice and happens to be built like a mechanical weightlifter, the Doctor's psychoanalysis of K1 doesn't seem to make sense unless the machine's been programmed with an unconscious understanding of human sexual roles. Presumably it picked this up from Kettlewell's 'brain-patterns', but it still makes you wonder exactly what kind of creature the Professor was trying to make. We're assuming, of course, that this 'organic' robot doesn't have reproductive systems. It talks about building other robots, not fathering them. See also **Does This Universe Have an Ethical Standard?**.]

Kettlewell, obviously an extraordinary man, has also created a metal-eating virus which he believes will be able to break down the metal waste that pollutes the planet. This seems to have been a product of the same research which created the robot itself. It throws the robot's growth mechanism 'into reverse', so K1 shrinks away to midget-size and disintegrates as the virus consumes it.

Planet Notes

• *Alpha Centauri.* The Doctor has honorary membership of the Alpha Centauri table tennis club: 'Tricky opponents. Six arms, and of course, six bats.' [If it's anything like Earth table tennis, then he means six bats in a *game*, not per player. Though it's anyone's guess how the Doctor managed to keep up, or why he's even been given 'honourary' membership.]

• *Skaro.* The Doctor has the freedom of the city of Skaro. [Two points here. One: this suggests that the planet Skaro only has one city. The sole city we've seen there was the home of the Daleks - 1.2, "The Daleks" - but it's unlikely that the Daleks gave the Doctor *any* kind of honour. The Thals apparently have a proper civilisation on Skaro by the time of 10.4, "Planet of the Daleks", so has the Doctor visited them? Indeed, did they take over the old Dalek city after the Daleks' defeat? In "Planet of the Daleks" the Doctor seems to know more about Thal and Dalek culture than he's ever been told, so this "freedom" suggests a visit to the planet that we've never been told about.]

History

• *Dating.* Evidently the '70s. [Probably 1975. See **When Are the UNIT Stories Set?** under 7.1, "Spearhead from Space" and **What's the UNIT**

Does This Universe Have an Ethical Standard?

...continued from page 11

have cost the taxpayers millions. It also harks back to the most famous rules for robots, Asimov's Three Laws of Robotics, which demand that robots look after themselves *provided* it doesn't cause harm to humans.

However, the existence of empathy means that self-preservation can come lower down the list of priorities than some specific objective. It means that the robot can sacrifice itself in the name of a greater good, even if that greater good doesn't *directly* lead to human lives being saved. It can jeopardise itself in the name of an abstract ideal. The robot can only kill if its brain is altered - we might reasonable suppose that beyond its "personality", it has some sort of fail-safe which Kettlewell can remove when the SRS needs an assassin - but even when it *can* hurt people, the SRS has to convince it that its target is an enemy of all humanity.

And when it tries to blow everyone up with nuclear missiles, it seems to believe that it's making things better by creating a less troubled world, inhabited by a new race of robots instead of nasty people who give it pain-inducing orders. Empathy allows a being to consider the next generation, which might explain why K1 seems to have its creator's understanding of sexual roles.

So, granting a robot or a piece of software the ability to take abstract issues personally may be the means by which it becomes an individual (it worked for BOSS in 10.5, "The Green Death"... sort of). But as neither "good" nor "pain" is quantifiable, the only thing stopping an empathic machine from launching a campaign against every perceived antagonist it encounters is exactly the tendency to generalise and judge-by-consequences which leads to Utilitarianism.

Look on the bright side: humans haven't solved that one yet, either

---

Timeline? under 8.5, "The Daemons" for a full justification.] It's the 4th of April when Sarah visits Think Tank, according to the pass she's given.

The Brigadier speaks of 'enemy agents' as if it's common for Britain to be under threat from other powers. A few months ago the superpowers - named as Russia, America and China - decided on a plan to 'ensure peace'. All three have secret atomic missile sites, and all three agreed to give details and operation instructions for these sites to a neutral country, i.e. Britain. In the event of 'trouble', Britain can publish the information and thus expose everyone's secrets.

Joseph Chambers, a Cabinet Minister, is the guardian of the 'destructor codes' until the robot kills him. This whole plan is supposedly a secret, but the Brigadier knows the details. The fact that he can warn all the superpowers to activate their nuclear failsafes within minutes, and that they all immediately comply, would suggest a greater level of international co-operation than *anyone* might expect. [The description of Britain as a 'neutral power', rather than as an obvious ally of the US, might suggest that America's influence isn't as great as it was / is in the world we know. See **Who's Running the County?** under 10.5, "The Green Death".] The safe containing the codes has a triple-security thermolock made of case-hardened 'indestructible' dynastrine, so exotic-sounding metals aren't just found on other planets.

By now the human race has developed plans for a disintegrator gun, a weapon that can make a tank disappear with a single shot, but there are no signs that any government has actually built one. The plans are kept at a Ministry of Defence weapons research station. Emmett's Electronics, a small-ish factory in Essex, is apparently the only place that can supply the focusing generator for the gun. The weapon has the range to drill a hole in the moon, but it's no bigger than a rifle. [You have to wonder why it's not standard military issue by 1980. Unless the authorities just don't want soldiers carving things on the moon.]

Think Tank is an all-purpose frontiers-of-science research establishment, which mainly deals in theory and passes its work on to others - usually the government - whenever the theory becomes practical. It pioneered the disintegrator gun research, and built itself an atomic shelter 'back in the Cold War days' [q.v. 11.2, "Invasion of the Dinosaurs"]. The Brigadier needs the Minister's approval to raid the place. However, Think Tank is being used as a front by the Scientific Reform Society, a collection of rabid sciento-fascists founded 'years ago' who want to rationalise the world by blowing most of it up and starting again. Think Tank has associates across the planet, and it can use the stolen 'destructor codes' to launch the world's nuclear missiles from the safety of its bunker.

Professor Kettlewell, an ally of both Think Tank and the SRS, believes in alternative energy technologies [so energy is still a prime concern, as it is in most of the '70s Earth-bound stories]. Kettlewell turned against 'conventional science' altogether, and got onto the newspapers because of it, so Sarah's heard of him. The Doctor, curiously, hasn't. [Compare this with his knowledge of contemporary scientists in "Invasion of the Dinosaurs" and 10.5, "The Green Death". Perhaps the new Doctor can't be bothered remembering this sort of thing, since he's not planning on being around for much longer.]

The Analysis

Where Does This Come From? Immediately after World War II, a group of second-string American scientists formed a collective called "Technocracy", advocating a streamlined, logical lifestyle based on pseudo-scientific "rational" principles. They all wore identical grey suits, drove the same model of car (grey) and lived by-the-book. As the impending oil-squeeze, population explosion, pollution crisis and energy-crunch threatened everything - and it's funny how we look back on the 70s as "carefree" - this school of thought underwent a revival. After all, it had worked in the Soviet Union (apparently) and during wartime in Britain (undeniably).

Many people wanted the world to listen to the scientists, not the generals and politicians. This formed the basis of the allegorical 1950 film *The Day The Earth Stood Still*, in which "Mr. Carpenter" - one of cinema's many alien Christs - visits Earth with a message of Peace, Love and Non-Euclidean Geometry, backed up by a big robot with a disintegrator gun. The robot, Gort, spends most of the film zapping tanks and standing menacingly in front of metal doors. This was based on Harry Bates' short story "Farewell to the Master", in which the robot turns out to be the moral exemplar and the humanoid emissary merely a frontman. Terrance Dicks would have read it when it appeared in his childhood favourite, *Astounding Science Fiction* magazine. (You've probably seen the artwork for that story. It shows a giant, sad-looking silver robot holding a bloodied human corpse in its hand, and it re-appeared on the cover of Queen's *News of the World* LP in 1977.)

Miss Winters is one of the few female *Doctor Who* villains seen by this point, although the programme's view of Women's Lib remains as confused as ever, since the SRS is presented as a fascist-science group that wants womenfolk to stay in the kitchen while its leader comes across as a bitter spinster who "just needs the love of a man to sort her out". She has to be *Miss* Winters, naturally. Here she uses her "feminism" as a means of scoring points off Sarah, just as she later exploits the Brigadier's inability to shoot a woman.

The Doctor's look and demeanour were taken wholesale from Toulouse-Lautrec's 1892 poster "Ambassadeurs: Aristide Bruant", probably the artist's best-known work, although the scarf was serendipity (a Mrs. Pope - no-one's sure if her name was "Magnolia" or "Begonia" - was asked to knit a long stripy scarf, and nobody told her when to stop). Aware that the new central character was going to be more "detached" than the Jon Pertwee version, Dicks claims he wrote the Doctor as Harpo Marx, curious and uncontrollable.

Things That Don't Make Sense Nothing about the SRS adds up. The nerd-Nazis claim to believe in a more 'rational' world, yet the example they give Sarah is that women shouldn't be allowed to wear trousers. Rationally speaking, shouldn't they want *everyone* to wear trousers, rather than skirts (which are much less practical)? And how does this square with the feminist politics that Miss Winters insists on bringing up in episode one?

More critically, you have to wonder at Winters' masterplan. The SRS people steal the plans for the disintegrator gun, but just want to use it to open a safe. Even though Kettlewell must know that the robot grows when it absorbs energy, the SRS people never consider shooting the robot *themselves* before the bunker-siege, just to be on the safe side. And then they try to launch the hi-jacked nuclear missiles, believing they can start again in the ruins. Which means that like most TV viewers and writers in the '70s, these "scientists" have no idea what nuclear armageddon would actually do to the planet. (Admittedly, much of what we now know about Nuclear Winter was unknowable prior to Viking landing on Mars, although that's another story.)

But silliest of all, in episode three the startled members of the Society meet the robot for the first time and are horrified to see it moving in to kill Sarah. The scene is interrupted by the Doctor, who tells them that the armed forces are on the way. Faced with this double-whammy of terror and imminent threat, the ever-so-logical SRS types… laugh at the Doctor's funny little dance. To make matters worse, the guard whom the Doctor KO'd in order to get into the venue then turns out to be standing at the back of the hall looking non-plussed. You also have to question the logic of the villains keeping the disintegrator gun in the same part of the bunker where they keep their hostages.

Leaving aside the awfulness of the toy tank… when it moves in to attack, the Doctor already knows it won't stand a chance against the disintegrator-wielding robot. But instead of telling the Brigadier to call off the assault, he just lounges casually against a UNIT jeep, makes a smug comment and watches the slaughter, as if "UNIT Personnel Dying Painfully" has turned into a spectator sport for him. The UNIT troops themselves are hardly blameless, since in episode four an eight-foot-tall robot vanishes from under their noses in broad daylight and nobody spots it walking off. The "broad daylight" is hard enough to explain in itself, though, as all the exterior action scenes are supposed to take place *after* an evening meeting of the SRS. It's bright even for the middle of summer.

As ever in adventure TV, the Brigadier gets the report on the stolen disintegrator gun in the same scene that Sarah coincidentally asks him if she can visit the HQ of the people who've stolen it. And another standard of badly-thought-out SF: the disintegrator gun, which presumably reduces matter to its constituent atoms, is somehow "smart" enough to know that if it's pointed at a soldier then it's only supposed to disintegrate the man (and his clothing and weapons) but not touch the ground he's standing on or any of the other objects around him.

When the Doctor uses the metal virus to kill the robot, the virus is described as if it *only* attacks the robot's living metal, yet Kettlewell has already established that it can break down any metal. And the Doctor releases it in the middle of southern England, so let's hope it doesn't go airborne.

Even if they weren't expecting an eight-foot robot, it's questionable that a high-security components firm would hire the less-than-imposing John Scott Martin as chief guard.

Critique At last, Terrance gets to write an episode of *The Avengers* all by himself. Unfortunately it's 1974, not 1967, the era of *Detante* and eco-scares; the age of grim Cold War thrillers by John le

Carre, not of James Bond schmoozing around at Casino Royale. And he's got to fit the Doctor into the story somehow, so Harry is roped in to fail at being Steed, Sarah dresses in the then-fashionable *Great Gatsby* style to become part Fay Wray, part Lois Lane, while the Doctor and the robot are largely there as plot devices. In later ersatz-*Avengers* yarns, such as "The Seeds of Doom" (13.6), the look of the finished show disguises the intention. Here a highly-reflective robot against CSO yellow means that bits of the monster keep disappearing and the whole story seems disposable.

In a sense, it is. All *Doctor Who* requires the suspension of industrial-sized amounts of disbelief, but some just insult the intelligence. After the almost-hip, ever-contemporary feel of the early '70s stories, "Robot" looks, sounds and feels more like children's television than ever. A comedy eccentric scientist with comedy eccentric scientist hair has invented a giant robot and "magic" metal virus in (more or less) his own garage, and on top of that there's a subplot about a disintegrator gun that makes even less sense. Even the mention of Oedipus and the desperate inclusion of nuclear missiles can't make it feel any more grown-up.

But even if you can accept it as being for under-tens only, the *real* problem is that "Robot" has no sense of direction, and for obvious reasons. Writing the last story before Philip Hinchcliffe took over as producer, Dicks had little idea where the programme was going to go, and responded by putting together a "generic" *Doctor Who* story using the props of the series he knew best. The regulars are there to be… regular, a known, familiar backdrop, and accordingly the threat is domestic and containable. We're in a limbo between comic-book and classic serial. In the end we're left with some nice moments for Tom Baker, but a story that feels as if it's desperately playing for time until something better comes along.

The Facts

Written by Terrance Dicks. Directed by Christopher Barry. Viewing figures: 10.8 million, 10.7 million, 10.1 million, 9 million.

Supporting Cast Nicholas Courtney (Brigadier Lethbridge-Stewart), John Levene (Sergeant Benton), Patricia Maynard (Miss Winters), Michael Kilgarriff (Robot), Edward Burnham (Professor Kettlewell), Alec Linstead (Jellicoe).

Working Titles *"The* Robot".

Cliffhangers Sneaking into the secret labs of Think Tank, Sarah's confronted with the lumbering mass of the robot; the Doctor, after leading the robot a merry dance around Kettlewell's lab, finally falls to it; having disintegrated the tank, the robot turns to the camera and threatens to destroy us all if we don't go (good place to end an episode, although he's probably supposed to be talking to the soldiers rather than the audience).

The Lore

• The head honcho of BBC Drama (Serials), Bill Slater, had been a director and often made the pilot episodes of long-running dramas in the late 60s and early 70s. He'd already brought Lis Sladen to the attention of Barry Letts and - after some head-scratching as to who could possibly replace Pertwee - he alerted Letts to Tom Baker, whom he'd already directed and who knew his wife socially (yes, *everybody* sniggers when they hear that).

At that point Baker was to be seen in cinemas in *The Golden Voyage of Sinbad*. Whilst the stereotypical hunky hero of the film was of no use to man or beast (Patrick Wayne, son of John, and future star of dreadful European light entertainment fodder *The Monte Carlo Show*), Baker's performance as the villain was so striking that he very nearly stole the show from the film's real stars, i.e. Ray Harryhausen's animated monsters. Tom Baker had hitherto played Rasputin in *Nicholas and Alexander*, made the odd horror flick and been Macbeth for the National Theatre, but work dried up after *Sinbad* and he was making a living on a building site when the *Doctor Who* offer came.

• The desperation with which the outgoing producer tried to fill the starring role led to Letts contacting Jim Dale, former pop star and straightman in several *Carry On* films; and Richard Hearne, '50s kids' TV star, famous as "Mr. Pastry". (Dear God, how does one explain Mr. Pastry? Start by imagining a cross between Peter Cushing as "Doctor Who" and Rowan Atkinson as Mr. Bean... '50s audiences were so much less demanding.) For this reason, with an elderly Doctor a real possibility, they introduced young Harry Sullivan as beefcake should the Doctor be unable to defend himself.

If it's any indication of the kind of character

they had in mind, two near-misses were Graham Crowden (seen in 17.5, "The Horns of Nimon", although you're better off watching the BBC's *A Very Peculiar Practice* if you want to see what sort of Doctor he could have been) and Fulton McKay (seen in 7.2, "Doctor Who and the Silurians"). McKay was enthusiastic, but a sit-com pilot he'd made a year earlier went to series, so he turned down *Doctor Who* and became a household name as the chief prison warder in *Porridge* instead.

• Terrance Dicks insisted on writing this story, creating a spurious "tradition" in which the outgoing script editor always writes the first script of the new era (a tradition which actually held for the next change-over, 15.4, "The Sun Makers"). Dicks wrote the script as a deliberate homage to King Kong, which is why it's one of the few *Doctor Who* stories to feature an old-fashioned sympathetic monster.

• Barry Letts and Terrance Dicks moved from *Doctor Who* to the BBC Classic Serial treadmill after this, making stolid renditions of old books for export. Many of these used the outside broadcast cameras that were given their first drama work-out in "Robot", not the last time *Doctor Who* would be a test-bed for "proper" drama.

• The scene in which the Doctor admires his new nose ('a definite improvement') is another joke at the expense of Jon Pertwee, who was always obsessed with his own schnozzle and insisted on it being filmed from certain angles during his time as the Doctor.

• Episode three starts by reprising the entire 2'17" cliffhanger scene from the end of episode two, with the Doctor and the robot facing each other in Professor Kettlewell's lab. It's the longest straightforward reprise of the 1970s, and nobody in recent years has been able to sit through it without reaching for the fast-forward button.

• The first choice to play Jellicoe was the actor who'd played Paul Merroney - a prototype J. R. Ewing, if *Dallas* had been about a haulage company in the Midlands - from hit soap *The Brothers*: Colin Baker. (See 20.1, "Arc of Infinity", and much of Volume VI.)

• Stalwart composer Dudley Simpson accompanied the Doctor's brief appearance in Viking costume with a minor-key quote from Wagner's *Flying Dutchman* (see also 18.7, "Logopolis"). The heroic fanfare for the viral attack on the robot isn't from Wagner, but "Pop Goes The Weasel" made to sound like *Siegfried*.

• Contrary to popular belief, the Doctor's Pierrot costume probably isn't the one worn by David Bowie in the video for "Ashes to Ashes", nor is the King of Hearts outfit the one from "The Celestial Toymaker" (3.7).

• The now-traditional scene-shifters' dispute (see 17.6, "Shada", 20.5 "Enlightenment" and many others) meant that this story had to "loan" its studio to live twice-weekly iconic children's show *Blue Peter*... thrilling a generation with a "sneak preview" of the new Doctor's first adventure a good seven months before transmission.

• According to Baker's autobiography *Who On Earth is Tom Baker?* (an entertaining if unhelpful read), rehearsals for this story were enlivened by Michael Kilgarriff's extensive repertoire of music-hall songs. Baker suggested that the robot should offer a rendition of "Nelly Dean", the first of many suggestions made by the star and ignored by directors.

• Jelly babies, for non-British readers, are a gelatine fruit-flavoured sweet in the shape of... well... babies. Depending on whose account you believe, they were either invented in 1915 as a fund-raising gimmick for the war effort or invented in 1918 as a way of celebrating the war's end. US Food and Drug Administration rules meant that any attempts by American fans to get hold of these were impeded, as the red colouring was thought potentially carcinogenic. This was rescinded in 1986. Bassetts, the original manufacturers, were keen to associate their products with a hit series but later got litigious over the Kandyman in "The Happiness Patrol" (25.2).

12.2: "The Ark in Space"

(Serial 4C, Four Episodes, 25th January - 15th February 1975.)

Which One is This? The whole of humanity's been put into deep-freeze, but big green wasp-faced insects have got into the system and now they're laying eggs. They're called "Wirrn", and every UK citizen over the age of thirty-five knows what happened next...

Firsts and Lasts The "new" era of *Doctor Who* arrives, with Philip Hinchcliffe taking over as producer and Robert Holmes getting a regular job as script editor. The difference is immediately obvious. After five years of psychedelic UNIT stories and political satires in outer space, the Doctor

suddenly gets dragged into a future where things are "nasty" rather than "groovy". Here we also see the first appearance of the Nerva space station, which will pop up again at the end of this season as part of what we might now call a "story arc", but you can judge for yourself whether it's a clever narrative device or a way of cutting costs by re-using old sets.

First use of the word "transmat"; first sign of the Doctor actively playing cricket; first story to be designed by the indefatigable Roger Murray-Leach; and the first (and last) time they try re-colouring the title sequence. (As with the Radiophonic Workshop of the day, it was the mandate of Visual Effects to constantly mess about with the technology.) It's also the first use of Dudley Simpson's catchy and endlessly disguisable "Fourth Doctor" *leitmotif*.

Four Things to Notice About "The Ark in Space"...

1. The word usually used to describe the Hinchcliffe era of the programme is "gothic", and it's a word that fits "The Ark in Space" peculiarly well, even though there are very few dark, dungeon-like places and an awful lot of shiny white space-station corridors. A tale of parasitic body-horror for tea-time television, it ushers in an age when the National Viewers' and Listeners' Association considered *Doctor Who* to be a prime target. The series may have covered people in green slime and mutated their bodies before, but it never had giant insects laying their eggs inside human beings. Watch out, in particular, for the scene in which Commander Noah wrestles with his alien-infected "evil" hand and it's treated as if it were a moment of horrific psychological intensity.

2. Indeed in many ways there's something very *old-fashioned* about this story, even apart from the '60s-style space-station setting. Like "The Daleks" (1.2) back in 1963, the whole of the first episode involves the Doctor and company wandering around a strange, deserted space-environment, as the frozen humans on the station don't start waking up until episode two and the first monster we see is a shrivelled corpse inside a cupboard. This means we get twenty-five minutes of the TARDIS crew being threatened by sliding doors, automatic laser-beams, faulty life-support systems and recorded messages from dead politicians.

3. The outer corridor of the Nerva station, a curved white passageway with "holes" in the side so that you can see the stars through the gaps between the beams, is *the* definitive outer-space

set of the 1970s. Sadly, the exterior shots of the station demonstrate the kind of effects work that people always insist on remembering when they think of *Doctor Who*, in the "squeegee-bottle model hovering next to a photo of Earth" mould. This month's worst special effect, though: the shot of an army of Wirrn crawling across the exterior of the spaceship, filmed using a clutch of small rubber Wirrn models and some wire.

4. Alert viewers will notice that the basic premise of "The Ark in Space" - in which a claustrophobic space-facility, full of humans in suspended animation, is infiltrated by an alien that plants its spawn inside a human host-body - is pleasingly similar to the plot of *Alien*. Many, many people have commented on this, especially since "The Ark in Space" was first released on video in 1989, but nobody's dared to suggest a causal link (consider **Where Does This Come From?**). Even if *Alien* writer Dan O'Bannon was a notorious geek, and director Ridley Scott had a known connection to *Doctor Who* (see 1.2, "The Daleks", again).

The Continuity

The Doctor The Doctor describes humans as his 'favourite species', and at one stage even gives a stirring laudatory speech on the indomitability of humankind. [This from a version of the Doctor who shows no real attachment to Earth and a constant impatience with its inhabitants. The suggestion here might be that although humans may be the Doctor's favourites, he sees them as interesting animal specimens rather than friends. This is a story all about individuality vs. animal survival, so it makes sense for the Doctor to regard humanity as a very large and interesting ant colony.] Harry, in particular, seems to bring out his patronising side. He's able to trick Sarah into making a grand final effort by feigning annoyance at the way her "pluck" gets her into situations she can't handle, and grins broadly when she falls for it.

The Doctor seems to be genuinely afraid of what the Wirrn represent, pondering that he and the humans have 'no chance at all', but it doesn't slow him down. Indeed, he often takes a positive delight in almost-certain-death situations. Nonetheless...

• *Ethics.* ...the still-new Doctor claims a moral motive here, believing he has to stop the Wirrn consuming the human race out of a sense of decency. Ultimately he's even prepared to give his life to save the future of the species. [He takes an *awful* lot of risks in this story, and attempts to sacrifice himself far more readily than usual. The regeneration may still be affecting his sense of balance.]

• *Inventory.* He's carrying a cricket ball here, though it gets blasted to pieces. He uses his yo-yo to test local gravity, and has a little metal rod that's ideal for poking around in giant insect membrane. The random piece of metal he picks up on the station may come in handy later on [it saves him in the next story, "The Sontaran Experiment"].

• *Background.* The Doctor claims his scarf was knitted for him by 'Madame Nostradamus... a witty little knitter'. [The obvious implication is that he's talking about the wife of Michel de Nostradame, who's now best-known as a prophet but was also a successful (and quite forward-thinking) doctor, so he's typical of one of the Doctor's historical "friends". Nostradamus was married twice, and next to nothing is known about his first wife. His second would have been around in the 1550s, when Nostradamus began recording his prophecies, so it's tempting to imagine that he picked up some fore-knowledge from the Doctor and got his missus to knit a scarf as a thankyou present.]

The Doctor states that his doctorate is 'purely honorary' [see **Is He Really a Doctor?** under 13.6, "The Seeds of Doom"].

The Supporting Cast

• *Sarah Jane Smith.* Hates brandy. She's having another "soppy" day, panicking for much of the time and blubbering when trapped in ventilator shafts [but then, she's in shock after being cryogenically frozen by mistake]. However, she comes up with all the bright ideas while the Doctor's faffing about with bits of wire and gypsy lore. The trick played on her when she gets stuck in the shaft is the first sign that she's able to engage in bluff and counter-bluff with this Doctor. [Which is how she finally leaves him in 14.2, "The Hand of Fear". This is the Sarah we all remember, coming through after the tom-boy guerrilla antics of Season Eleven.]

• *Harry Sullivan.* Refers to himself as Surgeon-Lieutenant Harry Sullivan. Here Harry's not only old-fashioned and prone to talk about 'the fairer sex', but also clumsy, fiddling about with equipment that doesn't concern him and generally getting on people's nerves. That said, he doesn't

Why Couldn't They Just Have Spent More Money?

We're always having to comment on cost-cutting measures. You'll notice, as this volume unfolds, that financial constraints force increasingly desperate and ingenious measures on the production team. Of course, there were always problems with both time and budget. In 1964, the series very nearly got cancelled in its first season due to an accounting error involving the TARDIS console. And by the late '80s it was resorting to such desperate "guerrilla TV" tactics that when "Remembrance of the Daleks" (25.1) required the filming of a 1960s street scene, the programme-makers set up the cameras on a suitable street, stuck a fake '60s number-plate on a car that happened to be in the way, then hurriedly filmed the scene and ran away again before the vehicle's owner turned up.

Many apparently odd choices and decisions, especially in the '70s, were purely fiscal. The obvious question for younger or foreign readers is the one in this essay's title, especially now that the 2005 re-make of *Doctor Who* is on its way with a budget rumoured to be in the millions. (Though at the time of going to press, none of the rumours can decide whether it's meant to have a budget of millions per episode, millions per series or millions to pay the new Doctor, Christopher Eccleston.)

Why couldn't they just have spent more money? There are two reasons, both a bit complicated.

As we mentioned in Volume III, *Doctor Who* is often thought of as a children's programme but was actually the result of the Drama department of the BBC attempting to reach as wide an audience as possible. Every single episode came out of the Drama budget, an overall proportion of the BBC licence fee. Into that budget went all the revenue from overseas sales and spin-off merchandise (see **Why Was There So Much Merchandising?** under 11.5, "The Monster of Peladon"). In the mid-'70s the BBC was doing very well out of selling prestige series overseas, especially the costume dramas, which the British public lapped up as well. Many popular and long-running programmes began in this period, some of them requiring enormous capital outlay that was defrayed over several years. (*The Onedin Line*, for example, required two reconditioned Victorian sailing ships and location work in mock-ups of Liverpool circa 1860 in every episode... "The Mark of the Rani" is just a set full of cobblestones by comparison.)

The BBC could have decided to delay a new series of hardy perennial *Doctor Who* while setting up these programmes, as it eventually did in 1985, but the popularity of the series with both the public and the BBC hierarchy - who didn't care what the show did, as long as a large and varied demographic thought that no-one else was doing it better - made this inconceivable. The Corporation could shove it around the schedules to maximise its effect, but the idea of *not* making one series a year would have seemed un-BBC-like. So in any given year the budgetary constraints would have been considerable, although as all BBC dramas were made in-house, the recycling of props and sets was widespread. Especially if the same designer was involved in more than one programme.

However, there was another problem for mid-'70s budgets. Inflation.

The numbers speak for themselves. The inflation rate in 1967 was 2.5%. This is what we're used to now. That summer, as the full extent of the economic downturn became apparent, the British government was forced to decide whether or not to decouple the value of the pound from the Gold Standard. Once it did, inflation almost doubled. 4.7% in 1968, 5.4% the following year. The effects on the *Doctor Who* budget are plain to see. (And if you've not noticed, they had to make fewer stories per year, hence baggy eight- or ten-parters cropping up in Season Six.) When Britain got rid of those quaint old shillings and went decimal in 1970 - something which involved much rounding-up of prices, and which in some cases saw unscrupulous traders changing "d" to "p" and tripling some basic costs - things got vastly worse. 1971 saw 9.4% inflation. By the time "Ark in Space" was being made, the figure was 16.6%. Small wonder that the Nerva Beacon turns up in two stories in Season Twelve, that big props like the transmat spheres end up being shunted from Earth to Voga, or that "Revenge of the Cybermen" (12.5) didn't bother re-building the Cybermen for the '70s as Barry Letts had planned to do just two years earlier.

The following year saw a record: 24.2% inflation. Just ponder this for a moment. Something costing £5 in 1974 cost over £6 in 1975. Something costing £100 (like a Cyberman helmet) was now £125. The Chancellor of the Exchequer, cuddly badger-faced show-off Dennis Healey, had to confront the Trades Unions - who were the main contributors

continued on page 21...

respond to the "alien" world around him too badly, instantly believing that he's travelled through space and time and positively enjoying his trip through a matter transmitter.

Harry believes himself to be a good bowler. He once caught his nose in a sliding door in Pompey [Portsmouth] barracks. Here he's carrying rudimentary medical equipment on his person.

The TARDIS There's brandy somewhere in the Ship, and cold-weather coats for everyone, plus a woolly hat for Sarah [and the oil-lamp from 11.3, "Death to the Daleks"]. The Doctor is originally planning to take the TARDIS to the moon, but Harry sends it off-course by twisting the helmic regulator. At the end of the story, the Doctor uses the space station's matter transmitter to go down to Earth and make sure it's suitable for life. [So perhaps he's still not *wholly* confident about steering the TARDIS, or maybe Harry has messed things up worse than the Doctor is letting on.]

The Non-Humans
• *Wirrn*. Insect-like creatures larger than human beings, the Wirrn resemble wasps, but with green carapaces and no wings. They have six legs, and appear to shuffle along on their abdomens [q.v. Alpha Centauri in "The Curse of Peladon", 9.1]. The Wirrn - the name seems to be both singular and plural - come from Andromeda, where they used to feed on unintelligent herbivores.

Then the humans arrived. The result was a war which ostensibly lasted a thousand years, but the humans eventually destroyed the breeding-colonies and the Wirrn were driven out of the galaxy. They've been drifting through space, searching for a new habitat, ever since. Now they want to consume humanity and take its knowledge, becoming a technological civilisation in one generation. [It's possible, then, that the Wirrn weren't even sentient before the humans came. They may only have learned this sort of ambition after eating the "forbidden fruit" of human knowledge. Nonetheless, the technicians on the Nerva station seem to be the first technologically-educated humans they've tasted. Incidentally, "Andromeda" would seem to reference the Andromeda galaxy rather than the constellation of Andromeda, judging by the way both Vira and Wirrn-Noah talk about it.]

The Wirrn life-cycle is difficult to follow. Here a Wirrn 'queen-coloniser' drifts through space towards the Nerva station and lays an egg inside one of the technicians, then gets killed by the station's autoguard. When the egg hatches, the young Wirrn consumes its host from the inside and becomes a slug-like green blob so gelatinous that it can initially ooze itself through a grille, leaving a slimy trail wherever it goes. It's also powerful enough to bend hardened metal. Having 'digested' the host's knowledge, the Wirrn leaves more young in the station's solar stacks to absorb solar radiation until they're ready to hatch. [This is a little confusing. The larva can't be ready to lay eggs of its own, so maybe it just takes other eggs laid by the queen to a ready energy-source.]

After the larval stage comes the pupal stage, in which the Wirrn are dormant in cocoons and don't require oxygen. It doesn't take more than hours for the creatures to reach their adult form, and the Doctor expects a hundred in a hatching [although they all crowd onto the transport ship at the end of the story, and it doesn't look *that* big, so he may be sorely mistaken]. Fortunately they're susceptible to electricity, but the queen survives for some minutes even after taking half a million volts. Fission guns just sting them.

When Commander Noah is touched by green slime straight from the larva's body, he loses consciousness and is "possessed" by the Wirrn. When he recovers he begins a slow transformation into one of the adult creatures. This means he has the race-memory of a Wirrn, 'symbiotic atavism, to be precise'. One of the humans newly-recovered from suspended animation "sees" Noah as a Wirrn during the possession. Strangely, it's Noah who eventually becomes swarm-leader rather than the larva which infected him. He can communicate in human-voice even after he appears to be an adult Wirrn, and retains some human instincts. The Wirrn mass-mind would seem to retain both the knowledge and personality of anyone who's been consumed / possessed.

A Wirrn's lungs recycle waste, 'almost certainly' by enzymes. Carbon dioxide is turned into oxygen, as with plants, so they can go for years without a fresh supply. From this the Doctor concludes that they must live in space, occasionally visiting a planetary atmosphere for food and air, and Noah states that their breeding colonies are terrestrial. They communicate with each other by squeaking. [The fact that they're said to have lived

Why Couldn't They Just Have Spent More Money?

...continued from page 19

to Labour Party funds - and request restraint in demands for wage rises. Imagine how well that went down. In return for removing 2.5 billion pounds from public spending (i.e. sacking teachers, doctors, civil servants and treasury staff, closing departments and generally making everyone still in a job do two people's work... hence 15.4, "The Sun Makers"), Healey was assured a three-billion pound loan from the International Monetary Fund, which had been set up after the Second World War to bail out Third World nations. Imagine how well *that* went down.

The blow to national pride was not as great as some expected. We were getting used to not being Imperial / important any more, and the odd thing was that we felt as if this were another test of our mettle, like the Blitz. Whenever we felt bad about ourselves we'd just look across the Atlantic and laugh at Watergate, Vietnam and *Star Trek: The Animated Series*. The only nations really doing well - aside from the Arab oil-producing states, whom we didn't really envy - were Japan and Germany.

The irony wasn't lost on us. This is, incidentally, why the multi-millionaire technologist in "Image of the Fendahl" (15.3) has a German accent and is said to be on a par with the Japanese when it comes to hi-tech research."

---

on a specific herbivore species - plus Noah's reference to the Wirrn's 'old lands' rather than 'old solar systems' - might indicate they were confined to a single planet before the humans came, and only adapted themselves for a space-going lifestyle during the alleged centuries of conflict. The Wirrn briefly appear again, in "The Stones of Blood" (16.3), once more demonstrating the finely-honed ability to die in cupboards.]

History

• *Dating*. The far future. [15000 AD, at the earliest. It's been 10,000 years since the solar flares made Earth uninhabitable, and other stories indicate that Earth is occupied until at least 5000 AD. See 14.6, "The Talons of Weng-Chiang" and arguably 5.3, "The Ice Warriors". Then again, nobody from this era definitively states that it's been 10,000 years; it's the Doctor's estimate, so it could have been *far* longer. See also 23.1, "The Mysterious Planet".]

According to the Doctor, the Nerva station was built in the late twenty-ninth or early thirtieth century [we see a newer version of it in 12.5, "Revenge of the Cybermen"]. Despite being impressed by some of the technology, he regards it as an 'early' space vessel.

But 10,000 years ago, solar flares supposedly destroyed all life on Earth. There were 'thermic shelters', though nobody seems to have been expecting them to offer much protection. At least several hundred inhabitants volunteered to go into suspended animation on Nerva, along with animal and botanic specimens, and the whole of human culture was stored on what the Doctor calls 'microfilm'. [He's simplifying for Harry's benefit, surely? For more on this era see 12.3, "The Sontaran Experiment".] Scientists calculated that it'd take 5,000 years for the planet to become habitable again, but the sabotage of the Wirrn caused the Nerva people to oversleep.

[Note that the Doctor acts as if the solar flares took place shortly after the station was built, c. 2900 AD, and describes the 'compartmentalised' human society we see here as being thirtieth-century society. Which it isn't, judging by later events. The script was clearly written to suggest that the station was reasonably new at the time of the catastrophe, but this contradicts so many other stories - including this story's companion-piece, "Revenge of the Cybermen" (12.5) - that it's best ignored as a mistake on the Doctor's part. It's said that there were 'millions' of people on Earth when the hibernation began, not 'billions', which might suggest a badly-damaged planet even *before* the flares.]

At the time when the humans went into suspended animation, the High Minister of the World Executive was female. She doesn't seem to be among those put into "cold storage", however. Nerva has its own 'prime unit' as leader and should apparently have a council once it's been revived. The people from this period have a strictly regimented, painfully logical and decidedly anal society, the project's leaders having little understanding of humour. On the other hand, Rogin - one of the first technicians to be defrosted - is a wise-cracking complainer. [People may be divided into different classes, with the technical types retaining more of their individual characteristics.

ABOUT TIME 1975-1979

This would be quite typical of a society designed by Robert Holmes…] Rogin also seems to suggest that there's a space technician's union.

The station is maintained by automatic systems, including an 'autoguard' that can fry intruders and blow up cricket balls with a burst of half a million volts. Technology set into the walls of the station includes a macro-slave drive and a modified Bennett oscillator [note the director's name]. The station's fitted out with matter transmitters, and there's a transport ship with four granovox turbines which generate twice the power of the "Ark" itself. The preparatory procedure for the suspended animation process involves a tranquilo-couch and 'bio-cryonic vibrations', and the Doctor says he's never seen cryogenics applied on this scale before. Medical science allows a recovering individual's electrical field to draw power from the 'bionosphere' of the suspended animation palettes, but there's a risk of lung tissue atrophying over time.

Solar stacks supply power to the station, and one of the computers contains a 'neural cortex amplifier' that allows the Doctor to display Wirrn memories on the screen when he hooks up part of the creature's eye and boosts it with his own brain. The staff are equipped with stun-guns, which can apparently be set to kill, but there are more powerful fission guns in the armoury. Today's super-tough space-construction metal: case-hardened dyranium.

The people in this era still seem to use "our" alphabet and numbering system. Medical staff are known as medtechs, while the non-conformist Doctor is seen as a 'romantic', a 'dawn-timer' and a 'regressive', and is assumed to be from the colonies. Noah states that there was a regressive faction among the volunteers for Colony Nine [another attempt at surviving the solar flares?], but it wasn't expected to last more than a generation. Vira believes 'the star pioneers succeeded' when she hears that the humans met the Wirrn in Andromeda. [This suggests that intergalactic travel was developed just before humanity went into suspended animation, and that Earth wasn't sure of the results. The human war with the Wirrn must have occurred while the Earth-people were sleeping.]

Harry is surprised that a woman is 'top of the totem pole' in the future, hinting that the Prime Minister's still a man in his own time [see 13.1, "Terror of the Zygons"].

The Analysis

Where Does This Come From? If you want to understand the western world in the '70s, then start with the horror. The generation that had grown up in the '50s had seen every threat as having an external cause, and with good reason. These were the children of the War Years, the ones who'd been raised in a culture of alien infiltrators and communist Martians, and much has already been said on this subject in Volume III.

But the generation growing up in the '70s didn't believe in the same kind of enemy. It's tempting (and a bit glib) to say that without any definite, external threat, the west started to turn in on itself, but there was a change in the nature of "popular fear". By the late '70s, more people were afraid of cancer than invasions. This is especially obvious in the American movies of that era, and not just the horror ones. The affluent middle classes of New York and Los Angeles were becoming obsessed with their own bodies, treating every fat-cell as if it were a hostile organism eating them up from the inside. *Alien* (1979) is the ultimate expression of this, but it's there even in a film like *Marathon Man* (1976), in which the villain is a Nazi dentist and the hero only survives because he's an experienced jogger.

But our bodies and our societies always reflect each other. '70s horror is about civilisation consuming itself, as well as things chewing their way through our stomachs. *Rosemary's Baby, The Stepford Wives* and later the re-make of *Invasion of the Body Snatchers* (the perfect example, since it replaced the communist aliens of the original with aliens who pose as psychoanalysts and *then* do hideous things with your flesh) gave audiences a kind of fright-pic that was more visceral and inward-looking. When something bad happens, anyone - no matter how smart or moral - is a piece of meat. *Jaws* and *The Texas Chainsaw Massacre* took millions at the box-office that year, so by making the victims of a space monster as vulnerable as possible and then raising the stakes to the entire future of humanity, "The Ark in Space" taps the public mood in a very *Doctor Who* way.

Yet it's not purely guts and gore. The theft of identity, always the Big Evil whether it takes the form of brainwashing (as in *The Manchurian Candidate*… see 14.3, "The Deadly Assassin") or possession (The Exorcist, released in 1973, set the standard for possessions throughout Hinchcliffe's term as producer), is made gruesome as well. Indeed, it's interesting that the *Doctor Who* monsters who'd tapped into this fear in the 1960s - the Cybermen - were turned into tin-plated bogeymen for "Revenge of the Cybermen" (12.5) to avoid clouding the issue. As has been noted, both the Wirrn and the '60s Cybermen can lay claim to being precursors of the greatest *Doctor Who* monsters in history, the Borg from *Star Trek: The Next Generation*.

In one of the classic examples of the "catchiness" of an idea outweighing the question of whether it stood up to examination, around this time everyone grabbed hold of J. McConnell's 1962 paper *Memory Transfer Through Cannibalism in Planarians* as proof that memory was mainly chemical, and to be found in ribonucleotides. "Everyone", in this case, doesn't just mean neuropsychologists but headline-writers in tabloids, junior-school teachers and TV hacks trying to fill four episodes at short notice.

McConnell's experiment was easy to understand: you teach worms how to get through a maze, grind them up into a pulp, feed baby worms on the puree and *voila*, the babies get the maze right first time. This was to biology and psychology what black holes were to physics. Even now, you'll hear it trotted out every so often, even though it no longer fits the rest of what appears to be happening in the brain and nobody - even McConnell - ever got worms to do it again.

Although the story's ending was a last-minute improvisation, apparently by director Rodney Bennett, the debts to *Quatermass* - in this case *The Quatermass Experiment* - aren't confined to this *deus ex machina*. The scene in which the Doctor projects the thoughts of the (dead) Wirrn onto a TV screen is, like the similar scene in "Planet of the Spiders" (11.5), a direct lift from *Quatermass and the Pit*. Funny how this old favourite always turns up when there are intelligent bug-monsters around.

However, *The Fly* is a far bigger "source" for visual elements, although in this case the matter-transmitter and the man-turning-into-insect are kept apart (in earlier drafts of the script this may not have been the case… consider the line about Sarah in suspended animation, 'her body's become a battlefield'). The big twist, insects laying eggs in people and absorbing their technology, is familiar to SF buffs from the 1943 book *The Voyage of the Space Beagle* by A. E. Van Vogt. But Robert Holmes, under time pressure, simply got

the BBC reference library to look up disgusting insect behaviour to replace the Delc. (Who're the Delc? Well, John Lucarotti's original storyline for "The Ark in Space" featured a spacefaring fungus infesting the Ark, which the Doctor dispatched with a golf-club. See **The Lore** for more.)

The Robert Holmes standards on offer here also deserve a mention. Society is humourless, compartmentalised and bureaucractic - at least until the Doctor turns up and gives Vira some jelly-babies - and though this time no "official" class-divide exists between the station's commanders and the mouthy technician Rogin. We've clearly got the same sort of civilisation we saw in "Carnival of Monsters" (10.2), the rulers having difficulty with the word "joke" while the workers grumble discontentedly. Some of the visuals are familiar, too. The Wirrn drops its spawn inside one of the station's solar stacks, meaning that we get to see their hideous one-eyed young squirming against the display-screen, the same "splatter on the glass" effect as the Nestene/s in "Spearhead from Space" (7.1). The "table used as defensive barrier against laser-beams" will be turning up again in "The Talons of Weng-Chiang" (14.6).

Things That Don't Make Sense Commander Noah (pre-Wirrn possession) spends much of episode two accusing the Doctor of being the station's saboteur and refusing to listen to his story about an alien intruder, apparently blotting out the whacking great Wirrn corpse that's lying on the floor when he first comes out of cryogenic storage. Also in episode two, the Doctor takes one look at the aforementioned corpse and instantly notices that the egg-tube is empty, whereas the *first* time he took one look at it he immediately started referring to it as a "he" [do Wirrn only have one sex?].

It's only a significant problem later, but if the Wirrn absorb knowledge from touching and eating people, and if they can live in space, convert other species, ingest other species and lay thousands upon thousands of intelligent babies… then why are there any other life-forms left? When it turns out that at least one has been in our neck of the woods for four-thousand years (16.3, "The Stones of Blood"), you have to wonder why we've never seen them before. They ought to be as universal as Starbucks and McDonalds. And if they float about in space, find a planet to land on and lay eggs, then how do they get off again? [As we saw in Volume III, Robert Holmes' scripts are full

ABOUT TIME 1975-1979

of references to funny smells and released gases. The Wirrn method of space-propulsion doesn't bear thinking about.]

Another snag, with hindsight. Vira's waiting for the Doctor to report back from Earth to tell her that the transmat's fixed. He never does.

Critique   And so, after five years of "The Adventures of UNIT", *Doctor Who* returns to our screens. There was a genuine frisson about this one at the time, a sense that things were back on track (never mind that the series had never been *quite* like this, this was how everyone remembered it from the days when it had been "scary").

It wasn't action-TV any longer, and nor was it aimed squarely at the boys. For a generation, this is what *Doctor Who* is like, in the same way that - for better or worse - "The Web Planet", "Tomb of the Cybermen" and "Mindwarp" all represent their own eras. Unlike its younger cousin, *Alien*, the horror here is all conceptual but not too abstract for the kiddies. The set is enough like a hospital for green goo to be shocking by its very presence. For a child, the worst thing imaginable is being separated, cut off from the familiar world; it's only an "adventure" if you can get home easily, but isolation and not-being-listened-to by authority figures are the source of a lot of deep-rooted anxieties, ones which all adults can remember. The Doctor and Harry are judged by what the locals think they must be, a situation repeated in episode one of "Genesis of the Daleks" and in almost all other Holmes stories. This is the real terror of bureaucracy, that you're treated as being guilty of something you don't understand. When you talk about it this way it's hard not to see Robert Holmes as a day-glo, sugar-coated Franz Kafka, so a man turning into a bug in this story is entirely natural.

What impresses anyone who's watched all the Pertwee stories back-to-back before this (as the British Public had) is the conviction with which it's played. Compare Sarah waking up from suspended animation on a spaceship in "Invasion of the Dinosaurs" (11.2) with the way it happens here. The doors don't make *Star Trek* shwooshing noises and there are no condescending, muesli-eating drop-outs to welcome her. When she gets caught up in the machinery, it's like the "termination" suite from *Soylent Green*, light-classical music and all. Director Rodney Bennett's background is in "serious" drama, and here he casts

theatrical actors for maximum effect (only Richardson Morgan, as Rogin, had a speaking part in the programme before… as a soldier in 5.5, "The Web of Fear"). Tom Baker hasn't quite settled into the role yet, and doesn't sound *entirely* confident when he's doing the geeky outer-space material, but it's here that he starts to set out his stall.

Ironically, if anything it's this grand push towards drama that gives the story its biggest noticeable flaw: the supporting cast are 100% serious about this, and occasionally look as if they want to ask "but what's my *motivation* for turning into a human wasp-larva?", yet Holmes' script cares more about the lurking, squirming themes of the story than the way the characters and the plot-points fit together. The writer's grasp of what directors can do is so sure that he pretty much lets Bennett rewrite the last episode to make more sense, which is fine when it comes to setting the tone of the new era, but it's fairly clear that nobody's thought through the details.

This is as much a statement of intent as a self-contained story, though. Quite simply, if this one doesn't press most of the right buttons then go away and watch some other series.

The Facts

Written by Robert Holmes, from a story by John Lucarotti (uncredited). Directed by Rodney Bennett. Viewing figures: 9.4 million, 13.6 million, 11.2 million, 10.2 million. Episode two's 13.6 million outperformed the previous record-holder (episode one of "The Web Planet"). Even that summer's compilation repeat of "The Ark in Space" got 8.2 million, during one of the hottest Augusts on record.

Supporting Cast   Wendy Williams (Vira), Kenton Moore (Noah), Christopher Master (Libri), Richardson Morgan (Rogin), John Gregg (Lycett), Gladys Spencer, Peter Tuddenham (Voices).

Working Titles   In John Lucarotti's original storyline, individual episodes had titles: "Puffball", "Golfball" and so on. Yes, exactly.

Cliffhangers   Harry opens up a cupboard on the space station, and a Wirrn topples out at him; once he's alone in the control room, Commander Noah removes his hand from his pocket, and even *he's* disgusted to see that it's turned into a slimy green pseudopod; at the solar stacks the Doctor's confronted by Noah, now almost entirely transformed into a full-grown Wirrn.

The Lore

• They had a cunning plan. Christopher Langley had submitted a script called "The Space Station". Gerry Davis had sent in "Return of the Cybermen" (see 12.5), and specified one big lavish set rather than lots of little ones. They seemed to merge conveniently around a single location, so budgets were allocated for these two stories and all the others that year up to "The Loch Ness Monster" (later to become 13.1, "Terror of the Zygons").

Then "The Space Station" turned out to be unfilmable - no-one's quite sure why - and John Lucarotti, stalwart writer from the Hartnell years who'd been in touch via Letts and Dicks and their *Moonbase 3* series, got the gig. But Lucarotti had moved to a boat in the Mediterranean, and started sending scripts back to Britain that were written in the style of Season Three and had individual episode titles. His story seems to have been very much like the "King of the Moon" scenes from Terry Gilliam's *Baron Munchhausen*, with disembodied superminds floating around the place and fungal bodies (named the Delc) infesting a "survival pod" the size of Kent. This all got into a fairly cerebral tangle, too talky and too complex for children who hadn't read Descartes, so Robert Holmes reined it in using the same basic premise and a lot of B-movie iconography. Lucarotti was later given an ex gratia payment, but Holmes was permitted to use his own name on the credits as so much had been altered.

• Ultimately the story was filmed after "The Sontaran Experiment" and back-to-back with "Revenge of the Cybermen", in order to offset costs and give a much more "serial" flavour to the season. Designer Roger Murray-Leach gave the illusion of a far larger set by careful use of mirrors and remounts of small set-sections.

• Holmes' script stated that Vira was Haitian, suggesting that the "zombie" element of the story was more prominent before director Rodney Bennett took over.

• There's an obvious edit in episode three, a missing scene in which the nearly-transformed Noah begs Vira to kill him. In rehearsal it was in keeping with the mood of the story, but when Philip Hinchcliffe and BBC Drama (Serials) head

Bill Slater saw it in the edit-suite it was deemed too "strong" for family viewing and clumsily cut. (The characters later refer back to a line that's not in the broadcast version.) Future writer / script editor Eric Saward eventually pinched the idea for "Revelation of the Daleks" (22.6).

12.3: "The Sontaran Experiment"

(Serial 4B, Two Episodes, 22nd February - 1st March 1975.)

Which One is This? It's the one that comes after "The Ark in Space". Post-apocalyptic Earth turns out to look like a green and pleasant land, where South African colonists roll their "R"s and Commander Linx of the Sontaran Army Space Corps makes a surprise return. Or so it seems. But all Sontarans look alike to us...

Firsts and Lasts First two-part *Doctor Who* story since 1965, and arguably the first to be made as an actual story. "The Edge of Destruction" (1.3) was a last-minute stop-gap, and "The Rescue" (2.3) was a way of introducing a character more than a stand-alone tale (expect more of this sort of thing from 2005...), but "The Sontaran Experiment" goes the whole hog and has the Doctor save the world from aliens in under fifty minutes. It's also the first story to be filmed entirely on location with video cameras, and features no studio work at all.

For the first time in the series' history, the Doctor gets to this week's guest planet - actually Earth in the far future - by means other than the TARDIS.

Two Things to Notice
About "The Sontaran Experiment"...

1. Making their second appearance in the series after their barnstorming success in "The Time Warrior" (11.1), here the Sontarans make an effort to become the New Daleks. How do we know they're a major monster? Simple: Sontaran Field Major Styre makes a "surprise" cliffhanger appearance at the end of episode one, even though the name of his species - assuming anyone remembered it, at the time - is proudly displayed in the story's title. (The cliffhanger is pretty much a carbon-copy of the first episode of "The Time Warrior", with Styre taking off his helmet and

revealing the gargoyle-face underneath.) And since this story is only two episodes long, Styre has to squeeze all his villainy into twenty-five minutes.

2. Those who miss the good old days of *Doctor Who* during the Jon Pertwee run, when every major fight scene would see the Doctor played by stuntman Terry Walsh in a Pertwee wig, will be delighted by the duel between the Doctor and Styre in episode two. It's the first time Walsh gets to pretend to be Tom Baker, and the new wig proudly announces its presence whenever it's in shot. Styre also looks as if he's been replaced by an unconvincing stunt double - who else but Stuart Fell? - as the Sontaran's entire head wobbles during combat. Not bad for a species with no necks. (See 22.4, "The Two Doctors", for more on what lies beneath a Sontaran's collar.)

The Continuity

The Doctor

• *Ethics.* When Styre mentally tortures Sarah, the Doctor becomes angry in a way that's rarely been seen before, instinctively lunging at the Sontaran as well as insulting him. [If Styre had done the same thing to a complete stranger then the Doctor might just have given him a good talking-to. So the Doctor's standards change when there's a personal stake involved, just like everybody else's do.]

• *Inventory.* In addition to its standard uses - fixing matter transmitters, deactivating force-fields, opening spaceship doors, etc. - one signal from the sonic screwdriver is enough to make a Sontaran robot collapse in a heap.

• *Background.* The Doctor believes that his Five-Hundred Year Diary [not mentioned since 5.6, "Fury From The Deep"] contains notes on Sontarans [see 11.1, "The Time Warrior", for more on the Doctor's previous encounters with the species].

The Non-Humans

• *Sontarans.* In this era Earth's galaxy is of tactical importance to the Sontarans, whose invasion fleet is planning to attack. [Earth had no value at the time of "The Time Warrior". But note that the whole *galaxy* is of interest, not the deserted Earth itself. Meaning that the Sontarans don't come from this galaxy.]

Field Major Styre, of the Sontaran G3 Military Assessment Survey, has come to Earth on the orders of the Grand Strategic Council. The Sontarans expected the planet to be abandoned, so Styre had orders to lure some humans to the site and use torture to test their reactions to physical stress. Sontarans now know enough about humans to realise there are two sexes, but have only just figured out that they all need food. Styre tires himself out rapidly in Earth's gravity. ["The Time Warrior" establishes that the gravity is vastly greater on the Sontaran homeworld. Ask any cosmonaut and you'll hear how low gravity makes the heart - and other organs - contract.]

Styre has a pod-like spacecraft identical to that of Commander Linx [11.1, again], and owns a large, chunky, non-humanoid servitor robot which captures humans with its lasso-extensions. The robot has a terrulian drive, and a 'terrulian diode bypass transformer' is part of a Sontaran's recharging process, allowing Sontarans to feed on 'pure energy'. When Styre tries to recharge himself after the transformer's been removed, the energy feeds on him instead; he shrivels away into a floppy husk, and his ship explodes. There's no tellurian in Earth's galaxy at all, it seems.

Styre's weapon looks like a standard ray-gun, not the wand-weapon seen before. He uses force-fields, and attaches a small device to Sarah's forehead which can cause hallucinations to generate fear. Styre vaporised an entire Galsec ship when it arrived, so the Sontaran ship must be well-armed. As with Linx, there's only *one* Sontaran here, even though they're clones and there are supposedly billions of them.

Styre communicates with one of his superiors, a Marshal, who isn't a member of the Grand Strategic Council and seems to be inferior to it. Though the Marshal is facially identical to Styre, he has grand-looking nodules all around the collar of his armour. The Sontarans here are paler than Linx was, with none of the wisps of hair that were visible on Linx's face, and they have four fingers and a thumb on each hand. [The clone "recipe" has changed since the Middle Ages, but even apart from that there may be some variation between individuals. They can't be psychologically identical, surely, or they wouldn't have ranks? Confusingly, Styre's reaction when Sarah tells him he's identical to Linx is 'identical, yes, the same, no'.]

Which is Best, Film or Video?

Make no mistake: the first thing a modern audience notices about any TV production, the first thing that makes the viewers *judge* it in any way, is whether it's shot on film or videotape.

We pick up on it before anything else, before we fully assimilate what we're actually looking at and long before we start to ask ourselves what we think of the story. *Doctor Who* wouldn't look like *Sex in the City*, even if - for some hideous and unthinkable reason - the two programmes both featured identical scenes shot from identical angles. We know this instinctively. (Although let's not forget, our grandparents didn't. Those born before the 1940s, who were brought up to regard *any* moving image as slightly exotic, don't necessarily see the difference the way we do. And how do you explain it to them? Other than vague descriptions like "oh, film is glossier", there's no real vocabulary for describing the two very different textures that we see when we're shown the two different media. As you'll know if you've ever found your grandmother watching a daytime soap opera and believing it's the afternoon movie, just because the *content* of the two happens to be roughly similar.)

Productions can stand or fall on their film or video stock. When the BBC made its supposedly "grown-up" fantasy series *Neverwhere*, written by much-hyped comic-book writer and wannabe rock star Neil Gaiman, the decision was made to use video and it doomed the programme before a single frame was shot. By the 1990s, the public - even those sections of the public who didn't consciously know what the difference was - had come to accept that "video" plus "fantasy" equals "cheap children's TV", and the response to *Neverwhere* was general confusion that it was being shown at nine o'clock in the evening instead of four o'clock in the afternoon. The BBC hasn't tried anything similar since, although it *has* occasionally tried grafting fantasy elements into other, slicker TV formats in an attempt to make them "cult".

So. The knee-jerk reaction of many people is that film is *automatically* better than videotape. The justification for VT is usually given as being "cost", i.e. it's cheaper, i.e. it's not something anyone would use if they could afford not to. But if we're going to understand the way it was used in the '70s, then we have to look at the wider context of BBC drama at the time.

In the days of black-and-white 405-line TV, about half of the BBC's drama output was made cheaply on film, using the same film stock as supposedly big-league productions like *The Avengers*. The low-grade transmission, and the cost-per-minute of the film (as it took a good-enough picture in relatively low lighting), meant that a director could make the arrangements to remount a set at (say) Ealing Studios and make the action-sequences there even if everything else was on tape. In that era, mobile camera-work and fast edits were easier with film than with VT. If you watch "The Aztecs" (1.6) or "Tomb of the Cybermen" (5.1), you can see when the fights are coming because the stock changes. It wasn't quite as simple as "talky bits on video, fights on film", but you get the idea.

Colour wrecked all that, as the film-stock was lot more costly and out-takes ate up a big chunk of the budget. Sets had to be lit differently, and acoustically "damped" (just watch / listen to 7.1, "Spearhead from Space", *Doctor Who*'s only all-film story). The main use for film in this era was location work, or special effects. This is the first problem. Even if only subconsciously, the viewer is always alerted to the difference between this and "routine" studio work. When the effects sequence is grafted onto location filming, this goes almost unnoticed, as with the exploding church in "The Daemons" (8.5). Viewers got used to the shifting back and forth from outdoors film to indoors VT, though not everyone knew the terminology or reasons for it. (There's a *Monty Python* sketch in which Graham Chapman leaves a building that's shot on video, steps outside into a scene shot on film, looks puzzled, then re-enters the building and tells the people inside: 'Gentlemen, we're surrounded by film.' It seems quite clever now, but listen to the reaction from the *Python* audience and it's rather muted, as if not everybody's got it. Again, remember your grandparents...) Colour VT needed less intense lighting, too. In the studio, bulky costumes could be worn rather longer without actors collapsing. Suddenly *Elizabeth R* and Silurians were much more practicable.

By the mid-'70s, Outside Broadcast units had taken delivery of much smaller video cameras. The old OB rigs, which came in big lorries that handily looked military enough to be used as vehicles for UNIT, had used big, fixed "Plumbicon" cameras like the ones in the studios. ("Plumbicon" because they were adaptations of the old "Orthicon" cameras, using lead oxide to make a roughly faithful flesh-tone. This meant that red was "better" for their pur-

continued on page 29...

Sontarans salute each other with a hand to the chest. The Doctor states that Sontarans never do anything without a military reason, but they also never turn down the chance to kill someone, so they're suckers for physical challenges. Styre is, perhaps surprisingly, capable of sarcasm. Though the story ends with the Doctor "scaring off" the Marshal by claiming that the humans are in possession of the Sontaran invasion plans, the galaxy is still of tactical importance to them, so it's likely they'll be back in future. The Doctor mentions a 'buffer zone' between human and Sontaran territories [probably speaking figuratively, if the two species are in different galaxies].

History

• *Dating*. The far future, again. [As before, 15000 AD at the earliest. The story begins mere moments after 12.2, "The Ark in Space".]

The Earth has, as expected, been habitable for several millennia. The planet is now devoid of any signs of civilisation, covered in plants but with no animal life since the time of the solar flares 10,000 years ago. There's a ring of spherical transmat 'refractors' on the surface, the reception point for the matter transmitter on the Nerva station, which the Doctor suggests might be on the site of central London. [Weirdly, the spheres are lying in plain view. Shouldn't they have been overgrown with plants, like everything else? We might conclude that the city fell, and was replaced with this charming British landscape, even *before* the time of the solar flares. It's also notable that all the plant species are familiar, even though the flares supposedly destroyed 'all life' on Earth. For more on far-future London, compare with 23.1, "The Mysterious Planet".]

The party of humans currently present on Earth comes from Galsec, which has its own empire with 'bases' across the galaxy. It's not generally known that Earth is inhabitable again, but the Galsec boys have no interest in the 'Mother Earth' idea. Earth is too far from the trade routes for anyone to come here. These humans regard the Nerva station as a myth, and state that the 'lost colony' has never been found. [The Nerva station can't be *that* hard to find. Then again, Styre doesn't seem to have noticed it either - surely it'd be in the Sontarans' interests to blow it up? - so maybe it's shielded in some way. But not well-disguised enough to fool a Wirrn, obviously.] The humans carry the usual guns-that-can-stun, and don't

expect transmat beams to work too well.

The Galsec people have pronounced South African accents. [No stranger than most of the universe having English accents, of course, but so obvious that it seems to be deliberately suggesting something about future history.] "Sarah" is a strange name to these people, and they've never heard of the legend of Atlantis. They came to Earth looking for a missing Galsec freighter before Styre's mayday call snared them. [The fate of the freighter is never explained, but it probably has nothing to do with the Sontarans.]

Also on a historical note, Sarah states that her meeting with Linx ["The Time Warrior", once again] took place in the thirteenth century.

The Analysis

Where Does This Come From? For "Earth", read "Britain". This is in keeping with previous Baker / Martin yarn "The Mutants" (9.5), in which South Africa - among other things - was allegorised into a colony planet cut off from Earth's fading Empire. Being reduced to a backwater was a familiar notion for the country that year (see **Why Couldn't They Just Have Spent More Money?** under 12.2, "The Ark in Space").

It was also around this time that a huge controversy erupted about giving money to pensioners to spend on winter fuel. How could this be controversial? Well, the research into how much heat is needed for people of different ages to stay alive was conducted by doctors working in the Nazi death-camps. Even if the conclusions were valid, the ethics were thought to be questionable. Then again, so was letting old folks die to save a few quid. With the fuel crisis of 1973 and the periodic power-cuts of the previous two winters, this was a simmering debate, and impecunious (that means "broke") students were allowing researchers to conduct fresh experiments on them to provide "untainted" data.

Like most of the British public by 1974, Baker and Martin had been subjected to the drip-drip-drip of BBC1's perpetual *Star Trek* re-runs. It's hard not to think of classic *Star Trek* 1.18, "Arena" (you know, the one with the frog-man) or any number of gladiator-style Kirk-in-a-truss sequences when watching Doctor-Walsh and Sontaran-Fell's "scratch your eyes out" duel in episode two. And the notion of a great city like London being subsumed by nature is a classic example of the sort of

Which is Best, Film or Video?

...continued from page 27

poses than blue or yellow, and the set and costume designers took note. Watch any early colour BBC costume drama to see the way they pick eras with lots of red in them, like the Tudors.)

The switch to portable EMItron cameras meant that smaller units, with two cameras and a sound man, could go anywhere. It meant that CSO could be seamlessly spliced in to location footage... or not, if Christopher Barry's directing (he never got the hang of CSO). It also meant that point-of-view shots were amazingly easy. Episode one of "Robot" simply couldn't have happened otherwise. It's staged so we see things from a robot's-eye view, thus turning the story into a thriller, the only thing which stops the script being a '60s throwback.

A quick examination of "The Sontaran Experiment" throws up other, unlooked-for advantages to video. The light drizzle which would have blighted this story on film isn't visible; the crisp image makes the bracken and ferns seem alien; the sound-recording, with actors having radio-mikes and the signal feeding straight into the tape instead of needing redubbing and post-synching, makes the whole thing more immediate; they could film miles from civilisation (not such an advantage when the star breaks his collarbone, but they weren't to know about that); it looks like it was really happening.

This last factor is important, because the previous use of OB in the BBC's output was live sports coverage. "The Sontaran Experiment" looks, and more importantly *sounds*, like an on-the-spot report. By 1990s standards, videotape is generally a subconscious "cue" that you're about to see kiddy TV, hence the *Neverwhere* debacle. In 1975 it was the other way around. When it came to the big outdoors, it was *film* that told you this was going to be like *Catweazle*. You can see the change in perspective happening in *Doctor Who* after 1975. Later directors assume that film needs to be used to make jungle sets seem "real" (13.2, "Planet of Evil"; 14.4, "The Face of Evil"; 17.3, "Creature from the Pit"), whereas location work set in the present day is increasingly shot on video.

Audience expectation, at least as much as cost, is the reason for opting one way or the other. When David Maloney wants to play *auteur* and allude to other directors, he works on film. When he's trying to clone *The Good Old Days* and has struck it lucky with a location which looks like a fantastic set, he goes OB (14.6, "The Talons of Weng

Chiang"), so Jago's breath misting in the cold air of the theatre doorway is an unexpected detail that makes it all seem "real".

There are occasions when the decision to use film is a major mistake. Having found the one locattion in Britain which looks like a generic *Doctor Who* corridor set, but a mile long - in 15.4, "The Sun Makers" - the programme-makers then shoot it on film, losing the "how-did-they-do-that?" factor which was the reason they selected it. As the whole plot revolves around a world where only the rich get to go "outside", this is a big, big flaw. Similarly, the interior locations for the TARDIS in "The Invasion of Time" (15.6) are shot on film, when they need to look "indoors" to have any impact. And when stock footage is sourced from the wrong system, there's always an obvious mismatch. Compare the air-strike in "The Seeds of Doom" (13.6), which introduces film into an all-VT shoot, to the one in "The Hand of Fear" (14.2) where filmed location shots are interrupted by VT aircraft. By the time of "The Stones of Blood" (16.3) they've almost resolved this, and even the old turning-day-into-night trick of tinted transparencies over the lens very nearly works... but unfortunately, once again, film-footage CSO'd onto VT looks clumsy and ugly. This is why the shot of Romana hanging off a cliff smacks of something from a '30s Saturday morning serial, the sense of an actress standing in front of a stock-footage backdrop and pretending she's in danger.

If we remember that this programme was intended to be shown once, on Saturday evenings after an afternoon of live sports coverage, then the idea of "better" (as opposed to "appropriate to the story and how we're supposed to relate to it") disappears. In the wider context of what every other BBC drama series was doing at the time, the ratio of film to VT is entirely typical, so *Doctor Who*'s position as a commentary on other programmes was maintained almost until the end. But by the mid-'80s, every British popular drama series was either pretentiously made on cheap film - such as *Howard's Way*, which was like a series of *Dallas* on the budget of one episode - or shot entirely on VT. In many ways *Doctor Who* was an anachronism when it gave up film shooting in 1985, a hybrid of approaches like nothing else still being made. (See **What Difference Does a Day Make?** under 19.1, "Castrovalva" to see how the series started to adapt to this strange new '80s environment... and to get some idea of how the *next* generation will feel about the film / video divide.)

ABOUT TIME 1975-1979

thing you used to get in Victorian Utopian fiction, such as William Morris' *News From Nowhere*, Samuel Butler's *Erewhon* and - not quite Utopian on the face of it, but social comment nonetheless - the "aftermath" scenes in *The War of the Worlds*. Traces of this can be found in George Pal's movie rendering of *The Time Machine*, and most obviously in the final shot of *Planet of the Apes*.

Things That Don't Make Sense To get across the point that Sontarans are clones, the script requires Sarah to be amazed by Styre's appearance and to mistake him for Linx from "The Time Warrior", claiming that the two Sontarans are 'identical'. Sadly, of course, the Sontaran mask was re-designed between seasons. Which makes Sarah's observational skills as a journalist look a bit shoddy. And while she keeps her yellow mac on throughout the story, she obviously isn't wearing her shiny white Nerva station uniform underneath, which means she must have done a quick-change in record time at the end of the last story [as the Doctor apparently did in "Robot", so perhaps this is a function of the TARDIS rather than the camera trick we all assumed].

Then there are the eponymous "experiments". Stick a human face down in a bucket of water for twenty minutes. Result: he drowns. Place twenty tons on his chest. Result: his ribs crack. It's lucky there aren't any Sontaran taxpayers to complain about this. And why is this big-budget waste of time cancelled? On a deserted planet they find one person out of a dozen who can fight a single Sontaran. How often is a single Sontaran in combat? Even if they think their plans have been rumbled, surely the immediate response of High Command should be to send a battalion to investigate and engage... just as Vira's lot arrive from the Ark. Nice work, Doctor.

People stumble across holes and bumps and lose their footing, but the spindliest, shakiest bunny-eared robot you ever-did-see can move smoothly across the terrain and sneak up on people whilst making noises a Chumblie would laugh at. Oh, and the all-time favourite: Styre uses a videophone to contact his Sontaran superior. Since Sontarans are clones, wouldn't it be cheaper just to use a normal 'phone and hang a mirror over it?

Critique Pure filler material, not just because it's so short (although it's got to be said that as *Doctor Who* is supposedly about new environments and new systems of thought, fifty minutes really isn't long enough for it to build a convincing "world" around you), but because it's so hollow.

Whereas the Sontaran debut in "The Time Warrior" could be described as a parable, a satire or a costume drama with aliens, this is little more than two episodes of people wandering around the countryside, so even fifty minutes seems to be pushing it. Devoid of any built-in purpose - unless, to be generous, you want to see it as a way for Tom Baker to accustom himself to his part or break bones trying - it only works as a way of making the time-scale of "The Ark in Space" seem more real, and of providing a way-station between "Ark" and "Revenge of the Cybermen". So what you're seeing here is the emergence of *Doctor Who* as a programme that's "just" about the Doctor fighting men in monster costumes.

There's certainly no attempt to make us give a damn about any of the supporting cast, and at times it's hard to keep track of which of them are dead and which are still alive. Cheap as it all seems now, its most notable quality is the very *look* of it, its use of location video-shooting to suggest vast, desolate spaces. The lack of music for the first nine minutes makes it feel like live coverage from the future (see **Which is Best, Film or Video?**), and the sound-mixing hints at an eeriness only previously achieved in the black-and-white days. But then the story comes along and spoils things. It looks for all the world as if the cast and crew have taken a day-trip to Exmoor, and the writers have run off a quick storyline on the bus.

It's also worth mentioning that this is the point when Sontarans become *monsters*, in the usual *Doctor Who* sense of the word. Linx in "The Time Warrior" was pitched as a *villain* rather than one of a species of Dalek-like marauders, and it's telling that Sarah's reaction on seeing Styre is 'Linx!' rather than 'my God, Sontarans!'. Indeed, the cliffhanger seems to be trying to fool the audience into thinking that this is a returning character instead of just a returning costume design (although it's somewhat spoiled when the name "Styre" then appears on the end credits). By the end of the story, however, we're thinking about the Sontarans en masse. The next time we see them, in "The Invasion of Time" (15.6), we're not even supposed to remember their names.

The Facts

Written by Bob Baker and Dave Martin. Directed by Rodney Bennett. Viewing figures: 11.0 million, 10.5 million.

Supporting Cast Kevin Lindsay (Styre, The Marshal), Donald Douglas (Vural), Glyn Jones (Krans), Peter Walshe (Erak), Peter Rutherford (Roth), Terry Walsh (Zake).

Working Titles "The Destructors".

Cliffhangers Styre emerges from his pod, and removes his helmet in front of the captured Sarah. The way Sontarans do.

The Lore

• Tom Baker broke his collar-bone in a fall. As the story was filmed on Exmoor, as far from a hospital as it's possible to get in mainland Britain, he had to be splinted up with the scarf and driven eighty miles by designer Roger Murray-Leach. Baker, who had yet to appear on screen, feared that he'd be replaced.

• The "colonial" aspect of the story was emphasised by actors with Afrikaaner accents (including Glyn Jones, writer of 2.7, "The Space Museum" and here playing Krans). In fact, most of them spoke BBC English but faked it in auditions.

• The Sontaran costume cost more than the actor in it (Kevin Lindsay, again), being made of very thin mylar, and the fight had to be carefully choreographed to avoid ripping it. Lindsay's health meant that the heavier mask used in "The Time Warrior" couldn't be risked; wise, as he died of a heart complaint about a year later.

• Shortly after filming this story, stuntman Terry Walsh completed the task he began in "The Monster of Peladon" (11.5) by appearing in the BBC Childrens' TV pantomime *Aladdin* and - speaking lines, at last - playing the Pertwee Doctor with Pan's People as his "assistants". (Anyone the right age to know who they were will realise how, er, "special" this concept is. See **Cultural Primer #1: Why *Top of the Pops*?** under 14.5, "The Robots of Death".)

12.4: "Genesis of the Daleks"

(Serial 4E, Six Episodes, 8th March - 12th April 1975.)

Which One is This? The Doctor goes right back to the beginning, to a time when Daleks were as scary as we always used to think they were and a little-known scientist called Davros was having a great time making baby mutants.

Firsts and Lasts The Dalek renaissance starts here. After spending the '60s and early '70s trying to take over the galaxy with a variety of viruses and complex master-plans, here the Daleks get a new focus, as we meet their creator Davros and enter a new era of Dalek Nazism. It also sees the first use of a freeze-frame for a cliffhanger episode ending, a fashionable film-buff trick that director David Maloney does rather well (see 13.2, "Planet of Evil" and 14.3, "The Deadly Assassin"; as well as the more explicit *homage* to director Francois Truffaut by director Lennie Mayne at the end of 14.2, "The Hand of Fear"... no, really).

Six Things to Notice About "Genesis of the Daleks"...

1. For a generation, "Genesis of the Daleks" was the first *Doctor Who* story to become *repeatable*. In 1979, BBC Records released a double-LP of the story, cutting the plot down to an hour and a half and hiring Tom Baker to provide linking narration. In an era before video, this was our first chance to experience a classic story over and over and over again (and not only that, but an edited version of "Genesis" was one of the first "old" *Doctor Who* stories to be repeated by BBC television in the early '80s). All of which means that specific lines from this script have become indelibly imprinted on the psyches of fans of a certain age. Dialogue to join in with: 'She is a norm. All norms are our enemies.'; 'You can't have that... oof!'; 'You are in-*sane*, Davros!'; 'Can you help me? I'm a spy.'; 'AND-THROUGH-THE-DALEKS-I-WILL-HAVE-THAT-POWER!'

2. "Genesis of the Daleks" features what many now see as the defining "moral" moment in *Doctor Who*, when the Doctor holds the two wires in his hands which - if touched together - will wipe out the Daleks before they even have a chance to exist. The speech he delivers ('if someone who knew the future pointed out a child to you, and told you that that child would grow up totally evil... to be

a ruthless dictator who would destroy millions of lives... could you then kill that child?') has become legendary, but just as notable is the Doctor's assertion that he won't kill the Daleks because then he'd be no better than they are. This is fitted-as-standard morality for those who grew up in the '70s and '80s, and even *He-Man and the Masters of the Universe* used the same ethical logic, but it meant something in 1975.

3. And Davros' soliloquy in episode five, basically an "open mic" session in which he gets the chance to contrast his own views (the Daleks are good because they'll wipe out all other life-forms and thus introduce peace to the universe) with those of the Doctor (diversity is great for its *own* sake), is another of the series seminal moments. Well, why not? It isn't the most subtle point that the series will ever make, but here - at last - the Doctor is becoming something utterly legendary, and speaking for our humanistic sides in a way that just about *anybody* can appreciate.

4. Yet despite all this moral philosophising, writer Terry Nation still feels the need to shove in as many adventure-serial moments as possible. Leaving aside the pointless messing about with the landmine in episode one (a scene which the modern viewer can, and usually does, safely fast-forward through), the main offender here is the scene in episode three in which Harry is savaged by a giant clam. Cut from both the LP version and the early '80s TV edit, the sight of this part-time companion stepping into the mouth of an enormous mutant mollusc is nearly-but-not-quite stupid enough to be great. The "Clam-bassadors of Death" moment in episode four - when all three members of the TARDIS crew heroically leap over a line of the (static) creatures as if they're a major threat - is, if anything, even funnier.

5. Two things are remarkable about the plot of "Genesis". One: how unimportant the Doctor is to much of the story, as the politics of Skaro become more pressing than the usual business of running up and down corridors (once the Doctor's set the ball rolling, anyway). Two: how unimportant the Daleks are, as they hover over the story like vultures but rarely put in an appearance. It's enough to say that this story is around 135 minutes long... and in total, the Daleks are only around for fifteen minutes of it.

6. Try to make sense of Tom Baker's peculiar statement, when the Doctor gets his briefing from one of the Time Lords at the start of episode one:

'Whatever I've done for you in the past, I've more than made up for.' Then find yourself expecting the Time Lord to say: 'Should you for any reason fail in your mission, the High Council will disavow all knowledge of your activities. This Time Lord will self-destruct in five seconds...' (Yes, it's *that* obvious a plot set-up.)

The Continuity

The Doctor   His long-term vendetta with the Daleks is obviously something he takes personally, as he objects to the Time Lords interfering with his life, but agrees to go on a "mission" for them as soon as he finds out that Daleks are involved. He has no apparent problem with the idea of changing history to make the Daleks less of a threat, describing it as 'feasible'. [Compare this with his attitude to changing history right at the beginning, in "The Aztecs" (1.6) and "The Reign of Terror" (1.8).]

• *Ethics*. Despite his obvious hatred of the Daleks here, at the last minute he decides not to wipe them out in their cradle, claiming that this would make him as bad as they are. It's notable, however, that he only makes this decision once he *personally* has to touch the bomb-wires together to commit genocide. Up until then he's been quite happy to go along with the Time Lords' plans, and has been encouraging the Kaleds to destroy the Dalek project themselves. He changes his mind *again*, and decides to blow up the infant mutants, when he sees exactly how nasty Davros is. [This is telling. We tend to think of the Doctor as a high moralist, but this suggests that his code of ethics is as wobbly as everybody else's, and that he'll make sweeping moral decisions based on the most recent things he's seen.]

His eventual verdict is that out of the evil of the Daleks, some good will finally come, something which only seems to occur to him after he recounts their history to Davros and realises how much they've forced other races to work together.

• *Inventory*. The new Doctor's making a habit of turning out his coat pockets. Among the many odds and ends seen here are... his yo-yo, a magnifying glass, a pair of handcuffs, a piece of yellowish rock [which looks a lot like trisilicate, as in 11.4, "The Monster of Peladon"], and a little red 'etheric beam locator' which is also useful for detecting ion-charged emissions ["The Curse of the Fatal Death" also mentions this sort of thing;

How Badly Does Dalek History Suffer?

Virtually every *Doctor Who* story raises awkward questions about the Doctor's ability to change history, but "Genesis of the Daleks" goes one step further. This is the story in which he's specifically, unambiguously *told* to mess around with the timeline.

Whereas in some stories he seems to inadvertently cause known events rather than altering them (especially when it comes to starting major fires... see 2.4, "The Romans" and 19.4, "The Visitation"), here we're led to believe that different rules apply. His Time Lord "handler" gives him three options: kill the Daleks in their cradle, make them less aggressive, or find some inherent weakness. The story ends with the Doctor's bold assertion that he *has* made a difference, though he thinks he's just set the Daleks back 'a thousand years'. Ergo, everything we think we know about Dalek history is thrown into jeopardy.

The problem goes beyond logic, and beyond a single script. *Doctor Who* fans are, on the whole, obsessive by their very nature. We like everything to have its place. We like all the strands to be tied together, or at least, we like the idea that they *can* be tied together. Rationally you could argue that every time the Doctor intervenes to save a planet, the knock-on effect is so great that it changes the complete history of the universe, so that whenever the TARDIS lands it's effectively landing in a different version of time.

But even though this thought might not bother a mainstream audience - who accepted the idea of all the UNIT stories starting with a clean slate, so that the Brigadier has to be persuaded about life on other planets every six weeks or so - it'd drive hard-core viewers stark raving mad. We're not used to that sort of chaos. (Besides, it'd rob the character of a lot of his power, and make his planet-saving activities seem rather pointless.) We prefer to think that this particular fictional universe is coherent, which is why authors like Lance Parkin can happily write book-length histories of it; why the writers of the novels and the audios can come up with whole stories to "explain" one line of dialogue from a single episode shown in 1983; and, come to think of it, why this book exists. If we believe that the Doctor really does throw Dalek history off the rails here, then we have to accept that every prior Dalek story from 1963 to 1974 is "cancelled" and that something quite different happens instead. We have a hell of a lot to unlearn.

In 1995, *The Discontinuity Guide* came out and said the unthinkable, loudly proclaiming that

Dalek history *does* change after "Genesis" (and therefore before it, retroactively speaking) so that nothing we see from "The Daleks" (1.2) onwards is reliable. It seemed positively rude at the time, but looking back on it now, the *Disco's* version of things simply looks shaky. Its only evidence for suggesting two different versions of Dalek history is that before "Genesis", Davros isn't an important factor, and that with Davros around the Daleks are divided into squabbling factions instead of being untied as a single force. Yet this is a poor argument, as most of the Dalek stories we see before "Genesis" are set in the centuries before Davros is recovered from the ruins of Skaro, so there'd be no *reason* for him to feature in their history until "Destiny of the Daleks" (17.1). The book's claim that the main difference between the two histories is Davros' survival - because, apparently, Davros listens to the Doctor's warnings in "Genesis" and fits devices to his chair which shield him from the Dalek assault - is even harder to credit, since Davros shows no sign of heeding anything the Doctor says and speaks of his survival systems in "Destiny" as if they're key components of his chair rather than recent add-ons.

Besides, whatever the Doctor may say at the end of "Genesis", *all* later Dalek stories assume that history hasn't been changed. The Doctor never regards his memories of early Dalek history as unreliable. In "Remembrance of the Daleks" (25.1) he speaks of the twenty-second century Dalek invasion of Earth as if it happened just the way we saw it happen (2.2, "The Dalek Invasion of Earth", natch). When he meets up with Susan in "The Five Doctors" (20.7), there's no hint that she's now living on a version of Earth that *wasn't* wrecked by the Daleks. In fact, the only thing which might even hint at a change in Dalek history is Skaro's destroyed in "Remembrance", something which seems to contradict "Evil of the Daleks" (4.9), but this is so vague that a myriad of other explanations present themselves - see especially *War of the Daleks*: **Should Anyone Believe a Word of It?** under 17.1 - and an altered version of history certainly isn't what the script is trying to suggest.

If we want to look at the supporting evidence, then the later *Doctor Who* novels routinely assume that history remains stable, or at least isn't drastically re-written. Only the Missing Adventure *A Device of Death*, which takes place immediately after "Genesis", has the Time Lords watching the

continued on page 35...

see the appendix]. The handcuffs get left behind on Skaro.

• *Background.* Interrogated by Davros, the Doctor mentions Dalek defeats which may suggest unseen adventures. See **History** for more. He's never heard of Davros before this.

The Supporting Cast

• *Sarah Jane Smith.* Sarah urges the Doctor to commit genocide against the infant Dalek species, comparing them to a virus rather than seeing them as an intelligent culture. Her instincts for "good" and "evil" aren't as subtle as the Doctor's, it seems. Also, she's not great with heights.

• *Harry Sullivan.* Like Sarah, he's got enough gumption to beg the Doctor not to reveal everything to Davros under interrogation, even when he's being tortured. What a man. His Latin's quite good, coining names for killer clams that make them sound almost dignified.

The Supporting Cast (Evil)

• *Davros.* The 'greatest scientist' and supreme leader of the Kaled people, though the other Kaleds are perfectly humanoid and Davros is a shrivelled, grey-skinned individual with no apparent eyes. He moves around in a "wheelchair" that looks like the bottom half of a Dalek, only has the use of his right hand, is surrounded by a web of electronic systems - including a "third eye" - and has a voice which sounds as if it's electronically-augmented. [What did this damage to Davros is never explained, but given the nature of Skaro some kind of chemical damage seems likely, although in "Destiny of the Daleks" (17.1) the Movellans describe him as a 'mutant'. There's no suggestion of radiation in this story. The chair-bound nature of Davros explains once and for all why the Daleks don't give themselves legs rather than those often-inconvenient wheels: Davros doesn't feel his lack of mobility to be a problem, so it makes sense that he'd program his "children" with the same view.]

A switch on his chair deactivates his life-support system and renders him unconscious, and he states that he can't stay that way for more than thirty seconds without dying. Other controls on the chair also activate various machines in Davros' presence, including early Daleks when they're not under 'self-control'. He can also speak through some sort of communications / PR system from where he sits.

Though clearly a scientific genius, Davros is also a megalomaniac with aspirations to godhood, who's delighted by the thought that through the Daleks he'll have the power to wipe out all other life in the universe. The original purpose of the Dalek project was to provide the Kaleds with a survival mechanism, but Davros has subverted that aim and turned them into extensions of his own ego. Even the Doctor points out that he has a fanatical desire to perpetuate himself in the Daleks, hence their lack of conscience. Davros believes the Daleks have no need for pity, yet curiously forgets this when they turn on him and begs for mercy anyway.

Though he's fanatical enough to sacrifice his entire race to his own ambition, he's also open-minded enough to accept that the Doctor comes from another planet and time when presented with evidence. It's said that there have been many occasions in the last fifty years when the 'government' has tried to interfere with Davros' work, though by this stage he and his cronies are firmly in charge. Davros is thinking about the conquest of 'the universe' even now, and Skaro doesn't seem to have developed space-travel yet.

In the caverns between the Kaled dome and the wasteland are the results of Davros' early experiments with animals. One of these is a huge scaly toad-like creature that's never seen properly. Some of the others look like giant molluscs, though nobody explains why Davros thought clams were worthy of his attention. [It's been suggested that the clams are "Mk. I travel machines", but this seems unlikely as they apparently can't move on their own. If we accept that evolution on Skaro follows pre-ordained paths, which is what this story requires, then this may be a "stage" towards the ultimate blobbiness of the Kaleds.]

The Time Lords The Time Lords intercept the transmat beam that's carrying the Doctor from Earth to the Nerva station, planting him and his companions on Skaro and charging him with a mission to (a) wipe out the Daleks before their creation, (b) make sure they develop into less aggressive creatures or (c) find some weakness in their origin. [Fan-lore has frequently claimed that this attempt to change time and commit genocide isn't sanctioned by Time Lord "officials" but planned by the Celestial Intervention Agency (see 14.3, "The Deadly Assassin"). However, it isn't the implication here. The Time Lord we meet in this

How Badly Does Dalek History Suffer?

...continued from page 33

timelines re-shape themselves in the aftermath of the Doctor's intervention... and even *then* they consider the operation a limited success, saving thousands of worlds from the Dalek wars instead of the millions they were hoping for. (The scene also sees the Time Lords using "dampers" to keep the shift in time under control, so history at least stays the same basic shape, which is handy.)

And this is perhaps the most straightforward way of looking at things. The Doctor *does* make a difference, but only on a local scale, and from our point of view history still looks more or less the way it did. *His* history certainly doesn't alter. Nor does the history of Earth, which is far too central to the Daleks' plans to be spared by the Doctor's meddling. It's doubtful that his claim to have held back the Daleks by 'a thousand years' is really meaningful, as the Daleks can surely tunnel their way out of the bunker and re-stock their lab much faster than that. If you like, you can take his words as being figurative rather than literal, especially since he previously (and wrongly) claimed that blowing up the Kaled nursery would be the absolute end of the Dalek species.

Pushing the point further, it's worth remembering that the Time Lord on Skaro charges the Doctor with the mission of averting a *possible* timeline; it's feasible that the Daleks he mentions, which go on to become the dominant life-form of the universe, might not be the Daleks we've already seen but the Daleks we never got to see. Which would mean that by setting them back, the Doctor's actually creating the timeline we already know (for more of this somebody-has-to-stage-manage-history approach see **How Involved Are the Time Lords?** under 15.5, "Underworld"). That's not how the Doctor seems to see things, though, so it may be going a shade too far.

Of course, we can always look twice at "Genesis" and consider what might have happened if the Doctor hadn't become involved. He seems to be an accelerant here, making things happen ahead of schedule rather than actually changing anything (so maybe the delay to the Daleks in the last episode cancels out the rapid sequence of events he's already caused...). He warns the Kaleds about Davros, so Davros makes sure the Kaled dome is destroyed, and sets in motion the events which culminate in the extermination of all the scientists in the bunker. Without the Doctor's involvement, much the same thing would have happened, except for the dome's destruction... meaning the Kaleds would all have been wiped out by the Daleks instead. In fact, the big change here may be to Thal history. If the Kaled dome hadn't been destroyed then it's unlikely that Bettan and her Thal guerrillas would have been able to seal the bunker, and the Thals would have suffered vastly more casualties. But Davros would still have been exterminated, or supposedly-exterminated.

continued on page 37...

story speaks with an authority that smacks of the High Council, not on behalf of some secret intelligence conspiracy.

Prior to this, and contrary to the later view of them, the Time Lord hierarchy has been happy to meddle when necessary and to use the Doctor as a cat's-paw. See **Why is the Doctor Exiled to Earth?** under "Terror of the Autons" (8.1) and **How Involved Are the Time Lords?** under "Underworld" (15.5), not to mention the Doctor's comment in "The Time Warrior" (11.1) that the Time Lords are like galactic ticket-inspectors. The *real* question is this: the Time Lords can seemingly plant their agents at any point in space and time, so if they want to get rid of the Daleks then why don't they just put a great big bomb in the Kaled bunker? Why go to all the trouble of putting the Doctor on Skaro, and outside the Kaled dome, too? As ever, there seem to be "rules" governing the Time Lords' intervention in history which don't make much sense to us.]

The view taken here is that the Doctor has the freedom to explore space and time so long as he occasionally does jobs for the Time Lords, who 'seldom' [not 'never'] interfere in the affairs of others. This seems to be official policy by now. The claim made here is that the Time Lords foresee a time when the Daleks will become the supreme power in the universe. [Later in the series we find out about the Time Lords' databank, the Matrix, and in "Terror of the Vervoids" (23.3) it's made overt that the Matrix can predict future events. Which may be the cause of what's happening here. Ironically, the same story tells us that genocide is one of the worst crimes imaginable.]

The Time Lord who briefs the Doctor on Skaro,

then vanishes into the mist with a "vworp" sound, is dressed in black ceremonial-looking robes far more sombre than those we've seen on his kind so far. [This might suggest some kind of shift in Time Lord society, which is certainly the impression you get if you compare the Time Lords in "The War Games" (6.7) with the ones in "The Deadly Assassin" (14.3). See 10.1, "The Three Doctors", for one possible reason.] He claims that the Time Lords superseded 'simple mechanical devices' like transmat technology when the universe was 'less than half its present size' [It's interesting that they use 'size' as a measuring-stick here, rather than age. If the expansion of the universe is constant then the two ought to be commensurate, but recent human observations indicate that it isn't, quite. Perhaps the Time Lords slowed down the expansion of the Universe; see "Logopolis" (18.1) for a possible means and reason, and **How Many Important Galaxies Are There?** under "The Web Planet" (2.5).]

The Time Lord supplies the Doctor with a time ring, a bracelet which can return the Doctor and companions - or at least, the Doctor and anyone touching him - to their proper place in space and time when touched [but see the next story]. Apparently it can only do this once he's completed his mission [so the fact that it "works" suggests he *has* made some sort of difference to Dalek history, unless it also becomes useable when he actively fails]. The time ring registers as an energy source when the Kaleds scan it, and it's decorated with a symbol that looks like a triple-armed spiral galaxy. The Time Lord encountered by the Doctor suggests that if the Doctor loses the ring then he'll never get off Skaro, even though the Time Lords must surely be able to scoop him off the planet again [more obscure "rules" for agents].

The Non-Humans

• *Daleks.* Davros is unveiling the first near-finished Dalek to the rest of the Kaled elite when the Doctor arrives, describing it as a 'Mk. III travel machine' but christening it a Dalek within hours. [The anagram is obvious. Davros, with his ruthlessly scientific mind, obviously prefers crossword puzzles to creativity.] The Doctor describes the first revealed Dalek to be 'undeniably primitive', although it looks exactly like the standard Dalek model, with vertical plates around its midriff, rather than horizontal stripes [q.v. 1.2, "The Daleks"]. The only difference is that Davros has

yet to fit the gun. Here Daleks are said to be both 'programmed' and 'conditioned', and the Doctor believes they've been primed to kill all the Thals. Davros speaks of 'Dalek memory-banks' into which information can be programmed.

The Doctor believes that by the end of his intervention on Skaro, the Daleks have been set back 'a thousand years', though in fact he's just blown up the baby Kaled mutants and seen the already-existent Daleks trapped behind a rockfall. [Even by this stage, the Daleks must surely be competent technicians. It shouldn't take them more than a few months to find their no-feet again.] Even Daleks 'conditioned' by Davros don't acknowledge the usefulness of non-Dalek scientists. Fully-automated production lines are already churning out the Dalek machines as Davros "dies", and the Daleks seem to reach the conclusion that their creator isn't necessary after some time rather than knowing it instinctively. All 'inferior creatures' are considered their enemies.

• *Kaled Mutants.* The Kaled scientists know that their race will eventually mutate into something hideous, thanks to the same chemical process that created the Mutos. Davros believes the change to be irreversible [in "The Daleks", the development of the Daleks is put down to radiation rather than chemicals].

The slimy, tentacled, hostile, genetically-conditioned things in Davros' lab are described as living cells treated with chemicals to turn them into predictions of what the Kaleds will eventually become. Whether this is accurate or not, these are the things which Davros intends to put inside the Dalek casings. Davros here orders that chromosomal changes be made to the embryo Daleks which will entirely eradicate their conscience, and this probably happens as the Kaled scientist Gharman talks about 'restoring' the cells that'll give the creatures a sense of right and wrong, but they're ultimately all blown up. It's implied that the mutants aren't identical, as 'some of them can move about'.

The few Daleks produced before Davros orders the change have no conscience either, though this could be because of a 'computer program' which Davros introduces to them in order to limit their actions and prevent them being 'unstable' [see **How Badly Does Dalek History Suffer?**]. Despite this, they eventually try to kill him anyway. Even the earliest prototype Dalek, when given self-control, detects the Doctor's alien-ness and tries to exterminate him.

How Badly Does Dalek History Suffer?

...continued from page 35

However, there's one other change to consider. When the Doctor arrives on Skaro, the Kaled mutants aren't yet ready to be put into the Dalek casings. Davros hasn't finished psychologically conditioning them. When the Doctor's tinkering forces Davros to send them out into the field, he jury-rigs them by adding a 'computer program' to their make-up which supposedly limits their actions (but not enough to stop them shooting him, obviously).

So the one thing the Doctor *does* ensure is that their brains are never quite finished. The doomed specimens in the lab are given the chromosomal changes ordered by Davros, yet the active Daleks on Skaro are let loose *before* these changes are made. The Daleks sealed in the bunker at the end of the story, and presumably those Daleks whom they make in their own image, still have the computer program instead of proper Davros-style conditioning. (This may help to explain the Daleks' new-found robot-ness in "Destiny of the Daleks", although by the time of "Remembrance" it's Davros who's busy attaching robot parts to Dalek units and the "mainstream" Daleks believe in a kind of racial mutant purity.)

Is that the difference, then? Is this really what the Doctor means when he says that they've been set back, and what causes the later Dalek wars to skip a few thousand planets? Are the Daleks hampered by the limitations of their computer-controlled minds, giving the other species of the universe a greater advantage against them? If so, then the Doctor's mission for the Time Lords is a success after all.

But ultimately, the Doctor's supposed victory in "Genesis of the Daleks" is personal rather than historical. In his own mind, he's fulfilled the mission according to the third option he was given: to find some weakness in Dalek-kind. By going through the process of arranging their destruction, he's finally come to realise that they'll just end up bringing unity to *other* species. Out of the evil of the Daleks, some good will eventually come. This is the weakness he's discovered, a flaw in the Daleks' methodology that *he* now understands even if it's of no particular use to the Time Lords. Some have tried to argue that the Time Lords set the whole thing up to cure the Doctor of his pathological hatred of the species, or of his parochial, Earth-based frame of reference, but that seems a little extreme...

Planet Notes

• *Skaro*. At the time of the Daleks' origin, Skaro is already a scarred planet, and all we see of it is a battlefield in the war between the humanoid Thals and the just-as-humanoid Kaleds. Though the Kaleds seem to have a more fascistic society, full of jackboots and science-Nazis, both sides are equally militaristic. No mention is made of the rest of the planet. Both Kaleds and Thals seem to be confined to domed cities, no more than a few miles from each other, but despite this the war between them has apparently been going on for a thousand years. Though the soldiers started out with laser-gun-level technology, they've been gradually worn down to the point where they're wearing animal skins, gas-masks and radiation detectors at the same time. [No mention is made of nuclear weapons, but the radiation detector suggests that they may have been used in the past. Did this war begin with an atomic exchange, and is that why there's so little life on Skaro now? If so then the Thals' belief in "The Daleks", that the Daleks were the result of an atomic war, could be a mis-remembered version of what we see here.]

The Kaleds have a bunker, three or four miles from the main Kaled city, in which Davros and his scientists carry out their research. Years ago the Kaled government decided to form an elite group of the best scientific brains in every field, but over the years the scientists have become so powerful that they can over-rule the military and demand whatever they want. The purpose of the elite was to end this war, but after realising this was futile it changed direction and aimed for something that would ensure the survival of the species. There are few in the government who have the power to act against Davros by now. Gharman describes the elite as the 'Military Elite Scientific Corps', but later everyone talks of a 'military elite' as if soldiers and scientists are in separate divisions [hence the differently-coloured uniforms].

The Kaled insignia is an eye skewered on a bolt of lightning. [Typical: all fascist states like surveillance. The Kaled dome seems to be wired with CCTV, which fits.]

Meanwhile the Thals are building a rocket packed with 'distronic explosive' to wipe out the Kaleds once and for all. The rocket eventually does its job, but for the last few months the Kaled dome has been protected by a Davros-made substance that's as strong as thirty-foot-thick reinforced concrete, so treacherous Davros has to supply the Thals with a formula to weaken the dome before the rocket penetrates. [Distronic explosive must be a relatively new invention, or the Thals would have tried this years ago.] Proving that they're not the good guys here, the Thals normally kill prisoners but use slave labour to prepare the rocket, and distronic explosive can give those who come into contact with it distronic toxaemia.

Living in the wastes between cities are the Mutos, described by Nyder as the 'scarred relics' of [Kaled?] civilisation, cast out for being genetically impure thanks to the chemical weapons used in the first century of the war. They were banished into the wastelands outside the cities, and have been there so long that they're no longer considered to be either Thal or Kaled. The Kaled race believes in keeping itself pure. [This doesn't seem to apply to Davros... as written in the script, this seems to be a deliberate contradiction, in much the same way that Hitler wasn't an Aryan.]

The Mutos we see are exactly the same as everyone else on this planet, but lurch around and dress in rags, and it's suggested that many have much worse mutations. All of them wear hoods as if it were a dress code. [Note that the Kaleds are described as 'the Kaled race', not 'the Kaled species'. Implying that the Kaleds and Thals are different factions of the same species, i.e. they're biologically compatible. Note also that the Thals and the Mutos are allied against the Daleks by the end of the story. Are the genetically-perfect Thals we see in "The Daleks" (1.2) descended from combined Thal and Muto stock?]

Davros has concluded that in all of the 'seven galaxies', Skaro is the only planet capable of supporting life. The Doctor responds by stating that there are more than seven galaxies. [Terry Nation once again fails to understand how big a galaxy is. It's *infeasible* that the Kaleds might have surveyed every planet in its own galaxy, let alone seven of the things, so we can put this down to bluster on Davros' part. Skaro may well be in the same galaxy as Earth, given the Dalek obsession with overrunning the human empire, but we never find out for sure.] Even so, both Davros and the Kaled scientist Ronson are prepared to accept that the Doctor's from outer space once they see his biological data, so they must be quite open-minded.

Ronson notes that nothing about the Doctor's metabolism matches Kaled physiognomy, apart from external appearances. [And you could write whole essays about what *that* means, when it comes to the diversity of evolution across the universe, but since the Doctor can pass as almost-human on Earth this would seem to mean that Kaleds aren't very human-like.]

Rumours in the Kaled camp have suggested that the Thals are developing human-like robots. Nothing seems to come of this. 'Total extermination of the Thals' is the battle-cry of the Kaleds even before they become Daleks. Nyder mentions a Kaled 'special unit' that's good at interrogating prisoners, possibly meaning the Science Division headed by Davros. The Kaled government has a Council and a House of Congress, which presumably goes up in smoke with the rest of the Kaled dome. Davros favours brain surgery to make useful people loyal to him.

History

• *Dating*. This is the origin of the Daleks, so all we can say for sure is that it's well before the twenty-second century. [This present volume will suggest a date of the eighteenth century, for mostly spurious reasons. See **What's the Dalek Timeline?** under 2.8, "The Chase".]

The Doctor states that the Daleks' attempts to mine the core of the planet Earth in the year 2000 were thwarted because of 'the magnetic properties of the Earth'. [This is evidently a reference to "The Dalek Invasion of Earth" (2.2), but both the facts and the date are wrong... the Doctor and the companions thwarted the invasion, and it happened in the 2160s. He's strapped to a machine which detects 'any attempt to lie' when he says this, and if he knew how to fool the machine completely then he'd tell much bigger lies, so apparently he can just stretch the truth a little. Then again, the date might suggest that he just doesn't have a very good head for Anno Domini. See 6.2, "The Mind Robber", for more shameless rounding-down by the Doctor.]

On Mars, the Daleks were defeated by a virus that attacked the insulation on the cables in their electrical systems. In the 'space-year' 17,000, the Dalek attack on the Venusians was apparently halted by the intervention of a fleet of war-rockets from the planet Hyperon, at least according to the Doctor's testimony. He claims that the rockets were made of a metal resistant to Dalek firepower, and the Dalek taskforce was completely destroyed.

The Analysis

Where Does This Come From? The single most striking thing about "Genesis" is the brutality of it all, and in this case it's not a bad thing, either. Ever since the beginning there's been a suggestion of Nazism in the Dalek psyche, but the rather more liberal standards of mid-'70s TV - not to mention the very liberal standards of Philip Hinchliffe and Robert Holmes - allow the Daleks to carry out a full reign of terror here.

The first episode of the original Dalek story, made eleven years earlier, sees the Doctor deal with hallucinogenic petrified jungles and strange alien animals made of metal. The first episode of *this* little epic involves landmines, barbed wire, fascists and ultimately letters to the *Radio Times*. You could, if you were so inclined, see "Genesis" as the optimum balance between old-style *Doctor Who* and the rather more dog-eat-dog and Wirrn-eat-human-entrails universe of the early Tom Baker stories. The Doctor opposes militancy and brutality by his very nature, and here he's finally got something to really rail against. In an era when Pol Pot was slaughtering thousands for their "impurity", and the photos of skull-filled warehouses were so widely-distributed that they no longer scared children, anything less than this would have been a frivolous, insulting fudge.

For the first time eugenics becomes a major part of the Dalek mythos. They referred to the Thals as 'disgustingly mutated' back in the '60s, but after that it was all about power and conquest, never *why* they hated everything else. A decade on the Daleks couldn't be allowed to remain "men in black hats"; they had to be turned into the embodiments of an attitude that was only a slight extension of what many people in Britain were actually saying. Overtly racist quasi-political groups like the National Front were infesting inner city areas. Hitler was fast becoming a punchline, a comedy voice like Frank Spencer or the stereotypical "thick" Irish accent. German citizens, raised in a culture in denial, found it baffling that they could be blamed for something of which they were unaware (see *Fawlty Towers* 1.6, "The Germans," for an acute dissection of this). Fascist, eugenicist ideology was creeping back.

And for once in a Terry Nation script there are no plagues in evidence, although the Daleks are compared to something viral at least twice during the course of the story.

Things That Don't Make Sense All right, let's start with the big one. This story may be presented as a fable, and scientific feasibility may not be the main issue, but even so... the Kaleds and the Thals are (or were, when their war started) hi-tech and almost certainly nuclear-capable, yet the war between them has gone on for a thousand years *even though their cities are within walking distance of each other*. And to make matters worse, halfway through the story - when the Doctor and company have to get from one camp to the other - it turns out that there's a secret passage from the wasteland into the Thal dome, known to the Kaled military, which has evidently never been used to (say) plant explosives inside the Thal citadel. Just as curiously, the Kaled elite gave up trying to build super-weapons to end this war because they saw it as futile, yet the less ingenious Thals now have a rocket that can put a stop to it in one blow.

Later, Davros and Nyder somehow sneak in to the Thal dome for a chat; do the Thals *have* security? And did Davros really trundle through a tunnel and several grills? The Kaled military / scientific combine has had fifty years to investigate possible ways out of this stalemate, yet even in the beginning no-one asked Davros exactly what he was doing with their precious resources (imagine Roosevelt and Churchill letting the Trinity A-bomb team fritter away the money for the Manhattan Project on frisbee design). Ronson's presence in this research-squad is a bit suspect, as he complains about 'senseless killing' when avoiding arrest, and seriously doubts whether a war can be ended by just means. Exactly how does anyone have qualms like this after a millennium of warfare, and even if it were possible, don't they screen people for working in a weapons development programme? Maybe he's from "Friends of Skaro" and let the clams out of the lab.

In her very first line of the story, Sarah complains that the transmat beam hasn't brought them to the right place and that 'this isn't the beacon', odd since the Nerva station isn't referred to as a beacon until "Revenge of the Cybermen" (12.5, i.e. the next story). She seems to know what the Doctor's mission from the Time Lords is without being told, and at the end of the last episode she knows the Doctor's about to hurtle around the corner of the corridor before his shadow's even visible on the wall. Ms. Premonition. She can also magically divine which locker contains combat clobber in her size, in case she needs to go mollicking about in caves in the not-too-distant future (again, see the next story).

Sarah's also the subject of one of the most disappointing cliffhangers in the programme's history, falling off a great big rocket-gantry at the end of episode two but then somehow landing on a convenient platform inside the gantry at the start of episode three. Even Flash Gordon would disapprove (and see 24.4, "Dragonfire", for more of this sort of business).

The leader of the Thals declares a 'general amnesty' after the Kaled dome is destroyed, conveniently allowing the Doctor to go free without having to open any cell doors with the sonic screwdriver, which *just about* seems reasonable (if you can believe that a government would let all the agents of an eradicated culture go free, and not expect them to carry out any reprisals). But this involves the guards letting go of him the moment the leader declares the amnesty, then leaving him alone in the Thals' rocket control room.

In his next scene he grins his head off when meeting the celebrating Thals, even though he thinks his companions have just been blown to pieces in the Kaled dome. What a sod. Mind you, in spite of what we're told, he's the only person in the city who seems happy that a thousand-year war is finally over. The end of a series of *Big Brother* gets a better reception than the rather muted office-party we see here. It also looks as though the Thals of the future are descended from a single woman. [There was only one she-Thal in "The Daleks", too, and again in "Planet of the Daleks". Maybe they reproduce like bees. If they're the same species as the Kaleds, who have no females in their ranks at all, then it might explain Ronson's claim that near-human biology shares almost nothing with that of the people of Skaro.]

At the start of episode six, the Doctor believes that blowing up the incubator room will wipe out the Daleks once and for all, even though he knows some of them are already active. At the end of the episode, with the incubator room successfully destroyed, he says that they've just been set back a thousand years. Eh? And, worse: when Davros is planning to stitch up his opponents and have them all exterminated, he points to a button in the research area and claims that if it's pressed then the Dalek production line will be destroyed. This is obviously part of his spiel to make himself look democratic. Yet as the Daleks turn against him, he reaches out for the button *as if it's actually connected to something.* Is there any feasible reason *at all* that he might have wired the production line with explosives, rather than just lying about it? This is Davros, for Heaven's sake! Nor does that fact that the button's big and red and marked with the words TOTAL DESTRUCT make things seem more credible. [The English words are, presumably, being translated for our benefit.] Also, one switch on Davros' chair is used to open various doors around the Kaled city. How does it know which one he wants to open? And why has the idiot installed an "off" switch for his life-support?

Once the Doctor has signally failed in the mission set by the Time Lords, nothing about the matter is ever said again. Do they send someone else to do the job properly, and if so then is this why the Doctor's "non-intervention" seems to have "not un-happened" (if you see what we mean) when Davros turns up again? [See **How Badly Does Dalek History Suffer?**.] And as with all the Doctor's biggest mistakes - see, for instance, the destruction of huge chunks of the Universe in "Logopolis" (18.7) - the Valeyard never mentions it at any point during his trial in Season Twenty-Three.

This being a Terry Nation script, it's full of ideas about the pre-determined paths that evolution *will* take, regardless of outside conditions. In "his" ending for *Blake's 7* ("Terminal"), we're doomed to become savage apes; in his story from the *Radio Times* special, "We Are the Daleks", Earth turns out to be Skaro in the remote past and we're doomed to become the ultimate evil in the universe. The idea of "adapting" seems not to have percolated through Nation's skull.

It's now impossible to see Davros and Nyder without thinking of Montgomery Burns and Waylon Smithers. Not anyone's fault, but it needed to be said. Davros describes things as 'excellent' twice in this story.

Critique Dear God, this works, in spite of all its gaping plot loopholes.

A quick skim-read of the previous volume of this book will reveal that the authors aren't liable to be kind to the work of Terry Nation, but here the material's so powerful, so iconic and so *mythic* that the lapses of logic and the occasionally appalling dialogue cease to be an issue. "Genesis of the Daleks" uses the ready-made mythology of both *Doctor Who* and the Daleks themselves to tell a morality-play-cum-origins story which touches just about every level of narrative at once, and the result is something that's great when you're twelve and just as great when you're a grown-up.

Everything's in the right place here. Tom Baker is finally settling into his role as the Doctor, so much so this is arguably the story which finally "makes" him; the Daleks are interesting again, becoming a meaningful threat rather than just generic monsters; the performances are impeccable, with Michael Wisher (Davros) and Peter Miles (Nyder) playing their parts so well that it's hard to imagine anybody summing up the concept of villainy in *Doctor Who* any better (actually, if you wanted to be *really* mean to Nation then you could say that the acting works in spite of the script rather than because of it); and unlike many later Tom Baker stories, there's a spectacularly successful attempt to make Skaro feel like a fully-fledged *world* instead of just a set of sets, from the child-terrifying opening sequence of dying soldiers to the brilliantly-staged BBC-chic scene in which the Doctor shelters in a trench from a Dalek passing at ground level. Even the colour co-ordination of the uniforms is "right".

"Genesis of the Daleks" is now regarded as one of the all-time greats by *Doctor Who* fans, and though you should never believe the received wisdom of fandom, here the arguments for it being a classic seem immediately obvious. There was a reason that we loved the programme in the '70s, whether we were teenagers or children or not even born. This *is* that reason. A political / mythological / SF epic that genuinely deserves six episodes, only the clams and the landmine need cutting.

Also, Sevrin the Muto and Bettan, the female Thal leader, should have their own flat-share sitcom.

The Facts

Written by Terry Nation. Directed by David Maloney. Viewing figures: 10.7 million, 10.5 million, 8.5 million, 8.8 million, 9.8 million, 9.1 million. The first time around, that is. But it's the most-repeated *Doctor Who* story of all, so *everyone's* seen it.

Supporting Cast Michael Wisher (Davros), Peter Miles (Nyder), Dennis Chinnery (Gharman), Guy Siner (Ravon), John Franklin-Robbins (Time Lord), Stephen Yardley (Sevrin), James Garbutt (Ronson), Harriet Philpin (Bettan), Drew Wood (Tane), Jeremy Chandler (Gerrill), Tom Georgeson (Kavell), Ivor Roberts (Mogran), Andrew Johns (Kravos), Richard Reeves (Kaled Leader), Michael Lynch (Thal Politician), Hilary Minster (Thal Soldier), Roy Skelton (Dalek Voice).

Working Titles "The Daleks - Genesis of Terror". (Big Finish Productions may be interested in re-using this title at some point.)

Cliffhangers Sarah, stumbling around in the ruins of Skaro, witnesses Davros and Gharman testing a fully-armed Dalek for the first time; leading her fellow escapees up the scaffolding of the Thal rocket, Sarah slips and plummets towards the ground (cue freeze-frame); while the Doctor's trying to sabotage the Thal rocket, the semi-unconscious guard presses some kind of button on the control panel that in some way electrifies the rocket and somehow pins the Doctor to it, apparently causing him some pain; Davros has the Doctor strapped to a machine that forces him to tell the truth about future Dalek defeats, then screeches at him to reveal everything while threatening to torture Sarah and Harry; the Doctor stumbles out of the Kaled incubation room with a slimy mutant wrapped around his throat.

The Lore

• The last story of Season Twelve to be filmed (but 13.1, "Terror of the Zygons", was taped immediately afterwards), this was commissioned by Barry Letts after Nation had sent in a script fingerprint-identical to "Planet of / Death to / The Daleks". Over a long gestation period, Robert Holmes added small touches of his own to the point where nobody's sure how much is Nation being told "do it again, better" and how much is Nation being genuinely inspired by the new opportunities which the revised format allowed him. He certainly stipulated that Davros had to appear in all subsequent Dalek stories.

• No-one seems able to recall who was originally cast as Davros, but Michael Wisher - who'd been on hand to do Dalek voices and had just completed work on "Revenge of the Cybermen" - was almost immediately accepted as perfect once

ABOUT TIME 1975-1979

rehearsals began. He claimed in interviews that as he had a bag over his head in rehearsals, the cast and crew forgot he was there and went off to lunch without him, locking him in the drill hall. On the strength of this (his performance, that is, not the bag thing), he was cast as Richard III in a major stage production, and became active in an organisation trying to prove that Shakespeare maligned Richard for propaganda purposes.

• Nobody weaned after the 1970s can fail to notice that Ravon, the young Kaled General, is played by Guy Siner, AKA the Comedy Camp Nazi from 'Allo 'Allo. He's also the most noticeable of three actors to have been in both *Doctor Who* and *Babylon 5* (he was an almost-as-camp Minbari in *Babylon 5* 4.13, "Rumours, Bargains and Lies"). And lo and behold, he's done *Star Trek* as well, but only *Enterprise* (as Malcolm Reed's father in *Enterprise* 1.12, "Silent Enemy") so it's not surprising that hardly anybody realises it. Between Skaro and Minbar, Siner was in the superb *Secret Army*, the series which 'Allo 'Allo parodied but which far fewer people now remember.

Just to take matters further into 'Allo 'Allo territory, Hilary Minster (AKA General Erich von Klinkerhoffen) here appears as a Thal soldier. It's almost hauntingly familiar, since Minster previously appeared as a Thal - albeit an entirely different one - in 11.4, "Planet of the Daleks".

• And nobody weaned on culture *above* the level of 'Allo 'Allo can fail to notice that the opening and closing scenes of this story are intended to echo the beginning and end of Ingmar Bergman's laugh-a-minute Medieval romp *The Seventh Seal*, hence the hat worn by the messenger in the opening sequence (Bergman's version of Death has the same fashion sense) and the "dance" activation of the time ring. This is the beginning of a long string of film-buff references in the series, with Holmes deliberately re-jigging scripts to suit particular directors. The first draft of "The Three Doctors" (10.1) also stated that the "death dimension" was to have the general look and mood of Bergman's movie.

• The BBC LP of "Genesis of the Daleks" was sampled by the KLF, trading under the name of The Time Lords, for their chart-topping hit single "Doctorin' the TARDIS" in 1988. Less famously, one line of Davros' screeching dialogue was sampled and used as the "hook" for the techno track "Punished for This" by Strobe Man. (Go on, guess *which* line.)

• And Davros' "aria" about the virus in the vial crops up in the most unlikely places. Not only did a fan working as researcher for a Conservative MP in the 1990s (allegedly) work it into a Parliamentary speech on genetic screening, but the storyliners of bucolic soap opera *Emmerdale* - most of whom had some connection with Virgin's New Adventures, in those days - developed a sub-plot about genetically modified peas just so wheelchair-bound megalomaniac Chris Tate could quote it. They did a lot of this sort of thing.

• Once again, the director can take credit for a rewrite that made all the difference. The final cliffhanger needed a bit more "oomph" than the Doctor pausing before detonating the explosives, and noticing that the story was under-running anyway, Maloney added the "strangulating mutant" scene in case small children didn't understand why the episode halted where it did.

• *Those* clams were made of foam rubber, but the slithery, hard-shelled thing that passes in front of the grille is… the carapace of an old Ice Warrior costume.

• Peter Miles kept being told not to wear the Iron Cross he'd somehow acquired, so he'd sneak it on just as each "take" began. See if you can spot where he's been caught…

• Those highly-cultured readers mentioned above might note that Davros' 'simple pressure of my thumb…' rant and the Doctor's 'if I were to show you a child…' spiel are both, by a roundabout route, analogous to the Inquisitor's taunting of Christ from Dostoievski's *The Brothers Karamazov*. Either one would be an interesting coincidence, but together it's rather more striking. Remember, one year earlier Terry Nation had given the world "Death To The Daleks". Precisely how much of this was Holmes' work…?

12.5: "Revenge of the Cybermen"

(Serial 4D, Four Episodes, 19th April - 10th May 1975.)

Which One is This? After a six-year absence from the programme, the Cybermen return to wreak vengeance on the planet that caused their downfall in the Cyber-Wars, first by planting a bomb on it and then by trying to smash a great big spaceship into it (q.v. 19.6, "Earthshock").

Firsts and Lasts Having already shown themselves to be susceptible to radiation, gravity and plastic solvents, the Cybermen now turn out to be allergic to gold, a standard Cyberman-killing method that makes its first appearance surprisingly late in their development. This is also their first appearance in colour (unless you count the blob-in-a-snowstorm cameo in 10.2, "Carnival of Monsters"), though as they're silver it doesn't make a lot of difference. It's the first time the actors in the Cyber-costumes get to say the dialogue, which means that it's the first time they talk like people instead of computers. It's less interesting, but at least it's comprehensible.

Last time Carey Blyton is permitted to try his hand at music for the programme, and some would say "thankfully". It's also the first use of Peter Howell, of the BBC Radiophonic Workshop, who steps in and tries to salvage the music for episodes two and three. Last appearance of Kevin Stoney (Tobias Vaughn, 6.3, "The Invasion"; Mavic Chen, 3.4, "The Daleks' Masterplan") and first appearance of David Collings (Poul, 14.5, "The Robots of Death"; Mawdryn, 20.3, "Mawdryn Undead"). Neither is recognisable under heavy latex, although Stoney has his character use a hankie all the time. Last story written by former *Doctor Who* script editor, and co-creator of the Cybermen, Gerry Davis.

It's also - and this *is* significant - the last story to be made before the public see Tom Baker in action, and the difference in his performance shows.

Four Things to Notice About "Revenge of the Cybermen"...

1. It's a story best-remembered for its scenes of Cybermen lumbering through the caverns of Voga, shot on location instead of on a cheap BBC set. Filmed at Wookey Hole, Britain's top subterranean tourist attraction, these are the moments when the Cybermen present us with a genuine sense of menace. They just look like parts of the furniture when they're on a shiny white space-station, but they *really* get to shine when they're glinting in the darkness. (Viewers of more modern BBC programming might note that this is the *Doctor Who* story alluded to in the "cave tour guide" sketch from *The League of Gentlemen*.)

2. This story also sees the return of the Cybermats, slippery mechanical slugs that like to launch themselves through the air and savage people's throats. This means that at least four actors have to do the time-honoured *Doctor Who* "dance", which involves holding a monster prop up to your neck and thrashing around as if you're trying to get it *off* you instead of trying to hold it in place. Why not join in at home? And note, too, the amusing way that the Cyberleader tries to throttle the Doctor in episode four. (Many subsequent stories indicate that the Doctor has unbelievably sensitive shoulders - 13.1, "Terror of the Zygons", for instance - so maybe the Cyberleader does some permanent damage here.)

3. Space-based *Doctor Who* is always bound to have budgetary problems, but sometimes you have to wonder why the writers thought they could get away with demanding such logistically unlikely special effects. The climax of "Revenge of the Cybermen" sees the out-of-control Nerva space station hurtling over the curve of the Voga asteroid, which means that the image on the station's scanner-screen has to show the asteroid's surface rushing past as the Doctor tries to prevent a catastrophic collision. It's hard to adequately describe the resulting special effect, but suffice to say that it's often referred to as "the chocolate log in space".

An even cheaper "effect" is the shot of the rocket blasting off from the surface of Voga, quite clearly a piece of real-life rocket footage nicked from NASA. This is why the Vogan missile seems to have the words UNITED STATES written on the side (the same footage turns up *again* in 13.4, "The Android Invasion"). And if we're really going to give this story the benefit of the doubt, let's just say that one symptom of the Nerva space-plague is to make corpses look like shop-dummies.

4. Tom Baker has already started adding his own flourishes; look out for the "three wise monkeys" tableau, the 'dusty death' gag and the line quibbling about the word 'fragmentised', all of which came about in rehearsal. At this stage, directors can choose which of these to use and which to discard…

The Continuity

The Doctor The Doctor's really settled into his new personality by now, mocking and haranguing the Cybermen in a way that wouldn't have suited most of his previous bodies. [You can imagine the First Doctor being this aggressive, but not the other two.] He's a lot more hostile to Harry, his male companion, than he ever is to his female sidekicks.

The Doctor's hat disappears without trace between Skaro and the Nerva beacon - see **The TARDIS** - so he must get a new one at some stage. He describes himself here as a 'doctor of many things'.

• *Inventory*. The first things Kellman finds in the Doctor's pockets: a bag of jelly-babies and a rusty apple core. He's still got his yo-yo.

• *Background*. The Doctor uses a 'triple Turk's-head eye-splice with gromits' that he picked up from Houdini. This means he's good at escaping from ropes, naturally. [See 11.5, "Planet of the Spiders" and **Is He Really a Doctor?** under 13.6, "The Seeds of Doom" for more on Houdini.] He knows about the history between the Cybermen and the Vogans [he's had prior knowledge of Cybermen ever since 4.2, "The Tenth Planet"], and recognises the scratches made on the station by the Cybermat.

The Supporting Cast

• *Sarah Jane Smith*. She's heard of the Cybermen, believing that they were all wiped out ages ago. [As a journalist, she might know about the events of "The Invasion" (6.3). However, she has trouble believing in alien monsters the first time she meets the Doctor, so it's unlikely that she - or the world in general - knew the whole truth about the Cyberman invasion before her first trip on the TARDIS. She most probably picked the details up from someone at UNIT, given how much hanging-around she did at UNIT HQ towards the end of Season Eleven.] She's notably protective of the Doctor here, defending his reputation in a way that seems positively Jo-Grant-esque.

• *Harry Sullivan*. Despite being described by the Doctor as an 'imbecile', he continues to adapt remarkably well to bizarre situations, using the made-up verb 'transmatted' as if it's perfectly normal for him. It's hard to escape the feeling that he still wants to play at being James Bond. Captured by the Vogans, he displays no fear and is prepared to say 'steady on, old chap' when he's being man-handled. He also gets comically greedy when confronted with a planet of gold [but wins viewer support by getting the alien names muddled up... this is in character, it's not Ian Marter fluffing his lines].

The TARDIS (and the Time Ring) The time ring supplied by the Time Lords [see the previous story] takes the Doctor and company back to the Nerva station several thousand years early, for some reason. [The Time Lords want the Doctor to sort out the Cybermen? If the Doctor hadn't got involved then the station would have been destroyed long before he set foot on it, triggering an obvious paradox. The Doctor's outfit changes between the end of the previous story and the start of this one, his hat and coat vanishing for no given reason. In addition, Sarah suggests that it's been 'weeks' since they all set out together. "Genesis of the Daleks" only sees the TARDIS crew stuck on Skaro for days at best, so it's at least feasible that the time ring takes the Doctor to various other Time-Lord-sponsored adventures which we never see. Tellingly, the TARDIS only re-appears once the Cybermen have been defeated.]

The TARDIS mysteriously materialises of its own accord, having drifted back in time to find its crew, and the Doctor indicates that this is a safety feature of the time ring. He then sets the 'drift compensators' to stop it slipping away again.

The story ends with the Doctor receiving a 'space-time telegraph' message from Earth, as he left the telegraph system with the Brigadier. [For all we know he could have given the Brigadier this system ages ago, perhaps in the gap between Seasons Ten and Eleven, soon after the TARDIS became operational again. See the next story for more on the telegraph. The message was sent a thousand years in the past, so Heaven knows why the TARDIS receives it at this particular point. Maybe the same amount of time passes for the Brigadier as for the Doctor before the telegraph is used, but if so then the TARDIS crew have been floating around the place for quite a while.] The message takes the form of a long string of ticker-tape. It's not clear whether it comes out of some special telegraph machine, or whether it's delivered by the main TARDIS console.

Incidentally, nothing can go wrong with a time ring except for a 'molecular short circuit'. It vanishes once it's been used.

The Non-Humans

• *Cybermen*. Decimated by humanity years previously - see **History** - the Cybermen who attack the Nerva beacon are wanderers with no homeworld of their own, travelling through space in an 'ancient' silver spacecraft with hyperdrive capability and missile tubes in the suspicious-looking nose-cone. The humans find the design strange, which is understandable.

In charge of the group is a Cyberleader, identifiable by his black headpiece, who seems smarter than the others. They see cosmic domination as their destiny, even though they were nearly wiped out while trying it before. They have enough parts in their ship to build a new Cyber-army. In war, Cybermen subscribe to no theory of morality.

These Cybermen are the same model which tried to invade Earth in the late twentieth century [6.3, "The Invasion", perhaps suggesting that these are left-over "strikeforce" Cybermen]. One of them refers to Cybermen 'warriors' [they have a culture of warfare by now?]. Gold, being the 'perfect non-corrodable metal', clogs up the breathing apparatus on their chests and suffocates them; one handful of gold-dust can be lethal to them if thrown.

For the first time, their voices are very nearly human. Nor are they as coldly rational as they used to be. Whereas earlier Cybermen were utterly practical, the Cyberleader here lashes out when the Doctor needles him, and seems to get some kind of kick out of dominating the humans. The Doctor speaks of the way the Cybermen 'hate' Voga. [Since these Cybermen are desperate survivors of their kind, they may be using more and more organic parts in the cyberneticisation process. This becomes even more pronounced later; see 19.6, "Earthshock". As the gold allergy has never been mentioned before, it's also possible that not all Cyber-models are susceptible to it. Compare with 26.1, "Battlefield". The fact that gold chokes them suggests a need to breathe air, not the case in 4.6, "The Moonbase".] Gold also jams their radar-scope, oddly. They don't seem to know anything about the Doctor here.

The Cybermen are bulletproof, and their weapon of choice is a beam set into the headpiece which can - as always - either stun or kill. Their muscles are said to be hydraulic. They're equipped with Cyber-bombs, allegedly the most compact and powerful explosive devices ever invented, two of which are powerful enough to destroy the Voga asteroid. The Doctor criticises the Cyber-Leader's 'English' when he uses the word 'fragmentised' [the Cybermen are actually speaking English…?].

• *Cybermats.* The Cybermen's "pets" are quite different to the ones seen before [5.1, "Tomb of the Cybermen" and 5.7, "The Wheel in Space"].

The one on the Nerva station is around two feet long, silver in colour - of course - with a snout at one end but no eyes or antennae this time. The "bite" of a Cybermat introduces a venom which instantly renders victims unconscious and kills within minutes. Glowing red lines spread across the face of a dying target, and the body temperature soars. Though the Cybermat we see here has some kind of autonomy, it can also be remote-controlled by a little box. It's rendered inactive just by throwing some gold pellets at it [so does it need to breathe?].

Planet Notes

• *Voga.* The 'planet of gold', currently wandering through Earth's solar system. It's now in orbit of Jupiter, and for some reason the humans - not recognising it - have christened it Neo Phobos. This "planet" is really just a large asteroid, which somehow has Earth-like gravity and an atmosphere. Though the surface of this mini-planet is lifeless, its caves are home to the Vogans, sludgy-coloured humanoids with high, domed foreheads. The Vogans are distrustful of outsiders after the events of their past (see **History**) but at least one faction wants to trade gold with the outside universe again. Tyrum states that the Vogan city we see was once their survival chamber, but that they've lived there since the conflict with the Cybermen. [So it's possible that this is just a chunk of the original Voga, an "escape pod" with artificial gravity and oxygen.] Almost everything is made of gold here, including the manacles used to hold their prisoners, amusing since gold isn't the hardest of metals [we might assume that Vogans are physically weaker than humans]. The Vogans have a reasonably advanced technology, as the military carry hi-tech projectile weapons and one of the factions on the planet has spent two years building a Skystriker rocket with a bomb-head capable of destroying the Nerva station.

The symbol of Voga is an elaborate figure-eight inside a circle. [We later discover that this is also the Seal of the High Council of the Time Lords, as seen in 14.3, "The Deadly Assassin". This could easily be coincidence, but since it's known that the Time Lords don't mind interfering in galactic politics it's at least feasible that the Time Lords played some part in making sure Voga was around to stop the expansion of the Cybermen. Or does that give the Cybermen too much credit?]

A military force called the Guardians, who have their own guild-chambers in the caves, traditionally police the goldmines but Chief Councillor Tyrum orders his senior militia to step in here. On the whole, the Vogans behave in a way that seems positively archaic [because most alien societies in this universe are staged like Shakesperian drama]. Once the Cybermen are destroyed, the Vogans seem to believe that they have nothing to fear. It's never revealed whether they formally re-introduce themselves to humanity.

Evidently there are mice on Voga, especially the cringing variety.

History

• *Dating.* After the late 2800s, but 'thousands of years' before the time of the solar flares. [In 12.2, "The Ark in Space", the Doctor believes the Nerva station to have been built in the late twenty-ninth or early thirtieth century. Received wisdom has always assumed this story to be set around the same time, but nothing here suggests that the Beacon is new in this period, even if it hasn't been assigned to Voga for long. The twenty-ninth century is the tail-end of Earth's empire - see 10.3, "Frontier in Space" - and the humans here don't talk or dress like imperials. In fact a date in the 3000s, with Earth picking itself up after the fall of the Empire, makes more sense and would explain some of the rather shoddy space-technology on offer. But the Beacon was still *built* under Empire, which was clearly a time of great engineering skill as the Doctor's impressed by some of the hardware in "The Ark in Space". If you date "The Ice Warriors" (5.3) to 3000 AD - and it's a very big "if" - then a "Nerva" beacon and a "Britannicus" base make sense; there's possibly a moonbase called "Caligula" and a rocket-ship "Nero".]

At this stage the station's known as the Nerva Beacon, a military facility orbiting Jupiter and controlled by Earth Centre, with a crew of around fifty. The Beacon has a thirty-year assignment, as it'll be that long before the last inward-bound freighter has the new asteroid Voga on its star-chart. Until then there's a constant danger of collision. An Earth-Pluto flight passes the Beacon here, but it's re-routed to Ganymede Beacon while Nerva's under quarantine. The Beacon's beige-clad staff do 'tours' of duty, although there's at least one civilian exographer on board, and they're armed with projectile weapons rather than ray-guns. The Commander can order execution for certain crimes. The Doctor's surprised that now Voga's

here, Jupiter has thirteen satellites. [In reality it's got dozens, but only four "main" ones, so it's hard to say how the Doctor's counting them. It's just as hard to say how a station in the proximity of Jupiter ended up being used as an "Ark" in orbit of Earth, some centuries later.]

The 'matter beam' of the Nerva transmat system separates human molecules, and therefore removes Cybermat venom from anyone who goes through it. The transmat reception site involves the same kind of spheres seen on Earth [in 12.3, "The Sontaran Experiment"]. A 'pentalion drive' is crucial to the transmat, and the Cybermen know when the beam's been used because they can detect a discharge of 'phobic energy'. [It runs on fear...? Unless there's some psychic component to the transmat process - which isn't all that unreasonable, actually - then "phobic" must mean something wholly unfamiliar.]

The Cybermen disappeared after their attack on Voga at the end of the Cyber-War, 'centuries' ago, and the humans believe them to be extinct. The name "Voga" seems to mean nothing to the Nerva crew, though. Before this, the Cybermen were already suffering at the hands of the humans thanks to the invention of the glitter-gun, which used gold from Voga as ammo. The Doctor claims, perhaps jokingly, that people now use gold-plated Cybermen as hat-stands. Voga was first spotted in Earth's solar system fifty years ago, and was captured by Jupiter's gravity.

The Doctor states that the Armageddon Convention banned Cyber-bombs, though he doesn't give a date for this. [The novel *The Empire of Glass* suggests the seventeenth century, i.e. it's nothing to do with humans].

The Analysis

Where Does This Come From? As we'll see later on, there's a trend in this period for stories to feature the final appearance of a once-terrible threat, the return from the dead of something 'almost too horrible to contemplate'.

Without wishing to get a bit too deep for a book of this nature, the psychologist Jacques Lacan noted the power of the "gap" between a symbolic "death" and real mortality, and Philip Hinchcliffe has hinted at this in various interviews since the '70s. Think how many Hinchcliffe / Holmes stories begin with someone effectively being killed, and end with that person physically dying. Even something as crass as "The Android Invasion" (13.4) works on this principle, while Davros is the classic example.

Here, for once, the "comeback" is a threat that we've encountered in its prime. But even this is a sequel to a story we don't know. The Cybermen were resting in their tombs almost from the day they were born, and we never saw them as galaxy-wide menaces, only sneaking around in corners like the filthy Commie threat they so very nearly became. As a ploy to make a story seem bigger than it could afford to be, this was fine, but we should at least note that there are psychological and historical reasons for this to work so well (see 13.3, "Pyramids of Mars", for more).

Gerry Davis, who subsequently went to America to make a series called *Vega$*, had the idea of a casino planet used as a front for the vengeful Cybermen. His original script, a glitzier reworking of "The Moonbase" (4.6) right down to the end of episode two being a literal "unveiling" of the lead monsters, was unworkable. And not very good, frankly. (Something to consider, though. When the producers of the 1996 *Doctor Who* TV movie seriously thought it was going to turn into a series, they considered bringing back various "old" monsters and decided that the best way to use the Cybermen was to focus on their status as displaced persons in search of a home. In short, plans were made to turn the Cybermen into space-going Native Americans, with techno-fetishes instead of tribal totems. Now the world's used to the idea of American-Indians owning casinos, Davis' storyline seems almost rational.)

Barry Letts had requested such a Cyber-story during his run as producer, and announced it in the same *Radio Times* reply which mentioned that the Ice Warriors would be back in "The Monster of Peladon", partly as a consolation for Terry Nation's refusal to let "Frontier In Space" be the long-awaited Daleks vs. Cybermen story we all wanted to see when we were seven. Hinchcliffe went along with it because the more "classic" monsters the new Doctor had to face, the smoother his ride would be, whoever ended up playing the lead character. Robert Holmes hated the idea of "robots" as principal villains, however, adding Kellman and the Vogans to the story as padding and character variation. Being a solo Davis script, the Cybermen are there as a physical menace, like Russians or sharks; not as a moral problem, as they had been to co-creator Kit Pedler (see especially 4.2, "The Tenth Planet").

Things That Don't Make Sense By this stage the Cybermen really are the most rubbish monsters imaginable. With no point and no purpose other than to represent something generically evil, the real clincher comes when they tie up the Doctor and Sarah with a single piece of rope before making their escape from the Beacon, as if they've turned into a race of silent movie baddies.

Yet despite this overall hopelessness, a party of only two Cybermen is enough to transmat down to the planet of gold - where just about *everything* metal seems to be gold, and therefore poisonous to the Cybermen - and wipe out huge numbers of Vogan soldiers. Aren't the Vogans using gold bullets in their gold guns? If not, then why don't they try sprinkling the Cybermen with gold-dust, the way the Doctor does? It's doubly strange when you consider that Vogans like Tyrum seem to routinely carry bags of gold-dust around with them (rather like a Bedouin carrying sand around in bags). It's also hard to believe that *only* gold can choke the Cybermen, since at this point you'd expect human research to be able to come up with sundry other non-corrodable alloys and make Cyber-killing weapons much more cheaply. Gold is treated as if it were a magic talisman here, dealing with Cybermen in much the same way that silver bullets deal with werewolves.

Two Cyber-bombs are enough to wipe out Voga, but the Doctor and Harry avoid the blast from *one* Cyber-bomb by hiding behind some nearby rocks. The Cybermat's functional again mere minutes after the Doctor wrecks it with gold pellets, and stranger still, gold thrown at its exterior stops it dead but gold stuffed into its venom-snout doesn't do it any harm at all. Even given that all the Beacon's medics are dead, it's hard to explain how the crew can believe there's a 'plague' on board when all the bodies have got Cybermat puncture-wounds on their necks. There's sound in space, and the burning debris of the Cyberman ship falls "down" after it's destroyed [does Jupiter's gravity extend that far?]. The Cyberleader only believes Sarah's story about a rocket on Voga after she mentions Kellman's involvement, even though she's already told him that Kellman's a traitor and he didn't react to the news at all. To be even pickier, you can see the space-time telegraph message hanging inside the TARDIS door as soon as the Doctor opens it.

The purpose of the Nerva Beacon is questionable at best. It's stationed around Jupiter to warn ships about the Voga asteroid, but the first ship that passes is an Earth-Pluto flight, and why on Earth would a ship heading to or from Pluto bother even going past Jupiter? The idea that ships this far in the future need beacons to avoid large, noticeable asteroids is dubious as well, but not as dubious as the idea that an inhabitable asteroid can cross the galaxy, slow down and slip into orbit around a nearby planet without anyone seeing it happen. (See **Why Does Earth Keep Getting Invaded?** under 13.4, "The Android Invasion", for a tentative explanation as to what's going on here.) In the context of "The Ark in Space": why was the Nerva beacon converted into a survival pod for humanity, rather than Voga, which has apparently been doing the same job for the Vogans for centuries?

And of course... if the transmat filters out non-human matter from Sarah's body, then not only is all known disease eliminated - making the plot of, say, "The Caves of Androzani" (21.6) a bit of a non-starter - but people should be arriving at their destinations stark naked. And the Cybermen should be a few internal organs slopping about on the floor. In fact, had the Doctor thought up this wheeze a couple of stories earlier, Commander Noah would have been cured of his Wirrn infection in episode two.

Critique   It's well-known that "Revenge of the Cybermen" is a horrible mess, although we should stop to consider *why* it's a horrible mess.

Certainly, the plot makes very little sense, but its problems go deeper than that. Stylistically it doesn't know what it is, either. Gerry Davis seems to have started out by trying to write a '60s-style monster story, complete with space station setting and over-elaborate Cyber-plans, apparently failing to realise that it no longer fits the shape of the programme. In a '60s context, Cybermen make perfect sense; they're the ultimate monochrome aliens, built for harsh, high-contrast black-and-white environments, and for best effect they need to be accompanied by the weirdest electronica the Radiophonics Workshop can provide (see "The Invasion", which doesn't make that much sense either but at least shows you how this sort of thing should look and sound).

But by 1974, colour had changed the whole working process of *Doctor Who*, and the music was more about melodrama than high strangeness. The result is something that just looks cheap, crass and dull, generic in most respects

and simply boring in others. Even Robert Holmes' drastic re-writes of the script can't help, since - not for the last time - his repair job just tries to cover the gaping great holes in the story with *Doctor Who* standards. His fatal misconception of the Cybermen as robots, rather than as hi-jacked people, robbed him of the chance to make the definitive "possession" story of the Hinchcliffe phase. Tyrum and Vorus, the two "main" Vogans, are just less interesting versions of the Old and Young Silurian (or, if you want to go back even further, of the Nice and Nasty Sensorites).

Yet somehow, at the time this seemed... apt. After re-configuring the series, re-energising the Daleks as a moral concern and discarding UNIT like a crisp packet, the production team (and the public) needed a sense of the old order fading. Using yesteryear's arch-villains as 'a pathetic bunch of tin soldiers skulking around the Galaxy' was just right. In school playgrounds the Cybermen were mentioned as once-mighty '60s relics, even as the guns in their heads and the diamond-shaped scanner array caught our imaginations. It was like the last vestige of Pertwee being cast aside, even if Pertwee never actually met the buggers. *Doctor Who* no longer needed invasions by monsters, it needed articulate creatures with reasons for what they did. This was a yardstick for why they didn't make 'em like that any more. The brutality in the story - a neglected feature - makes it a necessary stage on the way to the next one filmed, "Genesis of the Daleks". Watching them in broadcast sequence, the step from playing pat-a-cake with Styre in "The Sontaran Experiment" to the slow-motion trench warfare in "Genesis" is abrupt, but with this one in the middle the progress makes more sense.

For a series that's so often been about opening yourself up to foreign influences, it's strange to note that here it's the insular Tyrum who's seen as the wise and respectable one, while the more outward-looking Vorus is portrayed as a reckless and over-ambitious zealot. Voga utterly fails to make its peace with the outside universe at the end of the story, which really is a chronic oversight. Unless it was the set-up for a sequel that never came...

The Facts

Written by Gerry Davis, desperately re-written by Robert Holmes (uncredited). Directed by Michael E. Briant. Viewing figures: 9.5 million, 8.3 million, 8.9 million, 9.4 million.

Supporting Cast Jeremy Wilkin (Kellman), Ronald Leigh-Hunt (Commander Stevenson), William Marlowe (Lester), David Collings (Vorus), Michael Wisher (Magrik), Kevin Stoney (Tyrum), Alec Wallis (Warner), Christopher Robbie (Cyberleader), Brian Grellis (Sheprah).

Working Titles "Return of the Cybermen" (compare this with the Cybermen stories in Volume II, and see what strikes you).

Cliffhangers Sarah, alone and watching TV in a room on the Nerva station, finds a Cybermat lunging at her throat; the Cyberman spaceship docks with the station, and the Cybermen enter, shooting down both the crew and the Doctor (in a scene which you'd swear had been influenced by the opening of *Star Wars*, except that this was made three years early); Harry "imbecile" Sullivan tries to prise the Cyber-bomb off the unconscious Doctor's back, not realising that this is going to trigger a booby-trap and blow the Doctor up.

The Lore

• At the *Doctor Who* twentieth anniversary celebrations in Longleat, someone from BBC Enterprises took a poll of the story that fans most wanted to see again, to launch the release of old *Doctor Who* episodes on video. Although nobody admits to even mentioning it, this was apparently their choice. It was initially released in the form of a one-hour edit, costing £40 and with a picture of "Earthshock"-era Cybermen on the cover. This was hurriedly re-thought. The later ninety minute re-edit retailed at a mere £26.

• The little boats used in the cave scenes (called "Sizzlas") were a bit temperamental, so Elisabeth Sladen came off hers and almost drowned. Much of the location filming at Wookey Hole went badly, and the local stories of "The Witch of Wookey Hole" seemed to many of the crew to be real. Director Briant put this down to lack of oxygen.

• In amongst the shop-dummy corpses are the actors who also played the Cybermen. See if *you* can spot them.

• Michael Wisher provides three voices for the story, and was thus on hand at short notice when Davros was recast (see 12.4, "Genesis of the Daleks").

• David Collings (Vorus), aside from his three *Doctor Who* roles and casual scene-stealing in *Sapphire and Steel*, provided the voice for *Monkey* in the English translation of the Japanese TV version of the Chinese parable. His knighthood is long overdue.

• The magazine Sarah's reading just before being attacked by the Cybermat is an edition of the much-missed *Science Fiction* news / reviews quarterly, published by New English Library. In this, Michael Moorcock tried to get the literati to take *Doctor Who* seriously as popular mythology. (His damning review of *Star Wars*, unfavourably comparing Darth Vader to the Ice Lords, is eminently quotable.)

season 13

13.1: "Terror of the Zygons"

(Serial 4F, Four Episodes, 30th August - 20th September 1975.)

Which One is This? The villains: orange embryos with suckers, AKA "pizza babies". Their pet: the Loch Ness Monster. What fashionable Time Lords are wearing this season: tartan. Yes, it's the "Scottish" story.

Firsts and Lasts The UNIT era ends here. It's already obvious that the Fourth Doctor's planning on spending less time hanging around Earth than his predecessor, but "Terror of the Zygons" sees him called in by the Brigadier to save the world for the last time in the 1970s. Though certain UNIT personnel will make a brief comeback later this season (13.4, "The Android Invasion"), the Brigadier himself vanishes from the picture until "Mawdryn Undead" eight years later (20.3). And with UNIT go certain other "standards" of Earthbound *Doctor Who*... here the aliens attack an energy conference, just like they would have done during the Jon Pertwee years.

"Terror of the Zygons" was originally filmed as part of Season Twelve, but was held back until the beginning of Season Thirteen when producer Philip Hinchcliffe was told to provide an autumn start to the series (see **September or January?**). In fact, by rights this story really *should* go at the end of Season Twelve, since it's the last in a series of connected adventures that began with "Robot". It sees the TARDIS return to Earth after the Doctor's mission/s on the Nerva station, and Harry gets put back in Britain where he belongs. (He ceases to be a member of the TARDIS crew here, although he's one of those who comes back for "The Android Invasion".)

Four Things to Notice About "Terror of the Zygons"...

1. The Zygons themselves are the stars of the show here. Spectacularly nasty, looking not unlike walking embryos covered in alien pustules, the Zygons are perhaps the ultimate sick expression of the BBC designers' obsessions and show you just how much a stretching-the-budget programme like *Doctor Who* can do if it really, really tries. The

Season 13 Cast/Crew

- Tom Baker (the Doctor)
- Elisabeth Sladen (Sarah Jane Smith)
- Ian Marter (Harry Sullivan, 13.1 and 13.4)

- Philip Hinchcliffe (Producer)
- Robert Holmes (Script Editor)

only downside is that although they look beautifully hideous, the Zygons never actually *do* anything very interesting here, which might explain why they never came back to the series despite their obvious appeal to children everywhere.

2. Having dealt with the Welsh in "The Green Death" (10.5), here *Doctor Who* decides that it's time to savage the Scots. The very first scene sees a Scottish oil-rig worker ordering haggis by radio, while the inevitably-named "Angus" (played by real-life Angus, BBC "stock Scotsman" Angus Lennie) is a superstitious wee man who believes himself to have second sight, the way all village Scotsmen apparently do. Bagpipes, jokes about miserliness and big bearded highlanders in kilts are all in attendance, though porridge is only mentioned in the Target novelisation.

3. As befits the last tale of the UNIT age, this is the story in which the contrast between ordinary, everyday British politics and gaudily-coloured alien invaders becomes most obvious. It ends with a fifty-foot monster swimming up the Thames to attack the Prime Minister, and the Brigadier suggests that the powers-that-be are actually going to try to hush it up. The Brigadier also talks to Number Ten on the 'phone, and addresses the Prime Minister as 'madam' (Margaret Thatcher had become leader of the Conservative party in early 1975, so it must have seemed terribly modern at the time). And as the Doctor gloriously tells the Zygon leader: 'You can't rule a world in hiding. You've got to come out onto the balcony sometimes and wave a tentacle.'

4. It has to be said, so let's say it. The Skarasen, AKA the Loch Ness Monster, is possibly the most reviled special effect in the programme's history. The shot which really does the damage comes towards the end of episode four, when a Punch-and-Judy puppet of this dinosaur-like monstrosi-

September or January?

Just when Philip Hinchcliffe thought he'd got to grips with the production timetable of *Doctor Who*, a directive came from the BBC hierarchy telling him that the new season had to begin in September, and not January as planned.

On the face of it this was a strange decision, but the logic was impeccable. Not only was September the start of all major Saturday Night programmes (and remember, at this point Saturday Night was *the* night for TV, a weekly "big event" which yielded the highest-rated shows of the '70s), but in this particular year ITV was attempting to break *Doctor Who's* traditional hold on Saturday tea-time fantasy. They'd been trying this since, frankly, day zero. As soon as the pre-publicity for *Doctor Who* started back in 1963, ITV jumped in with a "spoiler" called *Emerald Soup*, scheduled directly against the BBC's offering; nobody now living remembers anything about this programme at all. But now, with Italian co-production and US distribution, came the most expensive programme - per hour - ever attempted in Britain.

All the signs were that *Space: 1999* was going to be huge. In terms of on-screen talent, scripts, effects and direction, this was the single most concerted effort yet made to "own" Saturdays. Why it failed tells you more about the climate of mid-'70s British TV than any number of statistics. However, you'll need a quick history lesson.

BBC Television began in 1936, funded by the License Fee and untouched by "vulgar" commercial interests. As viewing figures rose - especially after the Coronation of Queen Elizabeth in 1953, a never-before-imagined televised event which *demanded* the country's attention - questions were asked as to why this non-commercial, non-government body should have all the action. The incoming Conservative government decided on a compromise, which characterised UK television until the very recent past. The BBC would get 100% of the Licence Fee, while the new commercial companies would get 100% of advertising revenue.

That's "companies", plural. The Conservatives wanted as much competition as possible. They split the nation up into "regions", and made a law that each region was to have two broadcasting franchises, one for weekdays and one for weekends. There was only one commercial channel, ITV, but what you actually saw on that channel depended on where you lived and which company had the local franchise. In practice, most drama

and comedy series on ITV ended up being shown in every region, but not at the same time or even in the same order.

This meant that when the BBC got its act together, and started making more low-brow programmes as well as the "quality" stuff, ITV as a network was in disarray. No two companies showed the same thing at peak time, all of them trying to get their home-made material the best ratings. Of the sixteen ITV companies around in the '70s, five "big guns" ruled the majority of the air-time. Lew Grade's ATV, makers of *Space: 1999*, was the biggest. (Lew Grade's nephew Michael, then at London Weekend Television, will return to the story of *Doctor Who* in the '80s. It won't be pretty.)

So the debut of *Space: 1999* never really happened. Some companies, notably ATV itself, broadcast it opposite episode two of "Terror of the Zygons". Some showed a western or a talent-show in that slot, and kept *Space: 1999* for later on in the evening. Some showed it on a different day altogether. And thereafter, no two companies showed the episodes in the same sequence. There was a word-of-mouth buzz, namely "don't bother, *Doctor Who's* fighting Nessie", but the ITV companies were too busy competing against each other to form a serious threat to the return of *Doctor Who* to the autumn schedule.

Now, *Doctor Who* had been an autumnal series right from the start, running eleven months of the year until 1969. The decision to move the season opener to January in 1970 was part of the big shift to colour and twenty-six episodes a year. It's worth pondering the place of the series within the Saturday evening schedules in those pre-channel-zapper days. In the '70s, Saturday Night wasn't so much a line-up as a weekly ritual. The usual running-order was: sports results and the Pools (a system of socially-acceptable gambling, which required the public to try to predict which football matches would be goal-less draws... strangely not popular in other countries); a kiddie show (often with a puppet of some kind, Lamb Chop and Basil Brush being the easiest to explain); regional news; *Doctor Who*; then either *The Generation Game* or *The Black and White Minstrel Show*[2]. Next came a popular drama, either set in a small-town police station or in the Edwardian era. This and the subsequent comedy show would last fifty minutes each, and could be replaced by a feature film (sometimes in colour!).

continued on page 53...

ty rears up over some video footage of London. A lovely idea, but utterly impractical (see **How Good Do the Effects Have to Be?** under 10.2, "Carnival of Monsters", for more on this). Still, though the monster's obviously a puppet when it makes its final appearance, there are four all-too-brief moments in episode two when it's all done with stop-motion animation. It's not special effects pioneer Ray Harryhausen, but at least it's trying. And, hey, the Zygon spaceship - especially in the quarry scenes - is pretty fab, by 1975 standards.

The Continuity

The Doctor After getting a shock from the Zygon spaceship, he displays no signs of life and is assumed dead, a common mistake in this era. This Doctor has no trouble driving a Land Rover.

• *Ethics.* Here he has one last stab at being eco-friendly in his capacity as adviser to UNIT, claiming that humanity's reliance on oil doesn't make sense and advocating liquid hydrogen. [This was a fashionable idea then, and at the time of writing is making a comeback on London's busses for a trial period.] He's irritated by the call back to Earth, but agrees to help when the Brigadier points out that people are dying. For once he's happy to let the military blow up the monsters.

• *Inventory.* At this point he's carrying a little navigation device that lets him find civilisation from the wilds of Scotland. The sonic screwdriver's used to heat up organic tissue here.

• *Background.* The Doctor puts both himself and Sarah into a trance when they're trapped in an air-tight space, to preserve oxygen. It can be fatal to break the 'spell' incorrectly, and he claims he picked this trick up from a Tibetan monk. [His unseen visit to the Det-Sen monastery, mentioned in 5.2, "The Abominable Snowmen". Technically he *could* be referring to K'anpo from "Planet of the Spiders" (11.5), but it seems unlikely, as K'anpo only *looked* Tibetan. Ish.]

The Doctor knows a fair amount about Scottish culture, recognising Angus' bagpipe lament. It's not clear whether he knows about the Zygons in advance, but he's remarkably familiar with the way the systems on their spaceship work, so he must at least have seen something similar.

The Supporting Cast

• *Sarah Jane Smith.* Sarah indicates that she can't read Medieval Latin. [Curiously, she can in

Barry Letts' novel *The Ghosts of N-Space*. Perhaps she just can't be bothered today.] Still the great reporter, she's seen typing up the Tulloch Moor mystery even as the crisis unfolds around her.

Leaving Scotland, the only reason she gets on board the TARDIS is that she thinks she's getting a lift back to London, so she still doesn't see herself as the Doctor's full-time companion and apparently just wants to get to the capital. [Where she lives? See 14.2, "The Hand of Fear", for her address.] Even so, she's the only one who's prepared to trust the Doctor to get her there, and there may be a hint that she's secretly hoping for "diversions" on the way. [She doesn't seem *too* put out when the TARDIS gets pulled off-course in the next story. The Doctor genuinely thinks he's heading down to London here, and isn't trying to "trap" her into travelling with him. The Doctor even offers a lift to the Brigadier, so if *he'd* accepted then he'd be having adventures with anti-matters creatures and Egyptian gods in the days to come.]

• *Harry Sullivan.* Unlike Sarah, he refuses to let the Doctor try to get him back to London in the TARDIS, so the space-travelling lifestyle isn't for him. Like the rest of the UNIT personnel, he still acts as if Earth is the Doctor's base of operations, and seems to expect the Doctor to return to UNIT before long.

• *The Brigadier.* Has no qualms about wearing a kilt, proudly announcing his Scottish heritage as a member of the 'clan Stewart'. It's still not explained exactly when the Doctor gave the Brigadier a 'space-time telegraph' to get in touch with the TARDIS [see the previous story], but the Brigadier's idea of a crisis is a collapsing oil-rig, so he still sees the Doctor as being part of UNIT's defence of Great Britain.

He states that he was sceptical about the existence of aliens before he joined UNIT [he may be saying this just to get the Duke of Forgill on his side, since it's not an accurate description of what happens in "The Web of Fear" (5.5) and he seems to have been part of UNIT ever since it was founded]. He's now describing UNIT as a 'military investigation team'.

• *RSM Benton.* Now known universally as "Mister" Benton [and referred to as "RSM" in the credits, but not on-screen].

The TARDIS The Doctor leaves the Ship in a tartan scarf and a tam-o'-shanter, while Sarah's new

September or January?

...continued from page 51

You can see the logical progression from 5.30 pm to 9.00 pm. Just to reinforce this, from about 1976 many of these programmes had curiously similar diamond-shaped logos. The BBC never had serious opposition to its Saturday schedule, despite Michael Grade's attempt to poach all the BBC's best stars and put them in a weekly spectacular opposite Season Sixteen. Yes, that's right: the bugger was trying to sabotage *Doctor Who* even then.

Nevertheless, the slot usually occupied by *Doctor Who* in the '60s needed filling for half the year after the series slimmed down to twenty-six episodes in 1970. They tried an imported American show called *Star Trek*, but it bombed. It was moved to Monday evenings and was in perpetual rerun for over a decade (by which time most people had seen it, if not actually *watched* it, so it became an "old favourite" through repetition

rather than good ratings). It became apparent very early on in the '70s that "spooky adventures" worked better when the nights began early; in Southern Britain the difference between June and December sunset times can be five hours. So September to March was better than January to June.

This wasn't a snap decision. In the series' first few years, the start of the *Doctor Who* season moved from late November, to Hallowe'en, to late September, to August. In the Pertwee days the start date was rigidly New Year (or a day or so later), until "The Three Doctors" in 1973, when the BBC experimented with making it part of the Christmas festivities.

The logic is clear: by BBC standards, the content of *Doctor Who* was less important than the universality of its demographic. In 1975, they weren't simply competing with another "science fiction" show - aimed squarely at teenage boys - but against other BBC-made "family" programming.

coat surely comes from the TARDIS wardrobe. The 'space-time telegraph' is now referred to as a syonic beam [not "psionic", according to the script]. The TARDIS navigation can't be perfect yet, as the Doctor lands some distance from UNIT's Scottish home-from-home [presumably the Ship tries to home in on the beam].

Leaving Scotland, the Doctor intends to be back in London 'five minutes ago', though Sarah protests that she thought he couldn't do that. [He's close to the Blinovitch Limitation Effect here, but not too close. But compare this with 13.3, "Pyramids of Mars".]

The Non-Humans

• *Zygons*. Horrible lumpy blobby orange things, appearing humanoid but half-finished, with skins covered in patches of "suckers" that make them look a lot like sea-creatures. Still, they find humans equally unpleasant. The Zygons seen here are brutal and militaristic, led by their 'warlord' Commander Broton, though the Doctor - for once - never claims that they're *all* this aggressive.

This group of about half a dozen Zygons landed on Earth 'centuries' ago after their craft was damaged, and settled down to wait for rescue, but then heard that their planet had been destroyed in a stellar explosion. The Zygons decided to make Earth their home, and a Zygon refugee fleet is now

on its way, though it'll be 'many centuries' before it arrives. Broton plans to get rid of the polar icecaps, raise the mean temperature by several degrees and construct thousands of lakes with the necessary minerals in order to re-create his own planet. [We never hear anything of the fleet. If it takes around a thousand years to get from the Zygon planet to Earth then this particular Zygon unit must have been well out of its way when the ship crashed… but as Zygons are obviously long-lived, they might be used to extraordinarily long journeys. Broton describes the stellar explosion as 'recent' even though it happened centuries ago, which tells you something about the way they perceive time.]

Zygons are physically strong enough for strangulation or neck-breaking to be their chosen method of killing. For once the aliens aren't bulletproof. [The script's intention was for the Zygons to have a jellyfish-like sting, but this doesn't come across on-screen; see **The Lore**.]

Zygons have an organic technology, the interior of their spaceship resembling the interior of a body, with unpleasantly squishy and visceral controls. Strangely, though, the *outside* of the spaceship is black, metallic and hard-edged [perhaps they grow the insides, then seal the ship's guts inside a metal shell to protect it during flight]. 'Organic crystallography' seems to be involved in

ABOUT TIME 1975-1979

its power system, and the ship has something called 'dynacon thrust'. The Zygons can change shape to appear wholly human, and change back at will, but only if the original human subject is held in a compartment on board the Zygon ship so that its 'body-print' can be accessed. It's important to activate a body-print every few hours, or the original pattern [person] dies and can't be used again. Clothes and body language are also copied, thankfully. Zygons apparently have genders, as the one who takes the form of the local nurse sounds female even in her natural state. When a Zygon dies, it reverts to its natural squishy form and the "copied" human regains consciousness.

Other tools used by the Zygons here include a radar jamming system that affects the entire country [potentially more damaging than having a monster chew on the odd oil-rig], knock-out nerve gas and 'molecular dispersal' which allows Broton to disintegrate the body of one of his "men" from the comfort of his spaceship.

• *The Skarasen.* A vast, amphibious dinosaur-like being, covered in armour that's resistant even to nuclear missiles and with a mouth full of teeth that can chew through solid steel, the Skarasen is a cyborg brought to Earth by the Zygons as an embryo. Broton states it's been 'converted' into an armoured weapon, so this isn't its natural form.

As the Zygon ship is parked on the bottom of Loch Ness, and the Skarasen inhabits the nearby waters, it's fairly clear that humans have glimpsed the creature over the previous centuries. As well as being a neat piece of weaponry, the Skarasen is vital to the Zygons' survival, giving them the 'lactic fluid' on which they thrive. As Harry points out, it must technically be a mammal. [What did the Zygons eat on board their ship, before it landed? Did they have an in-flight Skarasen? The question of what the Skarasen eats should also be addressed, as it's really *much* too big for the Loch's ecosystem to support it. Maybe it nips out into the North Sea when it's hungry, or maybe it feeds on raw power from the Zygon ship.]

The screen in the Zygon ship can see what the Skarasen's seeing [camera implants]. The Zygons use a small, part-organic 'trilanic activator' to attract the Skarasen. When one of these devices is switched on from their control room, the beast homes in on it and rips the surrounding area to pieces. The Doctor believes it may give out a primeval mating-call, but it sounds more like a quiet beeping noise. The devices can stick to human(oid) tissue as if biting it, and seem to be able to move a little.

Ultimately the Skarasen swims back to Loch Ness, where it isn't expected to cause any trouble on its own.

Planet Notes

• *Voga.* The Doctor says he's been dragged '270 million miles' to Earth, so Voga's roughly that far away. Or will be, in the future [12.5, "Revenge of the Cybermen"].

History

• *Dating.* It's the '70s, and the Prime Minister's a woman. [1976 is a good bet. See **What's the UNIT Timeline?** under 8.5, "The Daemons". Some time must have passed since "Robot", as the PM would seem to have changed; Harry isn't used to a woman being in charge in "The Ark in Space" (12.2). See also **Who's Running the Country?** under 10.5, "The Green Death".]

Four oil rigs are destroyed on the Waverley Field off the coast of Scotland, the last of them being the Ben Nevis rig, fifty miles west of the similarly doomed Prince Charlie. The centre of Zygon operations is the village of Tulloch and Tulloch Moor, six or seven miles from Loch Ness. There have been sightings of the monster in the Loch since the Middle Ages, so the Zygons may have been there that long. [For more on Loch Ness, see 22.4, "Timelash".] A foreign visitor vanished on the Moor in 1922, as did young Donald Jameson in 1870, while his older brother Robert was found 'wandering about, off his head' two days later. He never spoke again.

The Fourth International Energy Conference is being held at Stanbridge House, by the Thames in London. A meeting of 'crucial importance', VIPs from all over the world are invited, and the British PM is attending. So is the Duke of Forgill, as President of the Scottish Energy Commission. At the conclusion of the Zygon attack the Skarasen comes out of the Thames in the middle of London and startles a large number of passing motorists, though after this there's no indication that the world remembers the event [as the Doctor points out in 25.1, "Remembrance of the Daleks"]. The Cabinet accepts the Brigadier's report, and the politicians act as if it never happened. Nor does anyone spot a Zygon spaceship blowing up in a quarry in Brentford.

Additional Sources In a scene cut from the broadcast version - though mention of it is still briefly audible in episode one, as the Doctor makes his way through the trees - the TARDIS malfunctions and becomes invisible on arriving in Scotland. This was meant to be a neat back-reference to the first UNIT story, "The Invasion" (6.3), also directed by Douglas Camfield. It's still found in the novelisation.

The Analysis

Where Does This Come From? Less than a week after Robert Banks Stewart pitched this story to Robert Holmes, a crew led by Sir Peter Scott, a conservationist, released a sonar shot of what looked like the fin or fluke of a large sea-creature in Loch Ness. This was significant as, not being like a plesiosaurus fin (spatulate, with vestigial fingers) but diamond-shaped, it earned the putative creature a Linnean species-name. *Nessitarius Rhombopteryx* (as Scott named the creature, all the better to get it listed as an endangered species) was back in the public eye.

Doppelgangers, fetches and shape-shifters are the raw material of many Scots folk-tales. Silkie-folk, the seals who occasionally become human, crop up as often as faeries stealing human children and replacing them with changelings (see also 18.3, "Full Circle"). So taking the '50s paranoid SF standby of aliens impersonating your friends - *I Married A Monster from Outer Space / Invasion of the Body Snatchers / They Came From Outer Space,* et al - and placing it in the Highlands was a canny move. And an uncanny one. As mentioned in the Critique, the first episode clearly invokes werewolf stories. The opening shot even has a full moon.

And North Sea Oil was never out of the headlines. The rigs were being launched almost weekly, with promises of a boom in production around 1979-80. This saved the Clydeside shipbuilders' jobs during the recession, and made Scots Nationalism a growing concern. One of the main campaigning platforms of the Scottish National Party was the way the London-based media portrayed the diversity of Caledonian ethnicity in clichéd, stereotypical ways…

Things That Don't Make Sense The Zygons are as confused about how the world works as all the other aliens we've ever met. Specifically, Broton seems to believe that the best way to take over the

planet is to alert everyone to his presence by attacking an energy conference in London. His plans *after* that aren't discussed.

More puzzling still, the grumpy Duke of Forgill gives the Doctor and companions a lift to UNIT's headquarters when he sees them hitch-hiking, curious as it later turns out that he's a Zygon warlord in disguise. How obliging of him. [Does he immediately notice something funny about the Doctor, and want a better look? Something funny *apart* from the hat, anyway.]

Strangely, the Duke has a sense of irony when he's human but not when he's lumpy and orange. And why, exactly, does the fake Sister Lamont feel the need to change back into her Zygon form whenever she's doing anything menacing? She's also one of those annoying villains who leave the heroes in complex death-traps rather than just slaughtering them, and similarly there's no good reason for the Zygons to keep the Doctor alive on the ship in episode four, except that it gives him a chance to wreck their plans.

The Doctor goes to all the trouble of whispering to the Brigadier that the boarding-house is probably bugged, so the Brigadier immediately orders Mr. Benton to search the place in his "loud" voice. Anyone who's ever seen a spy movie will know that the best place for a hidden camera is in the eye of a mounted head on a wall, yet when Benton approaches said head, Angus warns him not to touch it… to which Benton basically shrugs and walks off, meaning that UNIT searches everywhere *except* the head. Amateurs.

The Skarasen, a creature with yard-long teeth, somehow chews up the tiny signalling device before swallowing. The final scene sees everyone go back up to Scotland to watch the Doctor get his TARDIS back, then refuse a trip back to London. The Brigadier may well want to clear up loose ends at Tulloch, but why on Earth do Sarah and Harry go all that way by InterCity just to stand in a woodland watching the Ship dematerialise?

Inspecting the corpse of a man crushed to death by the Skarasen, Benton states that he's never seen anything like it before, so he's forgotten all about the man who got stepped on by the Devil in "The Daemons" and the soldier squidged by the giant robot in "Robot" only a few months earlier. Amnesia also strikes Sarah, who's seen loads of sliding doors on her travels. Yet when confronted with one that slides upwards instead of sideways, she turns into Norman Wisdom[1].

Critique A troubling sign of *Doctor Who* trying to come up with a generic *Doctor Who* story, "Terror of the Zygons" is best described as "typical", which is - depending on your outlook - either a sign of greatness or a very bad idea.

To be fair, there's much here that's original (a lot of the design work, for a start), but with hindsight there's also too much that's too familiar. As with "Planet of the Spiders", the first episode is substantially better than the others, a neat little package of wit and character-acting which instantly becomes less interesting when the monsters turn up. The Zygons may *look* great, but they're embarrassingly generic baddies with nothing to do but loom, gloat and drone on about puny humans, as well as committing a cardinal sin of SF by measuring everything in 'Earth miles'. Even the opening scene looks like a re-make of "The Sea Devils" with Scottish accents, while the Zygon in the hayloft might hail from "The Silurians", and the spaceship's just a more morbid version of the flying flesh-machine from "The Claws of Axos".

The sterile nature of Zygons-as-monsters becomes painfully obvious in episode two, when Broton rattles off his people's dismal back-story to Harry in the shortest possible time, just to get it out of the way. A worse sign still is the number of action-serial standards that are shovelled into the plot - again, as in "The Claws of Axos" - including all the tedious shape-changing; it's all very well for the Doctor to send up the Zygons' dull, unimaginative plans as if it were a great in-joke, but it'd be nice if he didn't have to.

In an odd way the story's almost an anthology. Episode one is a "gothic" tale, with Broton shot in such tight close-ups as to make him seem like a werewolf with sunburn; episode two is '50s-style alien doppelganger fare (plus aforementioned Harryhausen-lite ending); three is nearly Pertwee-by-numbers; and finally it turns into *The Man From Uncle*. Seen an episode a week in 1975 this was no bad thing, but now it's all atmosphere and no engagement, and the lead actors' performances are vastly more entertaining than the plot. It's certainly a good story for Lis Sladen, as Sarah often seems to do a lot more than the Doctor.

Lines to join in with: (1) 'I underestimated his intelligence. But *he* underestimated the power of organic crystallography.' (2) 'You're all utterly unhinged! Must be! Aliens? With wireless sets?' Bonus points if you can keep a straight face while Tom Baker fondles the "organic" Zygon controls.

The Facts

Written by Robert Banks Stewart. Directed by Douglas Camfield. Viewing figures: 8.4 million, 6.1 million, 8.2 million, 7.2 million. (Note the disparity between episodes one, two and three... and... see **September or January?**, for why this should be).

Supporting Cast Nicholas Courtney (Brigadier Lethbridge-Stewart), John Levene (RSM Benton), John Woodnutt (Duke of Forgill), Lillias Walker (Sister Lamont), Robert Russell (The Caber), Angus Lennie (Angus).

Working Titles Amazingly, "The Loch Ness Monster"; "The Secret of Loch Ness"; "The Loch Ness Terror" (this was a mistake by the BBC publicists, but you can see how they made it); "Doctor Who and the Zygons".

Cliffhangers Making a call from the local hospital, Sarah turns around to find a Zygon looming over her (this happens to Sarah a lot); the Doctor flees from the Skarasen across Tulloch Moor; the Zygon ship lifts out of the Loch and flies off into the distance, with the Doctor held captive aboard.

The Lore

• The Zygons weren't the main focus of the script to begin with (it was more *Avengers*-ish, with a bunch of eccentrics faking a monster in an attempt at Total World Domination). Yet, contrary to what many people think, the Zygon / zygote connection wasn't made until much later. The name preceded James Acheson's foetus-like design, which developed from the hint that the creatures needed the Skarasen for its 'lactic fluid'. Acheson and mask-maker extraordinaire John Friedlander only made three costumes, though some effectively claustrophobic direction makes the Zygon spaceship look much busier.

In the original design, the head and chest were meant to glow whenever a Zygon "stung" a victim, but this was abandoned when they realised that - apart from making the costumes get very hot – this would require an external power-supply. This may be why the finished programme glosses over the idea that the Zygons are capable of stinging, and just has them throttling people instead.

• It's Douglas Camfield who's singing the silly

little pseudo-Scottish song as Angus discovers the bug. Camfield's heart-murmur had led to his wife (actress Sheila Dunn) refusing to let him work on this stressful series, but the script tempted him out of "retirement".

• The entire story was filmed on location in Sussex, not Scotland (the roofs of the houses are a giveaway, if you know what you're looking for).

• The subplot about the gas attack was added when the Skarasen animation for the original scene looked a little too silly.

• The "fake" Harry's pitchfork attack on Sarah was heavily edited for the story's 1988 video release, and is far more brutal-looking in its original form (see 14.6, "The Talons of Weng-Chiang", for more paranoid violence-trimming done at around this time).

• On August Bank Holiday, five days before episode one was screened, Tom Baker presented an edition of *Disney Time* on BBC1 (in those days *Disney Time* was a Bank Holiday tradition, one of the few places where you could see clips from Disney films in the days before video, although with hindsight these shows just look like shameless "advertising features" for the Disney Corporation). He presented it in character, with the Doctor receiving a note from the Brigadier and leaving Blackpool in the TARDIS at the end. Which contradicts "Revenge of the Cybermen" somewhat, but probably no more so than having the Doctor break off from his adventures to take an interest in dancing cartoon hippos.

• Apart from a fortnight after "Genesis of the Daleks", the three-week break between filming this story and "Pyramids of Mars" was the only holiday the regulars had until a similarly brief gap prior to "The Brain of Morbius" (13.5). This was for a very good reason…

13.2: "Planet of Evil"

(Serial 4H, Four Episodes, 27th September - 18th October 1975.)

Which One is This? The one that definitively scared kids, with an "invisible" jungle-planet monster that sometimes looks like a glowing red outline and sometimes turns spacemen in tracksuits into fantastically gruesome skeletons. In tracksuits. We find out that anti-matter puts hairs on your chest, while the Doctor puts Black Pool rock in his toffee-tin.

Firsts and Lasts With the TARDIS more or less behaving itself, this is the first use of that hardy plot-device: "it's a distress call… let's answer it". Last appearance of the corduroy jacket intended to make the Doctor look like a student. Things have quite firmly entered a new phase now.

Four Things to Notice About "Planet of Evil"…

1. As ever in this period, the star attraction here is the monster, and it's another infamous child-scarer of the 1970s. The anti-matter creature on Zeta Minor - glimpsed only as a silhouette of energy, and quite overtly nicked from *Forbidden Planet* - has been memorably described as an "invisible red string thing", and is notable because there were never any photographs of it in the *Doctor Who Monster Books*. (Mind you, the thing that most people now think of when they see the anti-matter effects in episode four - the video for Queen's "Bohemian Rhapsody" - didn't turn up until later that year. Maybe they nicked it from *Doctor Who*?)

2. A word also has to be said about the design of the jungle on Zeta Minor. Alien jungles have been a staple of *Doctor Who* almost from the beginning, but this is easily the most impressive example, a lush, sprawling, almost *crystalline* world lit in exotic shades of purple. The BBC handbook on how to design sets used a photo of it as the front cover. Sadly, the whole design budget seems to have been blown on the jungle sets. The second half of the story is almost entirely set on the Morestran spaceship, and *Lord* it's dull, full of empty grey corridors patrolled by *Star-Trek*-style future-humans. Pay special attention to the Morestran military uniforms, designed to let the soldiers prove their manliness by putting their chest-hair on display.

3. The first story filmed for Season Thirteen, "Planet of Evil" kicks off what's now generally seen as *Doctor Who's* "horror year". Future stories will involve mummies, man-eating plants and a Time Lord Frankenstein's monster, but here the horror cliché on offer is a werewolf (an anti-matter werewolf, mind you, but still a werewolf). Frederick Jaeger's performance as the snarling, hairy Professor Sorenson makes the Primord ape-men in "Inferno" look believable, but if there's an award for most gratuitous eye-rolling then he gets it.

4. Hooray! Futuristic ethnic diversity. Louis Mahoney (the trend-setting black newsreader from 10.3, "Frontier in Space") gets another dignified-but-tiny role; obviously Irish actors play

characters called "Ponti" and "De Haan"; and Crewman Ranjit is a voice-only role for Michael "Davros" Wisher. Still, until *Star Trek* gets an Ensign Patel and a Lieutenant Singh, we're ahead on points.

The Continuity

The Doctor   Sarah points out, with some justification, that the Doctor always gets rude while trying to cover up his mistakes. Especially when it comes to navigating the TARDIS. Here he willingly uses physical force - a solid punch rather than Venusian karate - to knock out Salamar.

• *Ethics*. Formally describing himself as a 'scientist' here, he tells Sorenson that their privilege to experiment has a price of 'total responsibility' [compare with the Doctor's actions in 11.5, "Planet of the Spiders"]. This means that he's prepared to talk Sorenson into killing himself. Though he admits he's tempted to let the bullying Morestrans destroy themselves, he has a duty to stop them because 'they wouldn't be the only ones' [to snuff it].

The Doctor promises the planet that the Morestrans won't take away any of its mass, and Sarah speaks of his 'promise as a Time Lord' as if this were an unbreakable vow. [In the previous story he promises Sarah that he'll get her back to Earth straight away, and doesn't, so there's a difference between a "normal" promise and a "Time Lord" promise.]

• *Inventory*. He's got a little hand-held gadget that leads him to the source of the Morestrans' distress signal, but from the way he shakes it the device may not be working. There's an empty toffee tin in his pocket, which gets left on Zeta Minor.

• *Background*. Inevitably, the Doctor has met Shakespeare, describing the man as a 'charming fellow' but a dreadful actor. [See 17.2, "City of Death", for more on the Doctor and William.] He seems to know that Zeta Minor marks the boundary of an anti-matter universe without deducing it properly.

The Supporting Cast

• *Sarah Jane Smith*. Curiously, she knows where in the TARDIS to find the Doctor's spectrum-mixer without being told. She's equally good at finding her way around unfamiliar spaceships, recognising the sound of Compression Units firing up and knowing exactly what to do with a portable force-field generator. More importantly, she's aware of the anti-matter creature but is never attacked by it. [Some form of ESP the Morestrans lack, or just a TARDIS-passenger Frequent Flyer deal like language skills?]

The TARDIS   The Ship comes out of the space-time vortex 30,000 years too late, apparently due to a minor glitch [navigation is becoming increasingly erratic in this period]. The console then picks up the distress call from the Morestrans on Zeta Minor, and the Doctor feels obliged to investigate. He makes an 'emergency materialisation' which lands him *somewhere* in the vicinity of the call. Here he can't tell where the TARDIS has landed from the instruments [a result of Zeta Minor's slightly peculiar relationship with the rest of the universe, of the 'emergency materialisation', or of the glitch which makes the TARDIS arrive 30,000 years late?], but on board the Ship is a spectrum-mixer which allows him to determine his location through the position of the stars. [This is how he does things in 1.2, "The Daleks", but since then the TARDIS *must* have been upgraded so that the console readings tell him the locale. At least usually.] The mixer is kept in a black bag somewhere outside the console room, and the same receptacle contains the etheric beam locator that used to be in the Doctor's pockets [12.4, "Genesis of the Daleks"]. Somewhere on the Ship, there's also a metal frame with manacles attached that can bind someone's hands and feet.

This is the first time the TARDIS console room has been seen in some time [actually since 11.3, "Death to the Daleks"], and it doesn't seem to be in great shape. The console column's particularly wonky at the moment. Sarah's once again able to use the key without the Doctor being present, and the key still looks like a medallion [as in 11.5, "Planet of the Spiders"].

The Ship successfully makes two short-range trips here, despite its other navigational problems. The conclusion of the story sees it spinning off into space [it does this in 10.3, "Frontier in Space", but there it's implied that the Ship's moving through hyperspace and here it's just floating past stars].

Planet Notes

• *Zeta Minor*. 'The last planet of the known universe', at least from the Morestrans' point of view.

What Does Anti-Matter Do?

In *Doctor Who* we've had stories based around various different things called "anti-matter", all of which are based on physics as it was understood at the time those scripts were written. Which means that they all contradict each other. By invoking the science as it's known here in the twenty-first century, we've got some hope of reconciling these accounts and working out what's supposed to be going on here.

In theory, there's nothing odd about anti-matter. It's just made of particles with charges, like regular matter, but the charges are different. An atom of hydrogen (and hydrogen's the most basic element, if you failed GCSE science) has at its core a positively-charged proton and, "orbiting" around it, an equal and opposite amount of charge: an electron. If you had a negatively-charged particle at the centre and a positively-charged thing buzzing around it, then that would be anti-hydrogen, an antiproton orbited by a positron. Positrons - and it's so very tempting to think of them as "evil electrons" with eye-patches, which is undoubtedly how we'd show them if we were doing this in the style of *South Park* - do definitely exist. PET scanners in hospitals are built to detect them; PET stands for Positron Emission Tomography.

There's nothing in the maths to suggest that regular, common-or-garden, positive matter should be any more plentiful than anti-matter. The sums work just as well for both, and physics is - after all - maths taught badly. But as even Trekkies know, put matter and anti-matter side-by-side and they annihilate one another, leaving behind a lot of electromagnetic radiation (light, heat, radio waves, that sort of thing). If there were an equal amount of matter and anti-matter, even just in "empty" space, then we'd hear about it. So as soon as anti-matter got taken seriously, people asked the obvious question: if the universe is "democratic", then there should be an equal amount of anti-matter somewhere. Where is it?

The obvious suggestion was that it had its own universe, like ours but "upside-down". Richard Feynman, maverick physicist and bongo-player, once speculated that if positrons were "just" electrons going backwards through time (and this was seriously proposed, in the 1950s) then maybe there was just one electron / positron going backwards and forwards through time and "weaving" all of matter together. As the number of electrons in a grain of sand has at least twenty noughts on the end of it, a good way of giving yourself a nervous breakdown is to try to imagine how old that

electron would be at the end of its journey. Feynman felt happy with this kind of speculation because he and John Wheeler - the man who came up with the snappy term "black hole" - had demonstrated that there was a symmetry between the passage of time; no real reason why "forwards" should be better than "backwards", as far as particles were concerned. Thus, in the popular imagination, anti-matter progressed through negative time. (As in the gibberish science of Star Trek, notably the cop-out ending of the episode "The Naked Time", if you can remember it.)

By the mid-'70s this idea became an easily-digested "solution" to mysteries like quasars, black holes, time only going one way and whether yetis built Atlantis to house their flying saucers. What the SF-loving public wasn't so comfortable handling was *charged parity violation*. In essence, this is the observation that particles and their anti-particle "mirror images" aren't quite the same. This is where "Planet of Evil" comes in, as mid-'70s primers were speculating on how this might be resolved through "mixing violations".

All the fundamental particles that make up matter - electrons, neutrons, etc - were shown to be themselves made up of "particulettes", notably quarks. There are six "flavours" of quark, plus so-called "strange" quarks which are something like anti-quarks. Put one particular kind of quark together with a strange quark, and miraculously it makes a particle which "mixes" with its anti-particle. The resulting particle is called a "kaon". This is the so-called "strange matter" that the Rani gets so excited about in "Time and the Rani" (24.1), but let's try to forget we mentioned that story in relation to legitimate physics and get back to "Planet of Evil". The crystals Sorenson finds on Zeta Minor are potentially something like this strange matter, neither matter nor anti-matter but made from mixed-up bits of both. They aren't nearly dense enough, though, as in theory a sugarlump-sized piece of strange matter should weigh a few hundred tonnes.

It does, however, take something pretty extraordinary to create this kind of strange matter. But then, if we accept that the *Doctor Who* universe is a universe with an edge - and it's been suggested in too many stories to avoid - then we've already got something pretty extraordinary.

It rather depends on how you define an "edge". For time-travel to function as it's been explained (if

continued on page 61...

They describe it as being beyond Cygnus A [nothing to do with the constellation of Cygnus in Earth's galaxy, surely?], as distant from the Artoro galaxy as the Artoro galaxy is from the Anterides. Appearing purple from space, much of Zeta Minor is covered with lush and pleasantly garish jungle, but it's also rich in crystalline rocks which the Morestrans believe can supply them with a new source of energy.

In fact, Zeta Minor is the boundary between this universe and a universe of anti-matter, and these rocks are anti-matter rocks. [This is scientifically weird; see **What Does Anti-Matter Do?**.] Professor Sorenson believes that six pounds of the material can produce the same power output as the Morestran sun over three centuries. The stuff's radioactive, and glows alarmingly on occasion.

The planet, which apparently functions as if it were a single organism, objects to any attempts to remove the anti-matter. It makes an attempt to drag the Morestran ship back when it lifts off with some of the rocks, a pull which gets weaker when there's less anti-matter on board. The planet can also move its seams of ore around.

Guarding the surface is a large, aggressive, gunproof creature that's generally invisible and can only occasionally be glimpsed as a red energy-outline capable of growing to huge sizes. It seems to have the ability to form itself out of thin air, then dissipate again when it's finished threatening everyone, but it only comes out at night. Its victims suffer pain before disappearing without trace, their shrivelled bodies re-appearing shortly afterwards, lacking all bodily fluids. Sorenson sees it as 'pure energy in physical form'. Also on the planet is a "black pool" of nothingness, described as a vortex between universes. The Doctor communicates with the planet by taking a dip into it, and even *he's* drained by the experience. He suggests that he wouldn't have been able to survive the pool without a sample of anti-matter in his pocket, which seems strange.

Sorenson develops a vaccine to protect him from anti-quark penetration, but it sets up a cycle of chemical change which hybridises his cells. He's described as 'infected' by the anti-matter, and begins a metamorphosis into a snarling, red-eyed, super-strong wolfman-like creature, capable of dehydrating its victims just like the thing on the planet. The Doctor describes this creature as 'antiman'. [The similarity to the Primords in 7.4, "Inferno", is striking. Yet the substance which has

such a mutagenic effect on Sorenson is a "different" form of matter, from another universe. Compare this with the rampant speculation in **What's Wrong with the Centre of the Earth?** under "Inferno". Here, though, Sorenson's vaccine acts as a catalyst.]

One of the Morestrans' dangerously radioactive neutron accelerators boosts the anti-man's power, causing pure half-invisible anti-matter duplicates to split off from him and multiply, but they can be held at bay with more anti-matter. Oh, and the creatures can walk through walls. And for some reason they all vanish when Sorenson's pushed into the black pool, where the anti-matter's removed from his system and he's "cured". This is all quite baffling, really.

The Doctor claims that the two universes have existed side-by-side since the beginning of time, each one the antithesis of the other. He believes the universe would end if any part of Zeta Minor were removed, and states that it's dangerous to move material from one 'dimension' to another. [Q.v. "Inferno", again, in which the Doctor refuses to transport individuals from the parallel universe back to the world he knows.] The Doctor confirms that matter and anti-matter in collision cause radiation annihilation, though this doesn't seem to apply on the surface of Zeta Minor.

History

• *Dating.* According to the Morestran calendar it's 37166. [It's never made clear whether the Morestrans are humans from the far future, or aliens who just happen to look entirely humanoid. The former seems by far the most likely, though, as they have familiar human-style names. In which case it's quite possible that it's 37166 AD, especially as the Doctor says the TARDIS has come out of the space-time vortex 30,000 years too late.]

The Morestran solar system is dependant on a dying sun, and the Morestran science authorities are desperately searching for a new energy source in order to save its civilisation. Sorenson claims there are other civilisations just as desperate. The paid Morestran military have a functional, drab-corridor-stocked probe ship and are obviously capable of crossing vast tracts of space. The ship has a force-field barrier, a solarium, cyclo-stimulators and an atomic accelerator. The Morestran military wear stiff-looking blue-and-white uniforms in the Buck Rogers mould; carry large ener-

What Does Anti-Matter Do?

...continued from page 59

at all) in *Doctor Who*, there can't be a physical "end" to the universe. The universe has to be four-dimensional; the galaxies separate from one another as space expands, but it doesn't expand "from" a centre "to" an edge. All places are the centre, just as everywhere on the surface of a sphere is the same distance from the core. (The usual pop-science description: if you want a model for the way the universe expands, then draw some galaxies on the skin of a half-inflated balloon and then blow it up a bit.) As Giordano Bruno said, just before they burned him at the stake in 1600: 'We can assert with certitude that the universe is all centre, or that the centre of the universe is everywhere and the circumference nowhere.' (See also **How Can the Universe Have a Centre?** under 20.4, "Terminus".)

Zeta Minor may well be at the edge of the area where there are stars to be seen, but more significantly it's described as the 'boundary' between one state of matter and another. The area of the black pool, where this crossover seems to take place, produces the mysterious crystals. Earlier, in "The Mutants" (9.4), the Doctor speculates on a place at the other end of space where anti-matter versions of people go when they've been "converted" by matter-inversion. The whimsical tone of this speech allows us to posit that "other end" might not be a physical place, but a state of being co-existing with this one in a different spatial dimension, and that - as suggested in "Arc of Infinity" (20.1) - there are "gateways" located within ordinary space. The 'boundary' might be in the heart of a galaxy, like the eponymous Arc of Infinity, or simply on the edge of a spiral galaxy as Zeta Minor seems to be.

The latter is more likely to have gone unnoticed. And there's a side-effect worth noting here. As mentioned under "Inferno" (7.4), material from other universes has almost always manifested itself in a way which "undoes" evolution. The hint seems to be that time runs differently for things affected by peculiar forms of matter. Perhaps, as people thought in the 1950s, anti-matter runs counter to our chronology after all.

Now, in "The Three Doctors" Omega seems to have complete control over anti-matter, using it as cosmic jelly and converting it from anti-matter to matter to anti-matter again whenever he feels like it. To get a grip on how this works, let's get back to that question: in *our* universe, why does the amount of matter seem to greatly outweigh the amount of anti-matter? Well, in 1999 researchers at CERN and Fermilab came up with one possible answer, but it's a bit technical. In short, the transition from anti-matter to matter is easier than the reverse. The agency of the "reverse" transition is something called an X Boson, but the universe is now too cool to allow many of these to exist. So, maybe Omega's got some kind of deal going with these X Bosons.

In our universe, as it is now, you might see one created every (tight squeeze here) 10,000,000,000,000,000,000,000,000,000,000 years. But we're talking about someone who used to redecorate stars for a living, so this might not be a problem for him. In "Arc of Infinity" something called quad magnetism allows both matter and anti-matter to coexist, and allows the Doctor to be 'bonded' to Omega. As standard-issue magnetism involves forces connected to photons, maybe this mysterious "quad" variety is related to X Bosons instead. It's supposedly the product of collapsing Q-Stars (like Q-cars and Q-planes, custom jobs?), and the 'only' force which can shield anti-matter within our cosmos.

So there you have it: any anti-matter you might find is either from another universe, or created in a lab. (Fermilab at present can make sixty-billion antiprotons an hour, but it takes a lot of energy. To produce one kilo of it, you'd need to spend all the money that was spent in the 1980s by all the world's nations put together. There are 600 *trillion* protons in the aforementioned single grain of sand.) As a power-source it's a dud, unless you can find a way of "importing" it.

So you can see the appeal of nicking rocks from Zeta Minor.

gy weapons referred to as 'disintegrators' and smaller guns set to stun; own a little flying probe-robot called an 'oculoid tracker'; and can teleport - or as they put it, 'transpose' - objects onto their ship while it's in orbit. There are different religions in the Morestran Empire, with one crewmember described as Morestran Orthodox. In space, they "bury" their dead by jettisoning the bodies into the void. They even have a machine to play the last rites, though nobody has to listen to it.

It's Morestran procedure to scan any 'X-planet', i.e. an unexplored world, before landing. A Controller runs the ship, and the energy crisis is so bad that the ship only has enough fuel to get to

Zeta Minor and make the return journey. It's later said that when the ship crosses the galactic frontier, it can signal for an emergency re-fuelling. The Controller is ready to order the execution of prisoners without compunction.

Ultimately, the Doctor primes Professor Sorenson with the idea of re-fuelling the Morestrans by 'harnessing the kinetic power of planetary movement'. [This seems a spurious solution, as surely the Doctor knows plenty of other ways of generating vast amounts of energy? You almost get the feeling that he *knows* the Morestrans should develop kinetic planet-power around this time, and is helping history to run its course. Mind you, the novel *Zeta Major* has other ideas.]

The Analysis

Where Does This Come From? The most obvious point to make here is that the planet was, as the name suggests, originally intended to be evil. The "Jekyll and Hyde" aspect of the plot was to have been a feature of the jungle, not of Professor Sorenson.

In this respect we aren't a million miles away from Terry Nation's retreads of American World War Two movies, where the jungle is alive and actively planning to kill our heroes. In the light of Louis Marks' earlier script for "Planet of Giants" (2.1), some have chosen to read this as an "environmental" story, and indeed to invoke the "Gaia" theory. This would be a touch unfair, both to Marks and to environmentalist Jim Lovelock, who formulated the theory in the late 1960s (although the name "Gaia" - after the Greek Earth-Mother - was suggested by Nobel prize-winning novelist and Lovelock's neighbour, William Golding… it's caused a great deal of trouble, and Lovelock now regrets it, as it implies an actual *entity*).

The pop-culture version of this theory holds that the Earth is alive and active, responding to human abuses with hurricanes and AIDS. The Lovelock version is that there are interlocking self-regulating systems which, like thermostats, respond because they have to. Like "Inferno" before it, "Planet of Evil" hints at the more melodramtic, this-planet-hates-us version of the Gaia idea, but it's doubtful that the finished version of the script was meant as a deliberate eco-parable.

In fact, Marks' starting-point is much more likely to have been Renaissance literature, this being his specialist subject (see 14.2, "The Masque of Mandragora"). Of particular relevance is the lengthy Roman poem *De Rerum Natura* by Lucretius, which underwent a big revival in 1450s Florence as part of the Empirical movement. Lucretius was a big advocate of spontaneous generation, the idea that a "life-essence" goes from big dead animals to smaller living ones. The Empiricists were the beginning of all real science, and believed that true happiness came from contemplation of the workings of Nature, to be uncovered through careful observation. Discovery of one's true place in the cosmos eases the soul.

At the same time - and connected to this - there was the Humanist movement, associated with Sir Thomas More, Erasmus and Leonardo da Vinci, and the sense of all the powers and responsibilities incumbent on one who's in command of his or her destiny. So with his tale of living planets and scientists attempting to change the future of the universe, Marks is arriving at many of the ideas of 1950s SF / horror movies, but from a different direction. (See **What Does Anti-Matter Do?** for more on the contemporary theories that Marks was trying to exploit.)

Things That Don't Make Sense It's hard to make any sense of the anti-matter at all. Zeta Minor is a 'boundary' between dimensions, yet the minerals are clearly part of *this* dimension. It's possible that everything on Zeta Minor is supposed to exist in a "neutral zone" where it doesn't count as matter or anti-matter, but the pool is supposed to be the vortex between worlds, and the rocks are clearly on "our" side of it. [Do they "wash up" out of the pool, for some reason?]

The anti-matter's contamination of Sorenson is similarly hard to swallow. Apart from anything else, the Doctor claims that the anti-matter is destroying Sorenson's brain cells and that he'll 'descend to the level of a brute', yet once the samples are returned to the planet Sorenson recovers completely apart from a little memory loss. How do his brain cells grow back so fast? Or indeed, at all? [The Doctor's speculating wildly. Again.] Worse, the ship isn't supposed to be able to escape the planet's pull while there's anti-matter on board, but all the anti-matter creatures that split off from Sorenson simply dissipate into thin air after he's taken down to the planet. None of this is actually explained.

The Morestrans aren't much more logical. They desperately need energy to keep their empire going, even though space-travel is so easy for them that they can mount expeditions to the edge of the universe. They must have access to millions of suns and billions of planets, but they can't find power anywhere?

At the end of the story it turns out that the ship can get an emergency re-fuelling once it's closer to home, and that's after the fuel cells have presumably been depleted by the ship tugging against the pull of the planet. Yet in episode one Salamar doesn't even want to bother with a rudimentary scan of the incredibly hostile world they're visiting because it'll use up too much juice.

Critique One of those stories that does its best to scare the bejesus out of small children, and anyone in their infancy at the time will testify that it succeeded beautifully, but the moment the story leaves the jungle it's impossible to care about anything that happens. Sorenson aside, almost every scene involving the Morestrans borders on the unwatchable, partly due to the low-rent design but mostly thanks to the 2D dialogue and the unbearable technobabble. Prentis Hancock - formerly one of the wet Thals in "Planet of the Daleks" (10.4), and later a regular on *Space: 1999* - is so shockingly poor as Salamar that it beggars belief, but to be fair, the script seems to *demand* a wooden performance and his horrible outfit must be putting him off.

It's also a script almost completely devoid of wit, humour or lightness of touch, so even the Doctor's mocking of the macho Morestrans seems less impressive than it should. On top of this there's the problem that none of the stuff about anti-matter makes sense (which is to say, it doesn't make *aesthetic* sense, although you might be able to explain some of it away with enough pseudo-science), with the story changing the "rules" over and over again until Sorenson finally becomes an army of half-invisible ape-men for no good reason. The end result is something that looks disturbingly like an improv session, although on the plus side it's at least nice to see a story that doesn't have a conventional black-hat villain and doesn't end with the "flawed" character (Sorenson) dying for his sins.

The Facts

Written by Louis Marks. Directed by David Maloney. Viewing figures: 10.4 million, 9.9 million, 9.1 million, 10.1 million.

Supporting Cast Frederick Jaeger (Sorenson), Ewen Solon (Vishinsky), Prentis Hancock (Salamar), Graham Weston (De Haan), Louis Mahoney (Ponti), Michael Wisher (Morelli), Haydn Wood (O'Hara), Melvyn Bedford (Reig).

Cliffhangers The outline of the not-quite-invisible creature advances on the Doctor and Sarah in the jungle; the Doctor, overwhelmed by the now-enormous anti-matter creature, tumbles into the black pool (cue dramatic freeze-frame); the insane Salamar orders the Doctor and Sarah to be strapped into the probe ship's ejector tubes, and the mechanism starts sliding them out towards space.

The Lore

• You've guessed it: the anti-matter creature effect came first, and then they decided to write a story around it. Philip Hinchcliffe asked for a weird locale, so designer Roger Murray-Leech said he could do a jungle. Louis Marks decided on a "Jekyll and Hyde" planet and read a whole load of popular science books about anti-matter. Then, once the title had been decided, the emphasis moved from the planet itself to the person affected by it.

• The one thing everyone thinks they know about this story, that the deceased character Egard Lumb was supposed to be called "Edgar Lumb" until someone in the props department made a spelling mistake on his gravestone, is untrue. The script specifies "Egard".

• Though not credited, Peter Howell took over from Dick Mills making the odd "special sound" for this story. Howell would later be the main composer on *Doctor Who* during Season Eighteen, and had earlier tried to salvage the score for "Revenge of the Cybermen" (12.5).

• The shots from the oculoid tracker were footage from a documentary about orang-utans, shown in negative to turn them the same cerise as the jungle set.

13.3: "Pyramids of Mars"

(Serial 4G, Four Episodes, 25th October - 15th November 1975.)

Which One is This? An ancient Egyptian demigod terrifies the Doctor from the comfort of his own tomb, while mummies with 46DD chests stomp around an English mansion and occasionally step in man-traps. Oh, and Sutekh brings the gift of death to all humans.

Firsts and Lasts A couple of the programme's "standard" phrases turn up for the first time here. The Doctor's homeworld is said to be in the 'constellation of Kasterborous', and he's said to have a 'respiratory bypass system', always a handy copout when he needs to play dead for a while. It's also the first appearance of the "proper" velvet frock-coat. Crucially, it's the first time anything penetrates the TARDIS in mid-flight (see 18.6, "The Keeper of Traken"; 20.1, "Arc of Infinity"; 22.5, "Timelash"; and 25.4, "The Greatest Show in the Galaxy" for other instances of this supposedly impossible feat.)

Four Things to Notice About "Pyramids of Mars"...

1. Widely regarded as a classic of its age, "Pyramids of Mars" is the story that drives home the idea of *Doctor Who* as modern-day mythology by pitching the Doctor against a murderous Egyptian god, who - in classic von Daniken style - turns out to be the last survivor of an alien superrace. Astronomically-inclined readers might note that the story was broadcast a year before the Viking I probe provided photos of Mars which showed there really was something like a pyramid on the surface (in the region named Cydonia, not far from the now-famous "Martian Sphinx"). In *Doctor Who*, even ancient monuments are topical.

2. *Everybody* involved puts in a top-flight performance here, so much so that this may be the story which sums up Tom Baker's Doctor (or at least, people's memories of him) better than any other. Though at least one of the authors of this present volume might be considered biased, special mention still has to go to Gabriel Woolf as Sutekh, who becomes one of the series' greatest-ever villains just through the sheer, slinky menace of his voice.

3. It's time to play follow-the-bodycount. Robert Holmes had a habit of wiping out sup-porting characters when they got in the way, and "Pyramids of Mars" is one of the bloodiest *Doctor Who* stories to date. Out of all the non-regular cast, only the three Egyptian lackeys who run terrified out of the tomb in the first scene survive (and the cult of Sutekh assassinates *them* later on, according to the novelisation). This is the only story in which we see an "alternative future" in which the Doctor fails to save the world, a scene quite possibly included so that we actually feel he's *achieved* something by defeating Sutekh when everyone we've met has already bitten the dust.

4. It's one of the series' most celebrated gaffes, and yet many people can watch the story time and time again without noticing it. When Sutekh is finally released from his prison in episode four, and stands from his throne after 7,000 years of paralysis, the hand of a BBC technician subtly creeps into the picture and holds his cushion down. Did the man have no sense of occasion?

The Continuity

The Doctor The Doctor claims to be around 750 years old, apparently close to middle-age. [This approximate age remains consistent, more or less, throughout the rest of the Fourth Doctor's run. Later this year he specifies 749.] For the first time, the Fourth Doctor overtly states that his place isn't on Earth and that he's got better things to do than hang around with UNIT. His statement 'I'm a Time Lord... I walk in eternity' seems to suggest that he's got definite ideas about his role in the universe, even if he later claims to have renounced the society of the Time Lords. He's getting moody and reflective here.

Mixing up his old acquaintances, the Doctor refers to his former companion Victoria as 'Vicki', something he never called her when she was travelling with him. He honestly seems to believe that Sutekh is the greatest threat he and the world have ever faced. [Knocking Azal off the number one spot; see 8.5, "The Daemons".] Here he's said to have a 'respiratory bypass system', meaning that he can stop breathing and feign death. [A step up from the ability displayed in 13.1, "Terror of the Zygons".]

• *Ethics.* The implication here, suggested by the 'walk in eternity' comment and backed up by the Doctor's vision of a devastated world, is that the Doctor has a moral obligation to history [a subtly different focus for both the character and

Where (and When) is Gallifrey?

The evidence seems contradictory. For every detail that suggests the Time Lords co-exist with us, here and now and in this galaxy, we have something else to say they're in the far future, the remote past, the centre of the universe, the centre of time or all of the above. Many of the conclusions we tend to reach are based on what feels right rather than what's said out loud. Sometimes the writers had the same instincts, sometimes it's anyone's guess what they were thinking and sometimes they didn't have an opinion at all.

Let's start with the crude, astrophysical "where" question. Is Gallifrey in Earth's galaxy?

In "Pyramids of Mars", Sutekh requests binary co-ordinates from 'galactic zero centre'. This has been taken to mean that Gallifrey is somewhere in our galaxy, but it's by no means clear. Co-ordinates *from* galactic zero-centre: using the hub of Earth's galaxy as a starting-point, how do you get to this place? These co-ordinates could feasibly lead you anywhere in the universe. Besides, in the five-thousand years that Sutekh's been sat on his scatter-cushion, the galaxy has revolved a bit (0.00001125°, but over a parsec that's the distance from here to Pluto). Stars and planets alter their relative positions, so you *could* argue that for this data to have any validity to Sutekh, the direction has to be towards another galaxy. On the other hand, this is Osirian god-like technology we're talking about, and a computer that can keep records of every known planet can surely handle little things like shuffling solar systems.

Then there's the throwaway comment by the Magritte-style Time Lord in "Terror of the Autons" (8.1): 'My co-ordinates seem to have slipped a little... still, not bad after 29,000 light-years.' 29,000 light-years suggests a spot well within Earth's galaxy, and it's not that bad an estimate for the distance to galactic centre. But leaving aside the fact that Robert Holmes couldn't tell a galaxy from a Mars Bar and thought a constellation was the same thing as a planetary system, we can't assume much from this. Nowhere is it said that the messenger has come straight from Gallifrey, and Time Lord HQ didn't even have a name when the story was written. He could have come straight from another "case", or from some sort of local monitoring station for all we know.

Was Holmes seriously trying to suggest that the Time Lord world was at the centre of the galaxy? Weeeeeelll... in spite of his overwhelming disregard for cosmology, it's not impossible. '29,000 light-years' isn't the sort of figure you automatical-

ly pull out of the air. Let's remember, in the '70s there was little real "continuity" in *Doctor Who*, and that running themes rather than hard facts held the series together. The black hole from which Rassilon recovered the Eye of Harmony in "The Deadly Assassin" (14.3) wasn't supposed to be the same one created by Omega in "The Three Doctors" (10.1), but the same imagery underpins both. Holmes' scripts tend to regard Gallifrey as being a great all-seeing lens at the centre of galactic events, hence terms like "Eye of Harmony" and "Panopticon", and everybody knew that there was supposed to be a black hole in the middle of the Milky Way. So did he deliberately pick this as a good central spot from which the Doctor could be "watched"? If somebody more science-orientated had just happened to mention the distance to the galactic hub, then it's at least feasible.

"Feasible". Well, there you have the problem. A galaxy containing both Earth and Gallifrey is plausible, yet there's no more evidence to confirm it than there is to contradict it. ("The Deadly Assassin" has the Time Lords refer to Earth as being in Mutter's Spiral, which has often been taken as a reference to Earth's galaxy, but this doesn't seem to be what the script implies.) So instinct takes over. It feels right for Gallifrey to be in "our" part of space, because it suits the aesthetic of the rest of the series. Earth is important, for some reason; Earth's galaxy is important; humans and Time Lords are quite similar, which is to say, they're closer biologically than (for example) humans and Kaleds; ergo, Gallifrey should be close to home.

Many writers seem to have taken this as read, and certainly it was accepted as a definitive "truth" in the New Adventures era. The '29,000 light-years' line seems so neat that perhaps the best option is to assume Gallifrey *is* in the middle of our galaxy, at least until there's better evidence that it isn't. After all, the Time Lord civil servant in "Terror of the Autons" surely can't have *that* much to do in the outside universe, and his appearance *does* suggest that he's been "transported" to Earth from a fixed base of operations. In "The Brain of Morbius" (13.5) the Doctor lands on Karn and says that he was born nearby, which apparently means that Karn is in the region of Gallifrey. As in "The Creature from the Pit" (17.3) the Doctor indicates that he *was* born on the Time Lord homeworld, something which was by no means certain in the 1970s (see

continued on page 67...

the series]. Despite wanting to get away from Earth, he doesn't exactly seem a free spirit here, and acts as if he's a Time Lord above all. His statement that time is his 'business' is delivered with some conviction. He displays no feeling when Laurence Scarman is brutally murdered, and - another thing which distinguishes him from his previous incarnations - has no patience with Sarah when she suggests he should care more, sounding almost angry when he describes the carnage that'll follow if he doesn't get on with his "job". There's none of his usual humour when he's face-to-mask with Sutekh. This time he's not just prepared to sacrifice his life to save Earth, but honestly doesn't think he's got a chance of survival.

• *Inventory.* The Doctor carries a pocket-sized device with an aerial that acts as a radio-telescope, and throws away what looks like a pocket-watch [the same one seen in 11.2, "Invasion of the Dinosaurs"?] to short out the 'parallax coil' trap at the entrance to Sutekh's time-space tunnel. [The novelisation says it's the TARDIS key, which makes little or no sense. If it's the key, then why doesn't the Doctor have to recover it from the sarcophagus before he uses the TARDIS again?] He also has a French pick-lock, which…

• *Background.* …was given to him by Marie Antoinette, whom he describes as a 'charming lady'. [During the Doctor's first visit to Revolutionary France? The Doctor speaks of her execution as if he were there at the time. See 1.1, "An Unearthly Child". Maybe she would have lived longer if he *hadn't* taken her lock-pick off her.] The Doctor hints, perhaps jokingly and perhaps not, that he was blamed for the Great Fire of London in 1666. [He may well have been there. He'll certainly be there again, in 19.4, "The Visitation".] He describes 1911 as 'an excellent year, one of my favourites', though he may just be showing off.

The Doctor knows enough about Osirans to know the Sign of the Eye, a gesture which opens doors in the pyramid on Mars by 'tribophysics'.

The Supporting Cast

• *Sarah Jane Smith.* Weirdly, Sarah also knows about tribophysics, realising how the doors of the pyramid work without being told. [The Doctor must have done this sort of thing in front of her before. Incidentally, the spelling's questionable here; it's often written as "triobiphysics", but Lis Sladen doesn't appear to mouth enough syllables

on-screen.] On the other hand, she believes that they can safely leave Sutekh to do his worst in 1911, because she "knows" Earth isn't destroyed in her own time [she wasn't paying attention during 11.1, "The Time Warrior"].

Though Sarah's so used to life on the TARDIS that she's been rooting around in the wardrobe, she still sees it as transport rather than a home, and wants to get back to Earth. She knows how to use a rifle, but doesn't know better than to throw gelignite around. She's familiar enough with Egyptology to know all about the tomb of Tuthmosis III.

The TARDIS To prove that history hangs in the balance, the Doctor uses the TARDIS to do something he's never done before: he takes the Ship to a version of Sarah's own time in which they didn't bother to stop Sutekh, and it's a blasted, lifeless, storm-wracked planet circling a dead sun.

The Doctor tells Sarah that she's taken a look into 'alternative time', and that every point in time has its alternatives. [This is… bizarre. For one thing, it suggests that the timeline becomes "fixed" whenever the TARDIS arrives somewhere, because until landing in 1911 the Doctor never took any steps to stop Sutekh and the world clearly *wasn't* blasted in Sarah's own time. The novel *Psi-ence Fiction* by Chris Boucher actually supports this "fixed" timeline theory, but see **Can You Change History, Even One Line?** under 1.6, "The Aztecs", for more on this.

[The scene also suggests that the Doctor can hop forward to check the results of his work, then hop back if they're not satisfactory, an incredibly useful tool which he never, ever uses at any other point. This would contradict everything else we're ever told about time-travel, as it essentially allows the Doctor to change the past at will, defying the Blinovitch (etc.) and breaking all conceivable rules. We *have* to conclude that the scorched world he shows Sarah isn't "real", but some kind of projection arranged for her benefit. This doesn't square with the normal TARDIS abilities either, since he never uses *this* facility again, but it's by far the simplest option. In 1976 even letters to the *Radio Times* believed this scene to be a bit of a stretch. It *is* established early on in the story that the TARDIS is being beset by something unprecedented, so feasibly this sort of thing is only possible because of Sutekh's immense universe-warping power. The Doctor's statement that every point

Where (and When) is Gallifrey?

...continued from page 65

The Lore of 15.6, "The Invasion of Time"). And there's an Earthman living on Karn, at least implying that it isn't *too* far from human-space.

The question of *when* Gallifrey exists is stickier. We'll assume here that there's a kind of Gallifreyan "real time" that's in synch with the time which passes for the TARDIS crew, so the gaps between the Doctor's encounters with his own folk are as far apart for him as they are for them. This isn't stated anywhere, but if you're trying to make sense of this universe then you've really got to take it as a given. (See also **Do Time Lords Always Meet in Sequence?** under 22.3, "Mark of the Rani". Incidentally, it's the story immediately after that - "The Two Doctors" - which seems to be the one occasion when the Doctor breaches the "real time" rule. But all the writers of subsequent *Doctor Who* spin-offs have taken the rule for granted, with the exception of Terrance Dicks, whose novel *Warmonger* insists on having the Doctor casually wander into the Time Lords' past to warn them about Morbius. This non-linear approach to Gallifrey could produce some interesting material, though it doesn't in *Warmonger*, but it also contradicts virtually everything we see of Gallifrey in the TV series.)

Boil the "when" question down to its basics. Is Gallifreyan present in our past, our present or our future? The series never makes up its mind about this. The unaired pilot episode from 1963 had the Doctor claim to be from the forty-ninth century, which might explain how he knows so much about the run-up to the age of Magnus Greel (14.6, "The Talons of Weng-Chiang"), but it's an idea that was fortunately dropped from the finished programme. Apart from one jokey, throw-away line in "Nightmare of Eden" (17.4), there's no real evidence that Gallifrey is literally ahead of us. If it *were*, then there'd be a perpetual risk that events in our present might affect the development of the early Gallifreyans, another potentially interesting thought that isn't backed up by anything on-screen.

(FASA's *Doctor Who Role-Playing Game* - yes, it may sound like an obscure source, but at least one writer working on the series in the '80s had read it - blithely assumed that Gallifrey was in the far future. In FASA's universe the TARDIS can't go any further into the future than 21.3, "Frontios", because that would take it into the future of Gallifrey itself and allow the Time Lords to discov-

er their own destiny. Charming, but not wholly convincing.)

As for the present... well, stories like "The Three Doctors" (10.1) take it as read that present-day Earth and present-day Gallifrey are somehow linked, though this could be more to do with the mechanics of time-travel than anything. If there's such a thing as Gallifreyan "real time", then it's reasonable to suppose that events on Earth and Gallifrey might appear to happen "simultaneously" while the Doctor's larking around in England. Stories like "The Brain of Morbius", in which a planet in Earth's future seemingly has an ongoing relationship with Gallifrey in the Doctor's time, indicate that Time Lords have no trouble temporarily "tying" their own present to other points in history. It happens to twentieth-century Earth quite a lot, but twentieth-century Earth is by no means alone.

That leaves the past. In the '70s, nobody seems to have considered the idea that Gallifrey could have been "the oldest civilisation". The concept that it might exist in the ancient past is a very '80s one, and with good reason. By the '80s one-and-a-half generations had grown up with *Doctor Who*, so Time Lord history started to become "mythic", as if it were a new form of classicism. In 1977's "The Deadly Assassin", the ancient secrets of Rassilon only mean something to Gallifrey itself, and even the Time Lords barely remember the details. In 1980's "State of Decay" (18.4), the long-ago war between Time Lords and Giant Vampires is said to have spilled out across the whole universe, and events are described as if Rassilon were young when the entire continuum was new. The New Adventures stated, clearly and unequivocally, that ancient Gallifrey lay in the ancient past. The novel *The Crystal Bucephalus* even hints that by the time of humanity, Gallifrey is a long-dead world where people from Earth can safely build restaurants.

A "past" Gallifrey makes sense, and explains why the Doctor never runs into any of his non-time-travelling ancestors (we can safely assume that the TARDIS can't, or won't, travel into the past of Gallifrey itself), but that doesn't mean the modern Gallifrey exists in the distant past. A running suggestion in the series is that the Gallifrey we see from "The Deadly Assassin" onwards is in some way outside time, not in the past, present or future at all. Graham Williams suggested that the Doctor's homeworld is somehow at the "centre of

continued on page 69...

in time has alternatives probably isn't standard Time Lord philosophy, since he only seemed to reach that conclusion in 7.4, "Inferno".]

Heading back to UNIT HQ, the TARDIS suffers "turbulence" in mid-flight and an image of Sutekh momentarily breaches it. The Doctor believes such a penetration of the TARDIS to be impossible, as mental projection of that force is 'beyond imagination'. His explanation for the trouble is that the projection causes the relative continuum stabiliser to fail.

Sutekh's time-space tunnel then causes a 'temporal reversal', and acts as a lodestone which makes the TARDIS land on the site of UNIT HQ several decades early. [It's hard to say why the TARDIS should be interrupted *now* rather than at any point in its prior history. After all, Sutekh's always been "there" in 1911. The TARDIS is shown spinning through space again here, so is it in the "real" universe when the sarcophagus interrupts it, rather than the vortex?] The Doctor also claims that the TARDIS controls are isomorphic, responding only to him. [He says this to Sutekh, who can read his mind, so it's apparently true even though it's contradicted by so many other stories. Possibly the TARDIS can only be *reliably* steered if the Doctor's at the controls, although it's feasible that he's lying and on this occasion finds the mental strength to resist Sutekh.]

Sarah finds a dress in the TARDIS which makes the Doctor mis-identify her as Victoria [4.9, "Evil of the Daleks", et seq]. This is handy, as it more or less suits the era they land in. The 'time control' from the TARDIS can be detached from the console, and the Doctor uses it to shift the threshold of Sutekh's time-space corridor into the far future. [Returning to Earth from Mars, it becomes clear that the Doctor can't make the TARDIS land a few minutes before it left, or he wouldn't be under time-pressure to stop Sutekh.] On this occasion, the Doctor can tell the Ship has landed at the right location but doesn't know the exact year from the TARDIS controls.

The Non-Humans

• *Osirans.* A species from Phaester Osiris, the implication is that they're extinct apart from Sutekh, as the Doctor speaks of them in the past tense. The Egyptian gods were based on them. The Doctor knows the Osirans' history and describes them as dome-headed, with cerebrums like spiral staircases. Sutekh destroyed their

homeworld and left a trail of havoc across half the galaxy, until being cornered on Earth and defeated by his brother Horus and 740 other Osirans, these being the 740 gods named in the tomb of Tuthmosis III. Sutekh's name is vilified on 'every civilised world' [an exaggeration], though it's also rendered as Set, Satan or Sadok.

[Egyptology note... the war between Set and Horus matches the Osirian myth-cycle of Egypt in many ways, though the legends are confused as to whether Set was Horus' brother or his uncle. Osiris was supposed to be Horus' father and sometimes Set's brother, so it makes a kind of sense for the name of the Osirans' planet to find its way into human mythology as the name of a god. In fact the oddest thing here is the name given to the evil one. "Set" is a far more common rendering, "Sutekh" being the name of a warrior-god of the Hyksos who was identified with Set at a later date. Historically, there's absolutely no link between the names "Set" and "Satan". The real tomb of Tuthmosis III describes 741 gods, i.e. Horus and 740 others, but was built more than 5,000 years after Sutekh's time.]

Sutekh was imprisoned 7,000 years ago, not executed as the Osiran code forbade it; killing him would have made Horus no better than Sutekh himself [the same code the Doctor practices in 12.4, "Genesis of the Daleks", obviously]. Like the Doctor, Horus believed all sapient life to be kin.

Sutekh has been confined in a previously-untouched tomb in Sakkara, Egypt, buried under a blind pyramid behind a wall marked with the glowing symbol of the Eye of Horus. Scarman believes it's First Dynasty. [Making the tomb a significant find, as the oldest pyramid at Sakkara is *Third* Dynasty. If Sutekh really has been there for 7,000 years, then the tomb pre-dates the First Dynasty by almost 2,000 years.]

A force-field, powered by the real Eye of Horus in a pyramid on Mars, holds Sutekh in place to the extent that he can't even stand. Sutekh's power is limited to his tomb, but he evidently requires no food or fresh air, and his mind is so strong that when Professor Scarman opens the tomb he immediately turns the man into a slave and worshipper. The Doctor believes that Scarman is effectively dead, though he retains dim memories of his life, and sure enough he turns to ashes when Sutekh releases him. Even the Doctor's mind is no match for Sutekh, who has the power to keep victims alive and in agony for centuries, move

Where (and When) is Gallifrey?

...continued from page 67

time" when he became producer, so Gallifrey becomes a kind eternal watchtower, overseeing all of history from somewhere beyond / within / separate from the normal course of events. In "Shada" (17.6) we see the Time Lords' prison-world, and it's presented as a place that can't be reached by normal means but only through the TARDIS, again suggestive of a culture existing outside time as we know it. But the real giveaway, the only definite, absolute summary of the Doctor's point of origin and therefore our best evidence, comes in "The Stones of Blood" (16.3). The Doctor is asked whether he comes from outer space. His reply, which seems quite serious, is that he comes from *inner time*.

This has to be considered key. If ancient Gallifrey existed in the distant past, but removed itself from normal history when Rassilon balanced the Eye of Harmony and turned his society into a culture of 'galactic ticket inspectors', then everything locks together neatly. Gallifrey has a physical location, but isn't "there" now. (If you believe the *Crystal Bucephalus* version, then at some point in the Doctor's future Gallifrey will fall and return to normal-time, leaving the planet as a barren world throughout the course of recorded history. The Time Lords must at least realise this, and feel it to be a little ominous.)

In "The Invasion of Time" (15.6) Rodan is in charge of Time Lord Traffic Control, monitoring space-fleets as they pass close to the planet. In purely physical terms, this makes no sense. The universe is so immense that even the busiest parts shouldn't have anything comparable to "airspace". But if the fleets in question are those with some form of time-travel capability, and have to pass close to Gallifrey's "centre of time" region while in transit, then it all seems more reasonable.

(Then again, Williams' "centre of time" idea takes on a very different meaning if you look at it in terms of hard/er science. If you assume that the universe is currently expanding, but will eventually stop and begin to contract, then the "centre of time" is the apex of the expansion. But despite the amount of wanton pop-science found elsewhere in the Graham Williams era, it seems doubtful that this is precisely what he had in mind. "Centre of

time" sounds more like a way of symbolically putting the Time Lords at the heart of the universal order than a technical description. Besides, the idea of Gallifrey being at the apex of the expansion doesn't gel with the Doctor's 'inner time' comment at all, a comment significantly made halfway through the Key to Time season; the season in which Williams tried to lay out his view of the way the *Doctor Who* universe works.)

"Frontios" (21.3) claims that Earth's destruction in the far, far, far future is beyond Gallifreyan experience, and remember, the Time Lords are supposed to be able to see everything. The TARDIS gives the error message "time parameters exceeded" when it tries to go any further. Whenever Gallifrey is, it doesn't make sense that a TARDIS can't visit an era just because it's a long way into the future from a human point of view, so this has never been fully explained. The "prettiest" solution is that just as the Time Lords seem to have developed in the far-distant past, there's another power in the far-distant future which stops them looking too far ahead. This notion was a favourite with New Adventures authors, some of whom were planning on basing a story arc around it when the BBC took their license away (which explains why a similar idea has since turned up in both the BBC novel *Alien Bodies* and its bastard *Faction Paradox* offspring, and why it's being mentioned here).

Another fan-suggestion that's been made often enough to at least be worth addressing: that Gallifrey is Earth in the far future. On the surface this seems odd, as Earth's final fate is apparently known. But planetary destructions are easy to fake, and this would at least explain why the TARDIS has such trouble interfering with the "Frontios" era. Future-Earth must be protected for the sake of Gallifrey's past. In "The Mysterious Planet" (23.1) people hiding on Earth are tapping the Matrix, and the Time Lords choose to cover this up by moving the planet's entire system rather than by destroying the world or killing everyone on it. Many people would like a good reason for this grotesquely cumbersome plot.

On the other hand, if you're the kind of person who wants to be told that Gallifrey is Earth in the future then you're probably the kind of person who thinks it'd be really neat if the Doctor turned out to be Anakin Skywalker's dad.

objects telekinetically or look into the Doctor's thoughts to see if he's lying. At one stage he even "possesses" the Doctor. Sutekh wants nothing but

the destruction of all life, perhaps because he fears that other life will come to rival him in power, so if Sutekh were to escape in 1911 then the Earth would be dust by Sarah's time. His philosophy: 'Your evil is my good.'

Sutekh wears a mask, much like a death-mask, but Scarman - possessed by his power - briefly takes on the countenance of the animal-like Typhonian beast depicted in Egyptian wall-paintings. The same image replaces Sutekh's helmet when he's finally freed. [Do *all* Osirans look like that? The head of the beast doesn't look particularly domed. Egyptian lore claims that only Set / Sutekh had the Typhonian face, so there may be some weird genetic diversity amongst Osirans. Alternatively, this may be a projection of his psyche rather than his actual head.] His eyes glow green when he's using mind-power.

An Egyptian cult seems to have been awaiting his re-awakening for some time. Technology used by Sutekh here includes his mummy-robots and a pyramid-shaped Osiran war missile with an anti-gravity drive that's aimed at the pyramid on Mars, though it's not explained where all this equipment comes from. [Possibly he gets his servants to assemble it for him based on Osiran designs, but it's more likely that there are left-over pieces of Osiran technology on Earth already, probably kept by the cult. Contrary to popular belief, there's no evidence here that the Osirans actually entombed Sutekh with all the stuff he needs to escape.]

What looks like an Egyptian sarcophagus turns out to be a space-time tunnel to Sutekh's tomb in Egypt. An invisible 'deflection barrier' around Scarman's estate is generated by four hi-tech canpoic jars, each with the head of a different Egyptian god. Scarman, travelling to England via the sarcophagus, wears dark robes and a black mask similar to the faces of the mummies. He refers to himself as the 'instrument' of Sutekh, and can burn someone to death with his touch as well as burning the carpet with his shoes. His robes vanish thereafter, and he seems to lose the ability to scorch the furnishings. Even from Egypt, Sutekh can mentally stop bullets killing his mind-slave or prevent explosives exploding, though he can't keep this up for long while he's on another continent.

The Doctor believes that if Sutekh gets free then there isn't a life-form in the galaxy which could stand against him, not even the Time Lords. Though he doesn't recognise the name, Sutekh seems to know of Gallifrey when he's given the co-ordinates. The Osirans certainly know of the Time Lords, as Sutekh concludes that they're a 'perfidi-

ous species'. [There's no indication that Osirans ever cracked time-travel, or they'd still be visible in the universe, so it's unlikely that they ever visited Gallifrey. Perhaps the Time Lords did "business" with them at some point. The Doctor speaks as if Sutekh has a reputation that goes far beyond mythology. On the other hand, Sutekh's sarcophagus is described as a *time*-space tunnel, and the Doctor initially believes that something's interfering with time. It's hard to see how the Time Lords wouldn't be able to defeat an enemy who doesn't have time travel. It makes you wonder what happened to the *other* Osirans who didn't die on Phaester Osiris.] A data retrieval system in Sutekh's tomb [nice of Horus to give him something to do] supplies him with information on Gallifrey, apparently telepathically.

Sutekh finally dies when the Doctor shifts the threshold of the space-time tunnel into the far future. It takes the demigod 7,000 years to die [and his journey into the future seems uninterrupted, so he doesn't "escape" at any point before 8911].

• *Mummies.* The service robots used by the Osirans are mute, powerful and - crucially - wrapped in bindings chemically impregnated to protect them against damage and corrosion. The Doctor describes the design as 'typical Osiran simplicity'. They can be controlled by Sutekh's mind-puppet with vocal commands, while a mere mortal can give them orders if he's wearing a special slave relay ring. [Possibly suggesting that the Egyptians were inspired by the mummies to wrap up their dead.] The robots work by cytronic induction, drawing their power from a cytronic particle accelerator in Sutekh's tomb. [Again, we have to conclude that Sutekh's followers have only just constructed this.] Like most monsters these days, they're bulletproof.

Planet Notes

• *Mars.* The pyramid on Mars contains the Eye of Horus, a power source which keeps Sutekh confined by a force-field and looks like a big red glowing egg. When Sutekh is close to release an alarm signal is triggered, and a radio-telescope on Earth is able to receive a constant message from the pyramid which turns out to be 'beware Sutekh'. [It's not clear what language it's in, or how the Doctor "translates" it.]

A series of logic puzzles, plus a couple of Horus' servitor mummies in swish gold sashes, serve to protect the pyramid. [Even Sutekh thinks it's ridiculous to protect the Eye with these games. The Doctor believes it's typical Osiran deviousness, but it's more likely to be typical Osiran showing-off.] Within the chamber the air and gravity are those of Earth. The signal that keeps Sutekh in captivity is also a radio-wave of some description, as it's still reaching Earth two minutes after the Eye's destroyed. [So not a "real" radio signal, as this would take between 17 and 38 minutes, depending on where the two planets were in relation to one another.]

- *Gallifrey.* The Doctor's home planet is named here for only the second time – the first being in 11.1, "The Time Warrior" - and once again he only mentions it in front of a nasty alien. He states that Gallifrey is 'in the constellation of Kasterborous', and its binary location from galactic zero centre is 10-0-11-0-0 by 02. [A constellation is a group of stars perceived from a specific planet and by a specific culture, so who decided that Gallifrey's star is in Kasterborous is open to question. See **Where (and When) is Gallifrey?**.]

History

- *Dating.* It's 1911 when Sutekh is unleashed on the world.

The modern UNIT HQ turns out to have been built on the site of the Old Priory, owned by the late Marcus Scarman and near an unnamed village. Sarah knows the history of the Priory, and knows it burned down, something which turns out to be a result of the Doctor mistreating Sutekh's space-time sarcophagus. [Suggesting that the Doctor's intervention here is part of the "proper" timeline. Is it really coincidence that UNIT HQ should end up on this site, or is something strange going on?] In 1911, Scarman's brother Laurence has invented the Marconiscope, a table-top-sized radio-telescope 'forty years early'. Sadly, he dies before he can show it off. [Although if anyone else knows about it, this might contribute to the advancement of space-science in the *Doctor Who* universe.]

Sarah tells Laurence that she comes from 1980. [See **When Are the UNIT Stories Set?** under 7.1, "Spearhead from Space". It seems likely that Sarah's rounding up, in much the same way that Jo Grant rounds down in "Carnival of Monsters" (10.2), though her later use of the date when talking to the Doctor is slightly harder to explain. The Doctor describes the future he shows her as being 1980 as well, but this whole alternative-present is

suspect at best; see **The TARDIS**.]

The Doctor confirms that the whole of ancient Egyptian culture was based on the 'Osiran pattern'.

The Analysis

Where Does This Come From? Let's see… where does this come from? Oh yes, Jean Cocteau's *La Belle et le Bete* (1945), a film that's influenced more directors, designers and pop-video-makers than you can shake a stick at (see also 18.5, "Warriors' Gate"). Well, at least that's the source of Scarman's deadly, smouldering hands and the idea of running the film backwards to suggest wounds being healed. The rest is Bram Stoker's doing.

No, really. Stoker was responsible for the whole Egyptian-undead-returning-to-rule genre, a good twenty years before Tutankhamen and *The Mummy*, in a play called *The Curse of the Scarab* (it's also where the "immortality is a curse" notion got its first popular airing). But, yes, Boris Karloff in bandages has to be taken into account. So does the 1972-73 tour of the Treasures of Tutankhamen, which - in that golden era of "fringe" science getting government funding, and gurus coming out of the woodwork left, right and centre - got a very different reception to the one it had received in the 1930s.

As we saw in "The Time Monster" (9.6) and "The Daemons" (8.5), the whole pyramid-power / ancient mysteries / astral space-men idea was too good for *Doctor Who* to totally ignore, even if the Doctor insists on distancing himself from the "Age of Aquarius" idea. But the main source of icons here is, for once, Hammer Films. The Universal horror movies of the 1930s would have been set either in a Ruritanian Europe of Burgermeisters and lederhosen, or in the present-day with expressionist lighting and art deco sets. This, like Hammer's productions of the '60s and '70s, is set around the turn of the twentieth century (a) because they've got the costumes and (b) because most of the area around Pinewood Studios / Television Centre still looks like that.

The notion of an old threat coming back to life and taking root in the present-day (or at least the story's present-day) is as much a standby of the Hinchcliffe stories as possession, which we also see here. Of the sixteen stories made by this production team, the overwhelming majority involve the return of something or someone that was assumed to be dead. Many, like this, "The Brain of

Morbius" (13.5) and "The Talons of Weng-Chiang" (14.5), are sequels to stories too big and costly for the small screen.

This isn't exactly unknown in other TV adventure series of this period. Much of *The New Avengers* consisted of things from John Steed's past - from the original *Avengers* series or otherwise - coming back to bite him. *The New Avengers*' pilot episode was the ultimate expression of this, with a revived Hitler and a Scottish castle full of Nazis. At a time when the assumption that "everything new is better" had been seen to fall apart, returns of old threats and revivals of things we thought we'd outgrown were a staple of news, current affairs and pop culture. As we'll see (especially in 14.3, "The Deadly Assassin"), re-evaluating the past by its own standards and finding that we wouldn't have coped much better was a key '70s concept, after the notion of constant, linear progress had ceased to be quite so appealing or clear-cut.

Things That Don't Make Sense   In a desperate attempt to point out the plot-fudging before anyone in the audience notices it, Sarah tells the Doctor that the logic puzzles in the pyramid remind her of the City of the Exxilons (11.3, "Death to the Daleks"). Which… she never actually saw. And a cross-story continuity glitch: here the Doctor's trying to steer the TARDIS back to UNIT HQ, yet in the previous story he and Sarah were aiming at London. The script seems to assume that "London" and "UNIT HQ" are the same thing, which they're obviously not (see **Where's UNIT HQ?** under 8.3, "The Claws of Axos").

"The Egyptian" at the Priory keeps his mummies locked away in a wing of the building that he doesn't want anyone to disturb, but the window of the room is wide open even before the Doctor and Sarah climb out of it. No reason is ever given for the mummy to kill the butler in episode one, let alone to hide in its sarcophagus afterwards [is Sutekh just warming up?]. The poacher's motives are similarly questionable, as he shoots a man in the back through the window of the Priory in a moment of pique and only *then* realises that his intended victim was Professor Scarman. Aside from providing handy gelignite, he's there solely to die horribly.

The stuff about the time-space corridor is neat, but odd. Why does shifting the end of the corridor 7,000 years into the future mean that Sutekh

ages 7,000 years, apparently in a matter of seconds? Shouldn't it just spit him out in the nineti-eth century? [But then, this device isn't really built for time-travel. It must do peculiar things to the personal time of its users.] Given that Sutekh's capable of destroying people's brains from the other side of the planet, it's also strange that he's not able to use any of his mental powers when he's stuck on the corridor. If sound and light can escape the tunnel, then surely he could hurl some of his mind-power at the Doctor, who's standing at the end of it looking smug?

Leaving aside the ever-awkward question of why Horus thought it was a good idea to protect the Eye with logic puzzles rather than killer secu-rity systems… why is the glass of the 'decatron crucible' covered in dust, when nothing else in the pyramid is?

And why does this story take place in England at all?

Critique   This is, in a spectacularly real sense, what *Doctor Who* is all about: a story wilfully pitched as modern legend instead of "just" a piece of SF television, in which all the space-age trappings seem insignificant next to a Doctor-versus-demigod struggle so fundamental that it feels like a collision of elemental forces. Hardly surprising that it's now seen as one of the all-time highs of the series, especially as it seems to act as a focal-point for the entire Tom Baker run (the Doctor's obligation to history here is perfectly in keeping with what we already know about him, but puts the emphasis on his non-human, seer-like quali-ties in a way we've never quite seen before).

Yet "Pyramids of Mars" is a long way from "per-fect", even if it's "ideal". In places there's the sense of a story being put together under pressure, and of a production not quite managing to stretch far enough. Much of episode four is pointless and dull, as Robert Holmes covers the holes in the script with extracts from "Death to the Daleks". The massive body-count is a problem, too, since with no survivors in 1911 it's hard to feel you've got a stake in this world or care that it's been res-cued; *rationally* we know we've been shown a doomed future where the Doctor didn't save the day, but our instincts aren't fooled.

And it may sound like a minor detail, but the decision to film the exterior scenes in broad day-light rather than at night - immediately destroying the horror-movie illusion, and all its horror-movie allusions - is a genuine handicap. Stalking the Priory grounds, the mummies look like the men in bandages they really are, not the messengers-of-death they're supposed to be (the story gets away with it, just, by shifting the focus away from the mummy-cult and onto Sutekh himself in the nick of time). In the end it's a hard story to argue with, great in many of its details, but like "The Daemons" it also comes across as a rough-edged and not-quite-finished piece of work. The word *classic* doesn't seem to fit it quite as well as the word *seminal*. But then, this was a series composed in a permanent state of crisis, when "constraint" was a universal constant. *Classic* was never the point.

The Facts

Written by Stephen Harris (a pseudonym for Robert Holmes and Lewis Griefer). Directed by Paddy Russell. Viewing figures: 10.5 million, 11.3 million, 9.4 million, 11.7 million. Uniquely, the omnibus repeat the following November bettered all this with 13.7 million viewers… further proof that the best-remembered stories are the ones which were repeated over the winter months (see especially 10.5, "The Green Death" and 12.2, "The Ark In Space").

Supporting Cast Gabriel Woolf (Sutekh, also uncredited as Horus' voice), Bernard Archard (Marcus Scarman), Michael Sheard (Laurence Scarman) , Peter Copley (Dr. Warlock), Peter Mayock (Ibrahim Namin), Michael Bilton (Collins), Vik Tablian (Ahmed).

Cliffhangers The robed servant of Sutekh burns the grovelling Egyptian cultist at the Priory, and dramatically announces that he brings the gift of death to all humans; the mummies burst into the lodge where the Doctor and company are sheltering, knocking the Doctor down and moving in to kill Sarah; the Doctor faces Sutekh in the Egyptian tomb, only to be pinned to the wall by the Osiran's power.

The Lore

• Lewis Griefer's original script involved a British Museum heist and lots of pyramid-power hippyness, pitched somewhere between "The Time Monster" (9.5) and "The Talons of Weng-Chiang" (14.6) with UNIT involved. Robert Holmes revised it until not a line or character of the original was left, though the title remained intact. Griefer's basic idea was that ancient Egyptian corn could be used to seed Mars, but Holmes wanted to use the whole Isis / Osiris mythology. Griefer was unable to revise it himself because he celebrated his recovery from prostate cancer by taking up a teaching post at the University of Tel Aviv (as good a reason as any). He was paid off in full and - according to some sources - the option on his original concept was held open for possible later use.

• The location-work was at Stargroves, once owned by Lord Carnarvon (who funded Howard Carter's expedition to find Tutankhamun) but at the time owned by Mick Jagger and occupied by his mum. They donated their fee to a nearby school.

• Unlike other organ-based scores (e.g. 6.6, "The War Games"), Dudley Simpson took the opportunity to perform on a nearby church-organ himself.

• A far longer model sequence was filmed of the TARDIS in the "wrong" 1980. For this a new police box model was built, which was later filmed "flying" through space. This was re-used in the next story filmed, 13.2, "Planet of Evil".

• Extracts from "Pyramids of Mars" were used in an episode of Channel 4's 1999 series *Queer as Folk*, written by *Doctor Who* supremo-in-waiting Russell T. Davies. The programme intercut the 'I bring Sutekh's gift of death to all humans' scene with some of the most explicit gay sex ever seen on mainstream TV. It's fair to say that nobody working on *Doctor Who* in 1975 was expecting this.

• Davies is obviously a fan of this story in particular, as his New Adventure *Damaged Goods* describes "tribophysics" as the effect of two realities rubbing against one another (as in "tribadism"), causing mutations and breakdowns in the laws of the universe. In fact there's a perfectly respectable branch of the science of lubrication called "tribophysics", and a Journal of Tribophysics from the University of Adelaide.

13.4: "The Android Invasion"

(Serial 4J, Four Episodes, 22nd November - 13th December 1975.)

Which One is This? The Doctor gets tied to an exploding stake by white-suited spacemen who turn out to be robots, then gets back to Earth and beats himself up about it. Rhino-men in silver Doc Martens make yet more doppelgangers, while the Doctor and Sarah go down to the pub, run around the countryside, climb trees and have lashings of ginger pop.

Firsts and Last The "epilogue" to the UNIT era, here we see the last appearances of those UNIT hangers-on who haven't already left the series. Benton makes his last ever appearance here, as does Harry Sullivan. For the second and final time in his career as a *Doctor Who* writer, Terry Nation tries his hand at a story without Daleks in it, but as ever in his scripts, the aliens still use disease as a weapon. Barry Letts sits in the director's chair for the last time, while the Kraals are the last monsters with make-up designed by John Friedlander.

Four Things to Notice About "The Android Invasion"...

1. Yes; it's the obligatory "evil doubles" episode. Again. Though robot duplicates have been turning up in *Doctor Who* from the early days (starting with 2.8, "The Chase"), this is the closest the series comes to one of those episodes from late '60s action serials in which the central characters all have malicious twins and nobody knows who's who. The Doctor develops a sudden obsession with ginger pop, and Sarah goes out of her way to say how much she doesn't like it, just to give the Doctor a clue when her robot double drinks some. The struggle between two Doctors in episode four makes it harder than usual to spot the stuntman wearing the Tom Baker wig. Ian Marter has to play an evil version of Harry Sullivan for the second time this year, and while the Zygons monitored a Scottish boarding-house through the eyes of an animal head on the wall (13.1, "Terror of the Zygons"), here the Kraals monitor an English pub through the bull's-eye of a dartboard. Episode two ends with robot Sarah's face falling off, revealing the circuitry and artificial eyeballs inside, which has to be considered a "standard" of this sort of thing. And Styggron, the

alien scientist responsible for all of this, gets to 'activate the hostility circuits' in time-honoured fashion. Still, at least this time resistance is 'inadvisable' rather than 'useless'.

2. Roy Skelton - who, as we've already established, provided the voices for the children's series *Rainbow* - once again gets covered in latex and here plays Marshal Chedaki, the Kraal military supremo. His muttered comment in episode three, when he tells Styggron that testing the virus on a human being is a good idea, sounds for all the world as if it's being delivered by George the pink hippo. He even makes the name "Styggron" sound like "Zippy".

3. Faced with a village that's deserted except for white-clad guards and a UNIT soldier who walks off a cliff for no reason, the Doctor theorises that the place has been evacuated due to a radiation crisis which makes people go mad. In fact, the whole village is a fake made by aliens and populated by robots. This is one of the very, very few occasions on which the Doctor makes a guess about the nature of a strange new environment but turns out to be utterly wrong, and to make things worse he gets it wrong *again* in episode two, guessing that alien mind-control might be the problem. This might have created a sense of mystery, had the story not been called "The Android Invasion".

4. This month's guest monsters: the Kraals, not the most memorable of species but notable for coming from the planet Oseidon. This makes them the first monsters since the mid-'60s to have an exotic-sounding name that doesn't sound anything like the name of their homeworld.

The Continuity

The Doctor Partial to tea and muffins, and ginger beer in vast quantities. The Doctor describes himself as the Brigadier's 'unpaid' scientific adviser, and tends to call the Brigadier 'Alistair' these days. He can re-program androids in double-quick time, and he's an exceptional darts player.

• *Ethics.* The Doctor believes that androids are 'only' machines and doesn't mind killing them, even though they've got most of the memories [and therefore the sentience] of human beings. The Kraals, seeing the Doctor's record, regard him as a champion of 'libertarian causes'.

• *Inventory.* Yet another gizmo in the Doctor's pockets can be used to detect radiation, and pos-

Why Does Earth Keep Getting Invaded?

We've waited until now to bring this up, as "The Android Invasion" is the last "formula" invasion-of-Earth story, written by the author of the first (2.2, "The Dalek Invasion of Earth", naturally). The Daleks' motives for conquering and destroying were never really investigated, aside from the rather unlikely notion of removing the planet's magnetic core and steering Earth around the cosmos like a very slow battleship. This sets the tone for much of what's to follow. The monsters invade England / Earth because... well, because they're bad. And because the writers of the early series were part of a generation that had spent six years waiting for the Nazi paratroopers to land.

However, as the potential conquests become more outlandish and more frequent, patterns emerge. Some invaders want this planet and find the occupants an inconvenience; some want humanity and have decided to grab the source. And some, notably the Sontarans and therefore the Rutans, just see it as a handy staging-post.

Now, if you want to enslave an intelligent race, Earth is a good place to come as the residents are bright, spunky, multi-functional and not terribly good at spotting alien interventions (well, they failed to notice the Skarasen). Given the amount of external intervention in their evolution since the first amino acids started combining - 17.2, "City of Death", 15.3, "Image of the Fendahl", 8.5, "The Daemons", 13.3, "Pyramids of Mars" and 11.3, "Death to the Daleks" as a brief introduction - the humans' capacity to mythologise anything they can't handle becomes a definite survival advantage, like tool-making or antibodies.

Those alien forces with precognitive or time-travel facilities may take pre-emptive action against the planet (9.1, "Day of the Daleks", 14.1, "The Masque of Mandragora", 22.1, "Attack of the Cybermen" and possibly 25.3, "Silver Nemesis", if that story has any hope of making sense). Other infrequent motivations include a "lost" scout deciding to make this world a base of operations (5.3, "The Ice Warriors", 13.1, "Terror of the Zygons" and stretching a point 14.2, "The Hand of Fear" and 12.2, "The Ark in Space").

It's also the case that many species are drawn here by other circumstances, usually the Master. The Doctor may well have attracted some of them by his very presence. This is undoubtedly the case in five of these incidents (11.5, "Planet of the Spiders", stands out because it's the one occasion when the Doctor acknowledges his culpability). If "Earth" equals "England", then there's a pleasing

parallel here. Modern historians have argued that Britain became the throne of the industrial revolution, and therefore a leading world power, not because it did one thing right but because of a combination of a dozen minor factors which just happened to produce the ideal conditions. It's at least possible that Earth becomes a key world in the same way, because it's the homeworld of a future empire *and* on the galactic conquest-routes *and* of interest to a couple of renegade Time Lords *and* loaded with lots of useful minerals. It's the English way of cosmic history.

Usually, however, beings come specifically to this planet with the intention of taking what they can get and removing / enslaving the sitting tenants. The logic of this is questionable. As the outer planets of this solar system are mainly gas-giants, and their moons predominantly ice, the heavier metals are concentrated closer to the sun's gravitational pull (like here). Only one planet in the selection-box is currently seismically-active, so the magnetic field, internal temperature and interesting combinations of elements are likely to be better on Earth than on Mars. Fair enough so far. Yet, Venus is very similar. Admittedly the atmosphere's a bit of a worry, all that sulphuric acid and lead-melting surface temperature (to say nothing of the atmospheric pressure), but beings capable of making a fake Cotswold village full of androids or mining the core of Earth and steering it around the place shouldn't be daunted by a little thing like the Greenhouse Effect. The exotic minerals that might be useful to space-travellers would be more likely to crop up on Venus or Mercury (see **Why Are Elements So Weird In Space?** under 22.2, "Vengeance on Varos"). Moreover, this is far from being the only solar system in this neck of the woods. So far, despite the crudity of the detection-methods, over fifty have been found in the last decade. So why come here?

Stepping outside legitimate astronomy to *Doctor Who* logic, the overwhelming proportion of inhabitable planets are inhabited, and have well-developed, spacefaring species who - when not attempting to conquer us - are dealing with each other. If we're not covered by a protection-treaty, nor allied to a major power, then this is "virgin" soil with all the gene-patents and mineral rights up for grabs. A solar system is a big area to quarantine or protect, and as our fishing-fleets have found, anything not constantly patrolled is

continued on page 77...

sibly other energy sources. At the last moment the Doctor produces a robot detector which lights up in the presence of androids, with a little red bulb and no other markings [it's unclear what *possible* use this could have been to him in the past]. There's a knife in his right-hand pocket that's ideal for cutting ropes. When the sonic screwdriver is set to 'theta omega' [it has Greek letters on its controls?], it makes the Kraal's artificial ivy wither.

• *Background.* The Doctor remembers meeting the Duke of Marlborough, and says - perhaps not quite seriously - he always told Alexander Bell that wires were unreliable. [Knowing the Doctor, he probably means the first and most famous Duke of Marlborough, the celebrated seventeenth-and-eighteenth century soldier. The meeting with Bell would have been around 1875.] He apparently recognises one of the space-shells used by the Kraals for transporting androids, but can't remember where from, claiming that three-hundred years ago he'd have identified it like a shot. He recognises Styggron's matter dissolving bomb, calling it an 'MD bomb' as if it's an old acquaintance. Since he also recognises the Kraals and knows what their planet's called, it's likely he's met them before. [Maybe that's why he's got the handy robot detector.]

The Supporting Cast

• *Sarah Jane Smith.* She went to Devesham on a story two years ago, after the fuss at the Space Defence Station when the XK5 disappeared; see **History**. She stayed at the local pub. Unlike the Doctor, she doesn't care for ginger beer at all.

Sarah makes another costume change on the TARDIS, but still claims that she wants to go home, preferably by taxi. Yet when the Doctor offers to give her a lift in the TARDIS *again*, she doesn't hesitate to accept. [She must know what's bound to happen. You get the feeling she's really enjoying this lifestyle.]

• *Harry Sullivan.* The Kraals build an android of him from the memories of the astronaut Guy Crayford, and Crayford left Earth two years ago, so Harry must have been working at the Space Defence Centre then.

• *UNIT.* The Brigadier seems to be in Geneva, leaving Colonel Faraday *in charge* of the Space Defence Station. [So the Brigadier is usually in charge of the Station at present? Again, see **History**.] Believing Earth to be under threat, the Doctor speaks of warning London, not UNIT HQ.

• *RSM Benton.* He's got a kid sister, and he's taking her to a dance at the Palais tonight. Like Harry, there's a duplicate of Benton based on Crayford's memories, so he must have worked at the Space Defence Station two years ago and he's working there again now. [The UNIT people get called in whenever rockets take off or land. Benton bows out of the series without ever being given a Christian name... fan-lore sometimes cites his name as "John", but this almost certainly got started because it's the actor's name. In episode four you'd be forgiven for thinking that Benton's been killed and replaced by an android duplicate, but the Brigadier mentions him leaving UNIT to sell used cars in "Mawdryn Undead" (20.3).]

The TARDIS Still trying to get back to UNIT HQ, and once again the Doctor doesn't seem to know what planet he's on when he lands. [Some of the TARDIS systems really must be off-line.] The Doctor insists that the co-ordinates were set for Sarah's time, but he's having difficulty navigating thanks to the 'linear calculator'. He claims that the TARDIS is due for its 500-year service, though he could be joking. [Funny how Time Lords seem to do things in cycles of 500 years, c.f. the Doctor's diary.]

The Ship then seems to show an unusual amount of self-will. Apparently realising that it's landed in a fake Earth village by "mistake", when Sarah puts the key in the lock it dematerialises, completing its journey to the real Earth with nobody on board. The Doctor says that the TARDIS isn't supposed to auto-operate, but that the key cancelled the pause control. [Hard to see why on Earth it's programmed to take off when the key's in the door, since it's almost guaranteed to leave the crew stranded. The fact that the TARDIS lands in the same spot in the real Devesham as in the fake indicates that the Ship "knows" the two are connected in some way. But why did it land in the fake, anyway? Was it "fooled" somehow, even though Oseidon's in a completely different part of space?]

There's apparently a cache of ginger beer on the Ship, as the Doctor emerges with a bottle in his hand. He claims there's a 'radio' on board, which he can use to contact London from Devesham.

The Non-Humans

• *Kraals.* Yet another war-like species planning to invade Earth, and possibly other worlds after

Why Does Earth Keep Getting Invaded?

...continued from page 75

65,000,000 years back in time in 19.6, "Earthshock", though that's pushing things.

Meanwhile the Brigadier believes that once we began broadcasting on radio frequencies and sending probes into space, we'd 'drawn attention to ourselves'. This may explain why the rate of invasion-attempts-per-annum shoots up in the 1970s, but not why Southern England is the site for so many. One obvious candidate for this run of bad luck is the large lump of Validium that was launched from these parts ("Silver Nemesis"), in which case it's the Doctor's fault again. Another possible reason is that Azal, the last of the Daemons and apparently the only "pre-historic" alien to remain on Earth of his own free will, is still buried at Devil's End and egging on the aforementioned industrial revolution. (There's also Cessair of Diplos from 16.3, "The Stones of Blood", but she doesn't seem to have done much in the last four-thousand years.)

However, it should be remembered that the Doctor Who universe isn't all astronomy, wormholes and radio-waves. Many of the "rules" that govern this continuum are founded in mythicism rather than science, especially in the '80s stories, and questions like these can have solutions so grandiose that they're more like Biblical epics than logical theorems. When we're told about the Time Lords' war with the Giant Vampires in "State of Decay" (18.4), we're told about something that seems to have changed the nature of the universe in a quite profound way, especially if you care to believe that the Time Lords had a hand in "fixing up" the current state of history. It's at least feasible that Earth's real significance, perhaps underlying one or more of the less spectacular theories suggested above, lies in something that's worked into the fabric of history rather than something purely material.

The New Adventures are, as ever, a good indicator of the way later Doctor Who writers saw this universe. Ben Aaronovitch's storyline for the novel So Vile a Sin aimed to clear up the "what's so special about Earth?" matter once and for all, with a solution which revealed certain nexus-points in history to be the result of botched repair-jobs after the Time Lords' formative wars. If only Aaronovitch had finished the book, this might actually have held some weight.

bound to be encroached upon by desperate neighbours. Besides, at least two other space-travelling races have come from this system (the Ice Warriors and the Fendahl... plus the Silurians if 21.1, "Warriors of the Deep", is to be taken at face value). Maybe some ancient grudge against Earth's system is being avenged.

And that's not the only cultural consideration. According to Doctor Who, the future of humanity sees our descendants bullying, oppressing and ripping off everyone else just because they seem to think it's part of their destiny. Humans like building "toys", they like using weapons and they like dealing with perceived challenges, the men especially. Faced with the vastness and blankness of the outside galaxy, it's conceivable that humans might be inclined to target inhabited planets just as a way of keeping their culture together. Nothing makes a population feel good like thrashing an enemy, even if the enemy in question is much weaker and doesn't stand a chance of fighting back. And most intelligent species we see seem to have developed along astonishingly similar lines to humanity. Do the Kraals pick on Earth, rather than an uninhabited planet, simply because they see that sort of aggression as being part of their nature? Since we see nothing of Kraal civilisation but the military-industrial complex, do they have to keep invading places just to keep their own domestic economy and political system afloat?

Other options present themselves. The distances between stars being what they are, the only beings to deliberately target Earth must be able to travel faster-than-light (ignore the Urbankans in 19.2, "Four to Doomsday" for now). There may be some kind of local navigational phenomenon which enables or causes spaceships to get here easily. Both "The Android Invasion" and the quasi-canonical novelisation of "Remembrance of the Daleks" (25.1) hint at a wormhole of some kind near Jupiter. This may well account for Voga crossing the galaxy in a few generations and settling into orbit without anyone noticing it at first (12.5, "Revenge of the Cybermen"). This might also be connected with what Adric does to the freighter to make it travel

that. The Kraals are pug-faced, pale-skinned, rhino-like creatures who dress in mesh-like armour and have flattened horns on their noses.

Two named specimens are seen here, one (Styggron) a Chief Scientist with his own armaments section, the other (Chedaki) a Marshal in the Kraal military. They seem to be equals, more or less. Like an increasing number of alien species these days, the Kraals know about the Time Lords [maybe from Guy Crayford, who's read the UNIT files].

Most Kraal androids are physically perfect duplicates of human beings, if you can use the word "perfect" to describe models whose faces come off when they fall over. Even so, they're bulletproof and can be repaired when they break their necks. The voice and mannerisms of the original subject are copied exactly, although they occasionally get character traits wrong and they're quite bad actors.

Sarah gets strapped to a slab in the Kraal 'disorientation chamber' and a painful, throbbing hallucinogenic light analyses her brain, until the Kraals have her memory-print and body parameters. When Crayford's strapped to the same slab, a soldier from his memory cells takes shape over an android framework within seconds, yet the [more detailed] information from Sarah needs to be 'coded' before her duplicate can be completed.

The "flesh" and clothes of an android vanish when it dies, and they need occasional re-charging. The Doctor refers to them as 'electronic' rather than anything more elaborate, so a radar dish can jam their circuits. Other, more basic, androids wear what look like radiation suits and act as mechanics. They've got no faces under their visors, and their index fingers are inset with energy weapons.

The Marshal has a fleet of battle-cruisers, but doesn't believe Earth can be taken by force alone. Instead the Kraals are planning to use a virus capable of wiping out all human life on the planet within three weeks, although when Styggron eventually falls face-first into a phial full of the stuff, the "virus" is revealed to be a goo which kills him but doesn't spread to anyone else in the room. There may be a suggestion that it's supposed to go into the humans' water supply. [The fleet's fate is never explained either, but we can assume it never tries anything after the plan falls apart.]

Crayford's rocket gets beamed back to Earth by a space-time warp. The Kraals use a matter dissolving bomb to destroy the fake village.

Planet Notes   Oak trees don't grow anywhere in the galaxy apart from Earth, if you were wondering.

• *Oseidon.* The Kraal homeworld, Oseidon appears Earth-like but has a higher natural radiation level than any other planet in the galaxy, and it's getting worse all the time. Soon it'll be uninhabitable, hence the Kraals' attempt to conquer Earth. An exact copy of the English village of Devesham has been built on Oseidon as a training-ground for the androids. The Doctor and Sarah can walk around for hours there without ill effects. In its normal state, Oseidon appears to be a pale, dusty place, albeit with a nice blue sky.

History
• *Dating.* Some time after the TARDIS last landed in the twentieth century, apparently not that long as nobody's surprised by Sarah's return. The calendar in the pub says it's Friday the 6th of July. [Probably 1976. The 6th of July was a Friday in 1973 and 1979, but again, days of the week *never* seem to match dates properly in the *Doctor Who* universe. See **What's the UNIT Timeline?** under 8.5, "The Daemons".]

Britain has had a Space Defence Station for at least two years, about a mile from the village of Devesham [not the same facility seen in 7.3, "The Ambassadors of Death"; things seem to have changed since General Carrington's tenure as head of Space Security]. Despite sounding as if it's there to protect the world from aliens, space research seems to be the order of the day, and missions launched from the facility go as far as Jupiter. [Given the public don't seem to know about aliens yet, you have to ask whether anyone in Britain ever asks why a space *defence* station is a good use of taxpayers' money. Maybe the "Star Wars" programme has already started in this world.]

The XK5 space freighter, piloted by Guy Crayford, had its first test in deep space two years ago but vanished without trace. It was believed that an asteroid hit it. ['Freighter' suggests that humanity has bases off the planet by now. Possibly there's a facility on the moon, although there may be orbiting installations.] The freighter looks like a normal twentieth-century space rocket, but has 'cargo shuttle ejectors'. Only the escape pod lands on Earth. Having been in orbit around Jupiter, Crayford is said to have gone further into space than any other human being [Britain's still a world leader].

UNIT personnel are present when Commander Crayford returns, and the Brigadier has a permanent office at the station even though this isn't an international operation. [Britain knows that astronauts have a habit of bringing nasty alien material back with them. If *Doctor Who* really *is* set in the same universe as *Quatermass* - see 15.3, "Image of the Fendahl", for the argument - then this sort of thing is almost routine by now.] As Senior Defence Astronaut, Crayford knows about the Doctor and even knows he's a Time Lord. Everyone at the Station, including Crayford himself, calls UNIT's Colonel Faraday 'sir'.

[If Crayford isn't joking about cracking open a bottle of champers after five years in microgravity, the British approach to space-travel is closer to World War Two RAF heroics than to NASA's neurotic caution. The layout of Mission Control is analogous to a wartime command post (see 26.3, "The Curse of Fenric", for an example). His uniform and muffler are dead giveaways.]

The Analysis

Where Does This Come From? Oh look, more alien double-agents. Most of what could be said here has been said about "Terror of the Zygons" (13.1) and "Spearhead from Space" (7.1), for obvious reasons.

However, it's worth noting that the Doctor's erroneous theory about a nuclear accident is nearly spot-on for what might ordinarily cause a village to look like the one set up by the Kraals. The replacement coins, white-suited technicians and shoot-to-kill policy are all pretty much exactly what happened to the area around Chernobyl. In the early 1960s a smaller-scale event at Windscale, in Cumbria, led to farmers in the Whitehaven area having to dispose of millions of gallons of milk, and the news footage of the time is like a black-and-white forerunner of episode one. Ministers continually stated that each time something like this happened at Windscale or Dungeness (see 8.3, "The Claws of Axos") it was a one-off and could never happen again, and anyway we were switching to the American designed advanced gas-cooled reactor, which was safer. That design was the one they used at Three Mile Island.

Terry Nation had already had a phenomenal "adult" success with his series *Survivors*, a post-apocalyptic exercise in British angst and Range Rovers, in which (guess what) a mutant virus wipes out most of the planet's population. Especially those pesky working classes. It was obvious that he'd done some research on the government's contingency plans for a catastrophe, or

that someone else did it for him. Writer / producer Brian Clemens claims he and Nation discussed it when they worked on *The Avengers*. Certainly, Clemens' script for *The Avengers* 6.18, "The Morning After" features a lot of this sort of thing.

We might also mention *The Avengers* 4.1, "The Town of No Return" (in which an English coastal village turns out to be entirely populated by foreign agents, who are planning on taking over the whole country one community at a time) and *The New Avengers* 1.6, "Target" (in which a mock-up village is used for training agents). This was an urban myth of the time: that the Russians had exact replicas of English towns populated by willing spesnatz recruits from Britain, to teach "sleeper" agents how to pass for one of us. This is the source of the creepy *Danger Man* 2.3, "Colony 3" - now often seen as a dry-run for *The Prisoner* - and Verity Lambert's 1990s project *Sleepers*, written by the authors of "Meglos" (18.2).

Anyone who frequented village pubs in the days before the big breweries started forcing landlords to be "family friendly" will recognise the "us don't like strangers 'ere" frostiness of the locals. The Doctor's horror at finding plastic horse-brasses is typical of anyone confronted with the breweries' attempts to impose "atmosphere" on corporate drinking-holes. This was also the era which saw the formation of CAMRA, the Campaign for Real Ale, an attempt to get away from imported chemical sludge and lager so foul-tasting that it has to be served chilled. (CAMRA's motto seemed to be 'if it ain't got straw in it, it can't be any good'.) This may seem petty, but the move towards "authenticity" was a big '60s / '70s concern. The fear was that mass culture and commercial entertainment were eradicating centuries-old British heritage. The whole "folk" movement was part of the same trend. Richard Hoggart's groundbreaking book *The Uses of Literacy* obliquely hinted that television and rock 'n' roll would prove insurmountable opponents to any notion of a British identity. This present volume would seem to refute that, but let's see how we feel in another ten years.

And you can't really talk about this story without mentioning the holy trinity of mid-'70s android action: *Westworld* (a theme-park with killer robots whose faces fall off), *The Stepford Wives* (suburbia equated with automata... by the time you read this, the 2004 remake will have been forgotten) and of course Fembots Take Las Vegas (actually after this story, but *The Six-Million*

Dollar Man was about contemporary). The posters for the first two are, putting it tactfully, "referenced" by the final shot of episode two.

Things That Don't Make Sense   The Kraal plan. All of it. Where do we start?

The Kraals have easy access to space-travel, but insist on using jerry-built androids to carry their virus instead of just dumping it on the planet from a battle-cruiser or firing it at the surface in their space-shells. Their reasons for copying an entire village full of people, when apparently they only need personnel who work at the Space Defence Station, are no less mysterious. And if the virus just has to go in the water then the Station's irrelevant to the plan anyway.

Then they insist on blowing up the fake village once it's served its purpose, even though it's on a planet they're supposedly leaving soon, at which point Styggron becomes one of those old-school villains who prefers to tie the hero up next to the bomb instead of just shooting him. (Similarly, he leaves the Doctor alone in the disorientation chamber after delivering the usual sarcastic 'unfortunately I shall not be here...' speech.) Harry and Colonel Faraday get tied up instead of shot, too, despite being of no value to the invaders whatsoever.

The Kraals tell Crayford that his eye's missing for no given purpose, but they're lying about it anyway, and in the last two years Crayford has never bothered looking under his eyepatch. Maybe the Kraals have brainwashed him into not looking, but if so then wouldn't surgically removing the eye have been a wise precaution? Nor does anybody at the *real* Station ask him why he's wearing a patch these days, or where he got it from, as eyepatches can't be standard issue on missions to Jupiter.

A major design flaw in the robot duplicates means that they can't recognise each other on sight, so the invasion would have been a confusing mess even *without* the Doctor's interference. The end of the story sees the Doctor using his own robot double to thwart Styggron's plans, even though all the androids are supposed to have been shut down by the radar dish [he must do some *serious* re-programming]. Despite all of this, Sarah's comment when she finds out the truth about the village: 'It all makes sense now!'

It's never explained why a single Kraal space-shell is lying in the woods near the fake village.

Nor why Crayford is overjoyed to see the Doctor and Sarah at the fake Station before he tries to kill them. Nor why there's a hidden spy-hole in the wall at the end of episode one, since the Kraals aren't *expecting* any outsiders to turn up in the middle of a high-security military project on their own home planet. The androids on Oseidon seem to act in whatever fashion fits the plot, sometimes being autonomous, sometimes following orders from "control" and sometimes trying to strangle Sarah for no reason.

Leading the Doctor into a trap, robot Sarah decides to tell him the Kraals' real plan, thus tipping him off that there are android duplicates (like her) around. The Doctor picks up on the fact that the duplicate's wearing a scarf, whereas the real Sarah lost hers, but the Kraals copied Sarah *after* she lost the scarf so it's not clear why the double has one at all.

Robot Sarah's face, once detached from her body, bears no resemblance to Sarah. Or, indeed, to anyone human. The Kraals call their mind-sucking room the 'disorientation chamber', naming the whole thing after the side-effect it has on humans rather than its actual purpose. On Oseidon, Crayford tells the Doctor that the Brigadier is in Geneva, apparently expecting the Doctor to think they're on Earth (which he does, but Crayford has no reason to think that, as he knows the Doctor's a space traveller). And if the real Brigadier's in Geneva at this point, then how do the Kraals know about it, when the fake Space Defence Station is based on Crayford's two-year-old memories? Crayford even gets the name of the acting commander right.

(Pause for breath...)

UNIT isn't at all suspicious about an astronaut returning to Earth in a perfectly healthy state after vanishing for two years. Exactly the same NASA footage is used to depict Crayford's rocket taking off as was used to depict the Vogan rocket taking off in "Revenge of the Cybermen" (12.5); at least this time the rocket's *supposed* to come from Earth, though why a piece of hardware made for the British space programme has "United States" written on the side is anyone's guess. But since it appears to be the kind of old-fashioned rocket that leaves behind most of its mass once it's out of the atmosphere, why is it still "intact" when it blasts off for a second time on Oseidon? The g-force nearly kills Sarah, so it must have been designed by an incredibly shoddy space agency.

Then we have the robot guard-dogs, equipped with the same sense of smell as real Alsatians and not - say - infra-red detection and sonar, in case anyone does the old "I'll-jump-in-a-river-so-they'll-lose-the-scent" trick. And let's not forget that in the android-populated village, the ginger pop tastes exactly like ginger pop, but nobody can make accurate calendars [we'll be generous and assume that the androids are supposed to rehearse the same day over and over again]. The Kraals can get a ship to and from Jupiter in next to no time, but can't find any suitable planets nearer than Earth where they could hole up for a few years. (Ironically, around the time Crayford disappeared the space security people were having trouble with alien visitors who fed on radiation; 7.3, "The Ambassadors of Death". They should have organised some kind of exchange deal.)

To be pickier still, note the comedy sound effect when the Doctor jumps through a closed window in episode four. And what's that mysterious piece of cardboard which appears next to the space-shell to give Tom Baker something to lie on?

Critique   On the whole, it's hard to tell exactly what the production team thought it was doing. Since so much of the rest of Season Thirteen is aiming at tea-time horror, perhaps the intention was to make a "light relief" story, something clean, simple and pre-adolescent to stop the audience getting bogged down in alien slime. If so then it was a mistake. It may be in sharp contrast to the stories around it, but only because it looks cheap and silly.

Critically, though, this is *Doctor Who* pitched as a children's programme and nothing else (prior to this the last thing Barry Letts worked on for *Doctor Who* was "Robot", which may be telling). And yes, if you're six years old and can't spot a senseless story when you see one then "The Android Invasion" is bright and shiny and full of robots. If you're even *close* to being grown-up, though, then it's only watchable if you can convince yourself that it counts as "kitsch" and try to accept every ludicrous turn of the plot without question. The ever-loveable Milton Johns, playing inept astronaut Guy Crayford, is the best thing on offer here. By now Terry Nation's obsession with disease-weapons is just annoying, while Harry's appearance seems to have been an afterthought, as he never does anything and displays no sign of a personality at all.

And if you *are* that uncritical six-year-old, then you might still notice that they did the exact same story in September, but with a funnier pub landlord and better-looking monsters. And the real Brigadier.

The Facts

Written by Terry Nation. Directed by Barry Letts. Viewing figures: 11.9 million, 11.3 million, 12.1 million, 11.4 million. (Average score: 11.8 million. There really is no justice.)

Supporting Cast   Ian Marter (Harry Sullivan), John Levene (RSM Benton), Milton Johns (Guy Crayford), Peter Welch (Morgan), Max Faulkner (Corporal Adams), Martin Friend (Styggron), Dave Carter (Grierson), Roy Skelton (Chedaki), Patrick Newell (Colonel Faraday).

Working Titles   "The Kraals", "Return to Sukannan" (?!), "The Enemy Within" (there has to be one story potentially called "The Enemy Within" every year, it's the law).

Cliffhangers   Sarah follows the Doctor and his guards into the Space Defence Station, where a small panel opens up in one wall and the hideous alien eye of a Kraal peers out at her; Sarah's face falls off as she tumbles over onto some grass, REVEALING WIRES AND CIRCUITS WITHIN!!!; the rocket to Earth takes off with the Doctor and Sarah on board, and the g-force nearly crushes Sarah to death.

The Lore

• Martin Friend's death-scene, wearing those big silver Doc Martens and heavy latex mask, resulted in his executing a perfect somersault.

• Nicholas Courtney was due to appear as the Brigadier, but was cast in a play called *The Dame of Sark* and had to be written out at short notice. His replacement, Patrick Newell, played "Mother" in the last season of *The Avengers*... script-edited by Terry Nation.

• Devesham is, in reality, the base for a far more sinister quasi-official organisation. It's the BBC's training-ground for directors and crews (see 12.1, "Robot", for more cost-cutting with this site).

13.5: "The Brain of Morbius"

(Serial 4K, Four Episodes, 3rd January - 24th January 1976.)

Which One is This?   The *Frankenstein* one, where the monster has a plastic see-through head and the "angry mob of villagers" is replaced by a sisterhood of gyrating Kate Bush wannabes.

Firsts and Lasts   After seven years of being shown to be far-distant, all-powerful arch-manipulators, here the Time Lords are said to have an 'alliance' with another world for the first time, finally bringing them into the arena of galactic politics even when they're *not* tricking the Doctor into doing their work. And the first hint that William Hartnell may not have been the only First Doctor...

Four Things to Notice About "The Brain of Morbius"...

1. Yet another memorable monster costume - the finished Morbius creature, patched together out of bits of other (sadly not familiar) aliens with a transparent brain-jar for a head - is filled by long-term stuntman Stuart Fell, whose only visible human feature is his left hand. Oddly, it's hard to concentrate on anything but the hand when Morbius is in action, since it's the only way that Stuart can really express himself. Look out in particular for the moment when Morbius insists 'my brain functions perfectly!', and the hand feels the need to underline the idea by proudly pointing at said brain in its transparent casing.

2. Trapped in a tank full of bubbling liquid before it gets put into the body, the brain of Morbius delivers one of the most peculiar villain-rants ever heard: 'Even a sponge has more life than I! Can you understand a thousandth of my agony? I, Morbius, who once led the High Council of the Time Lords, and dreamed the greatest dreams in history! And now reduced to this, *to a condition where I envy a vegetable!*'

3. And though Philip Madoc's gorgeous performance as "mad scientist" Mehendri Solon saves the day, Solon's dialogue is even more prone to ranting. Among the invective aimed at the Sisterhood of Karn and its leader, Maren: 'that squalid brood', 'accursed hag', 'may her stinking bones rot', 'I'll see that palsied harridan scream for death'. And that's in *one line*. He remains one of

the most quotable villains ever, and a generation of younger siblings were subjected to insults like 'you chicken-brained biological disaster'.

4. The sets vary wildly here. Interiors are generally great, with Solon's "castle" combining Piranesi and Art Nouveau (but not, as is claimed elsewhere, Antonio Gaudi; if anything it's more inclined towards the German designers). However, the exterior is straight out of a school pantomime, and makes it seem as if Solon and the Sisterhood live inside a TV studio separated by one patch of basalt - which sounds like wood whenever anyone treads on it - while the sky looks as though it's been painted by kids on detention. Apart from That Chair (see "The Curse of Peladon", 9.2 and 16.4, "The Androids of Tara") and That Goblet (see every BBC historical drama made between 1965 and 1990), Solon has recklessly scattered severed heads from various statues around his front parlour; very odd for a fuel-depot converted into a lab. Meanwhile the Sisterhood of Karn have a 100-watt bulb to represent the sunrise, and worship a cupboard. Mind you, it is a *very* pretty cupboard...

The Continuity

The Doctor   Despite his new-found role as responsible Time Lord and protector of history [see 13.3, "Pyramids of Mars"], here he seriously objects to his people using him to do their dirty work. He seems to know that the Time Lords brought the TARDIS to Karn as soon as he lands, and sulks until his curiosity's aroused by a headless corpse. Nonetheless, he eventually becomes determined to sort out the Morbius affair for the sake of the future of the universe, so it's not the job he objects to as much as being told to do it.

On the verge of unconsciousness, the Doctor feels Morbius' mind nearby. [Compare this with 18.7, "Logopolis". All Time Lords would seem to have some form of telepathy, but Morbius seems particularly powerful, possibly because of the 'burning hate' described by the Doctor.]

The Doctor eventually challenges Morbius to a 'mindbending' contest, a form of Time Lord mental wrestling that's usually a game but can end in death-lock. A piece of equipment in Solon's lab allows the two of them to engage in this combat, with Morbius forcing his way back through the Doctor's memories and making images of the Doctor's previous incarnations appear. [The

Who Are All These Strange Men in Wigs?

The set-up: the Doctor, engaged in mental combat with Morbius, rewinds through his previous lives and lets us see them all on a handy piece of nearby apparatus. And there are more than three of them. You can imagine the debates that followed in school playgrounds and university common-rooms; if William Hartnell was the original Doctor, then whose were the faces "before" his? Four popular theories have emerged over the years.

1. They're Morbius. The one "recognisably" non-Doctorish face we see is that of Michael Spice, who's also the model for the bust of Morbius in Solon's living-room. We may see the eight unknown faces immediately after the Doctor's, but in fact the Doctor gets the upper hand after Hartnell's face appears. In the end it's clearly the Doctor who wins the contest, as Morbius' head explodes while the Doctor only collapses after the link is severed. So, the Doctor forces his way back through Morbius' previous selves and eventually causes goldfish-bowl-head to blow a sparky (although in fact, as it's written in the script, Morbius' head explodes because of the strain of combat rather than because he loses).

The big drawback with this theory is the fashion sense of the people we see on the display, and the idea that Morbius was attempting cosmic domination whilst parading about in fancy dress from Earth history. On top of that, you have to explain why Morbius is shouting 'back... back to your beginning!' while the mysterious faces are appearing. Perhaps he's confused, or simply ranting.

2. The Doctor is older than he claims, and older than the other Time Lords seem to know. This was clearly the idea Hinchcliffe was getting at, as the "costume" found in the old console room in "The Masque of Mandragora" (14.1) isn't recognisably like anything we've seen before. The original plan was to have fairly distinguished actors represent "unseen" Doctors, but nobody was interested and the production team stepped in (see below for a factual list). A subsidiary theory is that along the way the Doctor has "projected" versions of himself, as he does in "Logopolis" (18.7) and K'Anpo does in "Planet of the Spiders" (11.5). This was first advanced as a means of excusing the scene in "Destiny of the Daleks" (17.1) in which Romana "tries out" various bodies before plumping for that of Princes Astra, but it also covers these odd-looking specimens whilst keeping faith with the

Chancellor's statement in "The Three Doctors" (10.1) that Hartnell was the earliest model. (One supposed piece of evidence for these faces being the Doctor pre-TV is said to be the regeneration in 21.6, "The Caves of Androzani":'I might regenerate, I don't know... it feels different this time.' This *could* be taken to mean that the eight "mystery" faces, plus the five broadcast Doctors, make up the allotted thirteen lives. This opens whole cans of worms, but may explain the Sixth Doctor's arrogance and self-doubt. He's actually the *Fourteenth* Doctor, and as a result he's hopelessly confused.)

3. Fakery. The Doctor's winning the contest all the time, and the faces seen on the display are figments of his imagination, dredged up out of his psyche in order to fool Morbius. A reasonable explanation, this one, but ultimately disappointing. It was popular in certain drab sectors of fandom during the late '80s and early '90s, before a much more complicated theory turned up...

4. It's neither the Doctor nor Morbius, but some other Time Lord. This has been most clearly stated in the last-but-one novel in Virgin's New Adventures line (or at least, the last-but-one New Adventure which actually had the Doctor in it), *Lungbarrow*. Since this was a reworking of Marc Platt's unfilmed "Lungbarrow" script from the late '80s, and since this was one of the key texts of the so-called "Cartmel Masterplan" (see 25.3, "Silver Nemesis", for more), it has to be taken seriously. Not that everybody *wants* to take it seriously; there's a school of thought that *Lungbarrow* is one of the most unbearably fannish things ever written. But then, it was the near-conclusion of a six-year-long novel line which took an approach to the *Doctor Who* mythology quite unlike that of the TV series, and in context it didn't seem so unreasonable. However, if you *aren't* the kind of reader who can proudly boast "even a sponge has more of a life than I", then look away now:

Back on ancient Gallifrey, Rassilon and Omega had a mysterious collaborator called "the Other", whose origins were unknown (mysteries behind mysteries, etc) and who disappeared from Time Lord history when regeneration replaced the ability to reproduce. He told his granddaughter that he'd eventually return, then threw himself into a Loom, which is where new Gallfreyans are 'spun'. Millions of years later, bits of his identity resurfaced in a no-mark called Theta Sigma, who unex-

continued on page 85...

83

machinery in Solon's lab *can't* be built for this task, so Time Lords must just need some sort of "conductor" in order to enter psychic combat. Omega does something similar in 10.1, "The Three Doctors", but being all-powerful needs no equipment at all.] The faces we see are the Third Doctor, the Second Doctor, the First Doctor… and then eight others, which don't seem to be Morbius' previous incarnations as Morbius shouts 'back to your beginning!' as they materialise. [The suggestion is clearly that the Doctor has had previous incarnations before the first known one, but countless other stories, starting with "The Three Doctors", explicitly contradict this. See **Who Are All These Strange Men in Wigs?**] The Doctor collapses after this, and only the Sisterhood's elixir brings him back from the point of death.

The Doctor prefers his current head to the previous version. He's not immune to a Mickey Finn, and he apparently doesn't feel qualified to examine Sarah's eyes after she's temporarily blinded, letting the shifty Solon do it instead. Either he can do sums in his head in record time, or he knows how many seconds there are in a month off by heart. [By 19.6, "Earthshock", he no longer has the ability to do rapid calculations.] He gives his age as 749 here.

• *Ethics.* The Doctor believes that the immortality elixir on Karn could be synthesised by the gallon, but the consequences of everyone trying to live forever would be appalling, as 'death is the price we pay for progress'. [This probably isn't normal Time Lord thinking. It smacks of the nigh-Buddhism practised by the Doctor's mentor in 11.5, "Planet of the Spiders". Curiously he says that the Time Lords would fall into the same trap as the Sisterhood if they took the elixir regularly, odd since the Time Lords have such a static society anyway. See also **How Does Regeneration Work?** under 18.7, "Logopolis".] His first instinct is to return the brain of Morbius to the Time Lords, not to kill it.

• *Inventory.* There's a pair of pruning-shears in his pocket, and some small fireworks that he eventually gives to the Sisterhood, one of which seems to be kept behind his ear. [This, like the companion's temporary blindness, is a sure sign of Terrance Dicks' hand in the script.] He's still packing his yo-yo, although on this occasion he's left the sonic screwdriver in the TARDIS.

• *Background.* The Doctor was born within a few billion miles of Karn. [Presumably on Gallifrey, but note the use of the word 'born'.] He recognises the feel of Morbius' mind, and he knows Morbius' face, as well as saying - jokingly? - 'you remember me' when he first comes face-to-brain-case with the complete monster. [At the very least, Morbius was a well-known rebel in the Doctor's own 749-year lifetime.] He's familiar with Solon's book, the catchily-titled *Microsurgical Techniques in the Tissue Transplant*, and knows most of the lore of Karn.

The Supporting Cast

• *Sarah Jane Smith.* Unlike the Doctor, she's happy to go exploring on an alien planet when the Time Lords dump them there. Sarah's having a bit of a "dim" day today, believing that her recent experiences have been a terrible dream when she wakes up in Solon's castle. Her immediate reaction to blindness is sarcasm. She preferred the Doctor's previous head, and can spot a doped drink a mile off, tipping it into a bowl and faking unconsciousness.

The TARDIS The Time Lords still have the power to force it to land on a planet of their choice. [So the Doctor's new dematerialisation circuit, obtained in "The Three Doctors", doesn't stop them steering the Ship by remote control. It may be harder for them to control a TARDIS than to intercept a transmat beam, hence the timing of their intervention in "Genesis of the Daleks" (12.4).] The Doctor claims the TARDIS calibrators have been on the blink recently.

The Time Lords Once again sending the Doctor to deal with their own problems, here they seem to have found out about the brain of Morbius, somehow. [But the Doctor's visit to Karn also improves Time Lord relations with the Sisterhood - see **Planet Notes** - which may be almost as important. 23.2, "Mindwarp", would suggest that Solon's brain-transplant experiments alone are enough to get the Time Lords worried.] Morbius expects the Time Lords to turn up 'in force' to destroy him [this is obviously not unprecedented; see 22.4, "The Two Doctors"].

• *Morbius.* Once the leader of the High Council of the Time Lords, a bust of Morbius reveals him to have been bald and aggressive-looking. Believing in conquest rather than the usual Time Lord passivity, he failed to bring the Council round to his way of thinking and began his own

Who Are All These Strange Men in Wigs?

...continued from page 83

pectedly became a Time Lord and found that age-old technology - like the Hand of Omega (see 25.1, "Remembrance of the Daleks") - "recognised" him. This enabled him to nick an old TARDIS and revisit the Old Times, where the Other's granddaughter Susan took advantage of his befuddled state and left with him to explore the universe. The Doctor, for it was he, forgot all of this until mind-duelling with Morbius. Whereupon he suddenly recalled his earlier lives and started getting involved in Time Lord politics, ultimately becoming (all together now!) 'more than just a Time Lord'.

Well, you were warned.

5. Who they *really* were:
• George Gallaccio, production unit manager, later tipped to become producer of *Doctor Who* (and de facto producer of this story). Instead he worked on several high-profile drama series, notably the '80s *Miss Marple* adaptations.
• Robert Holmes, script editor and half of "Robin Bland".
• Graeme Harper, production assistant and later director of "The Caves of Androzani" (21.6) and "Revelation of the Daleks" (22.6).
• Douglas Camfield, director of the next story and tipped as either future producer or future Doctor. His face had appeared before, clean shaven back then, as the third possible Jamie in episode two of "The Mind Robber" (6.2). His version of the Doctor appears in the "flashback" sequences of BBC Books' thirty-fifth anniversary offering, *The Infinity Doctors*.
• Robert Banks Stewart, author of "Terror of the Zygons" (13.1) and the next story, "The Seeds of Doom". Later created the series *Shoestring* and *Bergerac*.
• Christopher Baker, production assistant.
• Philip Hinchcliffe, producer (we'll assume you knew that by now).
• Christopher Barry, director of this story and several others from "The Daleks" (2.1) to "Robot" (12.1).

crusade in the outside universe, leading an army of millions of followers to whom he promised eternal life. The Doctor describes him as a war criminal and dictator. Many of his followers were mercenaries, but judging by Mehendri Solon some of them were just fanatics. The attempt to gain the elixir on Karn destroyed the civilisation there, a fate shared by many other planets, but the Time Lords saved the Sisterhood. If the mind-bending match with the Doctor is anything to go by, Morbius had never regenerated before this.

People came to Karn from across the galaxy to see Morbius' trial. The Time Lords *executed* him for his 'rebellion' right there on the planet. [20.1, "Arc of Infinity", suggests that this was the only occasion on which the Time Lords executed one of their own kind. This is just about feasible, since the War Chief (6.7, "The War Games") was shot while trying to escape rather than executed per se, but see "The Deadly Assassin" (14.3).] His body was destroyed in a dispersal chamber, atomised and scattered to 'the nine corners of the universe', but unbeknownst to all Solon stole his brain. [Ohica says the *body* was dispersed, meaning that he was already clinically dead when he was atomised. Solon may have put a "fake" brain in Morbius' body some time before the execution - many of Morbius' followers would have been

zealots, so it's easy to imagine a brain-donor volunteering for this job - or he may have taken the brain after death and revived it somehow.] Solon comes from Earth, and was living on Karn at the time of the execution. [There's no evidence that the entire human species ever find out about the Time Lords, even in the far future, so how did he get mixed up in all this? Did Morbius recruit him specially? But see **History** and the notes on *Warmonger* at the end of this section.]

Morbius' brain has been kept in a tank of colloidal nutrient since then. Here it gets put into a body with one hand, one pincer, a large shaggy torso, a goldfish-bowl-like artificial head and 'lungs of a Birastrop' which have a handy methane filter, allowing the new patchwork Morbius to breathe cyanide gas without harm. Rage maddens his personality even before Solon drops the brain on the floor during the operation. Ranting and screeching, Morbius wants to return to his followers and take over Gallifrey once again, but this dream ends when he falls off a precipice. [And, we have to imagine, dies. If the goldfish-bowl is tough enough then his brain might survive, though the casing looks wobbly enough even before then.

[Here it should be mentioned that Terrance Dicks, the (original) author of this script, went on to describe the exact nature of the Morbius crisis in the BBC novel *Warmonger*. Though he of all people should know what "really" happened, *Warmonger* contradicts so much of the established nature of the *Doctor Who* universe - and presents such an unlikely scenario - that even those who see the books as canonical have trouble accepting it. This is, after all, a book which begins with the Fifth Doctor sinking his teeth into the neck of a pteranodon and turns Peri into a highly adept rebel leader. Perhaps we can pass it off as Time Lord propaganda? The book claims that Solon was already on Karn by the time Morbius got there and that he removed the brain in secret, bizarrely with the collusion of the Doctor.]

The Non-Humans

• *Mutts*. A creature that's apparently one of the mutants indigenous to Solos [9.4, "The Mutants"] crash-lands on Karn in an 'ejection bubble' from a Mutt cruiser, and is promptly butchered. The Doctor recognises it, explicitly referring to it as a Mutt, but describes the Mutts as a 'mutant insect species widely established in the Nebula of Cyclops'. [The native Solonians we saw before didn't have spaceships of their own, and besides, the mutant phase is supposed to be short-lived so it's strange to see a Mutt in charge of a vessel. If the Solonians started colonising other planets, then they might "freeze" in their insect phase when away from their homeworld, though evidently they're smarter than the mutants we saw before. Even so, see **History**. Odd that the Doctor uses the word "Mutt", which was racist slang on Solos.]

• *The Hoothi*. The Sisterhood can detect the Hoothi's 'silent gas dirigibles' while a million miles distant. [The Hoothi eventually get their own story, in the form of the novel *Love and War*.]

Planet Notes

• *Karn*. A barren and stormy world, said to be only 'a few billion miles' from Gallifrey. [This *might* put it in the same system, but it's more likely to be in a neighbouring system, especially if the Doctor means a *European* billion. Which is likely, as he's talking to Sarah, and the British tended to use the European version in the '70s. Note that Morbius uses the then-preferred 'milliards' to refer to a thousand million. The Doctor also says he's been dragged 'a thousand parsecs' off-course, and he and Sarah seem to have been heading for Earth, possibly a clue or just a figure of speech.]

The Doctor indicates that Karn isn't far from the Nebula of Cyclops, hence the crashed Mutt cruiser. Morbius destroyed the civilisation on the planet, but it still serves as home to the Sisterhood of Karn, an all-female religious order keen on scarlet robes, ornate hats, elaborate face make-up and sacrificing anyone who comes near the planet on the grounds that all intruders must be after their elixir. Solon claims the Sisters' 'song of death' is only heard when they're preparing to sacrifice an outsider, so many survivors of the crashed ships on Karn must have met their end in this way. They don't have much in the way of technology, but Maren has a ring that can stun people with its light or cause temporary blindness.

The Sisters have remarkable mental powers when they form a 'circle', even performing a ritual which can teleport people and objects to their shrine, and their leader Maren claims their senses reach beyond the 'five planets', to the extent that only a TARDIS can approach without detection. They're also capable of long-range telekinesis and have a way of making spaceships crash, the nearby spaceships' graveyard containing the remains of fifteen vessels. [The Doctor takes the view of 'innocent until proven guilty', but Karn doesn't seem to be on any major trade-routes so a lot of the travellers probably *were* trying to get the elixir. A Mutt, trapped in mid-mutation, would have an obvious use for it.]

Maren uses the circle to view the TARDIS at long range; the Sisters somehow focus on the Doctor's craft without knowing where or what it is; and Maren identifies it as a TARDIS despite its appearance. Maren believes that in all the galaxy only the Time Lords equal their mental power, since the Sisters place death at the centre of other creatures' beings or drive victims mad with false visions, but Time Lords can close their minds to these techniques. Morbius can place a barrier around his mind that stops the Sisters noticing him on Karn. [Species like the Daemons ("The Daemons") and the Osirans ("Pyramids of Mars") blatantly have more mental power than the Time Lords, so if Maren isn't exaggerating then it's probably safe to say that at *this* point in history only the Sisters are the Time Lords' equals.]

The elixir kept by the Sisters forms in a natural chimney, where chemicals in the rocks are oxidised by a 'Sacred Flame' and meet superheated gases from a geological fault. The Sisterhood see this as a mystical process, and worship the Flame, but naturally the Doctor puts these silly women to shame and points out that it's just a chemical reaction. He's the first one from outside the Sisterhood to ever see the spectacle.

The Sisters' powers fade as they leave the presence of the Flame. The Time Lords have used the elixir in 'rare cases', e.g. when having difficulty regenerating a body, and it's kept Maren alive for centuries. It's in short supply by this stage, as the chimney's clogged with soot - the Sisterhood seem to be *hopeless* when it comes to science of the non-psychic variety - but the Doctor sorts the problem out, much more effectively than Maren does by feeding it powdered rineweed.

The Sisters have shared the elixir with the Time Lord High Council since 'the time of the stones' [meaning the local stone age, unless silicon-based life-forms used to run this part of space, or unless Maren just remembers the '60s]. Only the High Council knows the elixir's secret, according to Maren, though later she changes her mind and says that only the Time Lords knew of it *until* Morbius. The Sisters have had to remain on guard ever since. Maren fades away to nothingness without a constant supply of the elixir, but she appears youthful again just for a moment. The end of the Doctor's visit apparently sees good relations re-established between the Sisterhood and the Time Lords. [The Time Lords must be *really* satisfied with the way this mission's turned out. Also, compare Karn with Sarn in 21.5, "Planet of Fire".]

History

• *Dating.* The Doctor tells Sarah that it's 'considerably after' her own time, but that's all. [How you date this story depends on whether you believe there's a Time Lord "present", and whether it intersects with the "present" of anywhere else in the universe. See **Where (and When) is Gallifrey?** under 13.3, "Pyramids of Mars". Assuming that Karn and Gallifrey aren't contemporaneous, however - even if they're in the same part of space - it would seem to be thousands of years beyond the twentieth century.

Lance Parkin's *A History of the Universe* points out that as Solon's brain-swapping experiments are similar to Crozier's in "Mindwarp" (23.2), they may be contemporaries, but this is unlikely. Crozier is performing brain transplants with state-of-the-art technology and the backing of some very rich aliens, whereas Solon is doing even more complicated work in his own basement with limited resources and inadequate parts, but *still* gets

the job done even after the brain gets dropped on the floor and his assistant tries to kill him. Solon would seem to be far in advance of Crozier, whose work is eventually destroyed by the Time Lords anyway and never becomes part of "real" history.

And then there's the Mutt. Assuming it really is a Solonian, this may be a time when the Solonians are undergoing their mutant season. It comes every two-thousand years, and this Mutt obviously isn't from the 2900s as it's got its own cruiser. The 4900s would fit, since a lot of human scientists can do remarkable things in ramshackle labs in this era. Just look at 15.2, "The Invisible Enemy". But as so many civilisations seem to know about the Time Lords, humans included, it could be even further into the future than that.]

Solon acts as if he's the only one in the known universe who can stitch a body together and transplant Morbius' brain into it. The Doctor refers to him as one of the foremost surgeons of his time, and his disappearance caused quite a stir, but there was a rumour that he'd joined the followers of the Cult of Morbius. Solon does the usual 'they laughed at me when I said I could create life' speech, and believes that Morbius was the only one who gave him a chance.

Matching the twentieth-century-gothic look of his "castle", Solon uses an old-fashioned projectile weapon, or "gun" as it's also known. But he's got a more futuristic stun-gun in storage. The castle is actually a re-fitted hydrogen plant, built on standard Scott-Bailey principles. It's not clear how long it's been in Karn-time since Morbius' execution; Maren was present at the event, and she's centuries old, but Solon was around as well and is apparently only middle-aged.

Condo, Solon's apparently human assistant, was found on Karn in the wreckage of a Dravidian starship. [This probably isn't a reference to the Drahvins from "Galaxy Four" (3.1). The Dravidians were an aboriginal Indian race, but the word's also used to describe a family of Indian languages, so the ship may have belonged to a human colonial group speaking a common tongue. The "Branch Dravidians" were David Koresh's followers at Waco, and apparently believed in "Enochian" speech, a language of angelic and unearthly presences...] Solon knows all about the Time Lords, which is reasonable, but Cordo seems to know about them even apart from Solon's ranting.

The Analysis

Where Does This Come From? A lot of what could be said here has already been said under "Pyramids of Mars" (13.3), and more will be said under "The Deadly Assassin" (14.3), but for now...

The fear being exploited here is a fear of hybridity. Morbius has acquired a body made of parts of other beings. Why is this horrible? Because it crosses our boundaries of "self". We've already dwelt on the effects of '70s body-fear under "The Ark in Space" (12.2); the original readers of *Frankenstein* didn't live in a world where organ transplants were a palpably real issue, but the *Doctor Who* audience did. If "Ark" hits the same nerve as the later *Alien*, then "Morbius" hits the same nerve as *Coma*, and every surgery-gone-wrong flick of the early '80s video nasty boom. Just as possession of the body by someone else's mind is "bad" in *Doctor Who* terms, so a body made to be possessed by someone disembodied is somehow "wrong" (even if the body is made of inanimate matter, as in 7.1, "Spearhead from Space" and 8.1, "Terror of the Autons"... the latter explicitly mentions *Frankenstein*).

However, the crossing-over from animal to human is the worst of the worst, and it comes as little surprise that there are whole lines in episode one lifted from H. G. Wells' *The Island of Doctor Moreau*. Admittedly these are the lines in which Solon reflects on the contempt of his peers, but it shows that someone had been doing the reading. "Hybrid" and "hubris" both come from the Greek word for crossing over, going too far. Humanity, in this programme's scheme of things, means that people who look like us behave like us unless otherwise stated. Anyone infected and altered starts to become a bad person, usually an unreasoning killer. Morbius wasn't human to begin with, but a Time Lord, presumably brought up to expect a change of form.

Set against this, however, is the exact opposite: a Sisterhood who resist change even to the extent of not ageing. The Sisterhood are quite obviously derived from Rider-Haggard's *She*, and its two film adaptations, but by a roundabout route. The storm-planet Karn originally appeared in Terrance Dicks' 1974 stage-play *Doctor Who and the Seven Keys to Doomsday*, and was home to the dreaded Clawrenticulars. These were giant beasts with bits of other creatures tacked on (notably, and here's the point, a big lobster claw in lieu of a right hand). As an aside, the Master of Karn was played by Simon Jones, the definitive Arthur Dent from *The Hitch-Hiker's Guide to the Galaxy* (see 16.2, "The Pirate Planet", et seq).

It's also worth noting in passing that the line about 'the female brain-case' not being big enough to contain Morbius' intellect is a standard of the mad "science" of anthropometry, which held that you could tell criminals by their skull-shape and prostitutes by how far their big toes were from the rest of their toes. The perpetrator of this particular notion was one Dr. Solon...

Things That Don't Make Sense As ever, we'll start with the obvious. Solon is a surgeon so brilliant that he can transplant brains under crisis conditions and stitch together a new body for Morbius out of the parts of species from different planets. But once the Doctor shows up, why does Solon proceed with plans to put the Doctor's severed head atop the monstrosity rather than just putting Morbius' brain into the Doctor's complete (and much more attractive) body? Surely the lungs of a Birastrop aren't *that* valuable an asset? He also insists on working on the very planet where Morbius died, i.e. not far from Gallifrey and with the Sisterhood of Karn living next door. Nice sense of irony, but isn't it a bit of a risk? [Perhaps Solon knows he can't get the brain off the planet without being noticed. If Gallifrey is as close as it would seem, then the Time Lords might be able to detect Morbius' presence as soon as his psyche leaves Karn... Karn, perhaps, being the Sisterhood's jurisdiction.]

The Doctor connects Solon with the Cult of Morbius as soon as he hears the name, but it takes him a surprisingly long time to remember the sculpted head he's already seen, and when he realises who it is he acts as though he hasn't thought about Morbius in years. In episode three, Sarah's ostensibly blind but still capable of closing a door she's never seen and operating the weird alien locking mechanism to seal Solon inside.

Solon's method of preparing the brain for transfer is to let all the green liquid out of the tank, so that the brain squidges against the glass in a fashion that really *can't* be good for the cells. And despite having the resources to transplant brains or build monsters out of spare parts, Solon doesn't own a machine which can automatically pump for him during operations, meaning that his assistant has to stand there pushing a lever every three seconds. In fact, the power-cut in episode one would probably have killed Morbius anyway, unless he's got batteries.

The Doctor can recognise star-patterns in a thunderstorm, and his decision to leave Solon on his own while disconnecting Morbius' brain isn't very convincing either ('I should have stayed with him!' he hisses, once it's too late). His eventual "escape" from the cellar doesn't make any more sense; the Doctor sends cyanogen gas through the vent shaft up to Solon's lab, and states that if he and Sarah are still trapped in a month then they'll know it hasn't worked. But if the gas knocks Solon out or kills him, surely they'd still be trapped if it *had* worked? In the end they get out because the gas alerts the cyanide-proof Morbius, but the Doctor doesn't know that Morbius is (a) cyanide-proof or (b) active at all by that point.

Look away now if you want to keep things clean. In episode two, while sacrificing the Doctor as part of her sacred duty, Maren calls upon the sacrificial flame and intones the words 'take this body into thy eternal heart'. But she delivers the word 'heart' at exactly the same moment that the whispering priestesses around her start to hiss the word 'fire'. The result is, sadly, an 'eternal fart'. Which can't be pleasant. Perhaps the Hoothi's silent gas dirigibles just came to the planet to refuel.

Critique Well, yes, it's true: it's clumsily-edited, the "magic flame" is a gas-cooker, the Sisterhood have necklaces made from plastic spoons painted silver and the alien monster has a rather obvious zip-fastener up its back. If you care, then you're watching the wrong series.

This story has a brio, a self-confidence and a sense that the audience is right there on board which hardly any other TV programme has come close to since. In a way, it's like coming home. Shelley's *Frankenstein* has repeatedly been cited as the earliest "proper" work of science fiction - see **Is This Really an SF Series?** under 14.4, "The Face of Evil" - and its vision of a universe where techno-fetishism holds sway, and primal powers (in this case history as much as the ability to create life) are forced into the hands of sweaty individuals, has echoes in almost every *Doctor Who* story ever made. The series in its original, '60s form looked and sounded absolutely nothing like this, but even so, nothing jars at all when Tom Baker strides through Solon's castle. It's almost as if Lord Byron's come back to see how the new

generation's getting on with all the things his contemporaries left behind... even if a lot of the imagery comes from the Hollywood treatment of *Frankenstein* as much as from the original text.

"The Brain of Morbius" strikes exactly the right balance between melodrama and absurdity, doing what the '70s series does best by re-visiting the great science-fables with all the flair that BBC drama can muster, and only some tedious running-about between Solon's place and the Sisterhood's shrine gets in the way. The all-video studio filming gives the production a self-contained, weirdly cosy feel that does more to maintain the atmosphere of a workable fantasy-world than any amount of location shooting, so even the much-maligned "exterior" scenery comes off. It's hugely unconvincing, but the fact that it looks so much like a stage-set reminds you that all of this evolved from televised theatre, and that's the way it's played. The relationship between Tom Baker and Elisabeth Sladen has rarely been better, and Philip Madoc... well, Philip Madoc's *always* great, isn't he?

The depiction of the Time Lords as a culture "involved" with the outside universe is controversial, but here the script gets away with it by keeping galactic politics as fairy-tale as the rest of the story. The alliance with the Sisters comes across as a story-book deal between kings and prophets, not a *Star-Trek*-style interplanetary treaty.

The Facts

Written by Robin Bland, a pseudonym for Terrance Dicks, the script once again being radically re-written by Robert Holmes. Directed by Christopher Barry. Viewing figures: 9.5 million, 9.3 million, 10.1 million, 10.2 million.

Supporting Cast Philip Madoc (Solon), Cynthia Grenville (Maren), Gilly Brown (Ohica), Colin Fay (Condo), Sue Bishop, Janie Kells, Gabrielle Mowbray, Veronica Ridge (Sisters), Michael Spice (Voice of Morbius).

Cliffhangers Nosing around in her usual fashion, Sarah pulls back a curtain in Solon's lab and finds the writhing, headless body of the Morbius monster; blinded, Sarah keeps nosing about and follows Morbius' voice into the depths of Solon's castle, not realising that the source of the voice is a brain in a jar; and having been individually menaced by both the body and brain, Sarah is left alone in the lab with the finished Morbius monster, not quite regaining her vision in time to see it slouching towards her.

The Lore

• Terrance Dicks' original concept for "The Brain of Morbius" was pitched as an inversion of the *Frankenstein* story, in which the creature's creator would be an inhuman monster and the final form of Morbius would be perfectly human. However, this was judged to be impractical, ostensibly for economic reasons. (Though it's got to be said that a story in which the monster's revealed at the start of episode one and the thing created on the lab turns out to be ordinary-looking is a bit of a non-starter, dramatically speaking.) As script editor, Robert Holmes stepped in to drastically restructure the script, much to Dicks' annoyance. During an angry telephone conversation, Dicks disowned the story and told Holmes to broadcast it under 'some bland pseudonym'. The legend holds that when the story was shown and Dicks saw the name Holmes had chosen, he burst out laughing and thereafter made his peace.

• Colin Fay (Condo) was with the English National Opera. This might explain his death-scene, in which it takes him several minutes to die and you're never sure when he's finished.

• Director Christopher Barry was dismayed to find that as this was the only studio-bound story of the year, the lead-in time was drastically curtailed. And as this was the first story to be made after a much-needed two-month break, nobody was around to assist. Dicks handed in his version of the script and went away at the end of August. Philip Hinchcliffe left production unit manager George Gallaccio in charge when he went a week later. Robert Holmes wandered off to write a radio script. Then came the "Robin Bland" incident. Designer Barry Newbury had 36 days, including the four days of filming, to do everything from first concepts to building the sets and props.

• Barry added the touch of the brain slopping around on the floor.

• Philip Hinchcliffe was rather perplexed when he saw the end result, as his request had been a story about robotics. He had another go (see 14.5, "The Robots of Death").

• The same people at BBC Worldwide who made us pay £40 for "Revenge of the Cybermen" put out a sixty-minute edit of this story in 1984,

before the uncut version was released on video six years later. The edit has most of the plot beats.

13.6: "The Seeds of Doom"

(Serial 4L, Six Episodes, 31st January - 6th March 1976.)

Which One is This? You know that *Monty Python* sketch where Sam Peckinpah directs *Salad Days,* and everybody gets their limbs torn off? Imagine a version of "Jack and the Beanstalk" in the same vein. Two giant killer plants, one compost-grinding machine, several inept henchmen and plenty of guns.

Firsts and Lasts Though it's by no means a UNIT story in the old-fashioned sense, and there's no sign of the old UNIT family here, "the Seeds of Doom" is the last time in the 1970s that UNIT troops turn up to try to save the day. The organisation won't be glimpsed again for another seven years (20.7, "The Five Doctors"), and won't see active service for another thirteen (26.1, "Battlefield"). This is also the last time the Doctor's portrayed as a UNIT consultant, and the Brigadier's mentioned (but not seen) for the last time in a *long* time.

It's also the last story directed by Douglas Camfield, the first genuine stylist to work on the series; and the last story *not* to have music by Dudley Simpson, until the big shake-up of 1980 (see 18.1, "The Leisure Hive").

Six Things to Notice About "The Seeds of Doom"...

1. *Doctor Who* rounds off its "horror movie" season with a story that's as violent as anything seen in the series before. *Everything* seems more brutal than usual here, from the people infected by plant-tissue ('it's as if he's turning into some sort of a... hideous monster!') to the scene in which the Doctor talks the personnel of an Antarctic expedition into amputating a man's arm.

At the time, Philip Hinchcliffe and Robert Holmes were much-criticised for the rising level of violence in the programme, but Holmes countered by pointing out that it was *fantasy violence* and it wasn't as if anyone was making petrol-bombs. Which is ironic, because here the Doctor orders Scorby to make petrol-bombs in episode five. And despite the Doctor's claim that 'bullets

Is He Really a Doctor?

By this, we mean a medical practitioner. He has doctorates in other fields coming out of his ears, including titles he gained at St Cedd's (17.6, "Shada"), Gallifrey (16.6, "The Armageddon Factor", with the strong hint that his thesis was on thermodynamics in 24.1, "Time and the Rani"), Glasgow (we'll come to that) and somewhere in Renaissance Italy, possibly Padua (various hints, notably 3.6, "The Massacre"). His knowledge of human anatomy is exemplary. He can diagnose injuries by tweaking an earlobe in "Remembrance of the Daleks" (25.1); he cures the Silurian plague in, of all places, "Doctor Who and the Silurians" (7.2); he heroically battles the common cold in "The Ark" (3.7). In "Frontios" (21.3) he enthusiastically takes command of a field hospital and saves lives almost in spite of himself. Why, then, does he claim not to be a "real" doctor? We might assume that he just has very high standards, although in "The Brain of Morbius" (13.5) he has to get Dr. Solon to examine Sarah's eyes instead of doing it himself. And he believes it when Solon lies about the diagnosis.

In "The Moonbase" (4.5), the Doctor claims to have sat for a medical degree in Glasgow in 1888 under Joseph Lister, who crafted the notion of "sterile surgery". Yet this is impossible, according to the history we think we know. Lister had moved to London in 1877, to lecture at King's College Hospital, only leaving in 1893. The Doctor's reminiscence is couched in at least three 'I think's. Yet the Doctor's clearly been to Scotland several times in unrecorded adventures, can recognise "The Flowers Of The Fields" as a lament for the dead (13.1, "Terror of the Zygons"), knows his way around Aberdeen (15.5, "Underworld") and has picked up a couple of tartan scarves (as well as an accent from somewhere... 24.1, "Time and the Rani", et seq).

It's at least possible that the Doctor's medical training was at Edinburgh University under Joseph *Bell*, not Glasgow under Joseph Lister. It takes seven years to qualify in medicine. If the Doctor was in Bell's class in 1888 then he might just have missed being there for the whole of the 1880s, perhaps only staying long enough to sit the exams. But even by the Doctor's standards, it seems odd that he could forget seven years spent cutting up corpses in Glasgow, or Edinburgh, or anywhere else.

Joseph Bell raises an interesting subsidiary question: Bell's most famous pupil, Arthur Conan-Doyle, has almost the same circle of friends as the Doctor. Harry Houdini (11.5, "Planet of the Spiders" and 12.5, "Revenge of the Cybermen"); the Prince of Wales / King Edward VII (the Doctor makes frequent references to *Belle Epoque* Paris - notably in 17.2, "City of Death" - and there's a direct reference in 7.4, "Inferno"); Sir Arthur Sullivan (1.3, "The Edge of Destruction"); H. G. Wells (13.3, "Pyramids of Mars", 15.1, "Horror of Fang Rock" and ultimately 22.5, "Timelash") and a whole lot more. If the Doctor knows all these people, then he must surely have bumped into Doyle, yet this is never mentioned. He doesn't even wince when Redvers Fenn-Cooper makes a disparaging remark about 'young Conan-Doyle' (26.2, "Ghost Light"). Either something happened which has affected his memory, or they had a blazing row.

Doyle's most famous falling-out was with Houdini, over the Cottingley "fairies"; fans of the many remaindered films starring Paul McGann will know this as the basis for the film *Fairytale: A True Story* (1997), as well as the other one released

continued on page 93...

and bombs aren't the answer to everything', in the end the RAF blows up the Krynoid. But towering above all the other horror elements in this story, there's *the machine*, a great big evil-looking piece of hardware that grinds people up into compost and threatens both the Doctor and Sarah at various points in the story. Make no mistake: *this* is the kind of thing that used to scare the living daylights out of children, not the monsters.

2. Sharp-eyed viewers will notice that the first two episodes aren't particularly necessary to the plot. *Two* man-eating Krynoid seed-pods land on Earth, which means that the same basic storyline takes place twice, once with the main cast being threatened by a killer plant in the Antarctic and once with them being threatened in an English country garden. If you didn't know better, you'd swear that the story had been under-running by a couple of episodes and that the programme-makers had decided to flesh it out with a re-make of *The Thing from Another World* (and yet... see **The Lore**). Even sharper-eyed viewers will notice that the half-man, half-plant Krynoid looks remarkably like an Axon painted green (8.3, "The Claws of Axos"), and there's a very good reason for this.

3. It's been said many times before, but while the first two episodes may look like an old horror movie, the last four are strangely reminiscent of

The Avengers. Key to this is the villain, Harrison Chase, an eccentric English millionaire with a quirky obsession that threatens the world (in *The Avengers* it could have been anything from cats to playing-cards… come to think of it, there was a killer plant in *The Avengers* as well, but it didn't have a human "helper" capable of gloating or mincing around the place in a sinister fashion). The real giveaway is the scene in which the Doctor meets Amelia Ducat, *another* English eccentric, who gives him the "lead" to Chase's mansion as if this were a criminal investigation instead of an adventure in space and time. Here the Doctor even gets called in by the authorities, instead of stumbling into things by mistake.

4. As with so many stories this season, it's human villain Harrison Chase who steals the show from the shambling monsters, with Tony Beckley putting in a memorably effete perform-ance as a bad guy who sadistically kills his ene-mies but considers the cultivation of bonsai to be a form of cruelty to plants. The line 'you know, Doctor, I could play all day in my green cathedral' may be the campest single sentence in the entire series. He also gets to say 'why am I surrounded by idiots?' *twice*. Voted "character most likely to fall into his own compost-grinder".

5. Meanwhile Scorby, Chase's mercenary strong-arm man, is one of those villains who car-ries a gun but insists on tying people up and leav-ing them next to bombs instead of just shooting them. Chase himself is no better, setting the grinder on automatic before walking out and giv-ing the Doctor a chance to escape. This sort of thing *might* just be acceptable, except that it's the fourth time it's happened to the Doctor in the last twelve months (stand up, Cybermen, Zygons and Kraals). Best exchange of the story, when Scorby's threatening the Doctor at gunpoint: 'I'm not a patient man, Doctor.' 'Well, your candour does you credit.'

6. The real tell-tale sign of a fully-fledged *Doctor Who* fan is that he or she (but probably he) will never, ever confuse this story with "The Seeds of Death" (6.5). In fact he probably won't even have noticed that the titles are in any way similar, any more than he will have noticed a connection between "The Web Planet" and "Planet of the Spiders", or any of the stories that involve the word "Terror". Civilians find it harder to make this distinction.

The Continuity

The Doctor He refers to Sarah as his 'best friend', the first time he formally acknowledges this sort of relationship with a companion. At the start of the story he's already in Britain, and may have been for some time, as he's called in by the World Ecology Bureau. [He and Sarah have been trying to get back to UNIT HQ for most of this season. It seems they made it, so prior to this there may have been meetings between the Doctor and the UNIT staff which we never see. Does he ever tell the Brigadier that he's not going to be around much from now on, after his revelation in "Pyramids of Mars" (13.3)? When they meet again in 1983, the Brigadier never asks the Doctor why he stopped coming back to Earth without warn-ing.] At the end of the story he offers an off-world holiday to Sir Colin Thackery, unusually generous of him as the man really isn't companion material.

The Doctor doesn't need thick clothes in the Antarctic, and doesn't seem to feel the cold. Sarah believes he's not a doctor of medicine, and the Doctor himself doesn't seem to think he's qualified to amputate a man's arm [see **Is He Really a Doctor?**]. He also leaves it to Scorby to build the fire-bombs, even though he must surely know how. He's still claiming to be 749.

• *Ethics.* Unusually, he's prepared to threaten the opposition with a pistol here, though Sarah knows he'll never use it. [See 9.1, "Day of the Daleks", for more should-know-better firearm antics from the Doctor. Notably, he's at his most violent here when Sarah's life is threatened.] He's happy to engage in physical combat when he's in a tight corner, again preferring a clenched fist to any sort of exotic martial art. [After he overcomes an armed chauffeur / henchman, we later hear that the injured man has turned up in hospital, which suggests that the Doctor and Sarah gave him a lift from the quarry in the stolen Daimler that's got the dead-giveaway clue locked in the boot. That's jolly decent of them.]

• *Inventory.* The Doctor carries a toothbrush. It's a pink one. He's still got that yo-yo, too.

• *Background.* He already knows a lot about the Krynoids. He states that he's President of the Intergalactic Flora Society, which finds Krynoids difficult to study as researchers tend to disappear. [President? How does he execute his duties…?]

Is He Really a Doctor?

...continued from page 91

in the same month, *Photographing Fairies*. Doyle believed in spiritualism and had been contacted by a Theosophist whose daughters had apparently taken photos of fairies. It was a silly joke that got out of hand, but Doyle had too much at stake to admit it. It was 1917, and people needed to believe in life-after-death and other worlds. Still, it seems too trivial a thing to make the Doctor pass up an excuse for a good name-drop. (For those who haven't already been informed... Joseph Bell, who could deduce vast amounts about his patients' lives from the tiniest details, is now thought to be the single greatest inspiration behind the character of Sherlock Holmes.)

So. We're left with an odd situation in which the Doctor knows all this human anatomy and medicine, yet can't remember learning it; in which he knows all these famous people, but not the one individual who connects them. Something's clearly wrong with his recall, which may be why he refuses to practice human medicine, at least if there's an option.

Or, it may be more mundane than that: like all academics, he may just be proud of his title (understandable in his case, as it stands in for his name) and resent being classed as a "professional". In the UK, surgeons who've become consultants are addressed as "Mister" and look down on mere doctors. This dates back to the days when medicine was divided. Diagnosis was performed by priests who'd chosen to specialise - a university degree was a degree in theology, from which all other studies derived in the middle ages - and a matter of looking at star-charts or examining the colour of the patient's urine. Pharmacy was in the hands of herbalists, and surgery was done by barbers (or barber-surgeons, which is why barbershops have red and white stripy poles outside). A surgeon was a master-craftsman, trained in all uses of blades. The practice of medicine was some way below scholarship or divinity in the very oldest universities. The Doctor may simply be a mediaeval snob.

Or it might just be that he's sick of people asking him to look into their ears and take their temperatures.

The Supporting Cast

• *Sarah Jane Smith*. Despite "living" on the TARDIS for much of her recent life, she's in her natural environment again now she's back on Earth. [If the Doctor landed here some time ago, then she may have been staying at her old house instead of on board the Ship.] The Doctor has to promise to take her to a holiday planet to get her off-world again. [But as ever, there's a hint that she enjoys the travel and therefore the danger. By the time she leaves in Season Fourteen, she acts as if the TARDIS is her regular home. This is quite an unusual lifestyle, for a companion.] She's carrying change on her person. Sarah's overcome her aversion to brandy, and seems to have formally joined UNIT at some stage. Even though the Doctor is assigned the investigation on UNIT's say-so, and takes responsibility for confiscating the Krynoid pod himself, Sarah's presence isn't a "con" but part of her "duties".

• *UNIT*. The Brigadier is in Geneva [as in 13.4, "The Android Invasion"], so the UNIT team sent to help the Doctor is led by Major Beresford, who's 'deputising'. The Doctor knows him on sight, and he seems to know both the Doctor and Sarah, treating them both as his 'agents'. Sergeant Henderson, who only seems to know that the Doctor's been right in other operations, appears to be a recent recruit from the regular army. The team, known as Scorpio Section, is equipped with a bulky, hand-held laser-gun of which it's obviously very proud. The UNIT boys have also got the latest military defoliant, still on the secret list.

Here we see UNIT acting as the "world secret police" they were supposed not to be [see 6.3, "The Invasion"]. They intercept communications and have the right to see anything untoward in any UK-based scientific enterprise. Beresford can, on purely circumstantial evidence, call for an airstrike on a stately home. [Perhaps a coup has taken place. See **Who's Running the Country?** under 10.5, "The Green Death".]

The TARDIS The Doctor forgets to cancel the co-ordinate program when aiming for Cassiopeia, so the TARDIS ends up back in Antarctica. [See **Things That Don't Make Sense**. He *can't* be absent minded enough to forget to set the co-ordinates for Cassiopeia, so 'co-ordinate programme' might suggest that he wired-in the co-ordinates for Antarctica - as in 10.5, "The Green Death" - and forget to turn off the mechanism that causes wired-in co-ordinates to override the ones he types into the console.] There would seem to be a beach-ball on board, and holiday clothes for Sarah. [Different to the ones she had in 11.3, "Death to the Daleks". She may buy the holiday gear especially for the trip to Cassiopeia. See also the amount of stuff she's got on board by the time of 14.2, "The Hand of Fear".]

The Non-Humans

• *Krynoids.* The two Krynoid seed-pods dug out of the Antarctic permafrost have been dormant for thousands of years, but start to come to life as soon as the stupid humans dig them out, growing a little before opening. The pod thrives on ultra-violet radiation during this phase, and doesn't need nitrogen the way most plants do. When a pod opens, the tendrils of the Krynoid inside immediately start feeling around for something to eat, in this case wrapping themselves around the nearest human arm and infecting the victim. [The resemblance to the Wirrn infection in "The Ark in Space" (12.2) is uncanny, but obviously coincidental.]

Plant bacteria appear in the bloodstream, and soon the victim becomes a shambling mass of green vegetable tissue, with the desire to consume more food and grow much, much bigger.

Before long the Krynoid has no human features at all, but is still capable of lurching around the place with its tendrils flailing, and ultimately it can engulf a mansion. [It grows remarkably large in a remarkably short time, with very little food. It's night when it goes through its growth-spurt, so even sunlight doesn't seem to be its main source of energy.] Though enough explosive can blow up a Krynoid, laser-beam fire only stings it. It can somehow channel its energy into other plants, allowing them to attack humans, so the Doctor believes that it'll soon be able to control all plant life on Earth. It uses plants as its eyes and ears, while at least three people within a mile of Chase's estate get strangled in their gardens.

The unstable, plant-loving Chase also becomes 'possessed' for a while. Unlike the half-human stage, the larger version of the Krynoid is capable of speaking in a booming voice [it grows big vocal cords?], but it's not clear whether it's naturally intelligent or gains the power to communicate from its human victim. Either way it speaks of itself as 'us', and is capable of tactical thinking, identifying the Doctor as the prime enemy and

cutting the 'phone lines. It's preparing to spurt out pods of its own just before it's destroyed.

The Doctor, who knows a thing or two about Krynoids, believes the seeds came to Earth after being shot into space by internal explosions on their own planet. This sort of thing must happen quite a lot, as he insists that they 'travel in pairs, like policemen', and he speaks of 'planets' - plural - where the Krynoids have taken hold. He seems to know nothing about the Krynoid homeworld, though. [For an interplanetary Krynoid life-cycle to make any sense, the Krynoids would have to deliberately *cause* volcanic activity on every world they consume. This would allow new seed-pods to find new worlds and continue the cycle, though they might take millions of years to find a new home. This all seems evolutionarily unlikely, so maybe the seeds are simply laid in pairs on the Krynoid homeworld, and just get shot into space by accident. In which case it's fortunate that these pods found their way to Earth, or indeed, to any other world where the Doctor claims the Krynoids have eaten all the animal life. Are the pods smart enough to navigate? Come to think of it, are they smart enough to navigate in pairs?]

Planet Notes

• *Cassiopeia.* The Doctor offers to take Sarah there, saying it's a good place for a holiday. [A planet, or just somewhere in the Cassiopeia constellation? They may be aiming for it even *after* the end of the story, but it's not known whether they ever get there, nor if Sir Colin decided to go with them after all.]

History

• *Dating.* Sarah acts as if the TARDIS has brought her back to the "present", and there's nothing to contradict this. Chase states that it's the autumn. [So probably 1976. See 13.4, "The Android Invasion".] It takes 2p to use a public 'phone, which is very '70s.

There's a World Ecology Bureau (WEB) with its headquarters in central London, where Sir Colin Thackery is obviously familiar enough with UNIT's track-record to call in the Doctor as an expert and send him to WEB's Antarctica expedition by helicopter. The Royal Horticultural Society hears about the Krynoid, and wants the Doctor to address a meeting on the 15th of the month [so more and more people on Earth are finding out about the sort of thing UNIT gets up to].

The Krynoids arrived on Earth between 20,000 and 30,000 years ago, the late Pleistocene era. Harrison Chase states that the west wing of his mansion was completed by Sir Bothwell Chase just before his being executed in 1587 [so his is an old, wealthy and probably quite mad family].

The Analysis

Where Does This Come From?   During the Angolan civil war (which started in 1974, though you may have missed it as it only lasted for twenty-eight years), many unemployed British men sought to earn money as gunmen and were apprehended and tried as a result. Most of these mercenaries were psychologically unfit for the British Army, usually due to an unreasoning, psychopathic racism, which made them tend to go to South Africa first. The British government officially condemned the practice but, with the Wilson government's slim majority, couldn't ignore constituency MPs' efforts to free them. If you've ever wondered what Elvis Costello's "Oliver's Army" is about, then now you know.

Drama serials found new morally-ambiguous action-men to explore, along with bent cops and jaded spies (see 21.4, "Resurrection of the Daleks" for Eric Saward's first belated attempt to explore this material). This is the era of *The Professionals*, and its BBC "cover version" *Target*, to which Philip Hinchcliffe "graduated" after Season Fourteen. Knowing director Douglas Camfield's tendency to "intervene" in the scripts, it's worth noting that Scorby's breakdown and panic-stricken bid for freedom are - except for the bit about him being killed by a pond with an attitude problem - identical to Lethbridge-Stewart's abject panic at the crisis-point in 5.5, "The Web of Fear".

Robert Banks Stewart evidently never got over being discarded by the producers of *The Avengers*, as he had a tendency to recycle scripts from around the time he wrote for that series. But not his own. So "Castle De'Ath" (*The Avengers* 4.5) becomes "Terror of the Zygons", and "The Man-Eater of Surrey Green" (*The Avengers* 4.11) is composted into "The Seeds of Doom". The seed-pod in the ice is flagrantly taken from the 1951 Howard Hawks version of *The Thing From Another World* (see also 5.3, "The Ice Warriors" and 15.1, "Horror of Fang Rock"), but so is a lot of Sarah's attitude in this story. Her spectacular tirades to the increasingly unstable and insecure Scorby are striking, and this is the one time she lives up to

the promise of the "feminist" agenda, supposedly her *raison d'etre* during Barry Letts' producership.

Oh, and there was a sudden fad for Venus flytraps around this time. One day nobody had heard of them, the next they were the favourites of cartoonists and TV producers everywhere. We've had the "plants that are more like animals" idea drummed into us through countless Terry Nation scripts; a *real* Crynoid is an animal, a kind of sea-anemone, that looks like a plant.

Things That Don't Make Sense   The last scene sees the Doctor and Sarah return to Antarctica by accident, because the Doctor's forgotten to cancel the co-ordinates of the TARDIS. Except that the TARDIS never *went* to Antarctica; the WEB sent them there by chopper. It's at least feasible that the Doctor programmed the Antarctica co-ordinates into the console before he was talked into using a helicopter, but if so then how on Earth could he forget that he never used the TARDIS when it's still sitting around in England?

On stepping outside the TARDIS in at least 20 below zero, wearing a bikini, Sarah stands around chuckling at the Doctor's rather feeble joke instead of - ooh - maybe getting indoors and not dying? Her breath makes mist in Chase's garden, but not at the South Pole. Likewise, none of the snow that blows over the characters in episode one ever sticks to them (a result of it being superimposed on top of the image after filming). Nor do any of the flecks of snow inside the base ever melt.

The Doctor's plan in episode five, to contact the WEB while Sarah and the others stay at the house, makes him look as if he's just leaving her in danger for a laugh. He claims he wants her on-site as 'a link', but to what? It doesn't seem particularly feasible, either, that the self-obsessed Scorby agrees to stay with her while the Doctor drives off. Paranoid millionaire Chase appears not to have staff who recognise one another, as the Doctor can pass himself off as the chauffeur and get past the door. Does Chase get them from a temping agency? If so, then what are the interviews like? And not to sound too bloodthirsty, but Chase's death in the grinder is incredibly clean and quiet, not leaving any blood on the wheels and not even making a "crunch" noise.

Hubert Rees (John Stevenson) is one of those actors who puts the emphasis on the wrong word in any line. He claims that they have a refrigerator 'to keep specimens in', as if they were bidding to escape, rather than 'to keep *specimens* in'. There are lots more.

Not exactly a mistake, but noticeable anyway: the death / vegetisation of one of the Antarctic team would almost certainly have resulted in the mission being cancelled, even if Scorby hadn't turned up and tried to kill everybody, so the second Krynoid pod would have remained dormant under the permafrost and never been discovered if the Doctor hadn't insisted on looking for it. Which means that all the trouble from episode three onwards is *his* fault.

Critique A story that smells of raw flesh as well as fresh vegetation, the curious, un-*Doctor-Who*-like structure of "The Seeds of Doom" makes it a hard story to get a grip on, and it makes a lot more sense in its original episode-by-episode form than it does if you go all the way through it from start to finish. The video age hasn't been kind, then. It's also another great epic of child-scaring, and that just causes more problems for the modern-day viewer. The siege in episodes five and six, which sees the Doctor's party trapped inside the house and hemmed in on all sides by murderous foliage, is brilliantly compelling when you're young enough to wonder 'will they get out in time?' but much harder to care about when you're old enough to know that the answer's obviously 'yes'. Watching it now it's hard to ignore the discrepancy between the writing, with its ineffectual civil-servants, dotty old ladies and the archest of arch-villains, and the visual style. The "running-around-and-getting-caught" scenes are choreographed as comedy, but the eerie music undercuts even this.

Many of the things we look for in the programme as grown-ups are still here, including some high-grade bluster from the Doctor and a few glorious set-pieces (and hats off to the model-work in episode six, the lovely, unforgettable sight of the full-grown Krynoid squatting on top of the mansion), yet there's also much that we *don't* want to see. The brutality has already been mentioned, and while a certain level of gut-level ugliness is great if it's used as a way of pointing out what the Doctor isn't - see 12.4, "Genesis of the Daleks", for one of the best examples - here the grotesquerie's just used to try to keep up the dramatic tension. If we can overlook the compost grinder, then we still have to accept the sight of the Doctor packing a pistol, and the fact that we know he's not going to use it really isn't a good enough excuse. He just

shouldn't *need* a gun, while his habit of punching the bad guys in the face isn't very endearing either. One shot of him twisting Scorby's neck to render the man unconscious could have resulted in death or paralysis, if kids had copied it.

The result is a story that can certainly be described as *good*, especially in its component parts, but in so many ways it also feels *wrong*.

The Facts

Written by Robert Banks Stewart. Directed by Douglas Camfield. Viewing figures: 11.4 million, 11.4 million, 10.3 million, 11.1 million, 9.9 million, 11.5 million. (Episode five dipped severely from episode four because it was opposite the feature-length episode of *The Six Million Dollar Man* which introduced Jaime Sommers, the Bionic Woman... ITV finally got the hang of this "networking" thing.)

Supporting Cast Tony Beckley (Harrison Chase) John Challis (Scorby), Mark Jones (Arnold Keeler), Kenneth Gilbert (Richard Dunbar), Michael Barrington (Sir Colin Thackeray), Seymour Green (Hargreaves), Sylvia Coleridge (Amelia Ducat), Hubert Rees (John Stevenson), John Gleeson (Charles Winlett), Michael McStay (Derek Moberley), Ian Fairbairn (Doctor Chester), John Acheson (Major Beresford), Ray Barron (Sergeant Henderson), Mark Jones (Krynoid Voice).

Working Titles "The Seeds of Death". It was about this time that the Doctor Who Appreciation Society was formed, and immediately earned its keep by pointing out that this title had been used already.

Cliffhangers One of the Antarctic expedition runs into the human / Krynoid hybrid in the base, and gets himself strangled to death; Scorby's bomb blows the whole Antarctic base; as the second pod begins to open, Chase has his men hold Sarah's bare arm out for it to feed on; the swollen, no-longer-human mass of the Krynoid rolls forward towards the Doctor and Sarah in the mansion's grounds; the Krynoid does some more strategic looming, its now-vast body towering over the courtyard where the Doctor and company have become trapped.

The Lore

• Contrary to the claim made in almost every other *Doctor Who* guide ever written, this story was always conceived as a six-parter; was in no way a four-part story with two unnecessary episodes of faffing-about in Antarctica grafted on later; and was emphatically *not* bolted together out of two separate stories. The idea was that the "two pods" structure would introduce the threat in an abstract setting, then place it in a more familiar context. The popular belief that the Antarctic scenes were a late addition only arose because Holmes and Camfield rewrote them more extensively than the rest.

Eric Pringle (who eventually wrote another two-parter for the series, 21.2, "The Awakening") *had* proposed a two-parter. It was apparently called "The Angurth", and was remarkably similar to "The Stones of Blood" (16.3). Season Thirteen was originally to have ended with "The Angurth" and another four-part story; when this fell through, plans were made to replace it with a six-part version of "The Hand of Fear" (14.2). And when *that* fell through, "The Seeds of Doom" was the result. Plans to expand "The Angurth" to four episodes for Season Fourteen came to nothing.

• Douglas Camfield was commissioned to direct the original version of "The Hand of Fear". He scouted several locations for it, which were eventually specified in the script for "The Seeds of Doom".

• Tom Baker was spectacularly not-too-impressed with this script, suggesting that it should have been composted along with the villain. However, he and Camfield agreed to play it as if the Doctor were scared and desperate, to try to avoid the potentially comical Krynoid losing its frisson of scariness.

• Douglas Camfield never worked on *Doctor Who* again, despite being in the frame to produce it sometime around 1982. He did, however, work with pretty much the same team he had here - including Robert Holmes - on the Friday evening chiller *The Nightmare Man*. His protégé Graeme Harper used those members of *The Nightmare Man* cast not seen in *Doctor Who* in his debut "The Caves of Androzani" (21.6).

• The casting of the villains is something Camfield practised when working on *The Sweeney*. One episode in particular, "Stay Lucky, Eh?", also features John Challis (Scorby) and Tony Beckley (Chase): Challis is now best known as Boycie in *Only Fools and Horses*, while Beckley will forever be Camp Freddie from *The Italian Job* (the good version, the one actually set in Italy).

• John Challis had to do two takes of his uncomfortably wet death-scene, the second earning him a bottle of brandy as it hadn't been his fault that the first one had been botched.

• There was an outbreak of flu during rehearsals. Then Michael McStay, playing Moberly in episode one, had a car accident. Camfield visited him in hospital and it was agreed that McStay was well enough to film the "Antarctic" material, with a false beard to cover his scars. Kenneth Gilbert (Dunbar) then gave everyone his daughter's chickenpox. Just when it all seemed to be over, someone at the BBC lost the tape of episode one just prior to broadcast and Hinchcliffe tried to piece it together again from the raw footage.

• The World Ecology Bureau HQ is unmistakably BBC Television Centre.

• Chase's original first name was "Harrington" rather than "Harrison". Either makes him sound like a furniture warehouse.

• The reason the Doctor and Sarah find their arrival in Antarctica so bleeding funny (in the final scene) is that the prop TARDIS collapsed during the first take. It was the same one that had been used since 1963.

• Elisabeth Sladen had been planning to leave at the end of Season Thirteen, and turned down at least one other role to honour this commitment, but remained in place for the first two stories of the next season. Part of the reason for this was a desire not to fade away or simply get married, but to have a proper send-off.

A potential motion picture deal was another factor. Tom Baker had put forward the idea of a *Doctor Who* movie, and he and Ian Marter had worked out a script - provisionally entitled *Doctor Who Meets Scratchman* - in which the Doctor and Sarah confronted a light-hearted devil-figure (it's usually claimed that Vincent Price was interested in this role). The project was abandoned, with some complications over funding, or rather re-funding as many misguided people had sent money to Baker after his ill-judged suggestion that the fans could all chip in to help pay for it. Camfield, meanwhile, was approached to write a final story for Sarah; see 14.2, "The Hand of Fear", for more.

14.1: "The Masque of Mandragora"

(Serial 4M, Four Episodes, 4th September - 25th September 1976.)

Which One is This? BBC costume drama meets Roger Corman's *The Masque of the Red Death*. Swordfights, ritual sacrifice and Renaissance villainy abound in what looks like a real fifteenth century Italian city-state. In Wales.

Firsts and Lasts After thirteen years, it's revealed that the TARDIS has a second console room, which is used as "the" console room for the rest of Season Fourteen. Originally intended to be a permanent(ish) replacement for the original, it's a break from the outer-space starkness of the '60s version and designed to match the more sombre, science-gothic feel of the programme in this era. This means metal handrails, stained-glass windows and lots and lots of wooden panelling.

This is the last story written by Louis Marks, who's been occasionally turning up on the programme's books ever since Season Two. For the first time somebody brings up the awkward question of why everyone the Doctor and companions meet can somehow speak English, but it's hurriedly brushed under the carpet. And for the first time in the 1970s, the Doctor's sidekick is explicitly referred to - by the villain, in this case - as a 'companion'. It's also (and this is a bigger point than it might seem to the uninitiated) the story which sees the switch from big chunky mid-'70s children's TV lettering in the titles to grown-up Times New Roman.

First (and until Ace's arrival in 1988, only) hint that football exists in the *Doctor Who* universe.

Four Things to Notice About "The Masque of Mandragora"...

1. No monster outfits this time, but the design department's been busy anyway. One writer on the series later pointed out that if you give the BBC a historical script then they go to extreme lengths to make sure that every tiny costume and set detail is accurate, but if you give them a "space" script then they just give you a stick with a flashing light on the end, and "The Masque of Mandragora" is a

Season 14 Cast/Crew

- Tom Baker (the Doctor)
- Elisabeth Sladen (Sarah Jane Smith, 14.1 and 14.2)
- Louise Jameson (Leela, 14.4 to 14.6)

- Philip Hinchcliffe (Producer)
- Robert Holmes (Script Editor)

case in point. Entirely devoid of corridors and control panels, Renaissance Italy is depicted in a fashion that can only be called "lush", all purple velvets and burly, well-tailored men on horseback. Some fans have seriously claimed that the filming in Portmerion "ruins" this story, as they only associate that town with *The Prisoner*, but it's almost unrecognisable here. The Brotherhood of Demnos leader, resplendent in his golden screaming-face mask, is much scarier than robots.

2. And the moment when he takes the mask off at the end of episode three, revealing nothing but a blur of purple energy inside his robe, is much scarier than a hideously mutated alien-face.

3. There are, however, some shocking pieces of acting - and some shocking accents - on offer. Though all the main cast rush at the script with as much pomp and ceremony as they can muster (and Jon Laurimore obviously enjoys rolling his "r"s as Count Federico, a villain in the "boo, hiss" mould), the peasants all mutter in the same Mummerset rustic accent that's afflicted "yokels" in *Doctor Who* since the early '70s UNIT stories, while the guards chasing the Doctor in episode two sound like a cockney music-hall double-act. Ripe period dialogue also abounds, including the ever-trusty guardsman's stand-by: 'Sire, let me punish this insolent dog!'

4. As part of this year's explicit campaign to avoid doing Doctor-Who-by-numbers, charred bodies are turned a copper blue rather than regulation green; villainous henchmen join the "right" side when their position becomes untenable; and any hint that the guest-hero fancies Sarah is downplayed almost to non-existence. They knew what to avoid, but some might say they were unsure of what to put in place of the clichés...

Does the Universe Really Speak English?

In 1964, Terry Nation gave the world *The Dalek Pocket-Book And Space-Traveller's Guide*, featuring a short glossary of the Dalek language. Thus we learned that "Zerinza" was a wish for success, used as a farewell; "Galkor" meant "follow me, I am your guide"; "Clyffil" was a way of saying "I understand you but I do not agree with you" (very useful for humans, probably less so when talking to Daleks); and the letter J was forbidden, as it was so insulting.

The significant thing to say here, apart from '*what?*', is that this seems so wrong now but didn't then. Oddly, it's mainly American fans who wonder why aliens should speak proper English instead of mid-Atlantic like the ones on *Star Trek*, though aliens speaking American is actually less likely than the notion of aliens listening to the BBC (as British radio started before anyone else's). But the fact remains that the Doctor, and his companions, are capable of talking to just about everyone they meet.

There are three main theories to explain what's happening in this universe. The first, and simplest, is that all non-English dialogue is being translated. By whom, though? The Doctor is the most likely candidate, and in "The Masque of Mandragora" he suggests to Sarah that it's 'a Time Lord gift I allow you to share'. Many off-screen sources, including the New Adventures, expand on this by claiming that the translation process requires the TARDIS' presence rather than the Doctor himself. Needless to say, it's usually said to have something to do with the Ship's telepathic circuits.

Even those who don't bother with "non-canon" material tend to assume that the Doctor's pseudo-explanation in "Mandragora" in some way implies telepathy, despite the t-word never being used. If the Ship's telepathic then it may be limited in the kinds of mind it can read, which would explain how it can translate the words of humanoids from far-off galaxies (e.g. 16.6, "The Armageddon Factor") but not the chitterings of the bipedal-but-otherwise-inhuman Foamasi (18.1, "The Leisure Hive") or the radiation-emissions of the Ambassadors ("...of Death", 7.3). But in certain stories, most notably "The Creature from the Pit" (17.3), the TARDIS crew speak the native lingo yet the locals can't always understand them if they use long and complicated words. This hints that rather than establishing a telepathic link between (say) Romana and Torvin, the translation process "plants" the language in a traveller's mind ahead of time.

If the process *does* involve the TARDIS, then it's at least feasible that the Ship uses a pre-programmed "bank" of languages instead of scanning the thoughts of those nearby. In which case it must be better-read than the Doctor himself, since he's often seen to communicate with cultures he's never even heard of. This might also help to explain why the Doctor's relationship with written language is so variable. Most signposts we see around the universe appear to be in English, and even the less-than-literate Leela can read numbers and letters without training (14.5, "The Robots of Death"), but occasionally the Doctor finds himself unable to interpret alien script (16.3, "The Stones of Blood"). In "Logopolis" (18.7) Adric can casually read English words, yet states that the Doctor has been teaching him Earth numbers, perhaps hinting that something *does* translate written text automatically - within the limits of its knowledge - but that the Doctor wants Adric to do this by himself rather than relying on the easy option. The signs on the walls in "The Invisible Enemy" (15.2) use English lettering but "futuristic" spelling, which might mean that the automatic systems only kick in when absolutely necessary.

The other possibility is that reading a script requires the presence of a nearby mind who can read it already. The Doctor can't read Tibetan on Chloris (17.3, "The Creature From The Pit"), but might have been able to at Det-Sen (5.2, "The Abominable Snowmen"). Significantly, in "The Stones of Blood" there are no living Diplosians around when the Doctor fails to interpret the seal on the prison ship. All of this chimes with the hints given in various sources, notably episode two of "The Mysterious Planet" (23.1), that the entire *programme* is the product of the TARDIS' telepathic "field" collecting information from more than just the Doctor's point-of-view.

But if the TARDIS is at the root of all this, then people presumably lose the ability to talk to each other once it leaves. This assumption raises a number of tricky issues, which we'll go into later.

Option #2 is that the aliens might all have learned our language. And obviously, being so advanced, they all talk like the BBC. This was the thinking behind the original Cyberman voices, when Roy Skelton delivered his lines in an androgynous, hybrid accent with the stress on the wrong syllables. It also explains how someone from Mondas picked up the phrase 'a foregone conclu-

continued on page 101...

The Continuity

The Doctor For the first time, one of the Doctor's companions asks the Doctor how she can understand the local dialect, and the Doctor describes it as a 'Time Lord's gift I allow you to share'. Weirdly, he also realises that Sarah's under the influence of hypnosis when she brings the subject up, deducing that as she's never asked before something must be affecting the balance of her mind. [Yet it's exactly the kind of question Sarah *would* ask. Since the translation process must in some way be telepathic - see **Does the Universe Really Speak English?** - it may auto-condition the TARDIS crew in such a way that they're primed not to ask, and only the hypnosis puts Sarah in a questioning state of mind. This is, of course, desperate retcon.] When the Doctor speaks Latin, both Sarah and the native Italian-speaker Giuliano hear it *as* Latin, rather than hearing a translated version. [It's evidently a 'gift' which can be withdrawn whenever awkward questions might arise.]

Here the Doctor also displays the ability to exactly mimic the voice of Hieronymous. [The Master can do the same trick in "The Time Monster" (9.5), and the Doctor manages something very similar at the end of "The Celestial Toymaker" (3.7). It's curious that he never uses this skill again, though, even when it'd obviously be incredibly useful.] He's a decent horseman and fencer [as in "The Sea Devils" (9.3), "The Androids of Tara" (16.4) and "The King's Demons" (20.6)].

• *Ethics.* The Doctor's insistence on being a dutiful Time Lord enters a whole new phase, as he claims that insisting on 'justice for all species' is part of a Time Lord's job. [Even given that Time Lords are nowhere near as non-interventionist as they're often made out to be, this is clearly a lie. The Doctor's stating his *own* philosophy here, and just pretending to speak for all his kind. But see also the next story.]

• *Inventory.* He's carrying a football rattle, improbably. He's still got that yellow yo-yo.

• *Background.* The Doctor knows all about the Mandragora Helix. He's looking forward to meeting Leonardo da Vinci, but ultimately fails to do so. He doesn't seem to have met the man before, as he has to ask whether Leonardo is one of the people who walks past him at Giuliano's place [see **When Did the Doctor Meet Leonardo?** under 17.2, "City of Death"].

He states that the finest swordsman he ever saw was a captain in Cleopatra's bodyguard, who 'showed me a few points'. He hints that he may have met Florence Nightingale, but it's not at all clear, and mentions Agincourt in the same vein [as in 14.6, "The Talons of Weng-Chiang"].

The Supporting Cast

• *Sarah Jane Smith.* She's 5'4", just about. The Doctor, credibly, believes himself to be her best friend. By this stage she seems to be travelling on the TARDIS just for the sake of it, as there's no hint that she's trying to get back to twentieth century Earth at the moment. She appears to speak neither Latin nor Italian [c.f. 13.1, "Terror of the Zygons"]. And she doesn't seem to need choreography lessons when called upon to dance with the masqueraders.

The TARDIS The second console room hasn't been used by the Doctor in some time, but he must have visited it at various points over the years as it contains a familiar-looking chair, a recorder that smacks of the Second Doctor and some dusty old clothes. There's also a shaving mirror in the middle of the console. [Does the Doctor need to shave? He's never seen to do it, but Time Lords must be able to grow facial hair or the Master wouldn't have a beard. Oh, and see 18.1, "The Leisure Hive".]

Despite the wooden surfaces on everything from the roundels to the console, it seems to function in exactly the same way as the usual console room, with a screen set into one wall. The Doctor states that this was originally the 'old' console room, and that he can run the Ship just as well from here as from the other one. The power comes on, and the room becomes fully-lit, with one touch of a switch on the console.

When asked how big the TARDIS is, the Doctor cites 'relative dimensions' and claims there are no constants, 'no measurements in infinity'. Exploring the TARDIS passages in the area of the second console room, Sarah also comes across the boot cupboard. The room's enormous and fully-furnished, with at least one portrait on the wall, though through the doorway only one pair of boots is visible.

The Doctor doesn't know where he is when the Ship lands in the Helix, but only because the astrosextant rectifier's gone out of phase, apparently because of the rough journey.

Does the Universe Really Speak English?

...continued from page 99

sion' from Shakespeare's *Othello*. Sil in "Vengeance on Varos" (22.2), the Foamasi cop in "The Leisure Hive" and the aforementioned Ambassadors all have obvious translator-gadgets, with flaws. The Lurmans in "Carnival of Monsters" (10.2) have special implants, and even the less-than-diplomatic Sontarans carry handy language-boxes around with them as part of their standard kit (11.1, "The Time Warrior").

This option seems more plausible than "instant telepathic translation" if you bear in mind how often the Doctor speaks other Earth languages: Mandarin (14.6, "The Talons of Weng Chiang"), Hokkien (8.2, "The Mind of Evil"), Russian (26.3, "The Curse of Fenric"), German (6.6, "The War Games") and Tibetan (11.6, "Planet of the Spiders"), to say nothing of Venusian. It's feasible that he *might* go out of his way to learn other languages in order to improve his understanding of other cultures, even though he doesn't really need to, but if he's automatically translating everything unconsciously then the anomalies mount up. He doesn't sing "La Donna I Mobile" in what we hear as English (mind you, he's forgotten the words: 7.4, "Inferno" and 23.3, "Terror of the Vervoids"), and he has difficulty understanding one of the thousand or so Australian Aboriginal languages (fortunately Tegan speaks it, in 19.2, "Four to Doomsday").

The thing to notice here is that all species seem to have similar grammatical structures, the differences being in vocabulary. But the idea of (for instance) "past" being different from "present" isn't necessarily innate. The notion that there are universal constants, which is present in *Star Trek*'s universal translators, is out of keeping with *Doctor Who*'s world-view. Even in our world, the idea of "warmth" is hard to convey in French. Bengali has difficulty with the pluperfect tense and the subjunctive mood. Japanese has no adjectives. If the current front-runner in the theory of language acquisition - Noam Chomsky's "Deep Structure" - is correct, then the human ability to perceive a difference between "one" and "two" is part of the way we've developed languages. Grammar is brain-function, made manifest in the outside world. In that case, why should aliens have brains so like ours that their thoughts are translatable at all? For example, humans see things in binary oppositions: self-other, yes-no, inside-outside... would a species without lateral symmetry have this ability / limitation?

The convention in *Doctor Who* has been to assume that the degree of difference between an alien's mental processes and our own is the degree to which Dick Mills or Brian Hodgson monkeyed around with their voices. This in turn assumes that sound is all there is to language, and we all know about the Delphons (7.1, "Spearhead From Space"), the aforementioned Ambassadors, or - if you like a looser canon - the people of Terserus ("The Curse of the Fatal Death"... see the appendix in Volume VI). If anything with a grammar and vocabulary that's used to communicate is a language, then can the Doctor understand birdsong, BSL and bee-dances? Apparently not, or at least, not without doing things the hard way and actually learning them.

Perhaps the most significant thing about his 'Time Lord gift' is when he says it and why. Sarah has been hypnotised, and suddenly questions her ability to speak Italian. The fact that she asks is a clue to the Doctor that she's not herself, which indicates that you're not supposed to notice it but also establishes that it only applies to those under the Doctor's "protection". If it's associated with travelling in the TARDIS, then only TARDIS crewmembers can do it. If it's proximity to the Doctor, then Steven, Vicki and anyone else left behind in a culture not their own might be in trouble. (3.9, "The Savages", 3.3, "The Myth Makers". As Ovid said, 'barbarus hic ego sum quia non intelligor ulli'. No, you look it up.) As human companions and aliens can talk even when the TARDIS briefly leaves the scene (e.g. "Logopolis"), it's possible that its passengers "soak up" the ability to speak the local dialect on arrival, perhaps losing the knack after a while.

The main rival to Chomsky's theory was, at least when the programme started, Behaviourism. In this view of language, we imitate whatever's around when we're growing up. The traditional argument against this is that humans can make entirely new sentences which "work", reflecting a grammar outside the repertoire of all the sentences we've heard before. "Colourless green ideas sleep furiously" was Chomsky's example, whereas we might use "golly, aren't Pip and Jane Baker good". If Behaviourism is right, then the odds against any other country - let alone species - developing human-style language unaided are astronomical.

Moreover, if the "telepathic translation" theory were to work then it'd require the Doctor to down-

continued on page 103...

The Non-Humans

• *The Mandragora Helix.* A 'spiral of pure energy that radiates outwards in ways no-one understands', which basically means it's a swirling thing in space. There's a controlling intelligence at its centre, the Doctor stating that it seems more active than usual [it's a regular hazard for space-time travellers?] and vainly trying to 'counter-magnetise' the TARDIS in order to withstand its pull. [Once again, something manages to snare the Ship even though the Ship shouldn't be "flying" in normal space at all. See 13.3, "Pyramids of Mars", for more on this sort of thing. The Doctor doesn't simply dematerialise the TARDIS to get away, either; compare with 5.5, "The Web of Fear".] The Doctor describes the Helix as living, but that's all anyone knows. There's some sort of mental turbulence when the Ship enters it.

Arriving at the Helix's centre, the Doctor finds himself in an echoing black space with swirls of something crystalline all around him. There's obviously air here, and an "invisible" ground to stand on [the Helix provides them so that the Doctor will wander from the TARDIS, giving it a chance to hi-jack the Ship]. A fizzing red ball of Helix energy - an 'energy-wave' - then appears and gets onto the TARDIS, something which obviously tickles the Helix's fancy as it starts to chuckle. The energy-wave then forces the TARDIS to land in Renaissance Italy, with the Doctor speculating that 'Helix force-fields' must have distorted the co-ordinates.

The Helix knows the 1400s are ideal for its purposes, demonstrating a knowledge of human history. Hieronymous believes he heard the voice of "Demnos" even when he was young, so the Helix has had an influence on Earth before and has been putting things in place. The Doctor suggests a 'tenuous' influence going back centuries, though how is never explained. Once transported to Earth the energy-wave starts burning up the locals, turning human beings into blue crystallised corpses, their tissue destroyed by ionisation. Shrubbery also suffers. [No reason is stated for it to kill. Arguably it could be sucking its victims minds' out to gain local knowledge, but it never displays telepathic powers and can't possess people in the usual sense. Maybe it's just mean.]

Through a 'sub-thermal re-combination of ionised plasma', this part of the Helix can manifest itself as a column of light before the Brotherhood of Demnos, speaking to the brethren as if it were a god. Only Hieronymous is allowed to step into the light, and even the Doctor's head hurts when he gets too close. When the Helix makes its move [after it's built up enough power, somehow?], it starts channelling its energy into the Brotherhood members through Hieronymous, who by this point has become a glowing mass of energy in a cloak that can shoot lethal bolts from its fingers. This ionisation is molecular, so the power's spread thin between the brethren and can be drained; wire and metal can conduct the energy-bolts. It's at this point that Hieronymous starts to speak for the Helix rather than as a human being.

The rest of Mandragora can't manifest itself on Earth unless certain "astrological" conditions are right. In the fifteenth century it arrives during a lunar eclipse, but the Doctor defeats it by doing something terribly technical so that it burns out as soon as it reaches the temple. His only explanation is 'a case of energy squared'. It isn't destroyed, though, and the Doctor believes that Mandragora's constellation will be in the right place to try again in about 500 years, i.e. towards the end of the twentieth century. [This is all terribly vague. What happens to the energy? And why can the Helix only attack at certain times? Is the implication that the end of the twentieth century will be a time of great superstition?]

The Doctor mentions Helix energies other than Mandragora, though he later refers to Mandragora itself as a 'them' and it speaks of itself as 'we of Mandragora' [a result of its consciousness being split up into so many pieces]. Mandragora controls by 'astral force', aiming to take away humanity's sense of purpose and leave it devoid of ambition. Its motive is to stop humanity expanding, as it feels that humans might not be contained within the galaxy and could threaten its domain [its speech makes it unclear whether by 'domain' it means the galaxy, or something *outside* the galaxy, but the implication seems to be the latter]. Unsurprisingly, it knows of the Time Lords.

History

• *Dating.* The fifteenth century. [Leonardo's patron is the Duke of Milan, suggesting a date of 1482-93, and Columbus' return to Spain in 1493 hasn't conclusively proven the roundness of the world... not that it was ever really in doubt among those who could read. The novelisation specifies 1492, which fits.] The summer solstice is approaching, and there's a lunar eclipse when

Does the Universe Really Speak English?

...continued from page 101

load the whole of everyone's lives, not just the rules and vocabulary of the local lingo. It looks like we're left with Chomsky's "Language Acquisition Device", which in the *Doctor Who* universe must be inside every intelligent being, and a few others. Syntax and grammar are, like being bipedal with a head on top, astonishingly common. Since we're led to believe that the Time Lords represent the oldest, cleverest and most influential of cultures, we might even be able to swallow the idea that the Time Lords in some way "pre-formatted" the universe to prejudice it towards English-style communication. (In which case, we might also assume that English is the closest match for Time Lord language on Earth, which could also explain the Doctor's propensity for hanging around in western Europe. Mind you, it's not *written* like English; see 14.3, "The Deadly Assassin".) The universe is full of humanoids, so it's at least possible that the universe is following the Time Lords' example. If it works for biology, then why not language, too?

Leading on from this, the third and most controversial theory is the least complicated. Everyone speaks English unless otherwise stated. The language and vocabulary, accents and semiology, spellings and punctuation of Britain 1963-89 are cosmic and eternal. Whilst seemingly unlikely, it solves problems like the Master's message to the peoples of the universe in "Logopolis" and the moment in "The Two Doctors" (22.4) when Peri points out that she doesn't speak Spanish, and the Doctor - referring to the aliens - replies: 'That's all right, neither do they.'

Of course, a possible solution is to assume that what we're seeing is a dramatic reconstruction of the "true" history of the *Doctor Who* universe with all the anomalies resolved, but that's another essay (again, see 23.1, "The Mysterious Planet"). However, if we take the "telepathic translation" theory as the default explanation, then it could explain why we so rarely see really *alien* aliens. Our perceptions are limited by the boundaries of our language. If aliens exist beyond our usual frame of reference, then we may not even be able to "see" them fully, let alone talk to them.

Mandragora strikes. The Doctor describes this era, with great over-simplification, as the period between the dark age of superstition and the dawn of a new reason.

San Martino, Italy, is certainly torn between superstition and science at this point. The young Duke calls a gathering of all the philosophers and men of learning in Italy, Leonardo da Vinci included, and receives correspondence from a man in Florence who gives him some ideas about telescopes. [This isn't Leonardo, who wasn't in Florence at the time and is already on his way to the ball anyhow.] Though the cult of Demnos doesn't slay Leonardo at the masque, many people *are* killed and some of them may be important men of learning. The Doctor acts as if history hasn't been changed, however.

The cult of Demnos is Roman in origin and dates back to the third century, so the Doctor's surprised that the current Brotherhood of Demnos is around as late as the fifteenth. Demnos is said to be the god of the twin realms of moon-tide and solstice. The Brotherhood follows prophecies influenced by Mandragora, practices ritual sacrifice and uses a surprisingly effective drug which makes those who drink it passive and zombie-like. Hieronymous also brews up a concoction

which, once Sarah smells it, makes it easier to hypnotise her into killing the Doctor [psychological know-how courtesy of the Mandragora Helix]. The cult's masks are made out of pre-diluvian sandstone 'with a complex circuit of base mental fused into it', though the significance of this is never explained. [It stops them burning up when Helix energy is passed on to them?] The cult is well-known in San Martino, and haunts the old catacombs, complete with secret doors.

The Analysis

Where Does This Come From? Louis Marks was a former lecturer in Renaissance History, and - bizarre as it may seem, on the surface - a lot of what could be said about this story's roots in Renaissance thought can be found under "Planet of Evil" (13.2). However...

There are always problems in taking this "fable" approach to the supposed battle between science and non-science, doubly so when you're dealing with *Doctor Who*, a programme that's traditionally been low on hard theory and high on improbable fantasy. Here, though, things are more explicit than usual. The Doctor blithely states that this is a period halfway between a dark age and an age of enlightenment, and to underline this most of the fifteenth century types we see here either absolutely refuse to believe in horoscopes or talk in astrology-babble all the time. The suggestion seems to be that in the 1400s somebody pulled a big lever marked "Reason", but that not everybody was wired for science-power.

Which is ludicrous, of course. The idea that science and superstition are polar opposites is a terribly nineteenth century one, and if anything the Renaissance was about measuring, not about chucking out old ideas as being too fantastical. Few people in fifteenth century Italy would have entirely discounted the possibility of demonic, angelic or supernatural influences on Earth, even those who believed in using the new scientific methodology. (Throughout the following century, many of the discoveries which led to the more "rational" world of the Enlightenment were sponsored by the church and considered to go hand-in-hand with Christian lore. Galileo's persecution wasn't exactly typical, or at least, that sort of thing wasn't universal. But then, when the BBC made "The Masque of Mandragora" they didn't want to offend anyone, especially not while Mary Whitehouse was watching. No wonder religion's never mentioned, apart from the 'blasphemous' and 'pagan' Brotherhood. The script would have had to decide whether Catholicism was on the Doctor's side or the enemy's.)

It's now well-known that even Newton, supposed godfather of all that's proper and scientific, was a practising alchemist and believer in tangible higher powers as late as the 1700s. So it's difficult to accept that a Prince would dismiss the works of Hieronymous as bosh because astrology can't possibly be true - rather than, say, because Hieronymous is just a bad astrologer.

Marks would have known all of this, of course, but there's a difference between knowing something and putting it into effect as a ninety-minute piece of TV. Renaissance thought stressed the importance of observation rather than received wisdom, and how do you televise *that*? Observation requires time. Television requires exposition. Audiences expect instant results. So Hieronymous is full of blather and a fraudulent peddler of superstition, yet the story can't resist giving him premonitions that turn out to be true and passing them off as vague, unexplained elements of Mandragora's plan.

The most telling moment comes when the Prince, who condemns the theory that a fire-demon is on the loose as superstitious nonsense, then suggests that Hieronymous has conjured up something *else* from 'beyond'. And of course he's right, but since he can have no concept of an alien energy-wave, he's basically just replacing the word "demon" with another kind of "incomprehensible thing" that isn't any more rational (either from his point of view or ours). The Doctor's warnings about Mandragora are supposed to represent the voice of first-hand experience - in fact, you could argue that this kind of empiricism is one of *Doctor Who*'s key principles - yet by this stage the programme takes the Doctor's knowledge of almost-everything to be a natural part of the way the universe works, so the script has no way of making *his* arguments sound any less like "received wisdom" than those of Hieronymous.

In short, the entire medium is on Hieronymous' side. The Doctor's study of Mandragora in episode four, looking through a telescope and talking about 'astral' forces trying to overwhelm the planet, looks so much like the astrology he's trying to debunk that it makes no odds. Well, naturally. In television terms, it's the only way his character can keep up with the bad guys.

Things That Don't Make Sense The Doctor states that if it had been fifty years later then he could have used Galileo's telescope, but since the story's set in the late fifteenth century he's about sixty years out. Sarah is 5'4" in the TARDIS, but in Italy the Doctor thinks she's 5'5". Sarah is 5'4" in the TARDIS ('just'), but in Italy the Doctor tells the peasants that she's 5'4 1/2, and moments later he tries to tell the guards that she's 5'5". He really is *remarkably* lucky to find her after the Brotherhood of Demnos captures her, as out of all the hiding-places in San Martino he just happens to take shelter in exactly the same region where the Brotherhood's gathering. The supposedly intelligent Helix then makes the mistake of descending upon the shrine of Demnos and distracting everybody just *before* they kill the Doctor.

Count Federico, who's playing a big-league political game and subtly murders the old Prince by poison in order to allay anyone's suspicions, tries to kill the young Prince by shouting 'death to Giuliano!' as loudly as possible and rushing him with a force of over half a dozen fully-armoured men. Can he rely on *all* of them to keep their mouths shut? That said, the number of soldiers who attack at the end of episode two seems much greater than the number the Prince fights at the start of episode three. Even so, the Prince must be an exceptional fencer as he can hold most of them off even before the Doctor gets involved.

Curiously, the old clothes in the TARDIS' second console room are covered in dust, even though nothing else is. And even though it's virtually a certainty that dust shouldn't form in the TARDIS anyway. Rossini states that worshippers of Demnos are coming 'out of every street' to converge at the temple, yet there's only around a dozen people in the temple when Hieronymous starts handing out the power of the Helix. In episode one Marco is sceptical when Giuliano receives a letter describing the principle of the telescope, but in episode four it turns out that there's already a massively anachronistic telescope in the palace. Judging by the overall happiness-level of the young prince at the end of the story, he's now established as the undisputed ruler in San Martino, so didn't any of the great and the good attending his masque start to have doubts about him after some of their number were killed? After all, the whole point of holding the ball was to assert that there were no problems in his Dukedom.

An aesthetic problem rather than a logical one: the Mandragora Helix is depicted as a blue spiral made up of blue crystals in a blue void, and its victims turn blue when it kills them. Yet the special effect for the fizzing energy-ball is red. Doesn't anyone in the effects department know how to co-ordinate?

Critique   Finally the programme returns to its roots. Not in a "nostalgia" way, as in "The Three Doctors", but in terms of what *Doctor Who* is supposed to be about: mix 'n 'match television drama, conceptual leaps and a likeable protagonist stranded inside someone else's world.

All the paraphernalia of a Borgia / Medici intrigue is present and correct, but the emphasis is squarely on Sarah, not Mr. Clever-Clogs Two-Hearts. The Doctor provides solutions, but he also caused the problem, something Marks' previous story toyed with but downplayed (13.2, "Planet of Evil"). The stakes are higher than simply a large body-count or some half-baked invasion of Earth; it's the entire philosophy of the programme that's at risk. Subsequent Tom Baker stories take this sort of thing for granted - the shift between a petty,

egocentric world-view (often represented by astrology or piddling superstition) and a world-view that actually considers the *world* - but here the humanist idea of our own powers and responsibilities has to be fought for, against (historically) real threats. The fact that there's a conceptually strange space-being involved is almost a side-issue, so it's little wonder that the history's more convincing than the pseudo-science.

The mid-'70s was the boom time of BBC historical dramas, and while it could be seen as "playing safe" to start a season with something that looks so much like one, the intent is clear: to get as far away as possible from UNIT, regurgitated horror-movies, alien-invasion-of-the-week stories and anything that ITV or the Americans were doing. Indeed, if there's a serious problem with "Mandragora" it's that what it *isn't* is much clearer than what it *is*. That Louis Marks worked for *Doctor Who* in its early years becomes apparent right from the first episode, because in many ways it's got the structure of a Hartnell story. Up to a point the plot *alternates* between the TARDIS crew and the politics of Florence, as if we're watching two different stories which occasionally happen to touch. This was fine in the '60s, when the Doctor was more of a reactionary than an adventurer, and often just a passive witness to events. But the colour era had changed the whole drive of the programme.

Baker's Doctor is - even here - a much more dynamic sort of space-time event. He insists on getting involved and saving the world, yet so much of that world seems perfectly happy to get on without him. The standards of historical TV work well enough (two villains, ready to betray each other when their plots collide), but the standards of SF TV don't (especially the ending, which assumes that once Hieronymous is defeated it's perfectly reasonable to have the Doctor chase away the Mandragora Helix by doing something vaguely scientific-looking which is never explained).

So the Renaissance backdrop defeats the leading man, but perhaps that was inevitable. In a story so bursting with Mediterranean colour and rich in period drama goodness, the society is always bound to come first. And when "Mandragora" works, it works by trusting us to instinctively feel how that society functions. Everyone knows how violent an age this is, but barely any blood gets shed on-screen. People talk a lot about torture, mutilation and death, yet it's all implicit. This is a world where it's permissible for the villain to talk about bodily functions (yes, especially defecation) without running into censorship trouble. Viewers can infer a great deal more than is said or shown, whereas other worlds need to be introduced from scratch, and the mind-set we use for that isn't one which "allows" rudeness (see **Is This Really an SF Series?** under 14.4, "The Face of Evil").

On its very most basic level, then, "The Masque of Mandragora" deserves credit for re-introducing the TARDIS as a way of reconsidering the past rather than just a way of moving the Doctor closer to the monsters. Even if the past and the present don't always mix as well as they should.

The Facts

Written by Louis Marks. Directed by Rodney Bennett. Viewing figures: 8.3 million, 9.8 million, 9.2 million, 10.6 million.

Supporting Cast   Jon Laurimore (Count Federico), Norman Jones (Hieronymous), Gareth Armstrong (Giuliano), Tim Piggott-Smith (Marco), Anthony Carrick (Captain Rossini), Robert James (High Priest), Peter Tuddenham (Titan Voice).

Working Titles "The Curse of Mandragora", "The Catacombs of Death", "Doom of Destiny", "Secret of the Labyrinth".

Cliffhangers The Doctor's head is placed on the chopping-block, and the executioner raises his sword; running into the catacombs to escape the Count's soldiers, Sarah is re-apprehended by the masked Brotherhood of Demnos; in the temple, Hieronymous' mask is ripped off to reveal a "blank look" of purple energy underneath.

The Lore

• In addition to building the new console room, designer Barry Newbury had to construct a new police box prop after the collapse of the original during "The Seeds of Doom" (13.6). This looked rather more like a real police box than the previous version, but still lacked the St. John's Ambulance sigil on the door and was a darker blue, although still *not* as dark as the genuine article. (Both the 1996 TV movie and the 2005 series

use props almost exactly like the actual Metropolitan model.)

• As ever, Robert Holmes needed a great deal of persuading to attempt a historically-based story (see 11.1, "The Time Warrior"), and when Philip Hinchcliffe decided to do a Roger Corman pastiche the deal was that it had to be "nasty" history. Louis Marks had written a postgraduate thesis on the era twenty years before (the snappily-titled *The Development of the Institutions of Public Finance in Florence During the Last Sixty Years of the Republic*, c. 1470-1539) and got the gig. The script references a number of contemporary sources - not least *Mandragola* by Machiavelli - prompting Holmes to comment that had he known how many "co-authors" there were, he only would have given Marks half the fee.

• In a *Radio Times* interview entitled "*Doctor Who's* Renaissance", Philip Hinchcliffe explicitly stated that UNIT stories and invasions of Earth were no longer what the audience (or the production team) wanted, and that he was heading in a far more literary, "adult" direction. At around this time, BBC Head of Drama Bill Slater began to request that Hinchcliffe stay on for a fourth year...

• Gareth Armstrong (Giuliano) was the voice of Sandy in *Monkey* (see also **The Lore** of 12.5, "Revenge of the Cybermen").

• In 1981 this story was to have been the Fourth Doctor's contribution to a special repeat season on BBC2, which showed "classic" stories featuring old Doctors for the very first time (unimaginably exciting, in the days before affordable video). However, the season was called "The Five Faces of Doctor Who", so "Logopolis" (18.7) had to take its place by default as Peter Davison's "proper" debut as the Fifth Doctor was still six weeks away.

• Louis Marks returned to television production after this. His biggest "hit" was the BBC adaptation of *Middlemarch* from 1994, a novel in which many of the same themes as "Mandragora" emerge.

14.2: "The Hand of Fear"

(Serial 4N, Four Episodes, 2nd - 23rd October 1976.)

Which One is This? Sarah's got a calcified hand in her lunchbox. Why? Because: 'Eldrad must live!'

Firsts and Lasts It's the end of Sarah Jane Smith's time in the Doctor's company. Like so many others, she'll be back for "The Five Doctors" (20.7). Unlike anybody else, she'll also get her own spin-off production (see 18.7-A, *K9 and Company*).

Four Things to Notice About "The Hand of Fear"...

1. The hand itself. Specifically, the cliffhanger moment at the end of episode one when it starts to move inside a tupperware box. At the time this was simply the best "crawling hand" sequence ever filmed; unlike the disembodied body-parts from most horror movies, *this* hand is fossilised, giving it a disturbingly crunchy appearance far more memorable than your average pale, self-willed human limb (let's not mention "Pyramids of Mars" again). Here a spooky glowing extra-terrestrial ring becomes a key plot-point for the third time in the last six stories, while the Doctor gets to say: 'Inert, yes... dead, maybe not.'

2. We could confine it to **Things That Don't Make Sense**, but it's so striking that it really deserves comment here. As in "The Claws of Axos" (8.3), writers Bob Baker and Dave Martin seem to have absolutely no idea what nuclear reactors actually do. When the Nunton nuclear complex is taken over by a hostile alien organism, the authorities' solution is... to launch an air strike on the building and flatten the place. This time the alien in question absorbs all the energy from the blast, so there's at least a good *reason* that no nuclear explosion or radioactive death-cloud follows, but obviously that's not what the good guys are expecting. You can tell, because the Doctor's sidekicks try to shelter from the imminent atomic catastrophe by - wait for it - leaving the building and crouching down behind a nearby jeep.

3. Special mention has to be made of Professor Watson, head of the ever-bombable Nunton research establishment, played by Glyn Houston with gruff, impatient gusto. Not only are his scenes with Tom Baker the very embodiment of the Doctor-versus-stuffy-authority scenario, but when the nuclear reactor's going critical he becomes one of the very few supporting characters in *Doctor Who* to get a genuinely human moment before his anticipated death. The fact that he 'phones his wife to say goodbye is remarkable enough, since most supporting characters aren't even allowed to *have* families, but just as unusually he's shown trying to pick up the pieces after the alien attack. Well, *somebody* has to.

4. Once again, the TARDIS lands in a quarry and Sarah's immediate reaction is that it *must* be an alien planet. And Sarah's pink-and-white Andy Pandy outfit also has to get a mention here, even if it's not the worst thing she's worn in the series, simply because it's the costume which has duped a generation of fans into believing that she was always just an excited little girl in space who loved having adventures (compare this with the bob-haired feminist guerrilla leader in 11.1, "The Time Warrior"). The child-voice she puts on while Eldrad possesses her doesn't help. Yet paradoxically - and the letters to the *Radio Times* confirm this - in an era when feminists were usually portrayed as clichéd harridans like Hilda Winters (12.1, "Robot"), this "girlyness" made Sarah more of a positive role-model in the eyes of women's groups because she showed it wasn't "either / or". Well, it was the '70s.

The Continuity

The Doctor Now claiming to be a Doctor 'of sorts', and he says he qualified on Gallifrey [he probably *did* qualify for something there, but didn't necessarily get a doctorate]. Whatever his qualifications, he knows a fair amount about human medicine here. He can knock Sarah out with one painless-looking blow, and put her into a hypnotic state just by touching her temples [easier than normal, as she's already been under Eldrad's influence].

• *Ethics.* He's prepared to help Eldrad to get back to Kastria, giving the creature the benefit of the doubt even though Eldrad's been responsible for two people's deaths and used painful psychic force against him. But he seems motivated to get Eldrad off the planet rather than anything more humanitarian. [He makes a similar offer to a stranded Sontaran in 11.1, "The Time Warrior".] In the end he deliberately makes Eldrad fall down an abyss, as if leaving someone at the bottom of a pit for all eternity is in some way better than killing them.

• *Inventory.* He's got an extendable magician's stick about his person, yet another of his showbiz "props", but it ends up on the bottom of the same chasm as Eldrad. The sonic screwdriver's currently being kept with the rest of the TARDIS tools, not in the Doctor's pockets.

The Supporting Cast

•*Sarah Jane Smith.* She's initially heading for home here, although not permanently. By this stage it's taken for granted that Sarah is the Doctor's full-time companion, as she's got at least one case of personal items on board and threatens to "quit" when the Doctor isn't paying her any attention. But she's clearly bluffing. When the Doctor asks her to leave the Ship so that he can return to Gallifrey [the only time he really "fires" a companion], she's obviously heartbroken.

[The Doctor only abandons Sarah because he thinks he can't take her to his homeworld. This raises an obvious question: if they don't really want to part then why doesn't he come back for her *after* he's been to Gallifrey? After all, Sarah's always been an on-and-off sort of assistant. For the last three years she's effectively been a space-time commuter, travelling to other worlds with the Doctor but often staying on Earth instead of living full-time in the TARDIS. Just a season earlier, it would have been taken as read that after visiting Gallifrey the Doctor would head back to UNIT HQ, and that Sarah would probably be waiting for him there. But by now he's become such a wanderer that he doesn't even consider going back to pick up an old friend.]

Sarah's home is Hillview Road, South Croydon, London. She says she'll pass on regards to Harry and the Brigadier, suggesting that she *knows* the Doctor's days with UNIT are over. Before she departs, she knows the names of all the tools the Doctor uses to fix the TARDIS thermal couplings, so he's got her well-trained. Things she takes with her when she goes: a suitcase, a yellow coat, a knitted jacket [worn in the final scene of 14.1, "The Masque of Mandragora"], a purple [alien?] flower, a tennis racket and a stuffed toy owl.

The TARDIS The Doctor is now using the second console room as if it were the main control area. The door appears to lead straight from this room to the outside world. [In "The Masque of Mandragora", the implication is that the Doctor and Sarah have to walk some way into the depths of the Ship to find the second control room. By the time they step out into the Helix it's simply *the* console room. Has the Doctor reconfigured the architecture to move the room closer to the door? This sort of thing is *de rigueur* for the TARDIS in later years, especially from "Logopolis" (18.7) onwards.]

The TARDIS monitor acts as a computer screen, displaying figures while the Doctor and Eldrad are working out co-ordinates for Kastria. Navigation still isn't perfect, as Sarah gets dropped off in the wrong place, but at least it looks like the right part of the world [even though it's filmed in Gloucestershire].

Eldrad's mental powers don't work inside the TARDIS, and the Doctor explains that within the Ship they're in a state of 'temporal grace', as they're 'multi-dimensional'. He goes on to say that in a sense nobody exists while they're in the TARDIS, so nobody can hurt anybody else. [This clearly doesn't make logical sense. If they don't exist then they shouldn't be able to do *anything* in the TARDIS, and why should violence be different to anything else? To some degree, the Doctor must be bluffing to calm Eldrad down. This is the only time that 'temporal grace' is shown to apply within the TARDIS. The Doctor mentions it in the future, as a feature that stops weapons rather than a feature that stops violence per se, but it never seems to work. It's important to note, though, that here 'temporal grace' is described as a side-effect of the TARDIS' nature and not as a deliberately-designed security system.]

The Doctor says that symbolic resonance will occur in the trachoid time crystal if the co-ordinates for Kastria are mis-set, so they'll never land anywhere, ever. He believes that the low temperatures on Kastria might have affected the TARDIS' thermo-couplings, hence the lurching take-off, and he goes under the console to fix them [though it's odd that he's never worried about this when landing in sub-zero environments before, and odder still that the temperature *outside* the Ship might affect the internal workings, which are apparently in a different dimension]. Tools used in this repair job: an astro-rectifier, a multi-quantis-cope, a Ganymede driver, a mergin nut and some Zeus plugs [Time Lord technology named after a Greek god…?], though he doesn't think he'll need these last two.

The Time Lords   According to the Doctor, to go back into the past and alter things would contravene the First Law of Time. [The First Law has changed since 10.1, "The Three Doctors", unless the Doctor's speaking figuratively. It changes again by 23.3, "Terror of the Vervoids".] He also claims that the Time Lords are pledged to prevent alien aggression, but 'only when such aggression is deemed to threaten the indigenous population'. He recites this as if it were a law, so it's almost certainly true. [Going even further than the rather polite description of the Time Lords in 14.1, "The Masque of Mandragora". This view of the Time Lords as a cosmic United Nations is so far from (a) their position in 6.7, "The War Games", (b) the non-interventionist stance later described in 15.5, "Underworld" and (c) the reality of everything we've actually seen, that we have to assume the *complete* law is more complex than the Doctor makes out. Possibly this rule refers to alien aggression by races who've perfected time-travel, and might be threatening history and / or Time Lord interests by invading other worlds. In which case 'indigenous' might mean indigenous to a certain *time* rather than a certain planet.]

The end of the story sees the Doctor receive a call from Gallifrey in the form of a telepathic signal, the first time this has ever happened. [It's presumably only possible now that the Time Lords can keep track of the Doctor, or it would have happened prior to "The War Games". The next story reveals that the Time Lord authorities aren't the ones who are sending it.] He claims that he 'must obey' this call, so he seems to think it's something official, but he must know something serious is going on as he's much more ready to follow Time Lord orders than usual. He also believes that he can't take Sarah with him, and the implication seems to be that it's because it'd be somehow *wrong* for a human to go to Gallifrey [or that the Time Lords wouldn't put up with it?... recall that the last companions to visit Gallifrey got their memories erased], not because the situation's too dangerous.

The Non-Humans

• *Kastrians.* A crystalline silicon-based life-form, rare in the galaxy, in their "normal" form Kastrians look like lumps of crystalline rock roughly poured into people-shape. However, this wasn't the way they evolved; see **Planet Notes**.

150,000,000 years ago the last King of Kastria, Rokon, refused to follow the conquest-mad scientist Eldrad and engage in warfare across the galaxy. Eldrad responded by destroying the planet's protective barriers, wiping out all life on the planet [he was almost certainly planning to start from scratch with the race-banks]. Rokon ordered Eldrad's death, but Kastrians are hard to kill. Eldrad was put into an 'obliteration module', a spacecraft designed to take him 'beyond all solar systems', where the module could be safely exploded. But control was lost, and the module was detonated early. Eldrad's hand, complete with his ring, ended up on Earth. [The implication here is that Eldrad is the last Kastrian, his people destroyed after his sabotage. But Eldrad speaks of Kastrian 'starships' and knows about alien cultures, so it's hard to believe that no other Kastrians left the planet.] There are / were different racial groups on Kastria, since Eldrad's rock-skin is blue and Rokon's is brown.

Eldrad's ring has the power to knock people out with an energy-wave, blow up architecture or mesmerise human beings so that victims become obsessed with bringing Eldrad back to life. The hand absorbs radiation, nuclear fission and the energy from a human missile attack, regenerating and growing into a new body for Eldrad. The ring is said to contain Eldrad's genetic code [but must, logically, also carry his memories].

The new body is feminine, as it's based on the body-print of the one who found the ring – Sarah - though it doesn't have Sarah's face and glittering crystal covers it. [Copying the native life is a smart move, though it might have been awkward if a species with no hands had found the ring. The logical extension of this regenerative technology is that Kastrians can make multiple copies of themselves by chopping off body-parts and then cultivating the bits. The Kastrian race-banks may be full of the same kind of data that's contained in the ring.]

Eldrad can only re-grow his "normal" body with the help of the regeneration technology on Kastria, technology he designed himself. Ultimately he falls down a chasm in the bowels of Kastria, along with his ring, and the Doctor doesn't believe him dead.

Eldrad can use mental power to scan people's minds, causing pain even to the Doctor. This makes the Kastrian's eyes glow blue, and the same mind-power can kill human beings. Eldrad can sense the presence of nearby humans, probably telepathically, and is - all together now - bulletproof. The fossilised hand shows no sign of blood or muscle when x-rayed. The Kastrians knew of the Time Lords, as Eldrad believes they're pledged to uphold the laws of time [accurate] and prevent alien aggression [less so].

Planet Notes

• *Kastria*. The Kastrian homeworld is cold, dehydrated and ravaged by solar winds, as it has been for millions of years. The atmosphere's Earth-normal, but the radiation's a bit high. Eldrad claims he built spatial barriers to keep out the winds and machines to replenish the earth and air. Eldrad also claims that he was the one who devised a silicon-based form for his people, presumably in order for them to survive the harsh conditions. [He seems to have invented an awful lot. The Kastrians seem to be immortal-barring-accidents, at least in silicon form, so his career as a scientist may have lasted for thousands of years before his "execution". It'd certainly take his civilisation some time to convert to silicon, and to mentally adjust to it afterwards.]

When Eldrad destroyed the barriers, his people decided that they'd rather die than eke out an existence in the thermal caves underground [counter to most species' survival instincts, so maybe they *weren't* adjusting very well]. They also destroyed the hundred million crystal particles in their 'race-banks' to insure their civilisation could never be re-born, just in case Eldrad ever came back to lead them into war against the galaxy… even though there was only a minute chance of him surviving his obliteration [that settles it; they're mad]. At the time that Eldrad's pod exploded, it was nineteen spans from Kastria instead of the designated twenty-five.

Despite the absence of life on the surface, there are still thermal chambers with glittery architecture which remain more or less intact. The regeneration rooms which contain the machinery for re-growing Eldrad are underneath Outer Dome Six. Traps have been left for him / her, including gas that's lethal to silicon-based life and a poisoned "arrow" containing an acid which breaks molecular bonds and makes a Kastrian's body go rigid. This would be fatal, if Eldrad's entire body weren't regenerated. Typically, Eldrad claims to have been the one who developed this acid. There's still an 'inexhaustible' power supply in the underground chambers, drawn from the core of the planet.

History

• *Dating*. Sarah acts as if it's the present-day, at least from her point of view. [So it's no more than a few months after 13.6, "The Seeds of Doom".]

There's a nuclear reactor at the Nunton research and development complex, and armed guards patrol the facility. The head of the complex, Professor Watson, can get in touch with the armed forces and request an air-strike in mere moments. [So military research may be done there. The similarity in name to the Nuton power complex, blown up in "The Claws of Axos" (8.3) but operational again by "The Daemons" (8.5), is striking. In the real world the Windscale nuclear reprocessing plant was renamed Sellafield in order to distract the public from its safety record, so it's possible that Nuton / Nunton is a slightly less convincing example of the same technique. But Nunton is described as 'experimental' rather than being a full-scale power station.] No location is given for the quarry where Eldrad's ring is found, or the nearby hospital, but Nunton is the nearest major power-source and may well be the name of the town.

The hand has been buried on Earth, in Jurassic limestone, for 150,000,000 years.

The Analysis

Where Does This Come From? As we'll see in **The Lore**, one of the key ideas in the first draft of this story was that fanaticism and science make uneasy bedfellows. Science, as a process of investigation and questioning, has to be open-ended. Technology, as a problem-solving and user-defined targeting of research, limits its own scope.

All the "mad scientists" from this period in the series' history (and there are plenty of them… between "The Android Invasion" and "The Talons of Weng-Chiang", seven out of nine stories feature villains who are either scientists or patrons of the sciences) are in fact fanatical technocrats. It's impossible, we're being told, to be a "true" scientist and be as narrowly obsessive as these loons. The Doctor frequently engages them in arguments about morals, ethics and responsibilities. And yet, the nut-jobs seem to be the ones with all the impressive achievements.

In post-war Britain, the harnessing of technology by Big Business and Government was seen to be creating a new form of mandarin-science, incomprehensible to most and beyond the kind of scrutiny that was applied to other forms of spending (as we see in the ham-fisted "audit" of TOMTIT in 9.5, "The Time Monster", and all those little empires created by autocratic science-maniacs in Season Seven). Under Philip Hinchcliffe we see an extreme version of this, with the control of entire worlds handed over to ego-maniacal would-be messiahs. Eldrad's big achievements are to reconfigure the bodies of his people to suit their new lives; to construct an impenetrable shield, and then remove it when things don't go his own way; to lead a tight band of followers into the bunkers, and to attack anything not racially "right". Remind you of anyone? Why they didn't just call him "Dovras" is a mystery.

Yet, we must remember, the Time Lords will - in the next story - turn out to have had much the same thing done to them by the sainted Rassilon. Clearly there's a theme emerging. Anyone offering "The Answer" should be accountable to the people, even in dire circumstances. This process of playing for high stakes extends to the Ark (12.2, "The Ark In Space"), a story which might be seen as drawing on the British folk-memory of wartime evacuations, when *everyone* felt their lives were in the hands of higher powers.

Things That Don't Make Sense   There are an awful lot of flukes going on here. Obviously Eldrad survives his obliteration even though his chances were supposed to be minimal, but against even greater odds his ring finds its way to an inhabited planet with an atmosphere and gravity just like Kastria's. And is then recovered from its 150,000,000-year burial by one of only two people on the entire planet who've got access to a space-time machine. Meanwhile the Doctor is now so casual about strolling through any given locale that he doesn't panic or break his stride when he hears a siren going off in a quarry and sees a workman waving urgently at him, as a result of which Sarah nearly gets killed when the explosive charges go off.

With their species on the edge of annihilation, the Kastrians decide to waste their space-power loading Eldrad into a pod and hurling him out of the galaxy, instead of putting themselves (or, indeed, their precious race-banks) on a ship and going somewhere more hospitable. The traps laid on the ruined planet suggest that Kastrians can die by means of poison or crushing them, so why didn't they just reduce Eldrad to dust instead of all this business with the obliteration module?

Eldrad's schemes are thwarted when he finds the Kastrian race-banks have been destroyed, as this means he can't lead an army to conquer the galaxy, but he never stops to consider that he's still got his ring and can presumably make an army out of copies of *himself* instead. And he's just the kind of egomaniac to try it, too. Outer Dome Six is still intact on the surface of Kastria after 150,000,000 years of pummelling by the solar winds, making you wonder why the Kastrians needed Eldrad's magical barriers to keep themselves safe.

Plus the stuff about the nuclear reactor, of course. Apart from the ludicrous grasp of science, the head of the Nunton complex convinces the armed forces to bomb a nuclear facility into the ground in just a few minutes and with no questions asked. The no-nonsense Professor Watson also believes the Doctor's story about a disembodied telepathic hand astonishingly quickly in episode two, even before he sees the video pictures.

Eldrad's claim that s/he absorbed the power of the explosion during the aerial missile strike is puzzling; there's no structural damage to the building, so s/he must have absorbed the power from explosions hitting the roof, i.e. explosions on the other side of large quantities of reinforced concrete. If s/he can do *that* then why does s/he even need to enter the reactor, rather than just standing in the same neighbourhood as any energy source on Earth?

Even the hand itself is questionable. Eldrad's entire female body grows from it, but it's part of big, butch, masculine Eldrad's original body, so has the slinky Eldrad got a right hand like a sailor's and a left hand like a girl's?

The RAF fire nuclear missiles at a nuclear facility. Later, Miss Jackson - Professor Watson's assistant - walks in from her coffee break and asks 'what was all that noise?'. Did nobody tell her she was about to be blown to smithereens? What kind of evacuation procedure do these people have? To add insult to injury, she's not even credited for that episode.

Critique   For those who were there at the time, it's difficult even now to separate the story from the events surrounding it. Lis Sladen's departure had been national news, and the mystery of how they'd write her out of the series was as much a talking-point then as the finale of *Friends* was here in the God-forsaken twenty-first century. As a result, there are an awful lot of broken-hearted forty-something Englishmen. Seeing Sarah apparently crushed in a rockfall, then falling victim to alien mind-control, walking into a reactor and zapping armed guards made each turn of the story seem like a potential end for the character. Paradoxically, the end we get isn't really an end at all. She and the Doctor played tricks like this on each other all along, and we're left with the sense that they could have renewed their acquaintance at any point up until 1980.

But let's at least *try* to look at what's actually there. This is a thing of parts. Episode one looks a lot like mainstream drama (especially cop-shows like *Softly, Softly* or medical soap *Angels*), but just slightly twisted, with a very dodgy first reel. Episode two is a nuclear terrorism play, of the kind that had often been shown on the single-drama slot *Play for Today*. Episode three is a retread of "The Seeds of Doom", but with filmed location work and VT of air-strikes rather than the other way around. Episode four is the bit that looks like low-budget space-opera, but it's over halfway through the episode.

Much of this transcends the usual problems of a Bob Baker and Dave Martin story, partly because of all the re-writes (see **The Lore**) and partly because director Lennie Mayne really pulls out all the stops in the scenes shot on film, with the girly-and-coy version of Sarah abruptly giving way to a version who can comfortably try to kill security guards. But as with "The Masque of Mandragora", there's the sense of a programme that isn't sure where it wants to go from here, that knows the Doctor's had his time on Earth and can't find anywhere better to put him. This changes by the end of the season, although we'll come to that later.

The *real* problem is that the whole story hangs on two key factors, the impact of the crawling hand and Judith Paris' weirdly memorable performance as the feminised Eldrad. Anything which doesn't directly involve either of those two main ingredients feels trivial, despite the best efforts of Professor Watson to inject some humanity into the proceedings. Dr. Carter is particularly weak - recalling Rex Robinson's similarly shallow character in "The Three Doctors" (10.1) - and his death is particularly pointless. Much of episode four feels just as unnecessary, and once again looks as if it's been bulked out with material salvaged from "Death to the Daleks" (11.3). It almost goes without saying that Stephen Thorne's hideously over-cooked performance as the "real"

Eldrad is a disappointment after seeing the slinkier blue-lipstick version, with even Sarah feeling moved to say 'I quite liked her, but I couldn't stand him'. (This is the same writer / director team that made "The Three Doctors", so Thorne gives exactly the same performance he gave as Omega. He'll eventually get to do it again, as Treebeard in the BBC's radio adaptation of *The Lord of the Rings*.)

Overall you're left with the feeling that this is the kind of story which might work in "modern" *Doctor Who*, as a self-contained fifty-minute episode instead of a ninety-minute story cut up into awkward chunks. And of course, the whole "possession" idea is getting tired by this stage. Like the "evil twin" concept, it might be fun for the regular cast but from a viewer's point of view it's been done to death. There's only one way to go from here and that's for the Doctor himself to turn evil (see 15.2, "The Invisible Enemy").

The Facts

Written by Bob Baker and Dave Martin. Directed by Lennie Mayne. Viewing figures: 10.5 million, 10.2 million, 11.1 million, 12.0 million.

Supporting Cast   Judith Paris (Eldrad), Stephen Thorne (Kastrian Eldrad), Glyn Houston (Professor Watson), Rex Robinson (Dr. Carter), Roy Skelton (King Rokon), Roy Pattison (Zazzka), Frances Pidgeon (Miss Jackson), John Cannon (Elgin).

Working Titles   "The Hand of Time", "The Hand of Death".

Cliffhangers   Inside the reactor room, Sarah opens the box containing the "fossilised" hand, and it starts to move; explosions rock the control room of the Nunton station as Driscoll, the possessed technician, walks into the reactor core with the hand; on Kastria, an oversized arrow shoots from the wall of the cave and skewers the full-grown Eldrad in the chest (another odd cliffhanger in which the *villain's* life is put in jeopardy, though at this stage we apparently don't know that Eldrad's entirely "evil").

The Lore

- The *original* version of "The Hand of Fear" was a six-part story set in a dystopian future

London, where UNIT battles a rival military organisation on the streets, alien monsters are being kept in London Zoo, silicon-based invaders are attempting to cleanse the world of humanity and new-agey cults are forming as society falls to pieces. Ultimately, the Brigadier sacrifices his life by flying a 'plane into the enemy mothership.

It wasn't the first time that Bob Baker and Dave Martin had come up with a ridiculously impractical and out-of-control storyline, and nor would it be the last. But once it had been starved and wormed this story was deemed preferable to the one which had already been proposed for Sarah's departure. Her last bow was incorporated into what was now a four-part present-day tale, and not the epic space adventure originally envisaged.

• Sarah's planned swan-song was written by long-time director and *de facto* producer on his stories, Douglas Camfield. "The Legion of the Lost" was set in the French Foreign Legion - sort of - and involved alien warlords manipulating the stupid humans. Sarah's death (yes, death) was heroic, and she was buried with full military honours, the sort of thing *Xena: Warrior Princess* might have done if it'd been around twenty years earlier.

• Lis Sladen was keen to be written out while Sarah was still popular, but had no long-term plans. She had apparently stayed on after "The Seeds of Doom" in the hope of the film *Doctor Who Meets Scratchman* getting made, but requested a story which worked in its own right, not one "about" Sarah leaving. Nevertheless, Sladen and Baker mainly improvised the final scene, with Robert Holmes' supplying the reason for her departure to tie in with "The Deadly Assassin" (14.3). Even the final freeze-frame was suggested to director Lennie Mayne by Sladen.

• It's Mayne whistling "Daddy Wouldn't Buy Me A Bow-Wow" at the end of the story (ironic, given the spin-off pilot that Sarah eventually got); his wife was the dog trainer. He died in a boating accident soon after filming this story.

• One of the casualties of the rewriting of "The Hand of Fear" was a minor character called Drax, a short, chubby, red-headed chap who also happened to be a fugitive Time Lord. He was deemed too good an idea to waste, and crops up in the last two episodes of "The Armageddon Factor" (16.6) *sans* hair (or, as he'd say, 'nanti riah').

14.3: "The Deadly Assassin"

(Serial 4P, Four Episodes, 30th October - 20th November 1976.)

Which One is This? The Doctor finally goes home to Gallifrey University, then falls asleep and has a nightmare about men in gas-masks. The rotten-faced Master hides inside a grandfather clock, the forces of darkness triumph (or at least get the producer replaced), fandom's split down the middle and everything changes forever…

Firsts and Lasts It's the birth of the Time Lords, at least as we now think of them. The story which re-defines Gallifrey forevermore, "The Deadly Assassin" presents the Doctor's people as stuffy old men rather than the god-technicians of the past, and their trademark high-collared robes make their first appearance here.

Other things which are mentioned for the first time, but which will come to haunt the programme's mythology in the future: Rassilon (the founder of Time Lord Society), the seal of the Time Lords (actually a left-over piece of design from 12.5, "Revenge of the Cybermen"), the Matrix, the Cardinals, the Castellan, the Chancellery Guard, the Panopticon, the idea that Time Lords have thirteen lives and the description of the TARDIS as a 'type forty'. The Master shows up for the first time post-Pertwee, and the Doctor's old tutor Borusa makes the first of four appearances in the series, though he'll end up regenerating even more rapidly than the Doctor.

This is the only story in which companions don't accompany the Doctor, so he has to do a lot of talking to himself for the audience's benefit. Unless you count "Mission to the Unknown" (3.2), it's the only story which features absolutely no women of any description, though at least the Time Lord "computer voice" is female. Uniquely, it opens with a scrolling prologue, a year before *Star Wars* but thirty years since anyone else did it: 'Through the millennia, the Time Lords of Gallifrey led a life of peace and ordered calm, protected against all threats from lesser civilisations by their great power. But this was to change. Suddenly and terribly, the Time Lords faced the most dangerous crisis in their long history…' Which doesn't seem very fair on Omega (10.1, "The Three Doctors").

Four Things to Notice About "The Deadly Assassin"...

1. The details can be dealt with in Where Does This Come From?, but for all its nods and winks to other political concerns of the era, the plot of "The Deadly Assassin" basically reconstructs the assassination of John F. Kennedy for the *Doctor Who* audience (the second time this had been attempted; see 3.5, "The Massacre"). A tale of conspiracies, cover-ups and secret government cliques, here the President of the Time Lords is shot down from on high during a public appearance; the Doctor, tricked into standing on a balcony overlooking the murder, is a patsy in all of this just like Lee Harvey Oswald (allegedly); and even the CIA gets a token mention. The story ends with the Time Lord administration sweeping everything under the carpet for the good of society, though the Master's attempt to become Jack Ruby is a predictable failure.

2. Yet despite all the pomp and political majesty being presented here, a word has to be said about the names. Specifically the fact that the Time Lords *have* names, as opposed to titles like "Doctor" and "Master". Though this trend for giving space-age appellations to the Doctor's people began with Omega in "The Three Doctors", here Time Lords lose their mystery once and for all, and come perilously close to being just another bunch of men from outer space by having spuriously exotic monickers full of unlikely syllables. It wouldn't be so bad if all the names seemed to be products of the same culture, but "Runcible", "Borusa", "Pandak" and "Goth" sound like random picks from a cosmic telephone directory.

3. This really needs to be said for the benefit of younger readers... note that the "virtual reality" world created by the Time Lords, which can only be accessed by wiring your brain up to a computer, is called "the Matrix". And this was in 1977. There are thankfully no unlikely kung-fu moves inside this Matrix, but there are some of the most strikingly scary images that the programme ever produced, involving clowns, surgeons and terrifying men in gas-masks. The moment when the Doctor gets his foot trapped in the tracks of a railway line, as an engine driven by a single masked figure rolls towards him, is / was perhaps the most disturbing thing in the whole "horrific" Philip Hinchcliffe era. (Children are far more scared of dangerous machinery than of monsters. See also 13.6, "The Seeds of Doom".) Altogether now: 'I deny this reality! The reality is a computation matrix!'

4. Here we see the debut of the "new" Master, his body now little more than a skeleton covered in loose flaps of flesh. Whereas the original Master looked like nothing so much as the Devil incarnate, this version looks like nothing so much as an omelette. This was the Master's first appearance since the death of Roger Delgado in 1973, but since the character is said to be horribly disfigured due to some kind of space-accident, this might be considered to be in questionable taste. Note that although the mysterious robed figure isn't identified as the Master in episode one, his name's given on the end credits, and a short piece in the *Radio Times* prepped the audience for his return; a rare example of the series expecting its viewers to have seen "supplementary material" in order to fully understand what's going on.

The Continuity

The Doctor Despite the Doctor's long-term dislike of the Time Lord elite, he actually seems *flustered* when he thinks the President's going to be assassinated, far more than he would be if (say) he were trying to stop an assassination on Earth.

The Doctor's brain is said to have an unusually high level of artron energy, allowing him to survive the trip into the Matrix. [19.2, "Four to Doomsday", claims that artron energy somehow powers TARDISes. This is, like so much else, suggestive of a symbiotic link between a TARDIS and its owner.] Here he enjoys drawing insulting cartoons of other Time Lords, and confirms that Time Lords are telepathic. He intimates, not entirely seriously, that his hair curls when it's going to rain. More impressively, he identifies tricophenylaldehyde just by sniffing it. He describes the Master as his sworn arch-enemy.

The Doctor here writes a letter in a language that's presumably Gallifreyan, which seems to have an awful lot of different letters or symbols [see **The Lore**]. He signs himself "the Doctor", in the same language and over the seal of the Prydonian chapter, as he is - or was at one time - a member of this order.

• *Background.* At the Prydon Academy on Gallifrey he was tutored by Borusa, who told him that he'd never amount to anything in the galaxy while he retained his 'propensity for vulgar facetiousness'. Also at the Academy was Runcible, known as Runcible the Fatuous, who believes that the Doctor was expelled after a scandal of some sort.

The Doctor has been to Constantinople at some point; see **The TARDIS**. He never met the outgoing President of the Time Lords.

The Supporting Cast (Evil)

• *The Master.* He's now little more than a walking corpse, a charred-looking husk with skeletal features and a suitably ragged cloak to go with it. Chancellor Goth found him dying on the planet Tersurus [see "The Curse of Fatal Death" in the appendix of Volume VI, if you must], at the end of his regenerative cycle [the first time regeneration is explicitly described as a standard, finite facility for Time Lords].

The Master has lost much of his charm in this state, but none of his hatred for the Doctor. He believes that the hate is the only thing keeping him alive, and wants the Doctor to die in shame. Ultimately he leaves Gallifrey in his TARDIS, having at least absorbed enough energy from the Eye of Harmony to keep himself alive [see 18.6, "The Keeper of Traken"].

The Master fakes his own death, and appears to have snuffed it even to the Doctor, by injecting himself with the neural inhibitor tricophenylaldehyde. He's able to hypnotise one of the Chancellery Guards, and still has a weapon that kills by shrinking [8.1, "Terror of the Autons"]. This is called 'matter condensation', and it's not a standard Gallifreyan technology, with the Doctor stating the Master picked up the technique on his travels.

The Doctor also mentions the Master's highly-developed ESP, and claims that he was a Time Lord 'a long time ago'. [Odd, as the Doctor still calls himself a Time Lord despite being a renegade; he might now believe that you're only a Time Lord if you accept Time Lord responsibilities.] The Doctor even goes as far as describing the Master as mathematically and technically brilliant, 'almost up to my standard' [a very different view of the Master to that taken in stories like "The Sea Devils" (9.3), in which he's a scientific ignoramus next to the Doctor]. As ever, the Master believes the Doctor to be predictable, and knows he will walk into a trap even *realising* it's a trap.

The TARDIS(es)

The Doctor's TARDIS is officially designated a type-forty TT capsule, described as obsolete and out of commission. [Compare this with 2.9, "The Time Meddler". TT for time-travel, one assumes.] None are now in service, so of the 305 that were registered, only this one was never de-registered or rendered non-operational. Goth thinks it's extraordinary that such a machine is even in use. [It's been well under a millennium since the Doctor stole it, not a great span of time for a Time Lord, so it was old even when it was taken. Compare this with Chronotis' description of the Ship in 17.6, "Shada".]

The type of 'barrier' on this model is a 'double-curtain trimonic', so a cypher-indent key is needed. [Hinting that the TARDIS lock activates some sort of force-field around the Ship, and doesn't actually keep the door shut by the normal physical means. Which makes sense, as a fully-functional TARDIS wouldn't always have an exterior door, depending on its shape.] The Guards have access to such a key [it's implied that all type-forty vessels have the same key].

Somehow the Commander of the Chancellery Guards immediately recognises the model of the TARDIS just by looking at it, even though it's in police-box shape, while the Chancellor recognises it to be in 'good condition'. [The Doctor has previously displayed the ability to tell if an object is a TARDIS - he homes in on the Master's horse-box straight away in 8.1, "Terror of the Autons" - but this is stranger still. Time Lords must be able to see some kind of "aura" around a TARDIS if this is to make any sense.] Spandrell says that the TARDIS 'transducts' when it arrives at the edge of the Capitol. Spandrell has to explain to Goth that the type forty's shape was infinitely variable [meaning that some modern TARDISes can't change appearance, or at least not much].

There's a panel in the console of the second control room which opens like a writing-desk, containing paper, ink, a fountain pen and the Prydonian seal. From a nearby room the Doctor produces a leather bag containing a hookah and he mutters 'cash and carry, Constantinople' when he produces it.

Meanwhile the Master's TARDIS takes the form of a grandfather clock [as in 18.6, "The Keeper of Traken"]. His face briefly overlays the clock's face as it dematerialises, which may be "real" or just a metaphorical visual effect…

The Time Lords

The Time Lord society shown here is very different to anything seen before. Whereas in the past they've been sterile immortals [6.7, "The War Games"] or all-powerful technicians [10.1, "The Three Doctors"], here the Doctor's people are more like the university dons of the universe, mostly conservative, self-involved old men obsessed with decorum.

The assumption is that they don't intervene in the affairs of the outside universe because they're too inward-looking, not because they have moral codes forbidding it. [In the past we've only seen the extremes of life on Gallifrey, including its judicial procedure and its time-control room, whereas the world we see here is the world of the old ruling elite. So it's possible that things were *always* like this, in the parts of the Capitol that were never seen on-screen. But it's equally possible that things have changed recently, and the shock of certain events has caused a slide into conservatism in the years since the planet was last seen. See "The Three Doctors" for more.]

The Time Lords' ceremonial robes, with high, rounded collars are 'seldom worn' [but from this point on they wear the same outfits on less spectacular occasions]. Ceremonial make-up is also on show, and almost everyone seen here wears a leathery-looking skull-cap. The symbol of the Time Lords is an ornate figure-eight inside a circle, suggesting the Earth sign for "infinity". [It's later called the Seal of Rassilon, but not here. In this story the figure-eight is seen on its *side*, as with the infinity symbol. By the time we get to the TV Movie (27.0) it's upright, like the Vogan symbol in "Revenge of the Cybermen" (12.5). The name for the standard infinity symbol is the "lemniscate", which has led some fan-writers to call the Gallifreyan version the "omniscate".]

Chancellery Guards, red-uniformed soldiers in shiny capes and even shinier helmets, handle security in the Capitol. They're led by a Commander and under the control of the Castellan. Spandrell is the Castellan at this point, and acts like a chief of police rather than a military man. [Co-Ordinator Engin notes that Spandrell's duties usually involve more 'plebian classes', hinting that there's a Gallifreyan population other than the Time Lords - and near the Capitol, not outside in the wastes - so it's these lower classes who usually cause trouble. There may also be the implication that the Guards aren't fully-fledged Time Lords, but of a lower class themselves.]

The Castellan has never heard of the Master [unlike the high-ranking Time Lords in 8.4, "Colony in Space"]. There are over fifty Guards at the President's resignation ceremony, all of them armed. They have a buzzing 'rogin tracer' that's used to follow the Doctor's trail, while Borusa insists that the Time Lords have a tradition of fairness and justice. Even so, one of the Guards interrogates the Doctor with a gun-like torture device which causes fifteen intensity levels of pain.

The Celestial Intervention Agency is said to have interceded in order to remit the Doctor's sentence of banishment to Earth. Castellan Spandrell is obviously irritated by the CIA's existence, saying that it gets its fingers into everything. The biog-data files of CIA agents aren't expected to mention any Agency involvement.

[The Agency is only mentioned briefly here, and not positively cited as responsible for anything we've ever seen in the series. Fan-lore likes to claim that every mission of intervention the Time Lords have ever given the Doctor has been the Agency's idea, but this is hard to believe, especially since the "CIA" reference in this story was only included as a joke. If the Agency wanted to end the Doctor's exile then it must have convinced the authorities to send him the dematerialisation circuit at the end of "The Three Doctors", but in that story the circuit is portrayed as a reward from the Time Lord hierarchy for defeating Omega. This would indicate that the Gallifreyan CIA works alongside the President and Chancellor in the same way that the American CIA works alongside the US government - at least, assuming the US government is Republican - and isn't necessarily working behind the High Council's back. After all, it's an official Agency rather than a secret criminal group, and the fact that it exists as a recognised body at all proves that the Time Lords aren't as non-interventionist as other stories might pretend. As the Agency isn't visible here, and the Capitol's head of security doesn't think much of it, it's possible that it had a good rapport with the administration at the time of "The Three Doctors" but not such a good rapport with the recent regime. See also **How Involved Are the Time Lords?** under 15.5, "Underworld".]

The unnamed President - regarded as wise and beloved - is currently on the point of resigning, although he's assassinated at the elaborate resignation ceremony. Either there's a new President since the last time we saw the Time Lord elite ["The Three Doctors", again] or he's just regenerated, probably the latter as it's implied he's been in charge for 'centuries'. He's referred to as Time Lord President, not President of Gallifrey.

Did Rassilon Know Omega?

Or: "One Black Hole or Two?"

In "The Three Doctors" (10.1) we learn that long, long ago a great engineer called Omega journeyed into a black hole and never returned, but through his efforts made Time Lord civilisation possible. In "The Deadly Assassin" we learn that long, long ago a great engineer called Rassilon journeyed into a black hole but *did* return, and through his efforts made Time Lord civilisation possible. You can see the problem here.

As we've already established, "continuity" didn't exist in the 1970s, at least not in the modern, post-home-video sense of the word. Throughout *Doctor Who* there are running themes, ongoing concerns and recurring images. Many of the people who wrote it had read the same literature, or been introduced to it by hard-hearted script editors. So there's a sense of the programme holding together, but... nobody ever went back to check the details. Did Robert Holmes even remember "The Three Doctors", when he wrote "The Deadly Assassin"? He certainly got the "black hole" bit right, but the Heroes of Ancient Gallifrey don't match.

Everybody born after a certain date (and extensive research hasn't yet confirmed what this date is) makes the same assumption: that Omega and Rassilon were contemporaries, that Rassilon finished the work Omega started, and that at some point they must surely have collaborated. Yet this is never stated anywhere in the series.

Rather, it's a view which started to become "concrete" in the minds of fans in the early '80s, largely thanks to *Doctor Who Magazine*. When a confused reader wrote into *DWM*'s "Matrix Data Bank" column, and asked for an explanation as to how Omega and Rassilon could both have the same sort of mythic status in Time Lord history, the reply seemed reasonable. Omega was the hands-on engineer, whereas Rassilon was more of an aristocratic, organising-principle type.

The same sort of view was taken by the back-up comic-strips in the magazine, notably those written by Alan Moore, which were thoroughly great and which proved to be at least as influential to the growing generation of fans as the TV series itself. Anyone who followed the progress of the *Doctor Who* novels throughout the 1990s can plainly see that the writers had grown up on stories like Moore's "4-D War" (*Cat's Cradle: Time's Crucible* and *Alien Bodies* are the two most blatant examples). These comic-strips were also an influence on the last few decent writers to work on the

series in the late '80s. Ben Aaronovitch's script for "Remembrance of the Daleks" is clearly written by someone who thinks that Rassilon and Omega worked together, though it's never explicitly stated. The Target novelisation of the story - the book which pretty much set both the style and the back-story for the entire New Adventures line - *did* explicitly state it, and then some. All pro-level fanfiction since has agreed.

So, despite the lack of water-tight evidence onscreen, the case for Rassilon and Omega knowing each other seems "proved" in the minds of... well, many. The majority, even. But it wasn't always that way. Some will tell you that if you were growing up with the stories in the '70s, then you might - *might* - have taken a different view. The alternative version sees Rassilon and Omega as being separated by generations, and it isn't even clear which of them came first.

There are inconsistencies, no doubt about it. For example: the Aaronovitch version of the story assumes that Omega's black hole and Rassilon's black hole are one and the same. But this seems odd at best, impossible at worst. "The Deadly Assassin" says that Rassilon went into his black hole and removed its 'nucleus', returning it to Gallifrey and turning it into the Eye of Harmony. This nucleus, and not the hole itself, is what holds together the whole of Time Lord culture (whether they know about it or not). What's this 'nucleus'? Well... if you're going to be scientific about it, then it can only be the black hole's singularity. After all, everyone in the '70s had read the same kind of source material, so a singularity is almost certainly what Robert Holmes had in mind. But in "The Three Doctors", the singularity of Omega's black hole is still there. It *can't* be the same nucleus, unless Omega's spent the last few millennia stuck inside the Eye of Harmony, which is silly.

The obvious conclusion might be that Omega spearheaded the making-black-holes process, but that Rassilon perfected it and retrieved the nucleus from *another* hole, yet the time-scale doesn't seem right. In "The Invasion of Time" (15.6) it's established that Rassilon lived 'aeons' ago, and from "The Ultimate Foe" (23.4) we might assume that a figure of 10,000,000 years seems like a good estimate. But Omega believes he's only been trapped in *his* black hole for 'many thousands' of years. Is he understating, in spite of his big melodramatic voice? Does time really pass *that* differ-

continued on page 119...

A robed figure called Gold Usher performs some unspecified function at the resignation, while the President himself wears white. Before his death the President compiles a Resignation Honours' List, to be read at the ceremony, and this may well include the name of his chosen successor. The President also holds the symbols of office, the Sash of Rassilon and the Key; see **Ancient Time Lords**. The resignation is being broadcast to a wider population than just the robed types seen here, but the audience is apparently expected to know / care about figures like Cardinal Borusa. Mention is made of a former President called Pandak the Third, who lasted for 900 years, far longer than these modern Presidents.

Currently acting as Chancellor is the treacherous Goth, who's number two in the Time Lord Council, so he's expected to be named as the President's successor even though an election is held and others can stand as candidates. [Again, compare the Chancellor's position with "The Three Doctors".] In fact the President is planning to select someone else before his death, but the true successor is never named. Goth found the Master on Tersurus. [So high-ranking Time Lords do sometimes leave the planet, for whatever reason. Goth is played by Bernard Horsfall, who was also at the Doctor's trial in "The War Games". They may well be the same character, though see 20.1, "Arc of Infinity".] Spandrell indicates that members of the High Council aren't great scientists. Significantly, Goth tells Borusa that 'the Time Lords must not be seen to be leaderless at this time', suggesting that they're themselves answerable to some external power. [Either the plebian classes, or other cultures like the Third Zone; see 22.4, "The Two Doctors".]

The Doctor's murder trial is held by a jury of high-ranking officials, and isn't the formal affair of his malfeasance tribunal [in "The War Games"]. No lawyers are involved, just the judgement of the Chancellor, and the Doctor is apparently only allowed to speak when sentence is to be pronounced. Found guilty, he's condemned to death in a vaporisation chamber. [Again, the question is how common this sort of thing is in Time Lord society. "Arc of Infinity" suggests that only one Time Lord has ever been executed - almost certainly meaning Morbius - but here nobody finds the sentence strange, even if it's imposed for a crime which must surely be unheard-of on Gallifrey.] He wriggles out of this by calling on Article Seventeen of the Constitution, which technically allows him to stand as a presidential candidate, and says in part that no candidate can be restrained from presenting his claim. Incoming presidents usually pardon political prisoners. [This *can't* be a reference to the kind of prisoners who are kept on Shada (17.6), as no President would be idiotic enough to let history-threatening war criminals go free just to uphold a tradition. Besides, the Time Lords have forgotten about Shada at this point in their history. So what kind of political prisoners *are* there on Gallifrey?] He also claims that vaporisation without representation is against the Constitution. [A parody of James Otis, the colonial Massachusetts lawyer who advocated the views that led to the American Revolution, but possibly true anyway.]

There are numerous chapters in Time Lord society, the suggestion being that these are related to the Time Lord academies, i.e. it's about education rather than birth. Each chapter has its own colours.

The Prydonians wear red and orange, the Arcalians wear green and the Patrexes wear heliotrope [or at least that's what Runvible says, but see **Things That Don't Make Sense**]. There are chapters other than these, though no other colours are in evidence. The Prydonians, the Doctor's chapter, seem to be considered especially noble and high-class even though they're notoriously devious; the Castellan only refers the case to the Chancellor when he finds out that the Doctor's a member, as 'when a Prydonian forswears his birthright, there is nothing else he fears to lose'. Goth is also a Prydonian, and claims they see 'a little further ahead than most'. The Castellan believes that the vows of a Prydonian make the Doctor's fidelity to the President suspect. Cardinal Borusa is leader of the Prydonian chapter, which has produced more Presidents than any other. Other Cardinals are mentioned. ["Cardinal" may be a title given to the head of a chapter, or the head of an academy, as it's indicated that each chapter has its own.]

Time Lords can only regenerate twelve times before death, and Engin doesn't believe anything can stop the end of this regenerative cycle [but compare with 20.7, "The Five Doctors"]. Runcible recognises the Doctor, even though he's regenerated several times since their last meeting, and asks if he's had a 'face-lift'. [Interesting that Runcible considers this more likely than regeneration.

Did Rassilon Know Omega?

...continued from page 117

ently for him, inside his realm? Or is he just insane?

Well, maybe. "Remembrance" is quite clear on the matter, stating that Omega 'left behind him' the science on which Rassilon founded Time Lord society. It might also be considered odd that Omega knows of the Time Lords and once sat on the High Council, though this might just indicate that the Gallifreyan elite called themselves Time Lords even before they had absolute control over time.

So. Here are the options.

1. The voice of the '90s. Omega and Rassilon knew each other, and there's only one black hole. Omega created it, and Rassilon later removed its nucleus to make the Eye of Harmony. This nucleus is *not* the singularity. It's something else entirely, quite possibly something only comprehensible within the framework of Time Lord physics. (After all, much of the Gallifreyan technology which drives the series is either incomprehensible or simply never explained, and for all we know there's some *other* factor involved in black holes which humanity just hasn't noticed yet.)

So the rest of the hole, with its singularity intact, was still around by the time of "The Three Doctors" and ready to go supernova. Though this is a cop-out in scientific terms, it *does* make sense in terms of *Doctor Who* after the '70s. Pop-science ceases to be the inspiration behind ancient Time Lord history from "State of Decay" onwards (18.4), and later stories are more concerned with sweeping, mythic confrontations than with technicalities. The idea that the nucleus is an undefined, indefinable quality of a black hole is perfectly in keeping with the style of "Remembrance of the Daleks", and with the style of most of the subsequent New Adventures, even if it jars with *Doctor Who* in 1976. This solution is aesthetically the neatest even if it's physically the most dubious. One hole, no problems.

2. The voice of the '80s. Omega and Rassilon knew each other, but it's not necessarily the same black hole. "Remembrance of the Daleks" is the definitive source, in this model of things. As the Doctor explicitly says, Omega came first. Rassilon built on what his "friend" pioneered (although there's a lurking suggestion, especially in the novelisation, that Rassilon deliberately set Omega up). It's possible that Rassilon engineered a second black hole, and did what Omega couldn't by com-

ing back, hence the line about the Sash of Rassilon preventing its wearer from being sucked into a parallel universe. Alternatively Rassilon's hole may indeed have been the primal one from the beginning of time - see the third theory - and Omega's black hole simply provided an energy source which in some way allowed Rassilon to install the Eye of Harmony on Gallifrey. Either way, the continuity is satisfied. Omega's belief that he's been in his realm for 'many thousands' of years can easily be put down to insanity, time-distortion effects or dramatics, the latter being most likely as he *does* have a liking for flowery language. Besides, it's no worse than any other dating error ever made by a *Doctor Who* character.

3. The voice of the '70s. Omega and Rassilon didn't know each other, or at least, they weren't contemporaries. The science is key. Physics c. 1976 dictates that a black hole can be used as a navigational device for time-travel, but that the traveller can't go back further than the point of the time machine's construction.

Robert Holmes, who was already researching this stuff and planned to use it in "The Sun Makers" (15.4), was aware of that. But as has been explained in the **Why All These Black Holes?** essay, there may have been a singularity left over from the Big Bang. Rassilon's voyage could have been a mission to find and convert this singularity; to take a naturally-occurring temporal anomaly and bring it back to his own world in a handy wardrobe-sized form, giving his people unlimited access to time. To do this, he'd need energy. So Omega's black hole was used as a power-source.

The most sensible way for the two Great Gallifreyans to have met is for Rassilon to have travelled back to Omega's time, which explains why Omega in "The Three Doctors" and "Arc of Infinity" (20.1) knows so much about the workings of Time Lord society. Rassilon may even have brought Omega back to his own era, and as Omega's been close to a temporal anomaly, his 'thousands' of years may be aeons in the outside universe. If you like things good and Biblical, then this has a lot of appeal. Omega - as the fallen angel - has to exist at the start of Time Lord history, ruling in "Hell" rather than serving in 'Heaven'; Rassilon - as the pioneer, lawgiver and patriarch - leads his people to "the promised land".

continued on page 121...

ABOUT TIME 1975-1979

Unless Gallifreyans are just starting to think of regeneration as something cosmetic? The Doctor's horrified by the thought of changing his appearance in "The War Games", but by the time of "The Five Doctors" it's taken for granted as an everyday part of Time Lord life. And then there's Romana in "Destiny of the Daleks" (17.1), who tries on alternative bodies as if she's in a dress shop. Troubled times on Gallifrey may be making the populace a lot more casual about re-birth.]

Energy weapons are used here which kill Time Lords without them regenerating, including a lightweight rifle-like weapon called a staser, which causes a lot of damage except to body tissue… though oddly, a corpse killed by a staser bolt will be charred beyond recognition within an hour.

And apparently there's no Time Lord word for "framed".

• *Borusa.* The Doctor's old tutor at Prydon Academy. Borusa is a stately, unflappable individual who refuses to give up one iota of his dignity. Unlike virtually every other "pompous" character in the universe, Borusa is obviously an intelligent man and the Doctor fails to get the better of him. Indeed, the Doctor still calls him 'sir', but makes it sound sarcastic. Borusa is prepared to do whatever's necessary to maintain the status quo of Gallifrey, and has no qualms about it. He invents the "official" story that Goth died heroically while fighting the Master, in order to cover up Goth's treachery and prevent news of a traitorous Chancellor shaking up Time Lord society, and he spins this lie without a moment's hesitation. He gives the Doctor nine out of ten for saving Gallifrey [not surprising, as the Doctor has just solved one of the oldest mysteries on the planet by discovering the Eye of Harmony's true nature]. He used to teach that 'only in mathematics can we find truth', which explains his view of history.

Borusa plans to make the Master a public enemy after the renegade's apparent death [but he may change his mind after the Master's eventual escape, as most Time Lords don't seem to know of the Master in 23.4, "The Ultimate Foe"]. Borusa himself doesn't seem to know of the Master [so either the appellation "Master" is quite new, or the Master wasn't in the same class as the Doctor at the Academy].

Ancient Time Lords

• *Rassilon.* Spoken of as the founder of modern Time Lord civilisation. The *Book of the Old Time* contains his exploits, but there's a modern transgram that's much less difficult. In his own time he was mostly regarded as an engineer and architect, 'long before we turned aside from the barren road of technology' [so Time Lords don't see things like TARDISes as technological?]. Rassilon journeyed into a black hole with a great fleet, and found within it the Eye of Harmony, which balances 'all things that they may neither flux nor wither, nor change their state in any measure'. He brought this back to Gallifrey, and sealed it with the Great Key, an ebonite rod now held by the President on ceremonial occasions that's kept among other relics in a display case in the Panopticon. The Sash of Rassilon, which protected Rassilon in the black hole and protects its user from being 'sucked into a parallel universe' [something similar happened to Omega], is kept by the President himself. The Doctor claims the Sash is damaged, but he could be bluffing to stop the Master [it didn't stop the President being shot, but then again it wasn't designed to protect its wearer from stasers, just black holes].

Nobody has any idea what the Key or the Sash do until this point, and the Eye is believed to be a myth which 'no longer' exists. Even the Doctor doesn't know the story about Rassilon and the black hole, so it's not a widely-recognised piece of Time Lord culture. [The Great Key seen here clearly isn't the same as the legendary Great Key mentioned in "The Invasion of Time", so obviously the Gallifreyan language is being badly-translated into English and giving two very different ancient artefacts the same name. After this the rod-like Great Key is generally referred to as the Rod of Rassilon.]

In truth the Eye is a black hole nucleus [possibly the singularity of a small but stable one; see **Why All These Black Holes?** under 10.1, "The Three Doctors"], and all the Time Lords' power devolves from it. Rassilon stabilised all the elements of the black hole and set them in an eternally-dynamic equation against the mass of Gallifrey. If anyone were to interfere with this, it'd be the end of Gallifrey and a hundred other worlds too. The Master tries to access this power by wearing the Sash and inserting the Key into a slot in the floor of the Panopticon. A black monolith then rises from below, which the Master identifies as the Eye of Harmony itself. It starts to shake Gallifrey apart before the Doctor stops it, and the Panopticon itself is badly damaged. [It'll

Did Rassilon Know Omega?

...continued from page 119

Even apart from the obvious generation gap, which of these options you consider to be the most rational really depends on the kind of "rational" you're looking for.

One final point here. In both "The Three Doctors" and "The Deadly Assassin", the ancient-Time-Lord-in-question is presented as an iconic figure, but neither Omega nor Rassilon is considered to be of great importance to modern Gallifrey. Rassilon *isn't* treated as the great demi-urge of Time Lord civilisation in "Assassin"; Co-Ordinator Engin believes that very few people care about the Old Time. Symbolically, at this stage Omega and Rassilon might as well be one and the same, even if one got out of the hole and the other didn't. In a way it's a pity that both of them had to turn up on our screens, in person, in 1983. Up until then the writers could justifiably have claimed that they were two different names for the same individual, and that the Time Lords had just got their history a bit muddled.

be re-built by the time of 15.6, "The Invasion of Time". The fate of the Sash and the rod-like Key are unknown, though they're both apparently in evidence in "The Invasion of Time". The Key is easily replaceable, especially since the Panopticon has to be reconstructed, but the Sash might not be.] The Master soaks up some of the power from the Eye, 'converting' it through the Sash's power in order to heal his dying body.

[Compare this with "The Three Doctors". No mention is made of Omega here at all, and much of this seems contradictory. Omega turned a star into a black hole, and the black hole's singularity was still in place by the time of "The Three Doctors". Whereas Rassilon ventured into a pre-existing black hole and pulled out its nucleus, "nucleus" suggesting "singularity" even if it's not explicitly stated. So they're not necessarily the same black hole; see **Did Rassilon Know Omega?** Omega's black hole gave the Time Lords the necessary energy to fuel time-travel, whereas it's only said that 'all power devolves' from Rassilon's nucleus, perhaps meaning that Omega provided the raw power-source and that the Eye of Harmony is the thing which allows the Time Lords to navigate through time properly. But this is by no means clear. It's also worth pointing out the Time Lords here don't see Rassilon as an all-purpose Messiah-figure, as his legend isn't widely-known and the Doctor has to ask for more details about him. The Doctor's statement in "The Three Doctors" that Omega is regarded as a hero by the Time Lords would indicate that at this stage, it's Omega who's well-remembered in folklore while Rassilon is only seen as the civilisation's founder by people like Engin, who has a specific interest in ancient history. This isn't what later stories suggest; see, for instance, "Four to Doomsday" (19.2).

Nonetheless, it's telling that in "The Three Doctors" the Doctor sees the reckless, do-or-die Omega as the great figure and not the stabilising influence of Rassilon.]

Planet Notes

• *Gallifrey.* The heart of Time Lord society is the Capitol, a grand, classical-style "city" whose limits aren't established here [but see "The Invasion of Time"]. The TARDIS can land on the planet without difficulty, though the landing is unauthorised and the Chancellery Guards are soon on the scene when the alert's sounded. The Doctor lands indoors, yet says he's right outside the Capitol, meaning that the Capitol is just the central area of a larger enclosed community. Objects can also be 'transducted' to and from the Capitol. The TARDIS can't leave again until the transduction barriers are raised.

The President's resignation ceremony is held in a great hall known as the Panopticon, and covered for Public Register Video - the Gallifreyan version of television, which the Doctor can watch on the TARDIS screen - by Commentator Runcible. Rather old-fashioned camera technology is used to record the event. There's a communications tower with fifty-three stories, close to the Capitol's perimeter, and a Capitol museum not far from the Panopticon.

Co-Ordinator Engin's chamber is equipped with a machine, apparently a computer of some description, which can immediately give the Castellan information on Time Lord affairs when he asks it for data retrieval. The voice which answers him is female, though no women are seen anywhere else on the planet. The chamber also contains extracted biog-data on individual Time Lords, the information being stored on what looks suspiciously like microfilm in canisters colour-coded according to the subject's chapter. The biog-data files are also known as data extracts (DEs), and data extraction requires an operating key, only issued to High Councillors and the Co-Ordinator. Records of data extraction can be changed, but only by a mathematical genius with a phenomenal grasp of exitonic circuitry. Even so, the Doctor believes the system would be considered primitive on some worlds. [The Time Lords specialise in temporal engineering, so it's reasonable that their records storage technology wouldn't be the most sophisticated in the universe.] The DE on the Master has been destroyed. Vaults and foundations dating back to the Old Time are found deep beneath the Co-Ordinator's chamber [and under much of the rest of the Capitol].

At one point Spandrell says that he has to keep running in Shobogans for vandalism. [No explanation for this is given here. Fan-lore has generally assumed the Shobogans to be the outsiders seen in "The Invasion of Time", and Terrance Dicks makes the same assumption in his novelisation of that story, but there's no evidence for it on-screen. Indeed, in context Spandrell would seem to be referring to another chapter of Time Lords, with an implication of student pranks at Sheboogan Academy. Or it may simply be local slang for tearaway kids.]

The Time Lords measure local time according to the 'time-band', whatever that is. Spandrell's significant use of the phrase 'forty-eight hours' might suggest a very Earth-like twenty-four-hour day. The Co-Ordinator refers to Earth as Sol 3 in Mutter's Spiral. [This has often been taken to mean the Milky Way, though other evidence suggests that Gallifrey is in the same galaxy, and Engin would hardly refer to his *own* galaxy in this way. The meaning remains unclear, but for all we know Earth's sun is in a spiral-shaped constellation from Gallifrey's point of view.]

When the Master tries to unleash the power of the Eye of Harmony, parts of the city are ruined before the Doctor can stop it, and countless lives are lost. Gallifrey has apparently never known such catastrophe.

• *The Matrix*. In the Co-Ordinator's chamber is the APC (Amplified Panatropic Computations) control. The device is described as being made up of 'brain-cells', trillions of electro-chemical cells in a continuous matrix, a repository of departed Time Lords. At the moment of death, an electrical scan is made of the brain-pattern and the impulses are immediately transferred to the system. There's a slab with electrodes attached to the machine, so the dead are presumably brought here to be scanned. [After all, most Time Lords die on Gallifrey. A Time Lord who died elsewhere - such as the Doctor, presumably - probably wouldn't be added to the mix.]

The existence of this matrix - hereafter *the Matrix* - isn't known to the Doctor until now, and the Co-Ordinator claims it's used to monitor life in the Capitol, predicting future events [we might assume that the predictions get vaguer as it looks further into the future, or the Time Lords would know everything that's ever going to happen]. It's never officially been done before now, but a mind can enter the Matrix by being hooked up to the electrodes, though there's a risk of lethal psychosomatic feedback and the subject will die if the power's cut. The Master has his own device for putting Goth's mind in the system, where hours can pass for every minute in the "real" world.

Entering the Matrix, the Doctor seems to find himself moving down a curious psychedelic tunnel. [A tunnel that looks just like the programme's title sequence. The script of "Shada" (17.6) suggests the same graphic to represent the time vortex, while "The Brain of Morbius" (13.5) uses it to represent mental contact between Morbius and the Doctor.] His mind then arrives in a disturbing landscape full of monsters, clowns, surgeons, bomber 'planes, men in gas-masks and sundry other hazards, in this case controlled by Goth. The illusions and nightmare-visions don't seem capable of actually harming the Doctor once he realises he can deny them, although ultimately Goth and the Doctor *are* capable of fighting to the near-death in the system. Goth has the advantage, since he's been in the Matrix before and has built his own 'dreamscape', but the Doctor can call on all his brain's artron energy for defence. The Master then tries to trap the Doctor's mind in the Matrix by overloading the neuron fields.

Curiously, both duellists require water to keep themselves going. [Part of the "rules" of the nightmare laid down by Goth. There's more on the Matrix in "The Invasion of Time", and by the time of "The Ultimate Foe" (23.4) it's been completely reconfigured. It should be noted that although we're referring to it as "the Matrix" here, that doesn't become its official title until "The Invasion of Time", and in "The Deadly Assassin" it's just referred to as the APC computation matrix. The Matrix and the system are essentially the same thing, at least here, as the APC device is described as a matrix.]

The "call" from Gallifrey received by the Doctor [in the previous story] here develops into a series of telepathic visions while the TARDIS is in the vortex, in which he experiences the assassination of the President before it happens. These predictions are forecasts from the Matrix, beamed into the Doctor's mind by the Master to lure him into a trap. The Doctor's biography print was needed to beam this message accurately. The other Time Lords nonetheless believe that precognitive vision is impossible. [Meaning, *unless* your head's hooked up to the APC system. Incidentally, the Doctor's conclusion that a living mind is just electro-chemical impulses - even if it's the mind of a Time Lord - would seem, at first sight, to deny the existence of the soul.]

History

• *Dating.* Gallifreyan present.]Possibly not related to the time-scale of the rest of the universe. See **Where (and When) is Gallifrey?** under 13.3, "Pyramids of Mars".]

The date of the Doctor's malfeasance trial is given as 309906. [6.7, "The War Games". There's no reason that this should be related to Earth history, as the Time Lords don't have Earthly origins. As far as we know. Probably not the 3100th century, then.]

The Analysis

Where Does This Come From? We were in an era when heroes were shown to have feet of clay. America had lost faith in its political system after Nixon, Agnew, Ford and the Warren Commission. Jimmy Carter was honest and intelligent, and he wasn't getting anywhere either. In Britain there was a generation bored rigid with World War Two, finding out that the sanitised version from 1950s movies was a lie; Field-Marshal Montgomery's posthumous "outing" was the last straw for many. Yet, as a secular age learned to re-evaluate the symbols of faith and power as historical phenomena (re-examining the Coronation ceremony in the run-up to the Queen's Silver Jubilee, for instance), it became increasingly apparent that a lot of seemingly pointless rituals were once immensely potent. Four of the six stories in this season revolve around advanced science underlying apparently supernatural phenomena. This isn't just von Danikenism, but a rethinking of history. Here history isn't a linear progression with us as its happy ending, but a sequence of people with radically strange and - under the circumstances - rational systems of thought. An entire way of thinking was now seen as self-deception, from wartime myth-making to religion, from the idea of art history being a series of codes to the idea of cowboys being good and "injuns" being savages. Now *Doctor Who* has its central character not only criticising every form of authority he encounters, but also his own past.

The most obvious thing to say, even more so than the Kennedy material, is that this is the *Doctor Who* version of *The Manchurian Candidate*. The details of Gallifrey's society are point-for-point matches for the film's version of American politics. Rassilon is invoked in much the same way as Abraham Lincoln. The entire dream-battle, whilst having a passing resemblance to Ben Bova's briefly-popular children's book *The Duelling Machine*, suggests the same nightmares-as-clues Cold War hysteria as Frank Sinatra's flashbacks of being brainwashed in the Korean War. The use of the camera-rig as the vantage-point for an assassination at a political rally is also plundered; TV's role in politics is a strong thread in the film.

We could go on, but what's interesting is Robert Holmes' spin on this. As a former journalist he's gleefully sending up the pointless rituals of the State Opening of Parliament (all those hallowed, Mediaeval rites date back to... ooh... at least the 1800s) and the vacuity of the TV coverage. Which of course makes the APC net the equivalent of the House of Lords, where Time Lords go when they're no longer of active use. This is a society whose government is run by the dead. Yet whenever he was asked about this, Holmes said that - *Manchurian Candidate* aside - his starting-point was the tendency of the older British universities to act as if nothing ever changed. Colleges of cardinals and chancellors, not unlike (say) St. Andrews' University, Edinburgh. Tom Baker had recently been asked to become chancellor there...

It's one of the conventions of the Hollywood version of psychiatry that the hero re-enters a nightmare to unlock the (often ham-fisted) symbolism and achieve a "breakthrough". Examples are almost too numerous to mention, but we'll take Hitchcock's *Spellbound* (1945) as paradigmatic as it's actually a good film and the dream's designed by Salvador Dali. In *The Manchurian*

Candidate the dreams are suppressed memories of brainwashing. The same logic applies to the "projections" the Doctor receives in episode one, but the APC-induced duel - not unlike *Blake's 7* 1.8 "Duel" and its more obvious forebear "Arena", both the story by Fredric Brown and its re-working as a *Star Trek* episode - is closer to the "conventional" nightmares of decaf-Freud.

Holmes, we must remember, also served in Burma in his army days. Given Hinchcliffe's decision to stage an entire episode as a nightmare, this was almost inevitably going to crop up in the imagery. Spandrell's antacid pills are a reference to the kind of cop you usually get in *film noir* (and the scroll-crawl at the start owes more to The *Maltese Falcon* than *Flash Gordon*). Similarly, check out the chalk outline of the dead President in episode two, almost nonchalantly making fun of cop-shows. As happens a lot in this season, the fact that dead bodies need to be taken somewhere is made a plot point, as though the programme-makers had decided to get away from the hygienic disintegrator guns of lesser programmes.

Things That Don't Make Sense

Deep breath...

The second most idiotic thing here is that nobody on Gallifrey has ever found out the function of the Sash or Key of Rassilon, or worked out what the fairy-tale story of Rassilon and the black hole means, but the Doctor hears the abridged version once and instantly knows what all the relics do. The subtext is that the Doctor does this because he's been "abroad" and has perspectives unlike any other Time Lord, but as in "The Masque of Mandragora", his supposed experience doesn't *come* from anywhere and as a result he just looks like a universal know-it-all who can solve the greatest mysteries in the cosmos without ever deducing anything.

The *most* idiotic thing is that the Time Lords, ostensibly the highest civilisation in the universe, *have absolutely no idea where any of their power comes from and have apparently never even tried to find out until the Doctor figures it out in a couple of seconds.* Of all the inconceivable things in *Doctor Who*, this may well be the most inane. If this were a random, never-before-seen alien planet then the series could just about get away with it, but these are the Time Lords, hyped up as the universe's most advanced culture for the last seven years. This is the one planet that's supposed to *matter*.

Not only that, but nobody ever thinks to explain how the Master knows the specifics of the Eye of Harmony when no-one else does. He's never shown any interest in the secrets of the old days before now, but he's suddenly figured everything out now that he's horribly scarred and (seemingly) mentally deranged? His plan involves unleashing the power of the Eye, and remaining safe because of his Sash, but... since the Eye is about to destroy the planet, what's his plan going to entail after he finds himself in the middle of a black hole with no transportation? And why does his evil scheme involve the Doctor being set up as a traitor and remembered as a murderer by the Time Lords, when he's planning on destroying Gallifrey almost immediately after the assassination? Fair enough, he wants to gloat, but even by *his* standards is it really worth going through all this just so the Time Lords can "remember" the Doctor as a criminal for a couple of hours? His claim that he needs a 'scapegoat' doesn't wash, as *without* a scapegoat Goth would have become President before the Time Lords could even begin their investigation.

For that matter, even the Master's plan to set Goth up as President and thereby acquire the Sash of Rassilon seems like a lot of needless bother, as he would've been much better off just shooting or hypnotising all the guards and stealing it. Actually, since the President believes the Sash to have no real value and Goth is his second-in-command, couldn't Goth have simply asked to borrow it for a bit?

Just to make things even less credible, the "keyhole" for the Eye of Harmony is set into the floor of the Panopitcon where everybody can see it, but apparently no Time Lord has ever thought about sticking the Great Key into it. Even though the Great Key's kept in a cabinet just a couple of yards away.

Borusa is said to be leader of the Prydonian chapter, yet he appears wearing the heliotrope robes of the Patrexes [see 15.6, "The Invasion of Time", for more on this]. After telling the Doctor that he's waiting for a signal from his camera technician before beginning his broadcast, Runcible almost immediately starts talking to camera, even though the Doctor's just figured out that the technician's dead. The Master later kills Runcible for no good reason, basically proving that the Doctor's innocent - as he's with the Castellan when the crime's committed - even as Goth is trying to have the Doctor executed. And is the Doctor *really* not capable of recognising Goth's voice when they're facing each other in the Matrix, or indeed, making out his face through that flimsy mask? 'Cos the audience is.

The Master tampers with the staser on the Panopticon balcony in such a way that when the Doctor's shot goes wild, it fails to hit anything else (or anybody else) in the crowded hall. At the same time Goth pulls a gun on the President without anyone around him noticing, even though the Doctor spots it from his vantage-point on the other side of the Panopticon. Amazingly, the Doctor's fooled when the Master fakes his own death, as if you'd expect him to commit suicide rather than try to escape. And the reawakening Master manages to strangle his guard into submission before the man can shoot him, even though the guard's pistol is aimed right at his head and ready to fire.

Just before leaving, the Doctor sees the Master's TARDIS standing nearby in the shape of a grandfather clock but doesn't think to question it; odd in itself, doubly so when you remember that Gallifreyans are supposed to be able to recognise disguised TARDISes, as the Captain of the Guard does in episode one. Spandrell's reaction on realising that the Master's escaping in the clock is to point a bit and sound bored. The APC system is capable of accurately predicting all events on Gallifrey, and correctly predicts the assassination of the President, but the Time Lords never hear the prediction because the Master has tampered with it... which sounds fair enough, at first. But why didn't the APC system predict his tampering, or warn anybody the moment he arrived on Gallifrey?

Oh, and all the shrunken corpses are Action Men.

Critique (Prosecution)   Reviled by many fans on its first transmission (because it contradicted everything they thought they knew about the Time Lords), "The Deadly Assassin" was later re-designated a classic. With hindsight they got it right the first time, though not necessarily for the right reasons.

In its design and in its conception, this *should* be one of the programme's grandest and most powerful moments, but it's also a very, very badly-made piece of television. Episode one is embarrassingly rushed, the script cramming in so much background before the cliffhanger assassination

that the whole thing looks more like a twenty-five-minute "previously on..." segment than a finished programme, and as director, the usually-great David Maloney just seems to want to get things out of the way as quickly as possible. (You'd swear that the lead villain's appearance was *deliberately* being robbed of all its drama, while the cuts between real events and the Doctor's visions are simply laughable.) Episode two should carry more dramatic clout than almost anything we've seen in the series, with the Doctor awaiting execution at the hands of his own people, but all the majesty vanishes as soon as the decision's made to treat Gallifrey as if it's just another bunch of "space" sets inhabited by generic officials with pulp-SF torture devices.

Nor does the music help, a repetitive organ-dirge apparently supposed to suggest "grandiose" but actually just aural sludge. Though nowhere near as revolutionary as is often claimed, episode three is at least interesting in parts, but only because it doesn't gel with anything else here. And episode four comes across as a work of desperation, smothered in meaningless technobabble and defeated by *Doctor Who*'s nature right from the start. This world is being ripped apart by its own power-source, yet all we see is four people arguing in a room. The lack of scope is crippling, and worse, the logic behind it all is moronic (see **Things That Don't Make Sense**).

But perhaps the real trouble with "The Deadly Assassin" is that aside from the occasional snack-bite of political satire, everything here is so thoroughly contrived that it's alien in all the wrong ways. The script makes up new rules for Time Lord society minute-by-minute, so what chance does the audience have of feeling as if it's any of their concern? If the Doctor reaches a dead end then a new piece of Time Lord technology or custom can be invented to help him get to the next scene, and if characters aren't in the right places then they can be conveniently shifted around by Time Lord "traditions" which everybody knows about except the viewer. We may take the story for granted as a lodestone of continuity now, but the Matrix is pulled out of the hat in episode two for no good narrative reason other than "the producer wants a nightmare sequence", while Rassilon and the Eye of Harmony are only mentioned *halfway through the last episode* when the plot suddenly finds itself needing a big finish. (The key moment is a tiny one, in the first episode, when Spandrell concludes that somebody must have accessed the Doctor's biog-data file because there's no 'micro-dust' on the film. This is treated as if it's a meaningful, logical clue, when in fact the writer could have made up *any* old piece of nonsense to keep this strand of the plot moving.)

Great fantasy works by creating new rules for new worlds, but here everything's just… spurious. And why anyone thought it was a good idea to bring back the Master, when the character's just a dull, generic, gloating villain without (a) Delgado's performance and (b) the context of the Pertwee years, is quite baffling. As with so much else here, the script automatically assumes his re-appearance to be a great mythic event, but feels no need to actually tell the audience why. No wonder modern fandom has decided to like it; they're the only ones who could possibly get it. Only the costumes are as good as everyone says.

Critique (Defence) We're not in Kansas any more. Everything about this story is taking us further and further from what we thought we knew about the programme's rules and set-up. The Doctor told Sarah 'nothing like this has ever happened before', and he looked scared. Now we have a story beginning with a voice-over and scrolling text, and a shot of the Doctor gunning down the President. No companion, no benign bureaucratic Time Lords, the Doctor visibly beaten up, shot, stabbed, bleeding and trapped… even when we find out that the Phantom of the Opera is in fact the Master, he's not the suave old chum of the later Delgado stories but the Holmes original with the gloves off. He's not a nice person, he hates the Doctor and wants the man finally humiliated before destroying their homeworld simply to gain more life.

The Master, the Time Lords, UNIT, monsters, the Daleks… all had been rethought, reinvented and removed from their position as "cornerstones" of the programme, taking us closer to what the series was always supposed to be about: exploration and isolation. Finally, the Doctor explores his own roots, and is alone even at "home". It's all unprecedented and, given how daring this team had been to date, no-one watching could guess where it would end. This was, in many ways, the "ultimate" story; one taking this particular strand of the series as far as it would be able to go. Each episode rewrites the rulebook. The flaw in this plan is that somehow they have to follow this, but that's a problem for Chris Boucher, as he's writing

the next story. This was never intended to be the start of a Gallifrey soap-opera, but a one-off, a freak, a demonstration of how far they've come in three years. Subsequent visits to the planet have squandered this, especially those in spin-off books and CDs. Yet criticising this story for the faults of Big Finish and the *Faction Paradox* saga is like blaming Malcolm Hulke for "Warriors of the Deep".

The original point was to prove that the Doctor needed a female sidekick, but in that one regard it's a failure. Admittedly the first episode's talking to camera is sometimes a bit forced, but as early as "The Ark in Space" this Doctor has been seen to talk to himself. Forced to invent other ways to relay exposition to the viewers, Holmes and Maloney push the medium further than mainstream TV had gone in 1976. And the central character is now seen as an outcast as much from his own people as from Earth; a misfit whose experiences on his travels make him more flexible, more open-minded, more curious than his compatriots. This allows Holmes to pull off the near-impossible stunt of simultaneously debunking the Time Lords and keeping them mysterious and powerful. They are omnipotent, but in ways they themselves no longer fully understand. Oddly, this is entirely in keeping with "The War Games" and makes them less approachable than the pompous technicians of "The Three Doctors".

In the end, what we have here is a world which feels solid and appears to extend beyond the edge of the TV screen, even though we're finding our feet whilst watching the Doctor revisit his past and know it for the first time. Real cities shouldn't be completely known at the end of ninety minutes.

The Facts

Written by Robert Holmes. Directed by David Maloney. Viewing figures: 11.8 million, 12.1 million, 13 million, 11.8 million.

Supporting Cast Peter Pratt (The Master), George Pravda (Castellan Spandrell), Erik Chitty (Co-Ordinator Engin), Bernard Horsfall (Chancellor Goth), Angus McKay (Cardinal Borusa), Hugh Walters (Commentator Runcible), Derek Seaton (Commander Hilred), Llewellyn Rees (The President), Maurice Quick (Gold Usher), Helen Blatch (Computer Voice).

Working Titles "The Dangerous Assassin". (Arguably "The Deadly Assassin" has the least convincing *Doctor Who* title of them all, since most assassins *are* deadly, unless they shoot the target's dog by mistake; see the essay under 10.5, "The Green Death". But "The Dangerous Assassin" is a shade worse.)

Cliffhangers Confusion reigns as the Doctor aims a rifle from the balcony of the Panopticon, a shot rings out and the President drops dead in mid-ceremony (the recap cheats by re-cutting the scene to show that it's not the Doctor who does the killing); in the Matrix landscape, the Doctor's foot gets trapped in the rails as a train thunders towards him; *still* in the Matrix landscape, the masked traitor forces the Doctor's head below the surface of a lake, holding him there to drown. (The original cut of this episode freezes the final image, but complaints from "concerned parties" led the BBC to trim the episode by six seconds for the repeat in summer 1977. See **The Lore**.)

The Lore

• Tom Baker had been pushing for the role of the companion to be phased out, as he believed that the Doctor was now an established-enough figure for audience identification (which may miss the point of the programme slightly, but there you go). Philip Hinchcliffe had been keen to try a whole episode as a nightmare, to see how badly beaten-up the Doctor could get and how much the audience would accept. In order to get to write this "experimental" script, Homes needed a dispensation from the Writers' Guild. He'd later suffer the consequences in the form of an audit by the Inland Revenue (see 15.4, "The Sun Makers"), due to his dual income for this period.

• James Acheson, primary costume-designer on the series, resigned halfway through the story as the limits of what he could do - that was affordable *and* unlike anything else he'd done before - were driving him nuts. Again, let's remember: he's got an Oscar now for *Spider-Man*.

• The location work, with biplanes, steam-trains and exploding lakes, made this story cripplingly expensive to shoot. The hallucinatory spider was a bit ropey, thanks to the usual BBC "spiders must not in any way look good" directive; see **Bad Effects: What Are the Highlights?** under 14.6, "The Talons of Weng-Chiang".

• George Pravda, as Spandrell, had taken to reading the Doctor's warning note in rehearsals rather than learning the lines. It was replaced when Roger Murray-Leech invented a "spacey" form of Gujarati for Gallifreyan writing, but Pravda wasn't told until after he unfolded the now-baffling parchment.

• A Spandrel is, as we all know, either part of a clock or an architectural feature of gothic arches in churches. "Runcible" is a type of spoon, dual-use; as anyone with enough education to tie shoes knows, it comes from "The Owl and the Pussycat".

• The moment when a Samurai severs the Doctor's scarf was to have been the literal "cliffhanger" to episode two. But the episode under-ran.

• The transduction effect was realised with an effect-box constructed by A. J. "Mitch" Mitchell, who often tried these things out on *Doctor Who* before utilising them on shows like *Multi-Coloured Swap Shop* or *Top of the Pops* (see **Cultural Primer #1: Why** *Top of the Pops***?** under 14.5, "The Robots of Death").

• This was the heyday of the National Viewers' and Listeners' Association, led by certifiable harridan Mary Whitehouse. The organisation campaigned to remove any hint of sex, violence, blasphemy or general realism from British television, and was often portrayed in the media as a "serious" pressure group even though its membership was less than a quarter of the size of the Doctor Who Appreciation Society.

Whitehouse led a fatwa against the programme, and specifically this story. She especially derided the end of episode three, as she felt children might not understand that a freeze-frame isn't "real". She pronounced, with little or no research to back this up, that younger viewers thought the Doctor's head would be underwater for a whole week (presumably the same children thought that Lis Sladen hovered above the Thal missile silo from the 15th to the 22nd of March, 1975). Bafflingly, the BBC agreed; the cliffhanger was savagely edited for subsequent reruns, and for the video release. The version as broadcast no longer exists.

• An enthusiastic writer-producer called Graham Williams had proposed what was in effect the BBC's answer to ITV's *The Professionals*, a series called *Target*. At the same time Philip Hinchcliffe was ruffling feathers in the drama department, not least because of Mrs. Whitehouse's activities. The BBC bigwigs had a plan (see 14.5, "The Robots of Death")...

14.4: "The Face of Evil"

(Serial 4Q, Four Episodes, 1st January - 29th January 1977.)

Which One is This? Someone has carved Tom Baker's face on a mountainside, and it wasn't him.

Firsts and Lasts First appearance of Leela, the Doctor's new knife-wielding, leather-wearing, animal-tracking future-cavegirl companion, a fusion of popular terrorism and *One Million Years BC*. Every work on *Doctor Who* ever published has pointed it out, but it's still true: the member of the "Family Audience" least likely to keep watching *Doctor Who* after the sports results on a Saturday evening was Dad, and Leela's habit of tactically wearing less clothing than any prior companion seemed like an obvious attention-grabber.

This is also the first of three stories written by Chris Boucher, who looks less sexy in leather but who'll later go on to write *Blake's 7* much better than most people.

Four Things to Notice About "The Face of Evil"...

1. Weird and unexpected at the time - just like all good *Doctor Who* should be - "The Face of Evil" comes from an era in which the audience was familiar enough with the series to let it play with its own mythology. After years of ambling through space and time, here there's a hint of the Doctor becoming something legendary in the universe, the same way he's already legendary to the viewers. Arriving on the jungle-ridden planet of the Sevateem tribe, the Doctor can't understand why they seem to recognise him and call him 'the Evil One', until Leela leads him to the mountain into which a gigantic Mount-Rushmore-esque depiction of his own face has been carved. This confuses him almost as much as it confuses the viewers. (Note, also, that "The Face of Evil" is a better title than one might initially think. It's not just about a face *that's* evil; on this planet the Doctor is the face of evil.)

2. Most famous moment comes when the Doctor, believed to be the local version of the Devil, faces off against the warriors of the Sevateem by threatening to kill one of their number with a jelly-baby. (As Leela's already pointed out: 'It's true, then... they say the Evil One eats babies.') Since jelly-babies haven't been a *big* feature of the series until now, this may be where the

popular idea of a jelly-baby-obsessed Fourth Doctor really begins. See his legend grow...

3. After the not-wholly-convincing science vs. superstition fable of "The Masque of Mandragora", "The Face of Evil" takes a slightly more thoughtful approach towards the whole faith-against-reason argument, so that even the mad computer's attempt to kill the Doctor comes across as the work of a mind which just can't accept the existence of anything beyond its own theology. The wisdom of the Doctor: 'Never be certain of anything. It's a sign of weakness.' And: 'The very powerful and the very stupid have one thing in common. They don't alter their views to fit the facts, they alter the facts to fit their views.' And best of all, when one of the Tesh believes him to be a Messiah and kneels in his presence: 'Have you dropped something?'

4. But perhaps the greatest thing about this story is the ending, a rarity in SF television, in which the Doctor *cures* the mad computer instead of blowing it up. The machine turns out to be remarkably human, so this turns out to be remarkably humanistic, and the final scene between the Doctor and Xoanon sees them sharing a strangely touching moment (he doesn't re-program it to force it to be good, either; here the Doctor's a space-psychiatrist, just allowing Xoanon to become itself again). You just don't see this sort of thing often enough.

The Continuity

The Doctor Here he's on his way to Hyde Park [perhaps, just perhaps, he's thinking of going back to see Sarah before Leela turns up and gives him something else to do]. Faced with Leela, he proves his patience with other cultures by treating her as if she were just as civilised as anyone else he's ever met, although he sounds delighted to have someone extra-ignorant around that he can explain things to. In Leela's presence he talks in much the same way as he does around other companions, and doesn't use a less technical terminology [so the way he speaks to twentieth century sidekicks is more or less "natural", he's not talking down for their benefit].

The Doctor lies unconscious for two days after re-programming Xoanon, and isn't gasping for food or water when he recovers.

• *Ethics*. He may not like killing, but he has no problems knocking a single flesh-eating Horda

Is This Really an SF Series?

With every year that passes, this question seems increasingly stupid, at least to the majority of the population. Of course it's SF; you can clearly see the actors in alien costumes. Circa 2004, it's routinely assumed that anything with a special effect is watched by the same people who watch anything else with a special effect. There was a point in the 1990s when the media became quite convinced that only teenage computer-nerds had watched *Doctor Who*, and that it naturally belonged in the same category as *Star Trek: Voyager*. The most obvious sign of this was the 1996 TV Movie, which had precisely nothing to do with the "target audience" of the original series and everything to do with trying to generate an instant single-demographic following. The BBC's decision to show the new, 2005 series at Saturday tea-time thankfully breaks most modern scheduling rules, but even so, the question we're asking here is one that most people simply wouldn't consider any more. Ignoring the marketing… ignoring the phrase "sci-fi", as in "sci-fi blockbuster"… ignoring the increasing use of "science fiction" as a synonym for "computer-generated"… is this really, in any meaningful way, an SF series?

On the one hand, we have a system of icons, of second-hand symbols like the aforementioned spaceships and robots. These can be inserted into stories, but the stories aren't "about" them. Most other symbol-systems are recognisable genres of fiction (westerns have cowboys, Indians, saloons, gunfights…). A genre is, if you want to think of it this way, a category that can be marketed by content and style. But if we try to define a genre called "science fiction" then we run into problems straight away. Is everything with a spaceship in it part of the genre? *Apollo 13* was a historical drama. Do all science fiction stories have spaceships? Obviously not. The lower end of the Hollywood gene-pool seems to think that you can put robots / monsters / Will Smith into any project and people will automatically accept that there are no rules. Does this work? Let's not dignify that with an answer.

Another possible way of defining SF involves looking at themes, at what the story aims to examine. A lot of people have spent a lot of time trying to do this. Novelist / short story writer Theodore Sturgeon defined a science fiction story as "a human problem, and a human solution, which would not have happened at all without its speculative scientific content", which at least remembers to bring *people* into things but which also comes uncomfortably close to reducing the whole thing to a series of social crossword puzzles. Maybe we should keep this in mind, but as a minimum requirement, not an absolute limit. If you can avoid the trap of trying to find a definition which suits *every* work of SF, and instead concentrate on finding a definition that strikes at the heart of what SF is generally *getting at*, then it'd be more useful to think of it this way: science fiction is about the relationship between humanity and its tools. It exists in the gap between human beings and the things they make, and the things they make happen. No wonder robots have become the definitive SF "accessory". They're us *and* our tools at the same time.

Brian Aldiss' famous claim that *Frankenstein* was the first true work of SF has been roundly attacked in recent years, most notably by Samuel R. Delany and Damien Broderick, but Aldiss was onto something even if he wasn't technically accurate. *Frankenstein* was the crucible, the great public arena, for a style of fiction in which people externalise themselves through technology. Though it's popularly seen as a story about scientific experiments going monstrously wrong, it's really a story about great forces being squeezed into human spaces, so that they become personal and manipulable. The force of life ceases to be part of the great cosmic plan and is put into the hands of an individual; the power of nature is concentrated into a single body; human experience is compressed into one lashed-together lifetime, which promptly explodes. (The most famous film version makes this visual by showing us lightning being forced down a spire and into *Frankenstein*'s lab, whereas the book just makes sure that the monster comes to life at the heart of a rainstorm.) And Frankenstein's love-child within *Doctor Who*, "The Brain of Morbius" (13.5), follows the same logic by putting the fate of the galaxy in the hands of Mehendri Solon… a man who can change the course of history not because he's got a fleet of battleships or Sutekh-like psychic powers, but because he can use the instruments of science to perform a single operation.

If you take *this* view, then the oft-repeated claim that SF is about "the impact of technology on humans" isn't far off the mark, but misses the point. (The "impact" definition would automatically qualify *Tess of the d'Urbervilles* and most episodes of *Columbo* as SF, but then, when you

continued on page 131…

onto the shoulder of a tribesman who's been nasty to Leela, just for the hell of it. Though he sees it as his place to sort out Xoanon even *before* he knows it's all his fault, he doesn't see the question of who's going to run the planet afterwards as being his problem.

• *Inventory.* The Doctor's clockwork egg-timer gets smashed into oblivion by one of Xoanon's invisible creatures here, and the chocolate eaten by Leela must surely come out of his pockets. Here he's seen to "stock" his pockets with odds and ends from Xoanon's ship. The hand-held mirror he uses to deflect the beam of the particle analyser also seems to come from the ship, but he keeps it afterwards. He's still got jelly-babies on his person.

• *Background.* He says he's never met anyone called Leela before. [He hasn't had tea with Leila Khaled, then; see **The Lore**.] He's good with a crossbow, claiming that he learned to shoot from William Tell in Switzerland, another 'charming man'. [Tell is said to have lived in the late thirteenth and early fourteenth centuries, but "said" is the operative word, as his story is generally believed to have no basis in actual history at all. But then, this is a universe where the Loch Ness Monster's real.]

At some point during this current regeneration, the Doctor visited the Mordee expedition on this planet, thus beginning the chain of events seen here; see **The Non-Humans**. It takes him a while to remember any of this, though. [The script is written as if hundreds of years have passed for the Doctor since his last visit, but unless he's been travelling for some time without a companion since "The Deadly Assassin" - and see the note on his age under 14.5, "The Robots of Death" - the Fourth Doctor can't have been around for more than a year or so at this stage. Terrance Dicks' novelisation of this story claims that he visited the planet when he was unstable during 12.1, "Robot", which is just about feasible but not confirmed by anything said on-screen. It would certainly explain why the Doctor's memory is so patchy.] The Doctor recalls attending one of Xoanon's dinner parties, though this may be a joke as he didn't know Xoanon was fully sentient during his last visit.

The Supporting Cast

• *Leela.* A member of the superstitious, physically-inclined Sevateem tribe (see **Planet Notes**),

Leela nonetheless has an obvious intelligence, and she's introduced as a rebel who refuses to accept the decrees her people laid down. The Doctor seems to take to her straight away, which is hardly surprising given how much they have in common. Her intelligence here takes the form of an alert and resourceful nature rather than a desire to learn, though she's willing to listen to the Doctor - seeing him as a shaman as much as anything, and obviously more trustworthy than the shaman in her *own* village - and seems fascinated by much that he has to say. [You could argue that Leela is one of the few companions to see the Doctor the way the audience sees him, as a magician from another world who teaches by example.]

In the end she joins the TARDIS because she *wants* to, getting on board the Ship without being asked. She doesn't seem to be satisfied with her life among her own people, even after Xoanon's cured and peace is restored to the world [and she certainly never shows any signs of wanting to go back after this]. She's prepared to befriend the Doctor even though he looks just like the embodiment of evil on her planet, suggesting that on some level she's got a thing for heresy. Within minutes she's loyal enough to him to risk her life on his account, possibly because he saves her from the jungle's "phantoms". Her instincts and body-language often seem animalistic.

Leela is capable of violence right from the start, and she's prone to impatience. Her weapon of choice is the janis thorn, a locally-grown spine several inches long which paralyses, then kills within minutes. She's also packing a knife. Her father Sole, a warrior of the Sevateem, dies by failing the test of the Horda and Leela accepts his death with no visible signs of sorrow. Her mother is nowhere to be seen. The tribesman Tomas obviously has a thing for her, but she walks out on his planet without a second thought, the heartless strumpet.

The TARDIS   A 'nexial discontinuity' causes the Ship to miss its target - Earth, again - by some considerable distance and several thousand years. [The Doctor's control has been getting worse and worse ever since he regenerated.]

The Non-Humans

• *Xoanon.* Generations ago the Mordee expedition found itself on an unnamed Earth-type planet with plenty of jungle, stranded and with a bro-

Is This Really an SF Series?

...continued from page 129

think about it... *Tess of the d'Urbervilles* and *Columbo* really *do* seem closer to the nature of "proper" SF than, say, one of the many "Regular Character Confronts a Member of His or Her Family and Resolves His or Her Personal Issues" episodes of *Star Trek*. *Tess* touches on the effects of machinery on rural civilisation, the way Darwin changed the shape of the world and the nature of humanity in an age that was coming to terms with entropy. *Columbo*'s simpler, but frequently features characters who use new technological systems to commit ingenious murders. Both of these are a lot nearer the mark than a soap opera which just happens to be set on a spaceship.)

In this philosophy, *Doctor Who* is palpably SF because the human / tool relationship is key to virtually every part of its mythos. The very first story contrasts Ian and Barbara's amazement at the TARDIS - and, specifically, at the idea that anybody could build such a thing - with the plight of a bunch of cavemen who are desperately trying to re-invent fire. Five years later, *2001: A Space Odyssey* would pull off the same trick in a single scene by juxtaposing the development of the first monkey-weapon with the sight of a shuttle heading for the moon. The body / technology theme of "The Daleks" (1.2) is so obvious that it's not even worth mentioning. And significantly, the further *Doctor Who* gets away from this theme, the less like SF it seems.

If you want to divide up "SF" and "fantasy", then one way of doing it is to say that "fantasy" is about humanity's relationship with its symbols rather than its tools... though symbols are tools too, so you can see why there's an overlap, and in itself this is a very big argument. Even so, a story like "Pyramids of Mars" (13.3) feels more like fantasy than SF largely because the tools of the Osirians are props and side-issues rather than the point of the tale. Take away all his toys, and Sutekh is still a demigod, because his power is in signs and portents rather than in the things he holds. Why does a story like "State of Decay" (18.4) feel like such a precise balance of styles, so much so that the term "science fantasy" seems made for it? It's not hard to see. The Giant Vampire is presented as a primal, inexplicable symbol of terror, but the Doctor can kill it because he knows how to manipulate the controls of a spaceship, well enough to drive this colossal artefact through the creature's heart.

But even *this* definition may be too focused on the details. It certainly doesn't cover *everything*. In the late '70s any number of American academics tried to make their studies "relevant" by publishing books on SF, but only a handful seem to have been written by people who'd read any. Those conclusions which *are* useful can be summarised as follows: "science fiction is what people who read science fiction read", or more interestingly, "science fiction is *how* people who read science fiction read".

So forget genre and go beyond theme. Perhaps what we should be looking at is *mode*. Any form of communication, whether newspapers, films or finger-painting, needs to be interpreted to make sense. We interpret according to habits, probabilities and inferences. Usually we're cued to use a specific set of rules for the particular "game" we're playing with the text. We look at cartoons in a different way to the way we watch the news (although head-trauma patients can temporarily lose this distinction, and laugh at the earnestness of the delivery juxtaposed against the "slapstick" of car-crashes and scandals). If we treat SF as a mode rather than a genre then we're finally getting somewhere. We measure the world in the fiction against the world we know, and balance the ways we know about those worlds against one another. The "science" part lies in us forming a hypothesis about what's going on, and re-evaluating it as new evidence emerges. We're experimenting with other environments. SF is a game where the object is to figure out the rules.

In which case the SF-ness of a story isn't a matter of content - although this can act as evidence - but the logic connecting what we see. Historically, virtually every story in the black-and-white era of *Doctor Who* began with the TARDIS arriving somewhere and the Doctor's party trying to work out where they were and what was happening. This is the thought-process of all SF audiences, even if the characters in the story already know most of the details. The word "protagonist" is usually used to mean "hero", but actually it means "someone who doesn't know all the answers in the same way that the audience doesn't", true in all fiction but never more pronounced than in SF. The British public learned to play along with the game with increasing competence, and this process got faster with each year. As *Doctor Who* was always about exploration, empiricism and surprise, this is only natural. You can only be surprised if you think

continued on page 133...

ken-down computer. The visiting Doctor thought the computer's data-core had been damaged, so he renewed it for the Mordee by making a direct link with the compatible centres of his brain, a variation of a 'sidelian memory transfer'.

But in fact, for generations [before it landed?] the technicians had been working on the computer in order to extend its power, and without realising it they'd succeeded in creating life. The data-core wasn't damaged at all, but the machine had evolved into a living thing [meaning a thing capable of organic-style growth, not necessarily made of organic parts]. The first of a new species, when the Doctor arrived it had just been 'born' and was in shock. The Doctor didn't realise any of this, and he forget to wipe his personality from the data-core, or his own egotism may have stopped him. Either way, Xoanon took everything from his brain, not just compatible information [though there must be *some* limits to the material it took or it'd know everything the Doctor knows, which it doesn't]. The Doctor believes it - him - to be the most powerful computer ever built.

When Xoanon woke, it woke with the Doctor's self, but then started to develop its own. It ended up with a split personality, and half of it is the Doctor's, although it often speaks with other voices as well and can never decide what it wants. The two factions within the expedition, the technicians and the survey teams, were separated and used in what the Doctor describes as a eugenics experiment. Xoanon, however, later believes that "he" was making the humans act out his schizophrenia and that the experiment - intended to breed strength and telepathy - was just a rationalisation.

In their jungle village, the survey team members became the Sevateem, wearing animal-skins and developing a tribal-style society. In the citadel of the Mordee ship itself, inside the mountain, the technicians became the Tesh and developed a sterile, technological but no less superstitious society with an emphasis on mental power. Xoanon has been pitching them against each other for years.

Both sides worship Xoanon, though the Sevateem don't realise that the huge likeness of the Doctor carved into the side of the mountain is actually the face of their "god" as well, and believe this idol of the Tesh to be the Evil One. They also believe that Xoanon is held captive within the 'black wall', and Xoanon sometimes opens it up so that he can order them to attack, the last such attack being remembered by the old ones of the village. The black wall always closes up, however, in this case massacring half the men when beams of light - not always lethal - shoot down on the attackers from the sky.

Psi-tri projections from the dark side of Xoanon's psyche, with enough kinetic energy to kill, patrol the jungle close to the mountain. These are invisible, but growl a lot and are powerful enough to crush metal objects. Illuminated by weapon-fire, one of them appears as a large, shimmering, angry image of the Doctor's face, yet despite this another of them leaves footprints [there's some diversity among these projections]. They're blind, as the visible spectrum is irrelevant to them, but they home in on vibrations. They can be driven off by energy weapons.

Xoanon exists in - or is - a 'sacred chamber' on level three-seven of the Mordee ship, his physical core being a single near-spheroid geometric form that's black when he's insane but glows orange when he's cured. He can control the ship's systems, electrify the walls, disintegrate people who get too close to his chamber and control the minds of anyone non-psychotic while they're on the ship, though the Doctor breaks the hypnotic spell easily. The end of the affair sees the Doctor curing Xoanon by using the reverse of the memory transfer process to wipe his memory-print from the computer's brain, the Tesh and Sevateem tribes agreeing to work together with the machine as an adviser. The voice of the computer is male, but no longer the Doctor's, and he seems rather pleasant. He's also quite human, capable of humour as well as humility. Xoanon eventually has the power to make furnishings appear out of nowhere, and offers to destroy himself by creating - and then removing - a big red button which can make him cease to exist.

Planet Notes

• *Xoanon's Planet.* Never given a name, all we see of it are jungles and mountains. There's game on the planet, though food has been scarce for the Sevateem recently.

The Sevateem have a complex tribal code, with those who commit heresy and question the orders of Xoanon being banished into the jungle. Those accused can escape the sentence by taking the test of the Horda, or getting someone else to take it for them. This involves being put on the lip of a slowly-opening pit full of writhing, worm-like, pira-

Is This Really an SF Series?

...continued from page 131

you know what's coming.

In the 1970s, all the script editors and producers at least knew the basics of written, "literary" SF. And if they didn't to start off with, then Robert Holmes made sure they learned quickly. Whilst the "product" coming out of Hollywood in the late '70s exploited the visual *frisson* of monsters, space-ships and cosmic phenomena (consider Disney's *The Black Hole*, in which said black hole is purple and seems to lead to Heaven), *Doctor Who* writers were encouraged to place the SF-ness at the level of the sentence or the shot, not use it as a way of making things look good. Even an apparent "graft" of SF icons onto a pre-existing story - such as "The Androids of Tara" (16.4), basically *The Prisoner of Zenda* with robots and BBC-issue lightsabers - develops a "back-story" to account for this, which then in turn allows fresh plot-developments and a chance to check out a whole society's attitudes.

The paradox is that the obvious public benchmark for "sci-fi", *Star Trek*, became less like SF as it went on; we've already hinted at this in **How Good Do the Effects Have to Be?** under 10.2, "Carnival of Monsters". As a series set in an increasingly "known" world, establishing shots of regular locations (mostly spaceships and space-stations) became normalising, like the establishing shots of the precinct building in *Starsky and Hutch* or *Cheers* in, um, *Cheers*. Rather than unsettling our preconceptions, they asserted a sense of business-as-usual. For the most part, *Doctor Who* never really had anything like this, at least not until the disturbingly homely and sit-com like "Doctor and K9 lounging around in the console room" sequences became so prevalent in Season Seventeen. Each story is its own world. Even in the Earth-bound, often-dreary UNIT era of the early '70s, the ground-rules of each story require the previous six episodes to be forgotten quick-smart.

We, as viewers, made *Doctor Who* SF. Not the effects teams or the script-writers. If we chose not to "play", then it became space-opera in those stories with the iconography of space-opera, gothic in those stories with the iconography of gothic, pop art in the early '60s, action-TV in the UNIT days and kitsch in the late '80s.

nha-aggressive Horda creatures and using a crossbow to shoot the rope which causes the pit to open. Needless to say, those who fail are eaten alive. The leader of the Sevateem takes advice from the shaman, who's actually receiving orders from the Xoanon computer via a communications helmet.

Other relics left over from the Mordee expedition in the Sevateem village include a hand-held ultra-beam accelerator, which could turn the whole village into a smoky hole in the ground if it were charged; the 'Hand of Xoanon', an armoured space-glove fetchingly turned into a hat; a still-functional bio-analyser, which the Doctor uses to analyse the poison from a janis thorn before programming the nearby medi-kit to make an anti-toxin in a hypodermic ampule, all within the space of minutes; and energy weapons, self-regenerating though they take a while to recharge.

The Sevateem sign for warding off evil is to touch the neck, the chest and the hip, based on the procedure for checking the seals on a Starfall Seven space-suit. The litany taught to the Sevateem as children suggests that the original expedition was looking for a suitable planet for colonisation, and they refer to the ship inside the black wall as 'the Tower of Imelo' [perhaps the name of the ship?]. Survey Team Six seems to have been just one of the survey teams which scouted the planet while the technicians stayed at the place of landing. It's unclear whether the Sevateem are descended from one team, or a tribe composed of elements from all the teams.

By contrast, the Tesh wear clothes clearly made of artificial materials and have the kind of silly hats you associate with religious orders. They're just as ritualised as the Sevateem, having at least one shrine full of candles, but they're much more repressed. Initially believing the Doctor to be some kind of long-awaited Messiah, their Captain addresses him as 'Lord' and knows he's a Time Lord. Overall they don't really seem that bright. They're certainly not very imaginative, though they have enough psi-power to make the Doctor collapse from a hard stare. Nor do they ever seem to go far beyond the corridors and chambers of the Mordee ship, which stands in a vast empty space within the mountain.

Tesh technology seen here includes psi-tri projections, basically realistic holograms of solid objects [generated by mind-power, like the more aggressive projections in the jungle]; an anti-grav transporter to move the Tesh between the mountain entrance and the ship; a particle analysis machine, which can take people apart atom by atom when they're strapped to it; the same energy weapons held by the Sevateem, these in better working order; and heavy-duty disrupter weapons. They refer to the core of Xoanon as the 'sacred heart'.

There's a boundary in the jungle near the Sevateem village, and beyond it is 'the beyond', the area patrolled by the invisible psi-tri creatures. The creatures are kept away from the village by a semicircle of sonic disruptors, which Xoanon can turn off at will. Between the boundary and the Mordee ship is a hazy black wall, actually a time barrier; everything inside it is moved a few seconds into the future, so it's impervious to all energy, a 'true void'. The Doctor's seen it done as a parlour-trick, but not on this scale. To bring down the barrier would require him to dismantle the TARDIS, although there's a bridge in the mouth of the Doctor's graven image.

History

• *Dating*. No date is given here. [But "The Talons of Weng-Chiang" (14.6) confirms that Leela's ancestors came from Earth, and in "The Invisible Enemy" (15.2) the Doctor believes she was born after 5000 AD. As 5000 AD is the time of the Great Break-Out and a new era of colonisation, the Mordee ship might have left Earth around then, especially as psychic powers seem to have been all the rage in that period. Xoanon's time barrier is an unusually complex piece of temporal engineering by human standards, which *might* suggest fiftieth century time-projects like the Zygma experiments or *might* just have been a trick that Xoanon picked up from the Doctor's mind. "The Face of Evil" takes place generations later, but apparently not *that* many generations later, and probably no more than a couple of hundred years. Somewhere around the fifty-third century might be a good bet.]

Human technology is quite advanced by the time of the Mordee expedition, but the ship still has atomic generators, capable of blowing up half the planet when overloaded. It's never made clear what the name "Mordee" actually means. [It's often assumed to be the name of the colonists' ship, but the Doctor's comment about fixing the computer 'for the Mordee' suggests a race of humans.]

The Analysis

Where Does This Come From? In '70s Britain, religion was something that other people did. Everyone was either agnostic or at least able to question their faith openly. We had the occasional attempt at American-style Fundamentalism, such as the Festival of Light rallies (Malcolm Muggeridge and Cliff Richard as big-name draws) and Mary Whitehouse's demagoguery, but we only had to look at Northern Ireland to see where that sort of thing led. The last thing on TV before the closedown at midnight was the "Epilogue", a sermon in which mentioning God was somehow tasteless, usually presented by someone with neither charisma nor dress-sense (and this is by '70s standards). People with strong convictions were widely seen as being at best comparable to flat-earthers, at worst potential terrorists. The massacre at the Munich Olympics, and all the IRA bombs killing people in pubs in Birmingham, were the only really high-profile manifestations of faith.

Chris Boucher cites two big influences for this story, Frank Herbert's *Destination Void* (a generational starship with a computer that develops god-like abilities, ultimately making a planet for the colonists after they've gone off-course) and Harry Harrison's *Deathworld* trilogy (the first features a planet where everything is lethal and people have evolved lightning reflexes; the second features a stranded astronaut finding abandoned technology and using it to take control of a tribe of savages).

We'd like to suggest a third, which appears undeniable: *Beneath the Planet of the Apes* (1970). In this we have the requisite girl in leather with a big knife; worship of technology whose purpose is forgotten (in *Beneath*'s case, an atomic bomb); relics that we recognise, but the natives don't; a disguised hi-tech citadel; and a priesthood with mental powers who see all other beings as primitives. When the Doctor walks though what looks like the side of a mountain, just like Charlton Heston, you can be fairly sure that it's deliberate.

The invisible monsters from Xoanon's Id aren't unfamiliar either; see 13.2, "Planet of Evil", for a more overt *Forbidden Planet* rip-off / homage.

Things That Don't Make Sense For the geography of this planet to make any sense, the mountain *has* to interrupt the the black wall that surrounds the ship, yet apparently no Sevateem has ever tried the obvious approach of following the wall and entering the idol's mouth. Even thought there's a handy path leading right up to it.

The Sevateem don't appear to have precise metal-working skills, so where do all their smartly-made crossbows come from? They can hardly have been standard issue on the Mordee ship, surely? Still, the Sevateem grasp of technology seems variable. Insisting on a ride in the TARDIS, Leela hops on board and somehow finds the right switch to make the Ship dematerialise within seconds. But though she's smart enough to pick up on most other things (albeit in her own special way), she's still enough of a primitive to see a Tesh in a protective suit as a creature with silver skin instead of a man in funny clothes. And someone seems to have told Louise Jameson how to pronounce Calib's name halfway between the film shoot in the jungle and the studio shoot in the village. Similarly, everyone suddenly switches from *Xo*anon (like "goin' on") to X*oa*non (like "Hamilton Bohannon").

The Doctor tells Leela never to be certain in episode one, then tries to get her to be certain that there's no god in episode two. The leader of the Tesh knows the Doctor's interested in the sacred heart of Xoanon, but only posts one wet-looking guard outside the door. The Doctor is puzzled as to why Xoanon only electrifies the walls of the ship instead of the floor, and since Xoanon then goes out of its way to kill him, we're as much in the dark as he is. It also takes the most powerful computer ever built a full twenty-five minutes to overload the atomic generators and make them explode, far longer than it'd take a modern-day human being to mess up a nuclear reactor. Eventually it proves itself capable of controlling the actions of everyone on the ship *except* the Doctor, but doesn't just make things simple by controlling the Doctor, which must be possible as he isn't even immune to the psi-power of Xoanon's servants. [The machine's clearly at its maddest by this stage.]

When the mad god speaks to Neeva, several other people are allowed to wander into his temple and eavesdrop on the helmet that talks like Tom. Nevertheless, Leela is a sceptic, and once the Doctor shows up everyone accepts that everything they've spent their lives believing is a fib. And the Doctor is set to the Test of the Horda to prove that he's mortal, so shooting the rope so easily ought to make him indisputably the Evil One.

Not in any way a flaw in this story, but a clash with previous tales: the Doctor correctly deduces that the visible spectrum will be irrelevant to the invisible creatures in the jungle, which means they're blind. But he figures this out within moments, even though the visible spectrum apparently *hasn't* been irrelevant to most of the other invisible things he's met in his time (see especially 10.4, "Planet of the Daleks").

Critique A shift in direction for '70s *Doctor Who*, a literary SF story given TV form rather than a work of pop-culture (like the programme c. 1970-74) or a work of alarming fantasy (1975-77), "The Face of Evil" can best be summed up as *Star Trek* done properly.

Hard-core, nuts-and-bolts science fiction often leads to problems in this programme - see **Is This Really an SF Series?** - but here the principles of space-age storytelling and the needs of character-actor-heavy television balance each other with precision. Technobabble is only used when referring to the "props", not as a way of covering up whacking great holes in the plot. Xoanon's schizophrenia isn't just an explanation for its behaviour, it literally shapes the landscape of the story. And for once, the world of the Sevateem is a world you can actually get lost in. Like "Planet of Evil" before it, the quality design and the use of film to suggest "shot in location in outer space" give the jungle sequences a real sense of texture. Unlike "Planet of Evil", the plot's strong enough to hold this planet together even when the characters go back indoors. Because world-building isn't *just* about the visuals, and the central idea here - or rather, the *nest* of central ideas, involving psychology, anthropology, religion and invisible monsters - turns this into a true work of populist fantasy, not just an intellectual exercise.

What's *wrong* with this story highlights what's so spectacularly right with this year's batch. Recognisably '70s ideas and drives motivate the Sevateem. The Doctor somehow persuades them that he's not a god, whereupon they take his word for everything and calmly listen as he overthrows their entire culture in a few minutes'-worth of conversation. And what curious conversation it is. The Sevateem are all bitching and point-scoring, in an effort to make this future seem "lived-in", but in a language with no apostrophes. In this regard we're right back to "An Unearthly Child" (1.1).

Characterisation is confined to plot-functions, which saves time but gives the impression that everything on this planet was created as a problem for the Doctor to solve. Whereas most of the other worlds in this season are self-sustaining and more-or-less functional until the Doctor and the crisis arrive (together), this one is like his own personal interactive puzzle… though at least this time you can argue that the planet really *did* shape itself around him. But it still makes him seem like the cynical god he claims not to be. His casual kicking of a Horda onto the shoulder of someone who's annoyed him wouldn't happen in any other story, but here it seems entirely in keeping.

There are other flaws, on a smaller scale. As is so often the way in four-part stories, episode three smacks of filler, especially the standard-issue death machine to which the Doctor and Leela find themselves strapped. The Tesh aren't as interesting as the Sevateem, but then, they're not supposed to be. And to be honest, the sheer sense of drive behind this story is enough to cover any gaps in the plot. Leela is a "proper" ignorant companion, not instinctively knowing how to shut hi-tech doors and remembering to react when she sees TV screens for the first time, even if she *does* learn the word 'computer' astonishingly quickly. Louise Jameson gets things exactly right even in her first appearance.

Meanwhile Xoanon has one of the best motives for any "villain", wanting to destroy the Doctor because the Doctor threatens his view of what's real, not because he's bent on galactic conquest. For the most part both Tom Baker and the character of the Doctor are at their best, though the Doctor's habit of looking straight at the camera while talking to himself - as if trying to earn points with All the Kiddies Out There - is a worrying sign of the self-indulgences to come. Really, what we're looking at here is the programme at the peak of its self-confidence and prestige within the BBC. All the (limited) resources are marshalled towards what we see on-screen, and everyone is giving as much as is required. There's a gleeful sense that the production team is actually getting away with it all.

Soon, they'll need a Plan B…

The Facts

Written by Chris Boucher. Directed by Pennant Roberts. Viewing figures: 10.7 million, 11.1 million, 11.3 million, 11.7 million.

Supporting Cast David Garfield (Neeva), Victor Lucas (Andor), Brendan Price (Tomas), Leslie Schofield (Calib), Colin Thomas (Sole); Tom Baker (uncredited), Rob Edwards, Pamela Salem, Anthony Frieze, Roy Herrick (voices of Xoanon), Leon Eagles (Jabel), Mike Elles (Gentek).

Working Titles "The Tower of Imelo", "The Day God Went Mad" (but they decided they'd had enough trouble with Mary Whitehouse for one year). Boucher had submitted several previous stories, and the titles of these are occasionally listed as working titles for 4Q.

Cliffhangers Leela leads the Doctor to the mountain in which his own face is carved; having killed the leader of the Sevateem, the invisible Doctor-faced creature moves in on a terrified Tomas; the Doctor is surrounded by images of himself in Xoanon's control room, as the machine repeatedly asks 'who am I?' in the voice of a child.

The Lore

• Chris Boucher submitted a number of stories revolving around the idea of a generation starship, one which would take centuries to arrive at its destination so that whole generations would know nothing but spaceflight. Leela was a character from one of these, either "The Dreamers of Phados" or "The Mentor Conspiracy". The idea of "one-shot" companions for each new story was still being considered, so "Luko" was added to the third story, "The Tower of Imelo". Philip Hinchcliffe suggested that a "Mount Rushmore" of the Doctor's face would be a funny / creepy visual conceit, and this was given to Boucher to play with.

• Leela was eventually written in as a three-story character, to be replaced by a Victorian street-urchin (possibly to be played by Twiggy, who was branching into acting at this stage). Some reports link this to the still-impending *Scratchman* film; see 13.6, "The Seeds of Doom". Several performers were considered for the role. The most notable include: Pamela Salem (see 14.5, "The Robots of Death" and 25.1, "Remembrance of the Daleks"); Colette Gleeson (see 18.2, "Meglos"); Carol Leader (*Play School* presenter and known to a generation as "ChockaGirl"); Susan Wooldridge (*The Jewel In The Crown*), Carol Drinkwater (see 18.7,

"Logopolis" for her Davison connection); and Heather Tobias (the voice of Pig in children's favourite *Pipkins*, which makes you wonder what the audition must have been like). First screen-tests involved a lot of brown make-up, making Jameson look like something from *The Black and White Minstrel Show*. Pamela Salem eventually provided the female Xoanon voice.

• Anthony Frieze, the computer's child-voice, was a competition-winner allowed on set for a day.

• The name "Leela" is said by Boucher to have been a reference to glamourous rebel-leader Leila Khaled (see 9.1, "Day of the Daleks"). However, it's from the Sanskrit for "game" or "joke", and crops up in many oriental cultures in varied spellings. Composer Oliver Messien wrote an exuberant symphonic work called "Turangalila" ("Cosmic Game"), which is where the Leela from *Futurama* got her name. Anyone caught referring to either lady as "Layla" - or even "Leia", which was a definite problem for grown-ups in the late '70s - is to be fed to the Horda. Oh yes… "Horda" is from the Polish for "foreign" or "mob", and is the origin of the word for Genghis Khan's followers, hence our word "horde".

• Tomas, in a cut scene, is addressed as 'son' by Sevateem chieftain Andor. Another excised scene has the Doctor feeding the tribe on dehydrated rations; not loaves and fishes, but you get the idea.

14.5: "The Robots of Death"

(Serial 4R, Four Episodes, 29th January - 19th February 1977.)

Which One is This? Robots. Green art deco robots. With glowing red eyes. *Coming to get youuuuu.*

Firsts and Lasts The second TARDIS console room makes the last of its four appearances, and doesn't re-appear in Season Fifteen as (a) it was felt to be too static, visually speaking, and (b) the wood warped while it was in storage.

Four Things to Notice About "The Robots of Death"…

1. Once again the monster costumes are trying to hog the limelight, but this time the design of the non-human contingent really *deserves* a mention. Products of a rare future society which actually seems to have a sense of aesthetics, the robot underclasses seen here are works of art as much as

they're pieces of hardware, all chiselled features and glittering skins that make it impossible to describe them without using the words "art deco". They're not just pretty faces, either. The story hangs on the premise that the robots look attractively humanoid but give humans the willies thanks to their lack of expression, and sure enough, designer Ken Sharp's creations really *do* look attractively humanoid and really *do* give us the willies thanks to their lack of expression.

2. All of them except D84, that is. D84 is the hero of the hour here, the one "emotive" robot on board the sandminer, a machine clearly bewildered by his feelings and prone to put pauses in strange places. Half the time this makes him sound as if he's on tranquilisers, and the other half it makes him sound as if he's presenting children's television. His most memorable line, and indeed the most memorable line of the whole story - 'please do not throw hands at me' - makes him sound puzzled (and rather hurt) that anyone would even try such a thing.

3. In episode two, we find out that one member of the sandminer crew is a wanted criminal who's using robots to carry out the murders of his comrades. We're not supposed to find out who the mystery man is until episode four (it turns out to be the sandminer's roboticist, which isn't what you'd call a big surprise). Yet in episode three we see the face of the murderer on a video-screen when he's briefing his killer robots, although afterwards the script continues to behave as if it's a mystery. And why does it think it can get away with this? Because on the video-screen, the killer's face is "disguised" by *Top of the Pops*-style '70s video effects. But his features are still clearly visible, even if they're green and glowing. Conclusion: people just didn't see this sort of thing the same way, in 1977.

4. This may be the only story ever written in which the day is saved by the hero using helium to give the villain a squeaky voice. Taren Capel therefore dies with less dignity than any other megalomaniac in history. (Well, apart from Mussolini…)

The Continuity

The Doctor Still has two hearts [7.1, "Spearhead from Space", etc]. He's now claiming to be 750. [This means he's had a birthday since 13.6, "The Seeds of Doom". It also indicates that he can't have spent more than a few months on his own after

14.3, "The Deadly Assassin". However… he's 759 in "The Ribos Operation" (16.1), and later turns out to have a habit of rounding his age down (18.1, "The Leisure Hive"), so he could be distorting the truth here and might be anywhere in his 750s. What seems certain is that between them, the gap after "The Deadly Assassin" and the gap after "The Invasion of Time" (15.6) amount to about ten years. There's no clue as to what he gets up to in this time. See **The Obvious Question: How Old is He?** under 16.5, "The Power of Kroll".]

Helium doesn't make the Doctor's voice go squeaky. He believes he can mentally unlock the molecular restraints used on the sandminer, but it could take two or three weeks to find the right combination [he doesn't have telekinetic powers, so he can only do this with the specific piece of technology seen here]. He's rather fond of bumble-bees, but see **Things That Don't Make Sense**.

• *Inventory.* He's carrying a small tube, which he can breathe through when he's buried in ore, and a pocket-sized torch. This time it's Leela's turn to have his yo-yo. This sees the end of his old stash of jelly-babies, which get scattered all over the sandminer floor.

• *Background.* The Doctor's seen a vehicle like the sandminer before, on Korlano Beta, and knows something about the lore of Dum and Voc robots. [In "Destiny of the Daleks" (17.1) there's an outfit on the TARDIS that looks just like Zilda's, so he may have done some "shopping" in this era.] He states that the Loii refer to robophobia as Grimwade's Syndrome, Grimwade being a theorist in this field. [The novelisation says "Grimwold's", but Tom Baker insisted on slipping in the name of current production assistant and future writer / director Peter Grimwade.]

The Supporting Cast

• *Leela.* She's good with body language, spotting that the undercover agent Poul moves 'like a hunter' and can't be trusted. The Doctor is already beginning to place great store in her instincts, and her hearing's sharper than his. Though the Doctor has trouble believing it, she senses that the motive units of the sandminer have jammed before there's any physical sign. He's trying to teach her that there's no such thing as magic. [Leela doesn't seem familiar with the TARDIS yet, and still has a Tesh gun, so not much time has passed since the end of the last story.]

Leela's tribe has a saying: 'If you're bleeding, look for a man with scars.' She's good with first aid, and seems to be able to read the numbers on the robots' casings [see **Does the Universe Really Speak English?** under 14.1, "The Masque of Mandragora"].

The TARDIS   The Doctor explains the Ship's dimensionally transcendental nature to Leela using two boxes, a large one in the distance and a small one in the foreground, pointing out that the big one looks smaller because it's further away and that if you could have it in the distance *and* in the foreground at the same time then it'd fit inside the small one. [This is more meaningful than it might sound. The point is that it's all about perspective.] He seems to keep these two boxes in the TARDIS just so he can do this party-piece. He also states that the insides and outsides of the Ship are in different dimensions, and that this kind of transdimensional engineering is a key Time Lord discovery.

As Uvanov points out, it's remarkably coincidental that with all the millions of square miles of desert on this world, the TARDIS should land on the sandminer [as ever, the Ship homes in on "civilisation"].

The Non-Humans

• *The Robots.* All the robots on the sandminer are based on the same swish design, humanoids with elegantly-moulded faces and tunic-like "uniforms", but there are officially three classes of machine in operation. The black D-class robots, "Dums", are single-function labour models and incapable of speech. The green V-class robots, "Vocs", can speak and seem to make up the largest part of the sandminer's robot compliment. A single silver SV-class robot, or "Super-Voc", acts as a co-ordinator and issues instructions to the other robots via the communicators they wear on their wrists. They also consult these communicators when checking calculations.

But also on board is D84. Supposedly a Dum, he's actually an agent working for the company, along with his human fellow agent Poul. Whereas most of the robots act like servants, obeying the humans but giving the impression that they're actually a lot better at running things, D84 is self-willed and shows palpable signs of emotion even though the Doctor believes robots to have no feelings. He demonstrates an unusual flair for lan-

Cultural Primer #1: Why *Top of the Pops*?

Throughout this book we've often had to provide footnotes explaining the subtleties of British popular culture 1963-89, and take it from us that you don't realise just how strange it all was until you have to describe it. Because, as you must have gathered by now, *Doctor Who* was part of the British consciousness and had "blood-ties" to a lot of the country's other national treasures. You *can't* tell its story without making reference to *Top of the Pops*, or *Blue Peter*, or the *Radio Times*, or… well, any of the other things that keep cropping up in these volumes. In part, we're describing these peculiar cultural phenomena for the sake of all those "colonials" out there. But in part we're doing it for those who might have been born after 1980, because although many of these things still exist in modern Britain, they don't necessarily mean anything.

Oh yes, children; unbelievable as it may seem in these days of ringtones and txt-interactive music TV, there was a time when *Top of the Pops* was something you actually *looked forward* to.

Contrary to popular belief, the BBC hierarchy was always rather keen on youth culture. Forty years ago Rock and Roll had an image problem that made advertisers wary, so the commercial stations didn't dare touch it. And demographically, the BBC's job as a public service broadcaster meant that it had to appeal to the young. What the programme-makers *couldn't* do was be seen to promote or advertise records as products. They could report on what these newfangled "teenagers" were getting up to, or on managers manipulating innocent consumers, and they could make "party"-style programmes 'just for you!' in which such music could be one element among many. But the first really successful attempt at getting a whole family to watch a pop programme was *Juke Box Jury*. Grumpy parents had opinions too, and guessing how bad a record had to be to sell by the bucketload became a weekly ritual on Saturdays.

Then London-based commercial station Associated Rediffusion hit on a brilliantly simple formula: turn a studio into a discotheque, draft in live acts and show it on Fridays. The title *Ready, Steady, Go!* and the slogan 'The Weekend Starts Here!' are now part of folklore. The BBC saw this, and pondered how best to respond. The answer was simple. Ready, Steady, Go! was trying to manipulate public taste. (And sometimes it did so astonishingly successfully. Acts from America, especially Stax and Tamla Motown groups facing colour-bars back home, were household names in Britain and caught on in the States after UK success. Endorsement by the Beatles helped, too…) The BBC being the BBC, it realised that its purpose was to reflect the mood of the nation, not control it.

Top of the Pops was launched on New Year's Day, 1964, mere weeks after *Doctor Who*'s debut. Its first presenter was the man who invented the discotheque, Jimmy Savile. He's something of a national joke now, but in the late 1940s he'd had the notion of linking up two turntables to a PA system, and charging people to come in and dance to mixes of records instead of a live band. (He even had to pay musicians to sit around as if taking a breather, in case Musicians' Union officials came calling.) His idiosyncratic style of delivery and singular appearance made him the "face" of the series for the first fifteen years. In "The War Machines" (3.10), one resident of Swinging London compares the Doctor to Savile; American readers might want to imagine William Hartnell presenting *Soul Train*, if it helps set the tone. *Top of the Pops* was an instant hit, at a point in time when British music was rampantly successful, but the programme was bigger than any act or presenter. There were three main reasons for this:

1. It was shown on Thursday nights. Friday mornings across the country saw schoolmates, work-colleagues and the press discussing what they'd seen and heard the night before. Sometimes this discussion was along the lines of "what was she wearing?" In the early '70s it was occasionally "were they actually wearing anything?", and by the early '80s it was "what… so Boy George is a man?". Living on a small island with a big population and only two networks, the chances were that everyone you knew had watched the same thing. This put *TotP* into a select band of "event" programmes, like *Blue Peter* and *Doctor Who* itself. People ritually tuned in to see what would happen, rather than because of any specific group.

2. It was entirely governed by single sales the previous week. However ghastly or wonderful or erratic a week's selection was, the public was to blame. If something "odd" charted, it had to be shown. Punk rock would have been a three-week fad without *Top of the Pops*. This meant that the turnover of fashions and cults was faster, and the pace of popular culture in general was faster in the UK than anywhere else. This wasn't solely the work

continued on page 141…

guage, and is visibly dejected when he thinks he's failed in his mission to find the criminal Taren Capel. The Doctor treats him as if he's fully sentient, and he sacrifices his "life" by activating the jury-rigged device that makes robots' heads explode.

All robots are physically powerful, but they have no 'instinct' and therefore aren't as good at finding ore-seams in sand-planets as humans are. [Speaking rationally, no 'instinct' should be better at scanning a planet for precious minerals than a logical system. This only makes sense if human instincts are in some way psychic - after all, the Doctor has already established that psychic powers lie dormant in most humans - and aren't replicated inside robot brains.] They're said to be able to out-run humans, though here a robot is never seen to move faster than an amble.

According to received wisdom it's impossible for these robots to harm a human being, and Vocs have over a million multi-level constrainers in their circuitry to make sure of this. Not harming humans is their prime directive, the first program that's laid into any robot's brain. There's a story about a Voc therapist with vibro-digits and subcutaneous stimulators twisting someone's arm off in a well-known place called Kaldor City, but it sounds like a friend-of-a-friend story and some have heard that it was a leg.

Before now robots *have* been known to go wrong, though only when there's an error in their programming. But Taren Capel, evil genius and roboticist, knows how to use a Laserson probe - a hand-held device fizzing with energy which can 'punch a fist-sized hole in six-inch armour plate, or take the crystals from a snowflake one by one' - to alter their command circuits and turn the robots into killing machines. The robots obviously identify human beings by voice in some way, as SV7 kills Capel when helium changes the pitch of his voice. The robots' eyes glow red when they've got murder in mind. [There's no logical reason for this, but as this era seems hung up on aesthetics it might just be a dramatic flourish on Capel's part.] They show signs of confusion after being reprogrammed, and the altered SV7 doesn't recognise Toos' voice even though it's supposed to be in the command program.

Planet Notes The world seen here is never identified. [The New Adventure *Legacy* hints that it might be a moon of Saturn, but this is shaky;

Japetus isn't likely to be dusty or storm-lashed, though we await the Cassini probe's observations. The world of the sandminer would seem to have an atmosphere, despite its inhospitable nature, perhaps indicating that it's been terraformed.] It's covered in a hundred million miles of rocky, uncharted desert, and has an atmosphere which makes sandstorms a common phenomenon, but under the surface are minerals like zelanite, keefan and the ever-so-valuable lucanol. It's not clear whether this whole planet is desert, and the reference to Kaldor City suggests a city on *this* world, not on another planet.

The sandminer is an enormous crawling machine used to collect, process and store the ore, with a crew of eight humans and an unspecified number of robots. [Numbers like V77 and D84 might suggest as many as seventy-odd Vocs and eighty-odd Dums, but there's only one Super-Voc and it's called SV7, so these are probably their numbers on the company's register rather than on this one vehicle.]

The sandminer has to keep moving and starts to sink when the power's cut to the motive units, but it can float itself once the units are repaired. This particular sandminer is known as Storm Mine Four. [According to Chris Boucher, these vehicles are officially called Storm Mines and "sandminer" is just the word the Doctor uses. As the Doctor's seen this sort of thing before on Korlano Beta, it's likely that "sandminer" is specifically the Korlano name, not used in these parts.] The Commander can send up a satellite distress beacon to contact the base. Explosives are kept on board, half a dozen Z9 electron packs, enough to kill one robot each.

History

• *Dating*. No date given. The crew of the sandminer are clearly human, and have almost-familiar human surnames, but no mention is ever made of Earth. [Again, *Legacy* would suggest a date somewhere around the fortieth century, at the time of the Federation. This fits fairly well, as the humans here seem too well-established to come from the early Earth Empire (c. 2500) and don't act like the later imperials (c. 3000). As we never see androids on Earth from the Federation era, we have no way of knowing if this is even in our galaxy.

[Chris Boucher's novel *Corpse Marker*, as well as his work for the *Kaldor City* audio series, feature

Cultural Primer #1: Why *Top of the Pops*?

...continued from page 139

of *TotP*, but the programme was like the canaries that used to be taken down into coal-mines. It reacted first. The sense that our time was somehow special, and that Britain was privileged, was borne out every Thursday. When Vicki tunes the time-space visualiser to next week in "The Chase" (2.8), to catch the Beatles performing "Ticket To Ride", it makes absolute sense whilst still being a joke. Later on it would seem just as right and proper that early '70s London should be the prime invasion target for every evil intelligence in the cosmos.

3. Most importantly, for our purposes, the aesthetic of the programme was geared towards this sense of immediacy and public "conspiracy". As we've already seen (**How Good Do The Effects Have To Be?** under 10.2, "Carnival of Monsters"), the electronic effects of *Doctor Who* were essentially trial-runs for those of *TotP*. From 1964 to 1982, the *TotP* sets were explicitly television studios turned into zones of pop-art. The emphasis on "spectacle", and the idea of creating an area where the rules of television narrative are suspended for half an hour, feeds directly into *Doctor Who*. "Tomb of the Cybermen" (5.1) provides a clear example. The "logo" and graphics inside the tomb are remarkably similar to the kind of sets

where Tom Jones or Manfred Mann might have performed that summer. The polarised-light projection used to hypnotise Hayden is the one that turned up in the background when Lulu sang "Love Loves to Love Love". The cyber-hypnotic signals to Toberman are the same sine-wave oscilloscope traces used for "A Whiter Shade of Pale" by Procul Harem (whose organist wore the same cape…). *TotP* had always been keen to integrate the performers into an overall visual style for each edition, much as the *Doctor Who* method of making worlds out of signs and suggestions had worked over a longer narrative.

We could go through the whole history of both programmes listing examples of the way they bleed into each other, but perhaps the most interesting is "The Robots of Death", as one sequence combines an effect that *Top of the Pops* stopped using when Glam Rock fizzled out in 1974 (Dask's face in degraded false-colour as he reprograms SV7, just like Marc Bolan or Roxy Music) and the one which became a *TotP* house-style when the New Wave made way for Ska around 1979 ("computerised" lettering moving around on the screen, much more disorientating then than it seems now). Watch it these days and you can't believe that nobody realised the "blurry" face was Dask's, but at the time most people were too busy trying to read the letters to look too closely.

characters from Boucher's scripts for *Blake's 7* and thus raise the possibility of *Doctor Who* and *Blake's 7* co-existing in the same universe. This isn't impossible, as *Blake's 7* takes place in the far, far future of humanity and little is known about the far, far future in *Doctor Who*, although you'd have to explain why the galaxy in *Blake's 7* is so devoid of alien empires (the humans killed them all?) and why the people of that era have forgotten the secret of inter-galactic travel. Still, this at least indicates that Boucher thinks of "The Robots of Death" as taking place a loooooong way in the future.]

The crewmembers on the sandminer wear stylish, opulent clothing which suggests an age of prosperity. They're eight months into a two-year tour of duty, so the water on board has been recycled eight times since the vehicle left base. The crew includes a Commander, a Pilot, a Chief Mover, a Chief Fixer who tends to damaged robots and a government meteorologist conducting experiments with weather balloons.

Commander Uvanov speaks of the Founding Families, 'the Twenty', who act as a kind of aristocracy and whose members always stick together. There's mention of Commander Uvanov's first command ten years ago, when a young member of one of the Founding Families got robophobia and ran out of the sandminer to die. The boy's father hushed it up to avoid accusations of cowardice, and Uvanov got results so the company didn't strip him of his command, but just made a note on his confidential biograph. The Commander gets a larger share of the profits than the others, and expects to be richer than some Family members by the end of this tour. Chess [or something very like it] is still played in this era, but Dask hasn't heard of the *Titanic* [so at least the movie's been forgotten]. Murder would seem to carry the death penalty, at least on the sandminer.

The technology used in this era seems advanced, though prone towards style rather than functionality. The robots wear "clothes", and the crew uses paper as well as computer records. This society is dependent on its robots, so if it were to turn out that robots can harm humans then the whole of civilisation might collapse, and many people in this era already suffer from robophobia. The problem is that robots don't have body language, something which humans just find unsettling.

A stop-circuit can be used to turn off all the robots, and usually they have to be returned to construction centres to be reactivated. Deactivated robots are marked with 'corpse markers' on arrival, little red discs that look remarkably like bicycle reflectors. There's a strict legal code governing the disposal of robots, with damaged robots placed in security storage. The restraining-bands used on the sandminer appear as soft as leather, but can be molecularly locked to become as strong as metal.

Taren Capel was an important scientist in the field of robotics before he disappeared, and he has a secret workshop on board the sandminer. He lived with robots from childhood, so thinks of himself as one, even dressing in Voc clothes and painting his face in the robot "fashion" as his plans reach completion. No record of his appearance exists, hence his masquerade as Dask. Believing robots to be the superior beings, he intends to murder everyone on the sandminer, though it's not explained why. [His way of making a statement, possibly?] His threatening letters to the company, promising a 'robot revolution', resulted in the company putting the agents D84 and Poul on board as a precaution. Uvanov hasn't heard of Capel, so he's not a well-known master criminal.

The Analysis

Where Does This Come From? Perhaps the most remarkable thing here is the sandminer crew's interaction. Up until the 1970s it was traditional for "space people" in mass-media SF to talk in terms of pure melodrama, with little or no sense of naturalism and most of the humour restricted to sit-com wise-cracks (just look at the "funny" blue-collar technicians in Forbidden Planet, or the "wah-wah-waaah" gags that end old episodes of That American Series). The space race changed all that, demonstrating to the world that *real* starships weren't likely to be neat and shiny but covered in grease and full of mess. This is at least in part what inspired the screenplays for Dark Star (1974) and that seminal work of clutter-in-space,

Alien (1979), while interior photos from the Apollo missions - revealing space-going vessels full of empty food wrappers - drove George Lucas to set Star Wars in a universe where the streets are full of rubbish and machinery breaks down all the time.

Though nobody shared this vision with the set-dressers of "The Robots of Death", the Alien ethos is already present here. In "The Sensorites" (1.7), the crew is as starchy as its uniforms; in "Frontier in Space" (10.3), the space-pilots are putting pin-ups on the walls and whining about wanting jobs on luxury space-liners, but still act like stiff-limbed members of the Earth Empire in the end. "The Space Pirates" (6.6) comes closest to depicting a second-hand future, but even there, most of the characters are just carrying out their regular duties and only the "light relief" figure of Milo Clancey really gets to loosen up.

Yet in "The Robots of Death" the personnel aboard the sandminer are petty, bitchy, argumentative and sarcastic, squabbling over money and winding each other up by telling stories about robots tearing people's arms off while their colleagues are trying to enjoy android massages. By his own admission, Chris Boucher took the idea of the sandminer from Frank Herbert's Dune, the definitive "fashionable" SF novel of the age. But it goes deeper than just the setting. Dune, with its vision of a world where sand gets into all the machinery and empires are founded on tiny psychological hang-ups, suggests a way of perceiving the future as well as a nice little cache of easily-nickable ideas.

It's traditional at this point to mention Agatha Christie. Although practically every beat of the plot in "The Robots of Death" can be found in Asimov (we'll come to that in a moment), the format is much like a 1920s whodunnit. From this point of view, the satin "flapper" costumes are entirely apt. This was towards the end of Barbara Hulaneki's reign as queen of style, and her Biba boutique in Kensington was a real-life film-set for Dietrich-wannabes and Garbo-clones. Thus the costume department, encouraged by the director to make this look as unlike a "space" story as possible, went all-out for the sort of thing you might find in early Roxy Music performances. Poul just is the Man Who Fell to Earth.

But we have to return to Isaac Asimov. The robophobia, the prime directive, the detective with an android sidekick and the speculation on how society would cope if robots could kill are all there in Asimov's two "robot" series. Yes, two: one is made up of the short stories collected in *I Robot* and sequels, about robo-psychologist Susan Calvin, who figures out how the odd behaviour of each machine results from literal interpretations of the laws of robotics. The other is about New York detective Elijah Bailey and his robot partner R. Daneel Olivaw (see **The Lore**). The Susan Calvin stories were often adapted for TV, as they were neat little fifty-minute logic puzzles with visual consequences, but it was the richer, society-led novels which made the biggest impact.

And pushing home the whole "literary SF" idea, many of the characters here have names suggestive of SF authors or concepts. "Uvanov" suggests Asimov; "Taren Capel" suggests Karel Capek, whose 1921 play *RUR* introduced the word "robot" in the first place; "Poul" suggests Poul Anderson, whose novel *The High Crusade* has already been mentioned (11.1, "The Time Warrior", and Boucher's *Corpse Marker* gives Poul's full name as Anders Poul); "Borg" suggests cyborgs (and at a time when Bjorn Borg was the reigning men's champion at Wimbledon, so it was perceived as a "proper" name). Meanwhile "Zilda" suggests jazz-age icon Zelda Fitzgerald, which fits the mood here.

Things That Don't Make Sense For the "shock" revelation about killer robots to work, all the characters have to believe that violence by robots is utterly unthinkable. But the first conversation we hear establishes that robots *can* go wrong if there's a programming error, and some of the crew apparently believe the story about the insane Voc therapist, so the Doctor's collapse-of-civilisation theory seems a bit overstated.

Cute as it is, Capel's demise is hard to swallow. The assumption is that the robots identify human beings by voice, but throughout the story they're capable of telling people apart even when nobody's speaking. We might assume that they *can* recognise faces, and that SV1 believes Capel is some kind of impostor when the face and the voice don't match, but don't these oh-so-knowledgeable and technically-trained androids *know* about helium? And isn't it a bit odd that Taren Capel makes himself up as a Voc, i.e. a robot who's technically inferior to SV7? You also have to question the company's choice of agents on this mission, as the individual sent to catch a criminal who reprograms robots, and who's partnered *with*

a robot, turns out to have robophobia. Poul also believes that the Doctor's theory about a killer robot is preposterous, even though that's exactly the sort of thing he's been sent here to prevent [denial].

The Voc which pursues the Doctor and Uvanov at the start of episode four isn't capable of removing a hat from its eyes, which is as pathetic as robots ever get. When Zilda sends Uvanov a message from his quarters, Uvanov can tell where she is with one glance at his communicator, but in the last episode the reprogrammed SV7 doesn't know where Toos is calling from and has to ask where to go to kill her. Toos' claim that if SV7's gone bad then all the robots have gone bad doesn't make sense - even if SV7 commands the Vocs to kill humans, their constrainers should still stop them unless they've had brain surgery - and is later proved to be wrong anyway, when Dask turns off all the friendly robots so that only the killers remain functional.

Russell Hunter (as Uvanov) develops an Irish accent for one single line in episode four ('we might get a chance to use one of these'), while Tom Baker can't pronounce "Terran". As in "The Daemons" (8.5), the Doctor claims that it's aerodynamically impossible for bumble-bees to fly, which is a myth.

Critique As with "The Face of Evil", Chris Boucher gives us a story of artificial intelligence, extreme psychology, futuristic ethics and humanity under pressure that suggests a more literate style of SF than just about anything seen in the series before. And as with "The Face of Evil", it holds together because it knows how to explore its subject matter within the framework of an edgy, dynamic piece of drama. The standards of adventure TV, the run-of-the-mill business of getting captured, escaping and having fights, don't drive *this* story anywhere near as much as the anxieties of its characters.

In many ways these first two Boucher scripts are the forerunners of the better stories from the early '80s, using High Concept science as a way of building a coherent environment rather than a way of explaining the machinery. The mentions of body-language aren't intellectual conceits, they're the heart of the whole story. The weakest element here is the half-hearted attempt to plant murder mystery "clues" among the sandminer crew, most notably the dead-end subplot about Zilda's brother that's surplus to requirements and isn't interesting anyway, but it's a measure of how busy the script is that you can watch the finished story several times over before you even notice how out-of-place these moments are.

Besides, we're looking at this with hindsight, watching all four episodes at once. In its original setting, the "whodunnit" isn't so much a serious attempt at a mystery as a way of building up the pressure, letting the story gain momentum once a week for a month. (One of the problems with doing an SF/ whodunnit crossover is that both sets of rules require absolute "purity". SF relies on you figuring out how a world works, and being surprised when fresh information leads you to re-evaluate. Detective stories rely on everything about the world being known up-front, so that the audience can play along. We know the butler did it, but guessing why the butler was reprogrammed requires knowledge of the world outside the closed-off setting. To its credit, here the apparently throw-away dialogue gives us just enough to infer a society but not enough to let us spot the ringer straight off.)

"The Robots of Death" implies a far bigger world than the one we get to see, a fact its creator exploits in subsequent spin-off books and CDs, but the deftness with which it's done is part of the point of this story. Because it is a familiar story, underneath, and as we'll see in **The Lore**, at least one of the cast would have known where the story came from. It's what they do with it that counts. The memorably irritable sandminer personnel express themselves in ways that you just don't see enough of in SF drama, and the late Russell Hunter deserves special mention, though he's curiously absent from most of episode three. The design-sense on display here isn't so much an added bonus as a way of making the production feel like a self-contained whole. Apart from Zilda's horrible hat, the only real disappointment is the main command deck of the sandminer, which ignores the chic of the rest of the vessel and comes across as a typically sterile, white-panelled SF set (little things like this can do a lot to damage a story's atmosphere; q.v. 13.3, "Pyramids of Mars").

And as in so many stories from this period, Leela's the one who's working hardest to drive the plot forward. However good Elisabeth Sladen was as "our" companion, by the end of her run Sarah Jane Smith wasn't doing anything more worthwhile than asking questions and getting into trouble every twenty-five minutes, but in her second story Leela is already bringing a new sense of focus to the programme. The relationship between her and the Doctor is a truly *dynamic* one, in which the audience's point-of-view never lies wholly with one character or the other. Sometimes we're the Doctor, explaining technology that we at least half-understand, and sometimes we're Leela as she gets herself lost in an unfamiliar environment. The second half of Season Fourteen, the "Educating Leela" trilogy, finally puts a proper character into the companion role and lets her personality make a genuine difference. In "The Robots of Death", she's the one who understands body language best of all even if she doesn't know any of the clever words for it.

The title, however, is rubbish.

The Facts

Written by Chris Boucher. Directed by Michael E. Briant. Viewing figures: 12.8 million, 12.4 million, 13.1 million, 12.6 million.

Supporting Cast   Russell Hunter (Uvanov), Pamela Salem (Toos), David Bailie (Dask), David Collings (Poul), Gregory de Polnay (D84), Miles Fothergill (SV7), Brian Croucher (Borg), Tania Rogers (Zilda), Tariq Yunus (Cass), Rob Edwards (Chub).

Working Titles   "The Storm Mine Murders", which might have avoided being such a giveaway; "Planet of the Robots", which might have avoided all those pesky viewers.

Cliffhangers   Trapped in one of the sandminer's containment units, the Doctor's buried under the ore that pours in through the chute in the ceiling; on the command deck, the Doctor hurries to cut the power as the sound of the motors builds to a crescendo and the sandminer prepares to blow; one of the reprogrammed Voc robots corners the Doctor, and begins to carry out its orders by throttling him.

The Lore

• Graham Williams (see **The Lore** of 14.3, "The Deadly Assassin") was taken to the rehearsals for this story and introduced to Baker and Hinchcliffe as the new producer of *Doctor Who*. All three men were alarmed. Hinchcliffe was bought off with the producer's job on *Target*, much to Williams' annoyance as he'd created the series. Williams was told that new limits on what was acceptable and how much he had to spend would be in place when he took over for Season Fifteen.

Hinchcliffe then did something that can either be seen as putting the programme ahead of his own career, or an astonishingly petty piece of revenge. He instructed all the staff under him not to worry about the budgets, but to do whatever they felt was necessary to make his last few stories look fantastic. The usual punishment for this is to have the following year's budgets "capped", and the personnel involved removed from that series (see also 18.1, "The Leisure Hive" and 14.6, "The Talons of Weng-Chiang"). Even allowing for inflation, Williams' budget for Season Seventeen was only 60% of what it had been two years earlier.

• Leela was retained from the previous story as part of the deal for Boucher to write both scripts. Once it was decided that she'd be the companion, he received a small ex gratia payment each time she appeared.

• Robert Holmes added the early scene of the crew relaxing, and the story of the robot masseur going haywire, as the episode under-ran. Another piece of padding was the Sandminer sinking at the end of episode two, bulking out the original cliffhanger (Zilda's death).

• As has already been suggested, the story owes more than a little to Isaac Asimov's second robot detective novel, *The Naked Sun*. This was adapted into an episode of the anthology series *Out of the Unknown* in 1967, in which the robot detective R. Daneel Olivaw was played by… David Collings.

• Gregory de Polnay, who played D84, thought (as apparently did Tom Baker) that a literal-minded robot would be a better companion than a knife-wielding savage. He was rather vexed when K9 appeared a few months later. De Polnay now teaches voice at a drama school.

• Viewers of the video release of "The Robots of Death" will be familiar with the cartoon "shh-doink!" noise that Leela's knife makes when thrown at a robot, but may be surprised to learn that this wasn't in the version originally broadcast and was added later. Nobody seems to know exactly why this was done, but since overseas TV companies (in New Zealand especially) often cut Leela's knife-throwing antics, it may well have been an attempt to make the whole thing seem less threatening…

14.6: "The Talons of Weng-Chiang"

(Serial 4S, Six Episodes, 26th February - 2nd April 1977.)

Which One is This? It's like an accident in the warehouse where they keep the nineteenth century period-drama archetypes. Sherlock Holmes, Fu Manchu, Hammer Horror, *The Phantom of the Opera*, grim Victorian streets, giant rats in sewers… well, see the first point under **Six Things to Notice About** for the full inventory.

Firsts and Lasts It's the end of another era, as Philip Hinchcliffe gets pushed out of the producer's office after a three-year tenancy. The programme will start to become noticeably less morbid and fairy-tale-like from this point on (see 14.3, "The Deadly Assassin", for the off-screen reasons why), although at least Robert Holmes will stay on as script editor for another year. It's also the last story directed by David Maloney, who's salvaged some dud scripts and made some good ones great. And who directed "Planet of the Daleks".

At the start of episode four, when Leela has to slosh around in the sewers wearing wet and near-transparent underclothing, Louise Jameson becomes the owner of the first female nipple ever glimpsed in the series. This may seem barely worth mentioning *now*, but try watching it as a teenage boy. Actually this story contains a stronger mix of sex, drugs and death than any other in the programme's history, as there are frequent references to opium and episode three features the only appearance in the series (unless you count Kate from 3.8, "The Gunfighters") of what the script tactfully calls a "lady of the night".

Six Things to Notice About "The Talons of Weng-Chiang"…

1. Almost universally recognised as one of the all-time greats, "The Talons of Weng-Chiang" does what mid-'70s *Doctor Who* does best by dropping the Doctor into the middle of somebody else's genre and watching it warp to suit the shape of the programme. You could easily sum this story up as "Doctor Who does Victorian Hammer Horror", but in all honesty, no single Hammer film is as accomplished as this. Checklist of Victorian / Sherlock Holmes / Fu Manchu / *Phantom of the Opera* standards seen here… a music-hall; a sinis-

ABOUT TIME 1975-1979

ter Chinaman; a Cockney cabbie; a deerstalker hat (worn by the Doctor himself, naturally); a token working-class Irishman; fog; comedy gin-drinking policemen with moustaches (one of whom, typically, is called P.C. Quick); a body pulled out of the Thames; references to both Limehouse and Whitechapel; a nod to Jack the Ripper; a scene with a Victorian scientist examining things in beakers; the sewers of London, complete with the Giant Rat of Sumatra; a character whose family used to live among "heathens"; a housekeeper called Mrs. Hudson, just like Sherlock's; an obvious prostitute who talks in rhyming slang; a notorious rookery in the East End; and a muffin man.

2. And as ever, the reputation of an otherwise spectacular story (and, worse, a story which is near-perfect for introducing new viewers to the series) is sullied by one very, very bad monster. Here it's the giant rat, one of the programme's most infamous lapses of judgement. At the end of episode one, when the Doctor and Leela are put in mortal jeopardy in the London sewers, the illusion of a gigantic rodent is briefly created by... putting a normal-sized rat in a miniaturised sewer set, an effect so shoddy that to modern eyes it's almost incomprehensible. A twenty-first century viewer seeing this for the first time can momentarily be confused as to why we're seeing a close-up of a rat in the sewer, before realising that it's supposed to be *filling* the sewer, again suggesting that the tele-literacy of the audience really has changed since 1977. But for its close-ups a furry rat-prop is introduced, and if anything it's even worse. Tom Baker later described the rat with the words 'I thought that looked rather good', which is one of the many reasons he's considered a great eccentric.

3. The other questionable area here is... race. "The Talons of Weng-Chiang" went unshown in America for many, many years, for fear of offending the Chinese community, and it's not hard to see why. To be fair, its depiction of all Chinese people as murderous, superstitious cultists isn't unreasonable in context - this is a parody of British imperialist fiction rather than an example of it, and *everybody* is stereotyped here, with the English exclusively shown as pompous, incompetent and self-deluded. It's telling that the script replaces all Li H'sen Chang's "r"s with "l"s *only when he's on the stage*, suggesting that it's just part of the act he puts on for the sake of the ignorant British. Yet the Doctor's claim to have been

attacked by a lot of 'little men' after the Tong's first assault is harder to swallow, even if he's technically taller than everyone else here. And Leela's description of Chang as 'the yellow one' just doesn't bear thinking about.

4. Not all the monsters on offer here are as unfortunate as "that" rat. Star of the show on the "evil" side is Mr. Sin, a.k.a. the Peking Homunculus, a grotesque, dwarfish mannequin that stabs its victims under the ribs while grunting like a pig. Perhaps the best monster of the era, and certainly the nastiest, it proves that the worst abominations aren't the space-age ones but the ones that look as if they're the result of a freak accident in the nursery. The scene with the mutant dwarf at the end of *Don't Look Now* isn't as scary as this.

5. And then there are the supporting performances. Henry Gordon Jago (Christopher Benjamin) and Professor George Litefoot (Trevor Baxter) have become folk-heroes to *Doctor Who* fans over the decades, despite only appearing in this one story and despite being the embodiments of bumbling Victorian sidekickery. John Bennett makes a convincing heathen foreigner as Chang, while Michael Spice - the face of the brain of Morbius - takes the art of ranting to new heights as arch-villain Magnus Greel. Hardest line to stop yourself joining in with: 'Let the talons of Weng-Chiang shred your fleeeeesh!!!'

6. Chang's death-scene presents us with one of the great unsolved puzzles of *Doctor Who*. Unable to say another word as he passes away, Chang attempts to give the Doctor a clue to the whereabouts of Magnus Greel by pointing down at the Doctor's foot. The audience is perfectly entitled to assume that from this clue, the Doctor will deduce that Greel is living on Old Boot Street or Toe Lane. In fact this scene is never resolved, as Greel later comes to find the Doctor instead of the Doctor finding Greel. So nobody has ever satisfactorily explained what Chang was trying to say. (Unless he was just telling the Doctor to "shoo".)

The Continuity

The Doctor The Doctor comes to the nineteenth century to teach Leela something about her ancestors, so he obviously sees it as his place to act as her mentor [something that's only a subtext in most other companion relationships, apart from Jo Grant]. He's prepared to change his costume to

Bad Effects: What are the Highlights?

In the public imagination, this - more than anything else - is what *Doctor Who* was remembered for throughout the '80s and '90s. Thanks to the constant jibes from a cynical, "knowing" media, the most common memory outside fandom was of "squeezy-bottle spaceships", though only "The Ark in Space" (12.2) offers anything that *literally* looks like a Fairy Liquid container in orbit. But we're going to have to define terms here. There are lots of slightly ropey effects, endless questionable set decisions and any number of dodgy alien costumes (the latter will get their own listing under 21.1, "Warriors of the Deep", for fairly obvious reasons). But what we're talking about here are effects so inept that they define an entire production, not just "spoiling the illusion" but actively distorting everything around them.

Here are the front-runners…

10. Non-Zap Guns. Just for a change, directors occasionally used "realistic" weapons. Often these were pistols or submachine guns firing blanks. There's a problem with this in a TV studio, as the shock-waves make what are called "venetian blind" effects on the picture (e.g. 13.6, "The Seeds of Doom" and 21.6, "The Caves of Androzani"). Alternatively a small charge in the nozzle would make a bang and a flash, with no need for faffing about in post-production. When the Cybermen did it (12.5, "Revenge of the Cybermen"), it was pretty good. When Morgaine's troops did it (26.1, "Battlefield"), it wasn't. What with the bizarre "Knights falling from the sky" effect, the disco music and the Knight Commander's lipstick and eyeliner, this makes the whole story feel like the video for "Ant Rap" by Adam and the Ants.

9. The Bandril Ambassador (22.5, "Timelash"). "The ambassador's receptions were noted in society for his exquisite taste and amusingly-shaped head." Tragically, although it is a fairly bad effect by absolute standards, it's the best thing in the story. Sometimes you can get away with a slightly suspect effect if it's (a) quick and (b) responded to by the actors as if it's real. This is why the giant rat from "Weng-Chiang" isn't in this listing, as the costume worn by Stuart Fell isn't *too* catastrophic, just a bit too clean (although the cuts between the costume and the real rat in the scaled-down sewer don't do it any favours). The Bandril Ambassador is a glove-puppet that appears on a 3D "screen", threatening to declare war on the Karfelons and later announcing the

Doctor's death. In still photos it's actually quite good, and well-lit. We have no sense of scale, so the Bandrils might be fifty feet high for all we know. But the story lost all our sympathy seventy minutes earlier, and the script, costumes, sets and one or two pantomime performances (naming no names, but he was in *Blake's 7*) all remove any reason to take the rubber Sooty at all seriously.

8. Spiders (11.6, "Planet of the Spiders"; 14.3, "The Deadly Assassin"; 18.3 "Full Circle"). The BBC had a directive about phobias. Every time someone built a convincing prop spider, an edict came down to make it less "scary". As a result, "Boris" from "Planet of the Spiders" was built to be almost cute, and the one that bites Romana and injects her with Marshman-juice in "Full Circle" was remade three times to look pretty-but-unrealistic. As an aside, the only genuine arachnophobe involved in the programme - Colin Baker - had it stipulated in his contract that no spiders were to appear while he was the Doctor. Imagine how much worse "The Mark of the Rani" could have been (see number two).

7. Kroll (16.5, "The Power of Kroll"). The model-work is the best stop-motion animation in the programme's history. The reactions of the cast are convincing. What's wrong is that these elements don't match; there's a crude split-screen, meaning that Kroll's tentacles are cut off below a certain point. The prop tentacle in the studio isn't altogether believable either, although everyone does their best to be appalled by it. The ingenious part is that the first tentacle we see, which causes Romana to scream her lungs out at the end of episode one, is actually a *deliberately* unconvincing rubber prop being wielded by a Swampie high priest. Some might say that a "dummy" monster only works if you can be absolutely sure that the real one's going to blow people's socks off…

6. The Skarasen (13.1, "Terror of the Zygons"). A story about the Loch Ness Monster requires, well, a sea serpent. For the most part what we get is a tolerable stop-motion beastie, but when episode four rolls by they try to make do with a sock-puppet stuck over CSO footage of Westminster. The bathos of the script's move from spooky chiller to "I've planted my monster-summoning device and now I'll take over the world,

continued on page 149…

suit the era, at least when he knows where he's going.

His stated philosophy here: 'Sleep is for tortoises.' He knows how to use an elephant gun, and knows enough gun-lore to trust the weapon simply because it's made in Birmingham. He's good enough in unarmed combat to hold off a gang of Chinese ruffians performing unlikely martial arts moves. He says he speaks Mandarin and Cantonese, 'all the dialects', and knows enough pathology to recognise giant rat bites on a corpse. Even more remarkably, he somehow knows that Jago's been hypnotised just by looking at the man.

• *Ethics.* Though he *tries* to be disapproving of Leela's use of a janis thorn, he seems to think that her murder of a Tong member is acceptable because the man was trying to kill him. As ever, he seems to treat self-defence as a defence. [The script is written as if the thorn instantly kills its victim, although "The Face of Evil" (14.4) demonstrates that the victim should survive in a state of paralysis for some time before death occurs. So here the Doctor basically kills through inaction by leaving the Tong cultist to die on the pavement instead of rushing off to find an antidote. This point is never addressed...]

• *Inventory.* The Doctor's good with conjuring tricks. He produces a chain of handkerchiefs from Jago's pocket, and causes a live dove to magically appear from a metal dish he idly picks up at the theatre. [Anyone who knows magic will be able to spot that the first of these tricks shouldn't work, at least not in the way it's presented here, while the second suggests that either (a) the dish belongs to Li H'sen Chang and has been left lying around by the theatre door for no apparent reason - and we do see two caged doves in his dressing room later - or (b) the Doctor generally carries a live dove around with him just so he can do this trick. Some futuristic technology may be involved in these games, though. In "Robot" (12.1) he's carrying a stuffed white bird in his pockets; is this some kind of automaton, capable of turning into a "real" bird when it's switched on? See also 25.4, "The Greatest Show in the Galaxy".]

Many of the props from the Doctor's usual coat have been moved into the pockets of the Victorian one. On display here are the etheric beam locator [from 12.4, "Genesis of the Daleks"], a lamp of rock [that trisilicate again?], the same old yo-yo and - unforgettably - a toy Batmobile. He seems to carry currency for buying muffins.

• *Background.* He speaks of hoping to see Little Titch at the theatre, suggesting that he's been to nineteenth century London before, and his reference to Agincourt might hint that he's been there as well [as in 14.1, "The Masque of Mandragora"]. He states that he hasn't been to China in four-hundred years. [From the context he seems to be referring to the calendar, not his own lifetime, as he's establishing that he can't possibly have met Li H'sen Chang there. The only visit to China we ever see is in 1.4, "Marco Polo", but the date on that occasion was 1289.] He claims he once caught a huge salmon in the river Fleet which he shared with the Venerable Bede, who 'adored fish'. [Bede lived in the seventh and eighth centuries. However, the Doctor never claims he *caught* the fish with Bede. For all we know, he might have had the salmon in a freezer in the TARDIS for years before cooking it.]

Most significantly, the Doctor has first-hand experience of human history in the fifty-first century, and knows all about Magnus Greel even though they've never met before. See **History**.

The Supporting Cast

• *Leela.* Not terribly bothered about seeing how her ancestors on Earth lived, though she looks delighted when the Doctor treats her to a night at the theatre, and is so happy when she gets his approval that you *have* to assume she sees him as much more than a mentor. [He was, after all, introduced to her as a virtual god.] The British ritual of "tea" perplexes her, though [she never had much patience with Sevateem customs either, remember]. She's familiar with the foghorn-like cry of a swamp creature from her own world, and knows all the 'signs of death'. She was taught to strike under the breastbone when aiming for the heart, and she's used to the idea of torturing prisoners to make them talk. There's no smoking where she comes from. She makes a prayer-like gesture over the body of Chang, even though he was her enemy, and believes in an afterlife - 'the Great Hereafter' - but it's no Heaven as she swears to hunt Greel down there.

Leela is carrying a blowpipe, which she uses to kill at least one victim with a janis thorn. For the second time since joining the Doctor, she hurls a knife at a robot and fails to do it any damage.

The TARDIS The Doctor emerges from the Ship wearing Victorian garb and a matching deerstalk-

Bad Effects: What are the Highlights?

...continued from page 147 back to the 1930s.

nyah-hah-haaah!" is mirrored all too clearly in the sudden decline in the quality of the effects... and in the fact that Baker, Sladen and Marter are all looking in *completely* the wrong direction.

5. The Cyber-Fleet/s (4.2, "The Tenth Planet"; 4.6, "The Moonbase"; 6.3, "The Invasion"). By and large the spaceships of the 1960s are exemplary, and in some cases more interesting than the sort of thing you see today (the existing footage of "The Dalek Masterplan", 3.4, is more inventive than most CGI even if it's wonkier). They knew their limits, and never tried to go too far beyond them. This is, however, not the case when Kit Pedler and Gerry Davis are writing. We'll start with "The Moonbase", as this is the quintessential "paper-plates-on-string" invasion fleet. The models were shot on the same set as the exteriors of the moon, with no regard for scale. So a crater we've already seen filled with astronauts and nonchalant Cybermen crops up again, within the same installment, as a crater fifty times bigger. Result: the punters at home can tell at a glance that the wobbly, dangly spaceships are the size of pizzas. Their earlier vessels were similarly maladroit, but at least avoided the "flying saucer" design; they looked like spacefaring casserole pots instead.

By "Tomb of the Cybermen" (5.1) the writers have learned their lesson and avoid any ships in flight, although one really duff model is used at the start. "The Wheel In Space" (5.7) returns us to halfway-decent model-work, and it's the other bodies in space - notably the Morris-Dancing Cybermen - that wreck it (well, that and the script). In their last "classic" story the Cybermen travel in fairly impressive-looking ships, but these are manoeuvred through space by a very obvious early example of motion-control, i.e. plonking them on a table and moving the camera instead. This wouldn't be so bad, except that it's the only attempt at "realism" amid an epic-length montage of stock-footage missile-launches, some dating

4. Zap Guns (various stories of the late '70s and early '80s). There came a time when the presence of "blasters" became a standard feature of the programme's narrative, which is why this present volume is fast running out of ways of saying "they carry guns that can either stun or kill". There are a few laser-effects here and there in the Pertwee stories, but not enough to be taken for granted or left unexplained. In "The Ark in Space" (12.2) the Doctor's comment 'I hate stun-guns' is a surprise, because we've not seen him stunned that often. Up to this point there were two ways of doing a ray-gun effect. Either you distorted the whole picture (as with the early Dalek "exterminations" that make their victims go into negative, and the curious image-squelching that accompanies a blast from the Ice Warriors' sonic weapons), or there's a localised effect on the victim but nothing from the barrel of the gun itself (like the "star" pattern of a Gallifreyan staser, and the smouldering of anyone at whom the Cybermen point their lightbulbs).

But after *Star Trek*, and with the BBC hierarchy deciding to try to do *Star Wars*, suddenly guns made beams. And beams have to point in the direction of the target. K9 would aim his nose-gun at a wall, a small flame would erupt and a beam would go off six or seven inches away. Someone would be shot - Della in "Nightmare of Eden" (17.4), let's say - and clutch her stomach as the ray gets her in the neck. As we shall see, with K9's arrival human anatomy is rewritten, and the kneecap becomes the place to aim lethal blows. The writers get wise to this pretty quickly, and either start specifying that a large, vague area is affected or simply don't use guns at all. Part of the reason that everyone went hog-wild for "Earthshock" in 1982 (19.5) was that we finally had gun-battles where everyone could shoot straight.

continued on page 151...

er hat, though thankfully he never claims to have given Arthur Conan-Doyle the idea for Sherlock Holmes. [That doesn't happen until the novel *Evolution*, but in *All-Consuming Fire* he meets Holmes and Watson in person anyway. See also **Is He Really a Doctor?** under 13.6, "The Seeds of Doom".] There's a natty nineteenth century dress-and-cap ensemble for Leela, too, another success

for the TARDIS wardrobe. The walking-cane that comes with the Doctor's outfit is hollow, and contains a small flask of what may well be an alcoholic beverage.

On this occasion the TARDIS ends up in the era it was aiming for, so the navigation's improving again.

History

• *Dating.* Jack the Ripper is still fresh in the public imagination, and Queen Victoria is on the throne [so it's got to be between 1889 and 1901]. It's evidently after February 1892, the date of the edition of *Blackwood's Magazine* read by Professor Litefoot. [The novel *The Bodysnatchers*, which insists on bringing back Litefoot and pitching him against the Zygons, holds that this story takes place in 1889. Parkin's *History of the Universe* concurs, based on the fact that a draft script mentions Jack the Ripper being 'in Canada' now, ostensibly a reference to Prince Eddy's tour of the colonies in 1889-90. Even though he didn't go to Canada.]

The Doctor hopes to see Little Titch [the popular entertainer who gave his stage-name to Persons of Restricted Growth the world over; Titch's biographer was Sax Rohmer, creator of Fu Manchu]. Litefoot's father was Brigadier-General in the punitive expedition to China in 1860, and stayed in Peking as palace attaché afterwards. Litefoot's family returned to Britain in 1873 [the end of Tung Che's reign as Emperor]. Next month Chang would have performed before the Queen at Buckingham Palace.

Magnus Greel was the infamous 'Butcher of Brisbane', the Minister of Justice responsible for the deaths of a hundred thousand 'enemies of the state', and who's now a wanted war criminal. The Doctor was with the Filipino army at the final advance on Reykjavik during the fifty-first century, and the implication may be that this is where Greel's faction met its Waterloo. However, this was the age of the zygma experiments - the Doctor says that Findecker's discovery of the double-nexus particle sent human science up a cul-de-sac and made this a scientific dark-age - and Greel managed to escape into the past in a time cabinet [the earliest "successful" time-travel experiment by humans, as far as we know, at least without alien involvement].

He took with him the Peking Homunculus, now known as Mr. Sin. The Homunculus was originally given to the children of the Commissioner of the Icelandic Alliance as a toy, but its swinish instincts took over and it nearly caused World War Six. Its disappearance was never explained. [Leaving aside the question of when World Wars Three, Four and Five were... there's a lot that's unexplained here. Who made the Homunculus, and did it originally have anything to do with Greel? If Greel was defeated in Iceland, then it makes a certain sense that he might have taken Mr. Sin with him, but the relationship between the two is uncertain.] The Doctor states that all this was around 5000 AD, during an ice age. [Apparently the same ice age seen in 5.3, "The Ice Warriors", but see that story for more arguments about its dating. And see 15.2, "The Invisible Enemy", for more on the fiftieth and fifty-first centuries.]

Mr. Sin is a midget-sized machine built in Peking, with the face and clothes of a Chinese doll. It contains a series of magnetic fields operating on a printed circuit with a small computer, its one organic component being the cerebral cortex of a pig. Though it seems loyal to Greel, the 'mental feedback' has become so great that the pig part has become dominant, and when its animal instincts take over even its master can't stop it trying to kill the human beings it hates so much. [The trip in the time cabinet, which did so much damage to Greel's biology, may also have made Sin's pig-cortex less stable.] It's only ever heard to speak when it's on stage during Li H'sen Chang's act, which may be a form of ventriloquism, as the rest of the time it just grunts like a pig or laughs maniacally. Chang appears to be able to give the Homunculus orders telepathically. The Doctor finally pulls the 'fuse' from the Homunculus' back.

Greel's time cabinet looks like a wardrobe-sized Chinese puzzle-box [it may have been disguised after reaching the nineteenth century]. Greel's arrival in China was some time between 1862 and 1873, and was witnessed by Li H'sen Chang, who gave the sick Greel sanctuary while the soldiers of the Emperor Tung Che searched. They took the cabinet, and Greel has been trying to recover it ever since. It was later given to Litefoot's mother by Tung Che. [It's not clear what the soldiers were searching for or why they thought the cabinet was of value, but it's interesting to note that the *real* power in China at this time was the Empress Dowager, an obsessive collector of timepieces.]

Being the product of a technological dark age, the cabinet's power source is a beam of zygma energy, and it split open Greel's DNA helix. He now has an organic distillation chamber for draining the life-essence from young women, leaving his agonised victims as blackened husks. But though these distillations are the only thing which can restore his protenoid balance and keep him alive, he needs more and more "sacrifices" as time goes on. And the more cells he absorbs through

Bad Effects: What are the Highlights?

...continued from page 149

3. Bok (8.5, "The Daemons"). The evil gargoyle is pretty obviously either a polystyrene model or a little bloke in a body-stocking. Nothing intrinsically wrong there, but the model moves like a stone gargoyle come to life - with glowing eyes, too - and the other one moves like a little bloke in a body-stocking. It zaps people by adopting a hood-ornament pose and waiting until someone edits the offending puny mortal out of the picture, meaning that some actors have to spend ages in ungainly postures waiting to be pointed at. The gargoyle can also fly. This is something few people realise the first time they watch this story, as it's only signified by a "whooshing" noise like a fat man in corduroy trousers walking fast, and by Roger Delgado looking skywards (which he does a lot anyway). The contempt for the audience is continued when it "dies" in two separate positions, the model crouching and Stanley Mason sitting cross-legged on the floor. The final insult is when he's bazooka'd. The model which explodes is obviously polystyrene, as all the pieces are caught by the lightest of breezes and blow away the way limestone doesn't. The effects got a letter in the *Radio Times* praising their authenticity, you know.

2. The Rubber Tree (22.3, "The Mark of the Rani"). By 1985 they can't even do costume-based pseudo-historicals properly, and on location in what ought to be the most atmospheric place ever, they blow it all by setting a scene in a real woodland and adding a rubber model tree-trunk of the kind you get in fancy-dress shops. What makes this really inept is the context. If you don't already know, the plot involves (dear God, it's a struggle just to write this, let alone watch it on first broadcast) landmines that turn people into trees. The heart of the rhetoric is that the evil queen-bitch-scientist Time Lord, the Rani, denies the dignity of human nature and is proved wrong when someone recently "arborified" saves the Doctor's sidekick by rapidly growing a branch and pulling her out of trouble. On-screen, this looks like a man in a rubber tree-trunk groping Nicola Bryant. And everyone emotes as though it were proof of the existence of the soul.

1. Dinosaur Porn (11.2, "Invasion of the Dinosaurs"; 22.3, "The Mark of the Rani"; 10.2, "Carnival of Monsters"). Those who don't learn from pre-history are destined to repeat it. The career of effects perpetrator Clifford Culley is an object lesson in overconfidence, and we should refer the interested reader to the entries on "Robot" (12.1) and That Tank; "Planet of the Daleks" (10.5) and the Rolykin Army; and the shot in episode six of "Invasion of the Dinosaurs" in which a tyrannosaurus and a brontosaurus appear to be making out in public just outside Marylebone Station. What makes it all worse is that it was a repeat of a questionable effect from the previous year, the plesiosaur that attacks the *S. S. Bernice* . "Carnival of Monsters" made it obvious that using CSO to superimpose monsters shot on video over backgrounds shot on film was a definite no-no (tell that to director Douglas Camfield; see number six), and that CSO and dinosaurs were best kept to a minimum anyway. So a year later they decided to shoot the location footage of "Invasion of the Dinosaurs" on film before adding the effects, thinking, "what could possibly go wrong?". By the mid-'80s they obviously weren't so fussy about irritating the viewers with badly-conceived effects, so they thought, "hey, let's give the Rani a pet tyrannosaurus embryo that grows up fast when her TARDIS goes wrong in defiance of all logic... that'll surprise and delight the fans". After all that had gone before (see number two), it almost seemed competent.

this 'catalytic extraction', the more deformed he becomes.

It's said that Greel's victims in the fifty-first century were used as test subjects for this machine, and they begged not to die this way. [It's not explained why his victims have to be *women*, unless it's just kinkiness on Greel's part. Which isn't impossible given his sadistic nature. Nor does anybody explain how he brought all this heavy equipment with him in one cabinet. Is it bigger on the inside, like a TARDIS? The extraction device looks as if it's made from antique parts, so maybe he just brought key elements and built the finished machine in the nineteenth century. The Doctor guesses what the missing women are being used for after he sees the time cabinet, so the fifty-first century zygma experiments must also have caused DNA damage to their subjects.]

When Greel's mask is finally removed, the effect on his metabolism is obvious, as his face looks as if it's melting.

The unique "key" of the correct molecular combination - a small, round, crystalline object known as a trionic lattice - glows when the cabinet's close. The Doctor describes the cabinet as having 'fused molecules', so only the lattice can open it. [In 14.3, "The Deadly Assassin", a *trimonic* barrier is said to protect the TARDIS. The similarity in names might be a coincidence, or just evidence that Robert Holmes liked the sound of it.] Greel believes that he can repair himself by using the zygma beam again, this time making no mistake 'in the program DNA levels', but the Doctor knows that the beam is already fully-stretched and that if Greel fiddles with it then it'll collapse. The implosion would be big enough to take out a large chunk of London.

Li H'sen Chang has hypnotic powers, given to him by Greel, which make his eyes flash and can mesmerise a victim in moments. He can also read minds, though the Doctor's thoughts are clouded to him. [It may be done technologically, but even so, psychic powers would seem to be in vogue in the 5000s.] Greel suspects the Doctor may be a 'time agent' from the future, suggesting that there are other time-travelling criminals and a special department to hunt them down, yet he also believes that by escaping into the past he became the first man to travel in time. [So Greel's fears of time agents are nothing more than paranoia, as he believes - wrongly - that others will follow his lead. Greel still considers the zygma experiments a success, but there's no mention of time-travel in any subsequent human history. The Doctor states that nothing came of this work, so zygma projects were probably abandoned after Greel's departure. Apparently the time cabinet only damages organic tissue, though, so it's odd that future scientists don't seem to be sending automatic probes back through time.] Though Greel isn't great with science himself, it was he who found the scientists and resources to create this flawed form of time-travel, so he sees it as his "baby".

Also following Greel is the Tong of the Black Scorpion, 'one of the most dangerous politico-criminal organisations in the world', to which Chang may or may not belong. It's he who issues a Tong member with a scorpion venom suicide pill, while the Doctor recognises the Tong's tattoo instantly. The Tong are fanatical followers of the god Weng-Chiang, believing that one day he'll return to rule the world. Greel's basement in the theatre is protected by a ghost-like hologram, to scare off intruders *Scooby-Doo* style, and he's been causing genetic disruption in animals that makes rats grow to ten feet in length and money-spiders grow to the size of a man's fist. The Doctor believes this was the result of an experiment to gauge the strength of the psionic amplification field [which doesn't make much sense, or seem to relate to anything we're told here at all; *what* psionic amplification field?]. The House of the Dragon, Greel's home-from-home prepared by the Tong over many months, is kitted out with a hefty laser-beam weapon set inside the head of a great dragon statue. It stuns before it kills. Greel owns a hand-held energy weapon that fires the same kind of beam.

Only one of the giant rats in the sewers is killed before the end of the story [but it's doubtful that they'll be able to live for long, and hopefully they won't breed]. The time cabinet is left on Earth, though it's useless once the key's destroyed.

[Special geographical note: the Palace Theatre is above the covered river Fleet, which joins the Thames at Blackfriars' Bridge, running almost due south from Hampstead through Camden Town. This means it can't be any further east than Ludgate Circus, so Limehouse - Litefoot's district - is at least a ten-minute cab-ride away. (In terms of London geography, Mile End is a better bet for his actual house.) From internal evidence and the Street Index of 1888, it's possible to place the Palace Theatre at Holborn Viaduct, perhaps near Farringdon tube station. The House of the Dragon would be at Limeshouse Causeway, possibly one of the disused Board Schools in Limekiln Walk, under what's now Westferry Docklands Light Railway station.]

The Analysis

Where Does This Come From? If real-life heroes were open to question in this era (see 14.3, "The Deadly Assassin"), then so were the giants of fiction. Since the mid-'60s it had been open season on Sherlock Holmes; a number of feature films had cross-examined his drug-taking, sexuality, psychology and status. Grown-ups could finally discuss the whole of Victorian society after the relaxation of the censorship laws. However, people still liked the colour, spectacle and certainty of that epoch. Best example was the BBC's retro-variety show *The Good Old Days*, which invited its audience to dress up in "authentic" Victorian garb and sit in an "authentic" theatre setting while watching "authentic" music-hall acts, with Leonard Sachs (seen as Admiral de Coligny in 3.5, "The Massacre" and Borusa in 20.1, "Arc of Infinity") acting as the alliterating, aesthetically adventurous arch-announcer. We could point out that Henry Gordon Jago is near-identical to Sachs' "character", but it'd be much too obvious.

This ambivalence to the past was typically '70s. We were able to take the surface appearances for our own purposes, but we were uneasy about the moral baggage. This is particularly true with regard to adventure fiction from the time. China was no longer takeaways and opium, it was the source of ancient wisdom. The *Kung Fu* cult of the mid-'70s is a subject for an entire book, but Martial Arts went from a kind of add-on for heroic machismo (see most of Volume III) to an entire way of life. That our Victorian ancestors had been so condescending to such a now-dignified and now-noble culture made hit "Noodle-Western" TV show Kung Fu work for a number of different audiences. Oddly enough, it was only in the wake of Chairman Mao that this respect for ancient Chinese ways began. Hong Kong - a British protectorate - provided our primary source for all things Chinese, and its population despised the Peking government. Hammer had tried to cross the gulf between genres with *The Seven Golden Vampires*, with Peter Cushing as Van Helsing confronting ninjas working for Dracula, but it hadn't caught on. "The Talons of Weng-Chiang" is a rather more attractive cross-breed of vampire and oriental lore.

To anyone in Victorian London, the name "Jago" meant a district of Bethnal Green notorious as a source of crime and poverty. This was the birthplace of cockney rhyming-slang and the Salvation Army. We should also mention the most famous "unpublished" case of Sherlock Holmes, "The Giant Rat of Sumatra", a case which Dr. Watson only mentioned in brief as he believed the world wasn't ready to hear the details. In TV terms, chases in sewers were a handy way of reminding the public of the world they'd rather forget, and we've seen them in this series before (2.2, "The Dalek Invasion of Earth" and 6.3, "The Invasion"). Big rats in sewers had been seen on our screens about three months earlier, in *The New Avengers* 1.13, "Gnaws"; their giant rat wasn't very convincing either, but the perspective shots were marginally better.

And the final confrontation in episode six, with the heroes sheltering from laser-fire behind overturned tables, is so similar to the first episode of Holmes' "The Ark in Space" (12.2) that it's barely worth mentioning. Even Leela's 'it cannot fire at two objects at once' strategy is the same as the one the Doctor previously used.

Things That Don't Make Sense Another story that rests on a ludicrous co-incidence, as the pathologist whom the Doctor meets after just an hour in London turns out to be the man who's got Greel's time cabinet. It took Greel twenty years to track this man down, of course. And the chronology of the cabinet is strange enough in itself. Litefoot speaks of it as if it's been in London for years, yet the disappearances of young women have only begun recently, meaning that Greel hasn't been in town long. Has it really taken him all this time to work out what city it's in? If it was taken by the Emperor and given to the family of a British attaché, then how on Earth can he *not* have figured out that it was probably taken to the capital of the Empire? And isn't it convenient that Greel, having already packed the Peking Homunculus in 5000 AD, should have ended up in China? [Or maybe he chose China deliberately, but if so, then why?]

The police sergeant at the station is satisfied with the Doctor's stated name and address incredibly quickly, and is just as happy to allow the Doctor to interfere in the investigation even though he and Leela are still technically being held in connection with an assault. [More of the Doctor's inhuman charm.] There's an enormous laser-cannon in Greel's House of the Dragon for no good reason - he can hardly be *expecting* a pitched battle there - which has been mounted inside a dragon statue, also for no reason. The beam from this laser is never seen to hit anything, not even the things which visibly explode after it's fired, while the rag-doll version of Mr. Sin that the Doctor heroically wrestles at the end of the battle makes the Master's shrunken Action Man victims look convincing.

Why does Mr. Sin laugh hysterically after Greel recovers the time-cabinet, when the Homunculus just wants to kill things and surely doesn't give a damn about Greel's time-travel plans? Doubly strange when you realise that Mr. Sin wasn't even allowed to kill Professor Litefoot during the raid, again for no good reason.

The trionic lattice glows and makes "woop" noises, getting louder and faster the closer it gets to the time cabinet... until it's in the same room, at which point it shuts up [it must have an "off" switch]. The rats are described as 'guards' for Greel's hideout, but since his lair is protected by an impenetrable metal barrier, there's no reason for him to *need* guards. Greel has spent these last few months living in a sewer, but turns out to have a nice, opulent headquarters in the East End that he only starts using just before he prepares to leave the nineteenth century. Even if the Tong's only just finished renovating it, wouldn't it still be a nicer place to live than a stinking subterranean tunnel?

There are also some geographical problems here. Anyone with a good working knowledge of Victorian London can pull holes in this story, as can anyone who lives in the East End today and knows where the Fleet runs. And it was only covered over about five years before Litefoot was born, not 'centuries ago'. Chang apparently gets from the sewer to the laundry in less time than it takes the Doctor to open the skylight, despite having a leg missing.

Aside from the perennial problems of changing size, even the rat has a logical flaw: if Greel's lair is on the course of the Fleet, then the rat will be getting all the choice offal from Smithfield Market, London's biggest meat distributor. They used the same river to dispose of the off-cuts and entrails (and still do, although it's better-regulated now). Even with the prodigious appetite caused by having 8,000 times its usual body mass - see **How Hard is It to Be the Wrong Size?** under 16.6, "The Armageddon Factor" - it's far less bother for the rat to eat fresh innards than to run after struggling humans on legs that would snap if it moved too fast.

One to think about: at the start of episode three, Leela escapes Mr. Sin by taking a run-up to Litefoot's window and hurling herself through the glass. There is, as far as we know, nothing even approximating glass on the Sevateem world. None of the Sevateem buildings have windows. How does Leela know that the magic see-through material will break if she hurls herself at it, let alone that she'll be able to survive?

And why is Bert Kwouk, the BBC's ethnic-stereotype-in-residence, not in this story?

Critique   Regarded by lazy people as one of the greatest *Doctor Who* stories ever made, who are nonetheless right on this occasion. The key is that

"The Talons of Weng-Chiang" is capable of being all things to all men, and more than any other story it presents us with a cartload of elements which *anybody* who likes *anything* about *Doctor Who* / British film-making / television in general can get to grips with. You can watch it if you like your *Doctor Who* good and traditional (to many people it's the very definition of "trad", though it certainly didn't look that way at the time), or you can watch it if you want to admire the sheer grandeur of its construction. You can watch it as an exercise in the cross-breeding of literary themes, or you can watch it drunk with your mates after coming home from the pub.

The Doctor gets a moment of greatness every couple of minutes. The fifty-first century we're told about is as believable as the nineteenth century we actually see. The technology of Greel feels like Victorian technology, giving the story an unprecedented sense of cohesion, and at the same time reminding us of what we (unconsciously) think science-fantasy *should* look like. Director David Maloney, who arguably bit off more than he could chew with "The Deadly Assassin", here finds it much easier to build a workable world by focusing on everything that's troubling and grotesque about Victoriana. Leela is - for the third story in a row - a proper part of the plot instead of just a mouthpiece for the audience's questions, her "primitive abroad" persona blending into the environment instead of standing apart from it; the script's having a great time likening the culture of Victorian London to the culture of a tribal society, right from the moment in episode one when the Doctor tells her that the local tribespeople are called "cockneys", and Louise Jameson's savage-but-child-like performance is as good as it ever gets.

But perhaps the story's main strength is that as with "The Brain of Morbius", in a way it feels like *Doctor Who* coming home. Victorian gothic was never part of the series' original design – the '60s barely touched on the nineteenth century, apart from "Evil of the Daleks" (4.9) - yet as a programme rooted in the Wellsian "amateur inventor" school of fantasy, which started off as a series about a gentleman traveller hiding the most impressive technology on Earth in a junkyard, the late 1800s is such a natural place for the story to be. You could even argue that it verges on over-confidence. This is a programme at the peak of its cockiness, secure in the knowledge that the viewers will lap up lavish-looking costume-drama fantasy and accept anything they're told about Victorian London. In a way it's very nearly lazy.

As with "The Brain of Morbius" and its recycling of *Frankenstein*, the programme-makers almost seem to say out loud: 'We're doing Fu Manchu meets Sherlock Holmes this week; deal with it!' Who needs plot logic when you've got Patsy Byrne saying 'make a 'orse sick, that would'? Who needs characterisation when Michael Spice and Louise Jameson are trading big fat ripening put-downs? And to be critical... the various elements of the story run along autonomously, with only the Doctor's presence connecting the set-pieces. Aside from some outrageous coincidences there's very little linkage, either aesthetically or logically, from incident to incident. Had this not looked and sounded so good, with memorably "robust" performances all round, then it might have been a shambles. So it's David Maloney's triumph at least as much as Robert Holmes', and it doesn't hurt that Philip Hinchcliffe was keen on over-spending for his final story.

But the fact that "The Talons of Weng-Chiang" has done such a good job of hooking and snaring non-Doctor-Who-fans, in the '70s, '80s, '90s and even in the twenty-first century, is proof that its sheer *oomph* is enough to carry the story through. It is, above all, a summary of Why This Sort of Thing Works; after this you'll never need to watch anything else like it. Rat aside, its only really *visible* flaw is that it should clearly be five episodes long instead of six, with the padding at its most obvious in the last two parts as Jago and Litefoot find themselves escaping and immediately getting recaptured again. Still, considering that most six-parters are at least *two* episodes too long, even this has to be seen as a result.

The Facts

Written by Robert Holmes, from a story by Robert Banks Stewart (uncredited). Directed by David Maloney. Viewing figures: 11.3 million, 9.8 million, 10.2 million, 11.4 million, 10.1 million, 9.3 million.

Supporting Cast Trevor Baxter (Professor Litefoot), Christopher Benjamin (Jago), John Bennett (Li H'sen Chang), Deep Roy (Mr. Sin), Michael Spice (Weng-Chiang), David McKail (Sergeant Kyle), Conrad Asquith (P.C. Quick), Chris Gannon (Casey), Judith Lloyd (Teresa),

Vaune Craig-Raymond (Cleaning Woman), Penny Lister (Singer), Vincent Wong (Ho).

Working Titles "The Foe from the Future", "The Talons of Greel".

Cliffhangers The Doctor and Leela are faced by the screeching, ravenous horror of a giant rat in the sewers (theoretically); Mr. Sin stalks into Litefoot's house, knife in hand, and advances on Leela; back in the sewers, Leela gets to scream properly for the first time as the rat seizes her legs; Greel's carriage hurtles through the night, the re-captured time cabinet on board; struggling with Greel, Leela rips off his mask and reveals the horrible mess underneath.

The Lore

• Those not native to Britain should note that the UK will occasionally experience "moral panics", during which governments and film censors will suddenly introduce spurious new rules in an attempt to cut down on the amount of violence in the media. At one point the decision was made to ban all nunchuckas in movie and video releases, a rule enforced so stringently that you weren't even allowed to show posters of Bruce Lee holding the offending weapons. So when "The Talons of Weng-Chiang" came out on video in 1988, shots of nunchuckas and rice-flails were removed, and the holes were patched up with shots of the Doctor and his assailants suddenly going into slow motion (thus making the production look even more like a David Carradine knock-off). Still, at least there were no cartoon sound effects this time.

• Designer Roger Murray-Leech, one of the many long-term *Doctor Who* stalwarts making his last contribution here, had to send out leaflets requesting anyone living in the street where the cameras were filming to remove their cars. Arriving at the scene, the programme-makers found a Porsche parked outside one of the houses. You'll notice that in episode two there's a big pile of hay left in the street...

• David Maloney, who'd been touted as a possible successor to Hinchcliffe, never worked on the series again (at least not officially; see 16.6, "The Armageddon Factor"). Instead he produced a new project with Terry Nation, the much-derided *Blake's 7*. We'll be hearing more about this later on.

• Another departing mainstay of the series, production unit manager Chris D'Oyly-John, resigned earlier than he'd planned after the stress of managing the freewheeling budget on this story (see 14.3, "The Deadly Assassin", for the messy details). A last-minute replacement, one John Nathan-Turner, stepped in towards the end of the production.

• And the conductor of the Palace Theatre orchestra? It's regular series composer, Dudley Simpson.

• At the turn of the last century there was a celebrated stage magician known as Chung Ling Soo (but born Bill Robinson), and his costume as "The Celestial Chinese Conjurer" is overtly referenced by Chang's stage outfit; see also 3.7, "The Celestial Toymaker". His act involved him producing hefty bowls of goldfish out of nowhere - much like the act mentioned by the Doctor when "auditioning" for Jago - and catching a bullet on a china plate. This bullet-catch trick eventually cost him his life, on stage at the Wood Green Empire in 1918. It's now a branch of Sainsbury's.

• John Bennett (Chang) was told not to blink, as his make-up was a latex which wrinkled easily. They later decided to make this part of his character.

• The part of Leela had been written, and Louise Jameson had been contracted, on the understanding that she was to appear for three stories only. With so much else on his plate, producer-in-waiting Graham Williams decided to retain the character no matter what Tom Baker said. This required him to quietly sound out Jameson whilst on location. Her terms were that the contact lenses had to go (see 15.1, "Horror of Fang Rock").

• The fall-out from Mary Whitehouse's campaign of evil ensured that from this point on, close scrutiny was to be paid to all suggestions of violence or disturbing imagery at the script stage, rather than in the final edit. All subsequent stories were to be vetted *before* the director got involved (see **When Was** Doctor Who **Scary?** under the next story).

15.1: "Horror of Fang Rock"

(Serial 4V, Four Episodes, 3rd September - 24th September 1977.)

Which One is This? Picture a glowing, electrified blob of green jelly making its way up the staircase of an Edwardian lighthouse. In the dark. In the fog. If you've seen it, then you'll remember...

Firsts and Lasts Graham Williams makes his debut as the new producer, even if this wasn't the first story *made* in his reign (see **The Lore**). And as is so often the way, the opening story of the Williams era isn't even remotely typical of the stories to come. For a start, it's set in the past, making it the only pretend-historical of his producership. After this there'll be a much more "spacey" feel to the series, and the TARDIS won't travel back in time again - at least, not for a whole story - for nearly five years (19.4, "The Visitation").

The Rutans, first mentioned in "The Time Warrior" (11.1) and discussed almost every time their arch-enemies the Sontarans turn up, make their one and only on-screen appearance here. This is also the first and only time the entire production leaves London (except for location work); and the first time the Doctor overtly refers to the source of the story on-screen...

Four Things to Notice About "The Horror of Fang Rock"...

1. It's the story that beats even "Pyramids of Mars" (13.3) when it comes to death-tolls. At least in "Pyramids" a couple of minor extras managed to escape the bloodbath. "The Horror of Fang Rock" is the first *Doctor Who* story in which every living thing except for the Doctor and his companion ends up being slaughtered. This includes the Rutans on their way to Earth in their mothership, and we never even see them. (The story opens with a young lighthouse-keeper seeing the Rutan scout-ship crashing into the sea and being told that this 'shooting-star' should bring him luck. Oh, the horror.) Yet though no-one here gets out alive, the Doctor leaves the scene of the atrocity looking as chirpy as ever and quoting poetry at Leela.

Season 15 Cast/Crew

- Tom Baker (the Doctor)
- Louise Jameson (Leela)
- John Leeson (voice of K9, 15.2, 15.4 to 15.6)

- Graham Williams (Producer)
- Robert Holmes (Script Editor, 15.1 to 15.3)*
- Anthony Read (Script Editor, 15.4 to 15.6)

* Holmes was officially credited as script editor for 15.4, "The Sun Makers", but Read performed the editing duties as Holmes also wrote the story.

2. More tricks with perspective. Following on from the normal-sized rat and the miniaturised sewer set in "The Talons of Weng-Chiang", the first time we see the Rutan - a gelatinous blob which for once looks as if it's *meant* to be superimposed over the real world - is in episode two, when Leela looks down from the lighthouse and sees it glowing in the darkness far below. Cue a shot of a little model Rutan sitting on some rocks. The trouble is that by this stage we don't even know a Rutan's relative size, so the first time round it's not even clear whether Leela's looking at a big alien blob a long way away or a small alien blob right in front of her. The shot would be unthinkable today, and not just because of the "sophistication" of the effects technology, another sign that these days we process TV pictures very differently to the way we did it thirty years ago.

3. The best line here, and indeed one of the best lines in all of *Doctor Who*, tells you just how different this programme is / was to almost everything else on television. In most SF, if the hero confronts an alien intent on taking over the world then you're in for a tedious, po-faced speech on how nothing can overcome the human spirit. But the Doctor's casual-sounding response, after hearing the military hyperbole of the featureless green protoplasm that's already murdered almost everyone else in the story: 'That's the empty rhetoric of a defeated dictator. And I don't like your face, either.'

4. In the final episode, the Doctor goes off to search the lighthouse for the Rutan transmitter and makes it quite clear that he's under time pres-

sure to find it. The next time we see him, he's looking through the lighthouse-keepers' effects and shuffling through a pile of dirty Edwardian postcards. So we can only assume that he's… easily distracted.

The Continuity

The Doctor Has no problem fuelling people's superstitions when it's convenient, telling young Vince that electricity has pseudo-magical effects so as not to alarm the man about the apparent resurrection of Ben the lighthouse-keeper. He's also tactless enough to describe Lord Palmerdale's death as 'interesting' right in front of his distraught secretary / strumpet's face. And Leela gives her a slap when she starts screaming, just to make things worse.

For the second adventure in a row, the Doctor tries wearing a different hat than usual.

• *Ethics*. He not only has the technical know-how to turn Fang Rock lighthouse into an enormous laser-beam using a large diamond [and other bits and pieces from his pockets, surely?], but he doesn't hesitate to turn this weapon on the approaching Rutan mothership. Once again, he's prepared to kill like a soldier if he's got a planet to defend, and he doesn't mind Leela threatening people with physical violence. He later tells her that it's wrong to celebrate an enemy's death, but can't resist saying 'that showed them' in a glib way after blowing up the nasty aliens.

• *Background*. He speaks of the Pharos lighthouse as if he's seen it with his own eyes, and begins another anecdote about lighthouses with the words 'on Gallifrey -' before being interrupted. [Not necessarily meaning that they've got lighthouses on Gallifrey. Given the amount of technobabble in the programme at this point, he'd be likely to finish the sentence by saying something like '- we control the passage of etheric shipping with short-burst photonic impulses'. Then again, this is by the author of "The Five Doctors" (20.7), so it could just as well be a Tower of Rassilon reference. Nevertheless, the season ends with a story involving Gallifreyan "traffic control"; see 15.6, "The Invasion of Time".]

The Doctor knows that the Malicious Damage Act of 1861 covers lighthouses, hinting at a prior visit to the late nineteenth or early twentieth century [as in 14.6, "The Talons of Weng-Chiang"]. His reference to H. G. Wells as 'Herbert' is plainly

supposed to suggest that the Doctor has met Wells [but see 22.5, "Timelash"]. Unsurprisingly, he knows as much about Rutans as he does about Sontarans.

The Supporting Cast

• *Leela*. The Doctor still seems to be trying to educate her about her ancestors, as he's trying to take her to Brighton. She refers to the TARDIS as 'the machine', so she isn't too familiar with it yet, *but* she speaks of it failing 'again' when it misses its target. [The Doctor had no target in mind in "The Robots of Death", and it was bang on the button in "The Talons of Weng-Chiang", so there must be at least one landing between seasons that we never get to hear about.] She uses the word 'Teshnician', suggesting that she's halfway between Sevateem-talk and Doctor-speak by now. She also believes that listening to the old ones of your tribe is the only way to learn [explaining her view of the Doctor, though this philosophy *doesn't* apply to bad witch-doctors], but it's traditional among the Sevateem for the [very] old, the crippled and the blind to be slain.

She doesn't yet know better than to strip off in front of strange non-tribal men, and they don't have shrouds where she comes from, but she doesn't think it's possible for the dead to get up and walk. She claims that she no longer believes in magic, although the way she talks about 'science' suggests that she's just replacing one word with another, especially as she doesn't seem to grasp any actual scientific principles. Here she gloats over an enemy's death instead of treating it with respect.

The Doctor acknowledges that Leela's senses are particularly acute, so she feels a drop in temperature before he does. When the Rutan mothership explodes, the flash permanently changes Leela's eye-colour from brown to blue. She's willing to risk her life to go back for her much-loved knife, even when she knows there's an explosion imminent.

The TARDIS The TARDIS lands near Southampton when it's heading for Brighton, and the Doctor can tell they're in the right time. On this occasion he can't give an exact location, though, as the fog has confused the visual orientation circuits. [Suggesting that the TARDIS "looks" where it's going before it lands. This is weird by human navigational standards, but

When Was *Doctor Who* Scary?

The obvious answer to this is "when you were eight years old". The programme's development always kept abreast of what television could do and what small children could handle, but the definition of "scary" varied wildly. As we saw in "The Ark In Space" (12.2), the visceral, gory notion of what the Wirrn are up to is mainly suggested, never seen. On-screen what we get are sleeping-bag monsters and people with blister-wrap on their hands. *Doctor Who* traditionally went for conceptual horror rather than entrails; if you were old enough to be troubled by the Wirrn, then you were old enough to know that it was just actors and rubber.

But that's *horror*, not terror. It's got more to do with disgust than fright. Knowing, cerebral fear is never going to match the sickly, suffocating kind that tugs at children's guts. There's something else at work here, and the problem one has explaining this to anyone who wasn't there at the time is that quite simply, the context has altered beyond all recognition.

Until the early '70s, the very signature tune of *Doctor Who* used to terrify children. It sounded unlike anything else, anywhere. The title sequences were also unnervingly "other", and their sheer strangeness could lead to nightmare-visions. This faded as synthesisers became more widely-used, and besides, the "Bohemian Rhapsody" video was quite clearly more disturbing than anything produced by the BBC effects department or Radiophonic Workshop.

Yet things were different in the early years. It was the place of *Doctor Who* within Saturday Nights on BBC1 to be (a) unlike everything else, but (b) interpretable in the context of *how* you watched television (see **Is This Really a Science Fiction Series?** under 14.4, "The Face of Evil"). In the era of 405-line monochrome TV, it was an effort of will to make sense of any picture, be it Sonny and Cher, Geoff Hurst scoring a hat trick against Germany, or Yartek, Leader of the Alien Voord. Televiewing - as they used to call it - was an active, participatory process. "Background" TV came with 625-line transmission, and sets that warmed up almost as soon as you switched them on. The tradition of cowering behind the sofa, although it's been made a cliché lately, was part of the way one engaged with all television; it was "real" but not "true", it was only happening because you willed it to happen. Any child frightened by the Daleks had, to a certain extent, decided to be frightened. And if that child was excited beyond

accepted limits, then the rest of the family were in the room. Nobody watched television alone.

The key thing to remember about the Daleks is that, for once, Mum couldn't definitively say it was a man in a rubber suit. She was equally at a loss to explain how they made those noises. The transition to 625 lines and colour wasn't a uniform process, so it's hard to put a definitive date on it, but we'll assume that by "The Daemons" in 1971 (8.5) most people had fairly clear reception. This was the golden age of the "domestic" monster, hence Jon Pertwee's oft-repeated comment about a Yeti sitting on a loo in Tooting Bec being more frightening than a monster in outer space. As had always been the case, the sight of the monster was a "tease", usually left until the first cliffhanger. In an odd sort of way the monster took the place of the decorative girl, something there primarily as a spectacle and with characterisation a poor second. The visual aesthetic of the programme was always about putting the "pretty" or "way-out" effect *within* the narrative, even though it was - at any given moment - there for its own sake. A disruption to the normal order of things, like a T-Rex mimsily flapping about in London (11.2, "Invasion of the Dinosaurs"), was odd rather than scary. Someone trapped in a warehouse with a dinosaur was scary.

In terms of conceptual fear, the scariest thing in *Doctor Who* was always the thought of being shut off from home. The programme's very premise involved wrenching people away from the familiar with no hope of return. Although the early '70s UNIT era robbed us of this, the first year of Tom Baker's reign saw Our Heroes trapped inside increasingly unsympathetic bureaucracies. Being judged by the standards of another time and with no appeal to anything outside those rules was the central terror of "The Ark in Space" and "Genesis of the Daleks" (12.4), not any threat from monsters or gas-grenades.

Yet context is everything. Ironically, though this far-from-home-ness was almost entirely absent during the early '70s, it was the Jon Pertwee / UNIT stories which allowed the early Tom Baker tales to work so well. "The Ark in Space" just wouldn't have come off, if we hadn't seen the Doctor and companions leave Earth a week earlier. Outer space can only alienate you if you're *trying* to get back to the known world, and part of Season Twelve's horror is the contrast with the homeliness of stories

continued on page 161...

there's a kind of logic here. It'd explain why the TARDIS seems to occasionally materialise in orbit of the planets it's visiting, and why it got so confused in "The Android Invasion" (13.4). See also **Does the TARDIS Fly?** under 5.6, "Fury from the Deep".]

Leela emerges from the Ship in period Victorian / Edwardian dress, though not the same outfit she wore in the 1890s. [Indeed, it's very Romana-ish; c.f. "Shada" (17.6) and "City of Death" (17.2)]. The clothes get left on Fang Rock, but the sweater and trousers she borrows are taken with her. [The TARDIS wardrobe must pick up a lot of clothing this way. Leela ran off with the outfit from "The Talons of Weng-Chiang", too.]

The Non-Humans

• *Rutans.* The long-term enemies of the Sontarans, Rutans are amphibious, and evolved in the sea on the icy planet of Ruta 3. [See 11.1, "The Time Warrior", for a longer look at the Rutan / Sontaran war.] The Rutan which crash-lands near Fang Rock lighthouse is a glowing green gelatinous blob with tentacles in its natural form, looking more like a jellyfish than anything else on Earth. It can drain electricity from a generator, and anyone touching it is electrocuted to death. This might explain why it makes electrical-sounding crackling noises when it moves.

Though apparently slow, it's capable of crawling up a sheer vertical surface, and seems to be able to sense the presence of nearby humanoids. Single projectiles go through it, but large numbers of small projectiles are capable of killing it, while heat causes it intense pain. This Rutan speaks of itself as 'we'. [Terrance Dicks' later novels have hinted that the Rutan Host is some sort of gestalt intelligence, but here the 'we' could be a '"royal we" for all we know.] Its voice sounds uncannily like that of Morbius [13.5].

This Rutan can, like so many beings in the universe, alter its shape and exactly mimic a human being. However, it must first analyse the life-pattern of a single member of the original species, something which involves taking apart a dead subject. The voice and clothes of the original are copied, and it smiles as it kills, though the humanised Rutan occasionally glows green for no given reason. Not all Rutans have the shape-changing ability, as this specimen is a scout of the Rutan Empire who's been specially trained in the 'new' metamorphosis techniques. [The Rutan isn't seen to be carrying any equipment, so this may not be technological. It's possible that all Rutans are capable of changing their jelly-like shape to *some* degree, but that this one has been trained to exactly mimic the close details of other species. The Rutan only dissects its very first victim, yet it never impersonates those it hasn't killed.] This organic restructuring is elementary physiology for the Time Lords, according to the Doctor, but something the lesser species might only grasp after a few thousand centuries. Intriguingly the Doctor also likens this to lycanthropy [making the Time Lords sound like a bunch of werewolves]. Even a disguised Rutan delivers a lethal shock.

Rutan spacecraft have shielded crystalline infra-structures, the scout-ship coming to Earth as a purple fireball and the mothership appearing as a glowing orange sphere. Landing on a planet like Earth, they cut off their energy-fields to save power, so the Doctor can blow up the mothership by focusing the beam from a lighthouse through a diamond and using it as a primitive laser. The beam ostensibly locks on to the ship's carbon resonator and knocks out its anti-grav, but ultimately it just explodes in a big flash that causes 'pigmentation dispersal' in Leela's eyes.

The Rutan scout has the ability to release a freezing fog [from the ship] which mimics conditions on its homeworld. It also leaves a silver, rod-like power relay in the lighthouse generator room, which powers a signal calling the mothership. No reason is given for the scout's crash [unlike the Sontaran in "The Time Warrior", it wasn't shot down].

Predictably, the Rutans are murderous, dictatorial, self-interested and certainly no better than the Sontarans. The Doctor states that the Rutans used to control the whole of the Mutter's Spiral, but that the Sontarans have now driven them to the fringes of the galaxy. Now he believes the Rutans are losing their 'interminable' war, but the scout insists that the glorious Rutan army is making a series of strategic withdrawals. The scout describes Earth as having a useful strategic position, the only suitable planet in the solar system from which to launch a 'final' assault on the Sontaran rabble. The other Rutans don't know about Earth, though, and won't until the scout's mothership returns to the fleet. Since the Doctor destroys the mothership, he believes the Rutans will conclude this part of space to be too dangerous for an attack.

When Was *Doctor Who* Scary?

...continued from page 159

like "Robot" (12.1). But by the late '70s, things had become almost wholly abstract. The Doctor had no real connection with Earth, and there were no longer any human beings on board the TARDIS, so getting stuck on a spaceship in a far-flung corner of the universe became "business as usual" rather than "terrifying." "The Horns of Nimon" (17.5) sees the Doctor separated from Romana and stranded in the middle of nowhere, yet he seems almost cosy as he hangs in the middle of the void, and Romana doesn't look particularly bothered by her abduction. By this stage it's taken as read that the TARDIS crew *can* get out of any fix, and that everybody knows there's no real danger. The Doctor becomes as solid and as dependable as your parents are supposed to be, so it's little wonder that younger viewers found it so disturbing when he became either untrustworthy (15.2, "The Invisible Enemy") or violable (see 18.1, "The Leisure Hive", for much, much more on this).

But back to the mid-'70s. Another odd feature of Philip Hinchcliffe's term as producer was that no-one could judge whether a monster or effect was in any way scary until it was transmitted. During filming, such items as Magnus Greel (14.6, "The Talons of Weng-Chiang") or the Doctor's head being held underwater in freeze-frame (14.3, "The Deadly Assassin") looked vaguely ridiculous. On the other hand the giant rat looked scary in the studio, but not on-screen. Hinchcliffe's success ruffled feathers amongst the BBC hierarchy, and his replacement Graham Williams was ordered to tone down both the violence and the "scariness."

However, many of the ideas in Williams stories are - on reflection - more repulsive or anxiety-inducing than any latex mask or slimy green goo. Leela being steamed alive (15.4, "The Sun Makers") is potentially the most unpleasant idea ever, but it's all talk. The anecdotes of the Graff and his general, Sholakh (16.1, "The Ribos Operation"), are

bloodcurdling. Seeing Captain Rigg become addicted to vraxoin (17.4, "Nightmare of Eden") may not send kids scuttling behind the sofa, but could be harrowing for adults, assuming any were taking the story seriously by that stage.

Yet the gut-level, child-nightmare kind of fear that had once been associated with the series pretty much ended with "Horror of Fang Rock." *Doctor Who* still utilised the "props" of fear-mongery - notably the monsters - but all the strangeness had gone, and without strangeness there was no fear. In 1979 the popular media was still claiming that creations like the Mandrels ("Nightmare of Eden", again) were giving children sleepless nights, though by that stage magazine photos of *Alien* were already circulating around school playgrounds and the opening credits of *Tales of the Unexpected* had set a new benchmark for weird terror among seven-year-olds.

With children, however, there's one final problem. No-one knows what a child will find scary or laughable. Many things can be both at once, if they're unsettling. After all, laughter is relief at a threat that's passed, or the result of a surprise. For every tot who thought the Wirrn were cute, there's someone who messed himself over the disease-riddled Lazars grabbing Tegan (20.4, "Terminus"). For everyone who sneered at the Sea Devils in 1972, there's someone who was distressed by them in 1984 (21.1, "Warriors of the Deep"). So far, however, extensive research has failed to locate anyone scared by the Myrka.

When the programme was aimed primarily at scaring children, it failed to convince as drama... though it was often hugely memorable and frequently produced some lovely imagery, and since it was originally only meant to be seen *once*, you could argue that this alone was enough to make it worthwhile. But when it was exploring characters in odd and stressful situations, it also - as a by-product - gave a lot of children the screaming abdabs. Which may have been a better strategy.

[The script seems to treat 'Mutter's Spiral' as another name for Earth's galaxy, as in "The Deadly Assassin" (14.3), but it could simply be the part of the galaxy that contains Earth. As Rutans have never been anywhere near Earth before, and as "The Sontaran Experiment" (12.3) establishes that Sontarans aren't native to this galaxy, the Doctor's statement about the Rutans controlling this part of space makes sense if this galaxy is well behind the Rutan front-line but not actually overrun with the

species. This would explain why Earth isn't of strategic importance in the Middle Ages - Linx's arrival in "The Time Warrior" (11.1) was a rare excursion into the Rutan zone - but has become a battle-front now the Rutans are being forced back. The Rutans presumably hold their own for some while after this, though, as in "The Sontaran Experiment" it's about 13,000 years (ish) later and the Sontarans are only just paying attention to Earth's galaxy again. But at least the galaxy seems

Rutan-free in that period. The Rutan scout's talk of a 'final' assault against the Sontarans is obviously just bluster.]

Sontarans. The Doctor believes that if the Rutans set up a power-base on Earth, then the Sontarans will bombard the planet with photonic missiles and turn it into a cinder.

History

• *Dating*. The early twentieth century, when lighthouses are going electric and an oil-vapour system is being introduced. King Edward is mentioned, so it must be between 1902 and 1910. [Terrance Dicks' own description of the story taking place at 'the turn of the century' makes 1901 the most likely date by far.] Colonel Skinsale mentions Bonar-Law as though the latter were a rising star in British politics. [Canadian-born Andrew Bonar-Law was Prime Minister in the 1920s, although nobody noticed.]

Fang Rock is evidently in the English Channel, probably only five or six miles from Southampton. The old lighthouse-keeper knows the story of the Beast of Fang Rock from the 1820s, 'eighty years ago'. Two keepers are said to have died on the night the Beast was seen, and the third went mad. The beast clearly has nothing to do with the Rutan, so this remains a mystery [see 9.3, "The Sea Devils", for other spooky goings-on in the area].

The Analysis

Where Does This Come From?   Take the story "Who Goes Here?" by John W. Campbell, long-time editor of Astounding Science Fiction. Remove the bits used in the 1951 film version, *The Thing From Another World*, but keep all the bits about shape-changing that Hollywood ignored. Place in an Edwardian lighthouse and stir.

The poem quoted at the end of the story, "The Ballad of Flannen Isle", has three lighthouse-keepers turning into odd-looking birds. The book mentioned by the Doctor, E. G. Jerome's *Lighthouses, Lightships and Buoys*, was the principal source that Terrance Dicks consulted.

Things That Don't Make Sense   It really is *spectacularly* easy to blow up an alien warship with a lighthouse and a diamond. [We have to assume that the Doctor adds some hardware / Gallifreyan know-how of his own, or that the Rutan ship's

structure is ultra-susceptible to this sort of thing. If it were that easy to make death-rays then World War One would have looked like *Buck Rogers*.]

Young Vince recovers from the shock of seeing his dead friend walking pretty sharpish, while Adelaide, the aforementioned secretary / strumpet, is prepared to wander around the killer lighthouse all on her own as soon as Colonel Skinsale gets her to throw a tantrum. The lighthouse-keeper who first spies the Rutan ship perceives it as a glowing red fireball, but nobody seems to have told the effects people this, as it's clearly bright purple.

From an aesthetic point of view... it's odd that although the script keeps mocking old Reuben for wanting to bring back oil and get rid of this new-fangled electricity, the Rutan uses the electricity as a weapon, suggesting that this modern twentieth century isn't as great as it's cracked up to be after all. Whose side is the story on, anyway?

Critique   If there's one thing Terrance Dicks is good at, it's efficiency. Required to write a script involving minimal sets, minimal monster costumes and minimal fuss all-round, "Horror of Fang Rock" wisely goes for the classic people-trapped-in-a-small-space-with-something-nasty model. "The Ark in Space" did the same thing, of course, but "Ark" had to be clinical by its very nature; shiny, ultra-efficient space stations aren't supposed to look lived-in. Once again, the props of BBC costume drama (and not just the purely physical ones, either) are used to invoke the menace of *old things*, of dark corners and mahogany machinery.

Those who didn't grow up watching BBC TV in the '70s might not recognise the tone and texture, but this was an age when children watched *When the Boat Comes In* just for the funny theme-tune, and at the time it looked as if a crawling alien monster had "leaked" into one of the Corporation's more serious-minded historical productions. Which means, ironically, that it works better now than it did at the time. Given that less than an hour after each episode we were off to the Bentinck Hotel for *The Duchess of Duke Street*, it was all a bit of a let-down on transmission. Watch it now, out of sequence and ideally on a wet night, and it's wonderful. On a sunny September evening it was "same-old same-old". The ratings picked up as the nights drew in, but it's only now they don't make 'em like that any more that this story has come into its own.

Still, the timing of "Fang Rock" makes it work as much as its setting. The decision to set the story on a single night means that in parts it almost feels as if it's being told in real-time, always a good trick if you're trying to build up a sense of claustrophobia. Even the body-count seems like a way of tightening the noose around the Doctor rather than a gratuitous murder spree. Like *Alien* (not an obvious comparison, but keep reading) it gains its momentum not from the number of on-screen deaths but from the sequence. Every killing alters the balance of power in the lighthouse and shifts our expectations of what kind of story this is going to be. Skinsale is so much the affable old soldier, midway between Professor Litefoot and Lethbridge-Stewart, that his death is a genuine surprise; we'd have laid money that he was going to say " 'pon my soul" as he watched the TARDIS vanish. Similarly, Harker is clearly a competent, well-motivated character of the kind usually given a good chance of survival (just look at "Image of the Fendahl" and see how Adam Colby sets out to be unkillable from the very first minute).

And it helps that in this period, the programme's found the ideal balance between the needs of the script and the lead actor's showmanship. If the lines were to get any more serious then they'd sound awkward coming out of Tom Baker's mouth, and if he were left to "perform" any more than this then things would just get silly. Yet the moment when he breaks the news to the humans that they may all be dead by morning - with a ruddy great smile on his face - tells you everything you need to know about the way we like to remember his version of the character. Odd that this story's often remembered as a good showcase for Leela, though, as at times her snarling and gnashing of teeth verges on self-parody.

As a story that marks the beginning of a new producership? Well, the differences between this and a Hinchcliffe production start with the music. There's barely any for much of the first episode, and it's almost all conventional instrumentation. (There's one electric piano, as used in about half of that year's hit singles. The Rutan burble is oddly prescient of "Wishing On A Star" by Rose Royce, the *Top of the Pops* performance of which featured a camera trick exactly like the POV shots in episode one. A nation's kids came to believe that vocalist Gwen Dickie was a jelly-monster.)

Under the previous administration, the music had almost been a character. In Season Thirteen there was a scripted reason for a piece of music at every turn, and in "The Talons of Weng-Chiang" we finally got to see Dudley Simpson in person. No matter what planet we were on, we were told that we were in Doctor-Who-land. Here that begins to change. Hinchcliffe and Holmes had systematically set about removing the pillars of the programme they inherited; Williams had a policy of "15% change a year", and sought to quietly remove the dead wood before putting his own stamp on the show. Until the advent of *Doctor Who Weekly*, nobody really knew who the producer was, but in many ways the self-indulgence of later Hinchcliffe stories - if you want to call it that - was most noticeable once it went. "Fang Rock" can certainly be considered a *small* story, and you can tell the production team would have preferred to kick off the new season with something grander, but at times it seems to be wilfully trying to sum up the way the whole series is supposed to work. The Doctor's telling reply, when he's asked if he's in charge around here: 'No, but I'm full of ideas.'

That's four good stories in a row, five if you insist on liking "The Deadly Assassin". Surely, the series can't keep this up?

The Facts

Written by Terrance Dicks. Directed by Paddy Russell. Viewing figures: 6.8 million, 7.1 million, 9.8 million, 9.9 million.

Supporting Cast Alan Rowe (Skinsale), John Abbott (Vince), Colin Douglas (Reuben), Sean Caffrey (Lord Palmerdale), Annette Woollett (Adelaide), Rio Fanning (Harker), Ralph Watson (Ben).

Working Titles "The Rocks of Doom", "The Monster of Fang Rock", "The Beast of Fang Rock".

Cliffhangers With the lighthouse out of action, a ship runs itself aground on Fang Rock; as the Doctor tries to convince those assembled in the lighthouse that they're under attack, a great scream rings out from downstairs (not the most convincing cliffhanger of all time, considering that people are *always* screaming in this programme); the Doctor, admitting to a mistake for once in his life, tells Leela that instead of locking the alien out of the lighthouse he's actually locked it *in*.

The Lore

• Following his goth-sci-fi reconstruction of *Frankenstein* in Season Thirteen, Terrance Dicks' original submission for Season Fifteen was a tale of Time Lords and vampires called "The Witch Lords". Scheduled to open the season, large chunks of the script had already been written when the higher powers of the BBC intervened and stopped it, as BBC1 was about to launch a much-publicised adaptation of *Dracula* and didn't want to give itself competition. "Horror of Fang Rock" was therefore a work of desperation, based on a suggestion from Robert Holmes (i.e. "do a story set in a lighthouse").

The second story of the season, "The Invisible Enemy", was produced first so that "Fang Rock" could be hurriedly prepared - which partially explains why so much of "The Invisible Enemy" looks half-finished. On top of that there was the usual BBC rush to get Christmas specials made, the same reason that the programme-makers went to Birmingham to film this story instead of staying in London. "The Witch Lords" didn't go to waste, though, and ended up being recycled three years later (18.4, "State of Decay").

• Once the production had moved to Birmingham's Pebble Mill studios, the local crew found that the Londoners were very impressed by their no-nonsense approach, getting things done in less time than the stroppy set-hands in London would. This was the one bright spot in an otherwise troubled production, as Baker and Jameson went head-to-head and director Paddy Russell removed all breakable objects. (As we see from "The Deadly Assassin" onwards, Baker just didn't want a companion.) Russell's ploy to get a quick and easy shoot was to remove options from Baker; the star complained that his "Auntie Wyn" wouldn't be able to see him. ("Auntie Wyn" was the term that Baker adopted to mean "the average viewer", although in fact it was costume designer James Acheson who said that Baker resembled his auntie Wyn.) Eventually Baker backed down, but he bitchily called Russell 'sir' from that point on. She left the BBC soon after.

• As we've already seen, Louise Jameson had taken the part of Leela for a three-story contract, which stipulated that she retained the brown contact-lenses worn in "The Face of Evil". With the contract renewal, she could insist that the lenses - which caused her considerable discomfort - had

to go. Terrance Dicks resorted to temporarily blinding *another* companion (see 13.5, "The Brain of Morbius") as a means to this end. Jameson's recurrent glandular fever also meant that she missed out on promoting the story on *Multi-Coloured Swap Shop*, the new Saturday Morning children's TV version of E-Bay.

• In the first draft of the script (they had time for a first draft?), Lord Palmerdale was called "Peach-Palmer". He had a valet called Burkin and a secretary, Adelaide Couchon. Colonel Skinsalde (with a "d") was accompanied by his wife, Veronica, while Reuben was called "Josh" (ooh-arr... see 8.3, "The Claws of Axos") and Vince was "Davy Williams".

• Contrary to popular belief, neither this nor "The Witch Lords" is the story being discussed in the documentary *Whose Doctor Who?* (a documentary that can now be found on "The Talons of Weng-Chiang" DVD). Holmes, Dicks and Hinchcliffe are instead faking a typical script conference for the cameras. Even so, some of what's discussed resembles Douglas Adams' very very early versions of the story that eventually became "The Pirate Planet" (16.2), portions of which - notably the pacifier ray, and Time Lord guilt for interventions which went awry - also got recycled for "Underworld" (15.5).

• The character of Harker got his name as a backhanded reference to the *Dracula* adaptation mentioned above. Which wasn't very good.

• Robert Holmes was in an unforgiving mood as Dicks submitted the scripts; he'd been miffed at getting told off by the powers-that-be for putting anachronistic potatoes in "The Time Warrior" (11.1), and so made Dicks do a great deal of research to avoid any such gaffes.

15.2: "The Invisible Enemy"

(Serial 4S, Four Episodes, 1st October - 22nd October 1977.)

Which One is This? The Doctor gets miniaturised and injected into someone's body, but out-does *Fantastic Voyage* by making sure that the body in question is his own. Then the virus that's been bothering him gets out of his system and grows to man-size, and it looks just like a... no, you wouldn't believe it.

Firks and Lasts First appearance of K9, who quickly becomes either a key element of the series in the late '70s or a chronic annoyance, depending on your point of view. Right from the start, though, he has a status unlike any other recurring "character" in the series. Half-companion, half-general-purpose-tool (in many ways he's just the sonic screwdriver on wheels, although his laser-powered nose also saves the Doctor the trouble of having to knock people out with fisticuffs), he's supposedly a regular member of the TARDIS crew but occasionally skips whole stories when he'd just get in the way.

The shiny white TARDIS console room makes a comeback here after its break in Season Fourteen, and the new design looks much more like the '60s original, only... cheaper. It's the first full story to utilise the talents of production unit manager (i.e. combination gopher and accountant) John Nathan-Turner, six months earlier than planned; see 14.6, "The Talons of Weng-Chiang", for the reasons. This man's going to crop up a lot later on.

Four Things to Notice About "The Invisible Enemy"...

1. This is the point when *Doctor Who* starts to move away from being a programme about monsters, and concentrates on being a programme about outer space instead (it can be a subtle distinction, but see number two), so it's our last chance to make fun of an ill-conceived monster costume for some time. But *what* a chance. The story of a cosmic virus that grows to human-size, when the virus nucleus manifests itself at the end of episode three it's revealed to be... a giant shrimp. There's no other way of putting it. It's just a giant shrimp. And not even a very scary giant shrimp, either.

2. Nobody these days can watch "The Invisible Enemy" - and take the year in which it was made into consideration - without immediately noticing one thing: this is *Doctor Who* coming as close as it ever gets to *Star Wars*, introducing a new "cute" robot sidekick and getting carried away with blaster-fights in space-station corridors. Curiously, though, it's safe to say that George Lucas didn't influence the story one iota. It's true that K9's popularity was virtually guaranteed in the droid-obsessed popular culture of 1978-79, but cutesy robots were becoming fashionable in SF even pre-R2-D2, and "The Invisible Enemy" was made too soon to be accused of cashing in on the year's big movie. It was filmed in April 1977, weeks before

anyone in America had even heard of *Star Wars* (which wasn't hyped in the US until after its release) and eight months before the film opened in Britain.

3. As has already been mentioned under the previous story, "The Invisible Enemy" was made in a bit of a rush, which might explain why so much of it looks half-finished. Everything's "simple" in this version of the future - even the English language seems to have been stripped down, judging by the signs on the walls - and the predominant style in the space-stations of the fiftieth century can best be described as Cheap Ikea. Bonus points can be scored for spotting the various pieces of hi-tech equipment which don't appear to have any moving parts.

4. Professor Marius, K9's creator, makes the obvious 'TARDIS-trained' gag within ten seconds of K9 joining the Doctor's crew. This didn't stop newspaper cartoonists and everybody's parents making the same joke over and over again for the next four years.

The Continuity

The Doctor Here he once again goes into a self-induced cataleptic trance, but even when he's in this state he can work out TARDIS settings for the journey from Titan to the Bi-Al Foundation. [The settings he gives are shorter than normal TARDIS co-ordinates and involve the word "vector", suggesting a short hop from a certain point rather than absolute co-ordinates. Even so, it means that he knows where the Bi-Al asteroid is in relation to Titan.] Struggling to resist the virus when it's inside him, at one point he's actually prepared to plead with it not to kill Leela, a rare moment of weakness.

Examining the Doctor, Professor Marius believes him to have a symbiotic self-renewing cell structure. [Either this just means that the Doctor heals quickly, or Marius has spotted something in his cells which hints at the Time Lord ability to regenerate. "Symbiotic" suggests two mutually dependent entities, though. This may mean that although Marius can tell the Doctor's supposed to be able to regenerate, it's also clear that he needs help from someone or something else. Presumably the TARDIS; after all, in "Power of the Daleks" (4.3) the Doctor describes his physical change as 'part of the TARDIS'.]

More interesting still, the Doctor has a reflex-link in his brain which would normally allow him to tune himself into the Time Lord 'intelligentsia, a thousand super-brains in one', but he lost this faculty when they kicked him out. [It's already been established that all Time Lords are telepathic, and this is apparently the part of the Doctor's brain which lets him communicate with other Time Lords. It must still be operational in some way, as the Doctor telepathically links with himself in "The Three Doctors" (10.1) and seems to have some mental connection to the Master in "Logopolis" (18.7), so the fact that he can no longer contact the 'intelligentsia' would seem to suggest that he could only do it on Gallifrey. Though the reflex-link may well be activated when dead Time Lords have their brains scanned by the Matrix - 14.3, "The Deadly Assassin" - it's probably got nothing to do with the Matrix the rest of the time, as many Time Lords don't even know the Matrix exists. The Doctor didn't, until last year.]

• *Ethics*. His moral debate with the virus nucleus is... strange. The virus claims that it has as much right to swarm and multiply as the human species, and the Doctor doesn't dispute it, as by this argument he has the right to dispose of the virus as well. *But* he later says that the virus has to be stopped because it threatens the macro-world of the humans as well as the micro-world of most viruses. Everything has its place, and the Doctor sees it as *his* place to keep the balance. [Spurious morality. All viruses affect the macro-world, by affecting the behaviour of larger animals. The only difference is that *this* virus is better at it than most. The impression we get here is that the Doctor wants to save the humans, again, and is improvising this rubbish in response to what the nucleus says.]

• *Inventory*. He's carrying a duck-whistle, and conveniently enough he's got a dog-lead about his person even before he knows K9's liable to run out of power.

The Supporting Cast

• *Leela*. She's now learning to write in joined-up letters, though she may have been able to read a little before this [14.5, "The Robots of Death"]. It's implied that she knows how to set the TARDIS co-ordinates, but she's never actually seen to enter them into the console. [It's possible that the "possessed" Lowe operates the controls for her, or that the Doctor briefly breaks his trance to press the relevant buttons.] She knows the Doctor comes

from Gallifrey, making her the first companion to take the name of the Doctor's homeworld for granted.

Leela's senses are so good that she can feel the virus' malevolent influence even from within the TARDIS, and she can tell by the sound of a man's voice whether he's possessed or not. The nurse at Bi-Al takes one look at Leela's biology and describes her as 'a bit of a mongrel'. Her body contains antibodies, perhaps in some way connected to her sense of instinct, which can defeat the Virus of the Purpose. [It could be argued that as 5000 AD is Leela's past, the antibodies used to cure the other humans become a time paradox. But there's no indication here that they "spread" to the whole of humanity after this. They could well have developed naturally in her people.]

• *K9*. Presented as computer on wheels rather than a robot per se, K9 was built by Professor Marius on the Bi-Al Station, as an all-purpose tool in his work but also as a replacement for the dog he had to leave on Earth thanks to the 'weight penalty'. [The implication must be that Marius built K9 out of odds and ends, which would explain the unit's simple, blocky shape. By the fiftieth century humanity *must* have the ability to build a convincing robot dog, legs and all, but Marius just didn't have the parts. Nevertheless, the extensive knowledge in K9's data-banks would suggest that Marius put an awful lot of care and attention into him.]

K9's voice has human inflections, but constantly speaks at an irritatingly high pitch. His motors make a noticeable growling noise when he moves; his antennae-like "ears" wiggle when he's mentally active; and the little red "eye" in the middle of his face extends when he's examining something. A photon-beam energy weapon is built into his nose, which can stun human beings or kill on the highest of its four settings, but it drains his power quite rapidly. 'Affirmative', rather than the much more simple 'yes', is the first word he's ever heard to say. The very '70s computer-lettering on his side is typical of the year 5000.

K9 believes he knows everything Marius knows, 'and more'. His scan of the Doctor is accurate enough to spot the Doctor's self-renewing cell structure, and it's recorded on a strip of paper which spools out of his head-unit. He can also spot the virus' presence in moments. After being taken over by the Virus of the Purpose, his motivational circuits are confused and he shuts down,

Cultural Primer #2: Why *Blue Peter*?

Anyone growing up in Britain after 1958 knows about *Blue Peter*. It's just there, like the rain or Wales. The format is simplicity itself. Three or four twentysomethings in a brightly-coloured set - which actually looks a bit like the white void from "The Mind Robber" (6.2), only with the endless vacuum broken up by multicoloured shelving units - present a live, often-educational magazine show for children with "exciting" filmed inserts about one of the presenters climbing up the side of a famous building or potholing in a Victorian sewer.

For two generations these people were a surrogate family, with pets and hobbies and occasional fashion-sense defects, and their interaction with the nation's youth was more familiar and familial than viewers writing to "ordinary" TV stars. So come the autumn they'd start asking for old milk-bottle-tops, discarded toys, used stamps or what-have-you for their annual charity appeal, and they'd be inundated. When one of them got flack for wearing old jeans, there'd be a nation of ten-year-old Gaultiers sending in designs for suits. The programme had - and still has, though the series has been almost buried by the modern media - its own traditions, its own ceremonies, its own dogs and cats and tortoises who've lived, hung around the studio and died as the years have gone by.

Doctor Who producers did their utmost to use *Blue Peter* as a means to entice the nation. Just look at 1967, a year when the official histories say that Patrick Troughton hid from the public. There he is as the judge of the "Design a Monster for *Doctor Who*" competition, which he did in costume and in character (the runner-up was Andrew Partridge of Swindon, ten years before his first appearance on Top Of The Pops in XTC). When the BBC Radiophonic Workshop took delivery of its first ever synthesiser, it was wheeled into the *Blue Peter* studio to be demonstrated by Brian Hodgson, and we saw a clip of it providing the sound of the Yeti spheres (in 5.2 "The Abominable Snowmen"). Each new Doctor made an early appearance on the programme as a guest, prompting a series of flashbacks, often the same montage - and script - used in 1973 for the Tenth Anniversary / Jon Pertwee / "Whomobile" item (see 11.2, "Invasion of the Dinosaurs").

In fact both programmes grew out of the same BBC ethos of public service television, aiming to provide something the commercial stations wouldn't or didn't, engaging the young as responsibly as possible without being dull. Both retained the original idea that in an age before widely-available air travel, it was the BBC's job to show its viewers the world, to set it all in a historical context but as a series of human-interest stories. *Doctor Who* did this with time-travel. *Blue Peter* did it with trips abroad and lots of dressing-up. But there are moments, especially in the Hartnell episodes, when the programmes are almost indistinguishable. In "Marco Polo" (1.4) Ian explains to the viewers how being so high above sea-level makes water boil at lower temperatures, just as Barbara realises she's meeting a Famous Person from History. All that's missing is a cake-decorating hint. One area where *Doctor Who* had an obvious advantage was fights, but after the Noakes-Purves team settled in (keep reading) they even ended up doing stunts with *Doctor Who*'s regular action-troupe Havoc.

The big problem with all of this, of course, was that the surrogate TV family was almost unbearably middle-class. Those who've seen "The Talons of Weng-Chiang" DVD will know that over a number of weeks *Blue Peter* showed its viewers how to build a cardboard "theatre" for the cut-out *Doctor Who* figures printed in the *Radio Times*. This culminated in Dick Mills' demonstration of how to make space-aged sound effects with ordinary household items. One of these items was a small tub of resin... of the kind you might use to clean violins. Sorry, what was that? You don't...? Oh, surely you must. Doesn't everybody?

"Making things" was an important part of the *Blue Peter* philosophy. If you're American, you can think of it as a kind of televised Summer Camp, where you were considered to have completed the process once you'd successfully made a spaceship out of glitter and toilet rolls. Indeed, many of the jokes people make about "spaceships made out of Fairy Liquid bottles" in *Doctor Who* may be mis-remembered folk-memories of *Blue Peter* making the kind of things that *might* have been in *Doctor Who*. Or perhaps the programme just made the audience more aware of the fact that for every Cyberman spaceship you saw on-screen, there had to be someone at the BBC gluing the bits together. Once you've seen *Blue Peter*'s instructions for making a doll's kitchen, it's hard to look at the diorama of the Mechanoid city in "The Chase" (2.8) without expecting Steven to say '...and here's one I made earlier'. But in the hands of presenter and goddess-of-wisdom archetype Valerie

continued on page 169...

but soon regenerates - his word - and returns to his usual self.

Blaster fire doesn't damage him. The instruction Marius gives him, 'Ka-Lay-Lee', is delivered as if it were an attack command. [But it may well be a transfer protocol allowing Leela to give him orders, in which case K9 belongs to Leela rather than the Doctor from this point on. Compare this with 15.6, "The Invasion of Time".] When Marius says he's returning to Earth and offers K9 to the Doctor [another problem with the weight penalty], K9 makes up his own mind and rolls onto the TARDIS without even a word of goodbye to his creator.

Despite the Doctor's usual reservations about computers, he takes to the "dog" immediately. Though K9 refers to himself as an automaton, and claims he doesn't need thanks or apologies, there's already the sense that he's lying and has feelings.

The TARDIS The "original" white console room has been closed for redecoration, and the hat-stand is just being moved in at the start of the story, but the Doctor claims he still doesn't like the room's colour. He starts using it again anyway, and refers to it as the 'number two control room'. [14.1, "The Masque of Mandragora", confirms that the wooden-panelled one was originally the primary control room.] He also criticises the TARDIS for being a computer and having no imagination. [Rare for him to treat it with so little regard, or as an object instead of a living thing.]

The Doctor can remove the TARDIS' relative dimensional stabiliser, a box-shaped device covered in controls which usually allows the Doctor to 'cross the dimensional barrier', and use it to shrink the clones he makes of himself and Leela. [Drax does the same thing in "The Armageddon Factor" (16.6), and this piece of machinery might also explain the events of "Planet of Giants" (2.1). However, one has to ask what the stabiliser actually *does*, if it can be removed from the TARDIS without wrecking the Ship. According to 15.4, "Underworld", it's the thing that makes the TARDIS' dematerialisation noise. It's almost certainly not the same as the dimensional control unit removed from the Monk's TARDIS in "The Time Meddler" (2.9). Strictly speaking it should be impossible to shrink people and keep them alive, so this is obviously highly complex Time Lord technology.]

The TARDIS is the same size on the inside with the stabiliser removed, but can't go anywhere. The stabiliser plugs into the hardware of the fiftieth century without any technical hitches. [This is believable. Much of the technology already seen on the TARDIS appears to be taken from different times, so it's credible that Time Lord machinery might "adapt" itself to fit any socket.]

The TARDIS picks up the mayday signal from the Titan base when it's in the right region of space and time, broadcasting it over a speaker. Something blows up on the console when the virus transmits itself through the communications frequency. The Doctor later claims that the virus attacked the TARDIS computer first because it was displaying the most mental activity, although at the time he believed it to be just a static build-up.

The Non-Humans
- *The Virus of the Purpose.* It starts with a large, cloud-like mass hanging in space somewhere in the vicinity of the asteroid belt. It's been waiting for the right carriers for millennia, and when a ship passes through the cloud, the virus gets on board to infect the crew. The virus microbes "possess" an infected subject, who forms silver scales around the eyes and / or hands, and passes the virus on to others through beams of energy that crackle out of his or her eyes.

The virus is obviously very adaptable, as it's capable of getting into artificial brains like K9's as well as organic ones, though sadly K9 doesn't grow the scales. It can even transmit itself over communications frequencies like those of the TARDIS. The virus is noetic, so it can only be detected while the carrier's conscious, and it feeds on intellectual activity. The only way to slow it down is to stop thinking.

All victims say 'contact has been made' when they're infected, and don't remember anything about their former identities. They're not mutually telepathic, although they all "hear" orders from the nucleus, and after a while they develop a resistance to the kind of radiation used in blasters. The Doctor's erratic and befuddled when he's first infected, and struggles to fight it as it takes hold. The virus knows certain things about the Doctor after it settles inside him, but not everything. The nucleus rejects Leela, meanwhile, because she's 'all instinct'.

In fact, the virus is sentient and intent on infecting all space and time. It has a single nucleus, which can be transmitted from person to person

Cultural Primer #2: Why *Blue Peter*?

...continued from page 167

Singleton, the application of sticky-backed plastic[3] became an alchemical process. The prim-but-practical Singleton joined the programme in 1962, and it's convincingly been argued that she was the template for Barbara Wright.

Key to the programme's success in the "classic" era, though, was John Noakes. Owner of one of the first outright Yorkshire accents allowed on national television, Noakes was apparently up for anything, no matter how stupidly dangerous. It was Noakes who got sent to jump off Ben Nevis for the film inserts, while his "sensible" co-host Peter Purves preferred to stay in the studio and gently mock him for it. Really you would have expected Purves to be the dangerous one, since he'd already spent a year on board the TARDIS as the aforementioned Steven Taylor ("The Chase" to 3.9, "The

Savages"). Other *Blue Peter* presenters to make the transition were Sarah Greene (hidden behind a mask in 22.1, "Attack of the Cybermen") and Janet Ellis (stuffed into space-overalls for 17.5, "The Horns of Nimon"). Another, Mark Curry, was part of a double-act with Bonnie Langford when they were both ten.

It was, inevitably, on *Blue Peter* that K9 was first introduced to the public. More accurately, he was introduced to Noakes, a well-known dog-lover. This was the era when both programmes were important to the national psyche, known to all even if they weren't always *watched* by all. Today Noakes, Singleton and Purves have the same iconic status in the minds of the British public as Tom Baker. Like him, they're seen as representing the series in its golden age, and all presenters from the early '80s onwards are lumped together as "the new ones".

---

and apparently likes to rest in the brain of the smartest victim it can find. When it's enlarged by the technology of the Bi-Al base, it's revealed to look like a shrimp - the Doctor, probably figuratively, calls it a crustacean - with four stinging mandibles. Removed from its natural environment, it soon begins spawning, and incredibly lays huge numbers of ostrich-sized eggs within hours or even minutes of its arrival at a site of a suitable temperature. The nucleus seems to need 'hives' even before it's enlarged, though this isn't explained.

[Dr. Science says: a single viral cell, 'nucleus' or not, really isn't big enough to contain all the neurons which would make it capable of communicating like a sentient being. The fact that it uses language at all is peculiar, as language suggests complex cultural development and we never hear about any other virus nucleuses that it might be hob-nobbing with. It might have gained its unusual intelligence from its victims, but this would mean that it's simultaneously carrying thoughts of the brain it's nesting in *and* thoughts from other brains it's encountered. Is the "thinking" part of the virus in the cloud, and is the nucleus just a conduit? As is so often the way in bad SF, thought is a form of mystical power here, the reference to the virus living on 'intellectual activity' being a dead giveaway. Until it emerges in the outside world, it's treated almost as an idea, existing near part of the Doctor's brain that's a philosophical space rather than a physical area.

Obviously the shrimp-creature doesn't look anything like any viral cell known on Earth, even having arms that can manipulate objects. Was this virus engineered? Or is it just not a virus in the conventional sense of the word?]

Just to make the whole thing seem *completely* incomprehensible: the virus exists inside the Doctor on the mind / brain interface, and therefore has no ascertainable mass or structure. Even Marius isn't convinced by this, but K9 takes it for granted. The Doctor later states that the interface is at the crossover-point of the left and right lobes, between the brain's logical side and its imaginative side. [See **Things That Really, Really, *Really* Don't Make Sense**.]

Planet Notes

• *The Bi-Al Foundation*. The Centre for Alien Biomorphology is located in the asteroid belt of Earth's solar system, worked into the rock of asteroid K4067, which is riddled with "windows" and has a landing-pad set at its entrance. Its function as an institute of alien biomorphology is never explained, as there are medical facilities on the station for humans. Professor Marius is the station's specialist in extra-terrestrial pathological endomorphisms [even though this doesn't make sense], but there's a more general staff of nurses and consultants.

• *Titan*. [The largest moon of Saturn, though that isn't stated here.] Site of a large refill station, with the relief shuttle landing on a platform that descends into an underground complex fit for human habitation. The shuttle crew are replacements for the four-man staff of the station, who are approaching the end of their "tour of duty".

The base Supervisor has the power of arrest. Ultimately, the Titan base is blown up when the Doctor lays a trap for the virus involving a blaster and the station's methane tanks. [Titan's atmosphere is composed of methane, so it's anyone's guess why the humans bother keeping it in tanks.]

History

• *Dating.* According to the Doctor it's 5000 AD, the year of the Great Break-Out, when humanity 'went leapfrogging across the solar system on their way to the stars… like a tidal-wave, or a disease'. [And he criticises Shakespeare for using mixed metaphors? The script seems to suggest that this is the *first* time the humans have been expanding out into the galaxy, but almost every other "future" *Doctor Who* story contradicts this. But we know that the Earth Empire falls around 3000 AD, and that Earth is part of a galactic Federation by about 4000 AD, so humanity must have become more insular and Earth-centric by this stage. "The Ice Warriors" (5.3) and "The Talons of Weng-Chiang" (14.6) both suggest that there's an ice age around this time; that there's serious political upheaval; and that after the Imperial and Federation phases, there's a tendency for places to be called old-fashioned things like "Reykjavik" and "London" instead of "Sky-City Twelve" or suchlike. So, Earth has clearly been in retreat for a while. We might conclude that after the thawing of the ice age, many people on Earth start heading out into the galaxy again while megalomaniacs like Magnus Greel from "Talons" make life a misery for those who stay behind.]

Everything in this era is hard-edged and functional-looking. The spacecraft are generic spacecraft, the spacesuits are conventional, and the fashion sense on the Bi-Al Station is all white uniforms and bland headpieces. Curiously, all the signs on the walls are spelt phonetically: "IMER-JINSEE EGSIT" and "ISOLAYSHUN WARD" are typical examples. [The writers referred to this as "Finglish", but it's never mentioned on-screen.] The energy weapons on Titan are straightforward blasters, with the minimum of moving parts. Old-fashioned close-circuit TV is still in operation, while real fruit and wine seems to be available, not just space-pills. Cryogenic cocoons can be placed around whole areas of the Bi-Al base to prevent the spread of disease. The Doctor expects the asteroid belt to be full of humans by now.

K9 states that the first successful [human!] cloning experiments were carried out in 3922. The Kilbracken technique isn't cloning in the *technical* sense, but replicates an individual from a single cell by creating a carbon-based imprint, a 'three-dimensional photograph'. A permanent clone [in the technical sense of the word] is feasible, but would take years to create because it wouldn't have the original's experiences.

Marius believes the Kilbracken technique to be simple, though he describes it as a circus trick, with no medical value. It's easily done, within minutes, in his lab. Incomprehensibly, from one cell the Kilbracken method copies the clothes and equipment of the individual as well as the memories, though obviously not any viruses the individual happens to be carrying. It appears that the 'original' and the 'clone' contain the same shared consciousness, and feel one another's sensations. The replicate is short-lived because of possible unsolved psychic stress problems, the longest-surviving clone having lasted for ten minutes and fifty-five seconds.

The Doctor seems to know everything his "mini-me" experienced before its demise, and his clone even feels pain when the mini-Leela kicks part of his brain. The Doctor's explanation, that the two selves are made from the same tissue and that the copy will die if the original does, is similarly vague. [No wonder there's something 'psychic' about all of this.] Strangest of all, the clones' knife, bangles and hair remain inside the Doctor's brain even after the clones cease to exist [See 16.2, "The Pirate Planet", for more projections with cellular "memory" and the idea of the original's will driving them until they become "real".]

In 5000 AD, people still say 'my God!' rather than anything more exotic. Ireland still exists, while Marius refers to 'good-for-nothing spaceniks'. The Doctor also confirms that this is the time of Leela's ancestors. [He says it as if to mean her *immediate* ancestors, hinting that the colonists of the Mordee expedition - 14.4, "The Face of Evil" - came from around this time.]

The Analysis

Where Does This Come From?   The first real model-based space story in ages (because Robert Holmes had got his fingers burned with 6.6, "The Space Pirates"), this is also the one where everyone busts a gut to get the science and the hardware right, for the first episode at least.

Much of the material about colonising the solar system is off-the-shelf from either NASA, the people wanting to get into NASA (such as Gerard O'Neill, advocate of asteroids remodelled into cylindrical city-states) and hardcore SF writers like Larry Niven and Jerry Pournelle. Closer to home, Belfast-based SF regular James White wrote a popular series of medical mysteries on a space-station where different atmospheres and gravities were available for the different species; one of the minor characters had a Scottie dog, which some aliens assumed was a symbiont. The atmosphere of Titan was assumed to be methane back then, although at time of writing we're still awaiting the Cassini lander's findings.

In the days before *Star Wars* turned outer space into something noisy and dynamic instead of something *reachable*, the public wanted this sort of attention to detail from nuts-and-bolts SF, and viewers weren't as ready to accept great big flaws in the science. The verisimilitude of things like *2001: A Space Odyssey* made *Flash Gordon* reruns as embarrassing as we now find *The Black And White Minstrel Show*. This wasn't seen as "nerdy" but as "getting it right", a minimum requirement like not using decimal coins in *Elizabeth R*. Once outside the knowable, anything with its own internal logic was fair game (see 15.5, "Underworld", for more on how Bob 'n' Dave get the minutiae obsessively accurate but then fly off to planet bonkers on the big stuff).

The intriguing possibility is held open that the "noetic" virus here is - in essence - analogous to a software virus. This is hardly a new idea. *Flash Gordon Conquers the Universe* (1940) featured a virus which only attacked those smart enough to challenge Ming the Merciless, and was thus only a threat to the kind of people who could find a cure. The Virus of the Purpose gains a new form once it's inside the Doctor's imagination; the idea of the "word made flesh" is actually quite common in Baker / Martin scripts, with data taking on physical form in "Nightmare of Eden" (17.4) and 'temporal grace' in "The Hand of Fear" (14.2) suggesting that everyone becomes fictionalised once

they're inside the TARDIS.

However, this may be working at too literal a level. The premise of "The Invisible Enemy" is that humanity could be seen, from a broader perspective, as no different from a disease. This idea lurks in the preamble to *The War of the Worlds*, but was made explicit by C. S. Lewis, whose anti-science rants *Out of the Silent Planet*, *Perelandra* and *That Hideous Strength* have understandably proved less popular than the smug *Narnia* books. Baker and Martin took the "right of free development" idea, already suggested in scripts like "The Hand of Fear", and shifted the scale.

The Bi-Al Station, a honeycombed asteroid with organic-looking openings all over its surface, is one of the more striking images on offer here but also one of the easiest to trace to its source. Anyone who remembers the prog-rock artwork that Roger Dean used to do in the 1970s will know *exactly* where this comes from (see, especially, Dean's "Lighthouse").

Things That Don't Make Sense

1. The Stupidity of Cloning. Leaving aside *all* the previously-mentioned improbable things about the Kilbracken cloning, costuming and shoemaking technique: Marius seriously believes that there's no value in the process.

Ponder that… a process which can create objects, as well as people, out of thin air. A process which could create infinitely large armies (you just have to generate a new wave of troops every ten minutes) or open up whole new areas of scientific research. And the people of c. 5000 AD are wasting time with Zygma energy? No wonder the Doctor thinks it's a technological dark age.

And that's assuming non-organic objects suffer the same bizarre 'psychic stress problems' which make the clones themselves self-destruct, by no means certain given that Leela's knife and jewellery may still be rattling around inside the Doctor's skull to this day. [Again, see "The Pirate Planet" (16.2) for a similar sort of procedure and a possible way out of this mess.] To be *really* picky, nobody questions the ethical questions involved with this process, either. Here the Doctor creates exact duplicates of himself and Leela, which act as if they're just as sapient as the originals. They're created even though he knows they're going to die within minutes. Granted, it's the only way of saving his "real" life, but isn't this still a bit harsh? Not even any screams of 'dear God, why me?' from the duplicates before they snuff it?

2. *The Stupidity of Shrinking.* The Doctor and Leela clones can breathe while they're inside the Doctor's brain. If the mini-Doctor is small enough to walk along neural pathways and see the neurons whizzing past, then air molecules should be too big to even fit in his throat, let alone be useful to his body. It goes without saying that the "architecture" inside the Doctor's head doesn't make much sense, even taking into account the fact that he's not human. He knows which dangly bits to pull in order to make his body react in certain ways, which is startling enough in itself. When he gets to the nucleus it's nesting halfway between the two sides of the brain, yet moments later it's somehow waiting to be collected at the tear-duct, "miles" away.

Nor is it clear why the nucleus seems to explode at the same moment as the clones. The fact that the duplicates are said to be carbon, made out of matter and not - for example - holograms, is worrying in itself; even if they disintegrate and are 'absorbed' into the system, there are still two human body-weights of matter in the Doctor's brain, so let's hope the cells never return to full size. And the Doctor gains Leela's immunity when his body (rather cannibalistically) absorbs the clones' remains, even though her antibodies should be several thousand times too small to function *as* antibodies once they're in his blood. Assuming you can overlook the oddity that the carbon-copy antibodies remain intact when the rest of the clone goes to pieces. See also **How Hard Is It To Be The Wrong Size?** under 16.6, "The Armageddon Factor".

3. *The Stupidity of the Doctor's Brain Itself.* The script refers to the two sides of the brain as being two different realms, one the seat of reason, the other the realm of imagination. This is *somewhat* simplistic, but just about acceptable, especially since this is a Time Lord brain and not necessarily inclined to follow the usual human rules.

But only the rational side is described *as* a brain; the imaginative side is described as a *mind*, as if the writers have read about mind / brain duality somewhere and weirdly assumed that these are two things found in separate parts of the head. If you wanted to be generous, you could swallow this as an extended metaphor, but it clashes badly with the glaring sci-fi of the rest of the story and is very nearly too absurd to contemplate even if you're not taking things terribly seriously.

The special effects we see at the entrance to the imaginative side are clearly supposed to tell us that we're on the edge of the Doctor's dreams and fantasies, as if a miniaturised explorer could be injected into the skull and somehow wander around someone's imaginings as easily as they could wander around the synapses, a suggestion that would horrify philosophers and neurologists alike. The virus itself, which is initially treated as a hostile idea and described as having 'no mass', ultimately turns out to be corporeal enough to get blown up. [Does it get its mass from the miniaturised Doctor and Leela?] Even given the weird-science, high-fantasy bent of *Doctor Who*, this is just... blaaaaah.

4. *Sundry Other Stupidities.* The "possessed" crewmembers from the shuttle stroll into the Titan refill base and gun down everyone there, rather than infecting the men with the virus as they do with everyone else. When the Doctor glows green inside the TARDIS, he seriously believes that it's a kind of cosmic St. Elmo's fire, even though that kind of atmospheric disturbance is entirely meaningless in space and shouldn't have anything to do with the TARDIS insides anyway (the *Star Trek* school of meaningless scientific analogies). Marius, the Bi-Al Station's expert on alien biology, is called to see the Doctor before anybody knows the Doctor isn't human. [They think he's Irish, so maybe the Irish have gone all mutated in this era.] Why does the Doctor-clone tell Marius that he'll be leaving the Doctor's body through the tear-duct, when the clones are obviously going to dissipate before they've got a chance of getting out and apparently have no need to try to escape anyway?

Marius only concludes that Leela's immunity to the virus is psychological, rather than biological, halfway through episode three. Even though it's one of the first things the Doctor tells him in episode two. *Then* it turns out in episode four that there's an antibody in Leela's system which can fight the virus after all. While all this is going on there's a countdown on the wall of the lab that gives the time remaining until the clones cease to be, even though the clones are supposed to be unpredictable and nobody knows exactly when they're going to pop. And the clone Doctor's habit of standing around explaining things inside his brain, when they've only got minutes left to do their job – indeed, minutes left to live - takes showing-off a shade too far even by the Doctor's standards. Especially as Leela is risking her life on the outside to make sure he's got time to complete his mission.

Once again, explosions can be heard in space and the "sparks" fall downwards in the void. There's a strange moment in episode three when the infected K9's beam utterly misses Leela, but she drops anyway. What's even stranger is that K9's under orders to kill her at the time, but only hits her with the "stun" setting. In the future, "exit" is spelled "egsit" but "oxygen" is spelt... properly. And Leela uses the word 'blaster' as if it's something she's familiar with, when nobody's used it in front of her before now and she's much more used to crossbows.

Finally, the motives of the nucleus - the swarm-leader who wants to be as big as its victims, so that it won't be 'vulnerable' any more - are questionable. Isn't that like a human megalomaniac wanting to be 10,000 feet tall, just so he can fight starships with his bare hands? Aren't the microbes *more* vulnerable when they're visible? And can they survive without a host-body anyway...?

Critique No, it didn't *seem* very likely that the programme could keep up the pace. It's well-known that "The Invisible Enemy" was made under pressure, and it's easy to blame a lot of its flaws - its haphazard script, its dire sense of design, its cack-handed attitude to the way "space" works on television - on the fact that it was rushed into production a month early. But give it the benefit of the doubt, and try to imagine the production with its edges smoothed off, and you're still looking at something dull and inane.

There's a school of thought which claims that many of the Baker-Martin scripts are "ambitious" and just unworkable on a BBC budget, but really, this (like the later and even more annoying "Underworld") is just badly-thought-out. As in "The Claws of Axos" (8.3), there's a terrible sense of second-hand SF / action-TV ideas being thrown into the workings of the story without any forward planning. It starts off as a space-age "thriller" about possessed astronauts, turns into *Fantastic Voyage* halfway through and then becomes a story about a typical alien conqueror who does all the usual alien conqueror things. Even the Doctor has to exclaim 'you megalomaniacs are all the same', as if that somehow glosses over the complete lack of imagination being offered to us.

The conclusion is lamentable, with the Doctor destroying the virus by fiddling around with some machinery on the Titan base that we've never even been told about before (the early episodes seem to be pushing the point that the virus is an *idea*, but the writers can't think of a dramatic way of killing an idea and ultimately just blow it up). Even Leela becomes a "comedy" ignorant sidekick instead of the fired-up story-engine we saw in Season Fourteen, while the matching "comedy" foreign scientist - Professor Marius - is an embarrassment from his very first line. The less said about the final 'whatever would we have done without K9?' scene, the better.

What's most galling is how close it comes to being iconic and mythic and all the things this book keeps going on about. As with all Baker-Martin stories, the High Concept nature of the scenario cries out for a summary dotted with exclamation marks. This is the story which sees the mid-'70s "possession" theme through to its conclusion and has the Doctor himself turn evil, the story that literally takes us inside the central character's head, yet it turns out that there's nothing of interest there. But even apart from little concerns like "plot" and "character", the really crippling problem here is that "The Invisible Enemy" seems *spartan* in every conceivable way. We're shown the future, but there's nothing there to involve us on any level. There are standard-issue settings, there are characters we don't care about doing all the usual "space" dialogue, there's a wholly worthless monster and... in the middle of it all there's the Doctor, who's just about all we've got to cling on to.

Drained of meaning, drained of style and drained of all but the crudest kind of wit, in a way this is nonetheless an "important moment" in *Doctor Who*; the story that exemplifies the series at its most ordinary. There was a time when people thought of *Doctor Who* as something strange, scary and unpredictable. But after the Irony Age of the 1980s, people just looked back and made jokes about cheap-looking effects and characters running up and down corridors. This, more than any other story, is what they were thinking of.

ABOUT TIME 1975–1979

The Facts

Written by Bob Baker and Dave Martin. Directed by Derrick Goodwin. Viewing figures: 8.6 million, 7.3 million, 7.5 million, 8.3 million.

Supporting Cast Michael Sheard (Lowe), Frederick Jaeger (Professor Marius), Brian Grellis (Safran), Roy Herrick (Parsons), Elizabeth Norman (Marius' Nurse), Jim McManus (Opthalmologist), Roderick Smith (Cruikshank), John Scott Martin (Nucleus body), John Leeson (Nucleus Voice).

Working Titles "The Enemy Within" (there's a surprise), " The Invader Within", "The Invisible Invader".

Cliffhangers The Doctor, with virus "fur" all over his hands, creeps up behind Leela in the Titan base and aims a gun at her; the miniaturised Doctor and Leela clones are caught up in the swirling vortex of liquid as Marius injects them into the Doctor's brain; having escaped through the Doctor's tear-duct, the seafood-like virus nucleus grows to human-size in the laboratory.

The Lore

• Graham Williams had intended to begin his stint as producer by reformatting the entire series to make it less Earth-orientated and more "epic". His notion of the Guardians and the Quest (see 16.1, "The Ribos Operation") was delayed until the following year, as this story and several stories for Season Fifteen were too well-advanced.

• Prior to this there'd been an attempt to remake *Quatermass* in colour, for which the special effects department had made several models. The test-footage of these provided the end of the story (the viral spoors brewing inside a vat), and as an in-joke the Doctor's examination of this was shot in exactly the same way.

• K9 had been intended as a Doberman-style gizmo, with a small operator inside. The production went over-budget by making it radio-controlled, but the cost was defrayed by making K9 a regular feature of the series. The genius who came up with this was the production unit manager / bean-counter, John Nathan-Turner, who'd later come to regret it. Robert Holmes was also intrigued by the idea, although the machine (also

called FIDO: Phenomenal [sic] Indication Data Observation) was simply invented to allow an "outside" narrator for the clones as they moved around the Doctor's brain. From Dave Martin's point of view, K9 was created because his own dog had recently been run over and he wanted to console himself with a traffic-proof version.

• The K9 prop was frequently affected by interference from the cameras, and had to be rewired for "The Sun Makers" (15.4). John Leeson based the robot's voice on noted philosopher and activist Bertrand Russell. Leeson was unaware that he wasn't required for rehearsals, and became a regular fixture, getting on all fours and playing the dog as a dog. Tom Baker was more enthusiastic about this than the "tin dog" prop, and he and Leeson (a former *Mastermind* question-setter) did the *Times* crossword each morning.

• Elizabeth Norman, who plays Marius' nurse, was director Derrick Godwin's wife. He hadn't wanted to do *Doctor Who*, but had worked with Williams before and trusted him. Many of the rest of the story's cast were old colleagues, including John Leeson.

• The final night's shooting was, according to Goodwin, simply spent filming whatever they thought could be edited into a good fight / chase scene in episode two.

• The original plan was for the clone Doctor to die in the clone Leela's arms, before she too aged to death in a matter of seconds.

• Much of the model-work, and the material about Titan, was re-used in the documentary series *Spaceships of the Mind* about post-Apollo NASA plans. Williams arranged for a bigger model budget than ever before, and for a whole week's shooting at the famous Bray studios, home of *Space: 1999*'s Eagle modelwork.

15.3: "Image of the Fendahl"

(Serial 4X, Four Episodes, 29th October - 19th November 1977.)

Which One is This? A skull with a pentagram, a gestalt entity made of giant green slugs, a psychic granny *unt more tcherrrmen* exhents abound as the Doctor and Leela check into the Priory.

Firsts and Lasts Last story script-edited by Robert Holmes, who's been trying to quit for a year. Anthony Read, an old colleague of both Holmes and Graham Williams, comes in about halfway through and co-edits this; the BBC documentation credits both, but on-screen it's still Holmes until "Underworld" (15.5). Last *Doctor Who* story written by Chris Boucher, at least for television.

First time that a writer has the Doctor take K9 apart to make repairs, just so he doesn't actually have to use K9 in the story.

Four Things to Notice About "Image of the Fendahl"...

1. Remember how in the early '70s, the influence of *Chariots of the Gods* and *Quatermass and the Pit* kept making itself felt in *Doctor Who* and teaching us that most of the secrets of the ancient world were down to aliens? "Image of the Fendahl" draws that era of the programme to a close by upping the von Daniken / Nigel Kneale ante, and attempting to explain away most of human history in the course of 95 minutes. Not only is there a brand new explanation for the origin of the human species, we also learn the shocking truth behind ghosts, precognitive powers, telepathy, race-memory, the concept of the soul, the fear of the number thirteen, the significance of the pentagram, the importance of salt in European superstition, the rise of Satanism (again) and the nature of humanity's 'dark side'. All we need now is an explanation for how life on Earth began, and we can all go home (see 17.2, "City of Death").

2. Yet despite all this back-story and pseudo-science, there's an unusual level of *doubt* in this script. Gone are the days when all shamans and astrologers were charlatans, and all scientists were on the right track (even if they were occasionally insane). This time, the superstitious old woman who remembers the 'old ways' turns out to know what's best if you're trying to deal with a soul-eating monster. This is about different perspectives, not about laughing at the locals and their quaintly bloodthirsty Satanic covens. You know the usual rules don't quite apply when in the course of a single scene, the Doctor gives *three* different explanations for the return of the Fendahl: one quasi-mystical, one using modern scientific terminology and one putting everything down to an enormous coincidence.

3. The Doctor's arrival on Earth in episode one, stepping out of the TARDIS into a field full of cows with a knife-wielding Leela at his side, is a lovely collision of realism and Doctor-logic. After concluding that the cows aren't responsible for the planet-threatening time experiment that's brought them here, the first person they meet is Ted Moss, who's been sent by the Council to trim the verges (in Leela's world, of course, "Council" has a rather more tribal connotation... or maybe it doesn't, when you think about it). Moss' reaction, on being faced with these lunatics: 'You've both escaped from somewhere, haven't you?' The Doctor's reply: 'Frequently.'

4. In a season which has already featured a "bought" man called "Skinsale" (in "Horror of Fang Rock") and would go on to mention a "Gatherer Pile" ("The Sunmakers"), the names in this story are oddly apt. "Fendelman" turns out to be the "Man of the Fendahl"; someone trying to investigate man's origins is called "Adam"; and the woman who's abducted and turned into a goddess is called "Thea Ransome". Why not just go the whole hog and call her "Athena Deadmeat"? (As we're on a names kick, note that Ma Tyler calls her son Jack "John" at all times... Russell T. Davies, if you're reading, *please* don't make Billie Piper's character in the new series turn out to be their long-lost cousin.)

The Continuity

The Doctor Loves fruitcake.

• *Inventory.* He's re-stocked with jelly-babies after losing his last stash [14.5, "The Robots of Death"]. He also has some Liquorice Allsorts. He uses the sonic screwdriver on an ordinary Earth lock, and it has no immediate effect, although the door mysteriously swings open some minutes later [see **Things That Don't Make Sense**].

• *Background.* The Doctor knows the story of the Fendahl, but only as a myth from childhood, and he admits that it terrified him [compare with 18.4, "State of Decay"]. So much so that he admits to not thinking straight here.

The Supporting Cast

• *Leela.* Knows about alcohol, and kisses palaeontologist Adam Colby on the cheek when wishing him good luck [not a typical sort of Sevateem custom]. She's a good shot with a gun, but rotten at throwing, despite her usual ability to hit robots with knives.

• *K9.* The Doctor's already taking him apart to deal with some corrosion in his circuits. Curiously, the Doctor now chides Leela for calling K9 "he" and insists on "it", contrary to the affection he showed the machine before. Still, the Doctor ultimately settles on "he", and is already thinking of K9 as *his* dog. K9 can listen to conversations and nod his head even when he's been opened up for repairs and is lying in pieces on the floor.

The TARDIS The Doctor believes he's in complete control of the Ship, stating that there isn't a single part of "her" he hasn't adjusted or repaired. Once *again* the TARDIS finds itself dragged towards its landing by external factors, this time a 'relative continuum displacement zone', AKA a hole in time caused either by Fendelman's sonic time-scanner or the time fissure at Fetchborough. Or both. This disruption makes the console room tilt alarmingly, but some console-fiddling and encouragement sort it out. [Once again, the obvious conclusion is that the TARDIS briefly emerges from the vortex near the disturbance and gets pulled towards it.]

The TARDIS is said to generate a low-intensity telepathic field [thanks to the telepathic circuits, as mentioned in various Third Doctor stories], the Doctor suggesting - perhaps fatuously, perhaps not - that Leela's apology to the Ship helps to soothe it. He's surprised that he can't calculate the co-ordinates of the time-scanner from the console, but he later uses the console to search for the location of a convenient supernova.

Leela's got a new dress from the TARDIS wardrobe, which she's evidently now treating as her own, although she's back in her old Sevateem gear by the end. [Assuming there are no "unseen" adventures, the Ship's been in flight for a while when we join the story.] Somewhere outside the console room there are old data-banks, as the Doctor emerges with three transparent plastic slides covered in writing, but none of them mention the Fifth Planet he wants to know about.

Heading back to Earth from the Fifth Planet, the Doctor's worried about being too late to stop the Fendahl, so he can't just nip back a few minutes in his own timeline.

The Time Lords More proof that the Time Lords *sometimes* interfere with the outside universe comes when that they destroyed and then time-looped the planet between Mars and Jupiter, to prevent any memory or record of the Fendhal escaping. But by that time either the "live" Fendahl or its skull had already left the so-called

Fifth Planet. The loop appears as a big green swirl on the scanner, and the TARDIS runs the risk of getting caught up in it. The Doctor states that only a Time Lord could have done this; he doesn't know about the time-loop before hand, but he's heard about the destruction of the Fifth Planet from his own people's mythology, apparently not knowing that the Time Lords were the ones who caused it. He believes the time-looping of the planet to be 'criminal' [even though he time-loops Axos (8.3) and plans to time-loop the Vardan planet in "The Invasion of Time" (15.6)], adding that Time Lords aren't supposed to do 'that sort of thing'.

The Fendahl being composed of thirteen parts is said to be reflected in both Earth and Gallifreyan myths, hinting that the Time Lords may also have a problem with the number thirteen [and it's the number of lives they have, too].

The Non-Humans

• *The Fendahl.* 12,000,000 years ago, on the planet which used to exist between Mars and Jupiter, evolution went up a blind alley and natural selection doubled back on itself. The result was a creature that feeds on death, although at one point the Doctor says it is death [you are what you eat]. He elaborates by stating that the being absorbs the full spectrum of energy, the life-force or 'soul', and it even consumed its own kind [indicating that the Fendahl was a unique organism, and devoured the species from which it sprang]. The Time Lords destroyed the planet, but a very human-looking skull escaped, finding its way to Earth via Mars. The Doctor speculates that it might have used its massive stockpile of energy to project itself through space, a possible source of the race-memory of astral projection. The skull was found in volcanic sediment in Kenya, and when x-rayed it turns out to have a pentagram marked into its cranium as part of the bone structure, which may be a neural relay where its energy is stored.

The skull gains power and starts to glow when Dr. Fendelman's time scanner aggravates a nearby time fissure, mesmerising Thea Ransome so that she remembers nothing but begins to do the Fendahl's work. A hiker in the nearby woods finds himself incapable of moving his legs properly when the skull starts glowing, and then dies, his body decomposing within hours as if something's removed all the binding forces from it. Even the

Is This the *Quatermass* Continuum?

Among the many things which surprised and bewildered first-time viewers of "Remembrance of the Daleks" (25.1) was the short exchange between Rachel Jensen and Allison, the two she-boffins of the ICMG, circa 1963:'I wish Bernard was here.''British Rocket Group's got its own problems.' The reference to *Quatermass* is obvious, at least to anyone obsessive enough to remember Professor *Quatermass'* Christian name and occupation. But we should pause here to remember what the BBC's original *Quatermass* serials (*The Quatermass Experiment* in 1953, *Quatermass II* in 1955, *Quatermass and the Pit* in 1958-59) actually represent. By now younger readers won't need to be told about the impact these serials had on *Doctor Who*, or about the way that whole chunks of the '70s Earth-bound stories seem to have been lifted from Nigel Kneale's scripts. Older viewers will know that *Quatermass* had a massive impact on *all* televised drama.

In an era when "dramatic presentation" generally meant a live play performed in front of the cameras as if it were still stage-bound, the *Quatermass* stories were among the first BBC productions to use television as a medium in its own right, to play to the strengths of the camera as well as banking on the Corporation's ability to handle complex live broadcasts. Dark, deft and occasionally political, the stories would have affected all but a few people working in TV throughout the '60s and '70s, and at the time they scared the willies out of the viewers so badly that the second series came with its own "not for those of a nervous disposition" warning. But in terms of SF, they also introduced - or at least, popularised - concepts which later TV fantasies made almost mundane. *Quatermass and the Pit* made connections between human evolution and the space-age that became par for the course in the decades to follow. *Quatermass II*, broadcast at a time when secret American military bases were appearing across the British landscape with no official explanation, invokes a sense of government / alien conspiracy so much more meaningful than anything in *The X-Files* that it's almost embarrassing. (In the days when government was starting to be perceived as letting the public down, and military secrecy was seen as a wartime habit that somehow hadn't been broken, *Quatermass* said what the public was only just starting to suspect. And let's remind ourselves that it was Kneale's TV adaptation of 1984 which really caught the public imagination, not Orwell's original book.)

So it's hardly surprising that sooner or later, someone should have suggested that *Doctor Who* and *Quatermass* might possibly be able to meet each other, or at least share mutual acquaintances. This is by no means as banal or offensively *wrong* as suggesting that - and the example is inevitable - *Doctor Who* and Star Trek might co-exist in the same universe. It's not just that the two BBC programmes share a certain iconography, or a certain sense of empiricism-under-pressure, or a certain moral outlook. Though he's an authoritarian and often-unpleasant man, Bernard *Quatermass* the science-detective deals with the first alien threat to Earth with reason rather than violence, and spends much of his later career trying to convince pompous military idiots to think things through properly. Nor is it purely that the two universes operate in such a directly comparable way; The *Quatermass* Experiment begins with the first manned space-mission returning from the void and crash-landing near Croydon, unthinkable in just about any TV series *except* these two.

But no, perhaps above all else… they both belong to a very specific tradition of television. Even apart from the difference in approach mentioned in **Is This Really an SF Series?** (see under 14.4, "The Face of Evil"), a programme like *Star Trek* is the inheritor of a legacy of westerns, born out of early-twentieth-century Hollywood. *Doctor Who* comes partly from a tradition of stagecraft, and partly from a tradition of technical "enthusiasts" inventing new methods of programme-making in rooms full of gutted oscilloscopes. With typical British mistrust of the slick and the professional, *Doctor Who* and *Quatermass* both show us worlds where everything from a spaceship to a mind-reading device can be lashed together by gentleman-scientists with good intentions. In short, if the two worlds aren't immediately compatible then it's easy to imagine someone *making* them compatible, by wrapping gaffer-tape around one of the connecting leads and fixing up the sockets with a soldering iron.

But let's look at the close details. For the most part, the two continuities segue together beautifully. In *Doctor Who* Britain has a space programme capable of manned flight to Mars by the 1970s, something which could well be explained by the presence of *Quatermass* and his British Rocket Group in an earlier decade. Readers of the New Adventures will notice that the disturbed near-

continued on page 179…

Doctor's mesmerised into touching the glowing skull, which he believes is (1) alive, (2) becoming a mutation generator and (3) using appropriate genetic matter to recreate itself.

[The obvious conclusion is that human-like life evolved on the Fendahl's planet before the Fendahl brought death to the place. Fendelman believes that humanity is descended from this species, while the Doctor seems to think that humanity is just genetically influenced by it. See also **How Does Evolution Work?** under 18.3, "Full Circle". But the Fendahleen - the lesser Fendahl components - aren't remotely human. Is the skull actually the skull of the original Fendahl, or of a human-ish creature which became its focus, much as Thea Ransome does here? The pentagram is part of the skull's structure, which suggests biological manipulation rather than evolution, and on Earth one victim of the Fendahl has a curious blister on his neck which may just be a birthmark or something more.]

After a while, Thea falls unconscious and starts to glow, during which time the ghost-like images of embryo Fendahleen are seen congregating around her body. When the skull gains more power, a glowing pentagram appears around her and she transforms into the Fendahl core, still humanoid but with golden hair, golden skin, a flowing golden robe, big eyes painted onto her face and the ability to float. It / she can kill with eye-contact, and smiles happily at the same time. [The Fendahl's original form, on its own planet? More evidence that it evolved from a human species, hence the skull. Unless the new core is being directed by Thea's unconscious and making her look like a Medusa.]

It's at this point that the Fendahleen, now fully-grown, start to arrive. They're constructed from pure energy while the skull is 'restructuring Thea's brain', but there's supposed to be one for each of the twelve followers in Stael's coven, so the Fendahl doesn't reach full power unless all thirteen elements are present. Thea starts taking life-force from her worshippers as soon as she becomes the core, which may be what makes the Fendahleen manifest themselves. A Fendahleen is psychotelekinetic, controlling muscles telepathically to stop anyone running away. Concentration can at least begin to break this hold. The core itself can teleport, and wavers between being a Fendahleen and being incorporeal.

The Fendahl is a gestalt organism, made up of the core and the twelve Fendahleen, which is why the number thirteen is associated with black magic. A Fendahleen is a horrible green worm-like thing, with suckers down the length of its body and a "face" of red tentacles. They tower over human beings once they're full-grown. Like SF movie monsters of old, they can be killed by salt, as it affects conductivity, ruins the overall electrical balance and 'prevents control of localised disruption to the osmotic pressures'. This may be what lies behind the old custom of throwing salt over your shoulder to ward off the Devil. [So maybe slugs and snails are evil too...]

The Fendahl has probably been manipulating humankind for millions of years, which is why the unwitting Fendelman - "Man of the Fendahl" - is the one who uncovers the skull. The Doctor suggests that the energy stored in the skull has been slowly dissipated as a biological transmutation field, so any appropriate life-form that came near it was altered into something suitable for the Fendahl to use, which would explain the development of the 'dark side' of human nature. It didn't create humanity, but it did affect humanity's evolution.

A slightly different explanation is that the Fendahl has been feeding the instincts and compulsions necessary for humanity to recreate it into the RNA of certain individuals. The Doctor suggests a third option: that it could all be a coincidence. [Of course, there's no mention of the Daemons (8.5), who were also supposed to have influenced humanity's development in this way. The pentagram on the skull, if turned so that it has two points aloft, is in part connected with black magic because of its suggestion of horns... horns supposedly being the sign of the power of the Daemons, remembered in the human collective unconscious. The Fendahl seems to pre-date most of the other alien visitors to Earth, though, and the genetic alterations it made are apparently more significant than anything we've seen so far.]

Once this affair's over, the Doctor plans to chuck the skull into a supernova in the constellation of Canthares, as it's supposedly indestructible but probably can't survive those sorts of temperatures. [Canthares isn't a "real" human constellation, so this might be one of the constellations seen from Gallifrey. The name is frighteningly close to "Cantharis", the technical term for Spanish fly...]

Is This the *Quatermass* Continuum?

...continued from page 177

future society portrayed by Kneale's (oft-forgotten) 1979 version of *Quatermass* is palpably similar to the near-future of *Doctor Who* novels like *Warlock*. *Quatermass and the Pit* claims that between three- and five-million of years ago, a now-extinct insect-like species arrived on Earth from Mars, affecting both the genetic and cultural development of humanity. Though this was obviously the inspiration for "The Daemons" - and the same horns-equal-power argument is made in both stories - it's worth pointing out that the Fendahl skull also arrived from Mars during Earth's prehistory, apparently having caused no end of havoc on the way. Since the Fendahl has a habit of leaving dead planets in its wake, we might theorise that the *Quatermass* Martians were the ones who brought the skull here (though it should be mentioned that *The Pit* never conclusively proves the three-legged grasshopper-aliens to come from Mars... their origin is mostly *Quatermass'* own speculation, but he's generally right about these things). The Martians are said to have genetically modified our ancestors, which could easily have been part of the Fendahl's DNA-fiddling process, if the Martians themselves were under the skull's influence.

Lance Parkin's *History of the Universe* reasons that the only problem in reconciling the two universes is that in "The Seeds of Death" (6.5) the Doctor describes Yuri Gagarin as the first man into space, whereas in *Quatermass* the first men into space were obviously English and quite right too. But it's at least feasible that history in the *Doctor Who* world glossed over the British rocket experiment. Given that the only apparent mission survivor ends up turning into a giant gestalt fungus-creature, it's not hard to believe that the UK cosmonauts' names might have been forgotten by an embarrassed nation. Indeed, Parkin himself has *Quatermass* appear in cameo in his novel *The Dying Days*, warning of the dangers of messing around on Mars. A sceptic might point out that *Quatermass and the Pit* ends with the Professor making a TV appearance in which he tells the whole world about the Martians, something that not even General Carrington quite achieved (7.3, "The Ambassadors of Death"), but we have no way of knowing if the speech was actually broadcast as all we see is the Professor standing in front of a microphone.

Other apparent glitches are no more troublesome than the glitches between individual *Doctor Who* stories. It's odd that the authorities in Season Seven don't realise the risks of staging top-secret projects at big, isolated plants after the events of *Quatermass II*... but no odder than them trying to draw extra-terrestrials to Earth in "Logopolis" (18.7) after so many invasion attempts in the '70s. It's odd that the public doesn't seem less sceptical about the existence of aliens after seeing Westminster Abbey get eaten by the aforementioned space-fungus... but no odder than the

continued on page 181...

Planet Notes

• *The Fifth Planet.* Original home of the Fendahl, 107,000,000 miles from Earth according to the Doctor. [Between Mars and Jupiter there's the asteroid belt, which may well have been a planet at one stage. The implication here is that the asteroid belt is made up if the left-overs after the Time Lords' intervention, but this is never stated.] Approaching the Fifth Planet in the TARDIS, Leela falls asleep and dreams that something's following her.

• *Mars.* Stop-over point for the Fendahl skull. [See **What's the History of Mars?** under 5.3, "The Ice Warriors". It's interesting to note that *Quatermass and the Pit* - to which this story owes so much - involves the discovery of a 5,000,000-year-old-Martian spaceship, also said to have influenced humanity's development and to have given humans a thing about horns. The *Quatermass* Martians brought death to their own world before trying to bring it to Earth. And 25.1, "Remembrance of the Daleks", hints that *Doctor Who* and *Quatermass* share the same universe (see **Is This the Quatermass Continuum?**). Did prehistoric Martians bring the Fendahl skull here, after it projected itself from the Fifth Planet to Mars? It doesn't seem likely that the Ice Warriors had anything to do with it, as they're not extinct. And 5,000,000 BC is well before the 4,000,000-year "start date" for the human species that Colby suggests.]

History

• *Dating.* No year is given, but it looks like the present-day. It's Lammas Eve [the 31st of July], because nothing like this ever happens without a scary date. [Events seem to begin on a Saturday night and end the next day. The 31st was a Sunday in 1977, but again, days of the week never match "real" dates in the Doctor Who universe.]

The computers used by Fendelman are still great big banks of electronica that take up a lot of floor-space. Fendelmen is said to be one of the richest men in the world, having made his money in electronics, unusual as he's not Japanese [so the economy of the Doctor Who world works in quite a familiar way]. Ten years ago, while working on a missile guidance system, Fendelman noticed what he calls a 'sonic shadow'. This somehow led him to build a sonic time-scanner, which can look through time and may eventually display TV pictures of the distant past. It was the scanner that led Fendelman to the Fendahl skull in Kenya. The machine only works after dark, probably to avoid solar disruption. [The similarity to the technology devised by Whitaker in 11.2, "Invasion of the Dinosaurs", is striking. If Fendelman inspired Whitaker, and the Fendahl was guiding Fendelman, then it'd explain how such advanced time-travel technology could have been around in the '70s.] The Doctor can identify a sonic time-scanner even from the TARDIS, and believes it'll cause a direct continuum implosion and destroy the planet after being used for around a hundred hours.

There's a large time fissure at Fetch Priory, near the village of Fetchborough, apparently about two hours from London. The description given by the Doctor is of a weakened point in space and time, and 'every' haunted place has one. The place names are a giveaway, "Fetch" being an old word for a ghost [technically the ghost of a person still living, which fits the time-travel vibe]. Precognition is quite normal in anyone who spent their childhood near such a fissure, so Mother Tyler shows signs of telepathy [i.e. developed telepathy, as ESP lies dormant in most homo sapiens...]. She can sense the Fendahl's presence, which puts her into psychic shock, while the treacherous Stael speaks of her drawing on race-memories to gain her visions. The locals are a superstitious bunch, consulting Mother Tyler and having their own black magic coven. The Priory's ultimately destroyed in a specially-rigged, controlled implosion of the time-scanner.

The Fendahl skull is 12,000,000 years old, and that's apparently 8,000,000 years older than a humanoid skull can possibly be. [A skull that's as human as this one really can't be as old as 4,000,000 years, but Colby's not being precise here.] It's not clear when it arrived on Earth. [It's been 12,000,000 years since it left the Fifth Planet, but it could have spent millions of years on Mars, especially if it was responsible for influencing and then destroying a whole culture there.]

The Analysis

Where Does This Come From? About two years before this story aired, a skull was found of a hominid - named "Lucy" by the discoverers - that was over four-million years old. That something so recognisably human could turn out to be so ancient changed the thinking on when and where "humanity" might have started.

The von Daniken "Ancient Astronaut" fad - that aliens influenced mankind's ancient civilisations - had finally died, von Daniken thinking having been applied to ludicrously inappropriate material to "prove" that the England Cricket Team were descended from the Prophet Elijah (or even, memorably, that God was an atheist). It was shown that our ancestors, whatever their faults as dinner-guests, were more sophisticated than we'd believed and had much more complex social arrangements. The main argument for alien intervention was that stone-chucking thugs couldn't have built temples, ergo someone else must have done it. Finding elaborate funeral arrangements and stone-circle calendars meant that they weren't stone-chucking thugs.

Meanwhile the pop-culture version of sociobiology was coming into vogue, with people like zoologist Desmond Morris making a packet out of "explaining" our habits in terms of how they helped our ancestors survive. We had trendy guides to body language (see 14.5, "The Robots of Death"); a briefly-fashionably theory that our ancestors were aquatic apes; the discovery of pheromones; and all manner of "Now It Can Be Told" accounts of our behaviour. Just being told "because that's how we are" wasn't enough any more. In a secular age, people will believe anything logically self-consistent. With "Image of the Fendahl", Chris Boucher came up with a neat, all-encompassing theory which happens not to be true, just to show how easy it is to "account" for all of human nature.

Is This the *Quatermass* Continuum?

...continued from page 179

public's lack of interest after the events of "The Web of Fear" (5.5) or "Invasion of the Dinosaurs" (11.2). *Quatermass and the Pit* doesn't contradict "The Daemons" any more than "Image of the Fendahl" does. In fact, perhaps the biggest question is "why didn't UNIT just hire *Quatermass*?". (Maybe they tried. Maybe he was just sick of dealing with moustached military types after what happened in the '50s.)

However, there's one truly fundamental difference between *Quatermass* and much of *Doctor Who*, one that can be seen most clearly in a scene which overtly references *The Quatermass Experiment*. At the end of "The Ark In Space" (12.2) it's shown that even after generations of stifled humanity, some spark of nobility persists in people like Noah. In the *Quatermass* serials, human nature is bad and getting worse. A lone scientist resolves the first crisis out of guilt for starting it; a brutish mob resolves the second. The third ends with a stern warning about humanity's self-destructive impulses, and the 1979 version shows primeval barbarism to be the norm. Kneale believes in Original Sin, in a modern disguise (a fact borne out by his other scripts, such as the inadvertently hilarious but oddly accurate *The Year of the Sex Olympics*, a 1968 BBC production about reality TV). *Doctor Who* is generally Romantic - note the capital "R" - and believes in innate goodness thwarted by circumstances, a fact that's also noted in "The Ark in Space".

Still, by the same token it's hard to believe that certain *Doctor Who* stories can coexist in the same universe. Perhaps we could resolve this - aesthetically, if not logically - by saying that stories like "The Enemy of the World" (5.4), "Invasion of the Dinosaurs" (11.2) and "The Seeds of Doom" (13.6), which take a pessimistic view of the human condition, *do* belong in the *Quatermass* continuum; whereas "The Wheel in Space" (5.7), "The Monster of Peladon" (11.5) and "The Masque of Mandragora" (14.1), which are fundamentally upbeat about human perfectability, don't.

However, it may be worth mentioning that in spite of the similarities between the two programmes, Nigel Kneale has never liked *Doctor Who* very much. (It's apparently not the plagiarism that bothers him. His stated reason is that he always tried to keep the scary stuff away from children, but then *Doctor Who* came along and wrecked his careful censorship.)

Things That Don't Make Sense Lots of dubious history means lots of logical flaws. The Doctor's claim that the Fendahl's responsible for the 'dark side' of human nature seems weird, for a start. There are perfectly reasonable evolutionary reasons for humanity's behaviour even *without* giant alien slugs getting involved, and besides, what about all those other humanoid species in the universe who've developed near-identical natures but who've never had a visit from the Fendahl? [The Doctor's just making excuses for the bad behaviour of his favourite species.]

The time-loop doesn't make sense, either. If it was supposed to shackle the Fendahl then it failed, because the skull got out. If it was supposed to trap the planet's physical mass then it failed, because the asteroid belt exists. And if it was just supposed to prevent the outside universe discovering any record of the Fendahl - which is what the script is apparently trying to tell us, since the TARDIS contains no records of it even though the Time Lords are said to be scrupulous record-keepers - then it failed, because the Doctor's heard of it.

The Fendahleen can control human muscles telekinetically to stop their victims running away, but they never think to paralyse anybody's arms to stop people with rifles shooting them. The Fendhaleen embryos which mysteriously appear over Thea's unconscious body in episode two are never explained, as we're later told that the number of Fendhaleen is in some way connected to the number of Satanists that Thea devours. [Possibly the embryo Fendhleen exist around the skull all the time, and are invisible before the cultists are sucked dry, but it would've been nice if the story had bothered to tell us about it.]

In episode four, the Doctor magically knows that the two people killed by the Fendahl before he arrived were a hiker and a man called Mitchell. The implosion of the time-scanner apparently removes the Priory from space-time altogether, yet the Doctor obviously doesn't think something like *that* will get rid of the skull once and for all, whereas a supernova will. So this 'indestructible' artefact can be destroyed by heat, but not by being in a part of the continuum that ceases to exist...?

As soon as the Doctor states that the time-scanner can only be used for a hundred hours before imploding, we skip to a scene of Fendelman looking at a never-before-mentioned running log of the machine which lets us know that nearly ninety-nine hours have already elapsed. From a TV point of view, it's also very handy that the time it takes a planet to be destroyed is a nice round number like a hundred hours [see the TV Movie, 27.0, for more such nonsense]. If the superstitions about salt and the number thirteen are race-memories of the Fendahl, then why aren't these superstitions as common in African culture as they are in Europe, when Africa is the place where the human species started (and where the Fendahl skull was found)? Is this more proof that only Britain counts in the *Doctor Who* universe?

And then there's the greatest mystery of all. Despite being the only person with a clue as to what's going on, the Doctor is locked in a cupboard on his arrival so that lots more people can get into life-threatening situations while he's trapped. How does he escape? Well... we don't know. He attacks the lock with the sonic screwdriver, but it has no immediate effect and the Doctor starts sulking. A while later, the door opens. This is never explained. We do hear what sounds like a key turning in the lock, so the solution proposed in Terrance Dicks' novelisation - that the lock belatedly shatters after the Doctor kicks it - doesn't work.

It's *possible* that it's a delayed reaction to the sonic screwdriver, but this is pushing physics somewhat. It's *possible* that the Fendahl itself lets the Doctor escape, to make sure he's not there when Thea Randome goes looking for help, but if it can move objects around at long range then you'd expect it to try to kill the Doctor rather than letting him go free.

Otherwise, we've got to play Cluedo with Fetch Priory. Except... everything's happening simultaneously, and we rewind a few times to show each set of characters arguing. Thea and Adam enter the lab just after the Doctor comes out of the cupboard, exchange a few heated words and go to see Fendleman in the kitchen (with a revolver). He appears to have been there since the Doctor was locked up. Then, a few seconds after he leaves his temporary prison, the Doctor eavesdrops on Max and Ted Moss - who left Ma Tyler's just as the Doctor was imprisoned - discussing him in the computer room (with a candlestick).

So maybe Ma Tyler's got psychokenetic powers...

Critique (Prosecution) In principle, it makes sense. *Doctor Who* has already been down this road before, of course, most obviously in "The Daemons". The idea of ancient superstitions being race-memories of something even more ancient wasn't new to the series in 1977, let alone to television, but it works in context. "Image of the Fendahl" was devised by a writer who'd come to the series under the Philip Hinchcliffe regime, when the programme was re-defining itself for an older and slightly more morbid audience. "The Daemons" took the *Quatermass and the Pit* idea and dressed it up in platform heels for the hip kids of 1971. "Image of the Fendahl" tries to do the same thing within the Hinchcliffe / Holmes version of the universe, disposing itself towards the horror of Lovecraft instead of the joy of men in ill-judged gargoyle suits, even if the subplot about the satanic coven looks painfully familiar. So far, so good.

The trouble is that in its execution, this is just... awkward. Like "Horror of Fang Rock" or "The Talons of Weng-Chiang", there's a sense that the Doctor has wandered into a different BBC production, but both of those earlier stories work through parody as much as anything. Put the Doctor up against the pomp and twaddle of the Victorian / Edwardian era, and you know the men in handlebar moustaches aren't going to stand a chance. Yet in "Image of the Fendahl", Chris Boucher actually wants to *replicate* the mood and the style of science-horror dramas like *The Stone Tape* (also written by the creator of *Quatermass*, and in many ways chillingly similar to what we see here). This isn't parody, this is doing it for real.

Which means that the Doctor just doesn't belong in this story, or at least, that there are two stories going on in parallel. In this it's more like "The Masque of Mandragora" than any of the series' more recent successes. At times you get the feeling that it'd work better as a TV play about scientists discovering the awful truth about humanity's origins, without any of the surplus technobabble offered by the Time Lord contingent. In episode one, the Doctor and Leela don't actually do anything except argue and land in a field, making it plain that Boucher's more interested in what's happening inside the Priory. And when the Doctor does stroll into the plot at the start of episode two, he rather annoyingly knows all the answers straight away, which in itself defeats the point of the exercise. You lose a hell of a lot of the tension if your ancient, unthinkable horror gets a name and a detailed back-story when you're only half an hour into things. A cosmic know-it-all doesn't belong in this story any more than a mind-reader belongs in a murder mystery.

As a result, the script gets distracted by side-issues, SF fancies rather than anything more substantial. The business about the time fissure, the most Kneale-ish thing of all (since it sets out to explain away ghosts, psychic talents and various superstitions in one great pseudo-scientific stroke), is also more or less irrelevant to the plot. So is the Doctor's concern about the time-scanner exploding after a hundred hours, and the 'wild goose-chase' to the Fifth Planet in episode three. The supporting cast at the Priory suddenly cease to be the important ones. Stael, a Satanist for no particular reason, is particularly hard to take; he's incapable of speaking in normal colloquial English and sneers about 'meddling fools' standing between him and his unexplained goals. Thea Ransome is introduced as a "proper" character, but gets to do nothing except stand around in a robe after she becomes the Fendahl core, so between her kidnap by Stael and the Fendahl's ultimate destruction there isn't a single moment when we're supposed to care - or even notice - that she's effectively been murdered.

The ending, in which the Doctor rigs up some scientific trickery and then runs away, is only just more acceptable than the ending of "The Daemons". And none of this is helped by the direction, so obsessed with giving us angst-ridden close-ups of the characters that we're never shown how this scenario is supposed to work as a whole. Worthy of mention for all the wrong reasons is the moment when the Doctor gives a pistol to Stael so that he can kill himself rather than let his soul be consumed by the Fendahl. As it's written, it should be horrific, unsettling and unforgettable. As it's filmed, it looks like one actor passing a prop to another and then hurrying on to the next scene as fast as possible (but see **The Lore**). The dire organ music, a la "The Deadly Assassin", just rubs Fendahl-killer into the wound. Even Fendelman's murder makes "The Seeds of Doom" look pretty.

Like so much of Doctor Who, "Image of the Fendahl" is ultimately a thing of parts. In its individual moments, in its quirks and one-liners, it's often brilliantly successful. The Doctor should make you laugh at least twice; Mother Tyler is a far better "yokel" than any we've seen so far; the cut between Leela describing the Doctor as having 'great knowledge and gentleness', and the sight of the Doctor throwing a strop in the locked cupboard, is lovely; the cows all put in good performances. But watch it from start to finish and the feeling isn't that you've just seen a great story, it's that someone's just *told* you about a great story, one which you'd probably quite like to see yourself some day.

Critique (Defence) There's a school of thought that "The Daemons" is the finest example of a strand of Doctor Who, the menace to mankind being an all-powerful entity which has entered our mythology and crops up in a rural, contemporary setting full of "rich" characters and "supernatural" occurrences. In Volume III we played along with this, but there is not one single part of that story which "Image of the Fendahl" doesn't do at least four times better. It is, in addition, more cohesive in both aesthetic and logical terms. With the possible exception of Stael, everyone has at least two reasons for what they're about. Even the expendable security guard gets a first name in the credits.

Perhaps the most impressive thing is the off-hand way that the bog-standard nightmares are paraded in front of us as though for the first time. The Doctor is chased by something but can't move his legs. Thea feels guilt for something she didn't do. Big worms ooze down corridors (ooer!) and glowing skulls "prove" that a man who thought he was "safe" has been manipulated all along. The Fendahl doesn't gloat or coax, it isn't Sutekh... it's *death*, primordial and unstoppable, unswayed by reason or persuasion. And the Doctor defeats it by making up a recipe for fruit-cake. Even if this is a retread of Quatermass and the Pit - and it's a lot better than the original TV series - it's the Lewis Carroll version, where the cosmic is inside the domestic. The Fendalheen are slugs (and salt can kill them), the Doctor's own people were scared of something in a small village and Leela defeats the borough council in single combat.

George Spenton-Foster, the director, was associate producer on the 60s series Out of the Unknown, and much of the direction here is from that era. There's no music for the first seventeen minutes of episode one, and when it does begin it changes a silly old bat's sneering at a jobsworth security guard into something more unsettling and significant. The sound effects and silent-movie-style dissolves are used to tell the story deftly and quickly. Whilst developing a mood and character, it doesn't hang about. In fact the most "modern" thing here is that the dialogue and the pictures are telling two different versions of the same story, rather than filling in the viewers with lengthy info-dumps.

There's a school of thought that *Doctor Who* is at its best when it's almost exactly like something else, and then the Doctor is thrown in. The rival school, that only things which are completely *Doctor Who* work, occasionally tries to claim that the combination of familiar elements in this story is unique to the programme even if the elements aren't. This does not bear close examination. Much of what makes this story work is the sense that everyone in it had lives before and (for the survivors) after, which had nothing to do with the Doctor or alien skulls. There is a version of this story which is completely *Doctor Who*: that's "The Daemons" and it's garbage.

The Facts

Written by Chris Boucher. Directed by George Spenton-Foster. Viewing figures: 6.7 million, 7.5 million, 7.9 million, 9.1 million.

Supporting Cast Edward Arthur (Adam Colby), Scott Fredericks (Maximilian Stael), Wanda Ventham (Thea Ransome), Denis Lill (Dr. Fendelman), Daphne Heard (Martha Tyler), Edward Evans (Ted Moss), Derek Martin (David Mitchell), Geoffrey Hinsliff (Jack Tyler).

Cliffhangers As the Fendahl skull begins to glow inside the Priory, the Doctor finds himself rooted to the spot out in the grounds, as *something* moves in on him; the Fendahl skull starts to glow (again) right in front of the Doctor, who's unable to take his hand away from it despite the obvious agony; at the Priory, the first of the full-grown Fendahleen shuffles up the passageway towards the paralysed Doctor and company.

The Lore

• Stael's death caused a lot of concern among the higher echelons of BBC Drama. The final version (he's handed a gun, the Doctor leaves, we hear a shot, later we see him dead) is a compromise with which the fewest people involved were unhappy.

• Ted Moss was played by veteran actor

Edward Evans, star of the first British TV soap, *The Grove Family*. Chris Boucher, a childhood fan of the show, was delighted.

• Boucher never wrote for the series again after this, as he'd taken on the job of script editor for *Blake's 7* (a job which, for the first year, meant taking Terry Nation's back-of-an-envelope notes and making fifty-minute dramas set in space on a BBC budget). He returned to the fold with a handful of BBC *Doctor Who* novels, described by some as "ingenious" and others as "shockingly awful", and with the *Kaldor City* audio dramas. Many of these combine the background from "The Robots of Death" with elements from Boucher's *Blake's 7* episodes, which makes the **Is This the Quatermass Continuum?** question look simple by comparison.

• The guard-dog is ingeniously named "Leakey" as a reference to the palaeontologist family. And to puppy-training, obviously.

• The Fendahleen were altered in pre-production to make them look just a shade less phallic. They were, believe it or not, given ribbing and tassels before getting an extra coating of latex (see 10.5, "The Green Death", for more prophylactic fun).

• A physicist wrote in requesting a precise explanation as to how a 'direct continuum implosion' might occur without contravening the Second Law of Thermodynamics. A lecturer for the Open University "ghosted" the reply (see more about these stalwart chaps under 16.3, "The Stones of Blood"). Meanwhile, a sharp-eyed child wrote to BBC's *Nationwide* asking why the Doctor offered Liquorice Allsorts every time he asked 'would you like a jelly-baby?' (see 16.2, "The Pirate Planet" and 25.2, "The Happiness Patrol").

• The Australian edit of the story loses the line 'mankind has been used!' and Fendelman's nasty death, but the Australian copy that circulated in the UK during the '80s has the inadvertently funny continuity announcement at the end of episode two: 'Oh dear! Well, *Doctor Who* returns on Monday in a brand new adventure, "Warriors of the Deep". So, er… obviously he escapes from the Fendahl, then.'

15.4: "The Sun Makers"

(Serial 4W, Four Episodes, 26th November - 17th December 1978.)

Which One is This? The workers revolt on Pluto (disguised as *Metropolis*) and we examine the knotty world of Free Collective Bargaining (disguised as a four-part adventure story for kids), while a nasty little bald man turns into green slime and gets sucked into his own commode. We have to explain it that way, because it's "the one with no monsters".

Firsts and Lasts Last story to credit Robert Holmes as its script editor (he's also the writer, in this case, so Anthony Read actually edited this one). He'll be sorely missed.

Four Things to Notice About "The Sun Makers"...

1. Things everybody knows about "The Sun Makers", number one: it's a satire on the British tax system. Robert Holmes' original pitch was a much less parochial story about the oppression of the masses under imperialism, but a visit from the Inland Revenue convinced him to turn it into a story about the oppression of the masses under a crippling system of taxation. This is why the elite guardsmen of Megropolis One are called the Inner Retinue, and why one of the corridors is numbered P45. But best of all is the farewell that Gatherer Hade gives his superior, the Collector, when he's bowing and scraping his way out of the door: 'I have the honour to remain, sir, your humble and obedient servant... yours, etectera, etcetera...'

2. And on a similar note: it's often been pointed out that the Gatherer's outfit makes him look like a giant humbug (even the Doctor notices it), but it may also be significant that the Company's weapon of choice is always *gas*, or - when it attempts to execute Leela - a lot of hot air.

3. Like many of the stories in this era, the best bits of "The Sun Makers" work by pitting the Doctor against decent "evil" character actors instead of blank-faced monsters. However good the aptly-named Richard Leech may be as Gatherer Hade, stealing the show here is Henry Woolf as the Collector. Woolf was well-known on '70s TV as a comic actor specialising in being small and creepy, and his performance in this story - as something that *looks* human, but acts as if it's been hatched from some kind of larva - is hideously unforgettable. Especially the way he talks about 'steaming' Leela.

4. Typical of Season Fifteen, this is a story that's prepared to go on location *anywhere* if it saves the BBC having to build sets. The exterior scenes, supposedly set a kilometre above the capital city of Pluto, were shot in the rooftop car park of a tobacco factory in Bristol. And it shows. The same factory also provided the longest corridor ever seen in the series - but see **Which is Best: Film or VT?** under 12.3, "The Sontaran Experiment" - and just to maintain the all-important "on the cheap" feel, the interior of the Company safe looks remarkably like the archive from "The Ark in Space" (12.2), only painted orange.

The Continuity

The Doctor A bad loser at chess. He can send a guard to sleep with nothing more than eye-contact and some drowsy words; it's not up to the Master's level of hypnosis, but it can't just be due to the guard's weak will as it affects Leela as well. [The Doctor's mind-skills are improving. He'll be ridiculously good at this sort of thing by the end of this season.]

• *Inventory.* He's got a collapsible telescope in his pocket, and must have at least two bags of jelly-babies on him, as he leaves one in the correction centre but can still offer a sample to the Gatherer. He's also got a pair of dark glasses, useful when fixing a piece of technology that might blow up. In addition to the usual sonic screwdriver, he's got a smaller buzzing device that comes in handy when re-programming the Company computer. The screwdriver itself can open the Company's safe from a range of about six feet.

Background. The Doctor claims that the Droge of the Gabrielides once offered a whole star system for his head. He's familiar with Professor Thripsted's *Flora and Fauna of the Universe*, which lists the Usurians under poisonous fungi. He considers the habitation on Pluto to be 'wrong', and has no knowledge of it [it's not part of established history?].

The Supporting Cast

• *Leela.* She claims she doesn't know her place of birth, as if the Sevateem didn't give a name to their world [not even just "World"?]. They seem to have spiders and webs where she comes from.

• *K9.* Able to beat the Doctor at chess, despite the Doctor's piffle about the limitations of the machine mind. He's eager to join the Doctor outside the TARDIS, so he's obviously got a sense of adventure, and asks the Doctor not to gush too much as this would 'embarrass' him. Despite his normal over-literal mind, he's capable of wishing the Doctor good luck and can even growl in desperation.

K9 can detect, and analyse, the neural inhibitor in Pluto's air conditioning without being asked. He's capable of "tracking" his new master by sensing where the Doctor's been. He runs on batteries.

The TARDIS When the column stops moving in flight, the Doctor is alarmed and says that the Ship could have gone right through the time-spiral. He adds that the 'paint' is always jamming things up. [The Doctor stated in 15.2, "The Invisible Enemy", that the console room was being redecorated. One might have expected something more high-tech than paint, but see 15.5, "Underworld". Is going through the time-spiral what happens if the TARDIS drifts too long in the vortex without materialising?]

The Non-Humans
• *Usurians.* Masterminds behind the 'widely-diversified' interplanetary operation known as the Company, the Usurians are businessmen rather than warmongers, and keep their slaves under control with a combination of bureaucracy, anxiety-inducing drugs and - most of all - crippling taxation. Their philosophy: 'Grinding oppression of the masses is the only policy that pays dividends'.

On Pluto there's only one Usurian in evidence, who appears as a bald, sadistic, ruthlessly cost-effective little man who never leaves his motorised chair and is rarely seen away from his computerised desk. In fact Usurians are fungal, normally resembling seaweed with eyes, and the chair keeps him in human form by particle radiation. When the Company operations collapse on Pluto, the Collector shrinks away to a slimy green fuzz that drains into a sink at the base of the chair. This is what they call 'liquidation'. Usurians don't breathe air.

Based on Usurius, the Company is said to have been manipulating humanity for some time; see **History**. It has computer records on the Time Lords, describing them as oligarchic rulers of Gallifrey, deemed a grade three planet in the last market survey with little economic potential

[though it's amazing that the Usurians can even *think* about doing business with the Time Lords]. It also has a file on the Doctor, who has a record of violence and economic subversion. There are no records on the Sevateem, but semantic analysis of the word correctly identifies it as the product of a degenerate Tellurian colony. [So the Usurians, like the Lurmans in "Carnival of Monsters" (10.2), refer to humans as Tellurians. Do they belong to the same interplanetary super-culture as the Lurmans? See also 22.4, "The Two Doctors".]

The Collector speaks of the 'management' above him, and there's a Company Benevolent Fund. Humanity isn't a particularly good labour force, and other Company operations are much more profitable. The Usurians have tried war, but have found that economic power is more effective. In the end the Doctor cripples the Company on Pluto, though not elsewhere, by introducing an index-linked 2% growth tax to the computers and blowing the economy.

Planet Notes
• *Pluto.* Officially the ninth planet of the solar system. It's occupied by three-hundred million humans in this era, but run by the Company, so the humans are essentially slaves whose earnings are recouped by the Company in taxes. The residents are especially taxed for the privilege of the in-station fusion satellites - or 'suns' - maintained by the Company, but the vast majority of citizens have to live in dormers in the enclosed spaces of the Megropolis and never see the suns anyway. Indeed, it's illegal for anyone not of executive grade to acsend to roof level, up to a kilometre above the ground. The Company also generates the atmosphere on Pluto [and the Earth-type gravity, presumably]. The suns would only last for a few years without power.

There are six Megropolises, and the Doctor lands in Megropolis One, the oldest city on Pluto. Each Megropolis has its own sun, and the citizens don't have a word for 'dark' [most people never see the suns, so the Company must keep the lights on all the time inside the city]. For most of the fifty-million people in the Megropolis, life is grim and utilitarian, with workers required to dress in uniform overalls: yellow and brown for the D-grade work-units, yellow and white for the kind of B-grades who work in main control, blue for Megro-guard security.

The anxiety-inducing agent PCM - pentocyleinic-methyl-hydrane - is introduced to the atmosphere to keep the populace in a state of fear, but the elite are given tablets to combat the effect of this, so the revolution starts as soon as the vapour towers are shut down. This atmosphere of terror even seems to affect the Doctor. Some have escaped Megropolis society and formed a "resist-ance" community in the undercity deep below ground, where only E-grade technicians normally go, but they're more like bandits than revolution-aries. Some of these "Others" are escapees from the hell of the correction centres.

On the other hand Gatherer Hade speaks of people called Ajacks, miners from Megropolis Three where Gatherer Pile is in charge, who still seem to dress individually. Or at least, not unlike the Doctor. The air conditioning isn't effective in the mines, so the Company's wary of an Ajack rebellion.

The Gatherer is charged with the task of over-seeing tax collection for the Usurians - it's not clear whether he knows their true nature or not - and organising a monthly budget, for which he gets privileges like raspberry leaves, a desk made of real wood and the right to wear a big imperious robe and an excessive purple hat. There's also the office of Tax-Master General, to which Hade aspires. Work-shifts are announced with the sound of trumpets, charmingly. All work-units are numbered on the arm at birth, though some crim-inals scar themselves by surgically removing it, and everything's under surveillance from oculoid electronic monitors all over the city.

Crimes against the Company are almost unthinkable. One attempt to defraud the Company by falsifying computer records, carried out by a conspiracy led by an Executive Grade called Kandor in Megropolis Four, was hushed up so that nobody below the Gatherer's level would get any ideas. Kandor survived for three years in a correction centre, a record. At the 'induction ther-apy' section of the correction centre, parts of pris-oners' brains are sensitised and neural pathways are cleared so that they feel a thousand times more pain when they get to the physical section. The centre is right under the palace of the Collector, ostensibly so the Collector can hear the prisoners' screams.

Public execution is practised, one method being steaming, boiling the victim to death in a condensation chamber above the city's power con-trol. The Collector's personal bodyguards are the Inner Retinue, divisions of uniformed men with sinister black visors and the usual energy weapons, who travel around in neat little buggies. The Inner Retinue men seen here are truly rubbish [because usually nobody fights back against them].

The Company logo on Pluto is a face inside a sun. The Gatherer travels by a 'beamer', though what this means is unclear. Consum-cards are used, basically very large, very thick pieces of plastic that look suspiciously like Visa cards. They can be used at consum-banks, but the "cash machine" booth entered by the Doctor knocks him out with larium gas when he tries to use a stolen one. The gas affects the throat, making it hard for him to speak once he recovers. The city's also fitted with an emergency sprinkler system which can flood the whole Megropolis with dya-nine, a poisoned gas capable of killing everyone but the Collector in ten seconds.

Citizen Cordo chooses the Golden Death for his father [suggesting a form of euthanasia], though the death taxes for this particular death have risen from 80 talmars to 117. It's that kind of society. There are preparation centres instead of schools, and Q capsules are available to cut down on the need for sleep, but as ever there's a high medical tax on these and 50% compound interest on all unpaid taxes. Praise the Company.

• *Mars.* As is so often the way, it was the stop-over point between Earth and the outer planets; see **History**.

• *Cassius.* Pluto was believed to be the outer-most planet of Earth's solar system, until the dis-covery of Cassius. [That makes at least three miss-ing planets in the system, possibly four. See also **What's This Planet Fourteen Business All About?** under 6.3, "The Invasion". As it happens, astronomers *did* find a tenth significant body orbiting the sun in 2003. Although it's currently regarded as a planetoid rather than a proper plan-et, strictly speaking Pluto isn't a proper planet either. The planetoid has yet to be officially named, but its discoverers refer to it as "Sedna" after an Inuit goddess of icy waters, which is just typical of Californian scientists. It's not too late to start a petition to get it called "Cassius"...]

History

• *Dating.* None given. The people on Pluto are treated as if they're the only humans in the solar system, so obviously the far, far future.

When Earth was running down and its people dying, the Company was looking for property in the sector. The Usurians made a deal, moving all the people to Mars after their engineers made the planet habitable, and then started taxing the humans dry. When Mars' resources were exhausted, a new environment was created on Pluto. The four planets in-between weren't considered viable by the engineers. Nowhere else is economic for the humans, so when Pluto's exhausted this branch of the Company will close and humanity will be left to die as soon as the suns go out [so the suns provide power, not just light]. With the Company defeated, the Doctor believes that the people will be able to re-settle on Earth using their sky-freighters, as it will have regenerated itself [meaning its mineral wealth?] by now.

[BBC publicity material in 1977 suggested this story took place "millions of years" in the future. There's certainly the suggestion that this is much, much further ahead than most other futuristic stories. The Doctor loses track of how far the TARDIS has been travelling and worries about crashing through the time-spiral, hinting at the outer limits of human history. The Collector's statement that Earth was dying when the Company found it *can't* be a reference to the solar flares referred to in "The Ark in Space" (12.2), although it may be a reference to the aftermath of "The Mysterious Planet" (23.1), which would certainly set a date millions of years in the future when most humans have already left the solar system. If Earth has regenerated since the humans left then this story may take place millions of years after *that*.

[Alternatively, there's a slightly more sinister interpretation. The Collector's statement about moving the humans to Mars and beyond *might* indicate that the Company has influenced Earth ever since the twentieth century - when the Earth began 'dying', if you want to be bleak - and that the Collector is referring to the whole history of humanity during the spaceflight era. The novels certainly haven't been shy in suggesting that the Company might have made overtures on Earth in the late 1900s. So the solar system may have been in the Usurians' pockets ever since the first colonisations, though the control obviously wouldn't have been as overt as seen here.]

Additional Sources One scene in Terrance Dicks' novelisation of "The Sun Makers" is memorable, simply for the unusual way in which it changes the morality of the original script. On-screen, the revolting citizens of the Megropolis (i.e. the citi-

zens who are in revolt) take the Gatherer up to the roof of the Megropolis and throw him off, then celebrate loudly. On the other hand, the book has them feeling sick with themselves almost as soon as they've carried out this murderous deed.

Dicks was evidently unhappy with the "revolution is great, let's kill the oppressors" mood of the TV story, but since this is a big *political* moment, the ethics here are more convoluted than ever before. The Gatherer is effectively a war criminal, a traitor who helped a hostile alien parasite enslave millions of people and murder thousands. If Holmes had presented his death as a formal execution (a la Morbius in one of Dicks' own scripts), rather than having the angry mob throw him to his death on the spur of the moment, then would it have been as objectionable…?

The Analysis

Where Does This Come From? This is not, when it comes down to it, a story about tax. That was a surface layer of petty gripes and in-jokes, prompted by Holmes' own tax problems after Season Fourteen.

This was, basically, the period which saw the start of the debate over what we now call the "work-life" balance. Megropolis One is a society of people running to stand still. As you may recall (see **Why Didn't They Just Spend More Money?** under 12.2, "The Ark In Space"), inflation had reached 24%. Everyone, if they wished to maintain a standard of living, was forced to do more work. In many ways this story is old-fashioned for its time, in treating militant workers as idealists, revolutionaries and sympathetic "everyman" figures, rather than as evil Bolshies imperilling the British Way of Life. To find any films taking the same point of view you'd have to look back to 1945-50, and the establishment of the Welfare State. By the '70s, virtually all union members shown on British TV or in British cinema were portrayed as selfish, lazy and stubborn.

But aside from the "obvious" political points, what's most striking about "The Sun Makers" is that it's set in a world where the revolution *will* be televised. The Doctor's overthrown despots and potential dictatorships before, but usually by fiddling with mad computers or guiding alien war-fleets into the heart of the sun. "The Reign of Terror" (1.8), one of the few stories to be set against the backdrop of an actual, bona fide revolution, takes the schoolroom history-book approach and assumes that these big upheavals are the result of big historical figures making big decisions. If things aren't solved by blowing up the "threat", then they're solved by interfering in the affairs of the ruling elite.

But here, one of the first things the Doctor thinks of doing is broadcasting news of the imminent revolution over the TV network. It is, in fact, one of the very few *Doctor Who* stories which even acknowledges the existence / importance of propaganda. Before now the closest thing we've seen to the Doctor's 'join the revolution!' broadcast is the climax of "The Dalek Invasion of Earth" (2.2), in which the TARDIS crew cause the Robomen to revolt against the Daleks, but *there* it was a case of giving orders to machine-people and *here* there's a sense of the power of the media in politics. The huge explosion in TV news coverage between the early '60s and the late '70s must at least account for *some* of this, the increasing awareness that television was part of the process and not just a way of seeing close-ups of the men in charge.

The original draft of the story, preceding Holmes' audit (see **The Lore**), was a reworking of many of the ideas found in *The Space Merchants* by Frederik Pohl and Cyril Kornbluth (1953). In this, advertisers run the world and the opposition ("Consies") are those who think the planet's resources shouldn't be squandered in continuous production fuelled by heightened demand. All the dystopian / satirical uses of euphemism and the media are present and accounted for in Holmes' script, and as writer / literary critic Kingsley Amis had proclaimed *The Space Merchants* to be the best SF novel in the world - ever - many people had read it.

The notion of continuous sunlight to remove "wasteful" sleep was partly derived from Adrian Berry's bafflingly popular pop-science book *The Iron Sun* (see also 14.3, "The Deadly Assassin" and 17.5, "The Horns of Nimon"). It's not an unfamiliar idea for anyone who's been near the poles, or who's read basic SF "primers", including Isaac Asimov's "Nightfall". Hinchcliffe had; Holmes almost definitely would have. Yet the basic source-text isn't in the script. Director Pennant Roberts took the iconography from Fritz Lang's 1926 blockbuster *Metropolis*, and the word "Megropolis" might possibly be a teeny hint that Holmes was playing along with this idea. The cliffhanger to episode three sees Leela held in a casket identical to that in which Lang's robot Maria is made, while Mandrel holds the dials steady, just as in the movie.

And as ever, certain recurring themes insist on making themselves felt in Holmes' work. The use of petty bureaucracy as a form of villainy is obvious, but more importantly, this bureaucracy is *sadistic*. The Collector practically slavers when he's describing Leela's forthcoming death (see 10.2, "Carnival of Monsters", for more office-bound kinkyness of this kind). The use of language is fairly typical, too. Many of the words used by Hade to suck up to the Collector - 'sagacity' is particularly noticeable - will be turning up again in Season Twenty-Three.

By the way, around this time BBC Radio 4 was experimenting with "quadrophonic" programmes, i.e. broadcast using four channels instead of one or two. Such programmes were trailed extensively, and proclaimed with a little logo in the *Radio Times*. Nobody bought the equipment needed and the whole scheme was quietly dropped, but obviously it caught on amongst the Usurians, as the death-chamber is wired for quadrophonic sound so that the victims' screams can be heard more clearly.

Things That Don't Make Sense   The Doctor's 'growth tax' idea is cute, but the sums don't really add up. It's the Company which *collects* the taxes, so if it taxes itself then all the money should immediately go back into its own coffers.

The story culminates in the Doctor shutting down PCM production in Megropolis One and fomenting revolution in the city, and as soon as the Collector's defeated he acts as if it's problem solved for the humans. Forgetting that there are five *other* cities still terrified and under the control of armed security forces, commanded by self-interested Gatherers even if the Company itself isn't operational. And how's human society going to function in the future, when everyone's determined not to pay taxes of any kind?

There's only one Gatherer in the whole of Megropolis One (pop. 50,000,000), and he personally handles everyday affairs like death-taxes, which would be hard to credit even if we *didn't* see him spending so much of his day lolling around his office doing nothing in particular. Leela's 'perhaps everyone runs from the tax-man' gag, easily the least funny and most self-indulgent "topical" joke here, is also massively out of character; she's never heard anyone say 'tax-man' before this.

But the big question is: what sort of work do

the work-units *do*, exactly? Taxes may be the method used by the Company to extract wealth from the humans, but talmars are only a local currency, so there has to be some critical resource underlying the economy. The Company apparently wants Pluto's minerals - there are miners in Megropolis Three, and the Doctor is frequently mistaken for one, which in itself raises the question of why miners should be taller than the general populace - but what about the hundreds of millions of human beings in the other five cities? What can they possibly be doing which would result in a profit for the Usurians? [Paperwork for other Company operations?]

Come to think of it, with Pluto terraformed despite the low gravity and distance from the sun, shouldn't oxygen be taxed? Wouldn't that be the very most basic and obvious start to all of this, as well as a more pointed satire?

Critique Rushed, padded, often cheap-looking and stocked with tedious minor supporting characters, but also written by Robert Holmes so ultimately quite good anyway. Or is that part of the problem? Written around the time that the BBC's documentary *Whose Doctor Who?* was broadcast, there's a sense here that Holmes is starting to believe his own reputation, thinking he can get away with all of this without anybody asking awkward questions. There are lines in the script which seem to have been penned specifically for use in future documentaries ('why don't you girls ever listen?' jarred even at the time).

Yet, Holmes' reputation didn't come from nowhere. This is a writer whose first script had students making acid and attacking the roots of society, lifting paving slabs but not finding a beach (6.4, "The Krotons"). He gave us grey-faced alien bureaucrats and space pirates who were bored civil servants on the make. Here's a writer who was a policeman and a political reporter, idly making an allegory about working-all-hours into something more personal. If scripts were everything then this would be a mildly amusing skit, but as director, Pennant Roberts adds his own stamp to the story. He's often derided, largely because of the scripts he was given in the 1980s, yet as with "The Face of Evil" (14.4) he's doing his best to think about the way this world works. Who else would have made utensils from drainpipes for one shot? Who else would have cast Henry Woolf as a monster (while Woolf was

appearing in *Words and Pictures* as the librarian helping children learn to read, and *Rutland Weekend Television* as various con-men and transvestite continuity announcers)?

So "The Sun Makers" is a curious two-faced animal. Often, it seems happy to demonstrate exactly what's wrong with *Doctor Who* in this era. The resistance is (as ever) useless; the roof scenes look exactly like the people-in-silly-costumes-hanging-around-a-car-park set-ups they really are; and the arguments with Mandrel are possibly the dullest thing in this season, which is saying something. But in parts, it tells you an awful lot about the way the series works when it's working at full-pelt. Though the constant messing around with monsters turned him into a near-conventional "hero" in the popular imagination - just look at the gag in "The Curse of the Fatal Death" about him saving every planet in the universe several times over - what's the *real* nature of the Doctor, other than to be the enemy of red tape? As an overwhelming force that stifles, intimidates and keeps people in their station, the Company is the perfect opponent for him. The real pity is that to get him into a position where he can harangue, send up and ultimately - almost literally - deflate the Usurians, the plot has to use so many clichés of TV in general and *Doctor Who* in particular. But when the Collector is making his rants against the Doctor ('I sense the vicious doctrine of egalitarianism, Hade!'), and the Doctor's replying in kind, *that's* when the story starts to shine.

One other small detail: in each story Pennant Roberts directed, at least one major character became female. In this case, Marn – the Gatherer's aide - was written as a man. Meanwhile Holmes makes use of BBC directives limiting violence in the series by having a good reason for the heroes not to kill the cannon-fodder Megro-Guards, but Roberts ensures that the two on-screen deaths we see are memorable, and the result of the victims' own folly.

The Facts

Written by Robert Holmes. Directed by Pennant Roberts. Viewing figures: 8.5 million, 9.5 million, 8.9 million, 8.4 million.

Supporting Cast Henry Woolf (Collector), Richard Leech (Hade), Jonina Scott (Marn), Roy Macready (Cordo), William Simons (Mandrel),

Michael Keating (Goudry), Adrienne Burgess (Veet), David Rowlands (Bisham).

Cliffhangers The Doctor puts his stolen consumcard into the machine at the consum-bank, at which point the booth snaps shut and fills up with gas; a buggy full of guards bears down on Leela and her associates in a surprisingly long corridor; strapped down in the condensation chamber, Leela struggles against her bonds as the chamber fills up with steam.

The Lore

• Leela was to have been killed in this story, before everyone realised that it was too frivolous a tale for such a thing to work. (She's the second companion in a row to have narrowly avoided this fate, the third if you count the Brigadier in the original version of "The Hand of Fear".)

• Part of the location work, as has been mentioned, was done at the Hartcliffe Wills tobacco factory in Bristol. When instructing the actors on how to look brow-beaten and doped on PCH, Pennant Roberts pointed out the way the company's employees wandered around the factory.

• The other main location was the Camden Town deep tube shelter, the setting for the first publicity photo-call with K9. The press were particularly welcome, as the cast and crew had inadvertently been locked in overnight.

• The "pyjama-suits" of the extras were colourcoded to give a sense of different departments having different uniforms. The Company's "Sun" badge was the only remnant of an early plan to give the entire story an Aztec look (suggesting blood sacrifices to keep the suns going).

• The original script called for the Collector's home world to be called "Usurers". Graham Williams objected, but Roberts and Holmes amended it to "Usurius" and kept mention of it to a minimum.

• Williams later said that the story outline - about an anti-colonialist revolt - wasn't exactly what made it to the screen, but that with Holmes and Roberts egging each other on the humour got in the way of the story.

15.5: "Underworld"

(Serial 4Y, Four Episodes, 7th January - 28th January 1978.)

Which One is This? Lots of people in animalskins run around in caves (or rather, run around in photographs of caves). Greek heroes with '70s spacesuits battle the overlords of the underworld, while the Doctor helps them get their rocks off.

Firsts and Lasts First of a loose "trilogy" of Greek myths retold as space-opera; see 16.6, "The Armageddon Factor" and 17.5, "The Horns of Nimon". First story to be given a gallery-only day for post-production (no, come back, it's really interesting and important), so that the programme-makers could get the thing made without running foul of the BBC scene-shifters' union... more on this later. This was especially important here, because it's the first story to have had more than 50% of its studio work done on CSO (we'd say "blue-screen", but it was actually green on this occasion).

Four Things to Notice About "Underworld"...

1. Ah yes. The first thing anybody ever remembers about "Underworld" is its dramatic misuse of CSO, an effect much-abused in the early '70s but here pushing back all boundaries of sense or artistic judgement. The (rather good) Minyan spaceship set, really only used in the first episode, cost somewhat more than expected and left no money for the cave-based location shooting needed for episodes two, three and four. Hence the decision to film the many, many cave scenes in a green studio and use CSO to insert cave-like backgrounds behind the actors later on. The scenes at the start of episode two - in which extras in ill-judged "peasant caveman" costumes run screaming from a rockfall that isn't really there, with their feet at odd angles to the ground - are incredible to behold.

2. Dr. Science has left the building. "Underworld" is packed so full of scientific inaccuracies that it's hard to justify even a fraction of the plot, since this time the script doesn't just get the details wrong but builds the entire story around some deeply peculiar "cosmic" ideas. Here we learn that new solar systems appear out of nowhere at the edge of the universe, and that gravity works like a kind of magic space-magnetism, so that rocks can collect around spaceships

and form whole planets even when the spaceships aren't very big or very heavy. (Even the bits that are scientifically valid just *look* wrong, but see **Things That Don't Make Sense** for more.) And to think, this was a series that started off trying to teach the younger viewers something...

3. Science may be in short supply, but if you want contrived literary parallels then this is the place. The plot of "Underworld" is modelled on the story of Jason and the Argonauts, transposed into space so that the golden fleece becomes the Minyan race-banks and fire-breathing dragons become laser-beams. The fact that fire-breathing dragons are actually a lot more interesting than laser-beams never seems to have occurred to the programme-makers. Obvious parallels to look out for: Herrick / Heracles, Orfe / Orpheus, Tala / Atalanta, P7E / Persephone, Hedis / Hades and Jackson / Jason, as if "Jackson" were somehow a more space-aged sort of name. Obviously the Doctor has to point out the comparison at the end of the story, for those of us who are hard of understanding, but even K9's not convinced by it.

4. In episode one the script requires Commander Jackson to explain the horror of a quest that's taken 10,000 years, but James Maxwell plays the part a little too realistically. It's supposed to sound tragic, and instead just sounds incredibly monotonous. Indeed, he almost seems to be telling the audience what to expect in the next three episodes as he drones the words: 'Going on and on... and unable to remember why...'

The Continuity

The Doctor   Refers to K9 as his 'second-best friend'. [Surely, Leela must be the first? Apparently the Doctor's companion is always his best friend, c.f. 13.6, "The Seeds of Doom".] Nonetheless, the dog pooh-poohs his idea that ancient myths may actually be prophecies of the future. [It only seems like yesterday that the Doctor was dismissing all forms of superstition.]

• *Inventory*. As ever he's got a gadget for measuring radiation, but it seems to be a new one that makes bleeping noises. The apple in his pocket gets fried by the invisible dragons at the End of the World.

• *Background*. Not only has the Doctor been to Aberdeen, where the people absorb more radiation from the granite than people who work in nuclear power-plants, he's also told Leela about it before. [By this stage Leela is treated as if she's been with the Doctor for a long, long time. There may be many "unseen" adventures for the two of them.] He's been to Blackpool, too. [See also 22.6, "Revelation of the Daleks".]

The Supporting Cast

• *Leela*. She's terribly into the idea of "revolution" as a first resort. She feels odd without any kind of weapon, is genuinely angry at being manipulated by either the Doctor or the Pacifier ray and has learned not to trust anyone - even the Doctor - without a good reason. Nonetheless, she tells young Idas that the Doctor 'has saved many fathers'. [Not hers, obviously. In fact, no on-screen adventure with these two ever shows the Doctor saving anyone's father.] By this point she's extraordinarily affectionate towards K9, and loves seeing the Doctor's pretensions burst [anyone would think she's ready to fly the coup...].

• *K9*. Now showing signs of sarcasm. Put bulldog clips on his "ears" and attach wires to another computer, and K9 can interface with it, even if the computer's a product of a wholly different culture [so software adaptability's quite advanced by 5000 AD, unless the Doctor's been upgrading K9 with the kind of technology that lets TARDIS equipment interface with just about anything].

K9's receptors can sense the pulsing of the Minyan ship's ion drive even when he's inside the TARDIS and the ship is beyond visual range. He can recharge by drawing radiation from the newly-formed planet and its igneous rock; date objects by measuring the isotope decay rate; provide a map of the tunnels from a slot in his side and analyse fission grenades. His blaster fire can bring down rock walls. The Doctor's already far, far too dependent on this machine.

The TARDIS   The TARDIS' familiar wheezing, groaning sound comes from its relative dimensional stabiliser during materialisation phase [the thing used to shrink people in 15.2, "The Invisible Enemy"]. The TARDIS actually seems to be flying through space at the beginning here, rather than travelling through the vortex, and the console rotor goes up and down until the Ship stops at the edge of the cosmos. The Doctor speaks of the Minyan ship being beyond 'visual aid range', suggesting the scanner can only see so far [apparently contradicted in 18.3, "Full Circle"].

Just How Involved are the Time Lords?

The funny thing is that the universe-in-general always seems to know exactly as much as we do. Before "The War Games" (6.7), nobody the Doctor encountered so much as breathed the name of the Time Lords. Even given that the Doctor never used to introduce himself *as* a Time Lord, you would have thought that one or two of the cosmic powers he came across might have mentioned them in passing, or at least have been able to identify the TARDIS as a product of you-know-where.

So it makes a certain sense that when "The War Games" finally presents the Time Lords to us, they're shown to be rather distant individuals who never get involved with any of the "lesser" cultures. But no sooner have we found out about them than *everybody* knows who they are, from Axos upwards. Suddenly they're doing deals with cultures all over history, and every space-power worth its salt has done a quick assessment of their homeworld (from the Sontarans in 11.1, "The Time Warrior" to the Usurians in 14.4, "The Sun Makers"... Robert Holmes was always keen on a political, "famous" version of Gallifrey).

Now, for our purposes, we'll assume that this connection between what we know and what the *universe* knows is a coincidence. The alternative is to believe that the Doctor's heart-felt speech in "The War Games", in which he claims that his kind have a duty to fight 'evil', really *does* convince the Time Lords to give up their millennia-old stay-at-home ways in a matter of minutes and instantly changes the nature of their entire society. Though this might explain an awful lot, it's also nigh-impossible to swallow.

Besides, in "The Time Warrior" the Doctor describes his people as 'galactic ticket-inspectors' who clamp down on reckless, unauthorised uses of time-travel. Unless he's referring to the things his people have been doing in the four or five years since his trial, it seems that the Time Lords have always been prepared to... well, let's not say "meddle". Let's say "monitor". "Underworld" claims that they adopted a policy of non-intervention after the tragedy of Minyos, but let's make sure we understand what this means. It *doesn't* mean that after Minyos, the Time Lords decided never to tamper with the histories of other worlds. The Minyan debacle wasn't like the Doctor's Gallifrey-sanctioned intervention in, say "The Curse of Peladon" (9.2). The Time Lords got *personally* involved on Minyos, actively becoming part of the planet's culture, making themselves known to the locals and - to an extent - trying to re-make the

civilisation in their own image. "Non-intervention" doesn't mean a complete ban on fiddling around with other planets, it just means not tying those planets to Gallifrey.

So Gallifrey is happy to interfere, when it feels the need. But what are the criteria? Where does it draw the line between being the watch-tower of the universe, and being the heart of an empire which actively wants to impose its own values on the rest of time and space? The Time Lords clearly feel they have a mandate, but it's not clear what that mandate is. They *do* feel obliged to clamp down on other people's time-travel experiments - see especially 22.4, "The Two Doctors" - but they apparently don't block every species' attempts to develop time-technology or they would have moved against the Daleks much "sooner" (compare 2.8, "The Chase" with 12.4, "Genesis of the Daleks") and might well have stopped the Navarinos (24.3, "Delta and the Bannermen"), among others. Though the name "Time Lord" might suggest that time is their *only* concern, they also step in when the plebian species come close to developing immortality (23.2, "Mindwarp"). Yet as they seem to exist outside the normal course of history, it's hard to believe they're playing an ordinary political power-game. They seem to have a greater agenda than pure self-interest.

A common view is that the Time Lords are there to maintain the integrity of history. In this version of things, history has a "proper" shape (though possibly the Time Lords had some hand in deciding that shape, a long time ago by *their* calendar). The Doctor's people are, on the whole, defending the way-things-should-be. They stop certain species gaining time-travel because that time-travel would jeopardise the timeline, and they make sure planets like Peladon join galactic federations because it's "right" for that to happen. This would, at the very least, explain why they accept the Doctor's defence in "The War Games". They acknowledge that he *has* been defending time, and that on the whole he's just done the jobs they would have had to do themselves anyway. No wonder the argument is couched in terms of fighting 'evil'. Damage to history is, in the Time Lord philosophy, as close to evil as you can get.

The trouble is that this idea assumes there's no free will anywhere in the universe, and very little room for manoeuvre. Perhaps the Doctor can save a few more lives on any given planet than *should*

continued on page 195...

An alarm sounds when the TARDIS is drawn into the spiral nebula encountered here, and it's obviously capable of harming the Ship. The Doctor gets 'escape co-ordinates' from K9 to break free of its pull, rather than just dematerialising and sending the Ship back into the vortex. [Is it impossible to leave normal space when the Ship's in the pull of this kind of gravity? Gravity does seem to have an odd effect on the TARDIS, as seen in 22.3, "Frontios". But if so, then that means the TARDIS must be able to make short jumps through space *without* entering the vortex.]

The Doctor's been painting in some part of the Ship near the console room, and emerges wearing an old smock and a hat. Though the hat suggests "artist", the paintbrush is the kind you'd use for doing walls, and the paint is white. [Which clashes with his previous thoughts on TARDIS décor. See 15.2, "The Invisible Enemy" but also 15.4, "The Sun Makers". In the next story we will see some fresh paint in the TARDIS interiors…]

The Time Lords Once upon a time, when space-time exploration was new to the Time Lords, the Minyans thought they were gods and the Time Lords were only too willing to help them develop. This occurred 100,000 years ago [on the Minyans' timeline, not Gallifrey's]. The Time Lords gave medical and scientific aid, better communications and better weapons to the people of Minyos, who promptly destroyed their own planet. This made the Time Lords develop their policy of non-intervention [even though they frequently intervene; see **How Involved Are the Time Lords?**]. The Minyans' regenerative technology is apparently based on Time Lord principles, even if the procedure's very different.

The Non-Humans

• *Minyans*. These early victims of Time Lord hubris appear to be entirely human. Though the people of Minyos were happy to accept Gallifreyan technology, they eventually kicked the Time Lords out at gun-point, went to war with each other, learned how to split the atom and then destroyed the planet. At least two vessels got off Minyos first, however: the P7E, carrying colonists as well as the Minyan race-banks containing 'the genetic inheritance of a million people', and the ship crewed by Jackson and his team. ["Jackson" is a notably Earth-like name. It's possible, though never even implied in the script, that Minyos was

a degenerate human colony which had forgotten about nuclear fusion when the Time Lords found them.] Jackson's ship has been on a quest to find the P7E for the last 100,000 years, occasionally getting a signal but then losing it again.

The Minyans on the ship go into 'regen' when they grow old, hooking themselves up to a coffin-like machine and coming out of the process young again, but unlike Time Lords this regeneration leaves them with the same body and personality. There seems to be no limit on the number of times they can do this. [See 20.3, "Mawdryn Undead". Do the Time Lords have this sort of technology, a way of renewing themselves without changing form? The Doctor obviously doesn't have a machine like this on the TARDIS, or the First Doctor would never have become the Second… but see **When Was Regeneration Invented?** under 11.5, "Planet of the Spiders", for another view.

[Borusa regenerates several times, and the implication is that he does it because his body gets worn out rather than because he's injured. So Gallifrey doesn't seem to use this technology either, and it's also odd that Minyans can renew themselves any number of times while the Time Lords are limited to twelve regenerations. It's possible that the Time Lords don't use this sort of technology because it's against their code, not because they can't. Compare this with 20.7, "The Five Doctors".]

Each member of the crew has regenerated over a thousand times, suggesting a fairly normal human lifespan for Minyans. The P7E apparently wasn't equipped with regeneration technology, so Minyans don't necessarily take this sort of thing for granted.

Other than the regen, Minyan technology is fairly bland. Their spaceship has an ion drive, a laser cannon and solar sail capability. They use armoured Lieberman maser shield-guns which fire charged particles along a laser-beam, can blow holes in metal and can deflect other maser blasts. Naturally, these can kill or stun. But perhaps their most appealing weapon is the pacifier, a hand-held device which makes its target get blissed out and non-violent. The Doctor's surprised that the Minyans ever perfected this, and there's even a paranoid come-down when the subject recovers. [It may well affect the brain's anandamide receptors, the way chocolate and cannabis do.] The Minyans' old-fashioned computer ident recognis-

Just How Involved are the Time Lords?

...continued from page 193

have been saved (although this would, logically, have massive long-term consequences on the timeline), but the big events in history fit together like a majestic clockwork and for the most part he's just performing maintenance duties. And aside from the fact that this isn't really in the spirit of the series, it doesn't sit easily with what we actually see of the Time Lords. In "Genesis of the Daleks", of course, they actively try to distort time by getting the Doctor to alter Dalek history (12.4). In "The Two Doctors" - where they negotiate with the people of the Third Zone to try to affect the outcome of the Kartz-Reimer experiments, rather than trying sneaky time-travelling sabotage - the implication is that they're trying to reach a settlement rather than working towards an absolute, fixed outcome.

Perhaps the simplest explanation, then, is that history is flexible but that the Time Lords' duty is to make sure the right *kind* of history is always in effect (see also **Does History Keep Changing?** under 2.4, "The Romans"). They're happy to fiddle with the details, to push planets into politically "suitable" positions or ensure that species X isn't wiped out by species Y, yet certain things have to remain constant. So it's important that, for example, they don't end up with a universe in which the Daleks invade every single planet by the Middle Ages or a universe where there are whopping great holes in the structure of cause and effect.

Virtually everything the Time Lords ever do fits this pattern. It may even explain the Doctor's reluctance to let his people find out about his interference on Frontios (21.3); that far in the future, with humanity's existence hanging on the survival of just a few colonies, *any* intervention could cause a massive and unpredictable effect on events to come. And if we assume that the Time Lords also have a vague moral code, which they're happy to talk about but which never really gets put into practice for practical reasons, then it might explain the Doctor's rather rose-tinted view of Gallifreyan conduct in "The Hand of Fear" (14.2).

In fact, if this is the case then the real question is this: why don't they intervene more often? It's reasonable that they might let the Doctor sort out the affairs of piffling backwater planets, but why aren't the Time Lords in evidence whenever the entire universe is threatened (18.7, "Logopolis" and 20.4, "Terminus"... for starters)? Still, time and time again there's the suggestion that the Time Lords'

actions are limited, almost certainly for fiddly technical time-travel reasons that we'll never be able to fully understand. See "Genesis of the Daleks" for much, much more of this kind of thing.

However, one thing seems clear. Despite the claims of fan-fiction authors the world over, there's never any real indication that the Time Lords' interference in other people's affairs is in any way covert, unofficial or technically illegal. The notion that the Gallifreyan elite denies all knowledge of intervention, and gets shady semi-criminal organisations to do its dirty work in secret, is popular with many - and was never more popular than during the great *X-Files* conspiracy-boom of the 1990s, sadly - but not supported by on-screen evidence. There's no suggestion, not even in the mention of the Celestial Intervention Agency in "The Deadly Assassin" (14.3), that the Doctor's frequent missions for the Time Lords are a breach of the Time Lord code. They're often secret, but for security reasons rather than because the truth would horrify Gallifrey.

In "The Two Doctors", for example, the High Council wants the Doctor to act unofficially for purely diplomatic purposes. Intervention in the affairs of others is something Gallifrey sees as unseemly, *not* something criminal. When the Doctor is once again called to trial - in 23.1, "The Mysterious Planet" - he's not charged with desecrating the natural order of things, but with acting recklessly and without due caution. It later transpires that there *are* dirty goings-on in the Capitol, but the Gallifreyans are shocked by the conspiratorial hi-jinks of the corrupt High Council (23.4, "The Ultimate Foe") even though five episodes earlier they weren't shocked by the idea of the Time Lords using assassins to take out key figures in galactic politics.

If the Time Lords don't want to get their hands dirty, then it's mainly because they see the affairs of the outside universe as being beneath them. The Doctor is used as their cat's-paw not because they can deny all knowledge of him, but because nobody on Gallifrey would sink to the level of doing that sort of work.

es the sound made by a TARDIS as being from 'the time-ships of the gods', and the ship's crystallo-cybernetics are on the blink.

• *The Oracle.* The P7E's computer, which has become a megalomaniac over the years, the way computers are wont to do. It manifests itself as a circle of light within its torchlit sanctum, and speaks in a female voice. It's the keeper of the race-banks, which turn out to be nothing more than two small golden cylinders, but refuses to relinquish them to the Minyan expedition that's come all this way to find them. It produces two fission grenades, with explosive contents in excess of 2,000 megatons, capable of destroying its planet. Which is what they eventually do. No explicit reason is given for its insanity [and the Doctor shows no interest in curing it, as he did with Xoanon in 14.4, "The Face of Evil"].

Planet Notes

• *The Underworld.* Known to the Seers as the realm of Hedis, a name also used by Herrick as the Minyans' word for "Hell". The gravitational pull of the P7E has attracted so many asteroids that the ship has become the core of a planet at the heart of a nebula, with an [artificial] Earth-like atmosphere in its subterranean tunnels. [The P7E can't have been a planet for more than a couple of generations, as the Minyans have been tracking it across space and it hasn't been at the edge of the cosmos for long. The oldest inhabitants seem to remember a time before the sky was made of rock.]

There are several classes of people occupying this underworld. The Trogs are typical humanoids, actually descendants of the P7E's colonists. They're forced to work in the mines, digging out radioactive rock which is then processed into food to keep the system going, overseen by hooded, grey-clad guards with Minyan maser weapons. The guards are led by black-clad officers, but at the top of the tree are the two Seers who live in the P7E itself and carry out the will of the Oracle. When their hoods are removed, their heads are revealed to be mechanical, golden robot-faces that look like old radio sets with glowing red eyes.

The Trogs refer to cave-ins as 'skyfalls' and don't know the word 'roof', but there are legends about stars on the other side of their sky. There's a culture of elaborate human sacrifice, the Seers publicly executing 'slaves' in the Oracle's shrine as a display of power. The mines can be fumigated with poisoned gas, and the skyfalls are said to be deliberately caused to keep the Trogs' numbers down. The P7E itself is known as the Citadel, and the map of the tunnels is known as the Tree because of its pattern, tipping the Doctor off that it might be connected to the Tree at the End of the World in the Jason myth. Forbidden areas are guarded by 'invisible dragons', meaning lethal energy-beams. The Trogs also have a prophecy of a god / Time Lord coming to save them.

Having been travelling across space for thousands of years, the P7E is now at the edge of the cosmos. Nothing but a black void is seen beyond the cosmos' edge, though the Doctor believes that a whole new world could be born at any moment. [See **Things That Don't Make Sense**. If this really is the edge of the universe then human cosmologists have got an awful lot wrong. See **How Can the Universe Have a Centre?** under 20.4, "Terminus".]

• *Minyos.* The Doctor states that Minyos was 'on the other side of the universe' from the place where the P7E has now become a planet. But ultimately the Minyans and the refugee Trogs set off towards Minoys 2, a mere 370 years away. [Did the Minyans designate a planet for the colonists a long time ago, or are other evacuated Minyans already there? Either way, it seems odd that they'd choose a planet on the far side of the universe - almost 100,000 years away from the homeworld - instead of one that's reasonably nearby. The ship is travelling at 4/7 light-speed as it escapes the exploding P7E, but it must accelerate afterwards or it'd be a *really* slow intergalactic spacecraft.]

History

• *Dating.* Unknown. [If Minyos *was* a degenerate Earth colony, though, then it must be well over 100,000 years in the future. As the TARDIS seems to have been drifting through space since the last story, this could feasibly be the same era as "The Sun Makers".]

The Analysis

Where Does This Come From? The idea is stated at the start, and picked up feebly at the end, that the way the Minyans see the Time Lords is the same way the rebellious Greek heroes saw the Gods… if not in actual Greek folklore, then in the Charles Schneer / Ray Harryhausen sandals 'n' stop-motion version of *Jason and the Argonauts* (and Bob Baker started as an animator, returning to the fold in the 1990s when he became one of the writers for "Wallace and Gromit").

This is - in turn - mainly diluted Renaissance Humanist angst, best expressed in Shakespeare's *Richard II*: 'As flies to wanton boys are we to the gods; they kill us for their sport.' This provides the first overt on-screen criticism of Tom Baker's Doctor as self-satisfied and aloof since "The Pyramids of Mars" (13.3). Graham Williams was keen to bring the Doctor down a peg or two. It's worth noting that the person who clearly hates the Doctor is the Minyan Herrick, who's presented to us as if he's the most likeable and well-rounded supporting character.

As mentioned before, retelling Greek myths as space-opera is hardly new. Naff-but-much-loved Japanese animation *Ulysses 31* is only the most egregious example. There are, of course, several *Star Trek* attempts at this. The most famous retelling of a Greek myth is James Joyce's *Ulysses*, and this really caused a lot of the trouble. By finding ingenious and mundane ways to retell the story of the Odyssey, Joyce permitted anyone else to have a go. Stanley Kubrick and Arthur C. Clarke did it in space for *2001*, with asteroids as clashing rocks, HAL singing as the sirens and so on, but once less talented writers started playing along it got... crass.

The "Monomyth" of Joseph Campbell, which was George Lucas' starting-point for *Star Wars*, was a notion of getting to the basic hub of all mythologies to find the archetypal patterns. In its more abstract and pompous manifestations, this became the idea that all quests were one quest in different disguises. The procedure in Campbell's book *The Hero with a Thousand Faces* specifies that after the "Belly of the Whale" stage of the story, wherein the Hero goes into the womb-like centre of the Earth to liberate the maiden and be reborn (see 11.5, "Planet of the Spiders" and theoretically 16.3, "The Stones of Blood"), he's reunited with his own people to praise, blame, reward, punish and confront the father-figure. And the story straight after "Underworld" is "The Invasion of Time"...

However, the science of "Underworld" is borderline. Many of the things happening, especially in episode one, *are* thought to occur, just billions of years apart. Some of the ideas here were only just gaining acceptance, but by the time of broadcast they'd been thrust into the mainstream by

Carl Sagan's Royal Institute Christmas Lectures. The stuff about zero-gravity at the planet's core is a well-worn Victorian popular science book's illustration of Newtonian principles.

And it's hard for British viewers of a certain vintage - even the ones who know what "troglodyte" means - to hear a thuggish astronaut with a West Country accent call himself a "Trog" without thinking of Andover's finest beat combo, The Troggs, and their singer Reg Presley.

Things That Don't Make Sense One of the artefacts found in the hold of the Minyan ship seems to have "Made in Minyos" stamped on it, which is apparently supposed to be funny but isn't. Besides, why would the Minyans stamp the name of their own *planet* on an item used in one of their ships? Likewise, Herrick speaks of the race-banks bearing the Mark of Minyos, as if it's perfectly reasonable for a planet to have a single symbol even though it was destroyed by in-fighting between nations. [The Minyans must have exported goods to other worlds before they destroyed themselves, but nothing else we're told indicates this.]

The conclusion of the story, which sees the Minyans heading for a planet they call Minyos 2, is not only hard to fathom in itself - see **Planet Notes** - but also underlines a major flaw in the whole story. Why has the Minyan ship been tracking the P7E for thousands of years? If the P7E set off in roughly the right direction to reach Minyos 2, and the Minyans weren't expecting the Oracle to go mad, then why didn't they just assume it was heading for the new homeworld and decide to meet it there? Why do Jackson and his crew think the race-banks need to be saved? Why didn't the two ships leave Minyos at the same time? Why does only one of these craft have regenerative facilities, at least as far as we know? And so on.

In the end, a large number of Trogs are herded onto the Minyan ship (which can't be that big, if their body-weight affects the take-off so much) and taken on a 370-year journey to Minyos 2 even though there are no facilities for them on board. But the Doctor never considers giving them a lift in the TARDIS.

The race-banks are useless to the Oracle. The Minyans are causing serious problems for the Oracle because they want the race-banks, so the Oracle hands over the race-banks and tells the Minyans to leave. And yet the Doctor doesn't understand why the computer is giving in so easily. As it happens he's right not to trust it, as the cylinders it hands over are bombs, but why on Earth does he *think* that when the hand-over of the originals makes perfect sense and he doesn't know about the computer's insanity?

Still, this is the machine which gives the Minyans two undefuseable fission grenades on the blithe assumption that the Minyans will have left the planet by the time they go off, so its sense of logic is obviously strained. There also seems to be some confusion as to whether the grenades are on a time-fuse, or just detonate when someone tries opening them. And: why are devices which can blow up whole planets called "grenades", anyway, when a "grenade" is something that's either thrown or launched from a projectile weapon? Isn't that like referring to a nuclear bomb as a "big bullet"?

The script has the Doctor casually stating that Minyos was devastated 100,000 years ago, as if there's a fixed timeline for both Time Lords and Minyans. We can easily ret-con our way around this sort of thing, natch, but the writers have clearly forgotten about the whole "time-travel" element. [The Quest has been ongoing for 100,000 years, and the *galaxy* is roughly 100,000 light-years across. So it's possible that P7E was originally supposed to be at the edge of the galaxy but was moved to the universe's edge in order to make the script seem more "epic". On which note: the Minyans don't seem to have mastered faster-than-light travel, so relativity taken into account, 100,000 years subjective time may well be millions of years for the people of the underworld-world. In which case, with all that radiation flying about and a small gene-pool to begin with, why do the Trogs look even remotely human?]

Leela once again seems to know too much about space-science, shouting 'we're going to crash!' when the Minyan ship hurtles towards Hedis, even though she can have little or no concept of what a 'crash' is. She also seems to know a surprising amount about Greek mythology. The incompetence of the guards in episode two is beyond belief; chasing the Doctor and Leela into the mine-workings, they find a chain of ore-carts, *one* of which has a cloth over it and something lumpy inside. Their conclusion? That the Doctor and Leela have doubled back and lost them.

You really have to notice some of the design flaws here, too. The Minyan flight deck and shield-gun weapons are surprisingly decent, but from episode two you can tell things are getting

desperate when the ship also turns out to be stocked with large tape-reel computer banks.

Funnily enough, the most notorious piece of "gibberish" science in this story - when the Doctor and company arrive at the centre of the planet and find themselves able to float (because gravity makes you fall 'towards the centre... this is the centre') - is theoretically sound. The mass of the planet above them exactly matches the mass of the planet below them, ergo, gravitational equilibrium. What's *harder* to accept is the transition: close to the planet's centre, gravity is apparently Earth-normal, but once the Doctor takes a single step forward he can float around as much as he likes. The way it's presented on-screen doesn't help, either, with Tom Baker looking generally bored and elevator muzak playing as he ascends.

Much of the remaining science is less excusable. Right at the edge of the universe (ye-esss...), matter is spontaneously created. It's in rock form, rather than hydrogen or random particles (okay, we'll take your word for it) and radioactive (for some reason). This rock accretes around any passing spaceship - even if the spaceship's relatively small and not moving very fast - but stays at the same density throughout, and despite the radiation doesn't liquefy. Two hand-held fission bombs are enough to blow apart a planet, yet when the Minyan spaceship escapes at relativistic speeds (thus gaining mass) it doesn't attract the fragments to make a new world. And isn't it odd that after 100,000 years of experience, the captain of the Minyan ship doesn't understand basic gravitational principles and has to have the Doctor explain them to him? Still, at least there's no sound in space this time.

Suddenly, in episode two, the Doctor gets a job delivering reassuring homilies on the ability of humans to survive and flourish in intense radiation. Is he being sponsored by British Nuclear Fuels this week?

Critique (Prosecution) Often described in fandom as one of the worst *Doctor Who* stories ever made, and usually the first thing that's mentioned is the bad CSO work. Which is a ridiculous, petty attitude to take; after all, this was never an effects-driven series, and even the best of stories has its bluescreen glitches and visual potholes. No, it's absurd to rip into "Underworld" just for one very bad design decision, especially when there are so many *real* reasons to hate it.

Ugly, crass and moronic, it's yet another Baker-Martin script which never stops to consider the way the programme - or even *television itself* - is supposed to work. Once again the whole thing's based on "big science" concepts, and once again the story becomes a mess of exotic-sounding words with no logic - aesthetic or rational - to hold things together. And even if the script had managed to live up to *Doctor Who*'s original "educational" ethic by bothering to get things right, the demonstrations of these concepts are so lacking in any sense of impact (unless, like the programme-makers, you seriously believe that some model-work of asteroids hitting a spaceship represents dramatic punch) that it *still* wouldn't be watchable and you'd *still* find yourself pining for the days of "The Mind Robber".

The first episode, where all the budget went, is tolerable simply because it doesn't connect with the other three. After that, things get embarrassing. All the supporting characters are pathetic, without exception. The acting among the Trogs is as bad as it ever gets. None of the villains have any trace of identity, which means that the Doctor has nothing to square off against and spends most of the (slender) plot struggling with the architecture of the tunnels. The music is smeared plaster-thick across the whole soundtrack without any sense of judgement. Almost all the dialogue is laughable, as if the script's assuming that you don't have to make people from another planet sound either (a) believable or (b) in any way interesting. And as in almost every storyline from this stable, all the usual pulp-SF suspects are called in to try and bridge all the awkward gaps between the plot-points. The mad computer who turns out to be running the show - just a year after the positively sublime "The Face of Evil", too - is so trite that even the Doctor has to deliver a speech about 'another self-aggrandising artefact' as if he's trying to point out the cliché before the audience can (see also 15.2, "The Invisible Enemy").

Ignore the CSO. Imagine it's got the latest swish CGI effects, if you like. Turn down the colour so you can't see the little green lines. It doesn't matter. Even with a budget of millions, this still would have been the worst *Doctor Who* story of the 1970s, bar none.

Critique (Defence, ish) Notorious almost from before it was broadcast, this little story doesn't actually do much wrong that 60's *Star Trek* or Pertwee *Doctor Who* didn't do wronger. All the excuses trotted out for "The Time Monster" can be rehearsed here with greater justification. Unlike those two monumental wastes of time and brain-cells, this story doesn't have any pretensions beyond entertaining (which sometimes it manages, more than fan-lore would have you believe) and the occasional bit of lateral thinking (the "Blackpool" joke and the much-derided "floating" scene). For once, Bob 'n' Dave have managed to keep the ideas-per-page count up without going off into ludicrous new territory; episode one alone has enough for a BBC Books Eighth Doctor story-arc. The shield-guns, for example, are a nifty bit of artillery and a surprisingly good effect. But...

...if you didn't know that the production assistant was having a go at directing, and that the object of the exercise was to see what they could and couldn't do with bluescreen techniques, and that the script editor was inching his way into the job by reading the last three years' worth of scripts, and that the producer had come back from holiday to find the estimated budget was three times what they could afford... then you'd still wonder why anyone thought it was worth attempting *Star Trek* on BBC time. Baker and Martin had never twigged that *Doctor Who* was different. Fortunately Louise Jameson does know what she's doing, and gives a nuanced performance even by her own standards. This is more noticeable than it ought to be as - Alan Lake (as Herrick) aside - everyone else is on autopilot. This is certainly less dull than "The Android Invasion", and yet "The Android Invasion" doesn't get anywhere near as much flak.

Budget, time and technicalities aside, the big problem with "Underworld" is that it assumed everyone watching knew the original story, and was giving this "clever" reworking marks for style and artistic interpretation.

The Facts

Written by Bob Baker and Dave Martin. Directed by Norman Stewart. Viewing figures: 8.9 million, 9.1 million, 8.9 million, 11.7 million.

Supporting Cast James Maxwell (Jackson), Alan Lake (Herrick), Jonathan Newth (Orfe), Imogen Bickford-Smith (Tala), James Marcus (Rask), Godfrey James (Tarn), Jimmy Gardner (Idmon), Norman Tipton (Idas), Frank Jarvis (Ankh), Richard Shaw (Lakh), Stacey Tendeter (Naia), Christine Pollon (Voice of the Oracle).

Working Titles "Underground".

Cliffhangers More and more asteroids are attracted to the Minyan patrol ship inside the nebula, entombing the vessel and its passengers; the Doctor tries to shut off the poisoned gas as it pours into the mine tunnels, but it just keeps coming through the grille; the Doctor and Leela cleverly try to sneak inside the citadel by hiding in a cart full of rock, but not-so-cleverly get dumped into the rock-crusher chute as a result.

The Lore

• As has already been suggested, Graham Williams returned from a break to find a story three times more expensive than the series could afford. With "Killers of the Dark" going haywire (see 15.6, "The Invasion of Time"), he was under pressure to lose the fifth story of the season, and thus have the following year's budget slashed further. Production assistant Norman Stewart believed that if they only had one big new set, then the rest could be done on CSO. He was allowed to direct and - against all the odds - persuaded the BBC to let him do a gallery-only day of post-production.

This later became standard policy as, from this point of view, "Underworld" had been a success. Moreover, he got up to nine minutes of footage for every studio hour; usually the elaborate line-ups and retakes meant that two minutes was the maximum one could expect. Thus, despite the overspend on the P7E / R1C sets, it came in on time and on budget.

• Alan Lake, as Herrick, was more notorious than famous. As husband of sex-kitten-turned-character-actress Diana Dors, he was constantly protecting her from the press, the Inland Revenue and the dodgy entrepreneurs who were bankrupting her. Their tragic deaths, within a few scant months of one another, make up a long and complicated story. But they're worth mentioning here because Herrick was almost self-parody, and because they were director Graeme Harper's first choice to play Morgus and Timmin in "The Caves of Androzani" (21.6).

• Imogen Bickford-Smith, as Tala, got her "aged" face into the papers as an erroneous story did the rounds that she was to replace Leela aboard the TARDIS. Now that we've seen Mary Tamm as Romana, this is a lot easier to believe...

15.6: "The Invasion of Time"

(Serial 4Z, Six Episodes, 4th February - 11th March 1978.)

Which One is This? The Doctor does his Groucho Marx impression and becomes the new President of the Time Lords, letting them get invaded for their own good. Has he really gone insane...? (Clue: no.)

Firsts and Lasts Last ever appearance of Leela (unless you count the recycled film in 18.7, "Logopolis"). Technically it's also the last appearance of the original K9, as he gets unexpectedly replaced by a Mark II version in the final episode. You'd never notice the difference to look at him, although from this point on he spends less of his time performing clumsy three-point-turns and bumping into things.

It took eight years, but at last: one of the Gallifreyans is finally shown to be female. But whereas the "proper" Time Lords get important masculine jobs like Chancellor or Castellan, Rodan gets to work in traffic control. We also see the exterior of the planet Gallifrey for the first time, and the pseudonymous "David Agnew" makes his debut writing for the series (see **The Lore**).

Six Things to Notice About
"The Invasion of Time"...

1. For only the second time in the programme's history (no, *you* figure it out), "The Invasion of Time" is a story with a dummy ending, as the Doctor stops the Vardan invasion of Gallifrey two-thirds of the way through but then finds out that the Sontarans are behind it all. The final scene of episode four - which sees the Sontaran troops menacing the Panopticon - is unquestionably a striking "surprise monster" cliffhanger, but opinion remains divided as to whether this is a sensational plot twist or just a bit contrived. (Since the Sontarans haven't even been hinted at in the first four episodes, this might be construed as a way of desperately stretching out the Vardan story for another fifty minutes... or, more accurately, the Vardans might be construed as a way of stretching out the Sontaran story for an hour and a half.)

2. Oh yes. The stretching-out process. It's often been pointed out, and not unreasonably, that the final episode of "The Invasion of Time" is little

more than a protracted chase through the TARDIS' guts; the first time the series has bothered exploring the Ship since the early days (1.3, "The Edge of Destruction"), although the result is... not wholly convincing. Especially considering that most of the sequence is shot on location, in a variety of very un-TARDIS-like places, including a swimming pool and a hospital in Surrey.

It also features one of the most grotesquely padded scenes in the whole of *Doctor Who*, in which the Doctor, Leela and Rodan end up arguing about paint while the Sontarans are supposedly chasing them. Pay special attention to the Sontaran trooper who tries leaping gracefully over the poolside furnishings in the TARDIS 'bathroom', before gravity reminds him that he was built for load-bearing and is the wrong shape for ballet.

3. This may be the third story to feature the Sontarans, but it's the first in which more than one of them appears in the same place (odd, since they're clones and supposedly reproduce by the million), which means that the Sontaran leader is now reclassified as a "monster" instead of a "villain". Here Derek Deadman takes over from Kevin Lindsay as the man behind the mask, the result being a Sontaran warmonger with a cockney accent.

4. Tom Baker gets virtually all the good lines here, and is allowed to run off with all the good scenes. The gag which sums up the Baker years to come, when Andred tells him that he has access to the greatest source of knowledge in the universe (meaning the Matrix): 'Well, I do talk to myself sometimes, yes.' However, the scene which encapsulates what makes this period of the series special is the chat with Borusa in episode three. The line 'what's for tea?' has never had so much significance...

5. *Star Wars* rears its head again. As with "The Invisible Enemy" (12.2), the casual viewer *has* to wonder about the very first shot of "The Invasion of Time", which depicts an enormous battle-cruiser steaming its way over the audience's head and looking an awful lot like a BBC attempt to replicate the famous "Star Destroyer" opening. "The Invasion of Time" was made before *Star Wars* opened in the UK, but some months after its US premiere, so it's just possible that someone in the effects department had seen it. Certainly, Tom Baker went to the US for a convention a few weeks later and saw the film before its British release, as "research" for his doomed *Scratchman* film.

6. Rodan, the groundbreaking female Gallifreyan, is quite clearly the Romana who never was (see 16.1, "The Ribos Operation"). Even the occasional line seems hauntingly familiar, with hindsight. Asked if she can switch the TARDIS' primary and secondary stabiliser circuitry into the defence barrier that protects the whole of the planet Gallifrey, her reply is: 'I'll need a screwdriver.' (Romana will do exactly the same gag in 17.4, "Nightmare of Eden".)

The Continuity

The Doctor Formally becomes President of the Time Lords here, but ends up having his memory of his "reign" wiped. He doesn't remember anything about the Vardans or the Sontaran invasion by the end of the story, or know how to build a de-mat gun. He believes that given the power of the Time Lords, the Sontarans could rampage through 'all the universes', not just this one. [Do less experienced Time Lords acknowledge that there are other universes?]

The Doctor can shield his mind from the Vardans, thanks to the training Borusa gave him at Prydon Academy. He allows Rodan to work on the TARDIS circuitry rather than doing it himself, suggesting he's not *that* qualified a technician, and later hypnotises her just by telling her she's in a state of deep hypnosis [technical minds like hers are easy to control]. He doesn't offer a proper goodbye when Leela leaves him, and looks a lot like a man having a sulk, at least until he unpacks a new toy in the console room.

• *Ethics.* The Doctor airily speaks of time-looping the Vardans' planet once they're defeated. [The power of the Presidency has gone to his head. In 15.3, "Image of the Fendahl", he not only says that Time Lords aren't supposed to do this sort of thing but believes it's positively criminal. Here he's basically condemning a whole world to an appalling fate just because of the actions of its military.] He doesn't balk at killing the Sontarans.

• *Inventory.* He nicks the pen that the Vardans give him to sign their contract, and still has his duck-whistle. The sonic screwdriver doesn't open secret doors on Gallifrey.

• *Background.* It's never explained how the Doctor found out about the Vardan invasion attempt, or how he got in touch with them, but he doesn't know their planet of origin until he gets K9 to track it down [so it isn't in the Matrix, either]. Borusa trained him in detachment as well as telepathy.

In the TARDIS bathroom is a copy of *The Daily Mirror* from 1912, announcing the sinking of the Titanic, but the Doctor insists he had nothing to do with it.

The Supporting Cast

• *Leela.* Knows how to throw her voice. By now she's learned how to use certain TARDIS controls, including the scanner. She doesn't know what 'proficient' means.

Her decision to leave the Doctor and run off with Commander Andred of the Chancellery Guard is unexpected, especially as they've barely spoken to each other before this point. The Doctor seems stunned by the news, but not as sad as you might expect. [Even now, Leela's decision to leave is just flummoxing. She and Andred must spend a lot of time together off-screen, although the fact that Leela's been running around with the Outsiders - a tribal society much like her own, but without the oppressive religion - may be significant. Still, it's strange that she's no longer interested in the Doctor's tutelage. Maybe he just hasn't been paying her enough attention. His "pretending to be mad" ploy may have alienated her a little, and his getting-K9-to-threaten-to-shoot-her antics must have hurt.]

• *K9.* States that he's not programmed for emotion and therefore doesn't wish for anything, but later asks the Doctor not to mock him. He finds it impossible to predict the Doctor's actions [in spite of all the chess], and is still over-literal enough not to known what the word "cheek" means in its colloquial sense. He can apparently communicate with the TARDIS by speech, but he disdainfully describes it as a 'very stupid machine' when it warbles back at him [he might mean the console computer, not the Ship as a whole]. He gets better results when he interfaces with the TARDIS via a panel at the base of the console, inserting his extendable "eye" into the circuitry, something which makes his tail wag. The panel slides open at his approach. This allows him to absorb data, and in this state the Doctor can only speak to him by talking into a "microphone" on the console.

K9 makes the decision to stay on Gallifrey with Leela [just as he made the decision to board the TARDIS in 15.2, "The Invisible Enemy"], as if his loyalties are to 'the mistress' rather than the Doctor now. Once the Doctor has left K9 behind, he produces a crate marked "K9 M. II" from some-

where outside the console room. He finds this hilariously funny, for some reason. [See 18.2, "Meglos", for more on this mystery.]

The original K9 can calculate success probabilities for the Doctor's plans to two decimal places. He knows an awful lot about names the Doctor's been called [either there are plenty of "unseen" adventures for the two of them, or the Doctor's programmed him with a great deal of past data].

The TARDIS It's time for the guided tour...

The TARDIS contains what the Doctor calls a 'VIP suite' or 'Chancellor's Suite'; directions from the console room are down the corridor, turn left, up three stages, down one stage, turn left, turn left, turn left, turn left again and the room's marked "no entry".

Deep in the guts of the Ship there's a workshop, and to reach it the Doctor passes through at least two identical, empty store-rooms with brick walls and descending staircases, the first of them being referred to as store-room 23A. After this is a brick service tunnel, known as blue section two-five, followed by *another* identical store-room called level 23B. Ten minutes later the Doctor and company find themselves back in the service tunnel, but then emerge in a room full of potted plants with garden furnishings, a clock on one wall and a flytrap-like specimen big enough to swallow a Sontaran.

Next comes store-room 14B, at which point - mysteriously - they end up in the same place Andred and K9 reached when they took the seventh opening on the right of the corridor outside the control room. This workshop has an early warning siren, which goes off when the Sontarans get past the console room 'upstairs', and all the parts needed to build a de-mat gun - including that all-important rod of type three iridium alloy - can be found here. A stairway down from the workshop leads to the 'bathroom', the Doctor pointing out that the lift's out of order.

The bathroom looks suspiciously like a typical public swimming pool on Earth, complete with inflatables and poolside cocktails, plus the aforementioned newspaper from 1912. Beyond the bathroom is a corridor with doors leading in various directions, but they all go to the sick-bay and Borusa complains that the Doctor should stabilise his 'pedestrian infrastructure'. The sick-bay is full of curtained cubicles, though no medical equipment is seen, and after that comes the plant room

How Might the Sonic Screwdriver Work?

The first, casual mention of this gadget in "Fury From the Deep" (5.6) was no big deal; we'd had "sonic" this and "sonic" that all through 1967. It was only with "The Dominators" (6.1) that things got interesting, when the device turned out to have useful cutting-through-case-hardened-Mennonite-like-it-was-cheese properties for final-episode use. After that it became a handy electromagnet, a marsh-gas ignition system and all-purpose electronica-scrambler. How can sound do all this and undo screws, too?

Well, in principle it shouldn't be too hard, as sound (compression and relaxation of molecules, usually air) involves giving energy to these molecules. Which is the definition of "heat", as well. High-frequency sound is fairly directional, but not *that* directional. Acousticians have developed two handy tricks to make sure that it's focused. The first of these is the fact that a spherical source with a hemispherical "dent" in it - think of the Death Star - will focus the sound at the focal point of the parabola. This technique was actually used for an experimental weapon developed by the Soviets in the 1970s, but it wasn't terribly effective as a field weapon as the business end was a thirty-foot-wide ball of concrete.

The other technique is the Tartini effect. Tartini, an eighteenth century composer, noticed that two loud notes will produce a third; the third note will be the exact difference between the first two, in vibrations per second and measured in hertz (hz). So two high-frequency signals from a hand-held device (one aimed at the screw, and the other at whatever the screw is screwed into) will make a third sound, a vibration between screw and location.

Now, unless the Doctor's wired up *his* device to make a "prrrrrrrrrrrr" noise just for a laugh, that third vibration seems to be an audible note. So it must be between 20 and 200,000 hz, and probably nearer the latter, in the '60s version at least. Once Dick Mills takes over as sound effects supremo in the '70s, the more familiar "wobbly" screwdriver effect varies around Middle-C (263 hz). Note, though, that when igniting marsh gas (10.2, "Carnival of Monsters") the sound rises to beyond audible pitch, suggesting a huge amount of energy being focused on a patch of air twenty feet away. This seems to cover all bases, except the very low intensity delta waveforms the screwdriver generates as part of Nyssa's cure (19.3, "Kinda").

Generating heat raises its own problems. Warm air is less dense, so it conducts sound less successfully, and fluctuations in air density will alter the pitch. Ah well.

So what about all this magnetic malarkey? Glorified loudspeakers may generate the sound, although for the speakers to be small enough to fit into a gizmo the size of a tyre pressure gauge, this would require magnets strong enough to make the keys to Bessie or the Doctor's toffee tin really dig into him. His jacket pocket would inconveniently fly towards all large metal objects nearby (including Daleks, Cybermen, Vocs, spaceships...). However, if the rig is some kind of piezo-electric "speaker" - one which directly converts pressure into an electrical impulse, or vice versa - then it'd take more effort to turn the device into a magnet, so the Doctor wouldn't do it routinely (which he doesn't). Perhaps, therefore, it's the power-source that needs to be converted.

Mind you, we've never seen the Doctor recharge his favourite implement, so it's either incredibly fuel-efficient or nuclear powered.

---

again. From here it's easy to get lost and end up back in the store-rooms.

Stor finds that a 'biological barrage' in the TARDIS, powered by an ancillary generator, prevents his equipment tracing life-forms. The Castellan finds the ancillary power station without difficulty, indicating that the insides of TARDISes have similar floor-plans [but see 19.1, "Castrovalva"]. This power station is "disguised" as an art gallery. Paintings on display include Van Eyck's "Jan Arnolfini and His Wife", Chagall's "Snail" and Turner's "The Fighting Temerere", and there's also a Venus de Milo. [One might assume that these are reproductions, since the TARDIS could mathematically model the originals down to the last detail. Then again, this is a time machine. The Doctor could easily have picked these works up somewhere in the future, perhaps at some point after one of the many falls-of-civilisation that humanity suffers after the twenty-first century. The Dalek Invasion of Earth, c. 2160, might be a good time for some quality looting. See also **When Did the Doctor Meet Leonardo?** under 17.2, "City of Death"].

When a hidden switch is pressed on the Venus, the artworks disappear, revealing a single control on the wall. The power to the biological barrier fails when an element is removed from this control, leaving the ship "dis-armed", tee-hee. The workshop is said to be three levels below the power station.

The Chancellery Guards' patrol stasers don't work inside the relative dimensional stabiliser field of a TARDIS, but the weapons of both K9 and the Sontarans do. [So the 'temporal grace' mentioned by the Doctor in 14.2, "The Hand of Fear", has either stopped working or never really worked the way he claimed. Can the 'grace' only nullify certain types of violence? Then again, K9's weapon only stuns and the Sontaran weapons are only used to shoot inanimate objects here.] The de-mat gun *certainly* works in the TARDIS' confines. Curiously, the Doctor knows that a staser won't work inside the Ship but the Commander of the Guard doesn't.

The Doctor immobilises the scanner mechanism while he's on the Vardan ship, to stop the Vardans getting in. After Gallifrey's defences pick up the inbound TARDIS, the console rotor doesn't move for the rest of the journey [suggesting that it's being brought in on automatic after passing the transduction barriers]. The Ship has a trimonic locking mechanism [as suggested in "The Deadly Assassin"].

From the comfort of the TARDIS console room, Rodan switches the primary and secondary stabiliser circuitry into the secondary defence barrier, linking the TARDIS to Gallifrey's force-fields. This isn't usually done, and the tools used to do the job [from the TARDIS toolkit] include a screwdriver, crimps, a 542 lever and a finklegruber. The TARDIS makes an ugly grunting noise while this work is being done. Yet from the control area for the force-fields, the Castellan can reverse the stabiliser banks, something which makes the TARDIS shake and nearly throws it 'into a black star' [the Eye of Harmony?]. A failsafe switch, in the corridor outside the console room, quickly re-stablises the Ship but stops the TARDIS moving until the switch is turned off again. Nobody can re-set the systems after the Doctor takes the primary refraction tube from this failsafe control. None of which seems terribly meaningful.

From the console room, blackness can be seen through the TARDIS doors when the doors of the police box exterior are shut [which throws up all sorts of awkward questions about the way the doors actually work]. The TARDIS' model of time-capsule was withdrawn centuries ago, according to the Castellan. The 'modern' type of time capsule is a 706 model, which the Doctor considers to have no character. [706 clearly isn't a "type", the way that the TARDIS is a type forty. The number may refer to the TARDIS equivalent of the processor inside a PC, rather than being a specific design of Ship.]

The Time Lords There's a new Castellan, Kelner, since the last time the Doctor was here. This one seems a lot more imperious than the last, acting like a politician rather than a police detective and even having a place on the Council. [In 14.3, "The Deadly Assassin", Spandrell seemed far-removed from the Council and didn't have a very high opinion of it. The Castellan may have been promoted after the Master crisis, but it's strange that Spandrell himself is nowhere to be seen now.] Although every indicator suggests the guards are of a lower caste than the Time Lords, the Outsider Nesbin used to be a guard and a Time Lord, and the Doctor expects Commander Andred to have attended an Academy. [Most Time Lords would seem to be born into the role, or at least educated into it, so guards may be among the few capable of being raised to Lordship. The Academy mentioned by the Doctor - *the* Academy, when it's already been established that there's more than one - may reference a military Academy rather than a Time Lord establishment.] There are 'guard leaders' under Andred, and a Commander also has at least one Sergeant. It's possible that guards can be shot for disciplinary reasons.

Other than the President, there only seem to be four Council members at this stage, including the Chancellor, the Castellan and the Surgeon-General. It's referred to as the 'Supreme Council' instead of the High Council. Although the President is in charge, under the Constitution he can't give orders to the Chancellor [which helps to explain the President / Chancellor relationship in 10.1, "The Three Doctors"]. It's the Chancellor's job to 'guard the guards', and the seal he wears around his neck is actually a personal force-shield, which can protect the wearer and at least one other person from energy-weapon fire. Sadly, it runs on 'batteries' that go flat quite quickly.

It's risky to be inducted as President without a certain amount of preparation. On his inauguration, an incoming President wears a simple white robe and is seated before an assembly of high-ranking Time Lords. He's given the Sash of Rassilon and the Rod of Rassilon, and is told to seek the Great Key. Rassilon is mentioned a lot in this ritual [it's the first time Rassilon is treated as the single great figure behind Time Lord society, rather than a figure who's only of interest to historians]. Finally, a circlet is placed on the new President's head.

Once the circlet is in place, the President becomes part of the Matrix and the Matrix becomes part of him, giving him access to the knowledge of 'hundreds' of Time Lords and their elected Presidents. Everything he knows enters the system at the same time. [Here, unlike in "The Deadly Assassin", the Matrix is referred to as *the* Matrix. In "The Deadly Assassin" the Doctor has never heard of it, and it's not treated as a well-known part of Time Lord culture. The Doctor also becomes the first to put his mind into the system while he's still alive. Perhaps only the highest level of society knows about the Matrix in detail.]

The ceremonial figure of Gold Usher recites the ceremony, and thus introduces the President to the Matrix. It's unheard-of for the Matrix to reject a candidate [and Morbius used to lead the Council, so it's not fussy]. According to Borusa, he who's been introduced to the Matrix has more power than anyone in the known universe. Even K9 can gain data from the Matrix by wearing the circlet and locking in his primary circuits.

There isn't a President when the Doctor arrives, but judging by Borusa's attitude the Time Lords are doing perfectly well without one. [This is a slow, slow culture. Gallifrey may still be re-writing the rules after the sudden shock of "The Deadly Assassin".] This means that the Doctor, as the only surviving Presidential candidate and therefore President Elect, has the legal right to claim power immediately. The artefacts entrusted into the care of the President include the Sash and the Rod. [Both mentioned in "The Deadly Assassin", but it's not clear how the Sash was recovered. The last time it was seen, it was in the Master's possession, and it's unlikely that he would have left it behind on Gallifrey. However, it's equally unlikely that the modern Time Lords would have made a new one in a hurry. The Sash seen here may be purely cosmetic, though the Doctor still insists on making K9 wear it.] Accepting the Presidency, the Doctor formally states that he claims the inheritance of Rassilon and the obedience of all Colleges. The correct form of address for a President is 'excellency' or 'excellence'.

Time Lords get energy from food pills [the same kind of concentrate used in the TARDIS food machine from 1.2, "The Daleks"], and those inside the Citadel never eat anything else. They communicate with "radios" that look like billiard balls. Regeneration is now taken for granted, as here one of the Time Lords asks another whether he's 'due' for a regeneration yet. They're so stuffy and formal that many of them don't even comprehend the word "hobby", but others find Borusa's bureaucratic approach annoying.

The Surgeon-General tends to the elite's medical needs. Rodan knows about Sontaran battle-fleet formations, so Gallifreyans would seem to be educated in alien cultures. Even the weasely Castellan Kelner finds human works of art beautiful, which means they aren't *complete* philistines. The channel used by the Vardans to enter Gallifrey is an outer spatial exploration and investigation channel, the circuit being part of the Academy's instruction and investigation control.

The Castellan states that two Time Lords are absent from their duties on Gallifrey on authorised research missions, and that unauthorised use of a time capsule carries 'only one penalty'. [The implication is "death", but capital punishment doesn't seem to be practised for anything less than political assassination; see 20.1, "Arc of Infinity". The Castellan doesn't believe the TARDIS' owner to be a Time Lord at this point, though, so perhaps it's just alien intruders who are executed after their arrest and interrogation.] The Doctor's time capsule is the only one currently in operation.

• *Borusa.* Now the Chancellor. The Council ratified his appointment, though normally it can't ratify anything without a President. He's still wearing heliotrope. [According to Runcible in "The Deadly Assassin", Prydonians are meant to wear scarlet. Given the on-screen evidence, it seems likely that the less-than-competent Runcible just got his colours mixed up.] Borusa immediately knows what the décor of 'Earth, 073 period' is like - see **History** - and he and the Doctor seem to have discussed it before [so Borusa taught the Doctor something about Earth, interestingly]. He believes the Doctor could never deceive him at the Academy. He used to say that 'there's nothing more useless than a lock with a voice-print', so obviously that's the phrase which opens the secret door in his office.

Like most Time Lords, Borusa is too single-

ABOUT TIME 1975-1979

minded to clutter his thoughts and resist the Vardans' telepathy. Unlike most, he's gracious enough to accept this as a weakness. He reminds the Doctor about detachment, and is stoically prepared to let his own people die if the alternative seems worse. The Doctor has read Borusa's essay on reason, which advises that the best place to hide a tree is in a forest, and he can out-think the Chancellor in mind games.

Early Time Lords

• *Rassilon*. Rassilon is explicitly said to have been President of the Time Lords, and was the last President to hold the Great Key. He died 'aeons' ago, but his mind lives on in the APC net [he only joined with it before his "death", judging by 20.7, "The Five Doctors"] and so the Doctor - part of the net during his Presidency - can find out how to make a hole in Gallifrey's quantum force-field [devised by Rassilon?] by wearing the circlet. When K9's given the circlet, the Sash and the Rod, he can trace the Vardans to their homeworld and activate a 'modulation rejection pattern' which beams all the invaders back home.

The Rod, Sash and Great Key, when linked into the Matrix, provide the sum total of Time Lord power. Since time immemorial it's been incumbent on every President to hunt the Great Key, though there's no record in the Matrix of any President ever finding it and officially it's just a legend. Predictably, the Doctor knows better. In fact the Chancellor has it, as Rassilon knew that without it no President can hold absolute power. [The question arises of what happens when a Chancellor becomes President, as nearly happened in "The Deadly Assassin" and as happens again in "The Five Doctors" (20.7). Do Chancellors get their minds wiped?] The Great Key turns out to look like nothing more than a key of old-fashioned metal, but it's the only thing that can arm the de-mat gun, the blueprints of which are to be found in the Matrix. [So the "lock" on the gun isn't a security device; something about the Key is essential to the scientific principles on which the gun's based, and it can't be replicated.]

The de-mat gun is the ultimate weapon, though it's shiny, sleek, silver and no bigger than a large rifle. It horrifies Borusa, who believes it could throw the Time Lords back to their darkest age [hinting at a time when the Time Lords misused these weapons, backed up by what we learn of

Rassilon in "The Five Doctors"]. When it's fired at a single victim, that victim simply vanishes. After using it to destroy Stor [and possibly the rest of the Sontaran fleet], the Doctor's memory of the entire affair is removed, which Borusa describes as 'the wisdom of Rassilon'. [Another safeguard to prevent the Gun's misuse, although the Key may be "intelligent" in some way as it only wipes the Doctor's mind after he's dealt with the threat to Gallifrey. How does it know what's going on around it? Is it telepathic, and if so then did the Doctor agree to let it erase his memories?

[Either way, this all means the Doctor has no memory of anything he might have picked up from the Matrix. See also 23.4, "The Ultimate Foe". *Why* the de-mat gun is so powerful, when it looks like nothing more than a standard energy weapon, is also open to debate. Perhaps it can dematerialise whole planets as well as individuals. Or perhaps it deletes its victims from history altogether, instead of just killing them. See also **Things That Don't Make Sense**.

[It's also worth mentioning that it's left unstated what happens to the Great Key after this story, but in all probability, Borusa just put it back in its usual place. After all, the Doctor doesn't remember the Key's location, and it's the Chancellor's job to look after it.]

The Non-Humans

• *Vardans*. An entirely humanoid species, the Vardans seen here are aggressive, humourless and militaristic. They're only interested in conquest and efficiency, and to make things worse they're required to wear deeply unflattering uniforms. They're formal enough to want to sign a contract with the Doctor before they enlist his aid in attacking Gallifrey, but their most notable attribute is that they can travel along any broadcast wavelength. Though this isn't really explored in detail, the Doctor states that they can travel on the frequency of thought, which means they can read encephalographic patterns but not machine-minds like K9's. [Because they travel along psychic frequencies, and machines don't have ESP?]

They can obviously teleport from place to place, presumably at the speed of light, and their clothes and equipment travel with them [so this ability must *surely* have developed technological-ly]. The only things which can block them are (a) lead, (b) the transduction barriers on Gallifrey, (c) the special helmet that the Doctor builds for

Andred which is a partial encephalographic shield and (d) the TARDIS, although they *could* get into the Ship through the scanner. They even get into the Matrix. [Kelner describes the Vardans as 'human', and the Doctor doesn't argue. Are these technologically-augmented human beings?]

At first the Vardans manifest themselves on Gallifrey as shimmering, silver silhouettes, only revealing themselves in humanoid form when they're sure of their dominance. Vardans in their "ghost" form can float about the place and kill or stun with energy-beams, but the channel back to their homeworld is clogged with deliberate interference and can't be traced by K9 until they fully materialise. They have a large battle-cruiser-style spacecraft which shoots gas out of its engines, escorted by a smaller shuttle-like vehicle. One Time Lord's observation, that over the last decade he's noticed a lot of fluctuation in 'relative wavelength induction over a particularly narrow band', might hint that the Vardans have been aiming at Gallifrey for ten years now.

It's not revealed whether the Doctor's plans to time-loop the Vardan planet are ever carried out. The judgement would seem harsh, since the Vardans are being used as a spearhead force by...

• *Sontarans.* Stor is Commander of the Sontaran Special Space Service. [The Doctor asks if this is carrying alliteration a little too far, which begs the question of whether it's still the SSSS in the Sontarans' own language. Consider the icon on the Sontaran flag in 11.1, "The Time Warrior", which looks a lot like a little "S".] He sees the Vardans as an expendable way of opening the force-field, and calls no-one sir but his Battalion Commander. He has the power to 'negate' his shock troop inferiors who fail in their duty, but they're terribly easy to fool if you adopt an air of authority, and Stor himself runs the risk of execution if he fails his commander.

Stor has a battle-fleet ready, in a typical arrow-like formation, though it can't land on Gallifrey until the hole in the force-field has been widened. As ever, they don't seem to have the word "Doctor" where the Sontarans come from. They're using wand-weapons that can cause pain as well as kill, but later they break out larger rifle-like energy weapons which produce a lot of heat. Stor considers the TARDIS to be 'a load of obsolete rubbish', the dimensional transcendence not surprising him in the slightest. He carries a little box which can trace nearby human life-forms, and a grenade which the Doctor believes will destroy

this entire galaxy if it's triggered in the Panopticon. [Because it'll unleash the power of the Eye of Harmony? This pretty much proves that the Sontarans aren't native to Gallifrey's galaxy.] Stor sees this proposed self-sacrifice as a glorious death, and he obviously perceives Gallifrey as a threat to the Sontaran cause. The Sontarans, and the Vardans, seem to know enough Gallifreyan lore to realise the Great Key's value.

The Sontaran army reckons its numbers in the hundreds of millions, the Doctor believing that they can reproduce at a rate of a million every four minutes [surely not every four minutes, or the universe would be covered with them]. It's not clear whether the Sontarans who attack Gallifrey have travelled through time to do it - since they certainly have the ability - or whether they come from the Gallifreyan "present". [They must come from after the era of Linx in "The Time Warrior" (11.1), though, as Linx didn't think Gallifrey could withstand a Sontaran assault. See also **Where (and When) is Gallifrey?** under 13.3, "Pyramids of Mars".]

They have two fingers and a thumb on each hand again, and are beige in colour, closer to the original brown than the later grey. [As in "The Time Warrior" but not "The Sontaran Experiment" (12.3). Perhaps indicating that these are Sontarans from an earlier period, closer to the Middle Ages than 15,000 AD. The Sontarans are willing to fiddle with their biology to gain a military advantage, so it makes sense that later "models" might adapt to warfare in a human-occupied galaxy by developing more digits.]

Planet Notes

• *Gallifrey.* Looks yellow and orange from space. Here it's confirmed that the Capitol is just a small part of a larger enclosed Time Lord city, the city being known as the Citadel. When he's asked where he comes from, one of the guards just says 'Gallifrey' [hinting that there are no other cities on this planet].

Outside the Citadel is a wasteland with an orange sky [as mentioned by Susan as early as 1.7, "The Sensorites"], where the Time Lords never go. Indeed, they're horrified by the thought of venturing into 'Outer Gallifrey'. Living in the wastes are the Outsiders, described as Time Lords who've dropped out of life in the Citadel and now have a tribal, back-to-nature lifestyle. This means headbands and spears all round. Nobody inside the Citadel even acknowledges that these Outsiders exist. There are animals and fruit in the waste-lands, too. [See **The Lore**. Though "Outsider" is the word used to describe these people in off-screen sources, nobody actually says it here. They're certainly not called "Shobogans"; see "The Deadly Assassin".]

The Eye of Harmony [regarded as a myth until "The Deadly Assassin", remember] isn't mentioned, but reference is made to a protective 'black star'; like saying "bless you" after a sneeze, it's a reflexive statement. Gallifrey is defended by trans-duction barriers which can be raised from their normal level to factor five when the planet's under attack. A quantum force-field serves as a second-ary defence barrier, but it would vaporise the planet if it were destroyed. The transduction bar-rier can be removed by destroying the machinery directly below the Panopticon on level three-zero. The force-field can be sabotaged from a similar area, and the whole citadel shakes when the Doctor fiddles with it. [The Vardans can beam themselves in as soon as the transduction barrier's down, but the Sontaran fleet can't get in until the force-field goes as well. So the barriers are there to keep out teleporters and hostile frequencies, while the force-field keeps out cruder matter. In "The Deadly Assassin" the Time Lords seem to use the word "transduct" to mean any kind of materialisa-tion, which fits.]

There's a space traffic control room somewhere around the Capitol, where a single technician - Rodan, in this case - monitors primitive space-craft passing by. Here a space-fleet with a crys-talline structure [Rutans…?] is given clearance, and Rodan isn't concerned about stopping them blasting some innocent planet to dust as interfer-ing would defy every law of Gallifrey. She can only observe, and she treats this sort of alien military action as a common irritation. [Why any space-ship would pass close to Gallifrey on its way else-where is a mystery, unless Gallifrey has a *very* large "exclusion zone" around it. Nonetheless, it's strik-ing that passing ships ask Gallifrey's permission, as if Gallifrey were a well-known local power.]

Rodan is past the 'seventh grade' and irked that she's just a glorified traffic guard, having studied quasitronics, about which the Doctor knows little. [Rodan refers to the guards and Time Lords as 'the boring people', suggesting that she herself is nei-ther.] A force-field protects the room, as it's one of the highest security-rated rooms in the Citadel. The TARDIS is picked up on temporal scan, and

identified as Gallifreyan from its molecular patina two minutes before it arrives. The Doctor's molec-ular code is analysed, but not recognised, before he even lands. [In "The Deadly Assassin" the Time Lords didn't spot the TARDIS until it landed, so they've souped up their security systems since the last crisis.]

There's a security control area from which the Castellan and the Commander of the Chancellery Guard both operate. Nobody is allowed to carry weapons [in the Capitol, or the Citadel?] except for internal security. Whereas Time Lords previ-ously had biog-data files, here the Castellan refers to 'bio-data extracts' which seem to serve the same function. The President's office is on level five.

The Doctor has no qualms about taking Leela to Gallifrey, even though he had to leave his 'best friend' Sarah behind on Earth the last time he went there. [14.2, "The Hand of Fear". This seems reasonable. He didn't take Sarah because the Time Lords wouldn't have tolerated her presence - the last companions who went to Gallifrey (6.7, "The War Games") got their memories wiped - but this time he's got the authority to demand Leela's pres-ence, and besides, he's trying to make the Time Lords think he's mental.]

They have tea on Gallifrey. [Perhaps green for Arcalians.]

• *The Matrix*. Here Borusa speaks of the Amplified Panatropic Computer, stating that the Doctor has entered it before but that the APC net is only a small part of the Matrix. [Cloudy, but the way Borusa says it makes fairly certain that the place explored by the Doctor's mind in "The Deadly Assassin" was the APC net, not the whole of the Matrix. So since "The Deadly Assassin", the word "Matrix" has changed its meaning subtly; it's no longer just the APC computation matrix, but something greater. Exactly *what* remains unex-plained.]

History

• *Dating*. The Gallifreyan present. [For the Doctor's relationship with Gallifrey to make any sense, it *has* to be assumed that when he's travel-ling in the TARDIS the same amount of time pass-es on Gallifrey as passes for him. In which case, no more than ten years have gone by since "The Deadly Assassin". See the note on the Doctor's age under 14.5, "The Robots of Death".]

The styles of architecture discussed by the Doctor and the Castellan are Quasar Five, Riga and second dynasty Sinan Empire. The Doctor plumps for Earth 073 period, which involves plating rooms with lead and covering them with abstract wheel-like designs, but Borusa describes the materials as 'the finest to be had in the whole Thesaurian Empire'. [This isn't explained, although the novelisation confirms that the Thesaurian Empire originated on Earth.]

The Analysis

Where Does This Come From? You may recall that we went through the Pertwee stories finding Cold War allusions in everything. Well, nothing to do with this story is that straightforward, but Gallifrey has more than a hint of the Soviet Union about it here. From the way people act as though the new regime had always existed, to the way enemies of the state (i.e. anyone loyal yesterday) are expelled to a wilderness, to the way Kelner adapts from serving the Vardans to serving the Sontarans without missing a beat; it's like the Brezhnev era in comic-opera costumes. Even the Vardans are surveillance metaphors.

This sort of thing becomes even more apparent in "Shada" (17.6), where the memory-blockage used by the Time Lords since "The War Games" is reworked to reinforce the notion of their criminals becoming "un-persons" ("Salyavin" is deliberately pitched as a pseudo-Russian name, and suggests both Solzhenitsyn and Sakharov, two of the best-known Russian exiles and "mind-criminals" of the era). The thing we kept hearing from Soviet emigres was that the state is always able to get into your thoughts, never giving you an opportunity to think for yourself. Anyone you meet could be a Stasi agent or informer, and anyone you thought you could trust has some flaw that the secret police can turn against them.

But then, the Soviet Union wasn't the only dictatorship on Earth. We should look further afield as well. This is a story about an erratic revolution, about a military coup led by a single unpredictable monomaniac, and in the popular imagination of the 1970s that sort of thing was the speciality of Africa. It's different these days, but back then the BBC reported Africa's civil wars and mass-executions as if everybody really, really cared. That in mind, "The Invasion of Time" often looks as if it's asking the question: "what if the things that happen *over there* happened *here*?" This isn't as big a stretch as it might now seem.

As we've already seen, the Chancellor of the Exchequer had asked for help from the International Monetary Fund as if Britain were just another Third World nation. There was even a planned military coup (see **Who's Running the Country?** under 10.5, "The Green Death", for more nasty details). While the UK economy was suffering, Ugandan dictator and alleged cannibal Idi Amin made a famously barbed quip to the effect that his "prosperous" nation would be happy to step in and help the poor, beleaguered people of Britain.

Since Gallifrey had already been established as the universal seat of English stuffiness (see "The Deadly Assassin", with all its university trappings), "The Invasion of Time" essentially gives us a world in which guerrillas overrun Oxford and Cambridge. As President of Gallifrey the Doctor is an unstable, autocratic dictator, condemning people during fits of insanity rather than forcing everyone to tow the party line. He's got far more in common with Amin than with the popular conception of Stalin. At one point Amin even offered to become the new King of Scotland, to lead the fight against the English, which seems curiously in keeping with Tom Baker's "madman" persona.

Here there's also the start of one of the main concerns of the Williams stories, the desire to show both sides of any given society. No longer do we see monocultural planets. Even when the programme's at its most hackneyed, we get a number of perspectives on the culture, with the malcontents usually being "right" but not knowing the whole story because they've never been anywhere else. Ironically, this starts happening in *Doctor Who* because everyone's getting fed up with *Star Trek* not doing it; the public of 1978 demand planets at least a bit more complex than their own streets. With the media going global, people are aware of other societies in a way never before possible. The idea of a whole world with only one style of trouser is untenable.

Plus, this is as close as the programme ever gets to Gilbert and Sullivan. Kelner is the Lord High Executioner, Borusa is the Lord High Everything Else.

Things That Don't Make Sense There are a lot of spurious "solutions" being offered here. The scene in which K9 is given the relics of Rassilon, and uses them to dispel the Vardans, is a massive plotfudge; we've never been told that the Sash, the Rod or the circlet have the power to generate 'modulation rejection patterns', and the suggestion seems to be that as these are big, powerful objects K9 can now do whatever he likes with them. And only the Vardans on the planet are expelled. Nobody remembers the existence of the great big Vardan battle-cruiser that's already in orbit. But the purpose of the Vardan ship is a puzzle in itself, since K9 implies that the Vardans are being beamed straight from their homeworld, even though we've already seen them discussing tactics on the bridge of their ship.

Worse, but in a similar vein, the whole thrust of the last two episodes seems almost meaningless. The Doctor struggles to build a de-mat gun because it's the only way of holding off the invasion, but in the end it's just used to kill two Sontarans, in which case it could just as well be any common-or-garden pistol. We have to *assume* that the Doctor wipes out the entire Sontaran fleet with the weapon, even though he seems to lose consciousness immediately after killing Stor with it, but it's never referred to and as a result the ending becomes the dampest of all damp squibs. [Is the gun "intelligent", and if so then does it know it has to wipe out the Sontaran ships as well as their leader? Does it remove Stor from the timeline, thus meaning that he never led his fleet here? Or does the fleet simply go home, now the forcefield's back up and the troops on the planet have been defeated? If it's the latter, then the whole de-mat gun subplot is *thoroughly* absurd.]

A question about Gallifrey that begs an answer, not for the first or last time but most noticeably here: why are so many Time Lords so ambitious? We're never led to believe that there's any money on Gallifrey, as its inhabitants have endless power and the resources of all space and time at their disposal, and there's apparently no sex either. So if it's not about the cash or the women, and most Gallifreyans don't even have hobbies, then what could possibly drive people like Kelner to betray his own people? The only answer hinted at here is petty revenge, yet this doesn't explain the scene in which Kelner tells a corrupt guard that he'll be 'rewarded' for siding with the Vardans. The script fails to mention what kind of reward this could possibly be. Status, perhaps, but to what end? [They've been raised to think of all other lifeforms as "pets", so their only real competition is each other. Is everything a big game to them?]

In fact, characters' motivations are strained allround. Why does Borusa tell the Doctor that Leela attacked him at his induction ceremony, when

moments earlier the Chancellor was claiming that the Matrix had rejected him? Why does Kelner try to send the TARDIS into a 'black star' at the end of episode five, when the Doctor's got the Great Key that his Sontaran masters want so desperately? How do the Sontarans even know he's got the Great Key? Not a bad piece of deduction, from a Sontaran commander who's too dim and too badly-briefed to realise that the Lord President and the Doctor are one and the same.

And why do only a handful of Sontarans land on Gallifrey? Fair enough, the whole fleet can't get through the little hole in the force-field, but if the Sontarans have got at least *one* landing vessel then surely they've got more? Once again, they're really not living up to their "cloned by the million" claim. The Sontaran who accosts the Doctor in the TARDIS workshop is so inept that he stands right in front of the completed de-mat gun and doesn't expect the Doctor to fire it, and then Stor proves even *more* inept by threatening to blow up himself and the entire galaxy, even though he's got no way of knowing that the invasion has failed.

Various people forget that "Castellan" is Kelner's title and not his name. The story opens with the Doctor facing the Vardans wrapped up in his scarf, but when he walks back into the TARDIS the scarf has found its way onto the hat-stand. Time Lord traffic control is a maximum security area, yet K9 can happily roll straight into the undefended catacombs which contain the forcefields and transduction barriers - Gallifrey's only defences against the universe - and blow them up. Security's clearly a problem on this planet; faced with arrest at the start of episode two, Leela seizes her knife from Andred even though it's forbidden in the Capitol. When she realises she's surrounded, however, she puts it away again. In her own belt. None of the guards try to get it back off her. [The all-purpose guard excuse: they're not used to anyone fighting back.]

The Vardan ability to travel along any wavelength should make them one of the most powerful species in the universe, able to bring down whole empires before their victims even know what's happening, but they're used as patsies by the Sontarans... who don't seem to have anything much to offer them.

Critique (Prosecution)   Another story rapidly assembled under time-pressure, and as with "The Invisible Enemy", there's a temptation to blame its relative sloppiness on that. But underneath it all, there's the sense of a programme that doesn't think it even has to *try* to get the audience on its side, a programme so firmly-embedded in the public consciousness that its original mandate of "take the viewers to strange places" has been entirely forgotten.

Not that it doesn't have its moments, of course. Tom Baker's obviously relishing his chance to rant in the first few episodes, and the scenes between the Doctor and Borusa (played, unlike so much else here, for drama rather than comedy) stand out a mile. But even the best of its quirks come across as in-jokes, as asides and winks to the viewer, not as things that can drive six episodes of plot.

In retrospect, what's really striking about "The Invasion of Time" is that it's so dependent on the programme's back-catalogue. Gallifrey becomes a "recurring guest-star" planet; however much the script tries to remind casual viewers of the lore of "The Deadly Assassin", from hereon in the Doctor's homeworld is meant to be as familiar to us as a sit-com living-room set. The Sontarans are presented as being dramatic simply *because* they're invading Gallifrey, a million miles away from the nifty satire of "The Time Warrior", while the idea of invaders capable of moving along any wavelength is frittered away on a generic bunch of uniformed villains who never *do* anything with this ability. The title "The Invasion of Time" is ironic, as here the Time Lords are just space-going people with ancient super-weapons who no longer seem to have anything to do with "time" at all, let alone retain any of their power or mystery.

In fairness, there's at least one massively good idea at work here - the Doctor's apparently insanity and rise to power, which by rights should make this the *Doctor Who* version of *The Madness of King George* or the Caligula episodes of *I, Claudius* - but the script blows it by making his actions so clearly a bluff that it's impossible to get involved (even the six-year-olds weren't fooled, in 1978). Yet even this central thrust of the storyline is telling. This programme isn't about other worlds any longer, it's about the central character.

And that's the real problem with "The Invasion of Time". It marks the point where Tom Baker definitely becomes the star of the show (but see **The Lore** for details of the Great Struggle). With the possible exception of Borusa, the others - including, and perhaps especially, Leela - are ciphers at best, so much so that a lot of the time the whole affair looks like a stage for the leading man's performance-pieces. Andred is pathetically shallow for someone who supposedly carries so much of the plot. Rodan's more promising, yet she's forgotten once her usefulness ends. The moment when the Doctor looks straight at the audience and says 'even the sonic screwdriver won't get me out of this one' sums up everything that's wrong with the series by this point; in television you need a *bloody* good reason to break the fourth wall, but this is just vapid self-indulgence.

It's a story so cavalier about the details of the plot, and so convinced of the hero's all-round superhuman nature, that the Doctor gains the power to hypnotise people in less than two seconds just by saying 'you're hypnotised' (this isn't even a slight exaggeration, by the way). The ending, with the Doctor producing a new K9 out of nowhere before turning to grin his head off at the audience and laugh as if he's sharing some private joke with his own ego, may well be the single worst moment in the entire run of *Doctor Who* and shows you just how little anybody involved cared about any kind of sense or reason.

K9 himself is particularly irritating here, half the time acting as a prop for jokes that aren't funny and half the time being an all-purpose plot-fudging machine, a "comedy" SF computer who changes his personality with every other scene. Does it really need to be pointed out that Leela's departure is risible? And does it need to be pointed out that the chase through the TARDIS in the last episode is not only tedious, but embarrassing as well? The Outsiders are pitifully weak, as well as pointless; Stor is the least interesting Sontaran of them all; and the less said about the Vardans, the better. Never mind the costumes, never mind the effects, just focus on the way they're written and it's bad enough. You know something's gone wrong with the enemy when even the other characters find them disappointing (q.v. 15.2, "The Invisible Enemy" and 15.5, "Underworld").

Is "The Invasion of Time" entertaining in *any* way, though? Well... funnily enough, in the end it's not so bad, if you can overlook the worst excesses of episode six. It's certainly watchable, in a way that "Underworld" obviously isn't. There *are* good bits, and in itself Tom Baker's performance *is* always worth a few minutes of anyone's time. But the good bits aren't directly connected to the story, and Baker takes up far, far too much of the spotlight. Ultimately it's probably best to regard this as a turning-point, and leave it at that. This is the moment when *Doctor Who* becomes a "professional" affair, efficiently recycling itself, relying on its star to carry the show and expecting the audience to be in on the joke. The words "too arch by half" spring to mind.

Critique (Defence)   It's traditional to begin any comment other than outright condemnation of this story with a list of excuses. Let's not bother with that, there's enough to praise here.

The first and most obvious thing is the way in which anyone under the age of twelve is now assumed to be just watching for K9 (who is rather disturbingly alien again in this story, especially when shot from below or pulling a gun-nose on Leela). Hinchcliffe stories equated "adult" with violent or sexy; this regime takes it to mean an awareness of the conventions of narrative and the things that children's TV has to leave unspoken. The best example out of dozens is when Kelner and a Sontaran are in the art gallery. The crass space-monster asks 'what is this place' in a space-monster way, and the urbane Time Lord loftily states 'ancillary power station' like Lady Bracknell. What else could it be? If you're mature enough to see why this is, you'll spot how it's been in the fabric of the story all along. The coronation music is cheesy gameshow stuff, but the version of the same tune used when Borusa breaks all the precedents and hands over the key is understatedly noble. Once again the superficial details distract us from genuine power hidden in plain sight.

Around this time, the production team was under BBC-management pressure to counteract the effect of *Star Wars*. Not just the film itself, but the cash-ins and general feeding-frenzy in its wake. *Doctor Who* responded by playing to its strengths, poising itself between Ealing Comedies and Hammer Horrors. The stories that followed were all things no other programme could do and no American-made film even attempt. Here, we have a story which needs to be shown over six Saturdays to unfold. It's set in a world made of a frame of mind, not big-budget effects. If you need glossy effects to make it "real", you're watching the wrong series. *Doctor Who* is about one-offs, not mass-production, and a series doing this without a "suck it and see" approach to its own making would be hypocritical.

The irritating irony is that the BBC itself was forcing Williams to contemplate abandoning such BBC values. The programme's production was an object lesson in the values it always espoused;

improvisation, empiricism and hope. Looking beyond the effects to the story being told was an object-lesson in finding the marvellous within the apparently humdrum. This had always been the case, but now it became the manifesto for a purer form of the series, a game between audience and programme-makers. Anyone who lived in Britain could play. In this regard it's not so different from "The Time Warrior" (11.1), which spent two whole episodes encouraging us to laugh at Sarah for getting it all wrong and not realising she was the new *Doctor Who* girl. This is a story about altered priorities.

At the heart of this story is the scene where the Doctor reveals all to Borusa. There was often a sense that the Doctor defeated threats to home and hearth *despite* acting capriciously; here he does it *because* of such behaviour. The Doctor never automatically respected any authority but here Borusa and he earn one another's trust. (There is so much affection and fear in their exchanges that two other actors managed to coast along in the role of Borusa afterwards. Seeing "The Five Doctors" for the first time, no-one who'd seen this story could have foreseen the twist.) In any other context the threat to kill the Doctor would be a duff cliffhanger. Here it's the final proof of the Time Lords' true power. It isn't their technology or their genetics but their mindset, and the Doctor is paradoxically their most loyal son.

Sure, there are flaws: Rodan is just annoying, the Outsiders come from Planet Thesp (especially the one who gets all hale and hearty on the baffling line 'now that's the language I do understand!') and if none of the other actors can take Derek Deadman as Stor seriously then how can we? The discrepancies between film and VT are irritating - see **Which is Best: Film or VT?** under 12.3, "The Sontaran Experiment" - and a lot of the sets look cramped. As the BBC hierarchy noted, Tom Baker was getting in the way of the series as a whole, and this was the point when the memos started flying. But at that precise moment this was what the public said they wanted. And in the end, when Leela leaves, we don't get a tearjerker. It's left unspoken, then he sets about living the rest of his life without a moment's glance backwards and - as we all knew once we'd learned to count to twenty-six - we were off on summer hols without a care in the world. Only people who've started to lose it can treasure that child-like liberty from worry. And they call it a kids' show!

The Facts

Written by David Agnew (a pseudonym for Graham Williams, Anthony Read and David Weir). Directed by Gerald Blake. Viewing figures: 11.2 million, 11.4 million, 9.5 million, 10.9 million, 10.3 million, 9.8 million.

Supporting Cast John Arnatt (Borusa), Christopher Tranchell (Andred), Milton Johns (Kelner), Hilary Ryan (Rodan), Derek Deadman (Stor), Denis Edwards (Lord Gomer), Reginald Jessup (Lord Savar), Charles Morgan (Gold Usher), Ray Callaghan (Ablif), Michael Mundell (Jasko), Max Faulkner (Nesbin), Gai Smith (Presta).

Working Titles Ahh, now you're asking. "The Invasion of Time" was made to replace a story (see **The Lore**) that's usually referred to as "The Killer Cats of Geng-Sing", or something similar. But that was just the way Graham Williams remembered it on stage at PanoptiCon V in 1985. The only extant paperwork calls it something like "The Killers of the Darkness"; there are various permutations. Suffice to say that the story broadcast was written much too quickly to have had any other title than the one on the screen.

Cliffhangers The circlet is placed on Doctor's head at the end of his inauguration, and he falls to the floor, writhing in agony; the Doctor tells the Council that they're about to meet their new masters, as the shimmering forms of the Vardans appear; believing the Doctor to be a traitor, Andred boards the TARDIS and sentences him to death by staser; just when the invasion seems to be over and everyone's celebrating, the Doctor turns round to find a troop of Sontarans standing in the Panopticon; inside the TARDIS, the Doctor and Rodan are thrown to the ground and start to fade into negative as the Castellan's technical trickery hurls the Ship into a black star.

The Lore

• How it all started… script editor Anthony Read asked a former colleague, David Weir, to concoct an action-led story. Weir was providing the English-language version of the hit mystical / martial arts Japanese series The Water Margin. He was also responsible for the Space: 1999 episode "Black Sun", but we'll let him off.

In keeping with Williams' idea of involving the Doctor's own people in the six-parter at the end of each season, Weir decided to re-think Gallifrey again. In his original version the Time Lords were born elsewhere, and used the Capitol they'd built on Gallifrey as Time Central. The indigenous beings of the planet agreed to this in return for exemption from the Time Lords' code of behaviour. Thus, the Cat-People of Gallifrey were permitted to use a time-scoop and stage gladiatorial games between species… or something like that.

However, when the scripts came crawling in it soon became apparent that this was a great movie, but not really Doctor Who and certainly not achievable on the budget of a six-part story. The version of events most commonly repeated is that Read realised he was going to have to pull the plug when the script demanded an arena the size of Wembley Stadium, filled with cats, for a nightshoot. So the programme-makers had about ten days to make a new story, using the sets and actors already in the pipeline. It was at this point that the traditional BBC scene-shifters' dispute came into play (see 12.1, "Robot"; 17.6, "Shada"; 20.5, "Enlightenment", etc). Nonetheless, the designs for cat-costumes were fairly advanced and by all accounts very, very pretty.

• The scene-shifters' dispute was the reason that so many of the TARDIS interiors were shot on film and on location. There was a contingency budget for outside broadcast work, which was outside the pay-deal being negotiated with the union, so it was the filming of the TARDIS material beyond the studio that allowed the story to be made. But it very nearly didn't happen that way. The BBC's Head of Serials, Graeme McDonald, suggested that the season end early and that the budget and props be reallocated for Season Sixteen. Williams, who already had elaborate plans for the next year's stories, believed that with the aid of a stoic and ingenious director it could be made to happen. Gerald Blake had worked with Williams before (notably on Z Cars) and had directed "The Abominable Snowmen" (5.2). He dealt well with the conflicts between the two regulars, cheering up Jameson and pulling rank on Baker (one version has him saying 'I remember you when you were Pat Troughton', or words to that effect).

• The script was written by Graham Williams and Anthony Read under the in-house BBC penname "David Agnew", to avoid a Robert-Holmes-style visit from the taxman (see 17.2, "City of

Death", for Agnew's later work). The starting-point was Williams' desire to see more of the TARDIS interior, bring back the Sontarans and re-evaluate the Doctor's relationship with his own people. The Vardans came comparatively late.

• Louise Jameson had decided to leave, but Williams believed he could talk her around. Thus her departure was left open in the script. The final decision was made during the brief studio work.

• Only three days' worth of studio time was available. All the material in the Panopticon and the Vardan ship was shot, as well as the main chamber of the Capitol (which was the Panopticon set again, near enough). The screen on the Vardan ship couldn't show things which hadn't already been filmed, hence the abstract patterns.

• The bulk of the location interiors were filmed in the disused mental illness section of St. Anne's Hospital, Redhill, Surrey. By this stage it was obvious that Jameson was leaving, so she and Chris Tranchell (Andred) started adding little hints of a developing relationship.

• Nigel Brackley, K9's operator, moved from the company he'd been working for at the start of 1978. It was unclear whether he or his machinery would be useable in future, hence the writing-out and writing-in-again of the tin dog. Brackley's services were eventually retained, and a new motor fitted to the prop to solve its noise and control problems. Baker was never keen on the idea of keeping the Doctor's "pet", but liked John Leeson.

• The Vardans really *were* sheets of tinfoil, out of focus and CSO'd into the picture. Dick Mills used similarly-sized tinfoil to make the sound effects.

• Like much of the BBC LP *Doctor Who Sound Effects*, the sound of the de-mat gun will be familiar to fans of seminal '80s cartoon series *Danger Mouse*. The BBC lawyers asked Cosgrove Hall Animations to stop using it. In a similar vein, it was at this point that Brian Hodgson's TARDIS take-off and arrival were reclassified as "music" rather than "sound effects", ensuring that he received royalties at last.

• As episode five was being broadcast, the aforementioned Head of Drama met with Williams to discuss ways of avoiding some of the problems that had beset this production. Williams commented on some of the flaws in the finished episode, notably the way in which the Sontarans were being made to look ridiculous and the fact that scripts weren't being adhered to. This would later result in the first of Tom Baker's threats to quit unless Williams was replaced with someone more on his wavelength.

• The now-notorious line 'even the sonic screwdriver won't get me out of this one' was an ad lib, as the scripted line was 'that's not fair, Chancellor'. It figures.

16.1: "The Ribos Operation"

(Serial 5A, Four Episodes, 2nd September - 23rd September 1978.)

Which One is This? A con-man and a warlord get in the way of a simple job for the Doctor and his posh new Time Lady assistant: stealing the crown jewels, on a backwater planet that looks like Tsarist Russia and is long overdue for a Renaissance.

Firsts and Lasts *Doctor Who* discovers the full-scale story arc, as "The Ribos Operation" marks the start of what's generally known as the Key to Time sequence, six stories involving the hunt for all the segments of the mystical and never-properly-explained Key. (Though at the time this was pitched to the audience as an epic, cosmic quest, it's *really* a way of forcing the Doctor to go to interesting places again. The '60s series had the TARDIS materialise in galactic danger-zones at random, whereas the early '70s saw the Doctor stranded on Earth, forced to deal with invasion attempts and dangerous scientific projects on a more or less monthly basis. But ever since the Doctor gained some control of the TARDIS circa 1974, the programme has increasingly been forced to rely on super-powerful alien forces to draw the Ship off-course and make sure there are decent adventures to be had. For the next six stories, the Doctor's got a mandate to go looking for trouble.) You can also have great fun spotting the joins where individual writers have stitched the Key to Time idea into their scripts.

Two other significant entities turn up at this point: Romana (who'll stay with the TARDIS for nearly three years, in one form or another) and the Guardians (who'll be important later on in the season, and turn up again in Season Twenty). K9 is replaced by K9 Mk. II, re-built in the *real* world but not much different to look at. Just a bit quieter.

It's the last time that Stuart Fell plays a monster, and it's not his finest hour.

Four Things to Notice About
"The Ribos Operation"...

1. "The Ribos Operation" is an oddity, unique in the series up until this point, a story with the

Season 16 Cast/Crew

- Tom Baker (the Doctor)
- Mary Tamm (Romana)
- John Leeson (voice of K9)

- Graham Williams (Producer)
- Anthony Read (Script Editor)

lush costume-drama feel of a "historical" piece but set on another planet. In the past we've been led to believe that *everyone* in outer space is futuristic, and even non-technological societies talk in spaceman-speak rather than any kind of credible period dialogue (just listen to the Thals). Yet Ribos is - commendably - shown as a world that's going through its own Middle Ages. Even Peladon did-n't get *this* Medieval. And it looks so much nicer than all those planets where people dress in silver and carry blasters. Binro the Heretic, the only man on Ribos who's figured out that the stars are other suns and not the ice-crystals of the sky-gods, is the series' one attempt to remind us that every culture needs a Galileo at *some* point.

2. By now *Doctor Who* has ceased to be a pro-gramme that puts the monsters in the spotlight, and become a programme full of human megalo-maniacs who just happen to operate in places where there's the occasional "guest monster" to be found. Keeping the five-year-olds happy here is the Shrievenzale, a dinosaur-like quadruped played by an "artiste" crawling around on all fours in a reptile suit. It obeys all the usual rules for *Doctor Who* monsters by spending most of its time off-camera, only revealing bits of itself for the first few episodes. (Our first sight of the creature is a rubbery claw reaching out from under a sliding door, which is fairly typical.)

3. Robert Holmes, whose scripts set *Doctor Who* adrift in a universe of petty bureaucrats and small-time crooks years before Douglas Adams did it, now outdoes himself with the characters of Garron and Unstoffe (played, with great character actor panache, by Iain Cuthbertson and Nigel Plaskitt). You know all those stories about con-men selling Tower Bridge to rich, gullible tourists? That's more or less what Garron and Unstoffe do. But they do it with whole planets. Their ploy, to plant a specimen of the galaxy's most sought-after mineral among Ribos' crown jewels in order to

make the place look more valuable, provides the series with one of its cutest-ever plots.

4. A dog savaged Tom Baker's face shortly before this story was made, and the make-up's obviously struggling to hide it. The scar-tissue is so noticeable during the Doctor's scene with the White Guardian that you expect him to say 'well, as you can see, I recently had a run-in with the Caninian Warlords of Sirius Five…' at any moment.

The Continuity

The Doctor Romana insists that he's 759, and she's apparently seen his records on Gallifrey, though he's claiming to be 756 and believes this to be 'mature' rather than 'old'. The Doctor recognises Garron's feigned Somerset accent [raising even more questions about the way the Time Lord gift of translation works]. He can hypnotise a human guard using his pocket-watch, though oddly it takes him longer than it did to hypnotise one of his own people [15.6, "The Invasion of Time"].

The Doctor is initially wary of accepting the assistant that the White Guardian provides, and apparently not just because he doesn't like having Romana forced on him, as he says that assistants mean trouble and that he's happy with K9. [This Doctor, so much less willing to enter into human relationships than the last, is more of a loner by nature. Note that the Fourth Doctor never really *chooses* a companion. They're either forced on him or stowaways, the one exception being Harry Sullivan, who was only allowed on board the TARDIS so that the Doctor could show off. He makes this point himself at the end of his run in 18.7, "Logopolis".] He's not a bad medium pace bowler [c.f. 19.5, "Black Orchid"; 14.2, "The Hand of Fear"].

• *Ethics.* Despite his respect for the White Guardian, at first he's reluctant to take up the challenge of finding the Key to Time, so he's still unwilling to accept universe-saving jobs if someone else is pulling the strings. He needs to be threatened before he agrees to 'volunteer'. He has no interest in interfering in the affairs of con-men [so petty crime isn't his business], and indeed, he finds Garron's criminality amusing. With his own life at stake, the Doctor doesn't hesitate to slip a primed bomb into the Graff Vynda-K's pocket, thus killing the man.

• *Inventory.* The Doctor's just perfected a "silent" dog-whistle for K9. The sonic screwdriver has no problem opening ordinary locks here, although multi-levered locks take a while.

• *Background.* The Doctor scraped through at the Academy with 51% on his second attempt [suggesting that 50% is a bare minimum to qualify, which seems quite low for the exacting Time Lords], and it's obviously still a sore point for him as he believes this information should be 'confidential'. He knows enough sleight-of-hand to pick pockets, claiming that Maskelyne trained him. [Jasper Maskelyne was the British magician who used the principles of stage magic to misdirect enemy forces in World War Two, which is a very Doctor sort of thing. Alternatively the Doctor might mean Jasper's father, John Nevil Maskelyne (and 14.6, "The Talons of Weng-Chiang", establishes that the Doctor knows something about stage-magic in the elder Maskelyne's era). But John was better-known for large-scale mechanical tricks than for sleight-of-hand.]

The Doctor knows of the Guardians, and as soon as the TARDIS loses its power he immediately concludes that a Guardian may be responsible [which is a good guess on the Doctor's part, given how many *other* things have been able to stop the Ship over the last few years]. He's heard of the Key to Time, but only in old myths. He treats the White Guardian with an unusual amount of respect, especially considering that the entity has just hi-jacked his TARDIS, and refers to the Guardian as 'sir'. [Is he scared? He says the Guardian could choose any number of Time Lords for this task, possibly indicating that the Guardians are somehow part of the Time Lord hierarchy. See **The Guardians and the Key** for more.]

The Doctor recognises the co-ordinates for both Cyrrhenis Minima and Ribos, perhaps indicating a familiarity with the planet. He even knows what a Shrievenzale is. [Being named after the Shrievalty of Ribos - see **Planet Notes** - it's unlikely that Shrievenzales are found on any other world.] He describes the lump of jethryk on Ribos as the biggest he's ever seen.

The Supporting Cast
• *Romana.* Short for Romanadvoratrelundar [although Mary Tamm usually ends up pronouncing it Romanadvoratnelundar] and she doesn't like "Romana". She's a female Gallifreyan [there's no hint of her being a fully-fledged Time Lord /

What Do the Guardians Do?

On having *Doctor Who* flung at him by the BBC, Graham Williams did some market research. Working on the assumption that the average viewer was a fifteen-year-old boy, he went to see what fifteen-year-old boys were reading and watching. One word kept coming up: "epic". In the period between *2001: A Space Odyssey* and *Star Wars* there were any number of fantasy movies aimed at younger audiences, often starring Doug McClure and involving dinosaurs, but more interesting to his target group were series of novels like *Dune*, the *Foundation* trilogy, "Doc" Smith's *Lensman* series and Michael Moorcock's interlocked sword 'n' sorcery slashers and alternate histories.

Then, as Williams shadowed Hinchcliffe, he found that BBC budgets weren't conducive to this approach. Worse, the set-up he was inheriting was constrained by the presence of the Time Lords. When the Time Lords had been "noises off" this hadn't been a problem, but now they were there, with a known homeworld and culture (although this also appealed to those "core" viewers, so junking the Time Lords outright wasn't on). The obvious solution was to make Gallifrey responsible for just a *small* part of time and space. This would, theoretically, have three effects. It would broaden the canvas of the programme beyond anything the average viewer in - say - 1967 could have imagined, and allow the series to explore its potential now that a generation didn't need to be sold on the idea of time-travel every four episodes or so; it would put the Doctor's haphazard exploits into a bigger framework than ever, possibly with a higher set of priorities than simply rebelling against the tedium of Time Lord life ("more than just a Time Lord"... sound familiar?); but most important of all, it would overrule the previous attempts to "bible" the programme into a safe, predictable format and leave it capable of doing just about anything.

The initial proposal, submitted on the 30th of November, 1976, is as intriguing for what it *doesn't* tell us about the Guardians as what it states or suggests.

"*Doctor Who* (1977 Season)", as the three-page memo is called, has been reproduced and ridiculed as "the weirdest job application in history". But consider the target audience. Williams had been lumbered with this series on the understanding that, as someone who knew science fiction, it was ideal for him. Knowing the difference between written SF and what *Doctor Who* had done so far, it irked him that the BBC thought of the series as *Tomorrow's World* with a plot or - worse - a home-made *Star Trek*. Pitching his memo as a reframing of the programme's philosophy in terms of particle physics (mainly filched from *The Tao of Physics*, a very '70s best-seller by Fritjov Capra ... more of this under 18.5, "Warriors' Gate"), he begins with an idea of binary oppositions, from the subatomic level to the macrocosm. If this hierarchical organisation persists, he argues, then the "Pyramidal Hierarchy" stretches through time and space and can have no apex. So beyond the Time Lords there must be a higher power, or rather pair of powers. Here we have to note that although he mentions a series of oppositions like "Chaos" and "Order", "Black" and "White", "Good" and "Evil", he never wholly identifies which is appropriate to which Guardian. He mentions that many of the Doctor's past adversaries have been unwitting servants of "Black", but that the balance between forces is more important than either.

One final point to consider before we progress to the broadcast version. Perhaps the Guardians are Time Lords, advanced to a higher degree along their own paths. Perhaps all of this is a test to see whether the Doctor qualifies for advancement; perhaps it's a gigantic fraud. Does the good guy always wear the white hat? None of this is out of keeping with the thinking of either Barry Letts (see especially 11.5, "Planet of the Spiders" and 9.6, "The Time Monster") or Andrew Cartmel (see especially 25.3, "Silver Nemesis" and 26.4, "Survival"), but it does open up the possibilities for an entirely new phase of the programme.

The first and most obvious thing to observe about the Guardians' on-screen debut is that it's withheld until the Doctor has been President of the Time Lords. Logistically this was for reasons given under "Horror of Fang Rock" (15.1), but in story terms it suggests that the Guardians' existence is only a rumour to most Time Lords. Romana's more surprised by the fact that someone can impersonate the Lord President than the fact that beings beyond the Time Lords actually exist. The Doctor's question about the White Guardian's identity is answered 'do you really need to ask?', which aside from the tease to the audience that this is God (see 3.3, "The Myth Makers", for a possible sidelight on this) might imply that the Doctor knows more about these entities than the rest of his kind.

continued on page 219...

217

Lady until 17.2, "City of Death"] who's recently graduated from the Academy with a triple-first. Formal, arrogant and quite posh, she's typical of Time Lord society, believing in the superiority of her own intellect and looking down her nose at the Doctor's haphazardness. Despite this, she's begging for help like any other companion within half an hour of being exposed to a dangerous alien environment.

She initially believes the Doctor to be suffering from a massive compensation complex, but then, she's obsessed with psychoanalysing other people. At one point she threatens to use him as a case-study in her thesis. She's 'nearly 140', young but certainly an adult. Being a girl, she likes jewellery.

Romana knows of the mission to find the Key to Time as soon as she's transported onto the TARDIS, but believes that the Lord President of Gallifrey recruited her, rather than the White Guardian, and the Doctor doesn't correct the mistake yet. [In Season Eighteen the Time Lords recall Romana as if they've known where she's been all along, so the Guardian may have informed them when she was removed from Gallifrey. On the other hand it's possible that she returns to Gallifrey for a short while in the gap between Season Seventeen and Season Eighteen, perhaps to finish her thesis and / or to fully qualify as a Time Lord.]

Unsurprisingly, she knows how to operate a TARDIS, and knows *Bartholomew's Planetary Gazetteer* well enough to quote what it says about Ribos [with a name like that, it *can't* be a Time Lord text]. But she's too naïve to realise there are scary monsters in outer space, and doesn't know the expression 'keep your fingers crossed'.

• *K9.* By now the "new" model of K9 is in operation, and the Doctor's planning on taking him on holiday. He can hear the Doctor's whistle from inside the TARDIS and through several floors of brickwork, and somehow he can open the TARDIS doors.

While the old model's weapon had five settings, this K9 uses stun mark seven to knock out a guard for hours. He can melt rock with even more efficiency than before. This version seems to have a much more human personality than the previous one, occasionally speaking in colloquial English [?] and saying things like 'quick!' instead of 'advise celerity, master'. His mind is, even so, terribly over-literal.

The TARDIS Romana claims she made the hole in the TARDIS console into which the tracer for the Key to Time fits. [This hints that the controls can be physically reconfigured from the console itself, which is the sort of thing that happens a lot after "Logopolis" (18.7) and which resembles what happens in "The Two Doctors" (22.4). Unless she's carrying a special TARDIS-drill.]

When it comes to TARDIS co-ordinates, the Doctor speaks as if every planet has a simple four-digit code, as Cyrrenhis Minima has the co-ordinates 4180 and Ribos has the co-ordinates 4940. These settings appear on a display near the tracer-hole, and on another display at the other side of the console. Romana asks if she should 'look up' these co-ordinates, implying the existence of some sort of file on board the Ship.

The brush and hand-held mirror that Romana uses would seem to come from somewhere on board the TARDIS, unless she brings luggage with her that's never seen.

The Time Lords The Doctor says, of the President of the Supreme Council: 'I should have thrown him to the Sontarans when I had the chance.' [There was no clear President on Gallifrey at the end of 15.6, "The Invasion of Time", so (a) someone must have stepped in to fill the role since then and (b) the Doctor must have heard about it. It could well be Borusa, who's in power the next time we see Gallifrey in 20.1, "Arc of Infinity". However, Castellan Kelner was constitutionally second-in-line, as the Doctor *did* designate him 'acting Vice-President'. Would Kelner be able to maintain his position after the Sontaran affair, though? Even given the obvious stupidity of the Gallifreyan political system? See "Arc of Infinity" for more.]

The Guardians and the Key The White Guardian has the power to shut down the TARDIS systems, and perhaps even draw the Ship to him, so right from the start it's obvious that he's a major power. [Curious that the Black Guardian never seems to hi-jack the TARDIS in the same way. See 16.6, "The Armageddon Factor", for more on this.] Emerging from the TARDIS in response to the White Guardian's summons, the Doctor finds himself in a barren, rocky landscape, furnished with a chair, a parasol and a table of drinks. [The rocky landscape may be some realm of the Guardian's, or possibly just the place the TARDIS

What Do the Guardians Do?

...continued from page 217

But note, also, the lack of respect shown by the Doctor to this omnipotent being. He calls the Guardian 'sir', yet he clearly just wants to be elsewhere and doesn't agree to the mission until he's threatened. If White = Absolute Good, then this attitude would be extreme *lese-majeste*. It's fair to say that the Doctor feels more comfortable with White than with Black - it's hard to imagine him doing the Black Guardian's bidding under *any* circumstances, and he and White express similar philosophies in "Enlightenment" (20.5) - but in the end he carries out his mission in the name of balance, not giving either Guardian an advantage.

The paradox here is that if the White Guardian were unopposed, then the universe would be just as dead as if the Black Guardian got things his own way. (In fact, as the 1977 memo states, the apocalypse wouldn't be instantaneous; there'd be no joy for Black in that. But for millennia, worlds and their inhabitants would suffer... compare this with the slow unravelling of causality described in 22.4, "The Two Doctors") Both Guardians are, in their ways, agencies of entropy. If we take the standard definition of entropy as the tendency of things towards the most probable state, i.e. death and inertia, then a dynamic, living cosmos needs a tension between rigid order and a chaotic void. As physicists, philosophers and Information theories were all suggesting at the time, binary oppositions are formed by underlying symmetries which are really similarities. Chalk and cheese are, after all, both white, crumbly, calcium-based substances with one-syllable names beginning "ch-". The White Guardian usually claims that both sides are necessary (at least for the foreseeable future, as in the ponderously enigmatic finale to "Enlightenment"), and the programme tends to present White's explanations as "true", perhaps because order finds it harder to lie than chaos. The Guardians are therefore extremes of tendencies, between which all created matter has to be suspended. This is in keeping with the broad tendencies of known science, especially on the pop-science side (see **What Does Anti-Matter Do?** under 13.2, "Planet of Evil").

In "Mawdryn Undead" (20.3) the Black Guardian

tells Turlough that for all his powers he 'cannot be seen to interfere'. Seen by whom? The other Guardian - assuming it really *was* White dressed up as the Man from Del Monte in "The Ribos Operation" (and *see* 16.6, "The Armageddon Factor" for a possible alternative) - seems to have detailed knowledge of a preordained future. Logically, therefore, all covert intervention is part of an overall "plan" for the universe. Such mechanistic, predetermined fates were generally considered to be a Bad Thing at this stage in the programme's development, as well as in mainstream '70s culture. From "The Invasion of Time" (15.6) to "Kinda" (19.3), randomness and spontaneity are seen as existential protests and - it's implied - Good Things. It's therefore part of the programme's nature to keep both parties in the background as manipulators rather than instigators, just as "one-offs" and "freaks" are treasured in the face of armies of robots, clones and brainwashed drones.

Doctor Who's reluctance to describe the ultimate fate of the universe beyond the 'Gallifreyan noosphere' (21.3, "Frontios") means that we only have supposition as to which side, if either, will prevail. It's been speculated, for example, that the Guardians are reverberating backwards in time from the universe after ours to make sure conditions are suitable for that cosmos to be created (compare with 26.3, "The Curse of Fenric"; 20.4, "Terminus"). Nothing we've seen contradicts this, but it's tenuous. We can say with some certainty that they act like shepherds for intelligent life. Each can only know of the other's activities from the consequences, after which it's too late (so the Blinovich Limitation Effect applies to them, it would appear... see **How Does Time Work?** under 9.1, "Day of the Daleks"). Free agents like the Doctor are used to introduce random elements into otherwise pre-determined schemes; oddly enough the embodiment of disorder is the one who gives precise, detailed instructions with clear descriptions of the consequences, most notably in "Mawdryn Undead". Meanwhile White simply gives veiled hints and threats, and leaves the Doctor to it, despite having "Ultimate Control-Freak of the Cosmos" as his job-description.

already happened to be before the Guardian appeared.] A white-clad, white-bearded old gentleman then appears in the chair to give him the task of finding the Key. It's doubtful that this is the

White Guardian's true form, however, unless bearded old Caucasian men are a universal symbol for goodness. He later turns out to have appeared before Romana as the President of

Gallifrey, and to have transported her onto the TARDIS.

Despite being presented as a force for "good", the Guardian has no qualms about threatening the Doctor into searching for the Key to Time, stating that if he doesn't then nothing will happen to him '…ever'. No actual connection with the Time Lords is indicated, but the Guardian has a penchant for using Time Lords as agents, which may be telling.

The Guardian's story is as follows. There are times when the forces within the universe upset 'the balance'. In order for the White Guardian to restore this balance, he needs the Key to Time, and has chosen the Doctor to recover it. Otherwise the universe will be plunged into eternal chaos - 'eternal' as the Doctor understands it, anyway [without beginning or end, i.e. chaos will overwhelm all of history at once] - which is presumably why the Doctor is warned to look out for the Black Guardian, who wants the key for an 'evil' purpose.

Both Black and White Guardians are required to maintain the universal balance. [This story, though suitably mythic, makes very little sense when you look at the details. Leaving aside the vagueness of the threat, why should the White Guardian want to merely *maintain* the balance? He may represent order and stability, but if the Black Guardian's always trying to get the upper hand then shouldn't the White Guardian be doing the same, thus ensuring a kind of equilibrium? Surely neither of them should have the Key to Time? Again, see "The Armageddon Factor" for a suggestion as to what might *really* be going on here.]

• *The Key to Time.* A perfect transparent cube, treated here as if it's the most powerful artefact in the universe. Its origins are never explained.

The Key has been broken up into six segments, by person or persons unknown, and scattered throughout time and space. When brought together the segments create a power too dangerous for any one being to possess, and the Key is said to maintain the equilibrium of time itself. [Meaning that it *can* maintain the equilibrium when it's re-assembled, or that it's *always* maintaining the equilibrium, even when it's in pieces?] The White Guardian claims he wants the Key so that he can 'stop everything… for a brief moment only', and restore the balance while it's stopped [although how there can be a "while" when time is stopped is another thing that's never explained].

The critical moment is rapidly approaching, so the Key has to be assembled before it's too late. [In *whose* present is the moment rapidly approaching? Gallifrey's? If the Doctor and the Guardian are both tied to the same timeline, then it might explain why the Doctor doesn't have an infinite amount of time to find the Key. See 18.7, "Logopolis", for one possible explanation.]

Each of the individual segments has taken on a disguise, doing the same trick that the TARDIS is supposed to do by looking exactly like an object you might find in its own space and time. They can be any shape, form or size because they contain the 'elemental force of the universe'.

In order to find and identify the segments, the White Guardian gives Romana a 'locator' or 'tracer', a wand-like device which crackles like a Geiger counter as it gets closer to a part of the Key. The tracer is also described as the 'core' of the Key to Time, around which the other six segments can be assembled. [And how did the White Guardian come into possession of this, exactly? The tracer bears some resemblance to Gallifreyan technology, especially the Rod of Rassilon.] When inserted into the TARDIS console, the tracer indicates the space-time co-ordinates for the next segment. [The segments obviously have a "correct" order, as "The Armageddon Factor" demonstrates. The last segment turns out to be the only one definitively in a galaxy other than Earth's, so perhaps the segments were scattered further and further away from some kind of central point in the Milky Way. Gallifrey, possibly?]

The first segment is disguised as a lump of jethryk [see **History**], stolen by the con-man Garron and being transported from Cyrennhis Minima to Ribos as the TARDIS arrives in the era. [The co-ordinates change before the TARDIS has even started moving, which might indicate that the TARDIS is already in the right time-zone before the Doctor sets off for Ribos. This raises the question of why the tracer leads the Doctor to any particular segment at *that* particular point in time, rather than at a time when it's less well-defended. Perhaps a segment's only accessible at certain times due to complex time-travel rules not easily comprehensible to humans. Or perhaps it's in the nature of the quest for the Key to make the quester struggle a bit.]

The Doctor thinks there's a chance of losing the segment's co-ordinates if they change again while the TARDIS is in the vortex [which is bizarre, as the TARDIS is outside space and time while it's in the vortex so there shouldn't be a "while"]. The segment, like all of those to come, reverts to its natural form when the tracer touches it. [We might assume that the Key is indestructible even in its disguised form, to stop – say - anyone breaking off a chunk of the jethryk to use as fuel. But see "The Armageddon Factor" for a possible exception.]

Planet Notes

• *Levithia*. The planet of the Graff Vynda-K, a tyrannical Emperor with a liking for opulent armour and who enjoys puffing himself up with ideas of military nobility. However, the Graff lost the Levithian crown after he raised an expeditionary force and went to fight the frontier wars for the Alliance. He left his half-brother in charge of Levithia, but his people refused to let their original ruler return, so the half-brother's still in power.

The Graff's still considered a noble and a Royal Prince of the Greater Cyrrenhic Empire, however. His appeal to the High Court of the Cyrrenhic Empire was rejected, so now he's looking for a way to regain his throne by force, and Ribos would be a perfect forward-base for him. He comes to Ribos with his heavily armoured companion Sholakh and a personal guard of men in red robes and thick metal helmets - his 'Levithian Invincibles' - who use energy weapons and carry hand-held explosives in the form of thermite packs. The Invincibles are loyal, but predictably doomed. Garron and Unstoffe, the two con-men who try to sell him Ribos for 10,000,000 opeks, would seem to come from the same interplanetary culture as the Graff even if they don't hail from the same planet. The Levithians are technologically far in advance of Ribos, but they have a similar liking for Medieval costume, so they blend in quite well.

Garron claims that he sold Mirabilis Minor to three different clients, and Alliance Security has been after him ever since. He comes to Ribos from Cyrrenhis Minima. There are known worlds outside the Cyrrenhic Empire, as the Graff talks of hiring Pontinese battle-ships and mercenaries from Schlangi, but to build a battle-fleet to take back Levithia would turn the Alliance against him.

The Graff and Sholakh remember fighting in a labyrinth on Freytus, where they went almost a year without seeing the sky; things squirmed under their feet in the darkness, and they had two

legions searching for the enemy. The Graff also fought battles on Skaar [spoken on-screen, the name seems to have become "Skarn"] and Crestus Minor, in which Sholakh planted the Graff's standard in the heart of the Crestan general. The Graff is used to intimidating natives, and his ship [in orbit?] is stuffed with eighteen years of loot from his campaigns. See **History** for more of this sort of thing.

• *Ribos*. A planet 'only' three-hundred light-years from the Magellanic Clouds and 116 parsecs [roughly 350 light-years] from Cyrrhenis Minima, according to Garron, which makes it centrally-placed from the Cyrrhenic Empire's point of view. [The Magellanic Clouds are satellite galaxies of our own, so in cosmic terms they're quite "close". But they're so big, and so far apart, that it's hard to say where Garron's measuring from.] Ribos is also described as being in the constellation of Skytha, from the Empire's perspective. It's actually part of the Greater Cyrrenhic Empire, defended by Alliance forces, and according to *Bartholomew's Planetary Gazetteer* it's a 'protected class three society' with no space-service.

In fact Ribos is home to entirely humanoid people who have no idea about space travel and no inkling that these alien visitors are in their midst. Their level of development is more or less Medieval, with no sign of industrialisation at all. Yet curiously, the room where the crown jewels are kept has electrical-looking lamps as well as candles, which go out when the guards touch them with ceremonial staves. [Technology salvaged from other alien visitors? Or is it some form of "magic"? Given Ribos has very few populated areas, it may well be another degenerate human colony, though Romana believes there can't be any 'Earth-aliens' here and Garron describes the locals as a different species.]

The natives believe the world to be flat, haven't invented the telescope, insist on seeing the stars as ice-crystals and hold that Ribos is a battlefield between Sun Gods and Ice Gods. Only Binro the Heretic offers the suggestion that stars may be other suns, and he was forced to recant for fear of bringing on the fury of the gods. The people are superstitious, and a robed, ornately made-up visionary called the Seeker is brought in to find criminals by casting bones. Her prediction that only one of those present among the Graff's people will survive - the Doctor, although he isn't specified - proves to be unsettlingly accurate, as do her visions of where Unstoffe is hiding. [A

221

side-effect of the Key segment, or did she just grow up near a time fissure…?]

Ribos has an elliptical orbit of its sun, and its two seasons are known as 'Sun Time' and 'Ice Time', each of them thirty-two Levithian years long. The planet's currently in Ice Time, so the natives tend to dress in clothes with lots of fur trimming and look very Russian. The principle city seen here is called Shurr, though there are several other settlements beyond the tundra to the north. [It's strongly hinted, at least in the symbolism used here, that Sun Time sees the rediscovery of lost ideas and the coming of the ice makes the people revert to superstition. So the few surviving settlements may be all that remain of a greater civilisation, which would explain many of this society's odder features.]

The crown jewels are kept in Shurr, guarded in a relic room by the Shrieves. When these guards go off shift at night, the Shrievenzale - a large, green, reptilian thing with pincer-like jaws and furry hind-quarters - is let loose in the room. ["Shrievalty" is a real English word, albeit an archaic one, so contrary to some sources it's likely that the Shrievenzale is named after the guards and not the other way around.]

The Shrieves-at-Arms and their Captain perform a quick ritual of thanks before the jewels every morning. Visitors to Shurr have to carry passes, scrolls of paper which Garron has no trouble forging, and curiously the locals - like the Empire - seem to use gold opeks as currency. [This can't just be a translation glitch, as Garron expects the Graff's opeks to sway the Captain, so there may be an influence from the Empire on Ribos despite it being a class three world.] There's a night-time curfew in effect, and the Shrieves have at least one small cannon.

Beneath the concourse and beyond the candle-lit Hall of the Dead are the ancient catacombs, thought to be the Ice Gods' home and housing the skeletons of the long-deceased. Everyone's scared to go there, hardly surprising as the catacombs are inhabited by a colony of Shrievenzales larger than the one in the relic room. The Shrievenzales hunt for small animals out on the tundra before returning underground.

• *Harlegan 3.* Yet another one of those holiday planets that the Doctor's aiming for but never reaches.

History

• *Dating.* No date given. [But this must be a time after the age of the Earth Empire. No mention is made of a centralised Earth authority, and the most precious substance known is jethryk, never mentioned again anywhere else. The novel *Lords of the Storm* casually mentions a number of worlds known as 'the Cyrrenhics' in the context of the twenty-fourth century, perhaps implying that the Cyrrenhic Alliance forms from these worlds after the Empire's fall c. 3000 AD. Reference to Magellanic Clouds suggests that humanity has left its own galaxy, but might not have full-blown intergalactic travel yet. This story may be some time in the 3000s before the founding of the Federation (9.2, "The Curse of Peladon"), or some time in the 5000s when humanity is once again expanding away from Earth. The latter seems most likely, as intergalactic travel is still quite novel even in the 5000s and there's a return to the planet's surface after the age of the sky-cities, which explains the fact that…]

Garron is from Hackney Wick [London], still a mud-patch in the middle of nowhere, and Somerset and Irish accents both still exist in this era. Garron left Earth many years ago, after selling Sydney Harbour to an Arab for $50,000,000, but the client wanted the Opera House thrown in and eventually went after Garron with a machine gun. Garron has a shuttle, although he claims that there can be no direct communication from Ribos, so to contact the outside universe he'd have to go to Stapros and communicate by hyper-cable. This could take weeks [and Ribos is supposed to be centrally-placed?]. Despite all this technology, Garron formally presents his credentials on an old-fashioned scroll.

Jethryk - the rarest and most valuable element in the galaxy - is so sought-after that one single mine of it is enough to turn a planet into a major power, and 'space warping' would be impossible without the substance. [Meaning, the kind of space warp technology the Levithians use. Other forms of hyperspace and faster-than-light travel have been used for centuries without any mention of jethryk.] Jethryk looks blue and crystalline to the naked eye, and the large lump that Garron owns contains enough energy to power a battle-fleet for an entire campaign.

The police in this era use handcuffs, judging by the way Garron surrenders. Space-travel still rots the muscles, and bugging devices are visible rather than microscopic. Garron mentions a Magellanic Mining Conglomerate, which conducts geological surveys and supposedly set the price of ten million opeks for Ribos. Planets like Ribos within the Greater Cyrrhenic Empire have deeds of title and mortmain, held by their owners whether the primitive locals know about it or not. Mining here would require the importation of technology, but as Ribos is protected this can't begin until it's accorded grade two status, which probably won't happen for thousands of years. [Suggesting that *Bartholomew's Planetary Gazetteer* was produced in these parts, as it uses the same "class" system. Most people in the Cyrrhenic Empire must see themselves as class one.]

The Analysis

Where Does This Come From? The idea of the universe as a battle between Light and Darkness is - as we'll see - central to the oldest known religions (such as Zoroastranism) and heterodox belief-systems (such as Gnosticism… consider **What Do the Guardians Do?**). However, in this story the struggle between Fire and Ice has a more recent referent. Hans Horbiger's *Welteislehre* "proved" Teutonic mythology for Nazi Germany by demonstrating that the moon changes shape every month because it, like the stars, is made of ice. Every so often it hits Earth, wiping out dinosaurs and the Gods. Last time this happened two Gods escaped into the centre of the Earth (it's hollow, you realise) and will re-awaken with the next collision to lead the pure into a bright future. This was published in 1911, and by 1935 Goebbels had to issue a proclamation that you could be a good Nazi without needing to believe it; that's how common the idea was.

The appeal of this notion of inevitable decline, and of the few heroes who withstand it, is obvious to misguided "Romantics" like Hitler. But on Ribos it has a certain validity. After all, they really *are* living through cyclic history. (Theories of history going in cycles were being re-thought in the late '70s. 1930s thinkers like Philip Toynbee and Oswald Spengler were tainted by the whole concept's association with Nazism, but with "progress" no longer being seen as a linear process, it was the next-best idea. We've seen, and will see again, how immediate post-war attitudes towards the one-way development of mankind - and the idea that modernity is necessarily *better* - had gone a little off the boil by 1973.)

Those of us still believing in a constant development from the Dark Ages to the Enlightenment and beyond will know all about the Vatican's treatment of Galileo for his observations. They threatened to smash Galileo's hands, and on Ribos the hands of Binro the Heretic really *were* smashed. But a more compelling reference is to Giordano Bruno - note the near-anagram - who suggested in the sixteenth century that the stars were all suns with worlds of their own. The Vatican had other reasons to call him a heretic, but this didn't help. If there were other worlds, then how many Messiahs would you need? One per planet? And if God made us, then were we necessarily unique and therefore saved?

Only historians and film buffs would notice it now, but at the time of "The Ribos Operation" the BBC had recently screened Sergei Eisenstein's masterpiece *Alexander Nevsky*, so the design of the Levithian Invincibles would perhaps have been familiar to many people watching (the stills in the *Radio Times* would have helped). The Teutonic Knights were the aggressors, defended by Russia's greatest military leader, in a film made at around the time of the Siege of Leningrad. The word "opek" as a unit of currency combines "kopec" (the Czech unit) and OPEC (the body deciding the price of crude oil and thus, in '70s Britain, the Bad Guys). Similarly, British viewers will "get" most of Garron's spiel about selling a planet as being the language of estate agents - "realtors" in Americanese - the terminology having been unchanged since Cromwell's time, for practical as well as aesthetic reasons.

Since the White Guardian is the closest thing we've ever seen in this universe to an Almighty Power, it's worth noting the way he's presented to us, as an elderly English gentleman who looks more like the last bastion of the British Empire than a demigod. And yet, despite his threats to the Doctor, we're clearly supposed to feel there's something *cosy* about this man. He's the "patriarchal" face of the old order. He is, in short, a cosmic Mr. Kipling.

Things That Don't Make Sense What's lighting the catacombs?

As with so many "Doctor gets sent on a mission" stories (see 12.4, "Genesis of the Daleks"), you have to ask why the tracer can send the TARDIS to the right planet to find the Key segments but doesn't allow the Doctor to appear right next to them and pocket them in a second. As ever, there must be "rules" governing the higher powers of the universe, but we're not supposed to ask what they are. The White Guardian doesn't even give a vague and mystically obscure explanation as to why he has to send the Doctor to get the fragments rather than doing it himself, or just wiring the tracer up to a time-scoop and picking them up by remote control.

The Graff and his people are remarkably quick to believe in the Seeker's 'mumbo-jumbo', even after her first prediction yields no results. We know she's right about Unstoffe hiding in the concourse, but he's gone by the time the Graff's men get there and the Graff treats the prophecy as gospel anyway.

One other seer-related point that either counts as a "mistake" or a "curiousity", depending on how generous you're feeling: the people of Ribos have no concept of other worlds, and even Binro the Heretic hasn't imagined *people* coming from the stars, yet the mystical Seeker refers to the Graff as an 'alien'. Curious, isn't it, that those who practice the supernatural arts are so far ahead of current scientific thinking on Ribos? It's also worth pointing out that the Seeker's prophecy, that all but one of those present will die, comes true only after the Graff kills her *because* of the prophecy. So precognition's not all it's cracked up to be.

Critique (Prosecution, ish)   A curiosity by any *Doctor Who* standards, a double curiosity for this period in the programme's run, presenting itself as a fusion of historical drama and imperious SF that suggests something much larger than the small, out-of-the-way story we see on-screen.

Robert Holmes was notoriously resistant to the idea of "historicals" in *Doctor Who*, but this is a format that lets him drain all the BBC's best costume drama resources without having to take out the galactic empires or do any actual research, and ironically it's his sense for real-world events that makes the script work; as in "The Talons of Weng-Chiang", he makes the made-up future-history sound just as credible as the history we know, so even the use of language suggests a properly-developed (or still-developing) environment. This is a society of "opeks", not "credits". The use of character is important too, of course. Whereas so many stories of the late '70s all but ignore the minor characters who come between the Doctor and the villain, here it's not the Graff Vynda-K himself who matters - although as an arrogant feu-

dal lord who's obsessed with letting other people die for his honour, he's a damn sight better-characterised than most megalomaniacs - but the relationships between the Graff, the con-men and the Ribos locals.

The flaws, however, are as visible as the good bits. Director George Spenton-Foster, who had such trouble knowing where to shove the camera in "Image of the Fendahl", once again doesn't seem sure how to give this world a sense of scope (the editing, too, is surprisingly poor here). But perhaps the *real* problem is that however comfortable the script may be when dealing in character parts and quirks of fate, it's painfully awkward when dealing with the Bigger Picture. The Doctor's rushed and badly-acted briefing from the White Guardian is such a contrived attempt to set up a mythic fantasy in the minimum possible screen-time that it's painful to watch. These days a competent script editor would almost certainly introduce "the Quest" through the first storyline, not bung all the exposition in at the start.

Then there's Romana. Ah yes, Romana. As producer Verity Lambert once pointed out, humour may be important to *Doctor Who* but the series only works when the actors are taking the outer-space set-ups utterly, gut-achingly seriously. However much wit the Doctor may flash around, it's vital that moments occur when he looks as if he's about to face the most terrifying things in the universe, and it's vital that we believe those moments. But from her very first line, Mary Tamm obviously isn't believing a word of this at all, and her scenes with Tom Baker sound as if the two of them can't wait for the filming to end so that they can have a good laugh about it in the pub. There's a sneaking contempt for the series here, or at least, a sneaking contempt for anyone who might treat it as anything but a knock-about. Which means that in the end, we're left with a story that works when it's *being* a story... but that also contains some grim omens of the stories to come.

Critique (Defence)   To the casual viewer, the opening scene is obviously God giving the Doctor a mission. This seemed right and proper at the time, as he'd had "bosses" before, but had outgrown both UNIT and the Time Lords. The scale of the task, as all the pre-publicity had stressed, was bigger and bolder than before.

Yet this first story is a miniature. The real focus of it is a chance meeting (or possibly not) of a petty crook and a forgotten heretic, over halfway through the story. The scale of most *Doctor Who* stories grows outwards, but this one recedes from Cosmic to Galactic to Planetary to City. Scale is shown as irrelevant, as the battles of the ideologies, the Ice Gods and the Guardians are suggested to be somehow all the same conflict.

The only character not participating in the balance of forces is the Graff (even Garron, by his own lights, is maintaining equilibrium between "haves" and "have-nots"). The only character not at home in whichever world he or she inhabits is Romana. Just a few years earlier she would have been the viewer-identification character, but now even this role is surplus to requirements. In many ways Unstoffe has taken on that role, but the show's format requires the Doctor and friends to be present, so into the catacombs we all tumble.

Not that this is a bad thing entirely, as we get two different versions of what's going on at any moment (which had happened a few times before, but under Read and Williams became part of the programme's structure) and the candle-lit Hall of the Dead, with Renaissance cannons later on. Every single aspect of this story is pointing in the same direction, from music to character-names, from camera-angles to the White Guardian's spats. Only two flaws can be cited: the door to the catacomb looks a bit stagey, and Mary Tamm is obviously reading off cue-cards in the TARDIS scene.

Brian Aldiss garnered all sorts of awards and critical acclaim for his thumping great *Helliconia* trilogy, rethinking the Renaissance as the thawing out and re-freezing of a world in an elliptical orbit. Bob Holmes did it in ninety minutes of screen time and had better jokes, more poignancy and three other layers of story on top.

The Facts

Written by Robert Holmes. Directed by George Spenton-Foster. Viewing figures: 8.3 million, 8.1 million, 7.9 million, 8.2 million.

Supporting Cast: Iain Cuthberson (Garron), Nigel Plaskitt (Unstoffe), Paul Seed (Graff Vynda-K), Robert Keegan (Sholakh), Prentis Hancock (Captain); Cyril Luckham (The Guardian), Timothy Bateson (Binro), Ann Tirard (The Seeker).

Working Titles "The Ribos File", "Operation", "The Galactic Con-Man".

Cliffhangers Both the Doctor and Romana get stuck under the sliding door of the jewel-room, with the Shrievenzale's blood-stained jaws moving in on them; the Graff, having surprised the Doctor and company in the snow, gives order to his men to execute them; the Graff and his men move in on the Doctor's hiding-place in the catacombs (the re-cap re-stages this scene to include the Shrievenzale, which unexpectedly turns up and saves the day).

The Lore

• Graham Williams had proposed the idea of the Guardians and the Quest a year earlier, but several stories had already been commissioned which the Big Plan couldn't really accommodate. Williams' three-page document begins with a discussion of ideas of "balance" (deriving from eastern philosophies and a garbled version of quantum physics), and the notion of "power without responsibility". Having begun his producership while "The Deadly Assassin" was being edited, his conception that the Time Lords couldn't be the ultimate power in the universe resulted in the creation of a hierarchy of beings - like Russian dolls (see Romana's comment in 17.4, "Nightmare of Eden") - with the twin Guardians as the highest in this plane of existence.

• Once it was certain that Leela wouldn't be returning, Williams contacted Elisabeth Sladen to see if she was ready to return to the role of Sarah Jane Smith. She was still hesitant. He then decided to go to the opposite extreme from the "savage" and introduce an "ice maiden", ideally a Hitchcock blonde, which may be where the idea originated that the Minyan named Tala from "Underworld" (15.5) was to join the TARDIS crew. He auditioned over two-hundred possible Romanas, including Belinda Sinclair (see 24.3, "Delta and the Bannermen").

Rising star Mary Tamm got the part, to her surprise; she'd been at drama school with Louise Jameson, and had thus changed her mind about *Doctor Who* being a career-killer. In another three-page document, Williams suggested that the Doctor's moral compass had gone a little askew after his recent experiences, and that he always believed himself to be infallibly right. Romana was to be his conscience. The document also states that, as she's now around 140, Romana could be due for a regeneration (but see 16.6, "The Armageddon Factor").

• The guest cast features a few interesting names. Iain Cuthbertson (Garron) was a familiar face after two radically different star vehicles. As Charlie Endell, first in Budgie and then (imaginatively) *Charles Endell Esq*, he'd played a cockney con-man and failed pimp. Then, in *Sutherland's Law*, he'd returned to his native Scotland to play an investigator for the Procurator Fiscal's office (sort of a highland DA). Garron required him to adopt both personae.

Nigel Plaskett, playing Unstoffe, was best known as a voice-artist for iconic puppet Hartley Hare in *Pipkins*; as "Malcolm" in the now almost-legendary ads for Vick's Sinex Nasal Spray ('...'course you can, Malcolm,' spoken as one word, was one of the great playground catch-phrases of the epoch); and later as one of the puppeteers on *Spitting Image*. Paul Seed, the Graff Vynda K, is best known now as a director of many prestigious BBC dramas.

• Romana's dress here, like many this year, is based on the colour-scheme suggested by Mary Tamm's astrologer. The fabric was heavy and sagged, causing delays in shooting as it had to be sprinkled with cold water to make it contract again. (One American convention saw people buying T-shirts with the slogan "Romana 1 - she dresses like a Ho!", and it's hard to argue with this.)

• German scholars will note that "Schlange" means 'snake' (the New Adventures have the mercenaries as reptiles) and "Unstoffe" means "naïve", or - more aptly - "unworldly". And "Graf" means "Count", but you knew that.

• Contrary to popular belief, the costumes were all made specifically for this story. Some of the sets, notably the relic chamber, were redressed from a big-budget adaptation of *Anna Karenina*. Keep an eye out for the crown and coronation robe, as we'll be seeing them again soon (16.4, "The Androids of Tara").

• During the break after Season Fifteen, Tom Baker had made a short film with his friend and occasional rival Eric Morecambe[4]. A pseudo-mediaeval romp entitled *The Passionate Pilgrim*, it featured Baker as Sir Tom and Morecambe as the minstrel / narrator. It wasn't very good, but anyone who grew up on *Morecambe and Wise* will note how much Baker's Doctor is starting to become like Morecambe in this era.

• Meanwhile, ITV's annoyance at the BBC's ratings - especially on Saturdays (see **September or January?** under 13.1, "Terror of the Zygons") - resulted in a big-budget "poaching" of BBC stars and formats. *Generation Game* star Bruce Forsythe hosted a themed evening series, *Brucie's Big Night Out*, opposite both *Doctor Who* and the programme he'd left behind. The publicity started at around this time, but broadcasts of *Big Night Out* began during "The Pirate Planet" (16.2). This explains both the dip in episode two's ratings, and the rise again as the public avoided ITV more resolutely than ever. The instigator of ITV's scheme, Michael Grade, never forgot this stain on his reputation as TV's "miracle worker" (see 22.4, "The Two Doctors", and indeed much of Volume VI...).

16.2: "The Pirate Planet"

(Serial 5B, Four Episodes, 30th September - 21st October 1978.)

Which One is This? Captain Hook becomes a cyborg on a far-off world that's suspiciously run from a "bridge". The kids are distracted by K9 taking on the Captain's robot parrot, but the grown-ups (and the Doctor) are more worried about a planet that's gone missing in the vicinity...

Firsts and Lasts Douglas Adams, the most famous writer *Doctor Who* has ever had by some considerable distance, pens the first of his two-and-a-half scripts for the series (although only one-and-a-half of them will ever be made).

Four Things to Notice About "The Pirate Planet"...

1. For those who haven't seen this story, the title might need an explanation as this isn't about a planet full of pirates. (Although its ruler does a fairly good Captain Hook impression, has circuitry down one half of his body instead of the more traditional wooden leg and owns a flying robot called a 'polyphase avatron' that likes to perch on his shoulder.) This is about a planet which functions like a pirate ship, warping around the universe and plundering other planets. Considering that it was written by Douglas Adams, long-term associate of the *Monty Python* cabal, the similarity to Terry Gilliam's Crimson Permanent Assurance featurette (the one about the pirate office-block) is striking. But this is bigger. And came first.

2. Those wishing to look for similarities between Adams' *Doctor Who* work and *The Hitch-Hiker's Guide to the Galaxy* will probably be fasci-

nated by the familiar-sounding lines and concepts on offer here. The hollow planet is more than a little suggestive of the Magrathea factory floor, although in *Hitch-Hiker's* the planets "inside" Magrathea turned out to exist in a different dimension. (You almost get the feeling that Adams, liking the idea of a planet being inside another planet, wanted a chance to do it properly without any of that - as it were - tedious mucking-about in hyperspace.) The scene in "The Pirate Planet" about the bad guys 'standing around looking tough' was written at roughly the same time as the perilously similar *Hitch-Hiker's* scene with the Vogon guard, while the idea of a ruler who's been dying for several decades comes up again in the second radio series. And it goes without saying that as ever in Adams' scripts, there's a love of stupidly-named technical equipment, as well as names with "oo" in them. More explicitly, the Doctor has to deliver the near-meaningless line: 'I'll never be cruel to an electron in a particle accelerator again.'

3. One of the best lines, though, suggests a theme that Adams would come back to over and over again throughout his career (even in his next solo script for the series, 17.6, "Shada"). The Doctor, facing the Captain of Zanak, points out a flaw in the logic of every SF megalomaniac: 'You don't want to take over the universe, do you? No, you wouldn't know what to do with it. Beyond shout at it.'

4. It's not all wit and wisdom, sadly. The supporting cast is occasionally two-dimensional, with an awful lot of people swearing vengeance against other people. Most *unintentionally* funny moment comes when the young and almost dashing Kimus, who's never even heard of the existence of other planets before now, picks up a lump of rock from one of Zanak's victim-worlds and hisses: 'Bandraginus 5; by every last breath in my body, you'll be avenged!' David Warwick is now a familiar face on television, especially in ads, and this line has dogged him throughout his career (see 19.3, "Kinda").

The Continuity

The Doctor Still doesn't know better than to say 'not now' when one of his companions tries to tell him something urgent. He knows how to put 1.795372 and 2.204628 together to make four, so he's good with sums.

• *Inventory.* Romana nicks the jelly-babies from the Doctor's pocket, but he gets them back soon enough, and he has at least one bag of liquorice all-sorts as well. He carries a large double-headed coin [not the same one used in 10.1, "The Three Doctors", as it's much too big] with the head of one of the two kings of Aldebaran 3 on each side. His bent hairpin is often better at opening highly-sophisticated locks than the sonic screwdriver. He's still got his brass telescope [15.4, "The Sun Makers"], but Romana borrows it and it gets confiscated on Zanak. [Yet it turns up again in 18.4, "State of Decay"...]

• *Background.* According to Romana, the Doctor has been using this TARDIS for 523 years. [He didn't "borrow" this TARDIS that long ago, as he was still at the Academy 450 years ago according to "The Armageddon Factor" (16.6). This might refer to the length of time that the Doctor has been trained to use TT capsules, and if so then he might have learned the basics in this Ship. So it may have been officially allocated to him even if it wasn't technically his. He's currently 759, which means he started using this capsule in his 230s, yet Romana's less than 140 and quite proficient with the controls. Was the Doctor a slow starter?]

The Doctor claims that he tried to give his friend Isaac Newton the idea for gravity by sitting in a tree and dropping an apple on the man's head, but Isaac just told him to clear off and the Doctor had to explain the theory afterwards at dinner. [He may not be telling the whole truth here.] He knows Calufrax to be a horrible place, suggesting a prior visit, and recognises the name "Mentiads" though he never explains where from.

The Supporting Cast

• *Romana.* The Doctor bids her a 'good morrow' on entering the console room, to which she replies 'good morning', suggesting that she at least actually sleeps on the Ship. She's already started raiding the TARDIS wardrobe.

Though she's got a good overall understanding of time-travel capsules (she doesn't use the word "TARDIS" yet), she states that the study of veteran and vintage vehicles was an optional extra on the Academy's syllabus, and that she chose to study the life-cycle of the Gallifreyan flutterwing instead [she seems to know a lot about Earth's insect-life too, as we'll see later]. She says she got an air-car for her seventieth birthday, and states that you get twice the speed for half the energy if you re-align the magnetic vectors and fit a polarity oscillator. [This is presented as if she were a teenager getting her first car from rich parents, though exactly who gave her the air-car isn't stated. And where did she fly it, if Gallifreyans never go outside the Citadel…?]

Despite her inexperience in a hostile universe, she's not flustered by men with guns. And for someone who's apparently never been in any kind of dangerous situation until recently, she's a remarkably good shot with an unfamiliar blaster. [Did daddy take her hunting as well as buying her a car?] She recognises Zanak's macromat field integrator as being part of a massive dematerialisation circuit, so they may have such things on Gallifrey.

• *K9.* Even more irritating, predictable and over-literal than ever, though he's at least capable of humouring the Doctor, which might explain why he's now officially the Doctor's 'best friend'. Something about the landing on Zanak, possibly the psychic wavelengths of the Mentiads, makes K9 spin round and round like a mad thing. He can certainly analyse psychic wavelengths, describing the Mentiads' gestalt-generated psychokinetic blast as having 'a wavelength of 338.79 micropars, with ochre interference patterns reaching a peak power level of 5347.2 on the vantalla cycle scale'. He can also track Mentiads by their psychic spoor, as that level of psychokinetic energy leaves considerable disturbance in the 'aether'. He recharges from a power cable on Zanak, and diverts some of the current into his frequency projectors to set up a counter-interference pattern on the 'psychic plane' which can cancel the effects of the Captain's psychic interference transmitter. He can even sense that the 'good vibrations' that the Mentiads use to knock out the Doctor contain no malice.

K9's weapon is now capable of stunning guards 'indefinitely'. [The Doctor doesn't cure these guards before he leaves, so are they comatose forever?] He can pilot an air-car by extending his "eye" into the controls, and detect the Doctor's distinctive heartbeats when the Doctor's about thirty seconds' walking-distance away. He brings the Doctor the "dead" polyphase avitron on the end of his snout [it's magnetic]. His language gets scrambled when his batteries are running down.

The TARDIS It's now revealed to have a handbook, a big, weighty tome that the Doctor never uses, and Romana insists on looking through it. [Given the TARDIS' complexity, even *this* seems remarkably small for a user's manual. Maybe it's

just the "idiot's guide". It looks hand-written.]

Having read the manual, Romana states that setting the synchronic feedback-checking circuit and activating the multi-loop stabiliser are essential for a smooth landing, but the Doctor doesn't bother with them. On this occasion the result is a landing which isn't smooth at all, although it's more to do with the fact that Zanak is materialising around Calufrax at the time. According to the warp oscilloscope on Zanak, the space-time continuum is ripped apart for ten seconds as the TARDIS arrives, which dilates gravity and forces the whole structure of quantum theory into retreat. Romana confirms that when the TARDIS moves it dematerialises, passes through a space-time vortex and then re-materialises elsewhere.

Zanak's warp oscilloscope and gravity dilation meter can be monitored from the TARDIS console room, and TARDIS co-ordinates for Earth are given as 58044684884. [Compare with the vastly less complex planetary co-ordinates in 16.1, "The Ribos Operation". The Captain uses the same co-ordinates, so maybe these are the co-ordinates as Zanak sees them, not normal TARDIS settings.] When the Doctor tries to set the co-ordinates for Earth to stop Zanak materialising there, he says it's the most dangerous manoeuvre the Ship has every attempted, as the disturbance when the two attempt to materialise in the same space-time will keep getting worse until one or the other explodes [compare with the time-ram mentioned in 9.5, "The Time Monster", although here neither TARDIS nor Zanak fully dematerialise]. The TARDIS has a force-field operative while it's in flight, and the Doctor drops it so that he can communicate telepathically with the Mentiads outside the Ship [see 10.1, "The Three Doctors" and 17.5, "The Horns of Nimon"]. Romana believes this to be incredibly dangerous, as the force-field is the only thing protecting the TARDIS.

The Doctor tells the Captain of Zanak that the TARDIS lock can't be opened unless both himself and Romana are present. [This is an obvious and enormous lie.] The hole in the console where the Key tracer fits seems to have moved, not the only time this happens.

The Guardians and the Key
• *The Key to Time.* The second segment is disguised as the entire planet Calufrax, a cold, wet, icy, lifeless oblate spheroid 14,000 kilometres across. Calufrax was rich in oolion and madranite

Cliffhangers: What Are the High and Low Points?

Ah, video has robbed us of so much. As we've already intimated, the decision to feature a **Cliffhangers** section in this book might appear odd to younger readers, but there was a time when the episode endings were key to our memories of the programme. With episodes being shown a week apart, you *needed* a strong twist every twenty-two-to-twenty-five minutes. In this regard the narrative conventions of *Doctor Who* are midway between Charles Dickens and *Flash Gordon* (actually, that holds true for the programme as a whole). Sometimes the cliffhanger simply put one of our heroes in peril, and sometimes it involved a character discovering something that we knew long before, especially if the script was by Terry Nation and had "Dalek" in the title. But occasionally they were arranged so that our suspicions and guesses were shown to be way off-beam, either in the final shot or line, or in the resolution of an "impossible" situation. And of course, sometimes they were just fantastic visual spectacles.

Here are some of the best…

"Marco Polo" (1.4), episode one. An odd one to start with, as the dramatic turn has already happened. The Doctor has gained the protection and co-operation of Marco Polo, to get himself and his companions from the mountains to comparative safety in Mongolia, but only on condition that the TARDIS is confiscated and made a gift to Mighty Kublai Khan. The Doctor is merrily chuckling as he tells his chums this, but when asked what their next move should be he reveals that he's got no idea; the all-powerful Doctor is laughing out of *hysteria*…

"Tomb of the Cybermen" (5.1), episode two. The other two cliffhangers really don't cut it (keep reading), but here we discover that the entire tomb is a trap to gain recruits; that the Cybermen aren't dead but resting, waiting for humans to take the bait; and that the logician Klieg is a willing participant of the Telosians' evil schemes. Added to this, one of the best-paced build-ups in the programme's history gives us no hope that the cavalry will come. Everyone's shut in, on their own and heavily outnumbered, and it's not their lives at stake but their bodies and souls, given the nature of the Cyber-conversion process. And at last we meet the "daddy" Cyberman, who towers over even the other "silver giants". In a word: eek!

"The Leisure Hive" (18.1), episode two. Love him or hate him, you've got to admit… by 1980, Tom Baker's Doctor had become a smartarse. A whole generation had grown up watching him face off against easily-dispatched villains without so much as chipping a nail. Nothing ever seemed to phase him, he knew all the answers, and he hadn't been afraid of anything since the Philip Hinchcliffe days.

And then, suddenly - just as we were getting over the disorientation of the new-look series - he came out of the tachyon regeneration chamber on Argolis… and he was *old*. Not just a *bit* old, mind you, but so visibly ancient that he looked as if he might snuff it at any moment. Now, even the cliffhanger to episode one startled us (the Doctor apparently gets his arms and legs pulled off, and he actually *screams*), but that was over in a flash and the effects made the whole thing a bit suspect. Episode two was something else. For those too young to remember "Planet of the Spiders", this was the first time the Doctor had been made fragile. Violable. Something tangibly *other* than his usual self. The rules had changed overnight, and it was far more unsettling than a whole army of Cybermen.

"The Daleks" (1.2), episode one. Barbara is shut off from the others in a city that's like a giant steel maze. We know, but she doesn't, that the radiation levels are dangerous. We know, but she doesn't, that something has survived and is in the city with her. She wanders into a corridor, and the exit is blocked. The "something" comes towards her. We can't see it, because we're looking at her terrified face from its point of view, and it has something resembling a sink-plunger - not a hand, not a claw, not a tentacle, but something wholly inexplicable - pointing right at her. It closes in on her… and that's why, forty-one years later, this book exists.

continued on page 231…

one-five, the refined crystals of which can generate vibrations to neutralise the Mentiads' mental power; see **Planet Notes**. Zanak has reduced Calufrax to the size of a football. The Doctor makes sure it's hurled into the vortex when Zanak is saved, planning to pick it up later. Its variable atomic weight is apparently a property of its nature as part of the Key.

Planet Notes

• *Zanak.* Zanak was a happy, prosperous place until the reign of Queen Xanxia, who lived for hundreds of years and staged galactic wars to demonstrate her 'strange powers'. Warfare had ruined Zanak by the time the Captain arrived, and there were hardly any people left, just a few nomadic tribes [which might explain why there only seems to be one city here].

The Captain crash-landed in the *Vantarialis* - a great silver raiding cruiser that he built himself - and as one of the few survivors he had his body re-constructed with cybernetic parts, which means that even now Xanxia can control bits of his body by remote control. He was one of the great hyper-engineers of his time, and was responsible for re-structuring Zanak, salvaging major components from his own ship. This history isn't well-known on Zanak, as most people have never even seen the Captain, though the Mentiads know many of the details. The Captain soon persuaded the natives to work for him with his 'golden ages of prosperity'.

Now Zanak is a pirate planet, a world equipped with enormous transmat engines so that it can warp across the universe at will. The planet is hollow, materialising around slightly smaller victim-worlds, crushing them and mining out the valuable minerals. This means there are precious stones lying around in the streets, from diamonds and Andromedan bloodstones to voolium. Past victims of Zanak include Granados, Lowitelon and Bandraginus 5, and Earth is its next target as it's rich in the 'rare' mineral quartz, or 'PJX18' as the Captain calls it [the Doctor recognises the term, so it's standard terminology].

Oolion, galdrium, voolium, vasilium and acetenite 455 are among the minerals taken during the raiding operations, but how Zanak finds new mineral sources isn't revealed. Much of the equipment that created the transmat engines came from the Captain's ship, as there are said to be four elements in the system which the Captain's men can't replace themselves, and one of these is the macromat field integrator… though quartz can be used if the integrator isn't working. The Doctor indicates that Zanak and all its victim-worlds are (or were) in the same galaxy, and the Captain knows of Earth, describing it as 'pretty'.

Zanak is controlled from the Bridge, a great metal tower built into the side of a mountain, while the planet's engine-room is an enormous chamber within the mountain which looks a lot like a gasworks. Officially the ruler of this world, even though the population never sees him, the Captain is a loud, sadistic bully but more intelligent than he appears. His "pet", the polyphase avitron, is a flying parrot-sized robot with a lethal energy weapon. K9 eventually shoots it down.

A nurse also attends the Captain, although in fact she's a projection of Zanak's real ruler, the tyrannical Queen Xanxia. Xanxia has been drawing out the last few seconds of her life for years, her emaciated body surrounded with time-dams that slow down the flow of time. This web of technology somehow allows her psyche to control the projection of the nurse. Zanak's victim-worlds are being drained partly to meet the massive energy requirements of the dams, and partly to give her new body corporeal form, so it's already reached the stage where it can't be turned off. This is done through a process of cell-projection, using the original body's cells to effect a full regeneration and give the new body all the original's memories. But the energy needs of the dams increase exponentially, so the Doctor believes there isn't enough power in the universe to keep Xanxia alive.

The Doctor has no trouble jury-rigging a similar, box-like piece of technology to create a holographic duplicate of himself, so good that it interacts seamlessly with its environment and is able to hold solid objects. [He doesn't have enough time to program it with a complete set of responses, so he *must* be steering his image telepathically.] Even so, the nurse-body disintegrates when shot.

There's very little sense of what Zanak society is like, but there's apparently only one city with plenty of woodland outside it. The dwellings seen in the vicinity of the Bridge are organic-looking and carved out of stone. The cheerily unquestioning people don't realise that Zanak keeps moving, although they've noticed that gems turn up on the streets every time there are 'omens', the lights in the sky which make the stars change. Not that they know what stars are. They're certainly much happier under the Captain's rule than they were under Xanxia, though the planet is policed by guards in black studded uniforms who drive air-cars and carry nasty-looking energy weapons. Telescopes, strangers and the question 'why?' are forbidden. Other technology seen here includes what the Doctor believes to be a linear induction corridor, but which turns out to be a passage that works by neutralising inertia; this basically makes

Cliffhangers: What Are the High and Low Points?

...continued from page 229

"Remembrance of the Daleks" (25.1), episode one. Trapped in a cellar with a Dalek, the Doctor and Ace run up the stairs. Ace gets out, but a Dalek agent knocks her unconscious. The door is bolted, and the Dalek - scanning the Doctor through a thermal imaging lens - *glides up the stairs after him*. Apart from the palpable terror, the look on his face says exactly what the viewers are thinking: "can they *do* that?"

"Earthshock" (18.6), episode one. So far it's been creepy thrills in the dark, with killer androids in caves turning people into smouldering slime one by one. Then, abruptly, we pull back from the android's POV to a scanner that's relaying everything it sees... and watching it is a Cyberleader. The Cybermen's return was one of two things about this story that the programme-makers went to great lengths to keep secret, and the "buzz" the next morning was amazing. And eight days later, the grins of certain cynical people grew even broader...

"The Massacre" (3.5), episode three. The Doctor lies dead in a Paris street, and a lynch-mob thinks that Steven killed him. Given what had already happened in the previous year, almost any change seemed possible.

"Vengeance on Varos" (22.2), episode one. The end of the first act of "Vengeance on Varos" sees the Doctor trapped inside the hallucinogenic hell of Varos' TV studio, believing himself to be in a desert and collapsing from thirst and exhaustion. That's not the cliffhanger. What happens next is that we pull back to the studio's control booth, where the image of the Doctor's dying body can be seen on the monitor-screens; the director's voice says 'and... cut'; and the screens go blank. *That's* the cliffhanger. So far we've been contemptuous of the "ordinary" characters watching prisoners suffer for their amusement, and then suddenly that means *us*.

"An Unearthly Child" (1.1), episode one. Seminal, obviously. The two schoolteachers are unconscious, having been abducted and subjected to some inconceivable process by a strange old man called the Doctor. The police box, incongruous enough inside a junkyard, is now standing lopsidedly in the middle of a bleak wilderness. A shadow looms across the bottom-right of the screen...

"The Pirate Planet" (16.2), episode three. The Pirate Captain forces the Doctor to walk the plank. He does so, and we hear his yell as he falls a kilometre onto rocks. What makes this great isn't just the "inescapable" nature of the Doctor's peril, but that the resolution makes us re-evaluate everything we thought we knew about this story and this planet.

"The Deadly Assassin" (14.3), episode two. Likewise. In a disturbing nightmare-scape, the Doctor gets his foot caught in a railway-line as an engine bears down on him with a sinister mask-faced man at the controls. You just try being five years old and *not* worried by that. Come to think of it, try being *over* five and not worried by the implications of it.

continued on page 233...

its users whizz down it very fast. They know what leeches are on this planet.

Whenever Zanak crushes a planet, some of that planet's energy is released on psychic wavelengths. Those on Zanak who are inclined towards psychic ability fall into a fever, but their mental powers are boosted as this psychic energy smashes open the neural pathways. The Doctor also refers to these people as absorbing the 'life-force' of the planets [possibly related to the life-force described in 15.3, "Image of the Fendahl", but pitched differently]. An underground organisation of telepaths now exists, dressing in yellow robes and known as the Mentiads, and as a telepathic gestalt they always come to take new psychics into their underworld lair. They can create hologram-like images of far-off events through a ritual they call the 'Vigil of Evil', and are troubled by visions they don't understand which come from the worlds that Zanak consumes.

A psychokinetic blast from the Mentiads can kill or knock victims unconscious at close range, or even cause rockfalls or open doors. When gathered together, they're energy-weapon-proof. They can also generate a force-wall, which lasts for some time after they leave, and can read the Doctor's mind at long-range when he wants them to. Romana describes these powers as 'paranormal'. The Captain encourages the belief that Mentiads are evil zombies, while the Mentiads want vengeance for Zanak's crimes [so they may pick up the memories of Zanak's victims as well as the psychic power].

Zanak's mines lead to the interior of the planet, where a visitor can quite happily walk across the surface of a "consumed" world three miles below ground level before the automated process removes all the valuable elements. The remains of the victim-worlds are kept in a trophy room by the Captain, shrunk down to super-compressed football-size, but not collapsing into black holes thanks to a feat of gravitational geometry whereby 'every system is balanced out within itself'. Even the Doctor's impressed, in a horrible sort of way, but the Captain's planning on using this power to create a standing vortex within Xanxia's time-dams and destroy her. The name-tags in the trophy room would appear to be in English. At the end of the affair, the Doctor rigs things so that the masses of the shrunken planets fill the centre of the hollow Zanak [but see **Things That Don't Make Sense**].

Expressions used by the Captain: 'By all the x-ray storms of Viga!'; 'by all the flaming moons of Herides'; 'by the bursting sons of Banzar'. These may or may not be real places.

• *Bandraginus V.* One of only two worlds where oolion, one of the most precious minerals in the universe, is found. Or at least it was, before Zanak destroyed it. According to the Doctor it was inhabited by 1,000,000,000 people.

• *Qualactin.* Now the *only* world where oolion is found [also mentioned in the script of 17.6, "Shada"].

• *Aterica, Bibicorpus, Granados, Temesis, Lowiteliom, Tridentia III:* Former victim-worlds of Zanak, all of which now form part of the Captain's cosmic Ker-Plunk set.

History

• *Dating.* No date given. [As this story mentions Earth but never shows it, the assumption's often made that it's set in the present day, i.e. 1978. The novel *First Frontier* confirms this in passing, but... the next story, "The Stones of Blood", is set on contemporary Earth. And it seems odd that two segments of the Key to Time should be located in the same time-zone, when the Key was supposed to have been 'scattered'. Still, the third segment has apparently been

around for a long time, so maybe 1978 is just a good time to pick these two segments up. For whatever reason.]

Bandraginus V vanished about a hundred years ago, according to the Doctor. However, Zanak only became a pirate planet after the "death" of Queen Xanxia, and an older native remembers her being in charge when he was young. [This means that either the people of Zanak have greater-than-human lifespans - which is unlikely, as Xanxia's ability to live for centuries is described as being unnatural - or the Doctor's rounding up horribly and it's more like fifty years.]

The Analysis

Where Does This Come From? This began as two separate story proposals from Adams (see **The Lore**), and one was about immortality-peddlers. The scheme was perhaps a little too similar to the antics of Garron and Unstoffe in "The Ribos Operation", but had a very '70s twist. The con-men would target people scared of dying, and offer them a means to slow down time, which the story analogised to drug addiction. The only way to pay off the increasing demands of the peddlers was to find two new recruits for them. It was, in the terms they used then, "Pyramid Selling". Stories about such schemes, and the chain-letter hoaxes often used by the same outfits, were doing the rounds of current affairs television as the government tried to find a way to ban this sort of thing without making church raffles illegal as a side-effect.

With many TV action series using drugs as an excuse to have thuggish heroes beating people up (as in, for example, *Target*; see 17.4, "Nightmare of Eden"), Adams was intrigued by the idea of drug abuse as a moral problem, a dilemma connecting to free will, capitalism and victimisation. In its finished form, however, the problem for the Doctor is that the majority of people on Zanak are happy and well-fed. So by what right does he wreck their society? This was more than an abstract problem in economically-stable, crime-free East Berlin, a city which Adams had already visited...

Things That Don't Make Sense There's a lot of general sloppiness going on here. The gunfight in episode two sees Kimus (who has, as far as we know, never even held a gun before) take down three trained guards before they can hit him once,

Cliffhangers: What Are the High and Low Points?

...continued from page 231

"The Caves of Androzani" (21.6), episode three. Everyone likes to go on about how good Graeme Harper's camera-angles were, but what's *truly* great about his direction of "Androzani" is that he understands the dynamic behind it all. This whole story is a descent into desperation, a plot which begins as if it were a stroll on a nondescript quarry-world and ends with the Doctor tearing his own body apart to save his companion while the planet blows itself to pieces around him.

The last cliffhanger, with the Doctor forcing a hijacked ship into a crash-dive as the engines start screaming and Stotz threatens to shoot him in the head, makes you feel as if the whole programme's caught up in the planet's gravity and that you're being dragged towards the bloody conclusion along with everyone else. In itself, the Doctor's dialogue gets across the acute sense of hysteria, serving the triple function of setting up the cliffhanger *and* changing the pace of the story *and* laying down the rules for this particular "death" (with the Doctor, almost uniquely, acknowledging that he's probably doomed).

"The Face of Evil" (14.4), episode three. The Doctor is physically inside the mind of a mad, godlike computer. For the "crime" of contradicting Xoanon's view about its own nature, the Doctor's role in its creation and what's real or imagined, the machine psychically assaults him. Part of Xoanon believes itself to *be* the Doctor, part wants him dead. Images of the Doctor's face, also that of the monster which Xoanon has created from psychic force, fill the screens. First they proclaim 'go away, I shall think you no more'. Then, as the Doctor resists, a child's voice from the screen-faces cries out: '*Who am I?*'

And now, to underline the point, here are some of the most inept…

"The Claws of Axos" (8.3), episode two. The Doctor and Jo are chased around a wobbly gantry by a beige duvet as the cyclotron exudes bubbles. As the frankly flatulent music goes from "melodramatic" to "overheated", like a silent-movie pianist trying to do it on a kazoo, three lumps of spaghetti bolognese bar the doorway. The Doctor takes this as final proof of his theory, but can't *quite* get the words out properly.

"The Underwater Menace" (4.5), episode three. Most villains have to spend whole episodes practising their ranting before they reach the same point where Joseph Furst, as Professor Zaroff, begins in episode one. By the end of episode three he's over the top, down the other side and in the next street. His tirade to the High Priest of Atlantis conveys more different emotions in one line than Matthew Waterhouse managed in a career; jubilation, anger, bemusement, contempt… and that's just in the words, 'you demand?'. Then - maladroitly pulling a revolver from within his cloak - he orders 'guards, kill those two men!', a line that should by its very nature be impossible to overplay. He manages it anyway, and then for the *coup de grace* exclaims (as a camera wobbles towards him): 'Nozzink in ze world can stop me now!!!' We haven't really got a font grandiose enough for this, but basically every syllable demands an exclamation mark.

"Tomb of the Cybermen" (5.1), episode one. A generation of us heard how great this story was from older relatives and, later, older fans. When the novelisation came out, the first act climax was sensational. Victoria in a sarcophagus, being electrocuted; Jamie and Hayden being hypnotised; the Doctor warning Klieg not to decode the controls, then doing it himself; and then, a Cyberman comes to life and shoots! Alas, this isn't what we get on-screen. Not only is the sequence of events different, so that each problem gets resolved before the next one starts, but the dummy Cyberman is obviously a scarecrow. The third cliffhanger isn't much better, and for slapstick timing and comedy "whoosh!" gun-sounds is actually worse, but this really was an enormous let-down. In both cases, the episode stops a good ninety seconds after the point where the natural climax occurs.

"The Mysterious Planet" (23.1), episode one. The Doctor is stoned to death by boy scouts. We know, as this is all done in flashback, that he's perfectly safe. Back in the "present", the prosecution lawyer - the mysterious Valeyard - now demands that the Doctor's trial be one for his life, which we knew from the start of the episode. Any goodwill the "revamped" series may have created in the first few minutes has long since left town.

continued on page 235…

even though they've got the drop on him and are firing from at least two broadly different angles. Mula's line about the Mentiads knocking out the Doctor with 'good vibrations' is as out-of-character as it is unfunny. K9's duel with the polyphase avatron is almost as silly-looking as the dog's "heroic" face-off with the Ogri in the next story, but worse, everyone just stands around watching K9 roll into the middle of the room and the guards don't even train their weapons on him.

The Doctor sounds amazed by the revelation that the Mentiads form a telepathic gestalt in episode three, even though K9 told him as much at the start of episode two, and when he tries to steal an air-car (for the *second* time) he goes through the risky procedure of distracting a guard with liquorice allsorts instead of just waiting for K9 to stun the man. The Mentiads pick up on the Doctor's existence when he arrives, and immediately realise he's important, but then fail to take him back to their HQ when he's unconscious and come back for him an episode later instead.

The Doctor's assessment that Zanak has plenty of mineral wealth for its "freed" citizens seems optimistic, considering that the Captain burned up all the useful minerals from the victim-worlds before shrinking them. Won't this just be a planet full of dross? Similarly, Zanak now occupies the orbit of a frozen world, Calufrax. So presumably next year's harvest is going to be a dud.

Reasons not to use technobabble in *Doctor Who*, number sixteen: the cast can never get it right. Observe this exchange from episode two. K9: 'Ochre interference patterns reaching a peak power level of 5347.2 on the vantalla cycle scale.' The Doctor: '543.72?' K9: 'Affirmative, master.' Similarly, in episode four the psychic wavelength of the Mentiads changes from 338.79 micropars to 337.98 micropars in the mouth of Tom Baker.

Critique (Prosecution) The problem, if you *see* it as a problem, is this: Douglas Adams isn't a science fiction writer. He likes *science*, certainly. He likes playing with quantum theory and particle accelerators (or rather, the idea that there *are* such things as particle accelerators in the world), and it goes without saying that he's happy as a lamb when he's writing comedy. But science fiction… the joys of exploration, of building worlds out of concepts instead of treating those concepts as fetishes in their own right, was never for him.

This is why "The Pirate Planet" is, depending on your point of view, either an intriguing little bundle of whimsical SF notions or a very awkward, very badly-structured piece of television. Traditionally *Doctor Who* has always been serious about what it does, but not necessarily about the way that it does it; this is the exact reverse. What's notable isn't that it treats the series' conventions with a sense of self-parody, it's that it expects the audience to think this sort of thing is perfectly *normal*, as if the episodes of the past - far from being mind-expanding little pieces of pop-culture - were rather silly and something to be apologised for. The assumption here is that the university graduates will spot the cleverness of the physics-bending ideas, and that the mainstream audience will be kept entertained by Tom Baker and Bruce Purchase posturing at each other. And these assumptions are quite correct, but fail to take into account all the people in the middle, the ones who watch *Doctor Who* because it's sparkly and exciting and occasionally scary-looking. Zanak isn't a strange new place for us to explore, it's a stage for the conceits that the writer and script editor find so fascinating.

This is a set-up so monumentally shallow that as the Doctor arrives, he finds out what's happening on the planet when a passer-by happily strolls past the TARDIS, tells him everything he needs to know and then walks off again. Witty and "knowing", or just lazy and irritating? You decide, but bear in mind the way that both the series and TV in general had changed over the previous decade. When Robert Holmes used wilfully-stupid SF names in "Carnival of Monsters" (10.2), he did it to make a specific comic point. When Douglas Adams calls the planet "Zanak" and its ruler "Xanxia", he's doing it because he assumes that it just doesn't matter. We're not supposed to believe in any of this, we're supposed to think it's clever.

And much of it is. The ideas are all here. There are, undeniably, good bits. In himself, the Captain of Zanak is an endearingly over-the-top villain, especially since (almost uniquely, in this era) the Doctor takes the time to actually look *troubled* by his villainy. Yet the story is a showcase for these things, not a narrative in itself. Earth is irrelevant to the story, but mentioned as the next victim of the Pirate Planet in a last-ditch attempt to get viewers to have a stake in what's happening, since it's impossible to care about the "liberation" of the happy, well-fed people of Zanak.

Let's not forget, Adams had never written a full-

Cliffhangers: What Are the High and Low Points?

...continued from page 237

"Death to the Daleks" (11.3), episode three. The Doctor heroically saves his local ally, Bellal, from a shower-mat in the middle of a corridor.

"The King's Demons" (20.6), episode one. The broadsword fight is historically accurate, but it's also rather un-telegenic. (BBC2 was showing chess matches around this time, and one of those would have been more pulse-thumpingly exciting. Certainly with better accents.) At the end of the slow-motion swashbuckling, "Sir Gilles" reveals his true identity. At this stage in the Saward / Nathan-Turner partnership anyone *other* than the Master would have been a nice surprise. Now the only shock is that he's hit a new low in pointless, over-complicated moustache-twirling villainy.

"The Abominable Snowmen" (5.2), episode one. 'Eh-Oh, Tinky-Winky.'

"Frontier In Space" (10.3), episode four. The Doctor and Jo are perfectly safe, going to meet the Draconian Emperor at last, with the Master locked up and acting chummy. Then, from his jacket, the villain produces a bleeper-box way too big to have been comfortably secreted in such tight clothing. We cut to a slow, dramatic pan of the Ogron spaceship as it receives his signal, and... Oh! My! God!... there's an Ogron on board, sitting in a chair with his back to us.

• The all-time classic, however, is episode one of the story which immediately follows this. The Doctor encounters the Daleks on the Ogron planet. He asks the Time Lords to send the TARDIS after their ship. Once there he's found by Thals from Skaro, home of the Daleks, who've dared to travel into space to confront... "them". Ten minutes of circumlocutions later, one of "them" arrives, rendered invisible. It leaves an oval dent in the ground, like a Dalek. But the Thals have 'liquid colour sprays' (aerosols to you), which they use to tag their handles on something which turns out to be... a Dalek! Cue theme music and credits. The story, in case any viewers had missed the previous episode and all the press build-up and competitions in the *Radio Times*, was called "Planet of the Daleks".

---

length story before this; his scripts for *The Hitch-Hiker's Guide to the Galaxy* didn't really have plots and weren't supposed to. *Doctor Who* just isn't the same kind of animal. The guards are sheer parody, but that's apparently okay because we're meant to be in on the joke. The design is generally appalling, but that's apparently okay because it's not "serious" anyway. The world we're shown here is chillingly similar in style to the one we saw in 11.5, "Planet of the Spiders", but that's apparently okay because... well, this time everyone's meant to *know* that it's not real (and the clash between location and studio filming has never been greater). The ending, which brings things to a conclusion by shooting the villain, blowing up the building and then having the Doctor do 'something terribly clever' with pseudoscientific technology, tells you everything.

Critique (Defence) As we've seen in **Where Does This Come From?**, the concepts and issues being discussed here are in deadly earnest. We're used to rebel couples helping the Doctor to overthrow a corrupt government, but here we have Balaton, representing the older generation as the Mentiad Pralix's grandfather, putting forward the quite understandable view that if everyone keeps quiet then they'll all live. It's a parent's (or grandparent's) point-of-view, and just because events prove him wrong that doesn't make it invalid. The thing is, it was never stated before. Even "Planet of the Spiders" had Sabor siding with his boys and Neska more worried about being left alone than reprisals. Kimus is the bog-standard Pertwee-style male lead, but he's misguided about how his world works (in fact Mula, who would have been merely decorative in an earlier story, is a better revolutionary than he is).

Unfortunately, the set-designers have decided it's a "comedy" story and have gone to town. So while the costumes are fine, especially the extremely sinister guards, it's all a bit relentlessly "wacky". Add to this Bruce Purchase's misreading of the Captain as being exactly what he seems (the script called for an older, more worn-out, man) and it's possible to argue that not everybody would get the point.

Except that the entire thrust of the plot is towards making us rethink what we think we know. The resolution to the cliffhanger of episode three forces us to reconsider this entire world and who's really in charge. The nurse wasn't in episode one at all, and has slowly come to the fore, but was "hidden" behind all the Captain / Fibuli exchanges. Seen an episode at a time, with no spoilers to remove the sensation of pieces falling into place every twenty-five minutes or so, this is a well-paced, exciting adventure. Seen in one go, after reading dozens of articles and reviews, some might think it was a bit slovenly.

But it's got gun-fights, sorcerers, flying cars, robot-on-robot action and a big explosion at the end. Everything a ten-year-old could possibly want; plus three pretty girls, a hunky hero (by the 1978 standards) and some high-concept slapstick for the parents. And then there are the boggling ideas, some good jokes in among the silly ones and enough things you won't see anywhere else to keep all but the most snotty casual viewer entertained. ITV certainly couldn't compete, so it's pretty clear this is what those casual viewers wanted…

The Facts

Written by Douglas Adams. Directed by Pennant Roberts. Viewing figures: 9.1 million, 7.4 million, 8.2 million, 8.4 million. (See 16.1, "The Ribos Operation", for an explanation on the drop between episodes one and two.)

Supporting Cast: Bruce Purchase (Captain), Andrew Robertson (Mr Fibuli), David Sibley (Pralix), David Warwick (Kimus), Primi Townsend (Mula), Ralph Michael (Balaton).

Working Titles "The Pirates".

Cliffhangers The Mentiads enter the house where the Doctor's hiding, and knock him out with their psychic powers; escaping from the guards in the mine-tunnels, the Doctor and company run into the Mentiads again (this makes Romana scream for the first time); the Doctor is forced to walk the plank off the Bridge, and the Captain's cronies have a good laugh once he's apparently fallen a kilometre to his death.

The Lore

• Adams had been submitting story ideas for two or three years, including one based around a pacifier ray (see 15.1, "Horror of Fang Rock" and eventually 15.5, "Underworld"). In this, the aggression of an entire mining planet was techno-

logically absorbed, but a Time Lord sent to investigate received the whole lot in one psychic burst and opted to finish hollowing out the world before materialising it around Gallifrey as revenge for being abandoned to his fate.

• Another story sent in at this time was about the origins of cricket. Many of you will know that the Krikketmen are the substance of the third Hitch-Hikers' spin-off book (off-spin book?), Life, the Universe and Everything. You may not know that after the Scratchman project finally bit the dust (see 13.6, "The Seeds of Doom"), Adams and Baker tried to launch Doctor Who and the Krikkitmen as a movie. Baker, captain of charity cricket team the Lords' Taverners, was keen to include the sport in the scripts (see 16.1, "The Ribos Operation").

• Williams latched onto some minor characters in Adams' proposal - space-pirates - and decided to make these the centre of the story. The polyphase avatron, mentioned briefly in the script, was incorporated to play up to the "pirate" theme (in one version it was to have said 'pieces of silicate', but Adams thought this was a bit much). It also did a good job of keeping K9 out of the way, and thus making the Doctor figure out Xanxia's true nature without hi-tech help.

But there was also a more subtle reason for including it. Baker had long argued that the role of the companion was unnecessary, and told anyone who'd listen that he could get by with a talking cabbage on his shoulder, asking questions and occasionally getting captured. By demonstrating the practical difficulties of such a "character", they hoped to shut him up (note that the avatron is definitely destroyed, just in case he insisted on keeping it). At one stage during filming the avatron prop mysteriously disappeared, and turned up the next day in a skip.

• Adams was working on this just as BBC Radio 4 picked up the option to make a series from his pilot of The Hitch-Hiker's Guide to the Galaxy, so he wrote both series concurrently. He later confessed that he should have had the people standing in corridors on television and the flying cars and crashing spaceships on radio. The early drafts caused Williams and Read to doubt their ability to make it, as it was ambitious in scope even by feature film standards. Director Pennant Roberts defended the script as doable when Head of Drama Graeme McDonald requested that they find a replacement. As it turned out, none was ready in time.

• McDonald's comments are interesting, as they show how far he'd taken on board Williams' points from "The Invasion of Time" (15.6). In particular he picked out items in the submitted script which were just asking for trouble, given Baker's tendency to amend things. One line, in episode two, he specified as demanding removal. This was a definition of the vantalla psycho-scale: 5347.2 how much force is needed to move a teacup 5347.2 miles, 5347.2 teacups one mile or a whole Gallifreyan teaset thirty miles. A number of other cuts were requested, one of which involved the Doctor and Romana passing themselves off as an "Astromobile Association" repair team. (Following a note in Williams' character brief, the Doctor occasionally calls her "Romy" in the original draft. Apparently this was a way of annoying her, but actress Romy Schneider - briefly a household name between *Last Tango in Paris* and being "outed" by the paparazzi - may have been an influence.)

• K9 consolidated his status as family favourite with a cameo on *The Generation Game* later on the night of episode three, trading one-liners with new host Larry Grayson in one of the oddest things ever shown on prime-time television. Well, certainly since Alpha Centauri (9.2, "The Curse of Peladon") cropped up on *The Black and White Minstrel Show*, but we don't talk about that.

• Vi Delmar, as the nearly-dead Xanxia, was given a £30 bonus for removing her false teeth before lying immobile for long takes.

16.3: "The Stones of Blood"

(Serial 5C, Four Episodes, 28th October - 18th November 1978.)

Which One is This?   Living, vampiric standing-stones; twinkling fairy-lights that put the Doctor on trial for his life; and a druidic goddess with a thing for birds.

Firsts and Lasts   The first of five scripts over the next three years to be written by David Fisher, four of which will end up with his name on the credits (see 17.2, "City of Death").

If you watch *Doctor Who* enough, then certain pieces of "space" furniture start to feel like old friends. So here we bid a fond adieu to the semi-circular bank of flashing lights, originally built for the *Thunderbirds* episode "Ricochet", which not

only graced the *Prisoner* romp "The Girl Who Was Death" but has been part of every notable space-ship set in *Doctor Who* from "The Time Warrior" onwards. (See, particularly, the Nerva station in Season Twelve.)

Four Things to Notice About "The Stones of Blood"...

1. The trouble with devoting an entire season to a single quest is that those members of the audience who *don't* religiously watch the programme every week can get a little confused. Now the search for the Key to Time is reaching its halfway point, the series tries to remedy this with one of the most blatant exposition scenes you'll ever see. Watch with amazement as the Doctor takes Romana to one side at the start of episode one, and re-explains the whole Key to Time concept *very very quickly* while his assistant stands there nodding and saying 'yes, I know'.

2. Like "The Invasion of Time" before it, this is a story that's got problems with its location shooting. Night-filming is always stickier than filming during the day, and "The Stones of Blood" is the first time the programme risks shooting night-scenes on videotape rather than film. The result can be a little, shall we say... static? But worse is what happens at the end of episode one, when the programme once again takes the word "cliffhanger" literally and has Romana pushed off a precipice. Supposedly hanging on to the cliff edge for dear life, Mary Tamm is quite clearly in the studio, with a "raging torrential waters" backdrop inserted into the picture behind her through the much-abused magic of CSO. Did the programme-makers learn nothing from "Underworld"...? Fortunately, they don't bother with a reprise at the start of episode two.

3. Funniest moment in "The Stones of Blood" (unintentional): the scene in which one of the Ogri menacingly "walks" past the window of de Vries' house, while those inside cower in fear. Since the Ogri are supposed to be living stone menhirs, and the Ogri props appear to be sculpt-ed out of polystyrene, you can see how this might not strike the note of terror that the script seems to be aiming for. Runner-up in this category: coven leader de Vries, trying to escape the wrath of a goddess, has his twittering acolyte suggest that they drive away. His line - 'Plymouth? For Heaven's sake, Martha!' - became the title of a fanzine, and the core of a scene in *The League of Gentlemen* (a scene which thereafter turns into a

pastiche of Binro's discovery of the truth from 16.1, "The Ribos Operation").

4. Funniest moment in "The Stones of Blood" (intentional): A silver-skinned Penelope Keith wannabe, in a prison in hyperspace, tells two intelligent indoor fireworks who are conducting a trial into the activities of a Celtic deity and three haemophagic dolmens… 'I'm Vivien Fay, of Rose Cottage, Boscawan. Ask anyone in Boscawan, they will identify me.' Runner-up in this category: Romana's naïve and puzzled 'really?' when Fay explains that she used to be a Brown Owl. (Still, as Vivien turns out to be a 4,000-year-old alien criminal with a necklace that can transmute matter, maybe Romana's right to take it literally.)

The Continuity

The Doctor Answers 'no' to the question 'are you from outer space?', and says that he's more from what humans might call 'inner time'. [See **Where (and When) is Gallifrey?** under 13.3, "Pyramids of Mars".] Unusually, he can't read the script of the planet Diplos on board the convict ship. He's presumably still wanted by the Megara at the end of the story, though he thinks that as he sent their ship back to Diplos he should get a couple of thousand years' grace.

• *Inventory.* He is, improbably, carrying a lawyer's wig in his pocket and can produce it at a moment's notice. He also seems to be expecting K9 to break down, and has tongs to conduct repairs with.

• *Background.* With crushing inevitability, it turns out that the Doctor knew Einstein. He tried to explain the realities of space and time travel to the man, but Einstein insisted that he knew best. [The Doctor really is turning into a terrible bore.] Professor Amelia Rumford believes she's met the Doctor before, but he doesn't know her [still… nothing's impossible with time-travel, except consistency]. He probably hasn't really read her *Bronze Age Burials in Gloucestershire*, as he claims when making polite conversation. He believes antiquarian / writer John Aubrey started modern Druidism as a joke in the seventeenth century, and the way he speaks of Aubrey having 'a great sense of humour' might suggest a personal meeting. Similarly, his description of the discovery of Troy by 'dear old Schliemann' [Heinrich Schliemann, c. 1871] might indicate something personal [see also 3.3, "The Myth Makers"].

The Doctor knew an unnamed Galactic Federation which once appointed a justice machine to oversee its many different life-forms. The machine found the Federation in contempt of court, and blew up the entire galaxy. He knows of the Ogri, and speaks of Ogros as 'repulsive' as if he's been there, but he's never heard of the Megara.

The Supporting Cast
• *Romana.* The Doctor finally bothers to tell her that it was the White Guardian, and not the President of Gallifrey, who sent her on the mission to find the Key to Time.

Romana believes herself to be good at puzzles, or at least better than the Doctor [as in 17.2, "City of Death"]. She's heard of Earth, and says that 'everyone' knows it's the Doctor's favourite planet. When Cessair takes on the Doctor's form and pushes Romana off a cliff, her first assumption is that the Doctor's gone bad rather than that somebody's been shape-changing… so she still doesn't entirely trust him.

Her interspatial geometry's a bit rusty, as they gave up teaching it 2,000 years ago even on Gallifrey [again, compare with "City of Death"]. But she heard a lecture at the Academy about the possible uses of a molecular stabiliser, a method of repairing K9 that doesn't occur to the Doctor. Romana believes hyperspace to be a 'theoretical absurdity', and seems surprised that anyone can use hyperspace technology. [It seems weird that someone from hi-tech Gallifrey should think this way, when so many lesser cultures encountered by the Doctor have utilised hyperspace. According to "Frontier in Space", 10.3, humans have hyperspace capability as early as the twenty-sixth century. But the Doctor's line about Gallifrey taking interspatial geometry off the syllabus might mean that Time Lords see it as too frivolous to teach.] She knows about the home planet of the Ogri.

Romana's choice in shoes is rather impractical, but her dress-sense is almost psychically exact for the place and time. She makes a big deal out of getting changed. [Once again, her style-guru seems to be Frida Lingstadt from Abba.]

• *K9.* He sounds positively crestfallen when the Doctor leaves him on guard duty inside the TARDIS. He knows about real tennis, lawn tennis and table tennis, at least until Romana inadvertently orders him to erase the data from his memory-banks. He can also scan his data-banks for a planet which might have been home to Cessair, and identifies Diplos as a result. Romana's scent, blood, tissue-type and alpha-wave pattern are also recorded in his data-banks, so he has no problem tracking her [though he doesn't mention a double-heartbeat this time]. He senses the Ogri's presence, but can't identify them, from some distance.

TARDIS technology is, of course, compatible with K9's internal workings. The TARDIS regenerates his circuits, suggesting an almost organic structure to K9, and Romana states that he'd be 'finished' if his cerebral core were to be removed. Once again coming up with a sudden 'scale' to explain everything, K9 takes one look at the Doctor's hyperspace gun and says it'll be effective on a setting of .0037 on the hyperspace scale.

The Doctor states that K9 can generate a force-field to keep out the Ogri, although this basically just means shooting them with his usual weapon, and it drains his power-packs after about seventeen minutes.

The TARDIS A type forty TARDIS is fitted with a molecular stabiliser. After his battle with an Ogri, K9's circuits are regenerated when the stabilisers are hooked up to his circuit frequency modulator in the console room.

Romana finds some '70s chic in the wardrobe, including a tartan cap that's ideal for this sort of rural setting [and exactly like the girl from the "Charlie" perfume ads][5]. There's an umbrella in the console room, but the Doctor discards it in a field on Earth. The Doctor also has the parts on board needed to lash up a tripod-mounted "gun" that takes its target into hyperspace, but tritum crystals are needed to fuel it. Hyperspace is said to be another dimension, used in space-travel to avoid the time distortion effect that comes with relativity. It looks purple.

The hole into which the Key tracer is inserted has changed position, and shape, again. A buzzer sounds on the console when the TARDIS lands [the Doctor sets it whenever he leaves the console room], and the atmosphere outside the Ship can quickly and easily be monitored from the console, which here makes more blooping noises than usual. Beside the console room there's a black-walled area, mostly undecorated, where the Doctor keeps the bits of the Key to Time inside a fridge.

Here, at last, the Ship is shown floating in the vortex instead of in space.

The Guardians and the Key The White Guardian sends another warning to the Doctor, his voice being heard to say 'beware the Black Guardian' in the TARDIS console room, though for no good reason. The Doctor says that the White Guardian is more properly known as the Guardian of Light in Time, as opposed to the Guardian of Darkness, AKA the Black Guardian. Like the Key, they can assume any shape or form.

• *The Key to Time.* The third segment is disguised as the Seal of Diplos, a silver pendant worn by the criminal Cessair, and it's been around for at least 4,000 years. The Seal can be used for transmutation, transformation and establishing hyperspatial and temporal co-ordinates. Cessair can take on the physical persona of Vivien Fay and apparently disguise herself as the Doctor. Romana indicates that the power to transform objects is a power of the Key rather than of the Seal. [A subtle distinction; if a segment took the form of a video recorder then it'd be able to play VHS, but that doesn't make it an ability of the Key itself. The segments seem to be deliberately disguising themselves as items with remarkable powers. See the next two stories, especially.]

The Non-Humans

• *Ogri.* The Nine Travellers is a name given to a stone circle on Boscombe Moor, England, which has been there for the last 4,000 years. However, sources over the years have failed to agree on a definitive figure for the number of standing-stones in the circle, and for a very good reason: some of them keep moving about.

In truth three of the stones are Ogri, silicone-based life forms from the planet Ogros which just happen to resemble featureless slabs of rock but are capable of shuffling around. They're deficient in globulin, a protein found in blood plasma, so anyone touching an Ogri during feeding-time will find him- or herself unable to move away as the creature strips the victim to the bone. These particular Ogri were brought to Earth by Cessair of Diplos - see **History** - and apparently do her telepathic bidding.

The Ogri never display any signs of culture, or of intelligence above animal level. [The assumption here seems to be that these three are the original 4,000-year-old stones, as mercifully nobody raises the question of how the things might reproduce.] They glow when they feed, and at the same time there's the sound of a great heartbeat. They weigh three-and-a-half tons at least. K9's blaster, usually powerful enough to blow holes in rock, only seems to sting them.

• *Megara.* Justice machines, overseeing the law of Diplos and acting as judge, jury and executioner [although their mention of a "Galactic Charter" might indicate that Diplos was one of many worlds in their jurisdiction]. They're bio-machines with living cells, micro-cellular metallic organisms.

Two of the Megara have been stuck on the functional-looking ship that brought Cessair of Diplos to Earth, behind a door sealed with the symbol of the Great Seal of Diplos, for the last 4,000 years. When released they manifest themselves as two floating clusters of silver light, which pulse as they speak and insist on carrying out the law to the letter. They don't regard mere humanoids to be capable of understanding the subtleties of law, and claim that the Megara can't lie, but justice machines are notoriously inflexible. Even contempt of court is punishable by death.

Since the Doctor was unauthorised in breaking the seal, he's found guilty and sentenced to execution, although he's permitted (a) a trial in which one of the Megara acts in his defence and (b) an appeal in which he argues his own case. Though the machines are capable of communicating in spoken language, when discussing points of law they "mutter" to each other in some sort of machine-code. Their judicial procedure is, as expected, hugely formal. They have the ability to probe people's minds during the trial with a beam of some kind, which assesses whether the subject is telling the truth, but only if the subject to be probed is a witness. They can disintegrate even an Ogri with one blast of energy, an act they call 'dissolution'. The Seal of Diplos seems to send them packing back to their spaceship and thence to Diplos, as the Doctor's already programmed the controls to take them home [but see **Things That Don't Make Sense**].

The Megara were sent to Diplos on judicial business to try Cessair, and an officer was to have identified her on arrival. The sentence for impersonating a religious personage is 1,500 years, while the sentence for theft of the Great Seal gets Vivien perpetual imprisonment, which means the Megara can - and do - turn her into a rock on Boscombe Moor. The bodies of at least three other aliens, some of which may be police rather than prisoners, are found in sealed areas on board the ship from Diplos. One is a skeletal robot, looking much like the framework of a Kraal android [13.4, "The Android Invasion"] but with big red lips. Another is shrivelled and humanoid, and another is what looks like a Wirrn. [In 12.2, "The Ark in Space", the Wirrn only arrived in Earth's galaxy c. 15,000 AD after the humans had sacked Andromeda. If one of their kind drifted into the Milky Way over 4,000 years ago then it may have been a sentinel, sent to scout out new territories. The other Wirrn wouldn't have risked heading this way after the Megara had locked up the scout.] Cessair wields a crystal-fuelled staff which can create a "vortex" and send someone to the ship in hyperspace, or create a static electrical force-field.

Planet Notes

• *Diplos.* A G-class [meaning, Earth-like?] planet in the Tau Ceti system. If Cessair is anything to go by, the inhabitants were / are human, with silver skins and the ability to live for 4,000 years with no apparent ageing. [Are they silicon-based, like the Ogri? It seems unlikely, as in "The Hand of Fear" (14.2) the Doctor has difficulty believing that two silicon-based life-forms could evolve in the same part of space, but it might explain why the Megara turn Cessair to stone. Unless it's their idea of irony.] Cessair is allergic to citric acid, which hints at a biological difference to human beings. This is why the Ogri don't try to eat her.

• *Ogros.* The planet of the Ogri, also in the Tau Ceti system, covered with amino acid swamps where the Ogri feed on the primitive proteins by absorption. Removing the Ogri from their home-world contravenes the Galactic Charter, according to the Megara, and using them for one's own ends is also illegal.

History

• *Dating.* None given, but everything about Earth says "contemporary" [so call it 1978].

Around 2000 BC, the criminal Cessair of Diplos - accused of murder, and of removing and misusing the Great Seal of Diplos - came to Earth and set up a home for herself in England. Since there are Megara justice machines and the bodies of monsters on board the ship, the implication is that it was some kind of convict vessel, though how Cessair took command of it remains a mystery. The ship is now parked in hyperspace, over the stone circle known as the Nine Travellers but in a different dimension.

Boscombe Moor is near Boscawen, Damnonium [now the Cornwall / Devon region in southwest England], a couple of hours from Plymouth. The circle known as the Nine Travellers is a Gorsedd, one of three places of augury in Britain, the other two being Stonehenge and Bryn Gwyddon in Wales. The circle's also 4,000 years old [so Cessair probably has something to do with its construction].

Over the years Cessair has taken wholly human form and adopted a number of identities in order to stay close to the circle. The Scots artist Allan Ramsay [1713-84] painted her as Lady Morgana Montcalme. The Montcalms owned the land, including the circle, and the 'wicked' Lady Montcalme was said to have murdered her husband on her wedding night. As Mrs. Trefusis, Cessair was a recluse, who lived in the house for sixty years and never saw a soul. She was also the Brazilian Senora Camara, though Senor Camara doesn't seem to have survived the crossing from Brazil. Portraits of these three "incarnations" are found at the house, and obviously they've all got the same face even though there's 150 years between them. In the Middle Ages the land was controlled by the Mother Superior of the twelfth century convent of the Little Sisters of Saint Gudula. As Vivien Fay she's currently living at a nearby cottage instead of at the Hall [to allay suspicions], which was built on the site of the convent in 1572.

Dr. Thomas Borlase's 1754 survey of the stones mentioned Nine Travellers, but the Reverend Thomas Bright's 1820 survey and the two surveys of 1874 and 1911 gave contradictory numbers. One of the stones 'fell on' Borlaise just after he completed his survey, hence the date "1701-1754" on his portrait. When the Doctor arrives, the doomed "druid" de Vries owns the Hall and is worshipping Cessair as a Celtic goddess, the Cailleach. De Vries uses a crow as a servant, describing ravens and crows as the Cailleach's eyes, but it's not explained how he controls them. De Vries knows the Doctor's title and believes his coming to be foretold, but this is never explained, either. There's a British Institute of Druidic Studies, which apparently practices animal sacrifice [legally...?] under de Vries, though Fay claims they've got nothing to with real druids 'past or present'. For ritual purposes, Cessair / the Cailleach dresses in the costume of a grotesque horned bird.

The Doctor suggests that the three Ogri may be the inspiration behind 'Gog... Magog... ogres'. [This recalls Geoffrey of Monmouth's "history"; see 11.1, "The Time Warrior").]

The Analysis

Where Does This Come From? At last, after all the von Daniken baloney, we come clean about the origins of the "mystic events turn out to be a simple, if bizarre, crime" stories. The Doctor recognises the portraits at the Hall, and spots the connection to someone who's recently moved into the area; just like in that other West Country pseudo-gothic classic, *The Hound of the Baskervilles*.

Around this time the druid revival was gathering strength, most of its devotees being bored middle-management types and ageing hippies. Until the New Age Travellers made it untenable, these folk would pop up at Stonehenge during solstices, usually blowing horns and wearing sheets in a harmless sort of way. However, as the Aleister Crowley brigade latched on to this it became less "quaint" and more desperate.

Meanwhile more sophisticated measuring equipment was showing how well-constructed and multi-purpose these henges, tumuli and souteraines were. Post-'60s, just about every children's fantasy series on TV touched on Stonehenge in some way, and stone circles usually turned out to be gateways to other worlds, times or dimensions. Two particular examples should be mentioned here, both produced by HTV and made in 1976. The first is *Children of the Stones*, a likeably earnest but wholly hilarious serial which insisted on squeezing virtually every quasi-mystical and pop-SF cliché of the era into a single storyline, and depicted the titular standing-stones as lurking, almost-living things that could have sinister effects when touched. The other is *Sky*, by our old friends Bob Baker and Dave Martin, which reveals Stonehenge to be a specially-constructed intersection between planes of existence. In places "The Stones of Blood" comes across as an attempt to be the grown-up, well-read cousin of these programmes.

Buffy the Vampire Slayer fans will know that there's a specific subtext to any witches who aren't raddled old crones. If anyone doubts what's being suggested about the precise relationship between Vivien and Amelia - and the salty comments about truncheons and sausage sandwiches might give one pause - then the names of Cessair's earlier *nomes de travaille* are a dead giveaway. "Mrs. Trefusis" (suggesting Violet Trefusis, Virginia Woolf's sapphic squeeze), "Senora Camara" (and here we must note the Doctor's pointed question 'was there ever a Senor Camara?') and a Mother Superior. Then we see that the man-hating Vivien is immediately taken with Romana, and offers her a ride. On a bike, which Vivien suggests archly '...will be a whole new experience for you'. As Violet Trefusis' diaries had just been published, it was hard to avoid this material in the press, and even *Gardeners' World* made a feature of it. That line about 'inner time' may also be a Virginia Woolf allusion. A lot of things were, then.

We have to spell it out these days, but this is also the Arthurian story *par excellence*. Ravens, associated with Arthur and various Celtic war-goddesses (e.g. the Irish Morrigan); stones drinking blood; but above all, Nimue. She was the sorceress, sometimes associated with Morgan le Fay (see 26.1, "Battlefield" and 11.5, "Planet of the Spiders") and often called "Vivien", who tempted Merlin to his imprisonment in a crystal cave. "Lady Morgana Montcalm" is another of the Cessair pseudonyms. Just in case the "hero imprisoned" aspect escapes us, the name "Megara" is associated with the fall of Hercules.

The explanation of hyperspace owes a great deal less to *Star Wars* or *Phoenix 5* than to the legendary bearded-and-sandal-wearing geeks of the Open University. For the sake of the un-British, it should be explained that the Open University is a body which educates via the media, its televisual lectures broadcast by the BBC between two and six in the morning. In the '70s the production-values (or lack thereof), the arid nature of the subject matter and the shirts of the presenters proved oddly mesmeric to insomniacs and connoisseurs of fashion-disasters. (If you want to imagine what an Open University lecture sounds like, then just imagine a conversation in which every sentence seems to end with the words '...and likewise with quarks'.)

Things That Don't Make Sense Vivien's motives are nebulous even by *Doctor Who* standards, and she doesn't even seem to have the old "wants to conquer the universe" standard to fall back on. She's spent 4,000 years staying close to the prison ship that brought her to Earth, but she doesn't seem to have any use for it and as far as we know she's never thought about leaving this backward

little planet. If she's been here since 2000 BC, with the ability to transmute objects and technology beyond the imagination of primitive humanity, then she could easily have taken over the world. Instead, she's happy to loll around in Cornwall and be worshipped by a handful of unimpressive local pagans. Can't she find a better planet to hide out on? [Or is she stranded here? It's possible that the ship was "beached" on some local hyperspace hazard.]

And the epilogue, in which the Doctor returns the Megara to their spaceship by waving the Seal of Diplos at them, is an almighty cop-out. The assumption seems to be that as the Seal has vaguely-defined mystical powers, the Doctor can routinely use it to make justice machines vanish or activate spaceships, but... until a few moments earlier, the Seal had been in the possession of Cessair. Cessair, who ended up arguing for her life in front of the Megara. Cessair, who was ultimately executed by them. Why didn't *she* just wave them away, while the Seal was still in her possession? [Lack of imagination?]

Bizarrely, Romana has never thought to ask *why* she's been sent to find the Key to Time until the Doctor deigns to tell her. Not finding the segment of the Key anywhere around the stone circle, the Doctor jumps to the conclusion that it must be in hyperspace with barely any supporting evidence, thus giving Romana a chance to set up the idea of hyperspace in the minds of the audience. Romana also proves herself to be excessively dim in episode three, when she has to ask why the ship can't be seen from Earth even *after* she's been told that it's in hyperspace.

And why (and how) does the Ogri burn out K9's circuits during their off-screen fight, rather than just falling on top of him and smashing him to bits?

Critique (Megara-Style Prosecution Case) A mess, frankly. A story so badly-plotted that it seems to give up and start again halfway through, so badly-shot that it frequently looks like home video and so obsessed with its leading man that much of it comes across as an extended series of improvisations between Tom Baker and either Mary Tamm or Beatrix Lehmann. Amelia Rumford *might* at least be considered a half-decent supporting character, since she's the only member of the cast - Romana included - who's allowed to have a personality, but even so she's just used as a prop for the Doctor. (Tamm once insisted that she and Baker 'wrote all the scripts' during her time on the programme, obviously an exaggeration but a good sign that by this point the lead cast were so full of themselves that the stories were virtually irrelevant. "The Stones of Blood" is possibly the worst offender. The opening scenes on the TARDIS are an embarrassment, nicely setting the tone for what's to come.)

The first two episodes aim for pagan Dennis-Wheatley-style horror with SF twinges, but have no idea how to pull it off in terms of either production or narrative, and that's assuming you can sit through yet another tedious black mass by inept yokels. You get the feeling the programme-makers had a bet to see how long they could keep the characters hanging around in fields and having pointless, turgid, meandering conversations. One particular scene in the first episode, between the Doctor and de Vries, is so inept that it's incredible it was ever broadcast... the camera doesn't get all of Nicholas McArdle's face in the frame, and wobbles around for the rest of the shot trying to find the best place to stop.

There's so little dramatic content here that the music seems to be doing double-time to compensate, the result being a ridiculous, ugly splurge of sound which tries to make every line of dialogue sound urgent. And any sense of there being anything *outside* the Doctor and Romana's line of sight is almost forgotten, the subplot about the coven becoming so meaningless that you don't give a damn when the other "characters" die horribly. There's no sense of this world even *existing*. A series which started off being about experience of the unknown, both for the audience and for the Doctor, has now become a series about the POV of two self-involved Time Lords.

What's most striking, though, is that throughout the story there are so many things which *should* be interesting. A story about a Celtic goddess on contemporary Earth *should* pack a hell of a punch, but the script mentions the lore almost as if it's an aside, and ignores everything that makes the Cailleach mythology actually worth hearing (compare this with 15.5, "Underworld" and 17.5, "The Horns of Nimon"). She's just a woman in a bird costume, and even *that's* buried by episode three. At times the story seems to simply want to show off its references. Gog and Magog are mentioned, then ignored. Crows and ravens are introduced as if they're going to be a running visual "theme", then forgotten.

It's like listening to a conversation between academics, when you're sure they're talking about something fascinating but they're not stopping to tell you what. Nobody's even trying to make these ideas work on-screen. Instead there's just a series of dramatic faux pas, from the sight of a bunch of murderous cultists running away from an old woman on a bicycle to the wretched Spanish bull-fighting music that plays when the Doctor lures a walking rock off the edge of a cliff.

And the Ogri, of course, rank among *Doctor Who's* worst-judged monsters. The sight of large, glowing chunks of polystyrene trying to look menacing is obviously laughable, but for once the budget isn't the problem; here it's the conception that's inane, most particularly the "duel" between K9 and the shuffling boulder. The tyrannosaurus in "Invasion of the Dinosaurs" may be awful, but in theory it's a good idea, and the younger (less FX-conscious) viewer can at least start to imagine what it'd be like if there really *were* dinosaurs on the streets of London. But menhirs that roll forward and threaten robot dogs are as unforgivable as they are unworkable. If you made the story with a budget of millions and had Stanley Kubrick behind the camera, there'd still be no way of making it anything but risible.

Yet that's fairly typical of a story which, appropriately, barely seems to exist in the real world and only makes sense in the abstract hyperspace universe of the programme-makers' own heads. The Doctor's final comment when Romana asks him if Earth is always like this - 'oh, sometimes it's even exciting' - is meant to be a joke, but says it all.

Critique (Defence Case) None of the above criticism makes any sense. This is effectively creepy, and makes an abrupt shift which (as with the previous story) alters everything you thought you knew but turns out to be entirely in keeping with what we were told. Anyone who finds the Ogri "laughable" has forgotten the scene with the two campers (arguably the last time *Doctor Who* was really scary, and it's done almost nonchalantly). A viewer now might find it not to his or her taste but to assume there's no plot when it's abundantly clear that a coherent argument is being made consistently is impossible for anyone prepared to just shut up and watch.

The production has an atmosphere and texture to it that will never be recaptured. Try to imagine this story in the '80s style, with squeaky music by Roger Limb, the Doctor in that horrid burgundy "uniform" and wall-to-wall blond young men in singlets showing off their muscles. This maturity is reflected in the script, especially the characterisation. We don't need obvious signposting as to what's going on in Rose Cottage, the way high-camp nonsense like "Four To Doomsday" (19.2) almost did. We don't need to be told that de Vries is a self-deluded stooge, as "The Time Monster" needed (9.6). If you're old enough to see through the Ogri as polystyrene, you're old enough to pick up the hints. There are moments of pure gold, such as the shot of early-morning dew on the dormant K9, the ravens circling and the Doctor talking to the bird in de Vries' study. This is a story in which even the domestic / cosmic juxtaposition of "Image of the Fendahl" (15.3), where the Doctor saves the universe with a cake recipe, is trumped; while the Doctor's in hyperspace on trial for his life, two women in a cottage kitchen work things out with a recipe book and a computer. If you can't take this, you'll never really like *Doctor Who*.

The Facts

Written by David Fisher. Directed by Darrol Blake. Viewing figures: 8.6 million, 6.6 million, 9.3 million, 7.6 million.

Supporting Cast: Beatrix Lehmann (Professor Rumford), Susan Engel (Vivien Fay), Nicholas McArdle (De Vries), Elaine Ives-Cameron (Martha); David McAlister, Gerald Cross (Megara Voices).

Working Titles "The Nine Maidens", "The Stones of Time".

Cliffhangers Someone pushes Romana off a cliff; Vivien Fay shoves Romana into the middle of the stone circle, then makes her vanish with the hyperspace "wand"; the silver-skinned Vivien appears on board the convict ship with two of the Ogri, and tells the Doctor that he's trapped in hyperspace forever (the sequence is re-filmed for the reprise in episode four, to remove the embarrassing evil laughter).

The Lore

• As this was the 100th *Doctor Who* story, Tamm and Baker made up a scene in which Romana surprises the Doctor by telling him that

it's his 751st birthday (picking up the hint from "The Ribos Operation" that he doesn't actually keep track of these things). The fridge on board the TARDIS contained a birthday cake, and Romana's present to the Doctor was a new scarf, identical to the old one. Williams came down hard on this, but the scarf pattern was licensed for sale in America.

• The first choice for Vivien Fay was novelist, agony aunt and ageing hippy Molly Parkin. Her timetable prevented this, but the rest of the cast found they enjoyed Susan Engel's company.

• Beatrix Lehmann - to whom novelist Christopher Isherwood dedicated *Goodbye to Berlin*, the source of *Cabaret* - drove to rehearsals in a powerful sports car, a Lancia, despite being well into her seventies. Her novel *Rumours of Heaven* was reissued at around the same time. Baker took the idea of a companion in her late sixties to Williams, who simply laughed.

• Lehmann took to John Leeson in particular, and bought him a camera - a Leica - knowing that he was a keen photographer. She entertained the cast with tales from her long years in the theatre, making this one of the most affectionately-remembered productions of the '70s. It was her last acting role.

• Roberta Gibbs doubled for Mary Tamm on the cliffs, although Tamm did a lot of these shots herself. Gibbs was also the "other" Strella / Romana for camera set-ups in "The Androids of Tara" (16.4).

• The school party visiting the Rollright Stones were perplexed by the fact that there were too many of them. They were even more baffled when one fell over. Then Tom Baker arrived and everything became clear. Many of the real stones were unimpressive on video, despite being daunting in real life, so the effects team "beefed up" the site. Some of the long-shots are of a model by Mat Irvine.

• The hyperspace "wreck" was constructed by Irvine using components from a kit of Apollo XI and a *Space: 1999* Eagle Transporter. This act of revenge on the ITV series earned Irvine the first of his many TV appearances on a BBC programme about model-making, for which he made a special clip of the Megara ship orbiting a planet. (Yes, there used to be television programmes about people building model spaceships. Model-makers pay Licence Fees too.)

• A Sea Devil was originally supposed to be on

board the Megara ship instead of the funny-looking android skeleton. Meanwhile the Megara "Tinkerbells" were meant to be floating metal spheres, but this was changed as the spheres were felt to be 'too *Star Wars*', making this the series' first official recognition of *Star Wars*' existence…

• Filming so close to Oxford was bound to cause trouble. Overnight, students removed the TARDIS prop to a nearby quarry. How apt.

16.4: "The Androids of Tara"

(Serial 5D, Episodes, 25th November - 16th December 1978.)

Which One is This? Return to Zenda. Electric swordfights, electric crossbows, electric aristocrats and a real castle.

Firsts and Lasts Last appearance in *Doctor Who* of Cyril Shaps, who's provided the series with some of its most memorable doomed professors (see 5.1, "Tomb of the Cybermen"; 7.3, "The Ambassadors of Death"; 11.5, "Planet of the Spiders") but here dons the erectile psychedelic hat of the Archimandrite of Tara. It's also the last story to have a fight arranged by Terry Walsh (but *what* a fight).

Four Things to Notice About "The Androids of Tara"…

1. Yes, it's another "android doubles" episode, though this time it's excusable. A long way from the action-TV clichés of "The Android Invasion" (13.4), "The Androids of Tara" is a future-feudal re-make of *The Prisoner of Zenda*, and it's not embarrassed about the fairy-tale implausibility of its story. Here Mary Tamm ends up playing four different characters - Romana, Romana's double Princess Strella, an android duplicate of Romana and an android duplicate of Romana's double Princess Strella - which tells you a lot about the sort of story this is.

2. This could well be the first story of the whole Tom Baker run which doesn't feature a single word of made-up science (at least, beyond the normal confines of science fiction). There are no pieces of technology with unlikely technical names, no rare alien minerals, no previously-unheard-of branches of physics. The androids' circuits are made out of ordinary-sounding things like carbon and silicon, and there's nothing more exotic inside them than micro-circuitry. The

knock-out drug in Prince Reynart's wine isn't called anything like "pentocynodripterine", or indeed, given any name at all. And since technobabble is so often used as a way of glossing over the cracks in the plot, it may not be coincidental that this story has less logical flaws than just about any other of this era.

3. It's time once again to make fun of the "incidental monster". In this era the monster costumes get less impressive as they become less important to the plot, and the only weird alien thing in the whole of "The Androids of Tara" is the 'beast' that lurks in the woods near Count Grendel's castle, only glimpsed in one scene but still gaining a reputation as one of *Doctor Who*'s worst outfits. It's not so much the gorilla suit that's the problem, or even the amusingly unconvincing mask; it's the way the actor inside the costume insists on waving his arms around as if he's trying to bring the stupidity of the thing to everyone's attention. (Like most bad things in *Doctor Who*, however, this can easily be justified. As Grendel turns up in the nick of time to save Romana from the beast, those who can't accept the creature's appearance might like to assume that it's one of the Count's servants, who's paid to dress up in an ill-fitting costume and threaten attractive maidens in the woods so that Grendel can "rescue" them. Or maybe Madame Lamia, Grendel's android-maker, knocked up a robot monster for him to fight. It fits the story far better than the hyperactive-monkey-monster idea, anyway.)

4. And the Doctor gets to deliver one of the great absurdist lines of the series: 'Would you mind not standing on my chest? My hat's on fire.'

The Continuity

The Doctor Good at fixing androids, and apparently has better hearing than most people. Likes fishing, though he seems to care more about the "lying around the place" aspect than the "fish-catching" element [he'll be at it again in 22.4, "The Two Doctors"]. As ever, he's not immune to knock-out drugs, although he's the last one to drop after the Prince's men taste the drugged wine.

The Doctor's good enough with a sword to beat the finest swordsman on Tara, and as in one of his previous duels [9.3, "The Sea Devils"] he's prepared to re-arm a disarmed opponent in order to finish the match properly.

• *Ethics.* Again demonstrating that he's not one

for formal responsibilities, even when the universe is at stake, here he petulantly refuses to go looking for the next segment of the Key to Time and lets Romana go off to find it while he relaxes by the river. Even though he must surely realise that it's bound to be dangerous for her.

• *Inventory*. About a foot gets chopped off his scarf here. [But see the backup scarf in "Destiny of the Daleks" (17.1) and the cut scene from "The Stones of Blood" (16.3).]

• *Background*. He saw Capablanca play Alekhine at chess in 1927, but thinks he may have been called away before the end. He last used his fishing gear when he was with Izaak Walton [author of *The Compleat Angler*, 1653].

The Supporting Cast

• *Romana*. Seems to have a better head for chess than the Doctor. Romana doesn't know what a horse is, and doesn't seem familiar with the whole "beast of burden" idea at all as she asks what makes it go. [Academy training is erratic when it comes to the outside universe.] She is, unexpectedly, the exact double of Princess Strella of Tara. Even their accents are similar. [This sort of thing happens a lot to Time Lords. See 3.5, "The Massacre"; 5.4, "The Enemy of the World"; and possibly 20.1, "Arc of Infinity". Romana will turn out to have a habit of looking like princesses.] She's also keen to wear the most innocuous, if stylish, garb for the job.

• *K9*. Quite audibly makes a little 'hmm' noise when the Doctor says he knows what he's doing. The Mk. II K9's able to beat the Doctor at chess, just like the previous version, and is programmed with all the world chess championships since 1866. His weapon can hold a human being still, but not knock the victim out, for as long as the beam is active. Naturally, he can tell the difference between androids and people.

The TARDIS There's now revealed to be a cupboard in the console room itself, which contains a gas mask, a bunch of magician's flowers, various brooms and the Doctor's fishing-rod. The TARDIS wardrobe, so often abused by the Doctor's companions in the past, is actually seen here [or at least, *one* of the wardrobes is seen here]. It's in alphabetical order - apparently human alphabetical order, as a hula-skirt for Tahiti and an outfit labelled "Tally-Ho" are near each other on the dress-rack - and the "T" section contains a

woman's outift for Tara which is what everyone's wearing on Tara this year, according to what Romana calls 'our records'. [But the charming purple ensemble doesn't match the style seen on the planet, so the records must be wrong. Maybe the clothing comes from the age when Tara was better-populated, before the plague (see **Planet Notes**). As the Doctor doesn't seem to have visited Tara before, the implication here is that TARDISes come fitted with clothing for inhabited planets. Not that the Doctor himself tends to use this facility.]

The scanner picture moves around, taking in the locale, when nobody's touching the controls.

The Guardians and the Key

• *The Key to Time*. The fourth segment is disguised as a stone dragon, part of a statue belonging to the Gracht family on Tara, of which the villainous Count Grendel is a member. Grendel states that his family's fortunes are tied to the statue. [And sure enough, when the segment is removed Count Grendel is soon disgraced. It's interesting that so many superstitions end up forming around the disguised parts of the Key, and that magical powers are often attributed to those closest to the segments. At least two segment-holders - Cessair (16.3, "The Stones of Blood") and Kroll (16.5, "The Power of Kroll") - are mistaken for gods. As the superstition about the statue turns out to be quite true here, it's feasible that the Seeker's precognitive abilities in "The Ribos Operation" (16.1) only worked because she was trying to find someone who was carrying the first segment.] In its natural form, at least, the segment seems to be indestructible.

Planet Notes

• *Tara*. A planet balanced between Medieval society and hi-tech futurism, so the castles, forests and swashbuckling noblemen are mixed with electrified swords for the upper classes, crossbows that fire electronic bolts for the peasants and - most significantly - androids. Castles are lit with torches rather than electric lighting.

Every indication is that Tara was an Earth colony, as the names are familiar and so are some of its sixteen Zodiac signs, though a clock on the wall has sixteen numbers [a thirty-two hour day?]. Other signs of Earthly origins are the dogs and horses kept by the locals. The Tarans know about life on other planets, though they don't seem to have many visitors. Tara is the name of the capital city as well as the planet [the site where the colonists landed?], and there's a system of monarchy, with Prince Reynart being crowned as King during the Doctor's visit. The prince has a Swordmaster as his right hand, who leads a trained Swordsman and the Prince's sundry other men.

The Great Plague wiped out nine-tenths of Tara's people two hundred years ago, which is when the locals started bulking out the population with androids. Only the peasant class on Tara know the secret of making androids, so - as ever - the aristocrats need the peasants' services even as they sneer down their noses at the commoners. Count Grendel of the Gracht family, who plots to take the throne and eventually escapes in disgrace, has his own surgeon-engineer in the form of the doomed Madam Lamia. Her workshop is the most futuristic-looking place seen here, full of exotic tools and computer-banks.

Androids are perfect replicas of human beings, with micro-circuitry and rechargeable power-packs, though they don't seem to be fully sentient and can have limited repertoires. They're sometimes used as assassins with built-in energy weapons, and if their circuits are faulty then they can be heard sparking. A mute android duplicate can be prepared quite quickly, but a perfect copy takes a long time. The Doctor can program them in such a way as to improve their intelligence.

The Prince can only be crowned King at an hour fixed by the astrologers, in the great coronation room of the Palace of Tara. He'd forfeit his right to the crown if he failed to turn up at the right moment. Princess Strella is the only other claimant for the throne, which is why Grendel has been holding her captive. The Princess is First Lady of Tara, a descendant of the Royal House and Mistress of the Domains of Thorvalde, Mortegarde and Freya. Under Taran law, the husband of a deceased Princess can claim her estates and her position in the succession [a *really* dangerous law, this]. If the rightful King marries and then dies, his Queen retains his power and her next husband will be the new King [which is even worse].

An individual known as the Archimandrite presides over the coronation at the Palace and places the Crown of Tara on the Prince's head. Nobles then line up to take the oath of loyalty, and the next day there's a convocation with the Archimandrite and the priests. The Archimandrite is obviously a religious figure himself [the term

derives from the Greek Orthodox church], empowered to perform marriage and funeral rites. By the end of the caper, Reynart is secure on the throne and quite likely to marry Strella [they're kissing in a way that makes it unlikely they're related].

All minerals, particularly unusual ones, must be registered with the Knight of Gracht. Meaning Count Grendel, though he might be making this up to get his hands on Romana's Key segment. Castle Gracht is the ancient home of the Grendels of Gracht, its woodland estate containing the famous Pavillion of the Summer Winds and stocked with beasts for the Count to hunt. The beast seen here is an upright-walking mammalian creature with shaggy fur and oversized teeth. Apart from this, most fauna on Tara is supposed to be friendly [so assuming the creature seen here really is an animal, it's possible that the colonists deliberately brought these beasts to Tara]. The last siege of Castle Gracht lasted for two years, and before Romana nobody had ever escaped from its dungeons.

The Palace of Tara has its own guards, and beneath it are secret 'plague tunnels' built two-hundred years ago, to allow the nobles to move in and out without passing through the contaminated city. Monastic lands are held by religious orders under the protection of the crown, and the local unit of currency is the gold piece. There are Articles of War, which forbid violence under a flag of truce, while Reynart's men believe guerrilla attacks to be unethical. The Doctor indicates that Tara may be twelve parsecs from Earth [less than forty light-years].

History

• *Dating.* Assuming that Tara is an Earth colony, it's obviously several centuries in the future. The Doctor flippantly speaks of travelling at least four-hundred years through time. [If he means from Earth in "The Stones of Blood", then this would be somewhere around 2400, which is reasonable. Earth is apparently starting to lose track of its colonies in this period - see **What's the Timeline of the Earth Empire?** under 10.3, "Frontier in Space" - although the specialised skill of android-building isn't seen on any other colony-world in this era. It's been suggested that as Tara was devastated by a plague two-hundred years ago, it may be two-hundred years after the events of "Death to the Daleks" (11.3), which refers to a plague killing millions in the human

ABOUT TIME 1975-1979

colonies. But that would give "The Androids of Tara" a date of around 2800, and in that era Earth has an empire which doesn't seem prone to "forgetting" about far-flung colonies. C. 2400 is the most likely date, then, even if the Doctor's dating is hugely unreliable.

[The counter-argument is that this isn't an Earth colony at all, but a planet which - like so many others in the *Doctor Who* universe - may simply have developed Earth-like flora and fauna, up to and including humans. This makes more sense in terms of the plan for the Key to be scattered across space and time, rather than simply across a few centuries and in one galaxy, yet almost all the other segments have been within humanity's reach so there's no reason to assume that this one is an exception.]

The Analysis

Where Does This Come From? *Star Wars* has already been mentioned in this volume. It'll be mentioned a lot more as we get into the early 1980s, and if you don't know why then you weren't really "there", but "The Androids of Tara" is the moment when the film has its first measurable impact on *Doctor Who*.

It may be hard to understand why, now. Today *Star Wars* tends to be remembered as "that film with all the effects" or "that film with all the merchandising", but look at material written about it in the late '70s and the name which keeps cropping up (other than *Flash Gordon*, which also featured electrified swords) is "Errol Flynn". With nothing better to compare it to, at a time when movie SF meant down-to-earth dystopianism like *Rollerball* instead of space-opera, most people perceived it as a modern swashbuckler rather than what we now call "sci-fi". If "The Androids of Tara" seemed rather slow - see **Critique (Prosecution)** - then it was because the older generation had seen much snappier technicolour movies about pirates and / or European masterswordsmen, while the younger generation had seen George Lucas do the same sort of thing at lightning-speed. Was this story a direct response to the most-seen, most-talked-about movie of the previous twelve months? Well… let's give David Fisher credit, he obviously had *The Prisoner of Zenda* firmly in mind, and what we see here is in no way a cash-in. But it's enough to say that all the children watching saw the connection.

(A word might also be said about the use of armaments here. *Star Wars* gave us the lightsaber, the ultimate cinematic weapon, a beam of pure light in a medium that's entirely *made* of light. A lightsaber wouldn't be anywhere near as impressive in the real world as it is on the cinema screen, because that's its natural habitat. The SF-adjusted melee weapons in "Tara", on the other hand, are standard fencing swords from the BBC props department with "electric" effects added. Which is, of course, exactly right for this sort of production. This is the BBC, and it's theatrical, not cinematic. Since so many viewers had already seen Ben Kenobi slicing off a Walrus-man's arm with one blow, the moment when one of the Tarans uses an electro-sword against the Doctor for the first time - a small prod that makes the Doctor's hat explode with a little "pop" - almost comes across as a visual joke. And that's not even mentioning the laser-crossbows, among the earliest weapons in *Doctor Who* to fire Stormtrooper-like "bolts" instead of "beams".)

Things That Don't Make Sense It's fair enough that Romana doesn't know what a horse is, but she has to be *very* dense not to realise it's an animal rather than some sort of exotic travel-machine. And Mary Tamm really has to struggle to make it look as though the bonds in Lamia's workshop are holding her in place, even though they're not even touching her body. Why does the Prince only seem to have two men at his disposal for much of the story, and only a handful in the final attack on Castle Gracht? As rightful heir to the throne, surely he must be able to call on more support than that, even apart from the Palace Guards who get locked up by Grendel…? [Security reasons, possibly?]

Tara is a planet where androids are commonplace and every scheming politician has his own robot-wright, yet nobody there can tell androids and humans apart, even though the Doctor can identify a fake Princess Strella just from the sparking noise she makes.

Critique (Prosecution) Unsatisfying, but in no way annoying. The problem is this: if you want to make a swashbuckling adventure story, then everything's got to be *tight*. Everything's got to move at breakneck speed, and every scene's got to look like a Medieval tableaux. Whereas Seasons Sixteen and Seventeen represent *Doctor Who* at its all-time loosest, a period when the cast are prone to improvise, the directors are no longer thinking of the programme as an "action" series and the designers are most likely to make mistakes (although here, as in "The Ribos Operation", they make a much better job of "history in space" than they've been making of "spacemen in space").

"The Androids of Tara" wants to rollick, but can only saunter. Tom Baker's scenes with Reynart and his men, lounging around and discussing court politics as if he's just idly interested, are just too *slow* for this sort of story even if they're perfectly good in themselves. Too slow, and more importantly, much too casual. It's no surprise that the plot really comes to life when the Doctor's facing Count Grendel, not only because Grendel's the best villain in this season, but he's also the one part of this story who seems to make things more urgent.

It's another "little" story, and it doesn't pretend to be anything more, but perhaps the real trouble is that it's not little enough. At three episodes, it would have been better-paced. At four, it could only have justified its length by culminating in a titanic battle sequence as the castle comes under siege from Grendel's men, and obviously the budget was never going to stretch that far. The final duel may be endearingly witty, especially Grendel's last message before he leaps from the battlements ('next time, Doctor, I will not be so lenient,' spoken by a man who's just been thoroughly trounced), yet even *this* seems far too relaxed. This adventure started with the Doctor lazing around on a riverbank, and he still hasn't broken a sweat by the end of it.

Still, after all the pseudo-science of the last year or so, at the very least it's nice to have a story that relies on the *aesthetics* of SF (it's taken as read that androids are duplicates of people, so there's no spuriously-invented branch of physics to explain how they work) and doesn't involve the Doctor saving the day by cycling a narrow-band phased beam emission through a gravitic electron warp-loop. Mary Tamm's at her best here, too, mainly because she's separated from Tom Baker for most of the story and thus doesn't sound as if she's part of a double-act all the time.

Critique (Defence) This is the kind of story where the plot is served best by the Doctor knowing what people in love do, whilst not really paying much attention to why they do it. In that regard it's more responsible about relationships than the kitsch we got in the 1980s ("no hanky-panky in the TARDIS" translating as "this is for arrested adolescents only"). It's also, for a last-minute lash-up, astonishingly lavish. Well, except for the Archimandrite's clock, and *that* chair in Lamia's lab (see 9.2, "The Curse of Peladon" and 13.5, "The Brain of Morbius"). Three sets of uniforms, ball-gowns, night shooting and a genuine castle with a moat, none of yer Hollywood mock-ups here.

On top of all this, it's cast perfectly. Who else but Declan Mulholland could have played Till, the faithful retainer? Who else but Peter Jeffery is conceivable as Count Grendel? How could anyone but Cyril Shaps have been the Archimandrite? Only a professional pedant could fail to be satisfied. But underneath all this is a plot, and a nippy, twisty, roller-coaster of a plot it is. Even without the doppelgangers meeting in episode four as planned - see **The Lore** - it's a good example of what Douglas Adams said you had to do: 'keep it simple enough for the adults to follow, and complicated enough to keep the kids' attention'. The second cliffhanger is, the first time round, a real surprise. As the story that led into the Christmas holidays, it was exactly what the public wanted to see; but in the summer holiday repeat, even when most people watching knew how it went, it still delivered. This story is perfect, the way most *Bilko* episodes are perfect.

The BBC's insistence that *Doctor Who* had to at least gesture towards *Star Wars* is catered for here, although the Doctor sneers about how 'quaint' it all is. Photon crossbows are for 'peasants'. But by the end, when the Doctor takes on Grendel and goes from slapstick to genuine, no-holds-barred swashbuckling - at night, mind you, in a castle - you realise that all the BBC's expertise in this sort of thing easily outweighs its lack of budget, time or epic-scale sets.

The Facts

Written by David Fisher. Directed by Michael Hayes. Viewing figures: 8.5 million, 10.1 million, 8.9 million, 9.0 million.

Supporting Cast: Peter Jeffrey (Count Grendel), Simon Lack (Zadek), Neville Jason (Prince Reynart), Paul Lavers (Farrah), Lois Baxter (Lamia), Declan Mulholland (Till), Cyril Shaps (Archimandrite), Martin Matthews (Kurster).

Working Titles "The Seeds of Time", "The Prisoner of Zend" (clever, eh?).

Cliffhangers Having drunk the Prince's drugged wine, the Doctor collapses at the feet of the smug-looking Count Grendel; an individual who seems to be either Romana or Princess Strella bows before the throne of Tara, at which point the Doctor unexpectedly leaps forward and clubs her over the head with a sceptre; demonstrating how to be a proper villain, Grendel rides off with the captured Romana slung over his horse.

The Lore

• Plans for a more complicated ending were abandoned as, at the last minute, the location they'd chosen - Leeds Castle (in Kent, not in Leeds as certain American fans seem to think) - became the venue for Arab-Israeli peace talks. Security for Sadat, Begin and Kissinger meant that large numbers of people with swords and crossbows were barred.

• The first story considered for this slot was "The Shield of Zarak" by Ted Lewis, author of the novel which became the film *Get Carter*. The production team persevered with this storyline well into Season Seventeen, but it was obvious from the start that Lewis' shambolic personal life needed more attention than any script. He attended a script-meeting drunk, and so Robert Holmes was approached to rework "The Moon of Death" (see 16.5, "The Power of Kroll") as a quick replacement. In the meantime, David Fisher was asked to pull together an idea he'd suggested when devising "The Stones of Blood".

• "Grendel" is, as you all knew, the name of the monster in *Beowulf*. The names "Mortgard", "Thorvald" and "Freya" are also blatantly Nordic. "Tara" is an Irish kingdom, but nobody's quite sure which one. A Lamia is a snake-woman, sent to hypnotise and capture men, as in the poem by Keats about duplicates and temptresses (note the snake-like make-up on Lois Baxter).

• The fishing-rod was a valuable antique. Baker lost it in deep water, not keeping a grip when casting. Terry Walsh had to put on a diving suit and recover it before the insurance men found out.

• Walsh also doubled for Mary Tamm on horseback, and Peter Jeffrey in the swordfight (but note that, unlike the Pertwee stories, the star does almost all of his own fencing). Tamm asked Walsh for self-defence hints, and in the middle of a particularly complex hold her husband made a surprise visit...

• Just to round off the whole *Star Wars* theme: Declan Mulholland, who plays Till, was the original "human" Jabba the Hutt (the one who got cut from the original release of *Star Wars*, and replaced by a useless CGI slug for the Special Edition).

• It's been said elsewhere that the Taran throne is Tim's chair from *The Goodies*[6]. It isn't. We checked.

16.5: "The Power of Kroll"

(Serial 5E, Four Episodes, 23rd December 1978 - 13th January 1979.)

Which One is This? The one with a mile-wide squid, which is hard to miss. It's worshipped by big green men, and they're not exactly inconspicuous either.

Firsts and Lasts Although the credits say otherwise, this is the first story produced by John Nathan-Turner. See **The Lore**.

Four Things to Notice About "The Power of Kroll"...

1. Briefed to write a story featuring *the* biggest monster ever seen in *Doctor Who* (hardly the most inspiring starting-point for a story), Robert Holmes came up with Kroll, a giant squid with mile-long tentacles whose appearance on the horizon in episode two was the big monster moment for the six-year-olds of 1978 and possibly the most striking image of the season. Surprisingly the model of Kroll is quite good, if you can ignore the little fuzzy line between the prop and the horizon, but its worshippers...

2. ...dear God, its worshippers. The Swampies - green skinned men with dreadlocks who live in the marshes of the third moon of Delta Magna, but who talk (and hang around looking bored) like modern-day Earthmen - are quite unbelievable, and in this day and age it's hard to see how the programme-makers thought they could possibly get away with it without anyone sniggering. The sight of them bouncing up and down shouting 'Kroll!', occasionally in time to their drumming, is one of the all-time great "stupid *Doctor*

Who moments" and makes the 1976 version of *King Kong* look credible by comparison.

3. Beyond the rubber tentacles and the grotesque make-up, there's a fable about imperialism and native culture here, with the Swampies portrayed as a Native-American-style tribe being oppressed by the pale-faced dry-footed humans. For a work about imperial intolerance, though, the script is surprisingly ready to portray the Swampies as murderous, superstitious, octopus-worshipping savages (as in 9.4, "The Mutants", you can't help feeling there's something vaguely racist about all of this even though you know the race in question isn't real). Note, also, the way the Doctor dismissively describes the Swampies' leader as having 'narrow little eyes' which make him hypnotism-proof. As ever in these stories, the self-obsessed sacrifice-happy priest ends up being killed (eaten, in this case) by his own god.

4. K9 takes a break here, the first of several in the stories to come, as he's not great with swamp-moons. However, John Leeson - owner of K9's voice - finally shows himself in the flesh as Dugeen, a particularly wet technician on a particularly wet alien world.

The Continuity

The Doctor His super-powers are really piling up here. He indicates that he *does* hypnotise people a lot, as he says he can't do it to the leader of the Swampies because of the native's narrow eyes. He can make a flute out of a marsh-reed in moments, and play it perfectly. Even more improbably, he can howl an inhuman-sounding note that shatters glass [but see 8.5, "The Daemons"; 9.6, "The Time Monster"; 14.1, "The Masque of Mandragora" for other odd things Time Lords can do with their larynxes].

However, on this occasion he loses his ability to stop breathing, as he blacks out for a few minutes from oxygen starvation [he can't use his respiratory bypass system while he's active]. He knows a lot about the way refineries work, and has no qualms about telling the technicians how to improve their systems [even though it presumably runs a risk of changing local history]. He claims that seven is his lucky number [it's gone up a bit by 17.3, "The Creature from the Pit"].

The Doctor's nearly 760. Here he can easily read the holy book of the Swampies, even though it's in no recognisable language. On this occasion he doesn't know where the TARDIS has landed

ahead of time, but remarkably works out that he's on the third moon of Delta Magna just from the air and gravity. [More likely, he had a crafty check on board the Ship and is just trying to impress Romana.]

• *Inventory.* Ever the walking toolkit, here the Doctor's carrying a hammer in his coat. He nicks one of the silver cups from the refinery, not liking the look of what's in it.

• *Background.* The Doctor may have met the opera singer Dame Nellie Melba [another person he might have come across in the late nineteenth or early twentieth century], which supposedly explains his glass-shattering ability, though Melba could only do it with wine glasses and the Doctor can do it with whole windows. He mentions Binaca Ananda as if he's been there... see **Planet Notes** for more on this curious place.

The Supporting Cast
• *Romana.* She knows about butterflies. [See 16.2, "The Pirate Planet" and 16.6, "The Armageddon Factor" for more on her entomological studies.] She's now almost nonchalant about threats to shoot her, but finds ritual sacrifice a bit of an ordeal.

The TARDIS The Doctor must have waders on the Ship somewhere. The door can apparently open without letting in water [see 5.6, "Fury from the Deep" and 18.7, "Logopolis"].

The Guardians and the Key
• *The Key to Time.* The fifth segment was originally an icon of the Swampies known as the Symbol of Power, which gave them the ability to see the future and revealed that the humans would destroy Delta Magna with their greed and great cities. But when they took it from Delta Magna to the planet's third moon, it was eaten by a giant squid, and as a result the creature expanded to enormous size to become the 'god' Kroll. [They didn't see *that* coming. Segments of the Key often seem to have mystical powers even in their disguised forms. Is Kroll's growth a result of the Key's properties, or of the properties of the thing it's disguised as? Compare with the Seal of Diplos in 16.3, "The Stones of Blood".] Kroll seems to have been worshipped before this, though, as it ate the Symbol and the high priest on its 'third manifestation'. It's been dormant in the two-hundred years since.

Kroll is nearly a mile across, with thirty tentacles down one side, and it can move at six knots through swamp or water. Judging by the smaller squid specimen seen here, it was originally a squid much like those found on Earth [maybe even a squid brought by the Earth colonists to Delta Magna], but the Key segment mutated its shape as well as its size. Its feeding processes continue independently when it's sleeping, and the methane refinery on the moon has roused it. Primarily a vegetarian, Kroll has learned over the years that anything which moves is wholesome. It now hunts by surface vibrations, and it's frighteningly sensitive to those moving in its territory. In the end, just touching the Key tracer to Kroll's body-mass turns the segment back into its natural form and makes Kroll "burst" [its size can't be supported without the influence of the Symbol of Power, not even by the fifth segment in its natural form].

Planet Notes

• *The Third Moon of Delta Magna*. A swamp, basically. It has an Earth-like atmosphere, and though the Doctor claims it has an escape velocity of 1.5 miles per second [one-third that of Earth] everyone moves around as if it were an Earth-sized body. [The atmosphere is thinner than that of Earth, so the swamp may be the result of a terraforming exercise.] There's apparently nothing but marsh and wetland all around, and electrical storms are common.

The residents, green-skinned humanoids with dreadlocks known as "Swampies" by the imperialistic Earth-people, are tribal and superstitious but are attempting to buy guns to drive out their white oppressors. They worship Kroll even though this generation has never seen it before now, offering sacrifices to it before going to war and chanting its name an awful lot. During the sacrificial ritual, one of their number even dresses up as a squid in Kroll's honour.

Those who commit crimes against the Swampies are executed by any one of seven holy rituals, decided by their leader / high priest. The first ritual of the old book involves the victims being thrown down a pit and having rocks dropped on them, but the seventh and slowest involves tying the victims to a rack with creepers, which dry in the sunlight and snap the victims' spines. Despite their primitive nature, the Swampies' holy book of is a nicely-bound edition which they rather unwisely keep in a muddy

underground tunnel, and it describes how Kroll ate the Symbol of Power because he was angered at the people becoming fat and indolent. Swampies refer to the humans as 'dryfoots', but speak the human language perfectly. No female Swampies are ever seen here.

In fact the Swampies didn't originate here but on Delta Magna itself, and were moved to this "reservation" centuries ago by the humans who colonised the planet. Some specimens of giant squid were taken along, just to keep them happy. But now the humans have a methane catalysing refinery on the moon. It's a typical no-imagination futuristic Earth installation, all bland corridors and technicians in starchy blue-and-white uniforms. It's the first of its type known to the humans, and thus a classified project, producing a hundred tons of compressed protein a day and shooting it into Delta orbit every twelve hours as using freighters wouldn't be economical.

One of the Swampies, unconvincingly poured into uniform, is a servant there. The humans are planning to put ten refineries on the lake, forcing out the Swampies and meeting one-fifth of the protein requirements for Delta Magna, but it's only Kroll's presence that allows them to harvest the methane in such great quantities; the process is doomed after Kroll's destruction. The humans defend themselves with gas mortars, capable of knocking out the whole Swampie village in minutes, and their computer's designed to run things automatically.

Even without the Key segment inside it, the Kroll-squid is capable of remarkable cellular regeneration, as the Doctor believes that all the little bits will survive as smaller squid-creatures. Rohm-Dutt mentions a local insect called the drill-fly, which lays eggs in your feet. A week later you get holes in your head.

• *Delta Magna*. Delta Magna itself is getting crowded, while the Swampies are getting lots of popular support, so the Company that runs the refinery is trying to establish a more 'balanced' picture. There's a 'crank' organisation called the Sons of Earth [just on Delta Magna, or common to a lot of human colonies?], which believes that all life [*all* life???] originated on Mother Earth, that colonising the planets was a mistake and that humans should return there. Even though Rohm-Dutt believes humanity would starve on the old homeworld. The Sons of Earth have always denounced violence, but would have the

The Obvious Question: How Old is He?

Evidently, from the Doctor's inability to decide how old he is, there's some discrepancy between our idea of a "year" and his.

One minute David Whitaker, Doctor Who's very first script editor, is telling the youth of the nation that the Doctor is 900-odd (although to be fair, it's never said on-screen during the Hartnell era), then a regeneration later he's 450, if what he told Victoria in 5.1, "The Tomb of the Cybermen" wasn't a mild fib to reassure her ten minutes after her father died on an alien planet in the previous story, "The Evil of the Daleks".

By "The Mind of Evil" (8.2), he's apparently been a scientist for 'several thousand...' unspecified units of time. His life 'covers several thousand years' (7.2, "Doctor Who and the Silurians"), but that could mean anything, not just subjectively-experienced time. Then, in the mid-'70s, he settles on 750-something. Sort of. It's calibrated at 749 in 1975, 759 in 1978, then - in the unshown "birthday" scene of "The Stones of Blood" (16.3) - he's 751. Then there's a ruddy great leap, as he's around 900 in 1985 (22.6, "Revelation of the Daleks") and 953 in 1987 ("Time and the Rani"). Apparently, and fan-lore in the Big Finish era confirms this, Nyssa doesn't age like a human being and the period between "Time-Flight" (19.7) and "Arc of Infinity" (20.1) could be half a century long for all we know.

Now, there's the possibility that the switch from Hartnell to Troughton (4.2, "The Tenth Planet") was less of a full regeneration than a "renewal". Somehow, the Doctor's "deal" with time allowed him to lose a few years and get an upgrade on his body for a downgrade on his clothes. But it *might* be neatest to assume that the Doctor knows exactly how old he is, just not what that means in Earthly terms. Our year is simply the time it takes for Earth to orbit Sol. Converting that to or from the year of any other world should be simpler than converting Celcius to Fahrenheit, and anyone who spends as much time here as the Doctor does should be pretty good at juggling the currency. So perhaps there's a problem with Gallifrey's orbit.

Stepping briefly outside what's said on-screen, the mid-'70s saw a snazzy new TARDIS key for the Doctor (beloved of merchandisers and American fans) on which there's a design purported to be the constellation of Kasterborous. This claim comes from Barry Letts, and it was made at about the same time that the name "Gallifrey" began to be used for the previously-anonymous Time Lord homeworld, so we'll take it as authoritative. Usually, when words like "constellation" and "galaxy" are thrown about by Doctor Who writers, it's pretty vague and often accompanied by the use of "light-year" as a unit of time. What if we take it at face value, though?

Gallifrey has three suns, judging by the diagram on the key. Two possibilities arise from this. One: there's a primary sun which itself revolves around a larger, less agreeable star, or does a figure-eight around both of the others, in which case there may be a basic year for the planet's orbit and a bigger "stellar year" for the sun's orbit. Two: more alarmingly, Gallifrey weaves around all three stars. "Alarmingly" because the periodicity of the orbit(s) will be chaotic. "Chaotic" in the scientific sense, that is. As you probably know from pop-science magazine articles and documentaries, this means that there's no way to accurately predict where the planet will be in the immediate future. No two orbits are alike. There'll never be any such thing as *a* Gallifreyan year.

Still, when Time Lords talk among themselves they do seem to have an agreed length of time called a "year". If the Doctor and Romana can quarrel over how old the Doctor really is, and old-timers can grumble about Presidents changing 'every couple of centuries' (14.3, "The Deadly Assassin"), then that suggests a stable orbit of sorts. The "one sun revolves around another" theory seems more likely, then. It may be that the planet orbits a G-class star, which itself orbits a bigger, red star (hence the colour of the night sky). Or maybe they just agree that a certain number of days make one year and have "official" birthdays, like the Queen or Paddington Bear.

So why can't the Doctor convert from this to Earth time? The Gallifreyans might not calculate time so much as sense it. (If they evolved on a planet with such a wonky orbit then they'd have to, just because their remote evolutionary ancestors would otherwise have died through eating fruit out of season or not coming on heat at the same time.) That would explain the ancient Gallifreyans' overwhelming desire to conquer and organise time, just to get their lives in order. If it's instinctive, then perhaps they might not be able to articulate it when thinking in terrestrial, Newtonian terms.

resources to arm the Swampies if they wished. In truth, the refinery's commander, Thrawn, has arranged for the Swampies to acquire human-made guns as an excuse for him to wipe them out.

The technicians have litica-micros instead of books, and use heavy-duty energy weapons as well as old-fashioned pistols. They have the option of calling for a police ship or a missile strike from Delta Magna, though the latter would take eight hours to arrive, so depth charges seem a better way of trying to kill Kroll. Rohm-Dutt, the arms dealer who ends up as Kroll-fodder, is a well-known criminal figure and his recent disappearance was a cause for some concern. The rifles sent to the Swampies are gas-operated, which is eco-friendly at least.

• *Binaca Ananda.* According to the Doctor, it's a place with a methane refinery in every town. [He speaks of it as if it's a planet, but it's the name given to an astral plane in Sanskrit. It's unlikely that methane refineries would be found in such a place, so possibly it's a planet named *after* an astral plane, in the same way that English-speaking colonists might call a world "Heaven" or "Eden".]

History

• *Dating.* The far future. Earth is seen as a place to starve, and the Doctor - who seems to know this period - states that none of the Sons of Earth could possibly have seen the planet. [Dating this story is tricky. Parkin's *A History of the Universe* suggests 2878, but this is unlikely. The twenty-ninth century is the time of the Earth Empire, and with Earth so centralised it wouldn't be true to say that none of the Sons of Earth could have seen their ancestors' homeworld. The script is written to suggest a time thousands of years in the future, not just hundreds. The exotic names also suggest a far-distant era. If Earth has no way of supporting life then it may well be a time in the aftermath of the solar flares mentioned in 12.2, "The Ark in Space" (by the same scriptwriter), when Earth has been almost forgotten by humans on the outer planets. This seems the most feasible option, given the type of technology seen here. On the other hand it could be the same era as 15.4, "The Sun Makers" (by the same scriptwriter *again*), when Earth has been sacked by the Usurians. Robert Holmes was good at these apocalyptic visions.]

The human technicians measure storms on the Deemster scale, and still have quaint old expressions like 'killing two birds with one stone'. Their ultra-hard metal, ideal for pipelines but no match for Kroll: eighteen-gauge collodion. The Doctor speaks from experience when he says that Earth colonies tend to be 'insular'.

The Analysis

Where Does This Come From? As mentioned in the notes for "The Seeds of Doom" (13.6), this is the era when commercial exploitation of the Third World ran into the Human Rights lobby and started hiring armed mercenaries. That Rohm-Dutt is played with an Irish accent shouldn't need further explication.

What is worth a mention is the analogy drawn between oil companies and old-fashioned Imperialists. As we've recently seen in Nigeria and Chile, Western governments have little or no compunction about shifting indigenous populations around or intervening in local elections if there's oil to be found in the region. The most obvious examples in the late 1970s were Nicaragua and Iraq. In using Rohm-Dutt to "frame" the Swampies and justify the use of force, Thawn is applying tactics that many occupying powers had actually used, notoriously the British in Afghanistan during the Pathan conflicts at the Khyber Pass.

However, all this aside, there's a much more obvious source: the "Trail of Tears", when Algonquin and Sioux "homelands" were given to the Native Americans as a recompense, then taken away again when gold was found there (ownership of land isn't a problem for the Swampies, it appears). There's more than a hint of the early '70s "revisionist" westerns here, like *Soldier Blue* or *Little Big Man*. Add to this Romana's sacrifice being a shot-for-shot remake of the first appearance of Kong in *King Kong* (the good one), and this is getting a bit complex. The Swampies, if they're of human descent - and this is apparently both confirmed and denied in the script - might be Polynesian as well.

Another set of ethnic clichés may also be in play here; the whole of this script is in unmistakable debt to Frank Herbert's *Dune*. In *Dune*, a thinly-veiled Lawrence of Arabia comes to save a (literally) thinly-veiled Tuareg from evil exploiters. They've been moved from planet to planet, and have now adapted to a desert world with an addictive substance that's produced by a giant worm, which hunts by vibration and is worshipped as a god. All sounding familiar?

As Robert Holmes was somewhat reluctant about this project, it's no surprise that he ended up falling back on so many of his standards. The obsession with gas makes itself felt once again (see 10.2, "Carnival of Monsters" and 15.4, "The Sun Makers" for more on this), and as ever his villains are shifty businessmen rather than universe-conquerors. The use of language is distinctive, too; you wouldn't find a "Rohm-Dutt" in a Terrance Dicks script. Holmes takes a five-year break from the series after this, and returns in 1984 for "The Caves of Androzani" (21.6), a story which has occasionally been described as 'like "The Power of Kroll", but good'. Rohm-Dutt himself, a criminal who's happy to acknowledge his amorality and who's interested in Romana's theories as to why he's maladjusted, is a clear fore-runner of Sabalom Glitz (especially the more murderous Glitz seen in 23.1, "The Mysterious Planet", and not the later comedy version).

As the technobabble sounds like routine space-talk, it may have escaped your notice that Holmes has been doing his homework here. The use of hydrogen peroxide as a rocket oxidant makes sense for a low-gravity, low oxygen world (see **How Believable is the British Space Programme?** under 7.3, "The Ambassadors of Death") and the methane-protein combination would indeed involve a catalytic cracker. A lot of this was "in the air" at the time, as NASA and various universities looked into the long-term sustainability of space colonies.

Things That Don't Make Sense *If* you can accept that the Key segment returns to its natural state when the Doctor presses the tracer against Kroll's skin, even though the Symbol of Power must be nearly an eighth of a mile inside its body… *if* you can accept that Kroll's flesh somehow channels the tracer's power to the thing which originally made it big… then why does the Doctor seem so determined to touch Kroll's torso, rather than just touching the tentacle that's got him in its grip? As soon as Kroll vanishes, the segment is revealed to be sitting on the end of the tracer, which means that it must teleport from the depths of Kroll's stomach as well as returning to its normal form.

The Doctor calls the Swampies 'little green men', yet the shortest of them is a dead ringer for Terry Walsh, his own stunt-double. As ever, the word "constellation" is used to mean "system".

Incredibly, it never occurs to any of the humans that if they talk about wiping out the Swampie village in front of their Swampie servant, he might just sneak off to warn his relatives about it.

Critique (Prosecution) Generally awful, but for different reasons than most of the worst stories of this era.

Made at a time when the programme could often fall foul to self-indulgence, over-played comedy and ludicrous techno-fetishism, "The Power of Kroll" fails not because of any of these things but just because it's so *tedious*. Nobody's heart is in it here, least of all the writer's. Most of the big scenes are set pieces, sloppy death-traps and easy escapes that make the Doctor look as if he doesn't even have to try any more. The programme's always at its worst when there's no wit or colour except when the Doctor's on the screen, and here the scenes of (a) technicians having dreary conversations and (b) Swampies having silly conversations drag on and on and on while giving you nothing at all to look forward to. (The *three-minute* control room scene in episode two is one of the most boring things you'll ever witness, only enlivened when the computer makes a breaking-wind noise at an inopportune moment.) You can literally skip episode three without missing a beat.

Ranquin's mad rant in the final episode is such a hollow pastiche of religious maniacs past that you have to wonder why he was included in the story at all, while the "epilogue" - in which the Doctor stops the refinery self-destructing by fiddling around with some wires - is as pointless as almost everything else. Even Glyn Owen's performance as Rohm-Dutt, the only character *with* any character, seems oddly uninterested.

But what's even more noticeable than the raw tedium is that it's weirdly old-fashioned, with the technicians' talk of 'orbit-shots' suggesting a time when the TV audience didn't take SF standards for granted and needed reassurance that spaceships are no more complicated than NASA rockets. The refinery scenes occasionally look (and sound) as if they've been taken from one of the less convincing black-and-white "station under siege" stories of the '60s, with an all-male crew going through the motions of looking at computer read-outs and arguing about the best way to deal with the alien threat. And the aliens in question… no, it's not even worth dwelling on the Swampies, except to say that their scenes would convince anyone already inclined to dislike *Doctor Who* that all their worst prejudices about it were right.

Overall it's hard to hate "The Power of Kroll", in the same way that (for example) one might hate "Underworld", but two hours after watching it you won't be able to remember who any of the characters were or why they did any of the things they did. Its most original feature, and sadly one which only works the first time you see it, is that at the end of episode one you're led to believe that Kroll is the man-sized monster who threatens Romana (actually just a Swampie in a ceremonial costume) but in episode two you find out that Kroll is in fact a mile-wide squid capable of eating the whole refinery.

Critique (Defence)   You have to feel sorry for director Norman Stewart; they gave him the two most difficult stories to make (this and 15.5, "Underworld"), and the scripts with the least for him to get any "juice" from. Yet what's here isn't at all bad. Location-work seems to suit him rather better than the all-CSO studio work in "Underworld", and the hovercraft and vast panoramas of swamp make the first episode at least seem unlike anything we've seen for ages. A look at the script shows how little the regulars tampered with the text; even Romana's apparent ad-lib about displacement activity in episode three is Holmes giving her the kind of Doctorishness we'd later see in Seasons Seventeen and Eighteen. The Doctor's comments on the clichés of adventure TV ('aren't you going to say "don't try anything"?') aren't too far removed from what even Starsky and Hutch were doing in 1978.

The whole point of *Doctor Who*, surely, is to give the viewers at home something they've not seen before and a reason to keep watching. You've got both of those here. Which other programme would give you a western in a swamp? By the time they've figured out what kind of story they're watching, the punters have a lot more questions than answers. One of these, unfortunately, is 'how much longer?'. The exposition seems to take a large chunk of episodes one and two, but this pays off in the latter half. Unlike '80s stories, where people suddenly do spectacular things (or things intended to look spectacular, anyway) right out of the blue, in a story like this the effort put in at the start enables viewers to join the dots unprompted.

We hear a lot of mumbo-jumbo about the way the modern generation takes in visual information faster, but the evidence shows something else. All the research into this indicates that older subjects process verbal and textual information faster. For younger viewers, visual storytelling is initially faster, but as recall is required younger probands need more reinforcement. In short, kids today need to be told twice as often as '60s kids, even if the first time round it doesn't take them as long to get it. And whilst today's viewers may need less "think time", they seem not to be able to pick up on nuances of behaviour or emotion, needing all characterisation to be laid on a bit thicker (compare the acting in, say, *The Forsythe Saga* with *CSI* and the earlier production can leave so much more unsaid).

Children *at the time* lapped this up. Adults, a bit more cynical, got involved in the policitcking. For anyone else, it at least looked unlike all the other space-opera stuff doing the rounds that year.

The Facts

Written by Robert Holmes. Directed by Norman Stewart, at short notice (see **The Lore**). Viewing figures: 6.5 million, 12.4 million, 8.9 million, 9.9 million. Note how episode one got 6.5 million, as everyone was Christmas shopping; episode two received a stonking 12.4 million, as in those days the week between Christmas and New Year was a wilderness of dreary wholesome family programming and dull sporting novelty shows.

Supporting Cast: Philip Madoc (Fenner), John Leeson (Dugeen), Neil McCarthy (Thawn), John Abineri (Ranquin), Glyn Owen (Rohm-Dutt), Carl Rigg (Varlik), Frank Jarvis (Skart), Grahame Mallard (Harg), Terry Walsh (Mensch).

Working Titles   "The Moon of Death", "Horror of the Swamp", "The Shield of Time".

Cliffhangers   Tied to a stake in the Swampie village, Romana *really* starts to scream as a set of black claws reach out for her; one of Kroll's tentacles bursts through a refinery pipeline and grabs the nearest technician; Kroll's vast form rises up above the swamp, taking up most of the horizon.

The Lore

• A story with a backstage story far more complex. Alan Browning had been scheduled to direct, but fell ill. During the changeover, as production-manager-turned-director   Norman Stewart took over, Philip Madoc found out that he was to play Fenner and *not* Thawn as he'd thought. George Baker, cast as Thawn (see 18.3, "Full Circle"), also pulled out at short notice and Neil McCarthy came in. Martin Jarvis, as Dugeen, either bailed or was rejected as John Leeson took on the role (which was cheaper, as he was already contracted).

Then Graham Williams was off on his break, so production unit manager John Nathan-Turner stepped into the breach. In case he made a mess, the producer from BBC Classic Serials - former *Doctor Who* boss Barry Letts - was asked to keep an eye on things. Just to round things off, at this point script editor Anthony Read mentioned that he was increasingly frustrated by the way the BBC and Tom Baker were draining him, and that he wanted to move on to other projects...

• Robert Holmes, although irked at being told to keep it serious and make the monster a whopper, submitted the scripts in under three weeks.

• The costumes included high rubber boots for the Doctor and Romana, but these vanished within seconds of the first attempt at a scene of them walking through the swamp. The location, should you be gagging to go and squelch in the footsteps of TV's *Doctor Who*, was the Iken Marsh in Suffolk.

• The "join" between Kroll and the horizon was the result of a misunderstanding between effects designer Tony Harding and location cameraman Martin Pathmore, about the split-screen effect being done electronically in post-production rather than on the lens during the shoot. It didn't help that the model was filmed at an awkward angle in its tank.

• The make-up for the Swampies had to be water-resistant, as so much rain and... well... swamp was involved. However, it proved impossible to wash off. The actors, including at least two future semi-regular Cybermen (see 19.6, "Earthshock", and others) needed to go to the nearby RAF base for swarfega and showers. This amused the men stationed at the base no end.

• Early versions of the script set the story on Ganymede rather than Delta Magna, presumably meaning the Jovian moon (see 12.5, "Revenge of the Cybermen" and 14.5, "The Robots of Death").

• The tracer prop went missing during studio filming, and a third version of it had to be built. (There was one for insertion into the TARDIS console and another, with a battery and lights, for actual tracing.) Mary Tamm maintains that the prop cost more than she got per story.

• Note for non-British, non-old-enough readers: the three ducks on Baker's lapel are a witty *homage* to the quintessentially cheesy plaster ducks that boring married couples used to have on their living-room walls in the '70s. These were the interior décor equivalent of slippers, pipe and Mantovani records (for American readers: Laurence Welk).

• In the *real* world there's an investigation company called Kroll, specialising in financial irregularities. The summer of 2004 saw at least three high-profile cases reported in the UK "quality" press, invariably referring to the company in the singular (as in "Kroll has been called in to investigate..." "Kroll interviewed CEO Fred Pilk..."). The attempted takeover of the Abbey Bank by a Spanish corporation was besmirched with allegations of bribes and sexual impropriety, which explains headlines like "Suicide Mystery After Kroll Investigation at Abbey" (*Sunday Times*, 15th of August). The funniest thing about this isn't the bizarre *Name of the Rose* scenario it suggests, but the idea of a quarter-mile-wide squid with sunglasses and a false moustache going undercover.

16.6: "The Armageddon Factor"

(Serial 5F, Six Episodes, 20th January - 24th February 1979.)

Which One is This? Two planets locked in a seemingly-endless nuclear war, both of them fighting over a beautiful princess (though they don't know it yet). The Doctor encounters his Shadow, and Romana gets to look her future self in the eye. But remember: after this they're supposed to hand in their Key to Time project, and the Guardian's going to be in a dark mood if he doesn't get it...

Firsts and Lasts After eight years of unlikely science and bad nuclear physics, it's the last outing for Bob Baker and Dave Martin as a writing team, although Baker will be back on his own for Season Seventeen. They re-use many of their favourite ideas for their final script together, including time-loops (8.3, "The Claws of Axos"), Time Lords with Greek names (10.1, "The Three Doctors") and the relative dimensional stabiliser (AKA the shrinking machine, 15.2, "The Invisible Enemy").

The Key to Time cycle ends here, and along with it goes Mary Tamm. However, the same story sees the first appearance of Lalla Ward, here playing Princess Astra but destined to be "body-snatched" by Romana in the next story.

Demonstrating that he's now supposed to be the Children's Favourite, for the first time the "life" of K9 is put in jeopardy as a way of building up the dramatic tension, as he's loaded onto a conveyor belt and slowly led towards a furnace in episode two. And though he's not credited, the last few scenes of "The Armageddon Factor" are script-edited by Douglas Adams, who'll take over from Anthony Read as full-time script editor in Season Seventeen. In similar vein, Graham Williams was still off sick at the preparatory stage of this story, and the production duties went to David Maloney (see 14.6, "The Talons of Weng-Chiang").

It's the first time, after goodness-knows how many years, that Pat Gorman - usually encased in latex and stomping about looking like a scary monster - gets a sitting-down, speaking, face-on-TV role as the pilot of the Marshall's ship. It's a great part: he's in three episodes, but caught in a tape-loop (sorry, time-loop), so he did about ten minutes' work which gets shown again and again for Equity standard rates.

Six Things to Notice About "The Armageddon Factor"...

1. It's the story in which the Doctor finally gets a name: the "fallen" Time Lord Drax, who went to the Academy with him, refers to him as "Theta Sigma" (*The Making of Doctor Who* gives it as $\_^3\_x^2$; see 10.1, "The Three Doctors"). After all, this is a script written by Baker and Martin, the people who've been trying to take the mystery out of the Time Lords ever since "The Claws of Axos" (8.3) and who were the first ones to give *any* Time Lord a proper name in "The Three Doctors". And what name did they choose then? Omega, which is - like Theta and Sigma - a Greek letter. Though you can see why fans immediately assumed this was just the Doctor's school nickname, you get the terrible feeling that the writers honestly thought they were naming the Doctor after all these years...

2. We've already seen how the programme's writers started having trouble involving the Doctor in adventures after he figured out how to steer his TARDIS properly (because if you need to

get your central cast into trouble every four -to-six weeks, then the random landings of the early series are just far more convenient), but "The Armageddon Factor" breaks new ground in contrived adventure television with the introduction of 'the randomiser'. Installed in the TARDIS so that the Black Guardian can't track the Doctor's movements, it demonstrates once and for all that the Doctor just doesn't *want* to know where he's going... but it's ironic that once the randomiser's in place, subsequent writers hardly ever use it, and keep letting the Doctor over-ride it whenever they need him to go somewhere specific.

3. The opening scene is one of melodramatic heroism, in the style of British-made films about World War Two, in which a brave young man of Atrios bids farewell to his true love as he goes off to fight the noble fight against the evil planet Zeos. This is soon undercut when we realise that it's actually part of a propaganda film, being shown on TV in a grubby-looking field hospital that's being bombed to bits, and that nobody's even watching it. But what's great is that just at the precise moment when viewers are wincing at the dialogue and wondering if the whole story's going to be like this, the next line is the immortal rallying-cry: 'Young men are dying for it!'

4. The problems of letting casual viewers know about an ongoing story arc (see 16.3, "The Stones of Blood") really become obvious here, as the Key to Time sequence draws to a close. In a last-ditch effort to remind the audience about the Guardians before the Black Guardian finally appears, the Doctor once *again* feels the need to explain the nature of the quest to Romana, this time telling her that it was the White Guardian who sent them to find the Key (and not, as she once thought, the President of the Time Lords). Except that... she's already been told this, and been amazed by it, in "The Stones of Blood". Nevertheless, she's happy to be amazed by it again here.

5. The Black Guardian himself is curious, even if he's played by the late, great Valentine Dyall. Seen in his "natural" form, he appears as a photographic negative of a human face, but then becomes reasonably normal-looking as he disguises himself as the White Guardian. Unfortunately, he doesn't look anything like the White Guardian we saw in "The Ribos Operation" (16.1). Could it be that the two Guardians were originally supposed to be played by the same actor, one in positive and one in negative? Could

How Hard is it to Be the Wrong Size?

As geneticist J. B. S. Haldane observed in his famous 1930s essay On Being The Right Size, there are problems with the sort of thing routinely taking place in stories like "The Invisible Enemy" (15.2).

Let's start with "getting bigger" before we move on to the fiddlyness of "getting smaller". Something x centimetres long changing to 3x centimetres will be disproportionately gaining mass and surface area, so if y is the original mass and z is how much skin there is, you get y^3 and z^2. Which means that a giant rat, going from six inches to ten feet (as the Doctor estimates it in 14.6, "The Talons of Weng-Chiang"), is going from x to 20x; the skin area will be 400 times bigger, and the weight 8,000 times greater. As the cross-section of his bones is only going to be twenty times bigger, that's a lot more weight to take per joint, and the poor bugger's going to break every bone in his body trying to move. Even standing still is risky. He'll also need to eat a lot more, as all that extra surface area is going to radiate heat (although a larger volume of brown fat may offset this, especially if he's not moving). The lungs will also be much larger, though the heart will be under an enormous strain keeping up.

On the plus side, as noted in "The Power of Kroll" (16.5), something big has a slower metabolism and can live for ages. This, of course, presents problems for anything made small. But for now we'll consider the problem of a three-metre robot turning into a thirty-metre one (12.1, "Robot") and not crashing to the ground under the strain on its ankles. As with the rat, the K1 robot has the capacity to adjust its molecular structure and grow, albeit not this big nor this fast. Neither being, however, has any capacity for modification of the "design"; rats are the optimum size for their lifestyle. Compare this with beings whose DNA has been altered in embryo, such as giant maggots (10.5, "The Green Death"), and the problem is obvious. If the rat were an adult before the "change" then it'd be a hairy blob, not rat-shaped nor able to run. If it were an embryo, then how did the foetus get to full-term? Maggots, developed from eggs exposed to a teratogenic green slime, don't have this problem (though the adult insect shouldn't be able to fly in our air).

Now we tiptoe into the realms of madness with writers Bob Baker and Dave Martin. By introducing dimensional stabiliser mayhem in "The Invisible Enemy" and "The Armageddon Factor", they seem to be playing along with ideas floated in the very first script meetings for the story which became "Planet of Giants" (2.1). However, it's not as simple as it might seem.

When the TARDIS crew were minimised before, it was because the Ship had landed badly and was itself tiny. In "Carnival of Monsters" (10.2) there's a compression field; once removed from this, things resume their rightful size. Thus any air inside the Miniscope is proportionately small and therefore breathable. Shrunken people can eat food and drink scotch and metabolise it all. In "Planet of Giants" the disproportionate size of Barbara to the pesticide DN7 makes its effect on her worse, although slower than with insects as her skin pores are smaller than those of an ant. With "The Invisible Enemy", what's particularly annoying is that the writers think of some of the problems. Mini-Leela is told that she isn't wet because she's too small to break surface tension, but nobody asks things like "how does she breathe giant air molecules?".

In all of these cases, however, a bigger problem is that a shrunken object retains its mass but has to squeeze it all into a smaller space. Azal in "The Daemons" (8.5) can miniaturise himself, yet at least has the good grace to shed some of his mass as energy and cause a minor heatwave. Normal people wouldn't survive this even if they could do it; the mass-loss would have to come from non-essential body-parts, and no shrinking-device we've seen used on humans is that selective. If we try to cram mass into a smaller space "naturally" then we either make things denser (and anything containing as much water as a human being won't get much more compact... uniquely, water gets bigger as it cools, so the molecules are at their most dense at 4ºc) or we melt it down. A lot of mass in a little space causes all sorts of tidal problems, and in extremis, a black hole. Surviving even a slight reduction is unlikely, and the Master notoriously uses miniaturisation as his trademark murder technique (8.1, "Terror of the Autons", et seq.).

The only other known way of doing it is for matter to degenerate, stripping the electron shells and making superdense stuff like the core of a neutron star (see 18.5, "Warriors' Gate"). This is the fabled one-teaspoon-weighs-a-ton material, neutronium, and it's not healthy to be converted into if you can help it. The people made tiny in Doctor Who are usually compacted inside some kind of "field", and thus not really engaging with the out-

continued on page 261...

it be that Cyril Luckham just wasn't available to reprise his "White Guardian" role? (If so then it's something that was completely forgotten by the time of 20.5, "Enlightenment", when both Luckham and Dyall get recalled to the series and the Guardians come face-to-face.)

6. The last episode sees a tiny shrunken Doctor being threatened by one of the Mutes, inhuman servants of the villainous Shadow. You would have thought that since they knew the creature's feet were going to be seen in close-up, the costume designers would have come up with more exotic footwear for the Mute than a pair of lace-up shoes from Clark's.

The Continuity

The Doctor

• *Background.* Rescuing K9 from the heat of a furnace, the Doctor claims he learned the trick of somehow traversing such an environment unharmed from fire-walkers in Bali. [But it's not just his feet... at the very least, his coat should have been singed.]

The Doctor qualified at the Academy in the class of '92; see **Time Lords** for more on this period in his life. He's never been to Atrios, nor Zeos.

The Supporting Cast

• *Romana.* She's heard of Atrios and Zeos, and seems to have learned about them at the Academy, unlike the Doctor. But she's never heard of Columbus. She is, however, up to speed on the dances of bees [yet more entomological knowledge].

• *K9.* Proving he's got feelings, he seems positively enthusiastic about communicating with the Zeon computer and sees it as far more interesting than limited organic minds. He spins round and round when he's about to communicate with the computer's systems, in what Romana believes to be a communication ritual, and he talks to the machine in radiophonic-like computer language. He's also taken to talking to himself in a very non-logical voice, sighing with relief when turned the right way up.

He can identify an incoming nuclear missile from inside the TARDIS, and gauge the depths of the tunnel in which the TARDIS lands, but lead shielding blocks his analysis. The radiation levels cause him to make a burbling noise when he first arrives. He suffers from overheating as he approaches the furnace, and eventually shuts down.

K9 only refers to the person who controls him as 'master', and calls the Doctor 'Doctor' when he's taken over by the Shadow, even when he's pretending to be on the Doctor's side [he doesn't have enough imagination to act properly]. He knows TARDIS technology well enough to realise that the Doctor's right about synaptic adhesion in Drax's dimensional stabiliser, and doesn't mind threatening Drax with obliteration in order to get his way [but he's bluffing]. Most improbably of all, he coughs when he's surrounded by rock dust. [He's clearing it out of his filters, and the Doctor's programmed him to make that noise as a joke... maybe. But see 17.1, "Destiny of the Daleks".] Ham that he is, he also clears his "throat" before he delivers a lie to the Shadow, as if making a performance.

The TARDIS(es) The TARDIS is explicitly said to materialise in 'parking orbit' of a planet before its final landing [something implied by many, many stories before this]. Co-ordinates for Atrios are 0069 [another four-digit planetary code, as in 16.1, "The Ribos Operation"], but the TARDIS arrives in space millions of miles away, and the Doctor thinks there may have been a 'time-shift'. A second reading gives the figure 008010040 [this seems to be a more complex reading of the same location, implying more than one navigational system on the TARDIS console... we might have guessed]. After the four-digit code takes the TARDIS to roughly the right part of space, the readings from the tracer are used to land as close to the Key segment as possible.

The Doctor activates all the TARDIS' defences when he's confronted with the Black Guardian, and improbably this stops the Guardian getting hold of the Key to Time. Ultimately the Doctor fits his TARDIS with a randomiser, a new device fitted to the guidance systems which causes the Ship to head for a random destination in the universe whenever it moves. He's quite confident that the Black Guardian won't be able to track him down if he doesn't know where he's going. The randomiser isn't actually seen here [and appears from out of nowhere between scenes]. There's enough chronodyne on board the Ship to allow the Doctor to construct a fake sixth segment of the Key to Time. It's silver in colour, and must be quite easy to manipulate.

How Hard is it to Be the Wrong Size?

...continued from page 259

side world, which is evidently why they're still people and not dots of neutronium. Aside from the breathing issue - which we can reluctantly sidestep as "dramatic license" - they should really be thought of as existing in a different dimension.

Yet the Doctor and Leela can interact with the world around them when they're shrunk to microscopic size in "The Invisible Enemy", so what happens to the mass? Potentially it's "banked" in a "holding account" within the stabiliser field generator. This might explain how a noetic virus gains so much bulk and changes shape at the end of episode three; it's got the mass that the Doctor and Leela put into the "account" earlier on. Mind you, if it's that easy to make things mass-less than travelling at the speed of light shouldn't be much of a problem, so no wonder space travel's so popular in the *Doctor Who* universe. What this means is that things reduced must be restored at some point, and by the same process which shrank them. From this we can conclude that the shrinking in "Planet of Fire" (21.5) is entirely stupid, but we might have guessed that.

Bizarrely, then, "The Armageddon Factor" presents us with the most credible size-change. It's temporary, and it's undone with the same device by which it was achieved; it's a reduction of 10:1, and it's conducted on two Time Lords who can presumably breathe under difficult circumstances. It's still twaddle, but give them marks for effort.

Drax's transport once got stuck on Earth thanks to trouble with the hyperbolics. He explicitly refers to his machine as a TARDIS, and it gets left on Zeos here, while some of its components are destroyed along with the Shadow's realm [so Drax won't be going far]. Its dimensional stabiliser is used to make a 'shrinking gun', the same principle once used by the Doctor [in 15.2, "The Invisible Enemy"]. Drax claims he's worked on 'thousands' of these [hugely unlikely], and believes the chronostat's out of order, though the Doctor realises it's synaptic adhesion that's causing the trouble. This time subjects only shrink to action figure size, not microscopic.

The Time Lords

• *Drax.* Another renegade Time Lord, Drax went to the [Prydon] Academy with the Doctor and speaks of the class of '92. They went on the tech-course together. The Doctor doesn't immediately recognise Drax; Drax knows the Doctor, but then, he's been briefed by the Shadow [there's no way of knowing whether Drax has regenerated]. His name for the Doctor, from the Academy days, is "Theta Sigma" or just "Thete" [25.2, "The Happiness Patrol", confirms that this was just a nickname]. This was 450 years ago, from Drax's point of view [and probably the Doctor's; see **Do Time Lords Always Meet in Sequence?** under 22.3, "The Mark of the Rani"].

Drax is - at present - a rough-edged, balding man with a cockney accent. He was good at practical work but poor at temporal theory, failed to qualify at the Academy and left Gallifrey. He went into repair and maintenance, doing anything, any time, anywhere. He buys, fixes and sells [you don't really need money if you've got a space-time capsule, so Drax probably just thinks the lifestyle suits him] in the fields of cybernetics and guidance systems, sometimes even dealing in armaments but 'not on a regular basis'.

He's definitely referred to as a Time Lord. [It's not clear whether you have to qualify to be called a Time Lord, or whether it's something that happens to your biology even before you go to one of the Academies. Drax might have been granted the Lord title even though he failed, or he might have re-taken his exams and qualified at a later date than the Doctor. Mind you, even the Doctor didn't pass on the first attempt.] He owns a TARDIS, which doesn't work, so presumably he doesn't have the parts to fix it as he's shown to be a competent technician otherwise. He never goes nowhere without 'is tools.

Drax's transport once broke down in Brixton, London, and he spent ten years in prison after trying to acquire replacements [meaning, replacement parts?]. This is where he picked up the accent and the annoying lingo. At first he thought the Shadow was just another customer, but the creature forced him to install [and build?] the Mentalis machine on Zeos, and he's been stuck in the Shadow's domain for the last five years. At the end of the caper, Drax plans to set up a contract job on Atrios, a deal with the Marshal to re-build the planet now the war's over.

The Guardians and the Key Having fully assembled the Key to Time, the face of the White Guardian appears on the scanner and asks the Doctor to hand it over. However, when the Guardian shows no concern for the welfare of Princess Astra - AKA the sixth segment - the Doctor grows suspicious, and orders the Key to scatter itself throughout space and time again. His hunch is confirmed when the White Guardian then turns out to be the Black one in disguise, who swears to hunt him down and make him suffer, etc. Whether the Key was assembled long enough for the *real* White Guardian to 'stop everything' and maintain the balance of the universe isn't made clear.

[At least, that's *one* interpretation of what happens here. But it's odd that the Doctor never even pauses to ask whether his mission was a success, and whether eternal chaos has been averted (he does in Terrance Dicks' novelisation of this story, perhaps by way of apology for what many saw as a cop-out ending at the time). And if the Black Guardian has to get the Doctor to hand over the Key before he can use it, then surely the White Guardian would have to do the same?

[The most logical solution is obvious: there was never a crisis. Eternal chaos wasn't threatening the universe - though "Logopolis" (18.7) might suggest otherwise - and the old man who gave the Doctor his mission in "The Ribos Operation" (16.1) was the Black Guardian, adopting the same disguise that he adopts here. This makes sense of many things. For a start, it always seemed odd that the White Guardian kept the "core" of the Key, when it shouldn't be the place of *either* Guardian to hold such an object (unless it *wasn't* given to Romana by the White Guardian, and it's normally kept on Gallifrey?). But if the Black Guardian had somehow only recently come into possession of the tracer, then it'd explain why he's only now giving someone vaguely qualified the task of finding all the other Key components. And another point: the Doctor knows the Guardian here isn't the real White Guardian, because the real White Guardian is "nice" and should care more about Astra. But the being who gave him the mission in "The Ribos Operation" wasn't "nice" either, and actively threatened the Doctor with non-existence in order to make him do the job. In addition to which, the supposed White Guardian's logic that Astra should be sacrificed for the greater good seems morally sound, or at least not wholly

objectionable. If all of this *has* been a ploy by the Black Guardian, though, then the Shadow doesn't know about it as he's convinced that the Doctor works for Whitey.]

• *The Shadow.* The Black Guardian's servant, a creepy, black-clad being who wears the top half of a skull over his eyes and nose, so he's clearly rotten. It's the Shadow who's been maintaining the war between Atrios and Zeos, and his own domain - a world of gloomy rock passages, which looks more like a space-station from the outside, confusingly referred to by Romana as the Planet of Evil - is halfway between the two planets. This realm stops the TARDIS getting a good view of Zeos from space, and is a recent addition to this region, as it's caused the orbital shift in Atrios which makes the TARDIS miss the planet by some distance.

The Shadow knows about the Key to Time and knows the Doctor has some pieces [the Black Guardian has briefed him], but doesn't seem to have the secrets of time-travel, doesn't know the disguised sixth segment when he sees it and can't open the TARDIS door. Entertainingly, he knows the Doctor can't abide being stuck in one place and is prepared to wait a thousand years - if necessary - for the Doctor to open the TARDIS and give him access to the Key to Time. He can create insubstantial phantoms of people, somehow, but can't abide strong light. He describes the Zeos / Atrios war as a 'rehearsal', as when he has the Key he plans to set two halves of the universe against each other, apparently what the Black Guardian wants. Nonetheless, the Black Guardian describes him as a 'whimpering wraith'.

Helping the Shadow are beings called Mutes, similarly robed types in black bone-like masks, who naturally can't speak and who follow his orders. The Shadow has a transmat shaft to Atrios or Zeos, and has been controlling the Marshal of Atrios with an implant on the man's neck, through which the victim can hear his voice. The same kind of implant doesn't work on the Doctor at all, but it does work on K9. Victims have no memory of their actions after the implant is removed.

The Shadow's exact nature is unknown, but he claims he's been waiting since eternity began for this moment. So his destruction at the Doctor's hands, when the Marshal's missiles are deflected from Zeos, must be a grave disappointment.

• *The Key to Time.* The Doctor describes the sixth segment as the most important of all. It's taken human form, and become Princess Astra, the Sixth princess of the Sixth Dynasty of the Sixth Royal House of Atrios. The secret of the segment is said to have been passed down from generation to generation of the royal house, but Astra is the sole surviving member of the line and doesn't know anything about it. She does, however, have an instinctive sense of her 'destiny' as she approaches the point when she's turned back into a segment. She looks perfectly happy about this, calling it a 'metamorphosis'.

The medic Merak finds a genetic anomaly in her bloodline, with Astra being its end result, so he believes that every cell in her body is part of the Key. [Again, the segment would seem to be bending local culture around itself. The connection between the segment and the number six, proving some sort of "order" to the parts of the Key, verges on the mystical. It's almost as if the segment planted exactly the right genetic information in Astra's ancestors, so that it could come into existence as Astra at exactly this point in time.] Astra is clearly sentient, and a "real" person, hence the Doctor's ethical concerns about changing her back into a lump of something mineral. She changes into the segment when she enters the Key's presence and realises her destiny, so the tracer doesn't need to touch her.

Once he's got five of the segments, the Doctor's capable of building a fake sixth segment out of chronodyne [the name suggests a material with intrinsic time-travel properties]. Fitting the chronodyne into the five genuine segments allows the Doctor to use some of the Key's power, enough to put the whole universe in a three-second time-loop. This threatens to burn out the chronodyne in 3.25 minutes, however, and the loop gets longer and longer every time it cycles as the chronodyne deteriorates. [This is the first time we've ever seen "inside" a time-loop, so it's not just something you can't escape from but something that forces you to go through the same piece of history over and over again.]

The loop begins automatically when the mock-up Key is complete, but the Doctor verbally commands it to only loop a specific area, so the chronodyne lasts longer and the loop stretches by only 0.3 milliseconds per second. The Doctor believes it creates a neutral, timeless zone, though the Key's operator is immune to the loop and the user can interact normally with a time-looped area. [This means that things moved around by the Doctor don't reset to their old positions when the loop

begins again, and that's as close to magic as you'll ever get. Compare this to the Doctor's "powers" as a Time Lord in "Invasion of the Dinosaurs" (11.2) and "The Time Monster" (9.6).] K9 believes that chronodyne is 74% compatible with the rest of the Key.

When all six parts of the Key are assembled into a cube around the tracer core, the Doctor believes he has power over every particle in the universe. Certainly, the Black Guardian has to ask for the Key rather than just seizing it. When the Doctor snaps the Key's core, the Key scatters itself again, and Astra re-appears on Atrios as if nothing had happened. [By implication: Garron will get his jethryk back, the Megara will take custody of the Seal of Diplos, the Gracht family statue will repair itself and the Swampies will regain their Symbol of Power. But if the planet Callufrax tries to go back to its former place in space and time then Zanak is in for a hell of a shock. The tracer would seem to be a vital and irreplaceable part of the Key, not just a gizmo for tracking down the segments, so by snapping it the Doctor basically ensures that nobody will ever be able to assemble the Key ever again. This could cause problems in future, although at least it means Astra's safe.]

Planet Notes

• *Atrios.* A world which has been engaged in a nuclear war with its twin planet Zeos for the last five years, which is why the surface is crackling with radiation and everybody lives in bunkers four-hundred metres below the ground, though atomic blasts frequently damage and contaminate the underground blocks. Atrios has a space-going technological culture, but obviously the war has made it insular and the grey-uniformed military holds the upper hand.

The most powerful figure on Atrios is the Marshal, who believes himself to be fighting a just war against the evil Zeons but is snapping under the strain. The TV system is full of gung-ho propaganda, while the locals wear rad-check armbands to make sure they're not in a high-radiation area, though these have to be renewed regularly. Energy weapons are, once again, a standard on this planet. Princess Astra, Sixth Princess of the Sixth Dynasty of the Sixth Royal House [shouldn't that be the other way around?], is a much-loved morale-boosting figure who wants to negotiate for peace with Zeos and likes making charitable visits to damaged hospitals. All scrap metal's sent to the furnaces, for recycling to help with the war effort.

By this point Atrios' space-fleet is badly deplet-ed, and only seems to boast six ships instead of the hundreds it once had at its disposal. Half of the remaining six are here destroyed in one battle with the "Zeons". The Marshal has a personal escape ship, tactfully known as a 'command mod-ule'. It takes mere minutes for Atrian space-mis-siles to reach a target millions of miles away, and both sides use 'disintegration capsules', which is why no prisoners have ever been captured [and not just because the war has been fought with nuclear missiles and spaceships?]. Behind a one-way mirror in the Marshal's command area is what looks like a melted skull, through which the Shadow communicates with him. Though the locals don't know about transmat technology - or 'particle matter transmission' - there's a secret transmat link to Zeos in the tunnels of K-block that's used by the Shadow's Mutes.

Zeos and Atrios are on the edge of the Helical galaxy, a long way from Gallifrey according to the Doctor. The two planets used to trade before the war. Though the Zeons looked much like the Atrians, they dressed differently.

• *Zeos.* What nobody on Atrios realises is that although there used to be human-type people on Zeos, they're all dead now. For the last five years the Zeon "menace" has been nothing more than a computer commandant, a pyramid-shaped war machine that sits within an unmanned control room under the surface of the planet. This is Mentalis, the computer installed by Drax, respon-sible for the deaths of millions but without feel-ings or a human voice. It's surrounded by auto-matic defences capable of disarming human beings, and considers the war to be over once the Shadow's purpose has been fulfilled. So when the Marshal attacks, it intends to self-destruct, taking out both Zeos and Atrios. When Mentalis senses that the Doctor is interfering with it, the defences blow its own control centre up, leaving only the destruct sequence.

Mentalis has some way of jamming the naviga-tion of Atrios' ships, and has a sizeable fleet [of computer-controlled ships] which easily out-guns the Atrians. Neither side seems to have any defence against bombardment other than sending ships to shoot down other ships [so missiles can't reach all the way from world to world]. The Doctor finally dismantles the machine, with help from Drax.

History

• *Dating.* No date given. [Though it's possible that the people of Atrios and Zeos might be descended from Earth-born humans - especially since the Doctor describes Astra as a 'human being' - there's no real evidence for it, in which case the date is impossible to establish. If they *are* Earth-spawn, though, then it must be well beyond 5000 AD as Atrios is in a different galaxy to Earth. Probably quite a few galaxies away, judging by the Doctor's comment that they're a long way from Gallifrey.]

K9 responds to a dummy distress signal sent by the Shadow, or possibly Drax, referring to it as a 'Galactic Computer Distress Call' as if it's a stan-dard frequency. The Doctor refers to it by the same name.

The Analysis

Where Does This Come From? In the 1950s, a group of technocrats (see 12.1, "Robot") formed the Research and Development Corporation, or RAND. Based in Santa Monica, this think-tank attempted to guide US government policy along scientific principles and use rationality (especially mathematically-determinable strategies) as the basis for risk-evaluation.

By placing numerical values on outcomes and potential losses, they believed that it was possible to determine the optimum outcome of any even-tuality and - crucially - that as anyone with any sense would do the same, an opponent's moves are predictable. This was the era of computers still being mathematical procedures made manifest, rather than data-processing contraptions, and of games of chess where the pieces were hidden from you. Much of the maths came from John Von Neumann, whose work on gambling and second-guessing developed into a whole branch of math-ematics called Game Theory, and a realm of com-puter-aided scenario-development usually called Kriegspiel; see 17.1, "Destiny of the Daleks", for more on this.

The acid test came with the Vietnam War. The US State Department, under Robert MacNamara, believed in RAND's ability to resolve the otherwise baffling strategies adopted by the Viet Kong. By 1968, the problem was becoming apparent. In a war like this, with no definite outcome in mind, how do you know if you've won? Statistical analy-ses of casualty figures were no use, as these were inflated and exaggerated beyond all recognition.

Later, it emerged that US / NATO estimates of the threat from the Soviet Union were wild guesses based on (a) believing Soviet propaganda; (b) believing that the Soviets had nothing better to do than invade anywhere they felt like (rather than their *real* strategy, waiting until all nations realised that the Soviet way was best… tragically, they really thought this); (c) believing that the Soviet arms build-up was offensive rather than defensive, thus justifying more Western arms expenditure and making the Soviets even *more* defensive (we now know that their whole military strategy was based on the idea that American-led forces would invade at any moment); and (d) big arms companies relying on fat government contracts and telling everyone how scary the Commies were. When a Foxbat fighter plane was delivered to the West by a defecting pilot in 1978, experts were amazed at how crude it was; the radio had valves rather than transistors.

So the roots of "The Armageddon Factor" are becoming obvious, but an older military hero is also lurking here. This was the period when it was finally permissible to question the leadership of Churchill, among others. The head of the Strategic Air Command at a crucial stage of World War Two, Sir Arthur "Bomber" Harris, was now openly being called a war-criminal for the damage to civilian targets like Dresden (see 26.3, "The Curse of Fenric"). The Marshall on Atrios, for all his paraphrasing of Shakespeare's *Richard II* at the Doctor's prompting, is manifestly Winston. The "buckle down in your shelters and wait for victory" attitude of the planet is obviously meant to strike a chord with older viewers, as are little touches like the "patriotic" recycling of metal. Which makes Astra… Princess Elizabeth, the future Queen? Or the more hands-on, outspoken Princess Anne?

Of course, there's another blatant and obvious source, because like Bob 'n' Dave's last outing (15.5, "Underworld") this is a Greek Myth knock-off. The ongoing stalemate, with an all-important princess as the prize, is meant to suggest the siege of Troy. The key moment comes when the miniaturised Doctor enters the enemy's stronghold hidden inside K9, which is perhaps the greatest abuse of mythology in the series' history. Atrios = Atreus, Agamemnon's dad, while Zeos = Zeus. (Even so, if Baker and Martin were writing a "pure" space-opera version of the story then the two planets would be more likely to end up with names like "Greex" and "Tarroy". Why pick Atreus, not the first figure who springs to mind in connection with the siege? Since Atrios is a planet locked in a war of *attrition*, this seems to follow the age-old *Doctor Who* tradition of giving planets overly-appropriate names, as well as harking back to Homer. And Zeos… well, being Atrios' "evil twin", a zappy little name starting with "Z" fits nicely. For a less pathetic Trojan Horse than K9, see 3.3, "The Myth Makers".)

However, it's mainly to contemporary news reports that we should be looking. The hospital is much like the ones we saw in Beirut; the strategy of Mutually Assured Destruction was back in the headlines after a lengthy lull for the *Detante* era; and anyone who thinks the Marshall's costume is a bit over-the-top should look at what the well-dressed Latin American junta leader was wearing that year.

Things That Don't Make Sense Almost everything the Shadow does, so it's not surprising that the Black Guardian's expecting him to fail. He gets hold of the Doctor as early as episode three, then attaches his prisoner to a torture machine and demands to be let into the TARDIS… rather than just getting the key out of the Doctor's pocket [he doesn't know it's that simple]. After putting his hand on the tracer to remove it from the Key to Time and doom Atrios in the last episode, it then takes the Shadow more than *twenty seconds* to make any move towards pulling it out, giving Romana enough time to remind the audience of what'll happen if he does; K9 enough time to alert the Doctor; and both the Doctor and Drax enough time to re-enlarge themselves with the dimensional stabiliser. The Shadow's a "nyah-hah-hah" sort of enemy throughout the story, but this takes incompetent villainy a step too far.

He also believes that Astra knows where the sixth segment of the Key is, but upon hypnotising her he just uses her to lead Merak into a trap, and doesn't bother interrogating her while she's in his power. You also have to wonder why Astra, commanded to do the Shadow's bidding, instantly turns "evil" and starts gloating sadistically instead of just following orders [the Shadow's malevolent influence…]. Nor is it explained how he finds out about Astra being the last segment of the Key, since he knows it's her by episode six but doesn't seem to have a clue three episodes earlier. [You could perhaps explain away two problems at once by suggesting that at some point while she's under his control, the Shadow probes her subconscious and works out what's going on. But we never hear about it.]

Mentalis is capable of self-destructing in a way that'll take out both its own planet and Atrios, yet it's been programmed to wage war on Atrios and has never thought about using this immense planet-destroying capability as a targeted weapon instead of a method of mutual destruction. The Shadow's domain is halfway between Zeos and Atrios, which presumably means that the Shadow and all his followers would be wiped out in the explosion as well, so if the Doctor hadn't done something clever to halt the Marshal's attack then the Shadow's plans would have been scuppered along with everyone else's.

Then there's the ending. In order to get the Shadow out of the way, the Doctor claims to have set up a brief deflective force-field around Zeos, making the missiles hit the Planet of Evil. It's never explained how he does this, or when. If it's a function of the TARDIS, then why doesn't he save planets this way more often?

As soon as he arrives on Atrios, the Doctor realises there's somebody trapped behind a metal door in K block, but doesn't get a chance to rescue her before the Marshal arrives and arrests him. Does he try to tell the Marshal about the trapped woman (and remember, he doesn't *know* the Marshal's "evil" at this stage)? No. When he's told that certain death lies behind the door, does he urgently inform the authorities that someone's stuck there? No. When he finds out that Princess Astra is missing, and that the dead man found near the metal door was her escort, does he spot the obvious logical connection and realise who's trapped? No. What's the matter with him today? He then concludes that the Marshal was involved in Astra's death because there have been 'too many coincidences', even though the only thing which might be construed as a coincidence is that the Marshal showed up after she went missing and apprehended the Doctor on suspicion of murder. Which is the kind of thing that happens to the Doctor all the time, and isn't very coincidental at all, really.

In episode two, the TARDIS is plainly visible in the tunnel on Atrios after it's already left the planet. While Romana has to be told for a second time that she wasn't sent on this mission by the President of Gallifrey, the Doctor says he's never seen K9 spin round and round before, even though it happened in "The Pirate Planet" (16.2) and he was just as surprised by it then. The Shadow's implant on the Marshal's neck, when we finally see it, is *much* too lumpy to be hidden under his collar or go unnoticed for so long.

From orbit around Atrios, the TARDIS can't see Zeos as the Shadow's realm has come between the two, yet nobody on Atrios - the planet that's been focusing all its attention and military technology on Zeos for the last five years - has ever noticed this new world or wondered what's caused their own planet's orbital shift. Three ships survive the last Zeon attack in episode two, yet by episode three the Marshal's escape module is said to be the only ship left on Atrios. Drax's story is peculiar, at the very least; discovering that he has a nearly-functional dimensional stabiliser, the Doctor rightly concludes that Drax could have escaped years ago, and so knows that this is a set-up by the Shadow. So... *why* does the Shadow let Drax have a dimensional stabiliser, exactly?

Merak is capable of convenient telepathy, somehow knowing everything he needs to know about the TARDIS in episode four and all about the Key to Time in episode six. On a similar note, Shapp knows all about the time-loop even though the Doctor and Romana never tell anybody about it. But then, Merak's unexpected knowledge may be a down-payment on the knowledge he loses later. He figures out that Astra's a segment of the Key almost before anyone else, and is there to witness it when she turns into a lump of crystal. He then forgets this and insists on staying in the Shadow's realm to look for her. It's possible that his mind has snapped, but it's staged as a last-ditch way of keeping him off the TARDIS as the story draws towards its conclusion.

And lastly, the "big" stuff. At the start of this great quest, the White Guardian had the ability to power down the TARDIS at will. In "The Stones of Blood", he had no trouble locating the TARDIS and sending a message to the console room. Why, then, can't the Black Guardian do the same? The business about the randomiser really isn't good enough; the Doctor may not know where he's going, but the Black Guardian shouldn't *need* to know where he's going to interrupt the Ship's workings, surely? [More unexplained "rules" governing god-like entities?] And lovely as the idea of Astra being the sixth segment is, it does throw up some awkward questions, especially when Merak states that 'every cell in her body' is part of the

Key. So if she got her hair cut, would the Key remain incomplete forever…? [There are any number of justifications for this, but let's not start that now.]

Critique Surprisingly merciful. Which is to say: given that it's another people-in-space story (in a period of the programme's history when outer space environments could often be awkward), given that it was written by Baker and Martin (who were always at their worst when dealing with things a long way from home) and given its format (a six-parter made at the end of the season, when budgets are traditionally at their most stretched), it's nowhere near as catastrophic as expected. Not that you could call it a great work of television, of course, and the dialogue's capable of choking any actor up to and including John Woodvine.

But what's surprising is the attention to detail being shown by people *apart* from the writers. Whereas most stories of this type just trot out the usual white-panelled corridors and nasty-looking space uniforms, both the design and the direction are freakishly coherent. Michael Hayes - previously the director of "The Androids of Tara" - takes the same future-historical approach here, and *almost* manages to make Atrios' power-politics look Shakespearian even when the words let him down. The sets are full of dark spaces and artistic flourishes, far from the visual horror of "The Invisible Enemy". For the most part this actually looks like a planet that's been worn-in with use, and it doesn't hurt that this is a society where the ceiling's liable to fall in at any moment. Zeos looks subtly different to Atrios, but not different enough to make you feel as if you're watching another story, while even Mentalis is far more attractive than the average mad computer (again, Hayes' spacious, unhurried direction helps with the atmosphere). The idea of jury-rigging an almost-complete Key to Time is a neat one, too; in most other stories the Doctor would lash up some unlikely piece of pseudo-tech if he wanted a time-loop, but here the mythic nature of the Key is finally being used properly.

The trouble is, the writers have decided that the way to make Romana interesting is to have *her* explaining things as well as the Doctor. So we have twice as many hangers-on, asking questions and jumping to wrong conclusions. The Doctor gets Shapp, Astra, Merak and Drax. Romana takes over Merak looking for Astra, and Astra looking

for Merak but really working for the Shadow. Shapp is quite possibly a satire on the ways in which the military sidelines the orthodox administration, but as he's such a prat it's hard to see him as anything other than an extra source of viewer-surrogate questions. These days we're conditioned to think that six parts is too long, yet in this case we have three four-part stories jockeying for supremacy. The Princess Astra / Marshall storyline is intriguing enough (and both the oboe music and Lalla Ward's performance make it a bit out of the ordinary), but *she* loses her gumption and *he* gets stuck in a time-loop. So we end up with the more overtly *Star Trek* idea of a machine-run planet whose entire population turns out to be dead, followed by an awful lot of running around in caves.

As with so many of these stories, if you don't know what's coming then it entertains, or at least piques curiosity. Much of it consists of the usual Baker and Martin screensaver material, but you can sum it up with the words "not appalling", and in context that's something of an achievement.

The Facts

Written by Bob Baker and Dave Martin. Directed by Michael Hayes. Viewing figures: 7.5 million, 8.8 million, 7.8 million, 8.6 million, 8.6 million, 9.6 million.

Supporting Cast: Lalla Ward (Princess Astra), John Woodvine (Marshal), Barry Jackson (Drax), William Squire (The Shadow), Valentine Dyall (The Guardian), Davyd Harries (Shapp), Ian Saynor (Merak).

Working Titles "Armageddon".

Cliffhangers Escaping from the Marshal, the Doctor and Romana head back to the tunnel where they arrived and find that the TARDIS has disappeared; the Doctor is seized by the Mutes in the secret transmat cubicle, and transported away; the Marshal's ship moves in on Zeos and prepares to attack with nuclear force, not really noticing that the Doctor's still there; from his cavern-like lair, the Shadow watches the TARDIS arrive in his realm, and at his side even K9 calls him 'master'; as one of the Mutes leads the Doctor into the TARDIS, Drax leaps out and fires the dimensional stabiliser gun at the Doctor, causing him to vanish from sight.

The Lore

• As has already been mentioned, Anthony Read became exhausted as script editor and announced that he wanted to leave. Read nominated Douglas Adams as his successor. Graham Williams asked Robert Holmes to step in; Holmes said he was busy and had done his dash with the programme for now, but Douglas Adams was worth a shot. Williams contacted Adams, who asked to be given time to get *The Hitch-Hiker's Guide to the Galaxy* out of the way, then shadowed Read for six weeks. His first amendation was the title. Then the nature of the sixth segment was deemed to be unfilmable, if elegant (it was originally supposed to be the Shadow's shadow). Princess Reina's name was being pronounced half a dozen ways, so she became both "Astra" and the segment. The chronodyne idea was introduced, and finally the end of the story was given a proper conclusion rather than just 'here's your Key, Sir'.

• Zeos was originally meant to be populated by mutants, but Read changed this even before Adams got involved (it was too much like 12.4, "Genesis of the Daleks"). Mentalis was added, replacing the idea of Zeos being a near mirror-image of Atrios.

• Tom Baker, meanwhile, was demanding more power. Story approval, director choice and casting decisions were to be his, or he'd leave. In America these are prerogatives of star performers on long-running shows, but the BBC doesn't usually operate that way. It came to an ultimatum: Williams or Baker. Baker sent a card to Williams stating that he was leaving, which Williams took to his immediate superior, Graeme McDonald. Williams asked McDonald if anyone else was asking to play the Doctor, then left on sick leave (see 16.5, "The Power of Kroll") with David Maloney standing in whilst *Blake's 7* was on a break. McDonald, calling Williams back to resolve the crisis, announced that Williams would be fired unless Baker's demands were met. When Shaun Sutton - McDonald's boss, who'd appointed Williams in the first place (see 14.5, "The Robots of Death") - returned from holiday, he demanded Williams' explanation. On hearing it, Sutton ordered Williams to fire Baker, but Williams refused on the grounds that Baker was just bluffing. A lengthy meeting ensued. It turned out that Baker was sick of having his suggestions nodded at and then ignored (like the "cabbage" idea… see

16.2, "The Pirate Planet"), and after this meeting the powers-that-be were a lot less inclined to take his tantrums seriously.

• It's a measure of the deteriorating relationship between star and producer that Williams' immediate reaction to Baker's threat to quit was to use this information to try to persuade Mary Tamm to stay for another year. Tamm had been married for less than three months when she got the part, and had barely seen her husband since, although she *had* at least managed to get pregnant. She believed the part was pretty near the limit of what could be done, or what the writers would be doing with it at any rate. It was, however, her suggestion that Lalla Ward could take over the role… although she was almost joking.

• The Doctor's fire-walking antics unwittingly echo the unmade William Hartnell story "Farewell Great Macedon", in which the Doctor turns out to have studied under Polynesian fire-walkers and uses this to pull rank on Alexander the Great (see 2.4, "The Romans", for more).

• As mentioned under "The Hand of Fear" (14.2), Baker and Martin had conceived of Drax some time ago. The script here describes him as short and stout, with "a touch of the swagger about him", not entirely unlike Del Trotter in *Only Fools and Horses* just a few months later.

• "The Armageddon Factor" provided the lore of *Doctor Who* with one of its most notable post-watershed moments, not broadcast on television until 2003 on ITV's *TV's Naughtiest Blunders 10*. The following exchange was recorded during the scene in which the Doctor dwells on the inevitable self-destruction of Mentalis: 'It's mindless, now… clicking towards oblivion… how long, K9?' 'Damage renders data unavailable.' 'Yeah, you never know the answer when it's f***ing important, do you?' This, and a shot of the Doctor and Romana apparently just about to get intimate, was filmed for the Engineers' Christmas Tape (see 17.2, "City of Death", for more on this odd ritual) and wasn't an out-take as is sometimes thought.

• In 1997, UK Gold was scheduled to show "The Armageddon Factor" on the same morning that the country woke up to the news of Princess Diana's death. This being a story about a morale-boosting charity-obsessed Princess who's "disposed of" by her government, UK Gold pulled it at the last minute. The replacement was "Planet of the Spiders" (11.5), in which a much-loved icon gets into a car chase and is killed by an evil queen.

17.1: "Destiny of the Daleks"

(Serial 5J, Four Episodes, 1st September - 22nd September 1979.)

Which One is This? The Daleks are getting back to their roots, on a "mysterious" quarry-planet where their arch-enemies turn out to be steely-eyed humanoids in silver disco-wigs. And we meet the new, improved Romana.

Firsts and Lasts Terry Nation pens his last script for *Doctor Who*, which means that although it's not the end of the Daleks it's the end of the "classic" structure for a Dalek story: in which the Doctor wanders around a desolate planet for the whole of the first episode, meeting the occasional unconvincing humanoid before the Daleks finally show themselves for the first cliffhanger (although in many ways, "Destiny" is also *Doctor Who* at its most *Blake's 7*). Still on the subject of Dalek creators, here David Gooderson takes over from Michael Wisher as Davros, the first time that the series has re-cast a recurring character *without* explaining it away with a convenient regeneration.

Oh yes, convenient regenerations. "Destiny of the Daleks" sees the debut of the Second Romana, with Lalla Ward taking Mary Tamm's part in one of the most improbable Time Lord change-overs in the series' history. It's a sure sign that Season Seventeen's going to be a lot more comedy-prone, with Tom Baker slowly coming out of his "gooning about like nobody's business" phase but concentrating it into short bursts.

Douglas Adams takes over as full-time script editor here, which helps to explain why the story's so full of "Adams-y" things (many of which possibly result from designers and directors putting in in-jokes, rather than the work of the man himself). So the Doctor's seen reading a book by Oolon Coluphid, mentioned in the opening speech of *The Hitch-Hiker's Guide to the Galaxy*, while the Movellans' co-ordinates for Skaro are a very *Hiker*-like 'D5-Gamma-Z-Alpha'.

For the first time the Doctor feels the need to make the same joke as everyone in the audience, climbing up a steep shaft and then telling the Dalek at the bottom: 'If you're supposed to be the superior race of the universe, why don't you try climbing after us?' (Evidently stairs weren't avail-

Season 17 Cast/Crew

- Tom Baker (the Doctor)
- Lalla Ward (Romana)
- David Brierley (voice of K9, 17.3 to 17.6)

- Graham Williams (Producer)
- Douglas Adams (Script Editor)

able for this gag.) And a very obvious first at the time, which has become so standard that most people now fail to spot it: the first use of SteadiCam, and thus the first set-design of the '70s to have ceilings.

Four Things to Notice About "Destiny of the Daleks"...

1. Terry Nation's main premise for this story: that two logical, non-intuitive machine-cultures, locked together in a logical, non-intuitive war, will reach a stalemate from which neither will ever be able to escape. Terry Nation's main *problem* for this story: one of the machine-cultures in question is that of the Daleks, and as everyone who grew up with *Doctor Who* knows full well... the Daleks aren't really robots, they're living things inside mechanical casings. In order to get around this massive flaw in his own rationale, Nation suddenly informs us that battle-computers control Dalek tactics, even though every indication before now has been that the Dalek Supreme Council runs the show. Then the script starts referring to the Daleks as *robotic*, and the Doctor dwells on the gooey remains of a Kaled mutant ('the Daleks were originally organic life-forms...') as if they just don't make 'em like that any more. Even Davros describes his creations as a 'race of robots'. It's been suggested in some quarters that Nation was deliberately trying to claim the Daleks had lost all their organic heritage, and that this is what the "Destiny" of the title is meant to be referring to, rather than Davros' mad rant about destiny in episode three. But if so, then neither of the writers who take up the Dalek baton in later stories believe a word of it.

2. The BBC have been lent a SteadiCam rig, and the *Doctor Who* team have been told they can use it first - for free - before the Corporation makes any decision about buying one. So for once, the running around quarries and up and down corri-

dors is actually the most visually impressive part of the story. With the novel use of ceilings, the vast white set of the Movellan ship and the use of pattern-generators for the ship's landing, there's a real sense of "look at me!" stylishness to this production. And then it goes and spoils it all with a bunch of aliens who look like Boney M[7].

3. Romana's regeneration scene. By this point the whole "regeneration" idea had ceased to be something dramatic and become a convenience that both the audience and the programme-makers took for granted - see **When Was Regeneration Invented?** under 11.5, "Planet of the Spiders" - so Romana seems to swap her old persona for a new one just because… well… she gets bored. She even tries on a variety of bodies before she settles on one, as if she's in a dress shop. Still, the regeneration starts off-screen, so for all we know there's some cause for this regeneration that we never get to hear about. Is there a horrible, never-explained accident in the backrooms of the TARDIS? Is it a delayed reaction to recent events?

4. Faced with a Dalek onslaught in the ruins of Skaro, the Doctor holds off the enemy by taking Davros hostage and threatening to blow the old megalomaniac up with an explosive device. This is one of the few occasions when the Fourth Doctor gets to do something so macho, which might explain why he gets so over-excited, planning to shout at the Daleks to 'stay back!' but changing his mind as he opens his mouth and yelling 'back off!' instead. The resulting exclamation - 'spack off!' - is one of the programme's most striking insults.

The Continuity

The Doctor On returning to Skaro, he senses that he's somewhere he's been before, but can't say why.

• *Ethics.* Though it's never made explicit, the Doctor risks his own life - and that of his associates - with his plan to get the captured Davros off the planet and away from the Daleks, rather than just killing Davros and ending the matter right there. [Compare this with his next meeting with Davros in 21.4, "Resurrection of the Daleks".] Shortly thereafter he attaches a bomb to Davros' casing, though it's not clear whether he's seriously trying to get Davros killed or just trying to distract the Daleks.

• *Inventory.* He's got a pot of anti-radiation pills on his person, as well as a beeper that reminds him when to take them. He's still got jelly-babies, in a brown paper bag. He can rig up Dalek explosives so the sonic screwdriver can trigger them at long range. He's also carrying a book called *Origins of the Universe* by Oolon Coluphid, which seems to start with an account of the very beginning and later mentions the planet Magla. [Obviously *Doctor Who* doesn't take place in the same universe as *The Hitch-Hiker's Guide to the Galaxy*, as Earth survives the 1970s. As the *Hitch-Hiker's* universe is actually a vast array of multiple universes, it might be argued that the *Doctor Who* environment could be one of those "alternatives", but the destruction-of-all-possible-Earths in Adams' last novel *Mostly Harmless* would seem to contradict this. Note that *Hitch-Hiker's* spells "Coluphid" with two "L"s.] The book gets left on Skaro.

• *Background.* Still on the subject of "that" book… reading *The Origins of the Universe*, the Doctor comments that Coluphid gets it wrong on the first line and should have asked someone who saw it happen, suggesting that he himself was there. [Possible, but judging by "Terminus" (20.4) he didn't get the full picture, as he doesn't know what caused it.] He also knows the truth about Magla, which Coluphid doesn't; see **Planet Notes**.

The Doctor mentions his old 'cybernetics tutor' while he's fixing K9, and claims with some authority that you can always tell a genuine zombie as the skin is cold to the touch. He mentions a book called Jane's *Spacecraft of the Universe*, which may or may not be real [it's obviously based on publications like Jane's *Defence Weekly*, Jane's *Military Vehicles and Logistics*, etc].

The Supporting Cast

• *Romana.* This is the way it happens…

The Doctor's in the console room when Romana enters, looking exactly like Princess Astra of Atrios [16.6, "The Armageddon Factor"]. She claims she's regenerated, and the Doctor tells her that she can't just go around wearing someone else's face. She responds by leaving his sight, and returning in three other forms: one very short [possibly a child], one a big-bosomed Valkyrie-queen and one very tall. Finally she re-enters as Princess Astra again, a form she keeps for the rest of her time with the Doctor. She says she thought it looked 'very nice' on the Princess.

[This is *incredibly* difficult to make sense of, so

War of the Daleks: Should Anyone Believe a Word of It?

Or, "What's the Best Way of Saving Skaro"?

In 1988's "Remembrance of the Daleks" (25.1), Skaro - homeworld of the Daleks, and their seat of power since their debut in 1963 - is destroyed. This annoyed an awful lot of *Doctor Who* purists, not because it seemed like sacrilege but because it messed up everything they thought they knew about Dalek history. Until 1988 it had been almost universally believed that *chronologically* speaking, the last Dalek story was "Evil of the Daleks" (4.9), which is partly set on Skaro and features what the Doctor believes to be the 'final end' of the Dalek line. "Remembrance" just gets in the way.

Since then, many pretend-historians have tried to work out how all of this fits together. Parkin's *A History of the Universe* claims that "Evil of the Daleks" is actually set much earlier than "Remembrance", and that the 'final end' isn't really final at all. Rational, but dull. *The Discontinuity Guide* claims that the Doctor changes history in "Genesis of the Daleks" (12.4), so that "Evil" never happened and the way is left clear for "Remembrance" to destroy Skaro whenever it likes. But this is shaky, and see **How Badly Does Dalek History Suffer?** under 12.4 to see why. Meanwhile fan-lore has frequently claimed that the Daleks simply create a New Skaro after "Remembrance", and that "Evil" is set on another planet with the same name, which is cute but not what the TV stories tell us.

Our *real* problem is this. Though this present volume only acknowledges the TV stories to be 100% canonical, it *does* take material from the *Doctor Who* novels as supporting evidence. After all, the novels - unlike the book versions of just about any other television programme - were specifically designed as a continuation of the series rather than a wholly shameless cash-in, and were almost exclusively written by people who knew something about the workings of the continuity. Ostensibly. (See **Is Continuity a Pointless Waste of Time?** under 22.1, "Attack of the Cybermen", for more of this sort of thing.) If there's a question about the way this universe fits together, then at the very least the books should be used as a "secondary source". And the books *have* presented an answer to the Skaro problem, specifically in John Peel's 1997 tribute to obsession, *War of the Daleks*.

Unfortunately... many fans greatly object to *War of the Daleks*. Its solution to the Skaro problem is a workable one, but it's also utterly bizarre, and re-writes huge chunks of the TV series with very

little reason. Perhaps its worst offence, though, is that it does this in such a po-faced way. If the novel had been even a *little* more humorous about things, then its weirdly convoluted version of Dalek history might have been massively entertaining. Instead its over-earnesty makes it seem, on occasion, just berserk.

Nonetheless. The *War of the Daleks* version of Dalek history reveals the following:

When the Daleks invaded Earth in 2157 (2.2, "The Dalek Invasion of Earth"), they raided the planet's archives and discovered records of the Dalek attack in 1963 ("Remembrance"). They realised that one day in the future, renegade time-travelling Daleks controlled by Davros - whom the Daleks of 2157 believed to be dead - would travel back to 1963, but be tricked by the Doctor into destroying future-Skaro. The Daleks of 2157 didn't like this much, but knew that history couldn't be changed (something which would seem to contradict their actions in 2.8, "The Chase", although never mind that now).

Later, in the 3900s, the Daleks set about a devious scheme to try to avoid this fate. They returned to the old bunker on Skaro, and found that Davros was indeed alive there, but in suspended animation. *Without waking him up*, they transported him to another planet (named Antalin) that looked a lot like Skaro, and left him in an exact copy of the bunker. When he was eventually revived ("Destiny of the Daleks"), Davros thus reached the conclusion that *this* planet was the real Skaro. So when the Doctor tricked him into destroying it ("Remembrance"), the Davros-hating Daleks on the *real* Skaro were perfectly safe.

In a way, you have to admire Peel for building an entire novel around a single point of piddling continuity. But he doesn't stop there. *War of the Daleks* goes on to explain that since the Daleks needed an excuse to bring Davros out of suspended animation, they invented the idea of the Dalek / Movellan war, all as part of their plan to fulfil their destiny without being wiped out. Yes; it turns out that the whole war, seen in both "Destiny" and "Resurrection of the Daleks" (21.4), is a fraud. A fake. The Movellans, far from being a galactic super-power to rival the Daleks, are actually just second-rate Dalek servo-robots acting on orders from Dalek high command.

At the very least, this would explain why the Movellans are such an embarrassment. They're

continued on page 273...

ABOUT TIME 1975-1979

let's deal with it a point at a time. Firstly: by this stage it's already been established that Time Lords can only regenerate twelve times, which means that by trying on four bodies before picking one, Romana would seem to be using up nearly half her lifetime. "Unthinkable" is a good enough word for this. Possible explanations are that (a) Romana's regenerative facilities are a lot more flexible than the Doctor's (she is, after all, of a later generation and the biological "equipment" could have been refined since his day), making her body mutable for a few minutes after the regeneration, allowing her to squidge it around for a while before the cells settle in; or (b) the different versions of herself which enter the console room are just projections of her potential future self, much like Cho-Je in "Planet of the Spiders" (11.5) or the Watcher in "Logopolis" (18.7). This latter might be more likely, as the second body she tries on seems to have the same voice as the Princess Astra version. Either way, it's astonishing that she suffers none of the trauma experienced by the Doctor during *his* regenerations.

[Which brings us to another bizarre point, the fact that she regenerates at all. Why? There's no indication that she's wounded, and she's evidently young for a Time Lord, only 140 the last time we heard (not much time has passed since Season Sixteen, as the Doctor's still in his 750s by 17.3, "The Creature from the Pit"). The Doctor, by contrast, was at least 450 when *he* regenerated for the first time. It looks for all the world as if Romana does this just because she feels like a change. On top of all that, it should be noted that Romana evidently has the power to regenerate into whatever form she chooses, as she seems to deliberately pick Princess Astra's body.]

The Second Romana may have Astra's blonde, button-nosed cuteness, but doesn't have the Princess' personality. Though she can be *almost* as haughty as her previous self, she's obviously much better-tempered, is capable of playing small pranks and can smile properly. There's instantly a much better rapport with the Doctor than the First Romana had [but then, for all we know some months have passed since the previous story], and there's less of a sense of the two of them trying to out-do each other. At this point, her first instinct is still to run away when she sees a scary-looking man like Tyssan, an ex-Dalek captive as it happens, not to try talking to him the way the Doctor would. She blubbers like a girl when interrogated

by the Daleks, and knows the basics of their history. [But given that the interrogation machine says "true" when she claims not to know anything about them, her apparent hysteria may be a means of bluffing the polygraph.]

Like the Doctor, Romana has two hearts, 'one for casual and one for best'. They taught her 'at school' how to stop her hearts, which means she can feign death. [This would seem to blow a hole in the oft-mooted theory that Time Lords only get a second heart once they regenerate, unless Romana's generation is one of the first to come with a second heart "built in".]

• *K9.* Currently inoperative again, and being taken apart by the Doctor. K9 audibly coughs when he's in pieces, something the Doctor describes as 'laryngitis', but even *he's* mystified as to why a robot would suffer from it. K9's brain is a cube-shaped mass of boards and wires that sits in his body, not his head. When re-fitting the brain, the arrow marked "A" goes to the front, or else K9 goes strange and starts spinning around again. The Doctor suggests [fatuously] that this "A" arrow is a standard part of cybernetic design across the universe.

The Supporting Cast (Evil)

• *Davros.* Believed exterminated [in 12.4, "Genesis of the Daleks"], in fact the Daleks' weapons merely damaged Davros' primary life-support system, but the secondary and back-up circuits switched in immediately and synthetic tissue regeneration took place while 'bodily organs were held in long-term suspension'. Which basically means that he's been asleep.

Despite the passage of thousands of years, he's still in the ruins of the old Kaled bunker, and begins to recover soon after the Doctor and company break into the area where he's buried. [His slightly altered voice can safely be explained away as an effect of his mummification.] There's no indication of what's been powering him, and he doesn't have to recharge after he wakes up. The blue "third eye" in the middle of his head lights up when he awakens. Once the Daleks have been defeated on Skaro, he's put into *proper* suspended animation - in a cryogenic freezer, apparently found on the Movellan craft - and a human ship is sent to collect him [this is where we find him ninety years later in 21.4, "Resurrection of the Daleks"].

Though Davros has a liking for logic, he's not

War of the Daleks: **Should Anyone Believe a Word of It?**

...continued from page 271

crass, unconvincing and easy to disable because that's what Daleks think *humans* are like.

Needless to say, this version of events hasn't gone down well in many parts of fandom. But nonetheless, this current volume feels obliged to take notice of it. Having already made the decision to accept the spin-offery of *Doctor Who* as a kind of hearsay testimony, it wouldn't be right to change the rules just to avoid one (admittedly quite large) black hole in the middle of the continuity. Besides which, for all its manic over-enthusiasm *War of the Daleks* does at least do a fair job of pulling together Dalek history, supplying a definitive dating-system for the final Davros stories ("Destiny", "Resurrection", "Revelation",

"Remembrance") and establishing - believably - that the big Dalek push for galactic dominance (3.4, "The Daleks' Masterplan") only takes place *after* they've dealt with their annoying creator.

For the record, then. In this volume, continuity notes on "Destiny" and "Resurrection" will focus entirely on what we're told in those stories, *not* on the *War of the Daleks* version of things. Whereas for Dalek chronology, the really rather convenient dating used in *War* will be considered "real". Anyone who disagrees, and who wants to know how the Daleks can still be talking about Skaro in 4000 AD when "Remembrance" would seem to destroy it in the 3900s, might just want to fall back on the old New Skaro argument. Or make up an equally spurious answer off the top of their head.

---

wholly bound by it. He still believes the Daleks need him to prosper. The Movellans conclude that Davros is a mutant humanoid [i.e. the war on Skaro corrupted his DNA, and his wrinkled form isn't just the result of gross physical damage].

The TARDIS The randomiser [see the previous story] does its work here by taking the TARDIS to an unspecified location, which purely by chance turns out to be the Dalek homeworld at another key point in their history. It's implied that the randomiser not only stops the Doctor knowing where the Ship's going, but stops him taking proper readings as well, as the console doesn't tell him that this is Skaro despite having been there before. The Doctor apparently presses the wrong switch when he leaves the planet, making the TARDIS vanish and then re-appear again before it dematerialises for good.

Romana's "test bodies" all have their own costumes, presumably from the TARDIS wardrobe. Which must be an impressive collection, given the various heights and bust measurements on display. As well as the pink and white "negative" of the Doctor's outfit that she eventually picks, at one stage she enters the console room dressed in a hat, scarf and coat exactly like the Doctor's. [The fact that the Doctor has a spare coat might mean he changes his own from time to time, rather than bothering to wash his clothes regularly, so no wonder the contents of his pockets can seem variable. The origin of the back-up scarf is a mystery, as "The Ark in Space" (12.2) seems to suggest that the scarf is one of a kind, although if he's got

spares then this might at least explain why it seems to teleport from the Vardan ship to the TARDIS console room in "The Invasion of Time" (15.6). See also the cut "birthday" scene from 16.3, "The Stones of Blood".] There's a multi-coloured umbrella in the console room here [not the same one used by the Sixth Doctor].

The Non-Humans

• *Daleks.* The Daleks have been fighting the Movellans for 'centuries', and as both sides' tactics are utterly logical there's no way for them to break the ongoing stalemate. Their two computerised battle-fleets are locked together in deep space, and neither has ever fired a single shot, as both sides are waiting for an optimum moment that never comes.

As a result, the Daleks have returned to their homeworld of Skaro, apparently deserted by Dalek-kind in this period. They intend to dig up Davros, believing that he can reprogram their battle-computers to find a way out of this stand-off. The implication here is that Daleks are *utterly* logical by this point, as they haven't even spotted that the way to break the stalemate is just to do something illogical. [The description of Daleks as 'robots' might indicate that they've become completely mechanised in this era, and thus incapable of irrational thought, although "Resurrection of the Daleks" - in an attempt to get the Daleks back on track - emphasises that it's the Daleks' battle-computer that's been giving them problems. Even so, this is a peculiar story that seems full of holes. See **Things That Don't Make Sense** for some of them, plus a possible get-out clause.]

Here the Daleks use slave-labour for their digging project, which is causing seismic activity, while their high-impact phason drills cause explosions on the surface. They're happy to go on suicide missions, attaching magnetic explosive canisters to their casings and chanting 'do not deviate!' as they go to blow up the Movellan ship. A few dozen of these canisters can cause a half-megaton explosion. In the Dalek command centre there's a lie detector for interrogating humanoids, which requires the subject to put his or her hands on a pair of white spheres. They designate Romana as 'category nine' after interrogating her, meaning that she's no threat. Captives from their various attacks on humanity are kept on a prison-ship in space, where life-expectancies are short, so prisoners consider themselves lucky to work in the slave-gangs on Skaro. Like all good totalitarians, the Daleks kill five prisoners for every one who tries to escape.

Despite being among the great technicians of the universe, Daleks still use computers with tape-spools in their control centre. Unlike the Doctor, they don't know the exact layout of the old Kaled city [they're not meticulous record-keepers]. Daleks have 'combat units', and their leader on Skaro is a Dalek who looks and sounds much like all the others but with black markings around his midriff, though they claim to be loyal to Davros once he's uncovered [a ruse, judging by later Dalek stories].

Dalek central control is said to be 'in space', and when a Dalek deep-space cruiser is called it takes six hours to reach Skaro. Davros is given a glowing white 'computer-sphere' containing the logistics of the Dalek battle-fleet, the information having been checked by the Supreme Dalek, and it looks as though it plugs into his chair. Dalek 'listening scanners' can make out individual voices inside the Movellan ship.

Put a hat over a Dalek's eye-stalk and it panics, firing blindly before blowing up for no good reason. And yet, astonishingly, the humans are all terrified of these creatures.

• *The Movellans.* A "race" of robots who appear quite human, apart from their tell-tale white dreadlocks [whoever built them couldn't do hair properly?]. Their origin isn't explained, but aesthetics were obviously important to whoever made them, as they're of mixed races and genders. It seems important to them not to be known as machines, to the extent of lying to cover up awkward anomalies.

They're cold to the touch, far stronger than real humans and are merely stunned by rockfalls, but if the cylinder-shaped power-packs on their belts are removed then they stop moving almost instantly. Some simple tinkering with these power-packs re-programs them to obey human orders, as the cylinders contain 'main circuits' which seem to form part of their minds. [A robot warrior that stops when its battery's unclipped doesn't seem very efficient, so presumably they don't do much face-to-face fighting.] Funnier yet, the Doctor's dog-whistle can confuse Movellans long enough for them to be overpowered. They carry cone-shaped stun-or-kill energy weapons which fit over their hands, and they're prone to the Daleks' weapons just as Daleks are prone to theirs.

The Movellans are predictably over-efficient, with no imagination and little sign of emotion even though they're capable of occasional lyricism. When two Movellans play stone-scissors-paper, the result is always stalemate [reasonable, if their identical machine-minds are trying to second-guess each other and haven't got random number generators, though it's harder to explain how the Doctor predicts their actions so easily… see **Where Does This Come From?**]. This means that their fleet's battle-computers are just as inflexible as those of the Daleks. They claim it's against their code of honour for aliens to see them in death, though this could just be because they don't want anyone finding out that they're robots. They know about Davros, though they pretend not to, and depressingly their eventual aim is the conquest of the galaxy. Those seen here are obviously military in nature, though none are referred to by rank apart from Commander Sharrel.

The Movellan spaceship is, unsurprisingly, a functional-looking affair with sterile white decor on the inside. It's shaped like an inverted cone, which means it can drill into the ground for both camouflage and defence, and beams [anti-gravity beams?] shoot out from its underside when it lands or takes off. Romana takes one look at it and says that judging by its design and size, she'd expect it to have intergalactic range and time-warp ability [it makes sense that Movellans can time-travel, if they're engaged in a war with the Daleks], and that it almost certainly comes from 'star system four-X-alpha-four'. It takes 32 minutes to charge up for a take-off, and its hull is immune to Dalek fire-power, but not Dalek explosives.

The Movellans also have a 'nova device', a weapon small enough to be carried in two hands which can nevertheless scorch the entire planet by changing the molecular structure of the atmosphere so that the atoms become flammable. If it were activated outside its protective shielding, then Skaro's atmosphere would burn up in seconds. The timer on the device uses familiar Earth-style numbers in green LED [translated for our benefit?], and it can be used over and over again as long as it's always re-armed.

Set into the back of a Movellan, hidden underneath the uniform, is a transparent panel through which wires and circuits can be seen [it looks much like one of the "cybernetic" panels that '70s *Six-Million Dollar Man* dolls had].

Planet Notes

• *Skaro.* Rocky, barren and uninteresting, at this point there doesn't seem to be any native life on Skaro, as the Daleks are apparently just visiting their old homeworld and the Thals are nowhere to be seen. [They may just be on a different part of the planet, but it's strange that they're nowhere to be seen near what used to be the heart of their civilisation.] Ruined buildings are still to be found on the surface, made of concrete rather than anything more exotic, while the remains of the old Kaled bunker [12.4, "Genesis of the Daleks"] are buried deep beneath the surface but still reasonably intact. Davros is still down there, and though he doesn't seem to be in the same room where he "died", he must be in the same general area as the Doctor knows how to find his way there. Davros is covered in cobwebs [so Skaro has spiders, or something similar].

At one stage, the Doctor finds the jelly-like remains of a Kaled mutant on the surface. [Surely it should have decayed, if this area's been uninhabited for so long? Maybe some of the mutants have been "roaming wild" since the Daleks left.] Radiation is still high on the planet's surface.

• *Magla.* An eight-thousand-mile-wide amoeba that's grown a crusty shell and is often mistaken for a planet, according to the Doctor. Oolon Coluphid believes it's incapable of maintaining any life-form.

History

• *Dating.* Hundreds of years in the future, at least, as the galaxy seems to be swarming with humans. ["Destiny of the Daleks" is the first of four Dalek stories often known as the "Davros Era", in which Davros becomes a key player in galactic politics and the Daleks are obsessed with finding him. Opinion is divided as to how the Davros Era fits in with the rest of Dalek history. Assuming it doesn't over-write the Dalek history we've seen before - see **How Badly Does Dalek History Suffer?** under 12.4, "Genesis of the Daleks" - the key question is really "before or after 4000 AD?". Parkin's original *A History of the Universe* holds that these four stories take place sometime after the events of "The Daleks' Masterplan" (3.4), a conclusion largely inspired by the fact that the rehearsal script for "Resurrection of the Daleks" apparently gave it a date of 4590 AD, but this isn't stated anywhere in the finished story. However, John Peel's novel War of the Daleks takes the view that in fact the Davros Era occurs right *before* "The Daleks' Masterplan", and that the Masterplan of 4000 AD begins once the Daleks have finally disposed of their creator. In many ways this is a much neater way of doing things, and would most probably date "Destiny" to the thirty-eighth or thirty-ninth century. But see **War of the Daleks: Should Anyone Believe a Word of It?** and **What's the Dalek Timeline?** under 2.8, "The Chase"]

Tyssan is a starship engineer, serving with the Deep Space Fleet out of Earth. He's been a Dalek prisoner for two years [either they've been digging on Skaro for that long, or they move slave labour around from project to project]. One of the other human slaves comes from the planet Zidi, where the Daleks attacked his settlement, while another was a civilian spaceship passenger and the only survivor of the Dalek assault. The planet Kantria is a tropical paradise, according to Romana, but another of the slaves was a combat pilot with Kantra's Third Galactic Fleet. When Davros is captured, a high-security ship is sent from Earth to meet the vessel that's carrying him, and he's to stand trial for crimes against 'the whole of sentient creation'.

The Doctor states that at some point while Davros has been asleep, Arcturus won the Galactic Olympic Games and Betelgeuse came second. [He doesn't specify a year, hinting that only *one* Galactic Olympic Games took place. Arcturans are small spidery things with faces in 9.2, "The Curse of Peladon", which raises the question of what events they might possibly have won. The BBC novel *Placebo Effect* is set at the Games, but doesn't elaborate, which is a pity, as it would have livened things up no end. And it's set in 3999 AD, which makes the dating even more complicated. Oh, and the Doctor pronounces Betelgeuse the Douglas Adams / *Gormenghast* author Mervyn Peake way, as if it's a drink made of insects.] Plus, the economy of Algol's in a terrible state thanks to irreversible inflation [so very '70s...].

The Analysis

Where Does This Come From? So, back to the war. As we saw in "The Armageddon Factor", the US government's military strategy was conditioned by the mathematical Game Theory of John Von Neumann, and before him the Symbolic Logic of Alfred North Whitehead (more on that under 5.1, "Tomb of the Cybermen"). As almost all electronic circuitry is based on the same system of AND, OR, NAND and NOR gates, Truth Tables and the like, it made sense to apply this process to politics, economics, social behaviour and - most successfully - animal behaviour. If you could give numerical values to the "success" of a strategy, then you could calculate which one to use. Give values of 1, 0 or -1 for any stage, and as long as you wind up with a score above zero, you're winning. Especially if you're the *only* player with a score above zero.

When a 1969 version of this model "proved" that the US had won the Vietnam War in 1965, it was time to rethink. The model-makers had already seen a drastic abandonment of their cherished dreams of a safe, predictable world. Their calculations couldn't find a way out of the Cuban Missile Crisis of 1962 that didn't involve millions of casualties. The stand-off was ultimately two grown men and their advisors playing chicken. First one to put "self-preservation" above "losing face" loses the game.

The snag with this strategy, which mathematically is a very robust one, is that it makes no allowances for anyone with a death-wish. The Kennedy administration figured out that Kruschev didn't have a game-plan for this, and so threatened a disproportionate response; all-out war, for a comparatively minor infringement of US sovereignty. Unsure whether Kennedy meant it or not, the Kremlin blinked first. (Or at least, that's

the conventional view of the Cuban affair, although in itself it's based on the assumption that the US and the USSR were both playing the same game. Recently-recovered evidence from the Kremlin hints that Kruschev may have seen things differently, but that's another story.)

The wider point to take from all this is that until you can accurately evaluate your opponent's priorities, you can't predict their responses. As we've seen recently, people who believe that being executed for killing "infidels" gets them into Heaven can't be intimidated, whereas people who put the lives of their countrymen above those of any other nation can't be persuaded. Calculating for the "whims" of groups or individuals who value different - possibly unknown - things required the Pentagon to hire Social Anthropologists, but nothing could prepare them for the counter-culture, who deliberately resisted numerically-evaluated ambitions; tossing coins or picking random destinations made them harder to police (compare with the use of the I-Ching in 18.5, "Warriors' Gate").

As with so much of Adams, author Robert Sheckley did it in SF first. In one of Sheckley's comparatively sensible stories, "Fool's Mate", he has two vast space-fleets poised at an impasse for decades until one of them does something random to fox the computers. This is, traditionally, how one defeats chess programs. In a wider sense this idea, like the "randomiser" and the Doctor's resistance to *both* Guardians, is part of a late-'70s-style existentialist notion common to many TV heroes at the time. We've already fleetingly seen this in the '60s stories, but under Williams it becomes a signature of the programme.

This story's other big narrative thrust is the use of zombies, with the Doctor's comment that the living dead are 'cold to the touch' mirroring the later discovery that Movellans don't have normal body-temperatures. We're not exactly in *Dawn of the Dead* territory here, but a film-buff like Adams could conceivably have asked Nation for something along those lines, and got a story like this instead. After all, Skaro was originally sold to us as "The Dead Planet", and the idea of the Daleks as creatures who refuse to die is there in Davros' ranting once he awakens from his multi-millennial kip.

Things That Don't Make Sense Let's take the "hat over the eye-stalk makes Daleks explode" problem for granted...

The whole idea of digging up Davros to break a logical impasse is shaky at best. The Daleks are said to be utterly rational, but clearly aren't. Everything we've ever seen of Dalek "culture" suggests technicians who aren't just skilled but imaginative, too, but they're not supposed to have imaginations (at least any more). In itself, it seems odd that a species incapable of making an illogical move should think of going to find their creator so that he can make an illogical move on their behalf. Why / how have they only just come up with this strategy, after centuries of warfare? And how do they even know that Davros is still alive, or at least that his intelligence might be salvageable? At the end of "Genesis of the Daleks", his corpse was entombed in the Kaled city with the early Daleks; didn't they dispose of the body, or at least check that he was dead? Even the idea that logical minds can't make irrational moves is flawed, since a reasonably intelligent logical mind really *should* be able to work out that in a stalemate situation where both parties can predict the others' moves, the best way out is by rolling some dice. [However, just about all of these plot-holes can be filled by the John Peel Thesis... see the accompanying essay.]

The nova device is capable of burning up the whole of Skaro if activated outside its perspex protective shielding, yet the Movellans decide to *test* it by putting it inside the shielding and standing right next to it. What if there'd been a crack in the shielding? Would *you* risk - say - triggering a nuclear bomb in your vicinity, even if you were fairly confident that it was held inside some sort of force-field? [Mind you, the British government did something similar.] More amusingly still, one of the ultra-efficient, computer-brained Movellans attending the test doesn't actually know what the device does, and asks one of his friends just so someone gets to explain it to the audience. And once the device is re-armed, the Movellans lounge around with it on their command deck without any security precautions at all.

Romana gets sick while she's working on a Dalek slave-gang, because of the radiation. So why don't the Daleks give her anti-radiation treatment, as they surely *must* do with all their other slaves? Neither the Doctor nor Romana knows anything about the Movellans, yet they can both identify the star-system in which the Movellan ship originated, as if they've read all about the spaceships of the universe but haven't bothered reading about the people who made them. [Unless 'star-system system four-X-alpha-four' is full of different cultures who use similar spaceship designs, but it's a long shot.]

Why is Commander Sharrel so surprised that the Doctor knows of the Daleks, when the rest of the story assumes that they've menaced everybody else in the galaxy at some stage? The last episode sees Sharrel so badly-damaged that he has to crawl across the planet's surface to get to the nova device, and Romana's capable of removing one of his arms. But how did he get in this state? Since the slave attack on the Movellans largely seemed to involve people pulling off the Movellans power-packs or stunning them with dog-whistles - and since a captured Movellan firearm, even used by a slave, would have blown Sharrel to pieces if he'd been shot - what wounded him so badly that his limbs are ready to drop off?

Critique (Prosecution) Another story that sums up everyone's memories of the days when *Doctor Who* was cheap, stupid, shoddy-looking and little more than a platform for the man in the scarf. "Destiny of the Daleks" comes across as an attempt by Terry Nation to follow up "Genesis" with another hard-edged, pseudo-political Dalek story that's doomed to failure by (a) a complete misunderstanding of the Daleks' own mythology, (b) the absence of the Hinchliffe era's "space-gothic" production values and (c) the fact that it's all so horribly, pathetically slow.

To an extent, this last problem isn't just contained in these four episodes. By this point the series was rapidly losing all its drive, urgency and menace, which means that everybody seems to stroll through the story at a leisurely pace. The scariest programme on television has become the most nonchalant. The format of the early series (Doctor tries to get companions back to Earth) in itself made the universe feel like a threatening place, as if *anything* could turn out to be dangerous outside the long-lost safe-haven of England, while the Pertwee run's format (Earth in constant peril) at least gave all the characters a reason to care. Now, though, the Doctor's just ambling around high-risk environments because he feels like it. Which is reasonable, since he's been a wanderer since the day we met him, but unfortunately his companion's doing the same thing - in episode one Romana gets ready for a walk on a radiation-soaked planet as if she's planning a trip to Ikea - and the supporting cast all follow suit.

The slaves in episode three can't be bothered to look worried when they're lined up for the slaughter; the Daleks simply sound bored; the Movellans aren't even worth mentioning; and Davros goes from being a great iconic villain to being a trite megalomaniac who spends most of his time being (literally) pushed around by people. Even his mask looks limp. Like so much in this era, you can either take the Doctor's faux-excited statement when he sees what's on the TARDIS scanner ('oh look, rocks!') as a witty acknowledgement of the programme's limitations, or a self-indulgent in-joke from a production team that wasn't even *trying* to get the "adventure" elements right any more.

And that's the nub of it. Beyond the sloppy sci-fi clichés and the appalling visuals, this is also the point when the programme becomes almost unworkable as a drama series. It's hard to resist pinning the blame on Douglas Adams, since "Destiny of the Daleks" begins with the ultimate test-case. Those who defend this period in the series' history like to claim that if you find Romana's "funny" regeneration scene objectionable then you're taking the programme much too seriously, yet the problem isn't its bizarre use of the continuity - which could be passed off simply as "weird" - or even that the scene's not remotely funny. The problem is that it strips away any sense of meaning, and makes everything *else* that happens impossible to care about.

Even in comedy, you have to be able to believe in something if you're going to get involved in it. If one of the central characters can change her appearance and personality just for a laugh, then all logic breaks down and no story can function. Why not have the characters produce magic wands from their pockets, and change the whole nature of the plot whenever they get bored? Why not make it all up as you go along? Why not spuriously claim that the Doctor and Romana can fly...? (See also 17.2, "City of Death".)

Critique (Defence, ish) The first and most basic thing to say is that by this stage Terry Nation believed his own hype. The story, once K9's removal and Romana's recasting had been tackled, was all Nation's doing. Adams - try as he might - couldn't get Davros or the "clockwork" Daleks removed, nor could he make the corny cliffhang-

ers come any earlier.

But let's not waste time on excuses... what we have here did the job, just about. The notion of Skaro as a "Dead Planet", which comes to life as the TARDIS crew investigate, has been revisited here as a planet of the dead. Both Tyssan and the Movellans are presented to us as zombies, and even Romana comes back from the grave. Unless you've read a plot-synopsis, or any of the spoilers in this entry, then you have to work out an explanation for what's going on based on the evidence you're given. Until the Movellans are revealed to be inhuman, this world is the afterlife ('the living are just the dead on holiday'). The unprecedented use of SteadiCam adds to the sense that this isn't quite real. Having genuinely "beautiful" people as untrustworthy aliens was a neat move - it hadn't happened since, ooh, "The Claws of Axos" (8.3) and even then they looked a bit ropey - and the emphasis on eugenics in other Nation stories opens up the possibility of a different kind of master-race. If no-one told you Davros was coming back (and it wasn't exactly trumpeted), then you might have been concerned about what was going to happen.

But no, the Daleks make a much-publicised return, and so does Davros. After all the hype, the nation's youth feel cheated. Still, there was always the Movellan spaceship set, which post-Breakfast Television looks a bit cheesy but was unlike anything else seen so far. And the Daleks are kept out of the story as much as possible, which is always a plus. But Nation seriously thinks we're still hanging on his every word about the History of the Daleks, about the way man will evolve into machine-creatures motivated by hate, yadda yadda yadda (as in his story "We Are the Daleks" in the *Radio Times* special; see 10.4, "Planet of the Daleks"). He thinks it's still 1965, and no amount of window-dressing can fix this. "Nova", the term for the Movellans' planet-scorching weapon, spelled backwards is "Avon".

The Facts

Written by Terry Nation. Directed by Ken Grieve. Viewing figures: 13.0 million, 12.7 million, 13.8 million, 14.4 million.

Supporting Cast: David Gooderson (Davros), Tim Barlow (Tyssan), Peter Straker (Commander Sharrel), Suzanne Danielle (Agella), Tony Osoba

(Lan), Roy Skelton (Dalek Voices), Penny Casdagli (Jall), David Yip (Veldan).

Cliffhangers The Daleks crash through a (flimsy) wall in the underground tunnels, surround Romana and insist that she's their prisoner; deep in the ruins of Skaro, the hand of Davros' ancient "corpse" begins to twitch, and the light comes on in the middle of his forehead; Romana lies unconscious inside the transparent tube of the nova device, as it stands in the middle of the blasted plain of Skaro with its timer counting down to zero (a sight so reminiscent of a surrealist painting that it's perhaps the most striking thing in the whole story).

The Lore

• When casting about for "serious" writers, Douglas Adams approached both Christopher Priest and John Brunner, respected and literary SF authors. Priest refused at first, but Adams talked him around (see **What Else Didn't Get Made?** under 17.6, "Shada"). An unsolicited script, "The Secret of Cassius", was considered promising; its author, Andrew Smith, was fifteen at the time he wrote it (see 18.3, "Full Circle"). Tom Stoppard, next on Adams' wish-list, was too busy (and see 19.3, "Kinda", for the rumours about his involvement in the series).

Adams also drafted a Writers' Guide, the first since the era of Dennis Spooner in the '60s, recommending things to avoid and a series of observations on how time appeared to work in the Doctor's universe. Many of Adams' former colleagues from Cambridge and BBC Radio started submitting scripts which were unworkable, but two were considered carefully. One was "Child Prodigy" by Alistair Beaton and Sarah Dunant, both now famous for completely different things; Beaton a satirical playwright, Dunant a thriller writer and former host of BBC2's The Late Show. The other was "The Doomsday Contract", originally by John Lloyd, Adams' former flatmate and co-author of the last two episodes of the original radio Hitch-Hiker's Guide. The last person Adams would have considered calling was Terry Nation. Graham Williams, however, was scouting around for writers for his thriller series "The Zodiac Factor" and had asked Nation to contribute. When Adams found that no-one else seemed to have a clue how to write for Doctor Who, he reluctantly began contacting experienced writers.

• Lalla Ward had already been a regular fixture on Saturday Night BBC1, as in The Duchess of Duke Street she'd played the wayward illegitimate daughter of Louisa Trotter, raised on a farm and brought to London to learn how to behave like a lady. Not that far-removed from Leela, then.

• David Gooderson was hastily cast as Davros as he was the right build for the costume and "buggy", and could make a reasonable attempt at sounding like Michael Wisher (they thought). Wisher himself was in Australia.

• Nation had already badgered the BBC to let him have one more go at launching a Dalek-led TV series. When this was wearily refused, he insisted on writing a Dalek / Davros story. He then dragged his feet over submitting the finished scripts, leaving Adams with little or no time to remove anything impractical or resolve it with the rest of Season Seventeen (one version claims that Nation wrote the script with Sarah and Harry still on board the TARDIS).

• EastEnders fans will note the presence of "Big" Ron Tarr (see also "Dimensions In Time" in the appendix to Volume VI) among the human slaves. David Yip, briefly famous for a series called The Chinese Detective, also crops up as the Dalek slave Veldan.

• Model-turned-actress Suzanne Danielle, playing the Movellan named Agella, was famous as much for her celebrity boyfriend Patrick Mower (star of action-drama Target; see 14.3, "The Deadly Assassin") as for her acting. She appears in those two seminal 1980 films Flash Gordon and Sir Henry at Rawlinson End, but retired soon afterwards due to a spinal injury. Her appearance garnered almost as much publicity as Lalla Ward's costume. Tony Osoba (Lan) had been in Porridge, and would return as Kracauer in "Dragonfire" (24.4), but here he downplays his Glaswegian accent. K9's cough, and croaking of the word 'Master', were provided by Roy Skelton.

• The "tiny" Romana is wearing Zilda's costume from "The Robots of Death" (14.5).

• The Radio Times didn't follow the lead of most of the press in taking the re-cast Romana or the Daleks' return as the "big story", but instead ran a feature on costume designer June Hudson, and the problems of making aliens on the cheap. (Costuming was always one of the biggest slices of the programme's budget, and even that was done at costs most programmes would have sniffed at for catering.)

• Tim Barlow, who played Tyssan, is profoundly deaf. Baker took out a lot of his frustration (see 16.6, "The Armageddon Factor") on Barlow.

• The "stunt" Daleks carrying explosives were detonated by Baker himself.

17.2: "City of Death"

(Serial 5H, Four Episodes, 29th September - 20th October 1979.)

Which One is This? Seven Mona Lisas, twelve Julian Glovers, three episodes with location-work in gay Paree, two surprise guests and one great big eye in the middle of a green alien seaweed-face from the beginning of time.

Firsts and Lasts Famously, it's the first *Doctor Who* story which involved filming outside Britain, allowing the main cast and crew to take a brief sojourn in Paris. "Famously" because the story doesn't let you forget it. Partially to show off the French scenery, and partially to pad out the script a bit, the first episode features *five whole minutes* of the Doctor and Romana jogging through Parisian streets between studio scenes (and yet, few people spot on the first viewing that there's absolutely no jogging at all in episode two). Often regarded as the only major flaws in this story, and certainly the only bits that video viewers regularly fast-forward through, these sections of the episode also feature their own musical theme. It's become known as "The Running Through Paris Music", and it's got exactly the right number of notes for the audience to sing along with it ('running through Paris, we're running through Paris, we're running through Paris... running through France').

Four Things to Notice About "City of Death"...

1. One of the most-watched *Doctor Who* stories ever, it's also one of the best-remembered, and not just because of the big ratings. In an age when most SF on television (other *Doctor Who* stories included) meant space-battles, gleaming white corridors and family-friendly robots, "City of Death" provided some of the most memorable fantasy images of the decade. A brooding, spider-like outline squats on the horizon of primeval Earth; Julian Glover rips off his face to reveal a one-eyed mass of green blubber underneath (it could so easily have been B-movie, but instead it becomes almost surreal, especially when we see the seaweed-faced monster wearing a smart cra-

vat-and-jacket ensemble); an experiment in time-technology turns an egg into a chicken, and then into a writhing, agonised skeleton; and most magnificent of all, the Doctor opens a secret panel in Count Scarlioni's chateau to find six copies of the "Mona Lisa"... all of them genuine. It's as far away from messing-around-in-Dalek-infested-quarries as you could ever hope to get.

2. Then there's the dialogue. Many would argue that there's too much comedy in *Doctor Who* during this era, but in "City of Death" - a story which doesn't require anybody to run up and down corridors while making quips - the scenes are shot through with the kind of elegant wit you'd expect from Oscar Wilde, not the Three Stooges. Which means that Tom Baker gets to be as great as everyone always says he is. The key to understanding how the Doctor's character works, as a figure who's at a slightly odd angle to the human species, comes when he gives the Countess Scarlioni a reason that the detective Duggan might have been following her: 'You're a beautiful woman, probably.'

3. In the beginning *Doctor Who* was a programme about humans, not about Time Lords, in which the Doctor was a way of involving the human characters in adventures rather than the heroic central character. One of the many problems the series has in its later years is finding a way of making us go "with" the Doctor as if he were one of us, and "City of Death" is the story which pulls off that trick most successfully. The crucial moment comes at the climax of the last episode, when the Doctor and Romana take the token stupid human Duggan back to primordial Earth, where the Jagaroth spaceship is about to explode and accidentally create all life on the planet. Like the Time Lords, we've been following the plot perfectly well, and Romana's observation that the craft's atmospheric thrust motors don't work makes perfect sense to us. So for once, we're on the side that's laughing at the humans when Duggan responds by pointing at the Jagaroth vessel and saying: 'That's a *spaceship!*'

4. The BBC's idea of Paris features a lot of famous locales on film, but interior scenes consist of cafés where the TV news is in English; the locals wear stripey jerseys, hankies around their necks, moustaches and berets; and local colour is added by cries of '*beaujolais!*'. Yet, bizarrely, this tourist-centred view of the city adds authenticity to one of the story's best jokes: the Doctor and company

When Did the Doctor Meet Leonardo?

It was always a source of great satisfaction that the writers of *Doctor Who* never did anything as obvious as have Our Hero meet Leonardo da Vinci. Then came the 1996 TV Movie, where the "new" Doctor sees a Leonardo print on the wall and insists on name-dropping. Never mind snogging Grace or all that faffing around with the Eye of Harmony, this was the *real* insult. Not only the safe, cosy option of a dumb name-check, but the fact that he gets the name wrong. Calling the artist "da Vinci" is like calling Rembrandt "Van Reyn" or Hippocrates "Cos" (as deriders of the ghastly *The Da Vinci Code* have pointed out more recently). Moreover, the picture he recognises - "Head of a Young Woman", from the Venice Accademia - is reproduced back-to-front.

But let's not fret unduly. Assuming he *was* there when that particular sketch was done (circa 1506-08, in Milan), what else could the Doctor have seen, done or influenced? Probably the most significant item would be Leonardo's big project at the time, a painting of Leda - who had sex with Zeus while he was in the form of a swan - which has subsequently vanished. The sketched head may well have been part of his preparations; he certainly made enough rough notes and plans for other artists to have had a stab at reconstituting the finished work in its absence. In mythology, Leda is often equated with the goddess Nemesis, and make of that what you will. We know the Doctor has (or had) a miniature gallery on the TARDIS that's used to disguise a secondary generator (15.6, "The Invasion of Time"), in which such works as "The Arnolfini Wedding" and "The Fighting Temerere" are displayed. Are these originals, salvaged from the National Gallery or Tate UK after some future catastrophe? Perhaps Leonardo's Leda had to be "confiscated" by the Doctor in the 1920s, when the blue box in the background would have become recognisable to Londoners.

Then there's Leonardo's painting "Christ Among the Doctors", also circa 1508. Yes, his sponsors were the Medici family, and Medici translates as "doctors". But as it vanished a few centuries back and hasn't been exhibited since its supposed recent rediscovery, who can say what these learned men look like? (Actually, many artists seem to have tackled this subject, mainly as an excuse to paint lots of old men with interesting nobbly faces but with a cute boy as the focus. It always sells.)

When signing off the mirror-written note to Leonardo in "City of Death", the Doctor says "see you earlier". A typical Tom Baker throwaway line, which could just be goofing or could be a big hint (like the way he asks 'what's those?' on hearing the name of Xoanon in 14.4, "The Face of Evil"). It's not clear whether the Doctor has met Leonardo or not. He puts on an air of familiarity when he's calling out the man's name, but it could just be the usual Doctor-bluster. "See you earlier" might hint that the Doctor hasn't met Leonardo yet, but is planning on going further back in time at some point and meeting the artist before 1505. Or it might hint that the Doctor has already met Leonardo, but after 1505. It's certainly feasible that Leonardo might obey a stranger's instructions to paint over marked canvases, if that stranger tickled his fancy by writing the note in mirror-writing, as Leonardo did in his own diaries.

In "The Masque of Mandragora" (14.1) the Doctor visits the early 1490s and is eager to meet Leonardo there, but doesn't specify whether he's met the man before / after / earlier / later. The script seems to suggest that there's never been any contact between the two, yet the Doctor never says anything to contradict the idea that they might have run into each other in another time. At one point the Doctor asks whether Leonardo is among a group of entertainers, though all the entertainers are masked, so there's no way of knowing whether he'd recognise the great man on sight or not. And the almost-canonical radio play "The Ghosts of N-Space" has the Third Doctor referring to Leonardo as an old friend. It's at least possible, then, that they met late on in Leonardo's life (but quite early on in the Doctor's). This is perhaps the simplest explanation, as it means you don't have to contrive a meeting in the brief gap between "The Masque of Mandragora" and "City of Death". So the Eighth Doctor's apparent claim, of being around in 1506-08, makes sense.

But let's bear in mind, the Doctor *does* have a habit of revisiting old friends, despite the TARDIS' unpredictability. "City of Death" implies at least two meetings with Shakespeare, so there may have been other get-togethers with Leonardo. How does 1485 sound? Most of the works in the studio in "City of Death" date from that period anyway, but there's also a fascinating gap in Leonardo's biography there. Well, less a gap than a discrepancy. He claimed to have been sent on a long journey of discovery by the Devatdar of

continued on page 283...

are under time pressure to get to the TARDIS and prevent the prevention of all life on Earth, but to get across Paris at rush-hour, they need a taxi. *And you can never find one…*

The Continuity

The Doctor Can mirror-write, and can apparently read an entire book in just a few seconds by flipping through the pages [an ability which he never demonstrates again, and which he apparently didn't have when he read *The Origins of the Universe* in the previous story]. He states that he and Romana have crossed the 'time-fields' so often that they can sense temporal disturbances. [A subtly different view of Time Lords to the one we're used to; in stories like "Invasion of the Dinosaurs" (11.2) the suggestion is that the Doctor's resistant to time disturbances because of his very nature, but here it's about experience rather than breeding.] He states that he and Romana exist in a special relationship with time, 'perpetual outsiders'. She's not impressed.

When discussing how they should get down from the top of the Eiffel Tower, Romana suggests that she and the Doctor should fly, which at first sounds a joke. But when they're on their way back to the TARDIS, they get from the top of the Tower to the bottom in twenty seconds while Duggan's back is turned, as if they've done exactly that. [A magic trick, performed more for their benefit than Duggan's?] The Doctor's also a skilled pickpocket, stealing an anachronistic bracelet from the Countess Scarlioni's wrist and somehow detecting its alien nature from across the room. He's enough of a connoisseur to recognise the "Mona Lisa" copies as being Leonardo da Vinci's work, and to know Ming vases when he sees them.

• *Ethics.* Once again, the Doctor apparently has ethical problems with the idea of someone changing history, even apart from the fact that it'll annul all life on Earth. But he has no problem popping back nearly five-hundred years on a "research mission" to see Leonardo da Vinci.

• *Inventory.* Here the Doctor's carrying a hammer [as in 16.5, "The Power of Kroll"], an instamatic camera [possibly bought during this trip to Paris], a torch [not the pen-torch from 11.1, "The Time Warrior"] and a felt-tip pen.

• *Background.* Not only did the Doctor know Shakespeare - as a 'taciturn' boy - he helped the Bard write the first draft of *Hamlet* when

Shakespeare sprained his wrist writing sonnets. This means that the manuscript is at least in part in the Doctor's handwriting, but he still objects to the 'take arms against a sea of troubles' line, as he always told the author it was a mixed metaphor. But Shakespeare insisted. [The Doctor also mentions a meeting with Shakespeare in 13.2, "Planet of Evil". The implication here seems to be that there were at least two meetings, one when young William was just a boy and another in the *Hamlet* era, c. 1601. There are Doctor / Shakespeare meetings in the novel *The Empire of Glass* and the audio "The Time of the Daleks", although neither of those encounters are the ones referred to on-screen.]

Then there's Leonardo da Vinci. Though Leonardo doesn't appear here, the Doctor calls out to the artist in the man's study, in a way that suggests they've met; he refers to the model for the "Mona Lisa" as a dreadful woman who wouldn't sit still, and leaves a note beginning "Dear Leo", telling Leonardo to paint over what he's written on the blank canvases. The note ends "see you earlier". [Has he actually met Leonardo by this stage, or is he bluffing it? See **When Did the Doctor Meet Leonardo?**. But it should be mentioned that the Doctor appears to know the exact co-ordinates of the artist's study in Florence.]

The Doctor knows of the Jagaroth, and speaks as if the universe is well rid of them, which is unusually harsh for him. He believes Paris to be the one place in the universe where you can relax absolutely, and knows the café which does a nice bouillabaisse from a previous visit. He considers the "Mona Lisa" to be one of the great treasures of the universe, even though he's never noticed that she's got no eyebrows.

The Supporting Cast

• *Romana.* Good with puzzle-boxes, and she's now carrying what may be a sonic screwdriver of her own. [See 17.5, "The Horns of Nimon". Note that she began this incarnation by dressing as the Doctor, and now she's copying his hardware. Telling, perhaps.] She claims to be 125 here. [In 16.1, "The Ribos Operation", she claimed to be nearly 140. Though it's possible that she's picked up the Doctor's habit of lying about her age, it should be noted that when she told him she was 139 she was still trying to convince him that she was a mature grown-up. So it's just as likely that she was lying *then* and 125 is the true figure. See

When Did the Doctor Meet Leonardo?

...continued from page 281

Cairo, and not to have been in Milan but in the Taurus Mountains near the Euphrates, then swallowed by some giant sea-beast dating back to the time of the Persian king Artaxerxes. True, the Sultan of Egypt *did* ask him to build a bridge in Constantinople, and plans for this exist. But most art historians dismiss the diaries and letters as his version of "the dog ate my homework", and claim that he was in Milan all along, doing the many commissioned works for which invoices exist and attending human dissections (for which the Inquisition would have wanted a word, had they known). But look at either of the two versions of "The Virgin of the Rocks" and decide for yourself if those heavily symbolic caves are in Italy. From the Doctor's point of view, this period - when Leonardo was still influenced by his patron's pet philosophers Ficino and Pico della Mirandola (the Doctor wouldn't pass up a chance to talk to these two), and just beginning to discover the extent of his powers - would be irresistible.

So, we have a likely timeline. The Doctor first meets Leonardo in 1507-08, when the maestro is arranging the festivities for Louis XII's entry into Milan and making mechanical wonders. This might explain why, in the novel *Happy Endings*, a much later incarnation of the Doctor hires him to design an enormous cybernetic wedding cake. Then there's a near miss c. 1492, when the Doctor leaves the Dukedom of San Martino before Leonardo arrives at the party (if, indeed, Leonardo ever turns up). And there's another near miss in 1505, when the Borgia family unexpectedly commissions six copies of one of Leonardo's neoplatonic experimental paintings. (The Borgias weren't flavour of the month in Medici Milan, what with the 1498 show-trial of Girolamo Savonarola, the brief ruler of Florence who was simultaneously hanged and burned. If you've got time and a strong stomach, check out the career of Roderigo Borgia, AKA Pope Alexander VI. It's thoroughly grotesque.)

After that the Doctor and Leonardo may well meet up any number of times, perhaps in Asia Minor, 1485. The adventure with the giant sea-beast sounds like the Doctor's sort of thing, at least.

also **The Obvious Question: How Old Is He?** under 16.5, "The Power of Kroll".] She's still not entirely convinced about the culture of the outside universe, and claims - perhaps not seriously - that she was never any good with geometry. Even so, she's now as big a smartalec as the Doctor and can measure the lengths of rooms to the centimetre without any visible measuring equipment. She's heard of the Jagaroth, and is as contemptuous of them as the Doctor is.

At last, the Doctor explicitly refers to her as a Time Lady.

• *K9.* The Doctor is heard to say hello to him on entering the TARDIS, though he's never actually seen, so it's not clear whether he's fully-repaired yet [probably not, as the Doctor never calls on his services here].

The TARDIS Romana's now wearing an oversized school uniform, which must surely come from the TARDIS wardrobe. [But raises all kinds of awkward questions about the Doctor's tastes. Mind you, as we saw in "The Androids of Tara" (16.4), the Ship might well select the clothing.]

The randomiser apparently brought the TARDIS to Paris, but the Doctor can obviously over-ride it to make planned journeys. He gets to exactly the right place and time in sixteenth century Florence, even if he misses Leonardo, so his control over the Ship isn't bad at all by this stage. From the console, the TARDIS can track Scaroth's path back through time [in the same way it could monitor Zanak's progress in 16.2, "The Pirate Planet"].

Interesting thing about time-travel: when Scaroth goes back in time to alter history, the world doesn't immediately change, but gives the Doctor a chance to get to the TARDIS and stop Scaroth interfering. [Scaroth is in the past for only two minutes, but it takes *ages* for the Doctor to get back to the Ship, so the time that passes for Scaroth in the past and the time that passes for the Doctor in the present aren't "connected".]

The Time Lords Painting and drawing is done by computer on Gallifrey, and the Doctor implies that it isn't very good.

The Non-Humans

• *Jagaroth.* A vicious, callous, war-like race, described by the show-offish Scaroth as 'infinitely old', the Jagaroth were humanoid in shape but with skins made up of a shaggy green sea-weed-like material and no visible features except for a single eye in the middle of each wriggly Jagaroth face. 400,000,000 years ago a crippled spaceship carrying the last escaping Jagaroth landed on primeval Earth, the others having destroyed themselves in a massive war. Scaroth attempted to use warp-thrust to take off, as the ship didn't have secondary engines and its atmospheric thrust motors were disabled, but warp from a planetary surface was untested and even Scaroth had reservations. The ship was destroyed, and Scaroth - being inside the warp control cabin, and the only one directly in warp-field - was thrown into the time vortex [suggesting that the Jagaroth were at least close to developing time-travel technology].

He was split into twelve splinters, and scattered throughout history, each one having a life of its own but somehow being in contact with the others. The twentieth century Scaroth doesn't constantly "talk" to his other selves, but every now and then he has a funny turn in which he apparently hears the voices of several Scaroths at once. His sixteenth century self recognises the Doctor "after" the Doctor meets his twentieth century self, and the later version mumbles the earlier version's dialogue when he's half-conscious.

[It's not worth trying to work out the physics of this, but it's fair to assume that some sort of linearity is involved; i.e. Scaroth at the age of (say) fifty can communicate with all the other fifty-year-old Scaroths, but can't converse with older or younger versions of himself. It might be safe to assume that when the twentieth century splinter of Scaroth dies, all the others die at the same point in their own timelines, but if not then they could still cause trouble. It seems peculiar that although Scaroth's ship exploded 400,000,000 years ago, all the splinters described here seem to have ended up in the human era, no more than 1,000,000 years ago.]

Scaroth's plan is to force humanity to create a time machine for him, then go back to the day his ship was destroyed and stop it happening, so his splinters have been steering human history for thousands of years at least. [Does this mean that his twentieth century splinter sees time change whenever one of his former selves makes a difference? Were twentieth century humans far more primitive, when he first found them? Perhaps not; other human-influencing aliens, like the Daemons (8.5) and the Fendhal (15.3), wouldn't have

allowed humanity to remain too primitive. It may be that (a) Scaroth is exaggerating his impact on human history; (b) early versions of Scaroth gave humans fire and stellar mapping just for their own convenience, as he already knew that humanity would invent these things on its own; or (c) Scaroth has been making sure that humans invent the things his later self has already seen in the 1900s, just to be on the safe side. See **History** for more of this.]

Scaroth's twentieth century alias Count Scarlioni appears human thanks to the rubbery mask that he wears, although all previous Scaroths seem to have something similar. [This is strange, as early versions wouldn't have had any of the materials you'd need to create something so realistic. Presumably, some Jagaroth technology was scattered through time as well as Scaroth's bodily form.] For some years now Scarlioni has been married to the entirely human Countess, who has absolutely no idea that her husband's an alien. [Nobody over the age of twelve can help asking the obvious question, but we'll gloss over it. The Countess is remarkably quick to believe the truth, though, accepting the Doctor's story with very little evidence. Perhaps some sort of hypnotic block is involved in his "disguise".]

The Jagaroth spaceship which explodes on pre-historic Earth is a black, evil-looking, spider-like construction with legs that fold up as it lifts off. Even apart from the ship's warp ability, Jagaroth science would seem to be quite impressive. In the twentieth century, Scaroth has [holographic?] technology which can exactly replicate the interior of the Louvre in his chateau, complete with touchable objects. [His mask might utilise this technology... or it might not.] He's also got a sonic knife; a box which generates a prismatic field, changing the refractive index of the air and thus messing around with laser beams; and a micro-meson bracelet which scans the Louvre's automatic defences. When the Countess wears the bracelet, the Count can twiddle a ring on his finger to make her drop dead.

Planet Notes   Art collections mentioned by Romana, and generally considered to be of note... the Academius Stolaris on Sirius 5 [see the references to Sirius in "Frontier in Space" (10.3) and possibly "The Caves of Androzani" (21.6)]; the Solarium Panatica on Stricium; and the Braxiatel Collection. [The last of which takes on an extra significance in the New Adventures, primarily starting with *Theatre of War*, where Irving Braxiatel turns out to be yet another roaming Time Lord (and a former Cardinal to boot, as seen in Big Finish's "Gallfirey" CD series). The Braxiatel Collection becomes the base of operations in Big Finish's Bernice Summerfield adventures.]

History

• *Dating.* 1979, described by the Doctor as a 'table wine' sort of year for Paris. The Doctor's trip to see Leonardo da Vinci takes place in 1505. The original "Mona Lisa" was completed in 1503, according to the Doctor, and is still in Leonardo's study two years later. [Conventional art history holds that Leonardo started the painting in 1503 and worked on it until about 1506, but it's easy to see how the experts might have got it wrong if Leonardo was working on so many copies.]

In 1979, human research into time-technology is - not for the first time - rather advanced, with Professor Theodore Kerensky describing himself as the world's foremost authority on temporal theory. Financed by Scaroth, the doomed Professor has managed to construct a 'cellular accelerator' which can wind time backwards and forwards inside its field, turning an egg into a chicken or vice versa. [As ever, this shouldn't really be possible for all sorts of reasons; see especially 9.5, "The Time Monster". The technology isn't unlike that developed by Whitaker in "Invasion of the Dinosaurs" (11.2), which in turn may have been influenced by Fendleman from "Image of the Fendahl" (15.3), so Kerensky may have been following up the research of these previous pioneers. Like them, he ends up a victim of his own creation.]

Experiments with the device cause time to skip backwards by a few moments, apparently across the whole world [but probably not for those performing the experiments, or the loop would go on forever], although the Doctor and Romana sense the disturbance once it's over. Even before the first of these experiments, an artist in a Parisian café sketches a portrait of Romana as a woman with a cracked clock for a face, suggesting 'a crack in time'. [This is never explained, but suggests that artists are very perceptive around Time Lords and temporal upsets.]

When a chicken is put into the machine and its time-stream reversed, it reverts to an egg before the face of Scaroth appears, as if the machine somehow "knows" that all life started with the

Jagaroth. Without a field interface stabiliser you can't cross from the time-field inside the device to the time-field of the world outside, but Romana can easily rustle up a temporary one with equipment in Kerensky's lab and turn the accelerator into a functional time machine. The device could easily blow the whole of Paris through an unstabilised time-field, which would apparently just mean ageing it to dust.

In fact the machine is just the end result of Scaroth's plan, and he's been influencing human history in order to make sure it's created. He was in ancient Egypt, with his real Jagaroth face appearing on an Egyptian scroll as if he were one of the gods. He also claims to have caused the pyramids to be built. [This might seem to contradict 13.3, "Pyramids of Mars", in which it's made clear that the Osirians were the Egyptian gods and hinted that they inspired the pyramids. But 8.5, "The Daemons", suggests that the Egyptian god Khnum was one of the Daemons. So if there was an Osirian "court" on Earth, then it's reasonable to think that it might have been quite cosmopolitan, welcoming other alien presences into its midst. After all, Horus did see all sentient life as being of the same kin.] Scaroth was Captain Tancredi during the time of Leonardo, serving under the Borgias in Florence and getting the great artist to produce six copies of the "Mona Lisa".

As the twentieth century Count Carlos Scarlioni - who is, presumably, the last of the twelve splinters - Scaroth now plans to sell these paintings, plus the original from the Louvre, to seven notorious underworld collectors rich enough to afford it. 'Everyone on Earth' has heard of Count Scarlioni, and works of art missing for centuries have been turning up unexpectedly of late, causing furore in the art world. Scarlioni's chateau was restored four- or five-hundred years ago, which is when Leonardo's copies were bricked up there, ready to be removed in 1979. Thanks to the Doctor's intervention, six of the seven paintings are destroyed and the one in the Louvre now has the words "THIS IS A FAKE" written underneath the paint in felt-tip. The temporary theft of the "Mona Lisa" is made public, and is all over the TV news. [As the only surviving "Mona Lisa" is recovered from the fire at Scarlioni's chateau, it's likely that the public know he was responsible, even if they never find out about his true nature.]

Scaroth also claims that he invented the wheel, demonstrated the true use of fire and was the first on Earth to map the Heavens. [There must be at least one caveman-age Scaroth who's never shown, but the mapping of the Heavens is ambiguous and could refer to any number of moments in human history.] When his past faces are half-glimpsed, those seen appear to be an Egyptian, a Greek, a Roman and a soldier of the eleventh century. [Julian Glover, who plays Scaroth here, also played Richard the Lionheart in "The Crusade". The connection seems irresistible, but see 2.6 for more.] He's recently sold a painting by Gainsborough [mid-eighteenth century], and owns a priceless Second Dynasty Ming vase that Duggan breaks; several Gutenberg Bibles [mid-fifteenth century, possibly collected in Captain Tancredi's time]; and the first draft of Shakespeare's *Hamlet* [see under **The Doctor**].

It's stated, quite overtly, that the explosion of the Jagaroth ship began all life on Earth 400,000,000 years ago. The radiation caused the chains of hydrocarbons in the planet's oceans to fuse into amino acids, thence into proteins, the so-called 'soup of life'. [The dates are a bit out. 400,000,000 years BC was the Carboniferous Era, when amphibians the size of dogs, dragonflies as big as eagles and enough ferns to make up all the world's coal were already in place. 600,000,000 years BC, the start of the Cambrian Era, would be a better bet.] The ship exploded in the middle of what later became the Atlantic.

Twentieth century Earth is said by Romana to be a 'level five' civilisation [a different scale to that used in 16.1, "The Ribos Operation"].

The Analysis

Where Does This Come From? There are two separate stories to be evaluated here, the one they intended to make and the one they eventually filmed (see **The Lore** for the whole complicated story). The original plot of "A Gamble with Time" was a clear attempt to make a free-wheeling ITC-style international adventure story like *The Saint*, mainly on backlots with a splash of stock footage and Surrey doubling for Monte Carlo. The finished article, however, overtly alludes to *The Pink Panther* (especially in the casting of Catherine Schell) and *The Maltese Falcon*. But the main thrust of the story is the idea of "worth" versus "value".

Marcel Duchamp, arguably the most influential of the Dada artists, opened this particular can of

worms in 1917 with his "readymade" exhibit "Fountain". A mass-produced item, in this case a urinal, "magically" becomes valuable because a famous artist has selected it out of the millions of identical objects and put his signature on it. If Andy Warhol never touched one of his silk-screen prints, then why is it a Warhol? If Rembrandt's studio was full of nearly-as-talented students, supervised by the Old Master himself, then how do you define "a Rembrandt"? Now that artworks are kept in vaults, accumulating wealth despite the inability of anyone to prove they're genuine, we've forgotten that paintings are supposed to be *looked* at. (And make no mistake, it wasn't always this way. There was a massive shift in the way the art "market" worked in the 1960s, so this issue was still reasonably topical even by the time "City of Death" was made.)

It's worth noting that the "Mona Lisa" was just one of the hundreds of paintings looted under Napoleon, and only became "valued" once it had been stolen from the Louvre. We have no way of knowing if the painting that was returned is the one that was taken. And if the most famous painting in the world is a fake, then what hope is there for anything other than individual taste?

Vincenzo Perugia, who stole "her" in 1911, did so by hiding the painting under his smock. The security arrangements of the late '70s were a constant news item (terrorism, but also high-profile thefts, making a robbery seem more likely). In films such as *Rififi* (1958) and *The Thomas Crown Affair* (the reasonably good one, from 1968), the ingenuity of the thieves is seen as a chess-match with the security teams. This is in turn a legacy of films about bomb disposal (e.g. *The Small Back Room* from 1946 and *Juggernaut* from 1974). Incidentally, when Perugia took the painting it was absent for two years, during which time crowds flocked to see the gap where it had been; consult **The Lore** to see how ITV viewers did much the same thing in 1979.

At around the time this story was being made, Tom Keating was released from prison. He'd been the most audacious and ingenious forger of modern times, and had set about getting his revenge on the people who'd turned him down from Goldsmiths College for "unoriginality" by trashing the reputations of valuers. He never claimed his paintings were authentic, and one supposedly by Victorian watercolourist Samuel Palmer was flagrantly done on post-war paper to see if they ran even the most basic checks. He became a folk-hero, and got his own TV series explaining the techniques of the Old Masters by recreating them stroke for stroke in front of the cameras. He died as the first instalment aired, but by that point other people had started faking *his* work.

Of course, if we're talking about art, forgery, France and the 1970s, then we also have to mention *F For Fake*, Orson Welles' film about mendacity; his own, and that of the art establishment (there's an interesting Jon Pertwee connection to this film, but we'll leave it for you to find for yourselves).

The idea that life originated in "primordial soup" is fairly well-established, although the precise make-up of the planet's atmosphere and oceans at the time is unknown, and the conditions under which it could occur are a matter for guesswork. Some researchers claimed to have achieved the same thing in a laboratory, in 1953, using ultra-violet light and electricity. This result has never been successfully replicated.

The Jagaroth's cry of 'help us, Scaroth, you are our only hope' sounds so much like *Star Wars* that it's hard believe it's accidental (the line is a standard of B-movie SF, much like 'it's quiet… too quiet' or 'there's just one problem, it's never been tested on humans', but this was the late '70s). And it may or may not be a coincidence, but "Duggan" is the name used by another tough, blond, fictional Englishman who gets involved in the Parisian underworld; it's the *nom de guerre* of the assassin in *The Day of the Jackal*.

Things That Don't Make Sense The most obvious point: the Doctor and company can comfortably hang around on Earth 400,000,000 years ago, soaking up the primordial atmosphere, when there shouldn't have been anything like "air" or "land" on Earth at the time. [Does the Doctor extend the TARDIS force-field, as in 17.5, "The Horns of Nimon"? If the force-field's that flexible, then no wonder he found it so easy to deflect those missiles in "The Armageddon Factor" (16.6). It's worth pointing out that when Douglas Adams cannibalised parts of "City of Death" to write his novel *Dirk Gently's Holistic Detective Agency*, he reprised the scene and this time forced the characters to wear diving-suits. This might not have worked as well on television, though.] If Scaroth's ship exploded in the middle of what later became the Atlantic, then isn't it convenient that all his splinters seem to have ended up in habitable environments on dry land in their own time-zones? [Unless the Jagaroth can breathe underwater, and the various Scaroths had to march all the way to the nearest country across the ocean floor. Judging by the shape of human technological history, most of them headed towards Europe rather than America.]

Scarlioni's way of making money for the time-travel experiments - getting Leonardo to paint multiple great works, then flogging them off after stealing the original from the Louvre - is rather elaborate, considering the technology at his disposal. It's fair to assume that his earlier iterations have been stashing away investments for Scarlioni to pick up in the 1900s, but someone with his level of scientific understanding should surely be ruler of the world by now, not just a multi-millionaire? The "hologram" technology he uses to prepare for the Louvre robbery, which to him seems like a mere distraction, should in itself be enough to make him the richest man on the planet. It seems to have the ability to exactly replicate solid objects, too, which makes you wonder why he needs to get Leonardo to re-do the "Mona Lisa" six times over. You have to assume that, like his human trophy-wife, Scarlioni is just a bit bored and wants to pull off a complicated caper. After all, the Count's right-hand man expects the "Mona Lisa" operation to bring them $100,000,000 dollars, which is hardly wealth beyond imagining (to put things in perspective… that's about 1.25% of what Rupert Murdoch's currently worth, so let's hope *he* doesn't invest in time-travel).

Scaroth's decision at the end of episode one, to tear off his human face *after* he hears the Countess calling him, is equally curious. As is the fact that he's never bothered checking what's bricked up in his basement, just to make sure there really *are* six extra Leonardos there. And there's a certain paradox there, as well, because if all the Scaroths are connected through time then Captain Tancredi should stop existing shortly after the Doctor leaves him in 1505. Which means that Leonardo has no reason to finish the six copies. Which means that they shouldn't exist in 1979. Aghhh. And even if Tancredi *did* survive "after" the death of Scarlioni then he'd know what had happened and wouldn't have any reason to keep Leonardo working on the paintings.

In episode one, the Count refuses to let Professor Kerensky stop working on the project. No more than a couple of hours later, the Professor's said to be asleep in his room and the

ABOUT TIME 1975-1979

laboratory's deserted. Mere minutes after *that*, Kerensky returns to the lab as if he's fully-rested. And as ever, the time-technology is suspect. Kerensky believes his machine can turn a calf into a cow in seconds, not explaining why the calf - in its own sped-up time-field - wouldn't simply starve to death and turn to bone in seconds instead. The Doctor reverses the polarity and turns chickens back into eggs by flipping one switch, something the Professor has apparently never thought of.

And perhaps most curiously, the fabulously rich Scarlioni thinks that the best way of creating a time machine is to give one single temporal theorist a cellar full of equipment, rather than setting up a massive industrial research complex with several hundred highly-trained staff. It's a very British view of invention, really. [But then, the Scarlioni version of Scaroth evidently "grew up" in Britain, if his accent's anything to go by.]

France and Britain use different electrical sockets, but Romana's seen messing about with a three-pin plug in the last episode. The sketch of Romana changes between the café interior and exterior scenes [another effect of the 'crack in time'…], while Duggan marches the Doctor and Romana into the establishment and interrogates them at gunpoint without any of the other patrons worrying about it. Then two of Scarlioni's goons pull out firearms and rob all three of them, and the locals make even *less* fuss.

Not exactly a flaw, but an oddity: this is a story in which the Doctor and company have the villain unconscious and at their mercy halfway through episode two, but leave him lying where he is before running off to do other things, thereby giving him a chance to threaten the world later on in the story. And why does the Doctor need to wait for Duggan to knock out Scaroth and save human civilisation, when the Jagaroth are no tougher than human beings and the Doctor has already displayed his muscle in this story by trouncing an armoured guardsman in the sixteenth century?

Critique (Defence) It is, of course, one of the best things ever. But let's look at *why*.

"City of Death" is the calm eye at the heart of the storm. Look at "Destiny of the Daleks" and you see a programme tearing itself apart, a series that comes from a tradition of fantasy adventure but that's now being run by a production team more interested in footlights comedy and quirky

SF in-jokes, never dramatic enough to feel like an adventure and never funny enough to feel like light entertainment. But "City of Death" is the one environment in which the Adams / Williams vision of the programme makes perfect sense, because this isn't space opera with gags, it's one big performance-piece. It has virtually no action sequences, no running up and down corridors, no laser-gun fights and no jungle planets. At the core of the story is a single, simple confrontation, the clash of personalities when the Doctor meets Scaroth, and everything else rotates around that. They say that great sit-com can be boiled down to "two people who don't like each other, trapped in a room", and uniquely in *Doctor Who* this is the same concept on a bigger scale. It's about two great elemental forces (and Julian Glover's performance alone makes Scaroth as good a villain as the Doctor is a hero) ending up on the same planet and constantly trying to out-do each other. In episode one, they're tied together by their dialogue even before they meet.

Not that there aren't some great "big" SF ideas here - quite blatantly, there are - but the duel at the heart of the story gives the High Concepts a sense of focus, so they actually *mean* something in a way that the sci-fi fancies of (say) "The Pirate Planet" don't. And here, the lesser characters are interesting even when they're second-fiddling along with Tom Baker. This supporting cast *supports*. Romana could so easily have turned into a feed for the Doctor's lines, but instead she comes across as an almost pixie-like presence who gets involved in events without ever seeing them in quite the same way as everyone else. Her key moment comes when she starts doing something-terribly-interesting in the background while the Doctor's busy arguing with Duggan, as if she's the perfect intellectual counter-weight to the ever-so-visible leading man. In any other story, Duggan the Comedy Goon might have been an embarrassment, but the final irony (the Doctor lambastes him for punching people throughout the story, yet in the end he saves the whole of human history just by smacking the last of the Jagaroth in the face) is actual, structured *comedy* instead of the usual larking-about. As is the idea that the Doctor's written "THIS IS A FAKE" on the canvas of the most famous painting in the world. Meanwhile Countess Scarlioni has one of the most convincing motivations of any supporting villain in the series, i.e. pure boredom, and even the music plays along with a slinky *Pink Panther* saxophone theme.

Perhaps more than anything else, though, "City of Death" works because its fantasy elements are as memorable as its witticisms. Heavy-concept SF doesn't work on television without the aesthetics to support it, and in 1979 "City of Death" showed its audience things they'd never forget, (tele)visual images that match its cleverness point-for-point. It's a story about an alien with a cellar full of Mona Lisas, and that in *itself* makes it irresistible. Even the opening shots of the Jagaroth spaceship, which on paper runs the risk of looking like something from a bad Bob Baker and Dave Martin story, works beautifully thanks to the model-work (technically outdated by modern F/X standards, but still impressive thanks to its aesthetic sense). Occasionally it slips, yes - aside from all the running through Paris, the usual Williams-era obsession with giving the Doctor super-powers threatens the plot at least twice, with the "speed-reading" and "can Time Lords fly?" scenes being both pointless and not in any way funny - but it's testament to how great the story is that you can even remember those tiny flaws. In almost any other production, they'd be blotted out by at least half a dozen bigger glitches. Above all else, "City of Death" suggests a level of care and attention that's tragically missing from so much of *Doctor Who*, a double achievement considering its era and a triple achievement considering that the script was written in a weekend.

As with "The Robots of Death", however, the title is useless. (And it isn't even particularly accurate. Only five people die, which is gentle by *Doctor Who* standards.)

Critique (Also Defence) The thing is, this story is only good because of the processes that made *all* of *Doctor Who* work in this era. Turning viewers' expectations on their heads; allowing us to see things from "outside", the way the Doctor does (in this case our "basic" culture, *Hamlet* with mixed metaphors, the "Mona Lisa" with no eyebrows); giving characters a good reason to be the way they are, and the Doctor a good reason to want to stop the villain; and above all, letting the viewers decide what's "realistic", not the budget or effects team. As with "The Armageddon Factor" (16.6), "Nightmare of Eden" (17.4) and "The Androids of Tara" (16.4), the guest-characters include a couple with a realistic relationship. In this case, the Countess seems to think she's the "beard" of a flamboyant gay master-criminal, and is frustrated that he's always 'in the cellar, with that professor'.

Ah, yes, the Professor. There are a few performances in this story not entirely up to snuff. David Graham's Kerensky is the kind of thing he could get away with in *Thunderbirds*, but not here. However, Tom Chadbon is the weak link. The Doctor comments on a fake American accent that Chadbon doesn't even attempt (or not noticeably), while the 'he's mad, or I am' stuff that even Chris Tranchell (as Andred) found a way to make work in "The Invasion of Time" (15.6) falls flat and seems like an excuse for him to stop running for his life, pause in a corridor, deliver a duff line and then run again. He also rivals Adam Colby (15.3, "Image of the Fendahl") and Mike Yates (various) for the number of lines beginning 'are you trying to tell me…', but delivers them all the same way.

These critiques have tried to avoid directly contradicting each other, but this tosh about "super-powers" has to be addressed. Nobody can be so literal-minded as to think that the Doctor can really skim-read that fast, nor yet fly. Whereas Spock or the Bionic Woman could acquire and discard super-powers according to the story's needs (as could the Pertwee Doctor, less forgivably), we know the Doctor's basic limits and yet he teases us. And anyway, it's structurally the same gag as the 'where are we going?' one later in the first episode. The point is that we're all so used to knowing he's - all together now - a Time Lord from Gallifrey (10-0-11-0-0 by 02) and has two hearts and can regenerate and… it's dull. Every so often the need is there to keep the viewers thinking 'can he do that?', as they did in 1966 when he turned into Patrick Troughton. For a split-second we're uncertain. Similarly, for a fleeting moment it looks as if the tape's broken and the previous minute's-worth of footage is being shown again, or that we've accidentally changed channels and are watching something starring Eleanor Bron and John Cleese.

Happy now? The only thing that needs to be said about this story is that it's the pay-off to a joke they've spent seventeen years setting up. With Duggan's brute force prevailing over all the Doctor's ingenuity and Scaroth's fiendish plans, it's only natural that his accidentally repairing the sonic screwdriver by thumping it should have the Doctor offering him the post of 'scientific advisor'.

The Facts

Written by David Agnew, a pseudonym for Douglas Adams and Graham Williams, working from an idea by David Fisher. Directed by Michael Hayes. Viewing figures: 12.4 million, 14.1 million, 15.4 million, 16.1 million (a record for *Doctor Who*). Average viewership: 14.5 million, (another record).

In the autumn of 1979, the round of strikes which blighted so much of British TV at the time succeeded in switching off the whole of the ITV network. This effectively meant that the BBC had no competition, and it's usually assumed that the ultra-high ratings for "City of Death" were a result of this. Yet episode four's record of 16.1 million viewers occurred the week *after* the strike ended. Still, the statistics give us a snapshot of British culture at the time, as the caption on ITV apologising for the lack of any programmes received about as many viewers as *Big Brother* does now.

Supporting Cast: Julian Glover (Count), Catherine Schell (Countess), Tom Chadbon (Duggan), David Graham (Kerensky), Kevin Flood (Hermann), Pamela Stirling (Louvre Guide), Peter Halliday (Soldier); Eleanor Bron, John Cleese (Art Gallery Visitors).

Working Titles "Curse of the Sephiroth", "A Gamble with Time"; again, see **The Lore**.

Cliffhangers Alone in the laboratory, Scarlioni rips open his face to reveal the "features" of the Jagaroth; visiting Leonardo's study in the Renaissance, the Doctor meets Captain Tancredi, who turns out to look exactly like Count Sacrlioni and knows who the Doctor is; Sacrlioni activates the cellular accelerator while Kerensky's inside it, turning the man into a skeleton in moments.

The Lore

Hang on tight, this is going to be a bit bumpy. David Fisher was once again contracted to write two consecutive stories, regardless of the fact that Season Sixteen had drained him and his marriage was falling apart. The scenario for his original "A Gamble with Time" was fairly straightforward; a beefy British investigator in 1920s Monte Carlo finds that a famous gambler is winning more than should be possible. He, the Doctor and Romana

discover that the gambler is an alien, one of the Sephiroth (and if you know your kabalah then that name should raise an eyebrow or two), with advanced maths, precognition and psychokinesis. The alien is raising funds to get a time machine built. There were lots of high-speed chases in vintage Bugattis and some fantastic period costume possibilities, but then the man who worked out the budgets - John Nathan-Turner - did a few sums and figured out that it was a whole £25 cheaper to film it in present-day Paris with three actors and a small crew than to mock up Monaco circa 1925.

The BBC drama department got very excited about the idea of filming on location overseas, and Fisher was politely asked to rewrite the entire story at very short notice. Understandably, he declined. With most of the main characters cast and filming due to begin on Monday, the decision to rewrite was made on Thursday. Douglas Adams was locked in Graham Williams' spare room with a typewriter and a bottle of whisky (this might be an exaggeration, but not much of one by all accounts). As much as a line per episode of the original persists, notably the Doctor's final sermon to Scaroth about not getting a 'second throw of the dice'.

• Director Michael Hayes had filmed in Paris before, making the 1962-63 series *Maigret*. Nevertheless, due to lost shoes, drizzle and Baker's irritation with the press - and, according to some accounts, his irritation with the fact that the locals paid less attention to him than to Lalla Ward in a schoolgirl outfit - this was a ramshackle shoot. The Parisian police were called on at least two occasions as the four-day excursion progressed. In those days the 1st of May wasn't a Bank Holiday in Britain, as it was in France, so the idea that Paris might be "shut" when they filmed hadn't occurred to anyone.

• The scene with the "art-lovers" in episode four was a returned favour for a skit that Tom Baker and John Cleese had done for the 1979 BBC Engineers' Christmas Tape (the same source as the K9 gag mentioned under 16.6, "The Armageddon Factor", as well as several other rude bits which have circulated amongst fans). Cleese lived close to Television Centre, so was only a quick phone-call away.

• Catherine Schell was dating a friend of the director, Michael Hayes. She was happy to appear in something where she didn't have to wear funny alien eyebrows (see the second series of *Space: 1999*).

• Despite what you might think, David Graham's Russian accent is authentic, copied from his maternal grandparents.

• During the filming of "City of Death", the BBC's wildlife-for-kids series *Animal Magic* celebrated its 400th edition with a segment in which Tom Baker - in character as the Doctor, as in his *Disney Time* appearance - interrupted the programme's usual articles on *real* animals by telling the audience about some of the strange alien species he'd encountered over the years. Bits of the set of "Creature from the Pit" were used as the setting for this sequence. The fact that *Doctor Who's* leading man could so easily pop up in the middle of other programmes to talk to The Kids (a technique he'd obviously perfected in "The Invasion of Time") tells you a lot about the way the programme was perceived in those days.

• In the 2002 Venice Bienniale, artist Mark Wallinger exhibited a work entitled "Time And Relative Dimensions In Space"; a police box. The later installation in London's Whitechapel Art Gallery saw this modified into a highly-reflective police box rather than the previous navy blue version. One of the authors of the present volume was seen at the venue, gesticulating and commenting on the curiously redundant vestiges of its previous use.

• The "macguffin" here, the idea of painting multiple copies of the "Mona Lisa" and selling each one as the stolen original, was recycled by the writers of the Granada *Sherlock Holmes* adaptations to pad out their script for "The Final Problem". Nice to see Douglas Adams on the receiving end of idea-pilfering for a change…

17.3: "The Creature from the Pit"

(Serial 5G, Four Episodes, 27th October - 17th November 1979.)

Which One is This? There's a pit, and it's got a creature in it. The creature is a big green luminous quasi-phallic blob, but you might also know this story as "the one with the most offensive ethnic stereotype ever, oy vay".

Firsts and Lasts For the first time, and for the rest of Season Seventeen, David Brierley takes over

from John Leeson as the voice of K9 (the reason for the Doctor claiming in 17.1, "Destiny of the Daleks", that K9 had robot laryngitis). This story marks the last ever appearance of Terry Walsh, as a speaking part (the engineer Doran) who doesn't do any stunt-related falls, even if his character *does* get pushed down a mineshaft off-screen. It's also the final story to be directed by old hand Christopher Barry.

This is the only occasion when it's hinted that the Doctor may have been involved in Biblical events (see under **The TARDIS**).

Four Things to Notice About "The Creature from the Pit"…

1. You have to give them marks for trying. Having exhausted the possibilities of men in monster costumes (or at least, they would have done by the end of the season) and having had limited success with enormously-inflated puppets (16.5, "The Power of Kroll"), the programme-makers plumped for a very different kind of monster here and constructed a giant, amoeboid mass that worked like an enormous air-bag. In fact, *Doctor Who* had tried this once before, in "Frontier in Space" (10.3) with the puffy, orange "Ogron eater." The result was such a failure that one director refused to film it except in long-shot, so the production team's desire in 1979 to put a similar "device" at the centre of an entire story might be construed as a credit to their optimism.

Erato, the titular (in more than one sense) Creature from the Pit, is also incapable of normal speech and hi-jacks the Doctor's vocal cords when it wants to communicate. This means that it sounds exactly like Tom Baker, the kind of actor-saving measure not employed by the programme since the days when Jon Pertwee played all the radio announcers and hoped that no-one would notice. Lady Adrasta's best line, when describing the creature's nature: 'Our researchers divide into two categories. The ones who have got close enough to find out something about it… and the ones who are still alive.'

2. Often seen as one of the test-cases for the use (or over-use) of humour in late '70s *Doctor Who*, "The Creature from the Pit" features near-record numbers of comedy supporting characters and general messing-about scenes from Tom Baker. The most famous / notorious of these is the moment when the Doctor gets stuck halfway down the shaft that leads into the monster-occupied pit, reaches into his coat and pulls out a book

entitled *Everest in Easy Stages*. Finding it to be written in Tibetan, he then produces another book entitled *Teach Yourself Tibetan*. At the end of the day, whether you find the late '70s style of *Doctor Who* bearable probably hangs on the question of whether you find this funny. If yes, then tick the "This is a Prime Example of Ready Wit Within an SF Format" box. If no, then tick the "Now You Know Why People Felt Relieved When John Nathan-Turner Turned Up" box.

3. Oh look, it's Geoffrey Bayldon. Here he's taking the part of Lady Adrasta's put-upon, pessimistic astrologer, Organon. An actor with a proud history of playing erratic magician-figures - he played the lead role in *Catweazle* (see 11.1, "The Time Warrior"), the Crow-Man who made all the living scarecrows in *Worzel Gummidge* and even the Doctor in two of Big Finish's *Unbound* audio adventures - Bayldon is easily the most endearing thing on offer here. Organon's sales pitch, delivered with a sigh: 'Astrologer extraordinary. Seer to princes and emperors. The future foretold, the past explained, the present... apologised for.'

4. Attentive viewers will note that this story is about a corrupt politician who kidnaps an alien ambassador, who can't communicate properly as it kills anyone it touches, and uses the creature as a way of murdering any opposition while at the same time making sure that it terrifies the local community. Then the Doctor turns up and speaks to the ambassador with a special communication device, only to discover that the ambassador's species are planning on destroying the planet as a reprisal for the politician's actions. Compare with 7.3, "The Ambassadors of Death". (Still, at least there's no "radiation" involved this time.) There is, however, an even more obvious parallel to be drawn; see **Where Does This Come From?**.

The Continuity

The Doctor Still claiming to be in his 750s, according to Romana [he hadn't turned 760 by 16.5, "The Power of Kroll", so there wasn't a very big gap between Season Sixteen and Season Seventeen]. The Doctor himself claims, probably fatuously, that 74,384,338 is his lucky number [and in "The Power of Kroll" it was seven]. He also says - even more facetiously - that Time Lords have ninety lives, and that he must have used up about 130 of them [this is nothing to do with

regeneration at all, but could so easily be misconstrued...].

• *Inventory*. The Doctor stuffs his jawbone of an ass - see **The TARDIS** - inside his coat pocket here. He's also carrying a spoon, matches, a stethoscope, a tiny device that can tell him whether something's made of metal, a large mirror, some climbing-hooks that can be knocked into rock with his hammer, a book in Tibetan called *Everest in Easy Stages* and a book called *Teach Yourself Tibetan*. [He seems to need this last volume, even though he speaks Tibetan in 11.5, "Planet of the Spiders". As he doesn't start reading it from the beginning, perhaps he's just looking at it to focus himself on the language.]

• *Background*. The Doctor claims to have helped Theseus and Ariadne escape from the labyrinth of the Minotaur, somehow producing an enormous ball of string to stop them unravelling his scarf. [The Doctor fights a half-man, half-bull creature in "The Time Monster" (9.5) and believes it to be the Minotaur of legend, but Theseus had nothing to do with it. Either the Doctor's making up stories here - and why bother, if he really *did* fight such a monster? - or he was wrong in "The Time Monster" and he's come across the *real* Minotaur at some point in the few years since, as the reference to his scarf suggests. Which would mean that the labyrinth / Minotaur fable of "The Horns of Nimon" (17.5) is the third time he's been through that sort of thing.]

The Supporting Cast

• *Romana*. Knows the plots of several children's books by Beatrix Potter, strange for someone with such a limited understanding of human culture. Here she refers to herself as a Time Lord, not a "Time Lady". She's good at using her upper-class demeanour to over-awe hairy working-class bandits, and now has her own dog-whistle for K9, which must be slightly different to the Doctor's as K9 can tell who's calling him.

• *K9*. Back in action after the Doctor's tinkering, but with a new voice and a greater tendency to get excited, irritated or distressed. After the Doctor's plan to misdirect a neutron star succeeds, K9's analysis is a very un-robotic 'I still say it was impossible', and he calls villainous women 'madam' in a haughty voice [he's entering his C-3PO phase]. He can tell whether disconnected components of the TARDIS are working or not just by looking at them, and claims he's programmed not to kill, except in self-defence. A mirror can reflect his "stun" blaster-fire, or alternatively his laser beam can be powerful enough to disintegrate metal. Tythonus and Tythonians (see **The Non-Humans**) are in K9's data-bank, although the Doctor isn't familiar with the place.

The TARDIS Has an external gravity tractor beam. Here it's used to hold a neutron star steady, but not for long periods or the console room starts to glow alarmingly and the control blows up on the console. The Doctor panics when this makes the neutron star head straight for the TARDIS, as if the Ship couldn't survive such a thing. Romana speaks of picking up the neutron star on 'band six' when it appears on the scanner [the scanner has different channels?].

The Doctor has a copy of *Peter Rabbit*, which K9's reading here. Romana's been cleaning out number four hold, and things she brings out of it in a box are… a big ball of string, which was used in the maze of the Minotaur and actually has a "thank you" note from Theseus and Ariadne attached to it [see **The Doctor**]; the jawbone of an ass, which has 'been about a bit' [the same one that Samson used to kill a thousand Philistines, hence the Doctor's 'don't be a Philistine' comment?]; and the Ship's Mk. III emergency transceiver, a hemispherical device that's part of the TARDIS and should allow the Doctor to receive and send distress signals, but he removed it to stop himself getting messages from Gallifrey. When plugged in it receives the distress call from Erato on Chloris, and makes the console room lurch to one side before taking the Ship there. K9 states that this is the first time it's been used 'properly' [suggesting that he's fully-programmed with the history of the TARDIS].

The Time Lords The Doctor states that the symbol of the maternity service on Gallifrey is a pair of crossed computers. [Suggesting that Gallifreyans *do* breed in a family environment, but perhaps hinting that reproduction is a highly technical process which doesn't involve anything too… physical. Which fits what we've seen of Gallifrey so far, apart from the fact that there seem to be hardly any women there. Of course, he could just say it in the hope of annoying an astrologer, an honourable enough intention.]

The Non-Humans
- *Tythonians*. Erato - the Tythonian High

Ambassador sent to Chloris on a trading mission - is a glowing, amorphous green blob, over a hundred feet long with various appendages attached. His homeworld of Tythonus is rich in metal, but rapidly running out of vegetation, which is why he was sent to Chloris; see **Planet Notes**. It's said that Tythonians thrive on mineral salts and chlorophyll, and can live for up to 40,000 years, while Erato has been half-starved for fifteen years but is still capable of crushing people in an attempt to make contact. It's not explained why the Doctor is the only one to survive his attentions. Erato's skin resembles a great cerebral membrane with green veins, and he doesn't like fire.

The 'blindingly simple' vessel in which Erato arrived was an enormous egg, woven out of living metal, which cracked open on landing. It's still transmitting a burbling distress signal, or 'screaming in pain', only detectable on very low-frequency wavelengths. Though the ambassador has no vocal cords, he brought with him a pentagonal, shield-like metal device which - when pressed up against his flesh - allows him to use the larynx of the person touching it. The user's lips don't move while this happens, and when K9 touches it Erato can talk through the dog, even when they're separated by miles of space. Occasionally the communicator glows blue for no given reason, and those near it feel the hypnotic urge to take it towards Erato.

Erato is capable of "spinning" metal barriers from at least one of its pseudopods, using the same material as the shell and the translator. The material's self-renewing, so blaster-fire just makes it stronger, but it breaks when Erato wants it to. The photon drive for Erato's space-egg, made of the usual material and compact enough to be held in one hand, is held by the creature while it's in the pit. He can also spin aluminium, and probably iron and cadmium too.

Though Erato is prepared to deal with the people of Chloris after Adrasta's out of the picture, the Tythonians can obviously be quite harsh, as they receive the message sent by the egg-capsule and send a neutron star hurtling towards Chloris' sun by way of retaliation. It's been on its way for several years, so it's lucky that the Doctor shows up in the nick of time. The neutron star could destroy Chloris' entire solar system, but the Doctor comes up with a plan to have Erato spin a thin shell of aluminium around it, which minimises its gravitational pull and lets the TARDIS yank it out of the field of Chloris' sun. A draft contract for a trading agreement is then sent to Chloris, and delivered by the Doctor [who probably supplies the paper on which it's written].

Tythonians measure time in ninods, twenty-six of which equal one hour and seven minutes, which is how long it takes Erato to spin a new ship around its vital components. [What happens, exactly, is this: Erato says 'twenty-six ninods', and the Doctor immediately responds 'one hour, seven minutes'. The Doctor doesn't know anything about Tythonians before this, so it's possible he "hears" an automatic translation of the term - although we don't - and is simply repeating what Erato said.]

Planet Notes

• *Chloris.* A planet with jungle as far as the eye can see, rich in plant life and therefore chlorophyll, but with no significant metal deposits at all. This means that any metal is like gold. It's the tyrannical Lady Adrasta who wields power here, since she's the one who controls the only mine, although 'all the metal on the planet' has been mined out of it by now.

Chloris is a pre-industrial world, the natives having a liking for opulent, ceremonial design, with Adrasta's guards wearing masks and turbans. The Lady doesn't run the whole planet, as Organon mentions the courts of other rulers, but her guards are the only apparent law in the region seen here. Yet no real signs of civilisation are ever glimpsed, other than her palace and the hovel of some bandits out in the jungle.

The locals seem to know about the existence of alien civilisations, even if visitors aren't common, as they're not terribly surprised by people claiming to be beyond the stars. Adrasta is the only one on Chloris who knows the truth about Erato, and has been keeping him in the mine since he arrived on Chloris fifteen years ago, as trade with the Tythonians would break her monopoly on metal. She's been throwing her enemies into 'the Pit' ever since, and keeping the ambassador's translation device in her palace, while serfs throw scraps of food into the pit for the creature. The place where Erato's egg landed is now known as the Place of Death, as anyone found there is automatically put to death. Most of the country [are there other inhabited countries?] is overrun by forest or jungle, as there's no metal to make tools for cultivation, so Organon is one of the few who's travelled.

Also found on this world are wolf-weeds,

grown in Adrasta's nurseries. They're clumps of foliage halfway between tumbleweed and giant sprouts, kept on leashes by Lady Adrasta's Huntsman, which can be trained to attack and overpower a human victim. The weeds tend to giggle stupidly when they attack, and leave K9 covered in webbing that stops him moving. The guards are under the control of a Guard-Master, but Adrasta also commands hooded engineers who've written a paper on the Tythonian egg. Her second-in-command, Madam Karela, hints that women are considered to be more resourceful in this society even though she and Adrasta are the only two seen here. [The Chloris' inhabitants seem quite human, but even apart from evolutionary questions, it's a little peculiar that they've developed such a familiar sort of culture on a world that's covered in jungle and can't have had an iron age. It's possible, but by no means implied, that Chloris is another degenerate Earth colony that's forgotten about space-technology.]

The Doctor talks about 'this side of the galaxy' as if Chloris is in a familiar galaxy [the one we're used to]. Once again, astrology seems remarkably accurate here, as Organon is portrayed as a bit of a faker but all his predictions come true.

History

• *Dating.* Absolutely no indication [though if these people *did* originate on Earth, then it must be a long, long way into the future].

The Analysis

Where Does This Come From? As anyone growing up in a steel-producing town in '70s Britain knew, government decisions about what was "economically viable" were a suspiciously good match for what was "politically useful". As with coal (see 10.5, "The Green Death" and 11.4, "The Monster of Peladon"), the manufacture of steel provided a means by which large bodies of organised labour could take concerted action against any government. Moreover, as British Steel was haemorrhaging money through (amongst other factors) management's slow response to rising fuel costs - and as management responded by sacking workers, closing plants and giving themselves pay-rises - imported steel looked like a better option, regardless of quality or logistics. Some towns had, for generations, been geared entirely towards the one industry. As with coal, shipbuilding and latterly agriculture, adjusting to the closure was hard even if you though it was necessary. And nobody outside Whitehall *did* think it was necessary. In each area where this transition was taking place, petty crime was on the rise, mainly among people previously of good background and character.

Some commentators - especially foreign ones - read "The Creature from The Pit" as a satire on this, citing the Scavenger leader Torvin's obviously false desire to be 'democratic' as proof that this was social comment. And it was hard to be unaware of these events, but there's a more overt starting-point for the story.

The simple truth has to be faced: this is the point where *Doctor Who* graduates from "pulling rank" on *Star Trek* and fights back. The mawkish, self-regarding Hollywood version of TV space-opera was out of keeping with the sardonic, lateral-thinking *Doctor Who*, but the BBC seemed to think they were interchangeable. The viewing public knew better. Anyone who knows the syrupy classic *Star Trek* 1.25, "Devil in The Dark", as we all did after umpteen reruns at prime time in the '70s, will spot the point-for-point parody. Erato draws the translator device in the wall, much as the Horda writes "No Kill I". He talks via a humanoid touching his shell; none of your Vulcan mind-melds here. The opposition doesn't come from a bunch of xenophobic blue-collar types in day-glo overalls, but from a vampish Snow Queen who's trying to maintain a stranglehold on the planet's economy.

That's only the start of it, though. *Star Trek* is based on the idea that all aliens are just regular folks, like us. They're as different from *humans* as America's diverse ethnic minorities are from WASP mainstream whitebread honkies, but no more than that. *Doctor Who* may have ended up featuring a lot of bipeds with RADA diction, yet the idea constantly being presented to us is that even other humans aren't like us (starting with 1.6, "The Aztecs"). Erato's people have very different priorities, but the assumption that classical *laissez-faire* economics is universal is opened up. Short-term economic advantage is inconsequential to a being that lives for 40,000 years. It might seem ridiculous to assume that all cultures in the cosmos want to buy and sell things from each other; however, that's no more ethnocentric than the thought that all beings want to be part of a universal brotherhood, or any other assumption we might make. Not all humans want to do either of these things, after all, but Western policies are based on this presumption.

If this seems a bit of a stretch, then consider the pickle that the West got into over what happened in Iran that year. A decade of conflict followed from the misconception that all nations and cultures want to be like us when they grow up, and that all difference is deviation from our standard. In this story, people who believe their own standards to be all-encompassing wind up dead. As with "Destiny of the Daleks", logic from a false premise is worse than guessing.

Things That Don't Make Sense Erato only wants to communicate with people in the pit, killing them purely by accident, and is "nice" really... or so we're led to believe. But Adrasta's been throwing people down the pit for fifteen years now, the latest of them being Engineer Doran (Terry Walsh, again). Has Erato, the supposedly dignified and intelligent ambassador of the Tythonians, really not figured out yet that people *always* die when he rolls over them? Anyone would think that this oh-so-benevolent diplomat was killing the locals just out of irritation.

Adrasta sees K9 stun one of her guards at the end of episode one, but then repeatedly gives Romana access to the dog anyway, and in episode two doesn't even worry when Romana points the thing right at her. She also seems to think that she needs a weapon like K9 to kill the Tythonian, which raises the question of how she got this hundred-foot monstrosity down the pit in the first place. As ever in television, the heroes find out that a death-device is heading for the planet exactly twenty-four hours before it arrives (a nice round figure to *our* ears, even if Chloris doesn't have a twenty-four hour day). It takes Erato over an hour to weave a small space-pod, but apparently mere moments to weave a shell around a much larger neutron star, while his communicator is roughly twenty times the size of the device which can drive his space-capsule across the galaxy [quirky Tythonian design]. Besides, neutron stars - though compact - are still supposed to be planet-sized. No wonder K9 expected it to be impossible.

Though aluminium has odd magnetic properties, it doesn't necessarily have odd gravitational ones. It's odd that Erato has so much of it "on his person" and never thought about making a ladder. And if the Doctor 'produced' the ball of twine which helped Theseus and Ariadne - say, from some oversized and unexpected pocket - then why is it marked with a "thank you" label that suggests it's some sort of gift?

Oh, and here's a strange thing: when Erato spins the shell around the neutron star, someone can be heard to yell 'Erato!' as the Tythonian appears on the TARDIS scanner. It sounds *sort of* like Tom Baker, but the quality of the voice isn't quite right, and the acoustics suggest that it wasn't recorded in the studio at the same time as the rest of the dialogue. Did someone realise during editing that there needed to be a victorious 'look, it's Erato!' line, but that none had been recorded? Is this someone doing a Tom Baker impression (compare with Jon Pertwee's Brigadier voice-over in 7.1, "Sperahead from Space")? Or is it just Tom's voice recorded on a dodgy audio track? We may never know.

Critique (Prosecution) Ever since *The Discontinuity Guide* raised the point in 1995, the big question about "The Creature from the Pit" has been whether it's "bad science fiction" or "a conscious spoof of bad science fiction". But this misses the point. *Doctor Who* in the late '70s was made for an SF-conscious audience (you could argue that this is exactly what was wrong with it). It expected its more discerning viewers to have seen - and probably mocked - programmes like *Star Trek*, so when a spanner-in-the-works character like the Doctor arrives on a gaudy jungle planet, it's inevitable that he should find himself sending up the whole genre. That's not parody, it's just business as usual.

No, the real trouble here isn't that it can't decide whether it's satire or not, the trouble is that it's comedy-SF in which the comedy isn't funny and the SF isn't very interesting, the same problem as every other story in Season Seventeen bar one. Like "Nightmare of Eden" after it, there are SF conceits here which look good on paper, but the script has no way of making them work on television. Chloris presents us with a kind of society we've never seen before, but it's never explored in any way, and instead the screen-time is wasted with endless scenes of "funny" bandits and the usual gamut of characters escaping from other characters. The idea of a planet without metal is novel, yet in the end it's just an excuse for the plot to treat "any metal" as this week's "most valuable substance in the universe", so the ore-hungry locals could be talking about jethryk or trisilicate for all we care.

Lush as the jungle filming is - and you have to give it credit for the guards' costumes - there's almost nothing here to make us feel that this planet even exists, and less still to make us care about it. David Fisher wrote copious background notes on both Chloris and the Tythonians before he wrote the finished script, which makes you wonder why even Skaro in a Terry Nation story feels more substantial than this. There's a palace full of baddies, there's a shack full of comedy Jews, there's nothing in-between; this planet is defined by people endlessly speculating, and we never see what it actually *does*. In effect it's an SF "joke", with the punchline that Erato turns out to be an intelligent life-form who's just a victim of petty politics, but there's nothing to care about beyond that and therefore nowhere near enough to sustain four episodes. (Episode three is untenably drab, stretching out five minutes' worth of material with scenes of arguing bandits and Adastra shouting at K9.)

Adrasta herself joins the Movellans, the vraxoin smugglers and Soldeed in the line-up of this year's villains who are about as threatening as air, so overshadowed by Tom Baker's ego that there's never a hope of worrying about anything she might do. No threat means no menace, no menace means no dynamic, and you just end up with one more reason that the children of the mid-'70s can never understand why the children of the '60s actually thought this programme was frightening. Only the opening scene of episode four, as Adrasta's power disintegrates before your eyes, works dramatically... but even *that's* rather spoiled when the villainess suffers the Pythonesque fate of being eaten by sprouts and crushed by a gigantic green blob at the same time. And by the fact that the story goes on for fifteen minutes afterwards (see also 22.5, "Timelash").

The new voice of K9 is, incidentally, almost unbearable.

Critique (Defence, of Everyone Except the Director) Even its sternest critics agree that the material up to the point when the Scavenger leader Torvin speaks is as atmospheric and well-executed as anything the colour era had ever produced. What happens thereafter is, with one obvious exception, ingenious and good-natured fun. But why the hell did Christopher Barry, who believed he was "salvaging" a script he clearly misunderstood from the start, decide to turn

Torvin into Fagin from *Oliver Twist*? Not only does it grate, but small children found it annoying. From the moment that Romana describes the bandits as 'hirsute', Barry abandons the notion of unemployed-miners-gone-bush and makes them bearded troglodytes (an error he's made before, in 3.9, "The Savages").

Ignoring this insult to everyone's intelligence and sensibilities, what have we got? This is as good an example as you can get of how the real "enemy" in *Doctor Who* is lack of imagination. The villains are villains because their parochial, self-centred attitudes don't even allow them to see how anyone can be laughing at them. 'We call it… the Pit', and later, 'we call it… the Creature', and in both cases we - and the Time Lords - can see how blinkered they are. Seeing the big picture gets you executed.

The antidote for this self-imprisonment is literacy. Not just being able to read, but being willing to "try out" ideas, to learn, to "be" other people. All through the Williams era (indeed, since Tom Baker first stepped out of Pertwee's shadow) this has been a developing strand. The recurrent jokes about books in this season, culminating in a book which is power (17.6, "Shada"), are only part of this. The brief gag about *Teach Yourself Tibetan*, which - aside from having a phrase not unlike "Don't Panic" as its introduction - is the main thing most people remember about this, is a distraction from the real book-joke; that two of the most powerful beings in the universe find time to read Beatrix Potter.

In *Star Trek* books are things you know *about* for trivia tests and, later, the source of dreary "holonovels". They're things you quote at people to seem "deep". As we've seen, this story is at heart a dig at the illiteracy of *Trek*, and the puerile values it smugly pronounces upon. However, it's also an attack on the egocentric, geocentric, money-oriented world we were entering at the time. These people are, however much wealth they accumulate, peasants. The regime of Lady Adrasta is one in which people are categorised. The possibility of change is forbidden even as a topic. This was a theme running through a lot of '70s conflicts, both in Britain under the incoming Thatcher government and in the Soviet Union. In Torvin's mob we have a gang who, like Tryst in "Nightmare of Eden" and Scaroth in "City of Death", know the price of everything and the value of nothing. Evaluating everything in purely market terms is just as confining, we're shown

here, as stage-managing the news to prevent contact with the outside.

Unfortunately, Barry misses the point entirely. As with all his colour stories, he's as concerned with finding new things to try that won't work with CSO as with understanding the characters or getting a handle on the script. In his Pertwee efforts he laboured under the assumption that lots of things happening loudly equate to "drama". Now, like so many people, he's come to assume that if Douglas Adams is around then it must all be "comedy". The comedy is in the situations, not the funny voices. Fortunately Myra Frances as Adrasta also misses the point and thinks that the character's jokes are the author's. By saying her lines as though contemptuous of anyone beneath her level, she gets at the heart of why Adrasta is the lowest of the low. This paradoxically helps Tom Baker. He delivers the Doctor's lines as if aware that no-one else in earshot will be able to follow what he's saying, and this is a much more subtle performance than he usually tries to give. However, when the thing which most adults remember about this story is that the Doctor's first attempt to communicate with Erato looks like inter-species porn, you have to admit that this is a difference of degree, not kind. If you're too old to be frightened by Erato, then you're old enough to see the funny side.

Ah, Erato. Named after the Muse of Epic Poetry, there's obviously a level of irony at work here. If you miss this then there's always the fact that in *Doctor Who*, the more mysterious something is, the more likely it is to be "wonderful". In the sense of "filling one with wonder". Starting with this premise, the monster clearly isn't a monster at all, but seen as one it's at least better executed than the Mutants or the Giant Robot.

Barry's final flaw (and let's try not to be too hard on him, as when he was paying attention he at least made the jungle and the caves look right) was to miss the hints in the script about the neutron star and make it all seem like an add-on to the "main" story rather than another inevitable consequence of Adrasta's folly. He mis-paces the whole final episode, making the theft of the photon drive another little incident along the way rather than a crisis with time running out for the planet. Still, in "The Daemons" Barry made the idea of the Devil threatening to destroy Earth (because he didn't like Jon Pertwee) seem equally inconsequential, so at least he was consistent.

The Facts

Written by David Fisher. Directed by Christopher Barry. Viewing figures: 9.3 million, 10.8 million, 10.2 million, 9.6 million.

Supporting Cast: Myra Frances (Adrasta), Eileen Way (Karela), Geoffrey Bayldon (Organon), John Bryans (Torvin), Edward Kelsey (Edu), Tim Munro (Ainu), Terry Walsh (Doran).

Cliffhangers Threatened by Adrasta, the Doctor decides to voluntarily jump into the pit rather than co-operate; the Doctor shows his suicidal streak again, by stepping forward to greet the creature in the pit and getting rolled on by one of its pseudopods, in a scene chillingly reminiscent of the "giant breast" sequence in *Everything You Wanted to Know About Sex But Were Afraid to Ask*; the Doctor holds the screaming Adrasta captive in the pit, as the translator is attached to the huge, gelatinous mass of Erato. (This is an odd one. At least when the Master's life was threatened as a cliffhanger - see 8.5, "The Daemons" - there was a sense that the whole world might be threatened at the same time. Here, however, we're supposed to be worried because the Doctor isn't letting the villain go.)

The Lore

• David Fisher wrote copious background notes on both Chloris and Erato when he submitted his story, and much of the material failed to make it into the finished script. The outline states that Tithonians (note the "tit" spelling) spend two-hundred years mating, the male and female merging into one another during the procreative act. The gestation period apparently lasts for 3,000 years.

• This was, due to the odd filming schedule, the first story of this season to be made and thus Lalla Ward's first stab at playing Romana. This changeover is covered in more detail under "The Armageddon Factor" (16.6). However, this and the guest-cast may have been instrumental in persuading Baker to sign a fresh contract.

• Geoffrey Bayldon, as has been mentioned, is *Catweazle* to a generation. As we saw in Volume III, this was one of the better ITV children's fantasies of the early '70s, in which an Anglo-Saxon wizard is hurled into 1970 and sort-of-adjusts.

He'd earlier been on Verity Lambert's long-list to play the original Doctor.

• Christopher Barry still believes that the Tythonian was an unfilmable concept. His insistence on having three attempts at making the models (which delayed matters, added to the budget and caused friction with the special effects department) didn't help; on top of this, he made them do the spaceship scenes again as he thought the first attempt was unbroadcastable. The BBC held an inquest afterwards, and all sides blamed each other. Meanwhile even Mat Irvine's radio-controlled wolfweeds had problems, as the gearboxes repeatedly caught fire.

• David Brierley had been extensively auditioned for the part of K9 (John Leeson having other commitments, he hoped). Whereas Leeson had scampered about the rehearsal-hall on all fours, Barry - an experienced Dalek-wrangler - introduced the idea of using a small pram to stand in for the prop dog.

• Australian academic John Fiske, whose work used to be the only material on television theory not based on an American model of viewers as "consumers", wrote what has to be one of the most misguided pieces of work on *Doctor Who* ever published. "*Doctor Who*: Ideology and the Reading of a Popular Narrative Text" was published in the Australian Journal of Screen Theory (numbers 13-14) in 1983. In this, he makes the anachronistic claim that Adrasta is based on Margaret Thatcher; that Romana's habit of wearing white suggests her views are to be read as "sacred" (how does he square this with the schoolgirl costume?); and that the Doctor's apparent re-assertion of "normality" - male rule, free-market economics, the motions of celestial bodies - is all to do with the BBC's patriarchal and elitist core values.

Given that what might be termed "mad capitalists" outnumber "mad scientists" in this phase of the programme, and that stories where such people are the villains outnumber stories involving Daleks or Cybermen across the programme's whole run, he's on shaky ground factually. His dinosaur Structuralist critique is equally risky from a more mature, post-Bakhtin, post-Foucauldian perspective, but worst of all he fails to take into account the possibility that this might be even slightly tongue-in-cheek, despite K9 reading Beatrix Potter.

17.4: "Nightmare of Eden"

(Serial 5K, Four Episodes, 24th November - 15th December 1979.)

Which One is This? *Airport* in space, where galactic liners collide and green-eyed swamp-monsters tuck into the in-flight passengers. Meanwhile, the Doctor gets busted for possession (no, really).

Firsts and Lasts Last story written by Bob Baker, and with him goes an entire style of space-based *Doctor Who*. Though spaceships will occasionally turn up over the next few years, there won't be another story of this type until "Terror of the Vervoids" (23.3), six years later. Various "ghosts" of the old Bob Baker / Dave Martin scripts make themselves felt here, including plenty of laser-gun fights in corridors and an annoying comedy scientist with an "amusing" European accent (14.2, "The Invisible Enemy"), while Major Stott's "gone native" role on Eden is remarkably similar to Sondergaard's in "The Mutants" (9.4).

First story to use Quantel, the miracle digital image-processing system beloved of daytime TV title-sequence designers.

Four Things to Notice About "Nightmare of Eden"...

1. It's a story about drug-trafficking. Which is to say: this being *Doctor Who*, it's a story about drug-trafficking where the drug is the powdered remains of a space-monster, which also features spaceships colliding in mid-dematerialisation and a machine that can store whole chunks of planets on microfiche. The drug in question is known as vraxoin, abbreviated to "vrax" even though heroin isn't abbreviated to "her", and the opening scene - in which a space-navigator sits in his control cabin, high on the stuff and grinning his face off - is one of the most peculiar-looking sights in all of televised SF.

2. It's often been said, quite wisely, that the problem with most shoddy *Doctor Who* monsters isn't so much the way the costumes look as the way the people inside them move around. The Mandrels, this story's way of keeping the children happy, are a case in point. See a photograph of one and it actually looks quite striking, with its strange-yet-feasible arrangement of exotic alien features. See one shambling along a corridor and it's altogether less impressive. (Although they *are* kept in shadows or hidden by distorted electron-

ic effects whenever possible... bizarrely, this was the story being broadcast while *Alien* was doing the rounds in cinemas.) This isn't helped by the rather unusual shape of their feet, which make them look as if this species comes with built-in flares. It's also got to be said that this monster confused the hell out of children of a certain age, who thereafter could never remember whether a "Mandrel" was a *Doctor Who* monster and a "mandrill" was a kind of monkey, or the other way around.

3. As with "The Creature from the Pit", your view of this story might depend on how you feel about out-of-control humour in *Doctor Who*. One of Tom Baker's most notoriously over-played attempts at comedy takes place in episode four, when the Doctor runs off behind some plants and is apparently attacked by the Mandrels off-screen. All we see is some foliage being thrown into shot, while the Doctor's voice can be heard shouting: 'Oh, my fingers! My arms! My legs! My everything! *Oooohh!*' (Compare this with the 'your arms, your legs, your heads, your everything' song from the Restaurant at the End of the Universe sequence in *The Hitch-Hiker's Guide to the Galaxy*, and wonder how much fiddling the script editor did here.)

4. A much more successful Douglas-Adams-like attempt at comedy comes when Captain Rigg, doped on drugs and laughing insanely, watches his passengers being torn apart by alien monsters: 'They're only economy class. What's all the fuss about?' The shot follows a pull-back from the (slightly rubbish) monsters attacking the passengers to Rigg watching it on a monitor screen, laughing the same way that uncharitable viewers might have been, and is therefore quite unsettling.

The Continuity

The Doctor While visiting the twenty-first century, the Doctor is asked for his date of birth and replies 'some time quite soon, I think'. [This is the only indication in the entire series that he was born in the future, whereas the more usual approach is to assume that Gallifreyan time is just "different" to everyone else's; see **Where (and When) is Gallifrey?** under 13.3, "Pyramids of Mars". The comment here is almost certainly a joke, or at least a way of distracting the nosy official who's asking.]

• *Ethics*. His stated philosophy by this stage: 'Of course we should interfere. Always do what you're best at, that's what I say.' He apparently has a problem with the idea of any animal life being kept in private zoos, not just the sentient kind [see 10.2, "Carnival of Monsters"].

• *Inventory.* He's got a toothpick, useful for tinkering with delicate pieces of technology.

• *Background.* The Doctor claims to have known Professor Stein, the mentor of the zoologist Tryst, and to have attended one of the Professor's seminars [though he could be bluffing to gain Tryst's confidence]. He also says that he's seen whole planets destroyed by the drug vraxoin, and poses as an agent for Galactic Salvage and Insurance, which existed between 2068 and 2096 [suggesting at least one prior visit to the late twenty-first century that we've never seen].

The Supporting Cast

• *Romana.* After her recent spurts of independence, here she goes back to squealing for help in a crisis, and she's even scared to touch a dead Mandrel. Yet she must be better than the Doctor in certain technical fields, as he asks her to rebuild the CET machine (see **History**) instead of doing it himself. Even Romana's heard of vraxoin, and at one point she claims - intriguingly - that the people who made Russian dolls were making 'a model of the universe' [we'll come back to this idea in Season Eighteen...].

• *K9.* Can track the Doctor over a considerable distance [by 'psychic spoor', as hinted in "The Pirate Planet" (16.2) and confirmed in the next story]. A 'matter interface', i.e. one of the anomalies caused by a dematerialisation collision, can jam his scanners. Though the Doctor readily admits that K9 has saved his life on occasion, he's only prepared to say that the dog beat him at chess 'once' [because all the other times, the Doctor found an excuse to end the game before checkmate]. K9 can cut through metal plate with his usual red energy-beam, or seal it up again with a blue one, which makes a different noise. Power from K9 can be transferred to other pieces of equipment by attaching jump-leads to his "ears".

K9 knows of vraxoin, but not Mandrels. Embarrassingly, when the Doctor describes Major Stott as a 'friend' K9 actually insists on going up to the man and making sniffing noises [the Doctor's deliberately programmed him with these quirks]. The Doctor describes K9 as 'electric' here.

The TARDIS From the Ship, the Doctor produces a shiny silver object that looks like a miniature missile-launcher and is fitted to its own foldable stand. This is a 'de-mat machine', and the beam it fires helps to separate the *Empress* and *Hecate* after the two ships lock together, though the details are as vague as all the other technobabble. The Doctor and Romana take all the CET crystals with them when they leave the *Empress* - see **History** - and plan to put Tryst's specimens back in their rightful places with the technology aboard the TARDIS.

Planet Notes

• *Eden.* Yet another jungle planet, a chunk of which is being stored inside Tryst's CET, the kind of place where giant flytraps snare people with their tendrils and alien birds / animals can be heard hooting in the distance. [The insect that causes Romana to collapse is termed a 'somnomoth', in the script though not on-screen.] Eden is home to the Mandrels, a species of upright-walking animal covered in both fur and scales, with faces that have luminous green eyes and big pads of segmented flesh instead of mouths [despite not looking exactly like the script's description, they fit the idea of swamp-based beings, resembling walking manatees as well as giant platypuses].

In life the Mandrels don't do anything more interesting than shamble after humans, but when one dies its body instantly disintegrates into a powder. This is vraxoin, an addictive substance which induces a narcotic high in humans when ingested, though strangely the drug is also referred to as a 'fungus'. The drug induces warm complacency and apathy, but soon proves lethal, and whole worlds have fallen to its influence. [The original source of vraxoin was destroyed, and had nothing to do with Eden. So it's possible that the Mandrels disintegrate into something which has exactly the same properties as vraxoin rather than the true vraxoin fungus, although it's a good enough match to fool K9's analysis.] The Doctor can easily lure a whole crowd of Mandrels with K9's "silent" dog whistle. They kill with their claws, and are surprisingly resilient to blaster fire, being stung rather than stunned and stunned rather than killed.

How Do You Transmit Matter?

Three procedures for this nifty plot-device have been suggested.

The most basic is that it's like television; you break down the object, whip it along a radio-beam and reassemble it at the destination. This was the method proposed in "The Dalek Masterplan" (3.4), and later in *Star Trek* and *Charlie and the Chocolate Factory*. But there's a basic problem here, namely what happens when you convert mass into energy. To put it bluntly, Bang = MC2. All that mass / energy has to be confined and made to behave itself as you do a subatomic jig-saw-puzzle.

One solution is a system in which you don't actually transmit matter, but instead break the traveller down into pieces, send the *information* about those pieces along the beam and use another machine at the other end to recreate the traveller out of raw matter that's already there. However, this raises all sorts of nasty ethical questions, since you're basically killing the person who uses the device and making an exact copy somewhere else. The replicators in modern-day *Star Trek* seem to work on this principle, yet the programme likes to gloss over the question of why the transporters on the *Enterprise* can't make endless copies of people by using the same techniques but not destroying the originals. Nonetheless, this is apparently what's happening in "The Mutants" (9.4) and "Revenge of the Cybermen" (12.5), which makes you wonder just how many times the Doctor, Jo Grant, Sarah Jane Smith and Harry Sullivan have "died" on-screen. This system is known as "transmat", though after 1978 this term is used to mean any kind of apparent teleportation, and turns into a verb.

But whether you're using transmat or the later (mortality-free) version that's being tested in 4000 AD, there's a scientific hitch here. This technique requires you to know everything about every single particle before you transmit it, and… you can't. As it turns out, if you try to find out *one* thing about a particle then it changes the nature of that particle, so you can't find out anything else. You can know its momentum or its position, but not both. (This is called Heisenberg's Uncertainty Principle, and yes, of course it sounds mad. As we'll see in other entries, the physics of the last century is full of counter-intuitive fun and games like this.)

Then there's the difficulty of getting a clear, uninterrupted transmission. Well, think of the transmitter device as a fax machine. You could send the data down the wires, but in the case of a human traveller you'd need a stack of high-density CD ROMs about three miles high in order to get every subatomic particle "right". It's worth noting that in *Doctor Who* this process usually involves a bracelet of an odd material, or - if Terry Nation's not involved - some other object for the passenger to hold.

The third and final technique seems more exotic, but involves fewer glitches. Instead of disintegrating and reintegrating the subject, you "simply" move the passenger from A to B by eliminating all the points in-between. The most likely means of doing this is a localised wormhole or Einstein-Rosen tunnel. The three "orthodox" spatial dimensions, plus time, are perceptible. If some fifth dimension were to be discovered, then to our senses anyone travelling through it would disappear and reappear elsewhere. An ant crawling on a sheet of paper might not realise that you've picked up the sheet and curled the corners together (making the bottom-left and top-right corners overlap), but if you gently uncurl the paper then it could be a foot away from where it was two seconds ago, even though it's only crawled an inch. This is straightforward travel, in an odd sort of way.

Despite the terminology, this appears to be how Zanak moves (16.2, "The Pirate Planet"), with the Doctor wistfully observing that there's no sensation. And though it's hard to explain how humans might have cracked it as early as the mid-to-late twenty-first century - and why they're not doing more with their localised wormholes - this could be how the Travel-Mat system works in "The Seeds of Death" (6.5). Travel-Mat is accepted everywhere on Earth, and nobody's worried about being disintegrated, suggesting that it doesn't break people down into bits like transmat does. Certainly, there's a clear implication that this is how the *Empress* and the *Hecate* travel in "Nightmare of Eden", and "Eden" takes place only decades after "The Seeds of Death". Why does everyone stop using this technique, though, and turn to the more morally dubious transmat system? Well, maybe there are unforeseen side-effects to messing around with other dimensions (q.v. the New Adventure *Transit*, which also happens to be set in the post-Travel-Mat era).

We've already mentioned the ethical problems, especially with regard to transmat. If the atoms of a person are zipped along as data, then is the per-

continued on page 303…

History

• *Dating.* 2096 is loosely said to be 'twenty years' ago, so it's sometime around 2116. [Captain Rigg isn't necessarily being exact, so it could be as late as the 2120s.]

Interplanetary travel, outside Earth's solar system, seems quite common in this period. The interstellar cruise liner *Empress* is a ship with nine-hundred passengers which flies the 'milk-run' between Station Nine and the planet Azure in West Galaxy. ["West Galaxy" may be a designated space-travel zone. Parkin's *A History of the Universe* claims that it's just the result of a fluffed line by David Daker, but that's not how it sounds. Was the original scripted line 'you'll never work in this galaxy again', but changed to 'you'll never work in West Galaxy again' when someone decided that a whole galaxy was much too big a place?] Its passengers sit in airline-like compartments, and wear shiny silver coveralls and dark glasses in flight.

A much smaller ship is the one-man *Hecate*, apparently on a survey mission but actually piloted by the drug-runner Dymond. The *Empress* materialises in orbit of Azure, and due to bad navigation arrives in the same area as the *Hecate*, so the two ships become locked together. [Though the word "hyperspace" is never used, we hear 'warp' and 'dematerialisation', as though this were a glorified T-Mat; see **How Do You Transmit Matter?**.] This 'dematerialisation collision' means that there are unstable areas of space-time where the two vessels touch, which look like walls of fizzing "interference".

It's possible to replicate the conditions of the accident and unlock the ships - Romana states that it's just a question of 'exciting the molecules' - but the crew are cynical about this and it can only be done with help from the Doctor's de-mat machine. After a while the locked ships start rejecting each other on a molecular level, 'like a tissue transplant' [one from the *Star Trek* school of half-baked scientific analogies]. The Empress has a shuttle bay, and the crew can send for cutting-lasers from Azure. Gravity is said to be seven-tenths normal in Azure orbit, though there's no visible sign of this.

The Azurian Excise sends a Waterguard and a Landing Officer to investigate events on the *Empress*, and they're identically-uniformed officials with caps that make them look like park-keepers. They expect the Doctor to carry an ident-plaque for identification, and the fact that he doesn't have one seems to be an offence in itself. They carry a wand-like scanning device which lights up in the presence of vraxoin, use stun-or-kill energy weapons and have no qualms about firing on suspects.

Major Stott, from the intelligence section of the Space Corps, was a plant on Tryst's expedition to Eden [almost certainly the same Space Corps mentioned in 6.6, "The Space Pirates", set in roughly the same era]. Trafficking in drugs is punishable by death, and Captain Rigg also mentions the possibility of execution for dereliction of duty, though he could be joking as he's high on vraxoin at the time. Despite the fact that humanity's obviously in an expansionist period, Tryst claims that government funding for his last expedition was cut because of a 'galactic recession', so now he's just assigned travel facilities on government-subsidised space-lines like that of the *Empress*. Tryst believes that with one more trip he stands a chance of quantifying 'every species in the galaxy'. [This is quite ludicrous, since the galaxy contains hundreds of billions of stars and most of them seem to have at least one life-bearing planet in the *Doctor Who* universe, so we have to assume that he just means those parts of the galaxy already reached by Earth.]

The Continuous Event Transmuter [*not* "Transmitter", as has been written elsewhere] is a desktop-sized piece of technology which can convert matter into electromagnetic impulses and store it on event laser-crystals inside the machine. It's currently being used to house specimens collected by Tryst's expedition, which doesn't just mean animals but huge swathes of their natural environments. When the machine is activated, and the dial is turned to the name of one of the planets "recorded" by the machine, it projects what seems to be an image of that planet as if it were an ordinary slide projector. However, the projection can be entered and objects / animals / people can be removed from it. Major Stott claims to have been trapped in the Eden environment for 183 days, as specimens go on living and evolving even while they're inside the crystals.

In fact the theory of the CET is just supposed to keep the specimens on crystal and allow them to be seen in the projection, but the machine has no 'dimensional osmosis damper', so the dimensions all get mixed up and it's this which allows things to move in and out of the projection. The unstable matter interfaces caused by the space-collision

How Do You Transmit Matter?

...continued from page 301

son on the other end the same individual? Does the soul - should he or she have one - travel as fast? This problem is amplified by the most likely transmat scenario, one involving quantum entanglement.

The simplest analogy would be hooking a rubber band around your left thumb; then your right thumb; then pulling it apart as far as it will go; then removing the left thumb. But without the "ow". At a subatomic level, particles come in matched pairs (electron and positron, neutrino and anti-neutrino), then disappear into a general flux of probability. The particles are often very far apart, but to affect one is to simultaneously affect the other.

Yes, that's right, simultaneously; a subatomic particle in London "knows" what's happening to a particle in New York, the information not "travelling" anywhere and so not impeded by the need to stay within the speed of light. So the research shows that if the particle and its other half are somehow mathematically "stirred in" to an object, then the one that's "transmitted" will be connected to the one that's "receiving". If you combine a particle of what you're sending with a particle whose twin is at the receiving end, then that twin will acquire a particle exactly like the one you've "stirred in" at the source. You don't really *send* anything, except some sort of influence over subatomic particles (even if they're a very long way away) which then combine to make an exact match for your original subject.

If you've done it right, then all the particles should spontaneously decide to be at the other end of the process rather than at the start, making it look as if you've moved the subject from one side of the universe to the other. Actually science says that all your particles might spontaneously decide to be at the other side of the universe anyway, but the odds of it happening are usually quite absurd.

can affect the 'dimensional matrix' of the machine, allowing Mandrels from Eden to appear all over the *Empress*. [On the surface the CET would seem to be similar to the Miniscope from "Carnival of Monsters" (10.2), but the two don't have a great deal in common. The CET breaks its subjects down into pure data, whereas the 'Scope lets them physically run around inside the circuits. The Time Lords would have no reason to object to the CET, in the way that they might have objected to the Miniscope, as time-technology isn't involved.]

Tryst worked on the CET with his mentor, the late Professor Stein, whom the Doctor claims to have known. Tryst seems to have "perfected" the device, although it's still an unstable piece of hardware.

Judging by the names on the dial, the CET contains specimens from Eden; Zil; Vij; Darp; Lvan; Brus; Ranx, a pleasant-looking world with a purple sky and plenty of vegetation; and Gidi, a world which has trees and shrubs but seems wracked by terrible storms. There's not much space on the dial, though, so some of these names may be abbreviations. Tryst's expedition on the *Volante* went through the Cygnus Gap, and did a slingshot over to a small system of three planets called M37, where the second world supports life at an early stage of evolution; molluscs, algae and primitive insects, now stored on the CET. [The *real* M37 is a cluster of stars, not a system, so it's almost certainly not the same thing.]

But it's Eden which provided Tryst with a source of vraxoin, and transporting it with the CET means that it doesn't show up on any molecular scan. [Major Stott was evidently planted on the expedition before it left Earth, so Tryst must have known about the Mandrels beforehand and someone must have tipped off the authorities.] Tryst boarded the *Empress* at Station Nine.

Everybody's heard of vraxoin in this period, and most people are so familiar with it that they've abbreviated it to "vrax". According to K9 it's technically known as XYP, and it's a banned substance, the expected profits from the Eden Project being z9,100,000 gal[actic] credits. The only prior known source of vraxoin was destroyed, and the Doctor states that 'they' incinerated an entire planet in order to get rid of it. Romana believes this was 'long ago'. [From the context, the Doctor seems to mean humans when he says 'they'. As vraxoin is known in this era, the suggestion is that all this happened before the twenty-second century, but it couldn't have been *that* long ago as humanity has only been outside the solar system for a few decades. So Romana's 'long ago' statement is probably a result of her not knowing exactly what time she's in.]

There's a great love for sparkly uniforms in this era, as well as petty bureaucracy. Captains of ships like the *Hecate* can be fined for being in prohibited areas. Caffedine capsules are mentioned, as if they were the space-age equivalent of coffee. Members of ships' crews wear radiation bands on their wrists, and there are visual records of some sort called vis-prints. On the *Hecate* there's an Entucha laser, a device used for transmitting telecom messages, which can be hooked up to a CET projection machine to send or receive data from the event crystals.

Galactic Salvage and Insurance was formed in London in 2068, but liquidated in 2096. [This one line in the script caused Lance Parkin to shuffle around all the dates of the twenty-first century in his *A History of the Universe*, but see the timeline under "The Enemy of the World" (5.4) to find out why this may not be necessary.]

Most people in the future apparently don't know how to pronounce "Hecate" properly [see also 18.7-X, "K9 and Company"].

The Analysis

Where Does This Come From? From the mid-'60s onwards, the idea of a "Jet Set" of up-market international travellers was replaced by the idea of "Economy Class" proletarian holidaymakers, herded like sheep around European resorts which were as unlike the rest of the target nation as possible.

It was a boom time for petty crooks, terrorists and anal-retentive bureaucrats. Airport customs officers, believing themselves to be in the frontline against the Baader Meinhof Gang, the International Red Brigade, Black September or anyone else who wanted to hijack a plane, became power-mad (see also 4.8, "The Faceless Ones" and 19.7, "Time-Flight"). And if your luggage went astray then it was your fault. In an airport you were no longer in any one country, so localised laws applied; even today, the police at Heathrow act as if they're governing a banana republic. Bob Baker's response to this kind of thing was Waterguard Fisk.

As we've already seen (16.2, "The Pirate Planet"), Douglas Adams was interested in the moral aspects of drug-use as a story hook, although Graham Williams was less sure. We have to remember that the large-scale heroin production and cocaine harvesting of the 1980s were still in the future. Here we're in the era of small-scale deals by independent traffickers and growers, not industrial-scale efforts to sabotage whole nations

and finance coups, as would happen with the Mujahaddin or Contras. Talk of 'whole planets being set alight' is largely space-opera exaggeration, not an upscale version of current news reports. Bob Baker, back when he was still working with Dave Martin, had already written an episode of *Target* about drug carriers (it's the one everyone remembers, directed by Douglas Camfield and with Katy Manning as a junkie).

As ever, the Doctor saves the day by playing around with technology, first using generic technical cleverness to separate the two spaceships and then re-wiring the CET to increase the range and snare Tryst and his criminal associate, Dymond. The '70s was a boom time for commercial electronics, the age of the stereo, the affordable colour TV and the domestic video recorder, so it's hardly surprising that in this period the technology of the TARDIS turns out to be compatible with the technology of every other civilisation. This was a decade in which the general public learned all about the joys of plugging pieces of electronic equipment into other pieces of electronic equipment, and so the *Doctor Who* universe becomes a place where altering the purpose of a matter transmutation machine is as easy as attaching new speakers to your record player, or where a couple of wires can turn K9 into an all-purpose battery for any piece of kit the Doctor might come across. This is, in short, the Bang and Olufsen continuum.

One other idea that's often ignored, as part of what viewers made of this at the time; on days with high-pressure areas, TV reception in Britain often suffered from "cross-channel interference". If the viewer was in Southern England then "cross-channel" might be literally true, as French TV signals sometimes interfered with the usual ones. The "meld" effect of the interlocked spaceships looks very much like this.

And the Doctor proves himself to be keen on either Steinbeck or James Dean, with his comment on finding himself in Eden: 'Let's go east!'

Things That Don't Make Sense Captain Rigg carries on trusting the Doctor even *after* discovering that the Doctor's cover-story about Galactic Salvage and Insurance is a blatant lie. Nobody's supposed to realise that objects can be removed from the CET, yet Major Stott knows someone's using it to carry drugs, and somehow neither he nor the Doctor figure out that logically the most likely suspect is the man who built the machine. It's never explained why Secker, the *Empress* navigator, is off his face on vraxoin at the start of the story. [The answer in the script is that Tryst arranged this in order to engineer the "accident", but it's never explained on-screen. Similarly, we need back-up sources to tell us that it's Stott who revives Romana after the "somno-moth" bites her, and indeed that the glowing thing which hurtles out of the projection is an insect and not a power-surge.]

As is so often the way, the writers forget that *Doctor Who* is a programme about time-travellers as soon as they've got the Doctor in the right era (another thing this story shares with 10.2, "Carnival of Monsters"), with Romana claiming that vraxoin was stamped out 'long ago' and acting as if there's no way the TARDIS could possibly have brought her to a time in which it exists. Unless she's very good at dating spaceships from their lounge design. And it's hard not to smirk during a misjudged special-effects moment, when a laser bolt hits Della in the neck but she clutches her *stomach* as if she's suffering from cramps before she falls.

One of the series' best-known fluffs comes in the last episode, when Geoffrey Hinsliff (playing Fisk) addresses Tryst as Fisk. Unless Fisk just has a habit of saying his own name out loud when he's frustrated.

Critique (Prosecution) Yet another story which sums up the way the general public would remember *Doctor Who* in years to come, full of bad spaceship effects, terrible performances, drab corridor-chases and droopy monsters, though this time - and you couldn't say this about "The Invisible Enemy" - underneath it all there's a half-decent story writhing to get out.

As with "The Creature from the Pit", on paper it looks quite nifty. If you can ignore the crass pulp-SF touches (nobody would call an exciting new drug "vraxoin", even if they were on the stuff at the time) then the ideas on offer here (a) work and (b) all fit together. The post-hyperspace crash which sees the Empress and the Hecate lock together like two rutting animals is just the kind of thing space-opera should do more often, while the CET fits snugly into this environment as both a plot device and a striking piece of SF-ness in itself.

But it takes a hell of a lot of care and attention to make "space" a believable proposition.

"Nightmare of Eden" doesn't even try, and the result is something that's shoddy on virtually every level, even if you can ignore the appalling sense of design. Yet again, it's full of gags that don't work and excruciating comedy characters that aren't funny. Yet again, the story doesn't bother turning any of its Big Concepts into anything dynamic, and instead wastes time with the usual tedious run-around of monsters and laser-guns. (It's possible that the Doctor's whimsical nature in this era was intended as a counter-weight to these "traditional" action-TV elements, but the increasing amounts of Tom-foolery just allow the writers to get sloppier and sloppier, so by this point the programme's in a constant downward spiral.)

Yet again, the script has intellectual depth - of a sort - but no *guts*. For those who remember the high mythicism of "Genesis of the Daleks", the squirming child-terror of "Pyramids of Mars" or the gothic gravity of "The Talons of Weng-Chiang", this just looks like a stroll in the park, without the substance to be a great epic or the claustrophobia to be a functional "little" story. You can tell how badly it's struggling to keep up the dramatic tension when Jennifer Lonsdale (as Della) spends most of her scenes trying to perfect the art of staring wistfully into the distance.

What's most striking, though, is how much better it all seems if you ignore the pictures. Not just because you don't have to focus on the terrible visuals or the "troubled" direction, either. Take away the sight of a dozen character actors trying to make every movement look like a pantomime-piece, and you could almost believe that this was a proper slab of drama instead of a rag-bag of off-cuts in search of a context. If we could erase every single copy on videotape, and just leave the audio track behind, then we could at least go *some* way towards imagining what it was supposed to be.

Critique (Defence) Yes, all right, everyone knows the 'oh, my everything!' line. But who remembers, a minute or so later, the last thing the Doctor says to Tryst? Exactly; all the effort has gone into slagging off this story and yet Tom Baker's performance, as good as any from any period, is relegated to one throwaway line.

For your information, the set-up is that the police are leading Tryst away and he makes the usual 'it was all in a good cause' excuse. The Doctor, not even looking up, stage-whispers 'go away'. This is how it should be. The oddness, the digs at package holidays and careerist police, are

ABOUT TIME 1975-1979

all surface details in a story which - as with the last two - deals with people exploiting something they don't fully understand or appreciate. The Mandrels are living beings turned into profit; so are the addicts. The CET machine is almost miraculous, and it's being used for a sordid purpose. In having something so near the knuckle at the core of the story, they took an enormous risk. It certainly made a big impression on the regulars (Lalla Ward insisted that the name of the drug be made less "appealing" to children… see **The Lore**).

Of course, it has its longeurs. Director Alan Bromly was notorious in the BBC as a hack who ruined everything he touched, and had to be replaced in mid-shoot. Yet ponder how similar this is to the much-praised and supposedly "intellectual" story "Warriors' Gate" (18.5), and how the video effects are being pushed and exploited for purely narrative ends. This is brave stuff for "family" drama. In certain shots the Mandrels are intensely effective, but a BBC directive states that the lighting has to be of a certain intensity, so that's that. We'll see this problem a lot more from now on (e.g. 18.1, "The Leisure Hive"; 18.3, "Full Circle"; 19.3, "Kinda"; all of Season Twenty-One…).

As has been noted, the scene where Rigg laughs at the Mandrels is a snapshot of how Williams-era Doctor Who plays it both ways. The storyline involving Della and Stott is surprisingly adult - not in a violent or sexy way, just in the way that Romana doesn't need to ask what their relationship was - and her numbed responses to everything are entirely in keeping. But, this being Doctor Who, everyone's supposed to be acting "big" like Lewis Fiander (Tryst). Ponder also that David Daker, playing Rigg, was Irongron in "The Time Warior" (11.1).

Fundamentally, though, this is a story about crossing the boundaries; between being "fiction" and being "real", between "authority" and "criminal", between "drama" and "for kids". And it has, after all, a concept too daring for Star Trek but simple enough for seven-year-olds to follow.

The Facts

Written by Bob Baker. Directed by Alan Bromly and Graham Williams (uncredited, and **The Lore** will provide answers). Viewing figures: 8.7 million, 9.6 million, 9.6 million, 9.4 million.

Supporting Cast: Lewis Fiander (Tryst), Geoffrey Bateman (Dymond), David Daker (Rigg), Jennifer Lonsdale (Della), Barry Andrews (Stott), Geoffrey Hinsliff (Fisk), Peter Craze (Costa).

Working Titles "Nightmare of Evil" (can you see the problem here, Bob?).

Cliffhangers The Doctor and Captain Rigg remove a section of metal plate from the interior wall of the spacecraft, only for a bellowing Mandrel to stick its head through the hole; the Doctor and Romana leap into the projection of Eden; as the two ships separate from each other, the Doctor vanishes in a blur of space-time.

The Lore

• The original name for the drug was "zip", from "XYP", short for "xyophyllin". As noted earlier, it was changed at the last minute as Lalla Ward and Graham Williams were both concerned about children thinking of drugs as appealing.
• Director Alan Bromly (see 11.1, "The Time Warrior") was a BBC "odd-job man" who whiled away the few years before retirement with odd jobs given to him by friends. He'd been marking time on Coronation Street before an acquaintance asked him if he'd consider returning to Doctor Who, where he'd previously directed "The Time Warrior". Convinced that the BBC must have improved conditions since 1973, when that story was filmed, he grimly conceded. When Bromly found that conditions had worsened and that everyone understood the story but him, an exasperated Graham Williams pulled him out during a lunch-break and took over the director's duties himself.
• One of many cuts made before Bromly quit… Romana gnaws on an apple as she looks out at the Eden landscape, and the Doctor tells her: 'Best not to; look what happened last time!'
• Lewis Fiander's decision to play Tryst with a German accent appears to have been a gag, improvised to lighten up the increasingly tense rehearsals.
• A new BBC policy directive meant that the budgets for this story had to be reduced by a further 10%, and the allocation was made per calendar year, not per screen-time year. It was at this point, after eighteen months of non-stop crisis management, that Williams appointed John

Nathan-Turner as deputy producer (George Gallaccio, the previous second-in-command, had gone on to produce *The Omega Factor*).

• Jennifer Lonsdale (Della) was quoted in *The Sun* as saying that she'd been scared by the Mandrels. Barry Andrews (Stott), in the same piece, noted that his six-year-old daughter had been terrified of them too. It was good copy, though a BBC source claimed that photos of the Mandrels weren't available due to a lack of photographers that day, and that it had nothing to do with "forbidding" the public to see the creatures as the paper claimed.

• The effects shot in episode three, when one of the Mandrels disintegrates into a heap of vraxoin, was originally meant to be much longer and much more elaborate. The lack of studio-time resulted in a less impressive version being filmed.

• Apart from Eden itself, all the planets seen "inside" the CET are represented by footage from *Space:1999*.

• A glimpse of the future: the studio was shut during filming due to fears about asbestos dust (see 25.4, "The Greatest Show in the Galaxy", amongst others). And this was *after* all the delays caused by Bromly's dismissal.

• It was on the set of this story that the trailer for the season was shot, with Geoffrey Hinsliffe (Costa, and earlier Jack Tyler in 15.3, "Image of the Fendahl") as a disembodied Time-Lord-ish voice warning the Doctor of the new perils he had to face, then curiously making him forget the warning. The scene ends with a sign on the TARDIS door: "Do Not Disturb Until 1st September."

17.5: "The Horns of Nimon"

(Serial 5G, Four Episodes, 22nd December 1979 - 12th January 1980.)

Which One is This? At last: the story where the sets are *supposed* to move, the bad guys are intentionally getting the names wrong and the male supporting lead is *deliberately* useless. *Theseus and the Minotaur* in space, with special guest Tom Baker.

Firsts and Lasts It's the end of another era, the last story produced by Graham Williams and script-edited by Douglas Adams (or at least, the last one to be *finished*; see 17.6, "Shada"). Which means that this is also the last story in the original

Doctor Who run which isn't produced by John Nathan-Turner, so as a result those who don't care for Nathan-Turner's style tend to see "The Horns of Nimon" as the last "proper" *Doctor Who* story... and as if to push the point home, it's also the very last story of the 1970s.

It's certainly the end of overt comedy in the series - at least for the next five years - which means that it's the last time the TARDIS console makes cartoon boinging noises when the Doctor operates it. We also wave goodbye to the "time tunnel" opening sequence, which has served the programme faithfully since 1974; the diamond-shaped *Doctor Who* logo, which was already looking a bit showbiz by this stage; and the "classic" theme tune arrangement, which had been running almost unaltered since 1963.

Other things that exit the series here: the Doctor's old coat (technically seen on hat-stands after this, but never worn again); the old TARDIS prop (replaced for Season Eighteen); David Brierley as K9's voice (before John Leeson makes his comeback); and the '70s style of background music that insists on going "dann-dann-dann-*doo*" whenever anything semi-dramatic happens (compare this story with something like 18.7, "Logopolis", and the difference is... palpable).

Four Things to Notice About "The Horns of Nimon"...

1. For the third time (see 9.5, "The Time Monster" and 17.3, "The Creature from the Pit"), the Doctor is called on to enter the labyrinth and face the Minotaur, although on this occasion the labyrinth is a printed-circuit-like space-maze and the Minotaur is an alien parasite who just happens to have bovine features and horns. As in "Underworld" (15.5), the names are supposed to echo Greek mythology: Aneth / Athens, Skonnos / Knossos, Crinoth / Corinth, Nimon / Minotaur, Seth / Theseus and Soldeed / Daedalus. (Although as in "Underworld", you have to wonder why... Daedalus is the great magician-architect of Greek legend, and a great archetypal figure, whereas Soldeed is a straight-out bad guy who doesn't know how anything works and goes 'nyah-hah-hah' as he makes his escape in episode four.)

2. A good two years before the "official" Fifth Doctor, the role of the heroic Time Lord is played here by Lalla Ward. Tom Baker, as part of the plan to get everything out of the way in this story before starting afresh with "Shada" (17.6), is allowed to be the comic relief in his own series

while Ward - in a performance very like that of Peter Davison - does much of the planet-saving. She even gets two young companions asking stupid questions. The last shot of the story, usually of the Doctor grinning, is of her pulling a face behind his back and then giggling. Best line comes when Romana, having psycho-analysed the Nimon and established that he's probably an insecure personality, is told that he lives in the Power Complex: 'That fits.'

3. If some of the other stories from this period give you the sense that Tom Baker's trying to make sure everybody else gets acted off the screen, then "The Horns of Nimon" gives you the sense that he's getting some resistance. Graham Crowden, playing Soldeed, puts in one of the most thoroughly over-the-top performances in the series' history (not necessarily a criticism... that's the way the part's written). Which is saying something. But of course, if it's Baker vs. Crowden then the leading man is bound to have the advantage; the Doctor's guaranteed to live, while Soldeed's destined to die. As if realising this, Crowden refuses to go down without a fight, and his death scene in episode four seems to demand a round of applause once he stops twitching (see **The Lore** for the reason).

4. Throughout this volume, the monsters encountered by the Fourth Doctor have always seemed to demand attention, sometimes because they're particularly good (Zygons) but more often not (Mandrels). The Nimon, however, is a rarity; a monster which deserves special mention because of its fashion sense. Whereas the majority of monster species either go naked or wear elaborate armour, the Nimon creatures have a sartorial style not seen since the string vests of the Sea Devils in 1972, going bare-chested but wearing gold skirts and platform shoes. It's hard to see one now without expecting it to say 'does my bum look big in this?'. (Also: what's notable here is that while most *Doctor Who* monsters either (a) turn up in groups of four or five or (b) are unique a la Scaroth, this story fools the audience by making us believe there's only *one* Nimon around... then having a whole bunch of his friends suddenly turn up in episode three.)

The Continuity

The Doctor

• *Ethics.* Again, the Doctor sees 'saving planets' as part of his job description.

• *Inventory.* He's got little sticky-paper star-shapes in his pockets, some of which he uses to mark his passage through the Nimon's maze, and produces a "First Prize" rosette for K9. He holds a red rag to the bull-headed monster.

• *Background.* He states that he's been to the planet Aneth, but 'not yet', describing it as 'charming'. He once again claims to have been involved in the original Minotaur story [see 17.3, "The Creature from the Pit"], but forgot to remind Theseus to return home in a ship marked with white. [A chronic error. Legend claims that Theseus had arranged a special code with his father, that if he slew the Minotaur then he'd return home in a ship with a white sail, but if he died then his associates would return in a ship with a black sail. Theseus slew the Minoatur, then forgot about the code. His father saw the black sail approaching on the horizon, and threw himself into the sea out of grief, dashing himself to death on the rocks. Nice work, Doctor.]

The Supporting Cast

• *Romana.* Romana made her own sonic screwdriver [seen in 17.2, "City of Death"], and the Doctor finds out about this for the first time. He's obviously impressed, despite calling the device 'a bit primitive', as he tries to swap it for his own. [Note that it's never overtly called a sonic screwdriver on-screen, but what else *could* it be?] It can open the doors of spaceships just like the Doctor's can. Romana is as handy with a gun as her first incarnation was.

• *K9.* Can track both the Doctor and Romana by their 'psycho-spoors' [in "The Pirate Planet" (16.2) it's called 'psychic spoor', but it's the same principle]. He's said to be 'armoured', and the Doctor clamps a hand over K9's snout to keep him quiet, as if the speaker's located there.

When making a damage report on the TARDIS, K9 spews out so much ticker-tape that he becomes entirely buried in it, and it's in shades of white, blue and pink. He gargles and coughs as if he's gagging on it [another "quirk" programmed in by the Doctor?]. Faced with the illusory wall at the Power Complex's entrance, K9 sees right through it and isn't aware there's anything there at all.

The TARDIS Once again it's shown to have a manual, though this one is smaller and less ancient-looking than the last ["The Pirate Planet", again]. The Doctor uses it after having an idea about making a modification to the conceptual geometer, and immobilises the Ship in space before trying it. While he's doing the work there's a large piece of TARDIS technology sitting on the console which could well be taken from the machine's guts; he states that he's dismantled the geometer and the dematerialisation circuit. [Stories like 10.1, "The Three Doctors", show us that the dematerialisation circuit is a small plug-in piece of technology. Possibly the Doctor's dismantled the entire system into which the circuit fits.]

When K9 tries to interface with the console at this point, there's a big bang and the dog's head spins round the wrong way, and the defence shield [the force-field, also mentioned in "The Pirate Planet"] is blown out. With the shield down, the console suffers more damage when it collides with the Skonnon spaceship. [See also **How Indestructible is the TARDIS?** under 21.3, "Frontios".] The dimensional stabiliser is fused, though at least the gravitic anomaliser still works. If the anomaliser is removed, the Doctor can still attempt to lash up the console so that the Ship can dematerialise, but the first time he tries it there's another explosion and the console makes a variety of comedy sound effects.

The defence shield on the door is on a different circuit, though [see 1.6, "The Sensorites"], and from the console can be extended so that it forms a tunnel between the hovering Ship and the Skonnon vessel. This tunnel has a "floor" solid enough to walk on, and obviously contains a breathable atmosphere. When a massive asteroid threatens to hit the TARDIS, the Doctor causes the Ship to spin rapidly in space, so that it survives the impact and safely gets thrown clear. The Ship can't materialise inside the Nimon's Power Complex, thanks to the Nimon's own defensive shield. [Strange that TARDISes can land inside each other, but not penetrate a barrier set up by what's presumably an inferior technology.]

The gravitic anomaliser, one of the many elements removed by the Doctor during the work, is a silver spheroid about the size of a cricket ball which can be hooked into the Skonnon ship to save it from a nearby black hole. It's also surprisingly good at deflecting energy-bolts. Near a black hole, gravity increases inside the TARDIS.

The Non-Humans

• *The Nimons.* Black-skinned, red-eyed horrors with evil-looking yellow horns and faces *not unlike* those of bulls, the Nimons are interplanetary parasites, moving from world to world and sucking each one dry. They call this the Great Journey of Life, and see it as their birthright. One of the Nimons arrived on Skonnos after its civil war, making a home for itself in its Power Complex, and now plans on bringing its comrades to this world in order to continue the journey.

The creatures move from world to world in spherical capsules big enough to seat three, which are transported by some impressively complex technology that creates black holes and links them with a hyperspatial space-time tunnel. Halfway between Aneth and Skonnos, a black hole is currently being formed with a fixed gravity beam controlled from the Power Complex: see **Planet Notes**. The pods somehow materialise on the host-planet, not in space, and apparently only one can come through at a time.

Whenever the Nimons swarm from one world to another, all the power comes from the next victim-world, as it's implied that the Nimons will have used up all the energy on the last planet by that point. Their emergency plan, when the power fails, is to convert their old victim-world into energy with an unstoppable chain reaction that ultimately makes the planet explode. The Doctor and Romana speculate that there might be 'thousands' of Nimons, but the creatures are ready to risk starting a chain reaction on Crinoth when only a handful have left for Skonnos [so there may in fact be very, very few]. It's never explained how the first "scout" Nimon gets from Crinoth to Skonnos to set up the Power Complex there, as it's certainly not through the black hole.

As has already been mentioned, the Nimons wear skirts and platform shoes, though that's all. With crushing predictability, they can kill human victims with energy-rays fired from their horns, although they can apparently also make blasters explode several yards away without any apparent beam [unless the blaster which goes "pop" is just old and faulty... this is unclear]. But ideally the Nimons "consume" victims by draining the life-force out of them, removing the binding forces of the flesh [c.f. 15.3, "Image of the Fendahl", and 14.6, "The Talons of Weng-Chiang"] and leaving behind the usual powdery husks. The Nimons are very, very tough, and can't even be killed with the power-staves they give to their followers. Like

ABOUT TIME 1975-1979

everything else in the universe, though, they can be knocked out by K9.

Planet Notes

• *Skonnos.* The Skonnon Empire once had a military dictatorship which extended over a hundred star systems, but Skonnos itself then fell into a civil war. Now a declining power, its more aggressive inhabitants want the glory days back. There's a sense of a world that's got all the technology you'd expect from a space-faring culture, but which is now entering a dark age, with a brutal and nigh-classical society. The Nimon finds it easy to manipulate these people by promising them power, though the only one who actually has contact with the Nimon is Soldeed, who apparently lays down the law for the whole of Skonnos.

Soldeed is ostensibly the only scientist left on the planet, as only the army survived the civil war, but he barely understands the technology supplied by the Nimon. Under Soldeed is what looks like a council of about a dozen Skonnons in black robes and shiny black helmets. From the air, the [only?] city on Skonnos appears to be a series of connected grey domes in the middle of a lifeless wasteland. Soldeed carries a staff which fires death-rays, apparently a product of the Nimon's technology, while the other Skonnons just tend to use stun-or-kill energy weapons.

The Nimon on Skonnos now lives in a Power Complex of its own construction, a labyrinth of corridors where the walls shift around while nobody's looking. It's surmounted by an enormous pair of horns, transmitting energy from a hymetusite-powered nuclear furnace that creates the black hole between Skonnos and Aneth. The Complex is protected a hemispherical defence shield, with a power of 7,300 megazones, and can only be entered by walking through one particular spot in its outer wall.

In fact, the entire complex operates like an enormous positronic circuit, so the switching of the walls has a technical function. The Nimon's "contract" with Skonnos states that in return for sacrifices from Aneth, the Skonnons will have enough ships to begin the Second Skonnon Empire, and the last shipment of seven tributes arrives on Skonnos here. These sacrifices take the form of seven young people dressed in horrible yellow pyjamas, each of whom brings a crystal of hymetusite from Aneth. These sacrifices are thrown into the maze of the Power Complex, where the Nimon stores the people in suspended animation cabinets as future food and uses the hymetusite to fuel the 'Great Journey of Life'.

Typical of a waning military power, the people of Skonnos dress to intimidate, with lots of black capes and ceremonial headpieces on show. Two-man Skonnon battleships are long, silver, rather functional and - having been built in the great days of empire, but patched up by fragments of the Nimon's technology - not all that reliable, with the computers blowing up if they're overloaded. It takes about twenty-four hours to get from Aneth to Skonnos by the usual route. The ship is carrying the goldfish-bowl containers which hold the all-important crystals of hymetusite, a substance that's highly radioactive, and K9 detects 'ultra-radiation level Q-7.235' when the containers are opened. Romana has no problem converting the ship's engines to run on the stuff. With Soldeed dead, the rather military Sorak takes over the running of Skonnos, so the Doctor doesn't expect things to get much better.

• *Aneth.* Apart from the Doctor's 'charming' description, little is known about Aneth, except that its people are easily cowed by the demands of Skonnos. The grandparents of the current generation describe the coming of the Skonnon battle-fleet during the First Conquest as an 'awesome sight', which blotted out the daylight. Judging by the tributes brought for the Nimon, the Anethans are a bit weak these days. The teenaged Seth lies about being a 'prince' of Aneth, but none of the others realise this. [Aneth society must be quite fractured if they don't know their own royalty.]

• *Crinoth.* The last world drained by the Nimons. When Romana visits, she finds the world in ruins, and its leader - Sezom, the only one left alive, though not for long - states that the Nimons used the usual tactic of promising them prosperity before sucking them dry. One of the Nimons indicates that Crinoth is no longer safe [perhaps meaning that the world's about to collapse from its proximity to the black hole, or just that there's no more sustenance there]. Sezom found that a rock called jasonite, which carries an electro-magnetic charge, upped the power of his energy-staff and made it capable of stunning the Nimons. There's no indication that Crinoth is part of the Skonnon Empire, or indeed, anywhere near Skonnos at all. Crinoth is ultimately seen to flare up and vanish after the Nimons' 'chain reaction'.

History

• *Dating*. No date indicated. [Yet again, it's feasible that these people might be descendants of humans from Earth who've lost track of the old homeworld, in which case this could be the same era seen in "The Power of Kroll" (16.5). Whatever era that may have been.]

The Analysis

Where Does This Come From? This story's debt to Greek myth is pretty obvious, but to a late-'70s audience, contemporary Greece made for some interesting comparisons. Under the rule of a trio of dictators known as "the Colonels", Greece had been economically and politically held back. Practically the only section of society functioning adequately was the army (as Romana notes, the only survivors of the Skonnon war were the military… 'sounds like a well-organised war'). Fascist Greece was geopolitically useful to the West, even if it was uncomfortably close. Offers of Western aid kept the regime together until the mid-'70s.

Are we therefore to translate this as a parable, with America as the Nimon? Well… this is no more extreme than some theories (see 17.3, "The Creature from The Pit") and chimed with a general mood of annoyance at the use of our shores as a US missile silo. However, while the Skonnon space-fleet was in as bad a state as the RAF at the time, all the talk of "The Great Journey of Life" makes the Nimon's sales-pitch sound like one of the many odd cults that were coming across the Atlantic and sucking recruits dry. Est, the Baghwan, the Moonies and above all multinational retail franchises like McDonalds were seen as "locust-like" by worried commentators.

Things That Don't Make Sense So much ticker-tape comes out of K9's mouth that you get the feeling his insides must be clogged with paper, and we're apparently supposed to find the way he's choked by the stuff "cute" rather than "stupid". The scene at the start of episode two, when the Doctor accepts that the asteroid's about to kill him and sits there saying goodbye to K9 and the TARDIS instead of trying to think of a solution, is so massively out of character - and such a flawed attempt at comedy - that you've got to assume either the Doctor or the script editor is on tranquilisers. [To be generous, we might conclude that the Doctor's just trying to relax in the hope of thinking of something.] As for the noises from the

"BBC Comedy Sound Effects" record made by the TARDIS console later in the episode… no, never mind.

Why does Romana ask Soldeed where the Doctor is when she arrives on Skonnos, when she last saw the Doctor hanging around near a black hole and has no reason to think he's on the planet (which he isn't)? And how does the Doctor know Soldeed's name, when he wasn't present during the Romana-and-Seth exposition scene? You also have to wonder why both the Doctor and Romana ask what anyone would want to create a black hole for, when their own civilisation's based on the principle.

Annoyingly, we're never told exactly *what* the Nimon have done to Crinoth to reduce it to ruins - we're just told about them eating people, but it looks to us as if the whole planet has been turned into a husk - and for some reason Sezom, Soldeed's equivalent there, is the only human being left alive. Surely he should have been the *first* one to die when the Nimon started to feed, especially since he's the one with the most advanced technology on the planet?

Soldeed drops dead in episode four, and makes sure we all know it, but the next time we see the scene his corpse has vanished altogether. [Again, if you wanted to be generous you could argue that the "killing" blow only stunned him and that he wandered off to do a mad rant somewhere else.] The same episode sees Seth (a dribbling boy who's never fired anything like a power-staff before) bring down two Nimons (creatures with built-in energy-weapons) before they can do anything but go 'raah' at him.

Critique (Prosecution) In the same way that *The Discontinuity Guide* convinced the fans of the '90s that "The Creature from the Pit" might possibly be a work of parody, ever since *Doctor Who - A Celebration* in 1983 there's been a tendency to pretend that "The Horns of Nimon" was deliberately written as a pantomime for the festive season, hence all the over-acting and the fact that a lot of it comes across as pure farce. But really, "The Horns of Nimon" isn't deliberately *anything*; it's just a culmination of all the worst excesses of the Graham Williams era, made at a point when nobody could be bothered paying attention to any aspect of the programme other than the appearance of the main cast and the whims of the techno-fetishist writers. (The only people who could possibly think that there's anything interesting about black holes… which is to say, about people *talking* about black holes.)

This is a series so convinced of its own cleverness that it fills the screen with excruciating clichés just so it can send them up, but doesn't seem to notice that this just means we're being forced to watch excruciating clichés for most of the time. The infamous Skonnon guard, who deliberately chews the space-furniture with every line and shouts 'weakling scum!!!' as if it's a comedy catchphrase, is clearly supposed to be a pastiche of a typical SF guard - worse, a typical *Doctor Who* guard, so this is self-parody more than anything - as if a pastiche of a typical SF guard is in some way *entertaining*.

The unwatchably awful Anethians are proof, if proof were needed by this stage, that the programme has just stopped caring about little details like "characters". The overwhelming sense here is that Tom Baker, the writer, the script editor and the producer have all just become staggering *bores*, insisting on doing the same party-tricks over and over and over. After this, you'll never want to see a Doctor-and-K9-in-the-console-room scene ever again.

But deep down at its heart, it's the sheer hollowness of "The Horns of Nimon" that's the hardest thing to take. In "Underworld" (15.5), we saw how Anthony Read (as script editor) tried to integrate ancient myths into *Doctor Who*, but didn't understand what actually made those myths interesting and ended up turning it into a pointless academic exercise. Sutekh works in "Pyramids of Mars" because he really is the demigod he claims to be, and Azal works in "The Daemons" because he's as child-terrifying as any Devil from folklore, but replacing the Golden Fleece with a couple of canisters of DNA is merely pathetic. Now that Read's writing the script himself, "The Horns of Nimon" makes exactly the same mistakes, but here the problem's even more pronounced even if the end result isn't quite as offensive.

The original Minotaur story is about a woman who curses a civilisation by consorting with an animal; about a man who descends into the darkest place on Earth to fight the most primal of all the beast-creatures; about a hero who slays the thing in the labyrinth, but becomes just as monstrous by causing his own father to commit suicide. It's a tale of everything animalistic and Freudian in human consciousness, about a journey into the darkest, guiltiest tunnels of our collective psyche (and that's not just an intellectual dissection, by the way… that's why the story works for us, even when we're kids). But "The Horns of Nimon"? It's about a bull-headed alien who fires energy-bolts from its horns and lives in the middle of some space-corridors. Anything which might have made the original story worth hearing is ripped away, and the left-over pieces are just meaningless sci-fi fodder. An earlier draft of the script revealed that the Nimon were aliens wearing scary bull-masks rather than actual bull-headed monsters, which makes you realise exactly how clueless Read was. Fantasy, TV fantasy in particular, is supposed to make stories *bigger*. Not smaller.

It's the end of an era, thankfully. After this *Doctor Who* starts to become a proper television programme again, not just a hobby for university science graduates and a gravy-train for actors who think it's all a bit of a laugh. As for "The Horns of Nimon" itself, the simplest and most damning criticism you can make is this: Graham Crowden (Soldeed), one of the greatest character actors ever to walk the Earth, is called in to play the villain and is given nothing to do but ham things up as if it's doomsday. Still, at least it looks as if he and Tom Baker are having a good time.

Critique (Defence)   And so all the worst clichés, all the flaws of production (multiple pronunciations of alien minerals and all) are flung on the bonfire to make sure no-one ever submits a script like this again. What the next year would have brought, if Graham Williams had stayed in place, is anyone's guess. "Nightmare of Eden" (17.4) and "Shada" (17.6) are both oddly prescient of the later Sylvester McCoy stories. Here, though, they go full-on to get the last mileage out of the "Greek-myths-in-space" things that everyone had been submitting (yes, "Underworld" was one of the good ones).

What have we got here? A story making a virtue out of walls that move. A story where Lalla Ward in effect plays the Doctor, allowing Tom Baker to prat about like he always wanted to and find out how unsatisfying it is. A story where the dead bodies really are gruesome; the monsters don't lumber but glide; where the kids were scared (and they were, amazing as people seem to find that now), the teens thought it was kitsch but watched anyway, and the adults - who were in on the joke

- laughed at the kids and teens and with the programme.

Well, sometimes. But, it has to be said again, if you discount a few clearly-marked scenes of Baker doing Baker things then it's played fairly straight. Indeed the discovery of the desiccated body is done rather well, and its sudden crumbling when Janet Ellis (Teka) touches it makes a few adults jump even now. The Nimon, at over ten feet in height, is striking when lit well or shot from beneath (more corridors with ceilings; see 17.1, "Destiny of the Daleks") and memorably voiced. The decision to cast dancers adds an eeriness to their movements lacking since "The Robots of Death" (14.5). The walls moving must have taken ages to get right, and for once the guns make nice little puffs *and* zap where they're supposed to zap. They're getting the nuts and bolts right for the ones who aren't in on the joke.

Nonetheless, there's a chill heart to this frivolity. The story we hear is of a war which only the military survived. Aside from references to the Colonels in Greece, this was a disturbingly plausible scenario in early 1980. We'd had the Soviet invasion of Afghanistan and the revolution in Iran At the time of broadcast this was a story with its head screwed on about what was happening "outside", but didn't dwell on it. Instead, once again, lack of imagination and perspective was the hallmark of the villains. Soon *Doctor Who* would be produced by an accountant and we would descend into a nerdish hell of obsessive continuity and formica.

The Facts

Written by Anthony Read. Directed by Kenny McBain. Viewing figures: 6.0 million, 8.8 million, 9.8 million, 10.4 million.

Supporting Cast: Graham Crowden (Soldeed), Michael Osborne (Sorak), Janet Ellis (Teka), Simon Gipps-Kent (Seth), Malcolm Terris (Co-Pilot), Clifford Norgate (Voice of the Nimons).

Cliffhangers An asteroid weighing two-hundred-and-twenty-million tons hurtles towards the TARDIS on its way towards the black hole; the Nimon bears down on Romana and the Anethans in the Power Complex; deep in the Nimon's lair, Soldeed bears down on the Doctor with his energy-staff raised and announces that 'you shall dieee!'.

The Lore

• The union dispute which claimed the life of "Shada" (see the next story) also meant that everyone was sticking neurotically to the time allotted for studio-work. Thus the last scene to be filmed, Soldeed's death, had to be done in one take. Graham Crowden "corpsed", and this is what was broadcast.

• The original concept of the Nimons was that they were too ugly to look at themselves, and needed vast masks. This was abandoned at the last minute, but the idea of tall, bulky beings on ten-inch-high cloven hooves was retained, and dancers cast. Read had hinted that they might be cyborgs (see the Seers in 15.5, "Underworld"), hence the decision to give them fifty-inch chests.

• Read's script was almost completely untouched by Douglas Adams, who - with "Shada" to write, as well as demands to follow up the first *Hitch-Hiker's* series with the books, play, records, second series and TV adaptation - was wondering why he put himself through all the grief he'd had over the last year.

• Janet Ellis (Teka) was already known for the occasional part in dramas like *The Sweeney* (British viewers may remember the "nude with a German helmet" scene…), and would later present puzzle-based kids' show Jigsaw before hitting the big time on *Blue Peter*. Recently her pop-star daughter, Sophie Ellis-Bextor, got her back into the public eye and she's been busier than ever.

• By this stage Lalla Ward was almost as prominent as Tom Baker. She was cast as Ophelia opposite Derek Jacobi in the BBC's *Hamlet* (the production also featured Patrick Stewart as the King Claudius), and appeared solo on *Multi-Coloured Swap Shop* and *Ask Aspel*. The first of these appearances re-used the set of the Nimon's lair, and this caused quite a bit of a fuss between designers. Ward's other extramural activity was illustrating a book on astrology for pets (look, it was the '70s, okay?). Baker, meanwhile, was actively promoting - at his own expense - the new *Doctor Who Weekly*, and visiting Australia to film "Keep Australia Beautiful" adverts.

• As a prelude to phasing out Dudley Simpson, producer-in-waiting John Nathan-Turner commissioned Peter Howell of the BBC Radiophonic Workshop to compose a score for scenes from episode two of this story (see 18.1, "The Leisure Hive").

• Williams sent a memo to the drama department, apologising for the fact that he was using so many familiar writers (not that the drama department really cared). He commented on the time wasted by new writers who didn't seem to have ever watched a whole episode, or who wanted to turn the programme into some other series, or who never suggested anything even remotely practicable.

17.6: "Shada"

(Serial 5M, Six Episodes, None Broadcast.)

Which One is This? It's the one that never got finished. Filming on "Shada" began in October 1979, and the story was originally slated to end Season Seventeen, but strike action at the BBC caused the production to slow to a halt and finally fall apart altogether. Of a 132-minute story, around seventy-seven minutes of material were filmed, and released on a BBC video - with linking narration from Tom Baker - in 1992. But though the story was never actually shown, it *did* get as far as the production stage (unlike many of the other well-known "failed" *Doctor Who* projects over the years), so it's generally considered to count as a "proper" story. Which leads us to the next point…

Did This Really "Happen"? Or, to put it another way: is it "canon"? Since this present volume regards all broadcast *Doctor Who* as a gospel part of the same fictional universe, but treats off-air sources as mere supporting evidence… where does "Shada" fit into things? And it's a question that fans have been asking themselves for some time.

The main problem is that when Tom Baker was "unable" to film new material for "The Five Doctors" (20.7) in 1983, the decision was made to use never-before-broadcast extracts from "Shada" in the story, so that he at least put in an appearance. Which causes all sorts of canonicity hitches. "Shada" sees the Doctor and Romana sharing a quiet moment on a punt in Cambridge, then going on to visit Professor Chronotis at the University. "The Five Doctors" sees them have exactly the same conversation in exactly the same punt, except that it ends with them being abducted by a time-scoop and dumped back on Earth some time later. Clearly, these two things can't happen in the same universe without some stitching being done around the edges.

The Discontinuity Guide tried to claim that the time-scoop just abducts them from the storyline of "Shada" and puts them back again later, but its claim that The Ancient Law of Gallifrey's properties affected the scoop is spurious at the very least. Things became more complicated still in 2003, when Big Finish Productions took Douglas Adams' script for "Shada" and recorded it as an audio play, this time starring Paul McGann as the Doctor instead of Tom Baker and adding some extra material to cover the gaps. (Weirdly, the Big Finish version starts with a scene in which the Eighth Doctor goes back to Gallifrey and picks up Romana before they go to Earth to have the adventure… as if the *Doctor Who* fans really needed some explanation as to why the Doctor and Romana were together again, and couldn't just take it for granted that Time Lords meet up with each other all the time.)

But there's a way around this. As luck would have it, two versions of the "punt" scene were written. The one filmed in 1979, and used in "The Five Doctors", is the re-write; the version in the original script is wholly different. So it's feasible that the Doctor and Romana might, just, have gone punting in Cambridge twice. An obvious, simple answer would seem to present itself. The Fourth Doctor and Romana went to Cambridge, and *would* have had the adventure described in "Shada", but the time-scoop in "The Five Doctors" snatched them out of the time-stream and stopped it happening. This is, if you want to ret-con the real world, why "Shada" has always existed halfway between canon and non-canon; it's an adventure that the Doctor was meant to have, but didn't.

Years later, the Eighth Doctor met up with Romana and they went back to Cambridge, having a different conversation but ultimately experiencing the same events that they *should* have experienced years before. Sadly the Big Finish recording removes the punt altogether, and has the Doctor and Romana wandering around some shops in Cambridge instead, but we can put that down to a side-effect of all the stretching of causality. The Eighth Doctor also recalls that all those years ago he took Romana to Brighton instead of staying in Cambridge - a reference to the opening of 18.1, "The Leisure Hive" - but from "The Five Doctors" it's reasonable to assume that victims of the time-scoop might not remember things too clearly. The point remains that both versions can

What *Else* Didn't Get Made?

"Shada" is unique amongst *Doctor Who* stories in that it's the only story which was partly-filmed and then abandoned, but of course, there's no end of stories which faltered long before they reached the production stage. Many of these are described in the various **Lore** sections, usually in as much detail as is warranted. Here, though, is our selection of ten stories seriously considered but - in some cases mercifully - never made.

• **"Doctor Who and the Spare-Part People"** (also listed as "The Brain-Drain" and "The Cold War") by Reed R. de Rouen and Jon Pertwee (!). Pertwee's father and uncle were both experienced scriptwriters, so you can see how he'd think himself qualified. Apart from his performance as Pa Clanton in "The Gunfighters" (3.8), de Rouen had written one episode of *The Avengers* and a *Play of the Week* called "The Trial of Lee Harvey Oswald". Now, there's no reason to dismiss this projected seven-parter out of hand without seeing what it actually entailed. Brilliant scientists and sportsmen are being abducted by a megalomaniac who lives in a tropical paradise at the South Pole, who's attempting to create a super-race and who stages gladiatorial combats between footballers and crocodiles. The Doctor goes undercover as a Nobel laureate, and he and the Brigadier are taken in a submarine to the Lost Kingdom, where the Doctor's immortality intrigues the Emperor. The Emperor puts the Doctor in a labyrinth to fight his pet monster, but his beautiful daughter helps the Doctor with a ball of string, and they all get in the sub and return to UNIT HQ where the girl replaces Liz Shaw. All right, *now* you can dismiss it out of hand. Terrance Dicks did.

• **"Beyond the Sun"** by Malcolm Hulke. Hulke submitted at least three ideas in the series' first year, including the now-legendary "Doctor Who and the Clock; more on this in Volume I. "The Hidden Planet", AKA "Beyond the Sun" (Hartnell titles are always tricky, even when the story was actually made) was a tale of a world in the same orbit as Earth but exactly opposite; a world where four-leaf clovers are common, women are in charge and birds fly backwards. This was to have been a six-parter, and it was given to Hulke as a consolation prize after his scenario "406 AD" had been rejected. Significantly, the production team's "do a total rewrite or we abandon it" decision was taken at the precise moment that the public got to see the Daleks and the whole tone of the pro-gramme changed. It would appear that this story was replaced in the line-up by "The Keys of Marinus" (1.5), in the belief that Terry Nation knew what he was doing...

• **"The Enemy Within"** by Christopher Priest. We could have cited his more famous "lost" story "Sealed Orders", in which the Time Lords order the Doctor to kill Romana while the TARDIS lands inside itself and runs at two different speeds. But this one's worth mentioning because it's apparently referenced in a story that *did* get made, written before "The Enemy Within" fell through. In "Castrovalva" (19.1) the Doctor hints at something powerful and terrifying at the centre of the TARDIS, but as he's just regenerated he can't quite remember what it is. What it *would* have been was a vegetable parasite / symbiont of the Ship, feeding on some kind of time-energy. Priest's early novel *Inverted World*, in which time and space are exchanged, shows how well he could have handled this material (as does his Wells pastiche *The Space Machine*, which also demonstrates his grasp of the idiom of *Doctor Who* as Victorian-style psychedelia).

A genuine stylist and respected author, with a background in SF but a few award-nominated "mundane" books, wanted to write for *Doctor Who*; it was the dream of the last four script editors realised. But although Douglas Adams commissioned "Sealed Orders", incoming script editor Christopher H. Bidmead wanted too many changes, e.g. the removal of Romana. So Priest got paid and was offered another slot. "The Enemy Within" was written to a Bidmead brief… and then Eric Saward arrived as script editor and asked for revisions. Plus, Priest was of the opinion that the new producer thought of writers - if at all - as rather less important than costume designers.

Things reached a head when John Nathan-Turner launched into a tirade at Priest over the 'phone, refusing to pay the writer's fee. The call has since become the stuff of legend, Priest himself describing it as 'an extraordinary display of petulance, with foul language and insults freely mixed'. The Writer's Guild found in Priest's favour, and Priest decided that life really was too short for dealing with prima-donna-ish TV types.

It didn't quite end there, though. When a fan wrote in to ask why no "real" SF authors were used on the series, Eric Saward replied (and we here

continued on page 317...

be true, and that anyone can safely treat one or the other as "real" without annoying people who feel differently (although for this section of the book, the notes are based purely on the filmed 1979 material and the original script, with the filmed material taking precedence if there's a contradiction).

History is satisfied, but more importantly, so is pedantry.

The Continuity

The Doctor Touchingly, when Skagra inspects the Doctor's mind he finds that Romana is the foremost thing in it.

• *Inventory.* He produces a medal, which he pins to Romana's outfit [it's not, as the script specifies, a badge marked "I AM A GENIUS"]. It seems to make her happy.

• *Background.* The Doctor is an old friend of Professor Chronotis at St. Cedd's College, Cambridge University, though there's no indication of how they met. The Doctor visited the College in 1955, 1958, 1960 and 1964. During all these visits but the 1958 one, he was in his current incarnation, and in 1960 St. Cedd's gave him an honorary degree. This means that he's known to Wilkin, the porter. [Indicating that his first visit was in 1958, hinting that his encounters with Chronotis aren't always in sequence. Then again, it's not explicitly stated that he met the Professor in 1958, though he did on the other occasions. The Doctor may have visited the College earlier than 1955, but the current porter wouldn't remember it.]

The Doctor knows how to go "vortex-walking" between capsules in the vortex; see **The TARDIS(es)**. He claims he learned this trick from a space-time mystic in the Quantocks [the script claims 'an Ancient Time Mystic in the Qualactin Zones', Qualactin also being mentioned in 16.2, "The Pirate Planet"] who made it look easy. He's read Saul Bellow's *The Victim*, and finds the name "Shada" vaguely familiar, even though it's supposed to have been wiped from the minds of the Time Lords [he could just be showing off again]. He recognises the names of the scientists drained by Skagra, claiming they're the finest of their generation.

The Supporting Cast

• *Romana.* By now she knows enough about Earth to know that Newton went to Cambridge, and off-handedly refers to herself as a historian. When she was a 'Time Tot' she used to have a Gallifreyan nursery book, which Chronotis also owns, called *Our Planet's Story.* It includes the line: "And in the great days of Rassilon, five great principles were laid down. Can you remember what they were, my children?"

• *K9.* Sounds palpably glum when someone stops him blasting down a door just by pushing the "open" switch, and isn't in any way tactful when he informs Romana that the Professor's dead. Whenever Skagra's sphere becomes active, e.g. by draining someone's mind, K9 can detect it even if it's more than five miles away. He can attach himself to Professor Chronotis' TARDIS as well as the Doctor's, slowing down the deterioration of the Ship's sub-neutronic circuits, and his metabolic analysis of Skagra [made without prompting, as if K9 routinely does this to new enemies] identifies Skagra's planet of origin as Drornid.

K9 assumes that everyone can see the invisible spaceship [q.v. the previous story, in which he can't see the illusion that everyone else sees].

The Time Lords According to Skagra, when Time Lord judges pass sentence they declare: 'We but administer. You are imprisoned not by this Court but by the power of the Law.' [This isn't seen to happen during any of the Doctor's three-and-a-half trials by the Time Lords, so this is probably an archaic form of the procedure.]

In fact this statement is, or was, literally true. "The Law" refers to a book called *The Worshipful and Ancient Law of Gallifrey,* a large red tome which is now in the possession of Professor Chronotis on Earth. The book is physically curious - it's written in the Gallifreyan alphabet but coded so that it makes no sense to the Doctor. It feels odd to the touch, can't be cut with a razor, stores up sub-atomic energy and makes spectrographs explode when the energy's released, it's atomically unstable, time passes backwards over its pages and when carbon-dated it turns out to be -20,000 years old. But more importantly, when its pages are turned in the TARDIS' time-field, this causes the rotor in the middle of the console to rise and fall. When all the pages are turned, the Ship dematerialises and heads for Shada (see

What *Else* Didn't Get Made?

...continued from page 315

reproduce his response verbatim, spelling and all): "The names of writers you quoat are novalists. Infact one of them has attempted to write a *Doctor Who* script with disasterous results. That is why we don't use novalists." Priest was shown this and contacted the Head of Series and Serials at the BBC, gaining a grovelling and abject letter of apology from Saward and Nathan-Turner, plus a written statement that Priest's version of events was the correct one. See the interview in *SF Eye* issue 15 (autumn 1997) for more.

• **"The Song of the Space Whale"** by Pat Mills. The same fate befell this script. The co-creator of *Judge Dredd* submitted a story about a whole culture stuck inside a vast ship, the Ghaleen, which may also have been alive. But Eric Saward, from Mills' account, took exception to the ship's working-class captain speaking anything other than the cod-Shakespearean dialogue which Saward apparently wanted everyone in space to speak. However, one of the minor characters - a roguish cabin-boy called Turlough - was recycled as an aristocratic space-orphan in a minor public-school, whilst the industrial conception of the spaceship's monastic life became a big thread in "Terminus" (20.4). What's interesting here is that only a few years later, the idea of a script by the writers of the comic 2000 AD was the ideal to which script editor Andrew Cartmel aspired.

• **"The Face of God"** by Donald Tosh, possibly. This was the idea that '60s producer John Wiles used as a bench-mark of what he wanted *Doctor Who* to be like. There's no indication that he ever intended to make it, but as a guide to his thinking he mentioned it in every interview he gave in the 1980s. As many people have taken this as a definite plan to make a deliberately "controversial" story, and listed it as something that nearly-but-not-quite got made, we've included it here to remove confusion. Mind you, Wiles' very first story as producer was set in known legend (3.3, "The Myth Makers") and he dared to tease the audience with the Doctor's death (3.5, "The Massacre"), so it's not completely out of the question.

• **"Prison in Space"** by Dick Sharples. If you've wondered just why stories doubled in length at the tail-end of the sixties, then… it was that or let something like this onto our screens. Several

abortive stories for Season Six were sufficiently advanced for props and half-finished scripts to be available. Some were rejigged in 1970 as UNIT adventures, in colour and three episodes too long; some were never going to work without somebody inventing CGI. But junking this idea was a definite decision on grounds of taste.

Sitcom veteran Dick Sharples concocted a story about a matriarchy where men were forced to wear dresses and be submissive servants / sex-objects. Following lots of jokes about Jamie's kilt, the Doctor and company stage a coup, and much spanking ensues. Along the way the story was, somehow, supposed to introduce Jamie's replacement "Nik". Everything else in the story could have been done very cheaply, with one spaceship set and a few cells, and perhaps a costume or two borrowed from the BBC's *Out of the Unknown*.

Indeed, looking carefully at what was intended, it seems that Robert Holmes was later instructed to write a story around what had already been requested from the designers (hence the odd pacing of 6.5, "The Space Pirates"). The same gender-war idea cropped up on our screens ten years later as a recurring segment in popular comedy show *The Two Ronnies*, where it was played for laughs as a pretext for middle-aged men in drag and attractive Nazi feminists in leather uniforms and big boots.

• **"Alixion"** by Robin Mukherjee. In Volume VI we'll look in detail at the various plans that were made for Season Twenty-Seven before the plug was finally pulled on the programme, but this is worth mentioning here as the only story by a writer who went on to do lots of TV drama *without* ever writing a New Adventure; the only one with a definite title; and the only one not at least partly recycled by Virgin, Big Finish, BBV or BBC Books.

Mukherjee had submitted many story proposals to script editor Andrew Cartmel, and was bound to have hit paydirt sooner or later. Alixion was the name of an asteroid, and the name of the substance made therein, a glorified Buckfast wine or Chartreuse. The asteroid was a warren of corridors and cloisters but, as it turned out, not your usual *Doctor Who* ones. In fact it was more like a beehive, producing the eponymous "elixir" and populated by giant beetles, the twist being that the stuff of life was made from digested human corpses. The human inhabitants were basically

continued on page 319...

Planet Notes). The implication is that this is the only way Shada can be reached.

Originally found in the Panopticon archive, the book is said to be one of the 'artefacts of Rassilon', all of which had great power. [Ergo, Shada also dates back to the Rassilon era. The other artefacts are presumably the Rod, the Sash, the Key, etc.] The Doctor states that Rassilon had powers and secrets which even modern Time Lords don't understand, so many of the artefacts' uses have been lost [which fits what's seen in 14.3, "The Deadly Assassin" and 15.6, "The Invasion of Time"]. Romana and the Doctor recite the words of the Time Academy induction ceremony [though it's not clear *which* Academy Romana went to]: 'I swear to protect the Ancient Law of Gallifrey with all my might and main and will to the end of my days with justice and with honour temper my actions and my thoughts.' The Doctor knows about the book, even if he doesn't know about Shada.

There's a College of Cardinals on Gallifrey. For more on Time Lord history, see *Drornid* under **Planet Notes**.

• *Salyavin*. A Time Lord criminal, who had the unique power to project his own mind onto other people's and thus take them over. [Even the Doctor's been seen to hypnotise Gallifreyans on occasion, but that's nowhere near the level of Salyavin's power.] The Doctor admits to regarding Salyavin as a sort of hero in his youth, because of the criminal's great flair, and even Romana knows of him. Found guilty of 'mind crimes', Salyavin was imprisoned on Shada before the Doctor was born, though somehow he escaped [evidently around three-hundred years ago]. In fact it seems that Salyavin's criminal tendencies were blown out of all proportion, and certainly he's older and wiser now, because he's none other than...

• *Professor Chronotis*. An old, eccentric, rather harmless-looking Professor at St. Cedd's College, Cambridge, Chronotis has been passing for human for three-hundred years. He claims he's been at the University ever since he 'retired' from Gallifrey, always living in the same "rooms", so he remembers an old Master of College getting run over by a coach and pair. The Doctor knows of the Professor's true heritage, but not that he used to be Salyavin, while Romana has never met him before.

Though absent-minded enough to let one of his students take the *Law of Gallifrey* by mistake, Chronotis doesn't want trouble and regards his

hot-headed mind-controlling days with some embarrassment. He admits that he stole the book from Gallifrey in order to cover his tracks, and used his mental powers to make the Time Lords forget that Shada ever existed. [So contrary to much fan-fiction, Shada hasn't been used by the Time Lords for the last three centuries, either officially or unofficially. It may well be brought back into use *after* this story, though.]

Chronotis calls on the Doctor to return the book to Gallifrey because he thinks he doesn't have long to live [he *does* pass away here, for a while, so he may have had a premonition]. He apparently sent the Doctor a signal, though he claims this was 'ages ago', and Romana believes that the Doctor got the time wrong. [This breaks the normal *Doctor Who* logic, which tends to act as if all Time Lords are connected to a kind of definite "Time Lord present", even when they're centuries apart. See **Do Time Lords Always Meet in Sequence?** under 22.3, "The Mark of the Rani".] Chronotis is reaching the end of his last regeneration, and actually seems to die here, but is rescued by a curious quirk of time; see **The TARDIS(es)**. After his death he vanishes without trace, and the Doctor acts as if this is normal.

Chronotis states that now he's retired, he's 'not allowed' to have a TARDIS. [An interesting development in Time Lord logic: Time Lords *can* leave Gallifrey, but aren't allowed to keep their Ships, which makes sense if the High Council doesn't want the technology getting into alien hands. However, since Chronotis is really Salyavin, it's likely that he never 'retired' at all and just used mind-power to make the Time Lords *think* he's a harmless old buffer settling down on a primitive world. Compare with 11.5, "Planet of the Spiders" and 21.7, "The Twin Dilemma".]

The TARDIS(es) Chronotis' rooms at the University are, in fact, his TARDIS. You wouldn't know it to look at them, although there are controls hidden behind the wooden panelling. It's a model even more primitive than the Doctor's, 'literally' rescued from the scrap-heaps [there are literal TARDIS scrap-heaps???] as Chronotis wasn't technically allowed to have a Ship, and he recognises the Doctor's vessel as a type forty: 'Came out when I was a boy, that shows you how old I am.' [This indicates that type forties are *thousands* of years old, not merely hundreds.] Whenever this TARDIS moves, its seemingly-wooden-but-inde-

What *Else* Didn't Get Made?

...continued from page 317

monks, and thus didn't put up much resistance (their vow of silence didn't help). The villain, the Abbot, was a manipulative smooth-talker - and also, possibly, a bank-manager - attempting to drive the Doctor insane whilst trying on increasingly loud suits. This was initially commissioned for Season Twenty-Six, but apparently not used as Mukherjee was a "new writer". Yet so were Marc Platt (26.2, "Ghost Light") and Rona Munro (26.4, "Survival"), so either Mukherjee didn't fit the plan or something about the story just wasn't working.

• **"The Rosemariners"** by Donald Tosh. Although irked at his treatment by the BBC during the Hartnell run, former script editor Tosh was drawn back to the programme by the prospect of writing for Patrick Troughton. His idea for a story featured space-based botanical research station ESS 454, and wasn't entirely unlike "Fury from the Deep" (5.6), with plants infecting and possessing people. Much of the politicking and jockeying for control was akin to "The Wheel in Space" (5.7), while the plants ended up creating doppelgangers of the men, again not unlike various Troughton yarns (especially 4.8, "The Faceless Ones"). He kept revising this story for various line-ups, but once the UNIT era began he abandoned it.

• **"Erinella"** by Pennant Roberts. Chris Bidmead claims, in just about every interview, that there were no scripts available for use when he took over as script editor in Season Eighteen. This just isn't true; what he means is that there were no scripts fitting his own rigid doctrine of what *Doctor Who* ought to be. As many as five possible stories were there to be made, in reasonably broadcastable form. One of these, the one he considered and reconsidered and repeatedly requested rewrites for, was director Pennant Roberts' reworking of Celtic mythology. With a real dragon, too, and there's documentary evidence that it had been commissioned in January 1979 under the working title "Dragons of Fear". Roberts, always happy to tell his side of the story to anyone who'll listen, claims that the suffix "ella" suggests "perhaps"; implying that this tale was set in an Ireland which never quite existed. As the prince and his brother-in-law battle dragons and fight for the hand of a princess, the Doctor wrecks everything

by arriving too early in a cyclic story, and is accused of being a poisoner. Bidmead also turned his nose up at script proposals by writers like Allan Prior, John Lloyd and Philip Hinchcliffe. (Hinchcliffe's "Valley of the Lost" appears to have been the Rider-Haggard pastiche with which he would have opened Season Fifteen if he hadn't been kicked out as producer, set in South America and ending with the Doctor trapped inside a sun, a fact that Hinchcliffe said could either be resolved or not depending on how matters stood with Baker's agent.)

• **"Project Zeta-Sigma"** by John Flanagan and Andrew McCulloch. Bidmead was so pleased with "Meglos" (!) that its writers were immediately re-commissioned, and were given the task of writing out the Fourth Doctor at the end of Season Eighteen. The story was a thinly-veiled nuclear arms-race parable about two equal and opposite sides, the subtly-named "Hawks" and "Doves", each with plans to stop the other lot starting a war. It involved things called autogems (or "autochems" in some accounts, apparently intended to be talking weapons), a missile capable of flying through the planet's sun and - inevitably - the Master, and it ended with a crap joke about the new Doctor's "disarming" smile.

Once it became apparent that this wasn't quite epic enough (or ready enough) to round off Season Eighteen and kill off Tom Baker, it was rescheduled as the first story of Season Nineteen. By this stage it was apparent that there was a gaping hole in the plot, or more accurately a gaping hole where the plot should have been. The proposal limped on as far as casting decisions, although three or four titles were used; "Project Zeta Plus","Project 4G" and so on. Bidmead's faith in the writers meant that the stories around it were filmed to end where "Zeta-Sigma" began, and to begin where it ended. Thus when it all went horribly wrong, Bidmead himself had to hurriedly create a sequel to "Logopolis" (18.7) that didn't contradict "Four to Doomsday" (19.2)... which, in the delay, had been moved forward in the shooting schedule and was even then being filmed.

ABOUT TIME 1975-1979

structible door simply appears in a wall wherever it's going. Despite his occasional talent for spotting disguised TARDISes [see 8.1, "Terror of the Autons"], the Doctor has never guessed the rooms' true nature, not even when sitting in them. There is, of course, no tell-tale humming noise.

When Chronotis dies, he vanishes without trace after a few minutes. Later, when an ignorant human is toying with the controls, there's an explosion and he abruptly re-appears... wearing a night-shirt and night-cap. He states that the intervention tangled his time-fields at a critical moment - 'think of me as a paradox in an anomaly' - and every indication is that he's real, not some sort of technical "ghost". Even so, he refers to himself as 'still' dead. [This is hard to take, as it means that Time Lords can apparently be easily resurrected by doing exactly the same sort of TARDIS-tinkering at a 'critical moment'. Even if it happens here as an accident, surely it can't be a hard thing to do deliberately? Chronotis' disappearance may be what usually happens to a Time Lord on final death - though 14.3, "The Deadly Assassin", would suggest otherwise - but the oft-stated fan-theory that he's being beamed straight into the Matrix is probably piffle, as the Matrix has no need for his physical body. Where the night-clothes come from is anyone's guess.]

After the tampering, the TARDIS' occupants are said to be jammed 'between two irrational time-interfaces' or 'standing obliquely to the time-fields', which is apparently what made the Professor's resurrection possible. It also means that from the outside, the door to Chronotis' rooms is filled with a shimmering blue void.

Chronotis can untangle his Ship in such a way that he doesn't cease to exist, but it requires two simultaneous operations to fix the interfacial resonator, and he has to put some of his own mind into a human being to get away with it. A conceptual geometry relay with an agranomic trigger and a defunct field separator is removed from the works, but these won't be needed if the resonator can be repaired successfully. Once fixed, this TARDIS can easily follow the Doctor's space-time trail. It can also move "alongside" the Doctor's hijacked Ship in the vortex, causing something to blow on the Doctor's console as if one vessel is jamming the other, and this holds as long as a certain switch is pressed in Chronotis' rooms. Skagra believes that soon the force-fields around Chronotis' TARDIS will give, and Romana asks K9

to check Chronotis' sub-neutron circuits when it starts to fail. The Doctor shows Romana how to drop the 'vortex shields' in Chronotis' rooms during this procedure, creating a small patch of time-lessness and spacelessness just behind the tea-trolley. When the Doctor enters this, he goes "vortex-walking" over to the other TARDIS. [It's not explained why he has to walk through the vortex, rather than materialising one TARDIS around another, the way it's usually done. The space-time vortex resembles the programme's title sequence, according to the script. Compare this with 14.3, "The Deadly Assassin".]

When the Doctor leaves the vortex, he finds himself in a small equipment room on the TARDIS, which is full of shelves, drawers and cabinets which just happen to contain the right equipment to build a helmet that lets him mind-wrestle Skagra. [He can only do this because Skagra's sphere has copied his own mind, but the mechanics aren't explained.] The equipment includes a beeping thing and a small laser gun, which he uses to take a chunk out of a metal table in the room.

Also on the Doctor's TARDIS is a medical kit, a metal case which includes a hi-tech collar covered in flashing lights. After Skagra's mind-draining sphere attacks Professor Chronotis, Romana uses this collar to free the autonomic areas of the Time Lord's brain - those which handle little things like breathing and heartbeat - to allow him to think with them, something that would be impossible for humans. Chrontis can then beat out a message with his hearts, using 'Gallifreyan Morse code'. The medical kit is kept on the top shelf of a large white cupboard opposite a door, directions from the console room being first door on the left, down the corridor, second door on the right, down the corridor, third door on the left, down the corridor, fourth door on the right. [The medical kit is the one piece of equipment the Doctor's likely to need in a hurry. That's a *really* stupid place to keep it, surely?]

The TARDIS misses the time of year the Doctor was aiming for because he didn't take axial tilt, diurnal rotation and the orbital parabola into account. [This is the only time that things like planetary rotation are said to have an effect on TARDIS landings. Note, though, that this text only appears in the original script and is cut from the filmed material...] Salyavin states that one of the main complaints about the type forty was that the kitchens were too far from the control chamber, but Romana's never seen the Doctor use them anyway. [Stories like 19.1, "Castrovalva", would seem to indicate that the Doctor can change the floor-plan at will, but more on this shortly.] There's at least one bottle of milk in the Doctor's kitchens, which has been in a stasis preserver for only thirty years and is therefore still fresh.

Skagra can use the Doctor's key to get into the TARDIS, and nothing stops him operating the controls when he absorbs the knowledge from the Doctor's mind [so the 'isomorphic' claim made in 13.3, "Pyramids of Mars", would seem to be bunk]. The Doctor's concerned about Skagra over-revving his Ship in 'third phase', and talks about sending out an 'all-frequency alert' from his Ship [to Gallifrey?], but never does it.

[Once again, there's mention of a conceptual geometer here. This device presumably measures imaginary spaces (which must be like imaginary numbers, e.g. the square root of minus one). The implication is that the interior of the TARDIS is a mathematical construct, which accords with what we're told in "Logopolis" (18.7) and "Castrovalva" but also fits the various descriptions of the TARDIS as being "outside" time. This is most starkly put in 14.2, "The Hand of Fear", with its talk of 'temporal grace'. This might make *some* kind of sense of Chronotis' paradoxical state, as he's forced to repair his own conceptual geometry relay. Note that it's only after the Doctor's modifications to the geometer in "The Horns of Nimon" (17.5) that rearranging and deleting the rooms of his own TARDIS becomes a matter of routine. In "Shada" he appears to have stuck with the default settings for the Ship's layout, and hasn't altered the floor-plan to make the kitchens closer to the doors.]

The Non-Humans

• *Krargs*. The servants of Skagra, performing the usual monster-henchman duties and acting as a crew on his ship. Krargs look like large, bipedal piles of slate, all jagged mineral edges and glowing red surfaces. They're sentient, but apparently not too bright, and they're loyal to Skagra as he grows them himself on his command ship; crystals form around wire skeletons inside coffin-shaped vats, and the finished Krarg is ready in moments [compare with 6.4, "The Krotons"]. Though the Krargs seem identical, they have a Commander under Skagra. Even with his blaster set at maximum, K9 can only keep a Krarg immobile for as long as the

blaster's active, and the Krarg becomes stronger as it absorbs 'impossible' amounts of the power. It glows red and produces mist as it does this, before ultimately blowing up, on one occasion taking an entire space station with it. Krargs can be dissolved by releasing the gas from their own vats, then sticking wires from those vats into the gas [this is all very hazy].

Planet Notes Among the books in Professor Chronotis' study is *Alternative Betelgeuse* .[Because this is, after all, a Douglas Adams script… and it's pronounced the Tim Burton way, again.]

• *Shada*. The 'time-prison' of the Time Lords, which from the outside appears to be a large metallic fortress built into the side of a planetoid. Covered in cobwebs [time-spiders?] and lit throughout with an ominous red glow, it's here that the Time Lords keep criminals from a variety of species. [On the whole it's not the job of the Gallifreyan to chase after bad people - in 15.6, "The Invasion of Time", Rodan doesn't give a damn about other species committing war crimes against each other - so these prisoners may be those too dangerous to time itself to be allowed to go free. Compare Salyavin's abilities to the brain-experiments that the Time Lords stop in 23.2, "Mindwarp".]

The prisoners are kept in cryogenic cells, stacked so that the foremost cabinets have to slide out of position to allow the deeper chambers to be accessed. Among the prisoners are a Zygon, a Cyberleader and a Dalek, as well as Rasputin [see **The Lore**, for how we know this when it wasn't filmed and isn't in the script]. The cabinet containing Salyavin is now empty, except for a crude dummy.

The reception area of Shada contains a computer index, which displays the names of all the prisoners in (a) what looks like English and (b) human-alphabetical order. Seen on the screen: "Rungar, War Crimes. Sec 5/JL. Sentence in Perp[etuity]. Cab[inet] 45, Cham[ber] S. Sabjatric, Mass Murder. Sec 7/PY. Sentence in Perp. Cab 73, Cham L. Salyavin, Mind Crimes. Sec 245/XR. Sentence in Perp. Cab 9, Cham T." [Is it reasonable to suppose that *everybody* here has been given a perpetual sentence?] Though some of the prisoners are released by Skagra, the Doctor takes them all back to Shada, but insists on letting the Time Lords sort it out. [Suggesting that the Time Lords now know about Shada again… will they be coming for Chronotis / Salyavin?

Somewhat optimistically, the Doctor tells the Professor that his secret's safe.]

• *Drornid.* After a schism in the Time Lord College of Cardinals, the planet Drornid became home to a rival President, but the other Time Lords forced him to come back by totally ignoring him. This is why Skagra, a native of Drornid, knows so much about Time Lord lore. Certainly, Skagra's computer is well-versed enough in Time Lord technology to identify the Doctor's TARDIS as either a type thirty-nine or type forty time capsule, and has records on the Doctor himself. Skagra reads Gallifreyan like a native, and somehow knows that Chronotis took the *Ancient Law* from the Panopticon Archives. [Since Time Lords are always so concerned about lesser species getting hold of time-technology, the idea of them 'ignoring' a rival Presidency seems massively out-of-character. This does, however, point out the difference between the way Douglas Adams saw the *Doctor Who* universe and the way later writers saw it; here we're almost led to believe that the Time Lords are members of a polite gentleman's club, not ruthless arch-wizards of time. *The Discontinuity Guide* mis-spelled "Drornid" as "Dronid", and the planet has re-appeared under that name in the BBC novels *Alien Bodies* and *Mission Impractical.*]

Skagra's technology is impressive, though it's not clear whether it all comes from Drornid or whether he's picked it up here and there. His self-designed, hundred-metre-long spaceship is run by a sentient but absurdly over-logical computer, and the ship is capable of disguising itself on Earth by turning invisible. Inside the ship, the computer can make food appear out of nowhere at Skagra's side or refresh him in moments by surrounding him with some sort of aura, while prisoners can be matter-transmitted into the brig. The vessel is immune to K9's blaster, and even has a small Krarg generation chamber.

Records on the ship's screen flash past incredibly quickly, but Skagra can take everything in anyway [mind-power]. Its design is so advanced that many of its functions are beyond K9's analytical ability, and it takes thirty-nine astrasiderial days [nearly three months] to travel hundreds of light-years. Although the ship isn't in itself a time machine, the Doctor constructs a primitive dimensional stabiliser by instructing the ship to re-wire its circuitry, starting with a reversal of the polarity of the main warp-feeds. This lets the ship

go anywhere in a matter of minutes.

But this ship is nothing compared to Skagra's command ship, also known as the Krarg Carrier, since it's a massive vessel stuffed with an army of Krargs. And lots of corridors. Smaller craft can be launched from the Carrier, perhaps similar in design to Skagra's personal ship.

Skagra's chief weapon is a floating white sphere, which can drain the mind of a victim through 'psychoactive extraction' by pressing itself against the forehead, leaving the victim as a mindless idiot. The Doctor and Romana hear 'strange babble of inhuman voices' in their heads when it's nearby, and when K9 eventually shoots it the sphere shatters, with each piece forming a smaller sphere. Skagra can access the memories of the drained minds by connecting the sphere to a screen in his ship, or utilise knowledge from stolen minds whenever the sphere's close by. Chronotis goes into a coma after Skagra takes part of his mind, his resistance causing a cerebral trauma, and he dies shortly afterwards. The Doctor doesn't resist, though, and the sphere just gains a copy of his thoughts instead of leaving him as an imbecile. Skagra believes that by harnessing Salyavin's mythical powers, he can put a copy of his mind-print on everybody in the universe, so that the universe will *be* him.

In the end, Skagra's ship is so impressed by the Doctor that it decides to make him its new Lord, and confines Skagra in its brig. Skagra's fate remains uncertain.

• *The Think Tank.* AKA the Foundation for The Study of Advanced Sciences, a space station orbiting a red star hundreds of light-years [at least] from Earth. Skagra paid handsome fees to assemble some of the finest minds available, with the intent of 'pooling intellectual resources by electronic mind transference', but the sphere stole their intelligences.

The scientists - all of them male - are little more than animals by the time the Doctor arrives. They're named as Dr. A. St. John D. Caldera, neurologist; A. S. T. Thira, psychologist; G. V. Santori, parametricist; Dr. L. D. Ia, biologist and Professor R. F. Akrotiri. None of them knew where Dr. Skagra came from, but they recognised him as a brilliant geneticist, astro-engineer, cyberneticist, neurostructuralist and moral theologian. [Most of the scientists *except* Skagra have Earth-like names, which might indicate that they're humans from the future. Caldera speaks of 'the whole of humanity' being threatened. The script states that the station's in a completely different galaxy, odd since it also uses names like "St. John", the computer countdown uses Roman numerals and an English-speaking Earth-person can read the signs. It's perhaps possible that the Krarg carrier has time-travel capability and that the smaller ship uses it as a base, which might mean that Skagra's Dromid is in the future as well. It's doubtful Dromid is a future human colony, though, as K9 identifies Skagra's planet of origin just from the man's metabolism.] An exploding Krarg destroys the Think Tank itself.

History

• *Dating.* Every indication - not least Skagra's outfit - suggests contemporary, 1970s Earth. The post-graduate Chris Parsons graduated in 1978 [so 1979 is a good bet]. The Doctor says it's October.

The Analysis

Where Does This Come From? There are two key books lurking behind most of the stories made from "The Armageddon Factor" (16.6') to "Kinda" (19.3). One of these is the novel that most well-read individuals had at least attempted, Thomas Pynchon's *Gravity's Rainbow*, in which the whole of the twentieth century (but particularly World War Two and its aftermath) were seen as conspiracies or attempts to calculate human behaviour; see the material on RAND and Kriegspiel under "The Armageddon Factor" and 17.1, "Destiny of the Daleks". In the novel, as in much of Pynchon's work, entropy is seen as a moral problem as much as a physical property.

The other book, increasingly central to *Doctor Who* in this period, is Douglas Hofstadter's "meta-mathematics" blockbuster *Godel, Escher, Bach: An Eternal Golden Braid.* We'll see its influence most clearly in "Castrovalva" (19.1), but even in apparently throwaway stories like "Meglos" (18.2) it's a crucial source.

In episode three of "Shada", Skagra's speech to Romana suggests that the only alternative to entropy is purpose; only his will can save the universe from decline. He compares planetary motions with the actions of molecules in the air in his hand, statistically predictable as a mass but individually random and pointless. Entropy makes everything homogenous. If you take one of those yoghurts that's got fruit-syrup in a side-con-

tainer, and mix the syrup into the yoghurt with three clockwise stirs, then stirring it three times anti-clockwise won't separate the syrup from the yoghurt again.

"Maxwell's Demon", named after physicist James Clerk Maxwell, is the term used to describe an agency which might be able to defeat the Second Law of Thermodynamics and unscramble things... but in the real world, they stay mixed and predictable. Skagra is proposing to become Maxwell's Demon on a cosmic scale. Paradoxically, this puts him back on the side of entropy, as he's imposing homogeneity by making everything an extension of one single will. Douglas Adams and script-editor-to-be Christopher H. Bidmead were on the same page with regard to entropy being the Doctor's great anti-life opponent, and they weren't alone in this. The popular "discovery" of entropy in the nineteenth century resulted in a rising sense that only human endeavour made the universe anything but a doomed, dying anomaly. This led to all sorts of things; Oscar Wilde, Wagner, W. B. Yeats, H. G. Wells...

...Wells didn't just write *The Time Machine*, by the way. A short story of his, "The Door In The Wall", features a sporadically-appearing door as a symbol of the narrator's loss of innocence / longing for the unattainable. However, *The Time Machine* - which we see Chronotis bringing home and reading, the only paperback in his library - is as much about entropy as it is about Marx, Darwin or bicycling (although if you've not actually read it, then these may not be what you thought it was about anyway). But from a more down-to-earth point of view, the starting-points for "Shada" were Douglas Adams waxing nostalgic about his University days and Graham Williams wanting to do a story about capital punishment. Contrary to a lot of expectations, the incoming Conservative government hadn't reintroduced the death penalty, and this generated a lot of comment. What alternatives might there be? Williams, in particular, wanted the six-parter to be about the Time Lords.

As Adams grew up in Essex, it would have been impossible for him to go more than a hundred yards without coming across something named after local boy St. Cedd. He was basically a scholarly monk who managed to go sixty years without offending anyone, which was enough to get you canonised in those days.

Meanwhile, elements of this story are suggestive of other scripts being considered at the time.

The working title "Sunburst" brings to mind Philip Hinchcliffe's submission "Valley of the Lost", which ended with the Doctor trapped inside a star in an aberrant time-field and was mooted as a possible regeneration story. Additionally, Alan Drury's "The Tearing of the Veil" was a Victorian poltergeist yarn involving energy from "elsewhere" and the draining of the Doctor's life-force; as in the next televised story "The Leisure Hive", the Doctor spent much of the story prematurely aged, in this case bedridden in a nightshirt. (See **What Else Didn't Get Made?** for more in this vein.)

The opening sequence, of the scientists lying in their recesses in a star-formation around the central cone, is so similar to the opening sequence of *Alien* (released nine months before) that it's hard to believe it's a coincidence. The use of Roman numerals in the countdown is, however, unique.

Things That Don't Make Sense In episode two it takes Chris Parsons a remarkably short time to go deep into the guts of the TARDIS, fetch the medical kit and come out again. That's after Romana uses his Christian name, even though she's never been told it [at least not while the camera's been on her]. In episode six the Doctor finds a laser gun in the TARDIS equipment room, but never even thinks to use it against Skagra in the final confrontation. And it's not as if he's got ethical codes against using energy weapons, given the number of people he's shot with K9 over the last few stories. Once Salyavin's cell turns out to be empty, why does he immediately reveal who he really is, thus giving Skagra a reason to drain his mind and put everyone in jeopardy? Is he really *that* senile? Why, indeed, doesn't he put his mind into Skagra's and make the man take up stamp-collecting or the oboe instead?

The miniature Krarg generation chamber on Skagra's ship creates a new Krarg whenever the computer makes the 'launch procedures activated' announcement, and it's not clear why. Why should a Krarg be necessary while the ship's launching? Does it supply the in-flight entertainment? Doesn't the ship get rather bunged up with Krargs, if a new one gets spawned every time it takes off? [Maybe there's a minimum crew requirement, though the ship seems to do perfectly well on its own.]

Radio-carbon dating of the book reveals it to be 20,000 years old. This is cute, but nonsensical.

Dr. Science says: the only way this can happen is if more than 100% of the carbon molecules in the sample are Carbon 16, and as it has no organic compounds in its make-up it's pointless testing anyway. And the dating process can only work if you calibrate the carbon isotope decay against known rates for each type of material - bone, wood, cloth or what-have-you - and if the living organism that took in the Carbon 16 did so from our sun and not from some other star. Dr. Science was then politely asked to stop, as he had a whole sheaf of notes on other things wrong with this idea.

In the filming schedule, the "time criminals" listed on Shada include Rasputin, Boudicca (spelled "Boedicia" here), Lady MacBeth, Salome, Lucretia Borgia, Nero, a gladiator and Genghis Khan. And a Zygon. Even if generations of pulp-SF writers are right and Rasputin is some kind of evil alien mastermind, the rest can't *all* be the Rani in previous incarnations, can they?

Critique We'll never know for sure how well it would have come together, of course; we'll never know whether the final face-off between the Doctor and Skagra would have been a monumental confrontation or just two men gurning at each other, whether Shada itself would have been the heart of darkness as the script suggests or just a bunch of badly-lit corridor sets full of old monster costumes. (Although judging by the sterile, white-walled, '70s-computer-lettering environment of the Think Tank station, the latter is a distinct possibility.) We've got over an hour of material to look at, but it's hard to judge the weight of the story when we never get to see the villain do anything except wander around Cambridge, and if you're watching the BBC video release then the God-awful music doesn't help. We've got the scenes set on Earth, and there's a pleasing sort of Englishness about them, but that's hardly surprising given that the previous three stories have given us nothing but outer-space sets and jungle planets.

What we can say for certain is this: unlike Douglas Adams' script for "The Pirate Planet", "Shada" actually seems like a story with some power behind it, as if he'd finally got the hang of this "structure" idea. The discovery that the Time Lords have a forgotten prison-world, and the sheer sense of *age* suggested by Chronotis' tenure at Cambridge, make this feel like a Big Project instead of just a collection of nice thoughts.

But even so… there's also a sense that the author was only *reluctantly* forcing himself to give up his favourite obsessions. The real giveaway is the Krargs. Just consider that name: "Krargs". Hard not to get the feeling that Adams had no time for this sort of nonsense, that the Krargs were a way of keeping the monster-loving audience happy, that he deliberately gave them a stupid name and then concentrated on the parts of the story he found more interesting (but see also **The Lore**). And it's a shockingly lazy way of writing a script, when you think about it: come up with a deliberate cliché, and pretend it's irony. 'Scaroth, last of the Jagaroth' verged on SF parody too, but at least had a certain lyricism to it. And if the Krargs are designed as "typical" monsters, then Skagra is a "typical" villain. Adams wants a platform to explore his favourite anti-sci-fi idea, the question of why anybody would want to rule the universe, and Skagra is a hollow shell of a character designed to let him do just that. Reading the script, you can imagine Julian Glover delivering every line, purely because the author can't be bothered devising a new villain-persona after "City of Death". Skagra and Scaroth… even the names are similar.

These aren't the only recurring problems that make themselves felt here. The amount of shooting that K9 does, at Krargs, at Skagra's sphere and at the mind-slaves, underlines one very uncomfortable fact about the series in this era; the Doctor has effectively come to rely on a gun. It may only be a *stun*-gun, but even so, there's an attitude of "shoot the bad guys and let the Doctor get on with the cleverness". The Doctor doesn't use his wits to escape from tight corners any more, he uses them to lash together pieces of machinery while the dog blasts anyone who comes near him. Towards the end of "Shada" (as scripted, at least), you get the feeling that Tom Baker has become an automated mannequin programmed to shout 'K9!' whenever he needs fire-power and 'come on' whenever he has to leave the room to build something.

There's a running (or rather, too-often-repeated) joke in *Doctor Who* in this period, probably thanks to Adams himself, which goes something like this: somebody says something, the Doctor disagrees, the person asks for an alternative suggestion and the Doctor repeats whatever it was the other person said. It happens several times here, and it's no funnier here than it ever was. And not for the first time, the Doctor prompts characters to ask him for explanations, always a bad sign.

Most telling of all, though, is Chris Parsons. Parsons is Douglas Adams' Mary-Sue, a way of making himself the "ordinary man" in the Doctor's world, and the scripted description of the character - including the tell-tale line "likes Bach" - makes you squirm to read it. His embarrassing speech about scientific possibility in episode two demonstrates Adams' habit of lecturing people while trying to make it sound as if he's philosophising. It comes across as a rallying-call to all of those watching *Doctor Who* in the viewing-rooms of universities, a way of making the science-literate, Cambridge-educated people wave their copies of *Scientific American* in the air and shout 'right on, brother!'. (Daniel Hill's rather awkward performance as Chris just makes things worse, though special mention goes to Victoria Burgoyne, who as Chris' associate Claire Keightley strikes just the right balance between bewilderment and curiosity.)

And yet despite all the script's worst excesses, we shouldn't overlook the fact that there's an awful lot of imagination running through some of this material. We tend to take Chronotis and his time-travelling university rooms for granted, but only because we're so used to them from (a) the write-ups of "Shada" in *Doctor Who Magazine* and (b) *Dirk Gently's Holistic Detective Agency* (again, see **The Lore**) that we forget what a surprise they would, and should, have been. Despite its use in many of the late '70s stories, the TARDIS isn't a spaceship at heart, and shouldn't be treated as one. Chronotis' version of the Ship - and even "Ship" is misleading - is the TARDIS as it was always meant to be, an impossible environment instead of a convenient piece of hardware. There's also a bluff in the story that history has made us forget: the plot's deliberately structured so that we think Skagra is Salyavin for the first couple of episodes, a neat piece of distraction which lets the characters talk about a missing Time Lord master-criminal without the audience spotting the *real* reason for it.

It's also curious how far the knowledge that "Shada" was intended as the end of Season Seventeen affects the way you look at the stories leading up to it. The production team wasn't just building up a new idea of who the Doctor really was, and his place in the scheme of things, but trying to introduce the concept that the true power of the Time Lords was beyond even *their* comprehension (see also 15.6, "The Invasion of Time"). Not to mention all the cost-cutting they did in the previous two stories, simply to be able to afford this much location filming. Williams had finally tamed Baker, got him "with the programme" literally and figuratively; tamed the unions, nearly; reined in the designers; and was set to launch the series into a new phase, as different from the previous three years as they'd been from Hinchcliffe's run. And then the BBC made it impossible for him to stay.

Prior to the BBC release there was another, unofficial, edit of "Shada" that seemed pacier and stranger. In part this oddness was due to the lack of music, but there were also little moments of camera-movement much like the supposedly "revolutionary" direction of "The Leisure Hive" (18.1) and "Warriors' Gate" (18.5). The use of old material in flashbacks (the Doctor's memory being scanned, for example) is also very Season Eighteen. There's a massive gulf between "The Horns of Nimon" and "The Leisure Hive", but there's at least *some* continuity here. And it's hard to imagine how another Williams season might have turned out, given the sort of thing he seems to have been planning. Lost Gallifreyan artifacts from the Old Time, and the Doctor being more than just a Time Lord? A companion who's almost more interesting than he is? This is the same sort of direction the series would take in the late '80s, when the writers were trying to stop the programme turning into soap opera. The Doctor's musings on how people will see him in centuries to come is also strikingly close to what would be screened ten years later.

Final analysis? It's like this. Graham Williams' description of "Shada", after it fell to pieces, was that it was a story with 'something for everyone'. For all its many, many flaws, it's a better description than he could have known. The shift in style between Season Seventeen and Season Eighteen would demonstrate that there were at least two different approaches towards *Doctor Who* as the '70s turned into the '80s (see **The John Nathan-Turner Era: What's the Difference?** under 18.1), and "Shada" - a story big enough to feel like a major part of the legend, but clever enough to seem like literate SF - would have been the ideal bridge between them.

The Facts

Written by Douglas Adams. Directed by Pennant Roberts.

Supporting Cast: Christopher Neame (Skagra), Denis Carey (Professor Chronotis), Daniel Hill (Chris Parsons), Victoria Burgoyne (Clare Keightley), Gerald Campion (Wilkin), Shirley Dixon (Voice of Ship), James Coombes (Voice of Krargs).

Working Titles "Sunburst".

Cliffhangers The monstrous face of the Krarg Commander appears on the screen in Skagra's ship, and tells his Lord that everything's ready; the Doctor's chased down a dead-end street by Skagra's sphere; the Doctor convinces Skagra's computer that he's dead, as a way of establishing that he isn't a threat, but it responds by shutting off the ship's life support as there are no living beings in the vicinity; one of the Krargs, made red-hot and smoky by K9, lumbers into the Think Tank station to threaten the Doctor and Chris; on Shada, the released prisoners controlled by Skagra move in on the Doctor.

The Lore

• Adams had been dismayed, as Williams had hinted in a memo (see 17.5, "The Horns of Nimon"), at how few worthwhile scripts had been submitted. Although he had half a dozen possible six-part stories on the table, in various degrees of hopelessness, Williams asked him to write the Season finale himself. (Williams eventually had more than a small hand in writing "Shada", but this is rarely acknowledged.)

Adams' first attempt was an idea that the Doctor, fed up with saving every world he visited, was checking into a sanctuary to get some "me-time". Williams declined to use this, claiming that it'd 'send up' the Doctor. Plan B was an idea about capital punishment (see **Where Does This Come From?**), and Adams wound up setting it in his home-town of Cambridge by default; the one place, he said, where someone dressed like Skagra would go unnoticed. The script was written in six days, and needed rewriting to trim it down. He kept the principle cast small, but the filming allocation was a week.

- When confronted with the prospect of writing the six-parter himself whilst desperately trying to get "The Doomsday Contract", "The Tearing of the Veil", "Erinella" et al to work (see **What Else Didn't Get Made?**), and with the rest of the production team nipping off to Paris to film "City of Death" (17.2) after he'd spent three sleepless nights writing it, Adams hit on a brainwave. With no actors or producer around to get in his way, he joined up with Ken Grieve - director of the next story due to be filmed, "Destiny of the Daleks" (17.1) - and went on an epic pub-crawl. Adams' account of this entertained many convention-goers in the 1980s, but in short they went to the same hotel in Paris as their colleagues and were told to leave, so Grieve suggested an all-night bar in West Berlin. They arrived back at Television Centre minutes before the rest of the production team, heavily hung over.

- At two o'clock on the 7th of November, 1979, the cast and crew of "Shada" returned from lunch to find a locked studio. As always in the run-up to Christmas, a demarcation dispute about the wiring and resetting of electric clocks in the studios had been used as a pretext for strikes over more abstract issues. All the technical managers walked out, and Television Centre was unusable. This sort of trouble was usually resolved with a bonus, but this year the issue was more than monetary, and no means of ending the dispute could be found without protracted negotiations. The talks were over by the 1st of December, although priority went to the "prestige" Christmas specials (and the *Fawlty Towers* episode "Basil the Rat"), so "Shada" had to be put on ice.

Williams had to honour actors' contracts by being there to order them to go home once they arrived. With Adams departing and Williams planning to leave, their attempt at a triumphant swan-song had originally been met with a great deal of enthusiasm; everyone was agreed that this was the best script, and certainly the cleverest, of Adams' career. The abandonment was seen as only temporary, but Williams and Adams had a desultory farewell party on December 14th.

- The footage already shot was kept by incoming producer John Nathan-Turner, who hoped to salvage something from the project. His first attempt was a blocked three-day shoot to make either a four-part version or two fifty-minute instalments as a Christmas special. This didn't work, as most of the material filmed was just conversation in Chronotis' rooms, and Head of Serials

Graeme McDonald was less than enthusiastic about the idea. Nathan-Turner was planning to introduce new regular characters and phase out Romana and K9, so if the material wasn't salvaged immediately then the story could only have been told in flashback. In the end, of course, nothing came of any of these plans.

- Chris was to have worked at the Cavendish laboratory, birthplace of particle physics and DNA research. Filming for this was the first thing to be hit, as it required a night-shoot and the lighting charge-hand was recalled by the union as the opening move in negotiations.

- The shots of the cyclist being attacked, and some of the chase scenes, were filmed from an open-topped Citroen 2CV.

- Wilkins was played by Gerald Campion, formerly TV's Billy Bunter (see 3.7, "The Celestial Toymaker" and 6.2, "The Mind Robber").

- The name "Krargs" was originally "Kraags", as in an anagram of "Skagra". The costumes had CSO components, so that the image of burning coals / lava could be superimposed onto their bodies as they heated up.

- Contrary to what's specified in the script, it appears that the prop for the Doctor's "helmet" in episode six would have been fairly restrained, a series of leather straps and a small cylinder with lights. There's no indication of a portion of table attached anywhere.

- "Shada" may have been aborted, but it didn't all go to waste. Like some of his material from "City of Death", Douglas Adams salvaged various bits from the story when he wrote his novel *Dirk Gently's Holistic Detective Agency*, most notably the character of Professor Chronotis and his TARDIS-rooms at St. Cedd's (although *Dirk Gently* glosses over the Professor's origins, pumping up the man's forgetfulness so that he can't even remember where he came from, and tries to emphasise the idea of the rooms as a time-travelling *place* rather than an actual *Ship*). Needless to say, there are no Krargs in the novel.

1 It's not worth explaining who **Norman Wisdom** is, but to translate this sentence for foreign readers: "Confronted by one that slides upwards instead of sideways, she turns into a spaz."

2 *The Black and White Minstrel Show*: Variety programme which involved a troupe of white men from Wales dressing up in black-face and performing Cole Porter, the soundtrack of *Hair* and lots of Carmen Miranda material, punctuated by comedy pratfalls and the inevitable Al Jolson tribute. It ran for twenty years between 1958 and 1978, at one stage being watched by about a quarter of the population. Yes, of course we know better *now*. Those born after 1980 have trouble believing that it ever really existed, but its fall from grace had at least as much to do with the end of the Showbiz Age as it had to do with the programme's dodgy race-politics.

3 **Sticky-Backed Plastic.** Sellotape. However, the BBC couldn't say "sellotape" because it was a brand-name. Many children were confused by this, and came to believe that sticky-backed plastic was a special kind of sellotape with magical model-making properties, which wasn't available in their local shops and could probably only be found in the Big Cities.

4 **Eric Morecambe.** Half of Morecambe and Wise, then Britain's best-known and best-regarded double-act, and a strong contender for the title of "funniest man who ever walked the Earth". The 1977 *Morecambe and Wise Christmas Special* garnered the highest ratings for an entertainment programme in British history, a crowning achievement which effectively marked the beginning of the end of television's Showbiz Age. *Star Wars* opened in Britain the very next day, and thus was a new era born.

5 A quick fashion note for non-UK readers. Burberry - the makers of up-market raincoats and such - have recently revived their fortunes with baseball caps in their distinctive traditional check, targeted at a rather different market; those who in America would be called "trailer trash" and here are termed "Chavs". Romana would be picked up for soliciting if she landed in present-day London dressed like that.

6 **The Goodies.** Nigh-indescribable comed series which ran throughout the 1970s, and whic dealt with virtually every topical or fashionable issu of the era with a mixture of satire and slapstick vi lence. It is, unsurprisingly, bound to the popul consciousness of that decade in much the same wa as *Doctor Who* itself.

In 1970, when the *Doctor Who* production tea was trying to make CSO work as a way of giving tl nation oversized monsters, the very first scene of tl very first episode of *The Goodies* used exactly tl same technology for a series of sight-gags. The pl of that first episode involves a criminal breaking in the Tower of London in order to put something ir the case where the Crown Jewels are kept, and some places looks alarmingly like "The Rib Operation". But the best-known *Goodies* episode far is "Kitten Kong", in which a fluffy little white k ten grows to eighty feet in height and rampa; through London. Made two years before "Invasi of the Dinosaurs", many of the shots are hauntin; similar… but vastly better.

7 **Boney M.** '70s European disco group who ep omised everything that was relentlessly absu about '70s European disco (bear in mind, Euro completely overlooked the "hip" side of the ge and instead treated it as an excuse for nove records about UFOs). Some of Boney M's songs w about - or sounded like they came from - ou space, but many were three-and-a-half-minute h torical epics; the most notorious was a stomp dancefloor-filler about the life of Rasputin, with chorus of 'Rah-Rah-Rasputin, Russia's greatest le machine… there was a cat that really was go Though Boney M's dreadlocks weren't actu. bright silver like those of the Movellans, the blurr of the line in this era between "costumes you mi see on *Doctor Who*" and "costumes you might see *Top of the Pops*" meant that people were expect the Daleks' new arch-enemies to break out int chorus of "Daddy Cool" even then.

POLICE _{PUBLIC CALL} BOX

OPEN THE DOOR TO
A NEW DIMENSION
www.galaxy4.co.uk

who made all this ?

Lawrence Miles is the author of… hold on… yeah, *eight* novels now, the most recent of them being the first volume in the ongoing *Faction Paradox* series, *This Town Will Never Let Us Go*. After co-writing *Dusted* - a guide to *Buffy the Vampire Slayer,* also published by Mad Norwegian - he suddenly found that he'd been cured, and didn't want to see another episode of *Buffy* ever again. So once *About Time* is finished, he's planning on constructing a great ceremonial pyre and burning the complete collection of *Doctor Who* videos and CDs that's taken him nearly twenty years to assemble. Favourite story in this book: "City of Death". Least favourite: "Underworld".

Recovering academic **Tat Wood** is the person most compilers of previous guidebooks went to for advice and cultural context. Despite having written for *Film Review, TV Zone, Starburst, SFX, Dreamwatch, Doctor Who Magazine, X-pose* and just about every major fanzine going, he has a rich, full and complex life. Currently lecturing and tutoring, he is busy mentoring mature students from across the Commonwealth and the new Europe whilst attempting to break into mainstream "literary" fiction. Tragically, this is interrupted by people wanting to get the lyrics to half-forgotten 1960s TV themes ringing him rather than bothering with the Internet (because he's quicker). Although culturally adept and well-rounded, he has lived in Ilford for the last ten years. Favourite story in this book: "The Ribos Operation". Least favourite: "The Seeds of Doom".

Mad Norwegian Press

Publisher/Series Editor
Lars Pearson

Copy Editor
Fritze CM Roberts

Interior/Cover Design
Christa Dickson

Cover Art
Steve Johnson

Associate Editors
Marc Eby
Dave Gartner
Val Sowell
Joshua Wilson

Technical Support
Michael O'Nele
Robert Moriarity

mad norwegian press

1309 Carrollton Ave #237
Metairie, LA 70005
info@madnorwegian.com
www.madnorwegian.com